Pirates of Venus

Carson Napier set out for Mars in a secret interplanetary rocket but found himself instead on a different world – the cloud-hidden planet of Venus.

Venus was a startling world – semi-private, semi-civilised. It was a place of unmapped oceans dotted with great islands; a world whose trees pierced the clouds and whose cities squatted on their branches; a planet whose inhabitants included men, half-men, and monsters, all struggling with each other for dominance.

Lost on Venus

In the Room of the Seven Doors, Carson Napier faced the choice of his life. Six doors led to terrible deaths – the seventh was the door of life. But for him, this door too would lead only to the new dangers of a planet whose beasts were more frightful than those of his native Earth. But Carson sought the rescue of the planet's fairest princess, and even though he stepped from one danger to meet another, he was determined to make good an Earthman's pledge.

Carson of Venus

Carson Napier, first Earthman to reach Venus, had to keep alert every instant of his stay on that world of mist and mystery. For its lands were unmapped, its inhabitants many, varied and strange, and he had taken an obligation to restore a native princess to her lost homeland. Across terrible oceans where dreaded sea-monsters dwelled, through deep forests where terror haunted every branch, and behind the walls of eerie cities where power-mad chieftains plotted uncanny schemes, Carson of Venus would fulfil his oath.

Also by Edgar Rice Burroughs

Tarzan
1. Tarzan of the Apes (1912)
2. The Return of Tarzan (1913)
3. The Beasts of Tarzan (1914)
4. The Son of Tarzan (1914)
5. Tarzan and the Jewels of Opar (1916)
6. Jungle Tales of Tarzan (1916, 1917)
7. Tarzan the Untamed (1919, 1921)
8. Tarzan the Terrible (1921)
9. Tarzan and the Golden Lion (1922, 1923)
10. Tarzan and the Ant Men (1924)
11. Tarzan, Lord of the Jungle (1927, 1928)
12. Tarzan and the Lost Empire (1928)
13. Tarzan at the Earth's Core (1929)
14. Tarzan the Invincible (1930-1931)
15. Tarzan Triumphant (1931)
16. Tarzan and the City of Gold (1932)
17. Tarzan and the Lion Man (1933, 1934)
18. Tarzan and the Leopard Men (1935)
19. Tarzan's Quest (1935, 1936)
20. Tarzan the Magnificent (1936, 1937)
21. Tarzan and the Forbidden City (1938)
22. Tarzan and the Foreign Legion (1947)
23. Tarzan and the Madman (1964)
24. Tarzan and the Castaways (1965)
25. Tarzan and the Valley of Gold (1965)
    (authorized sequel by Fritz Leiber)

Martian Tales*
1. A Princess of Mars (1917)
    (aka Under The Moons Of Mars, 1912)
2. The Gods of Mars (1918)
3. The Warlord of Mars (1919)
4. Thuvia, Maid of Mars (1920)
5. The Chessmen of Mars (1922)
6. The Master Mind of Mars (1927)
7. A Fighting Man of Mars (1930)
8. Swords of Mars (1934)
9. Synthetic Men of Mars (1938)
10. Llana of Gathol (1948)
11. John Carter of Mars (1941)

Pellucidar
1. At the Earth's Core (1914)
2. Pellucidar (1923)
3. Tanar of Pellucidar (1928)
4. Back to the Stone Age (1937)
5. Land of Terror (1944)
6. Savage Pellucidar (1963)

Venus
1. Pirates of Venus (1934)
2. Lost on Venus (1935)

3. Carson of Venus (1939)
4. Escape on Venus (1946)
5. The Wizard of Venus (1970)

The Land That Time Forgot
1. The Land That Time Forgot (1918)
2. The People That Time Forgot (1918)
3. Out of Time's Abyss (1918)

Other Science Fiction
The Moon Maid (1926) (aka The Moon Men)
Beyond the Farthest Star (1941)
The Lost Continent (1916)
The Monster Men (1929)
The Resurrection of Jimber-Jaw (1937)

The Mucker
1. The Mucker (1914)
2. The Return of the Mucker (1916)
3. The Oakdale Affair (1917)

Jungle Adventure Novels
The Man-Eater (1915)
The Cave Girl (1925)
The Eternal Lover (1925)
    (aka The Eternal Savage)
Jungle Girl (1932)
    (aka Land of the Hidden Men)
The Lad and the Lion (1938)

* Not available as SF Gateway eBooks

Carson of Venus
SF GATEWAY OMNIBUS

PIRATES OF VENUS
LOST ON VENUS
CARSON OF VENUS

Edgar Rice Burroughs

GOLLANCZ
LONDON

First published in Great Britain in 2014 by
Gollancz
An imprint of the Orion Publishing Group
Orion House, 5 Upper St Martin's Lane,
London WC2H 9EA

An Hachette UK Company

A CIP catalogue record for this book is
available from the British Library

ISBN 978 0 575 12920 7

1 3 5 7 9 10 8 6 4 2

Typeset by Jouve (UK), Milton Keynes

Printed and bound by CPI Group (UK) Ltd, Croydon, CR0 4YY

The Orion Publishing Group's policy is to use papers
that are natural, renewable and recyclable products and
made from wood grown in sustainable forests. The logging
and manufacturing processes are expected to conform to
the environmental regulations of the country of origin.

www.orionbooks.co.uk
www.gollancz.co.uk

CONTENTS

ENTER THE SF GATEWAY . . .

Towards the end of 2011, in conjunction with the celebration of fifty years of coherent, continuous science fiction and fantasy publishing, Gollancz launched the SF Gateway.

Over a decade after launching the landmark SF Masterworks series, we realised that the realities of commercial publishing are such that even the Masterworks could only ever scratch the surface of an author's career. Vast troves of classic SF and fantasy were almost certainly destined never again to see print. Until very recently, this meant that anyone interested in reading any of those books would have been confined to scouring second-hand bookshops. The advent of digital publishing changed that paradigm for ever.

Embracing the future even as we honour the past, Gollancz launched the SF Gateway with a view to utilising the technology that now exists to make available, for the first time, the entire backlists of an incredibly wide range of classic and modern SF and fantasy authors. Our plan, at its simplest, was – and still is! – to use this technology to build on the success of the SF and Fantasy Masterworks series and to go even further.

The SF Gateway was designed to be the new home of classic science fiction and fantasy – the most comprehensive electronic library of classic SFF titles ever assembled. The programme has been extremely well received and we've been very happy with the results. So happy, in fact, that we've decided to complete the circle and return a selection of our titles to print, in these omnibus editions.

We hope you enjoy this selection. And we hope that you'll want to explore more of the classic SF and fantasy we have available. These are wonderful books you're holding in your hand, but you'll find much, much more ... through the SF Gateway.

www.sfgateway.com

INTRODUCTION
from The Encyclopedia of Science Fiction

Edgar Rice Burroughs (1875–1950) was a US writer whose early life was marked by numerous false starts and failures – at the time he began to write, at the age of 36, he was a pencil-sharpener salesman – but it would seem that the impulse to create the psychically charged Science-Fantasy dream-worlds that became his trademark territory was deep-set and powerful. Once he began to write, with a great rush of built-up energy, within two years he had initiated three of his four most important series. He never stopped.

Certainly the first of his published works has ever since its first appearance served as a successful escape from mid-life burdens and frustrations. *A Princess of Mars* (1917), which was originally published February–July 1912 in *All-Story* as "Under the Moons of Mars" as by Norman Bean, opens the long Barsoom sequence of novels set on Mars (Barsoom). (Many of Burroughs's novels appeared first in magazines; we are giving only first book publications here). The long array of Barsoom tales established that planet as a venue for dream-like and interminable Planetary Romance sagas in which sf and fantasy protocols mixed indiscriminately as an enabling pretext and human men were preternaturally strong, due to the manly intensity of their native Earth gravity. *The Gods of Mars* (1918) and *The Warlord of Mars* (1919) further recount the exploits of John Carter as he variously befriends and battles various green, yellow and black Martians without the law, and wins the hand of the red-skinned (and oviparous) princess Dejah Thoris. The standard of storytelling and invention is high in the Barsoom books, *Chessmen* and *Swords* being particularly fine; but it has always been difficult for some critics to accept the Planetary Romance as being, in any cognitive sense, sf. Although Carter's adventures take place on another planet, he incontrovertibly travels there by magical means, and Barsoom itself is inconsistent and scientifically implausible to modern eyes. It is clear, however, that Burroughs's immense popularity has nothing to do with conventional sf virtues, for it depends on storylines and venues as malleable as dreams, exotic and dangerous and unending.

The Tarzan saga is just as much sf (or non-sf) as the Barsoom series. Though clearly influenced by H. Rider Haggard, Burroughs did not attempt to imitate one of that writer's prime virtues: Haggard's effort to embed his tales in a vision of history, even though (to modern eyes) his work seems almost dementedly dated, certainly in its imperialist assumptions about race. Allan Quatermain's Africa, even though it is romantically exaggerated, can distress modern readers; but Tarzan's Africa is a cartoon, and must be accepted as being no more governed by the reality principle than Barsoom. *Tarzan of the Apes* (1914), the story of an English aristocrat's son raised in the jungle by "great apes" (of a non-existent species) as a kind of feral child, was immensely popular from the beginning, and Burroughs continued producing sequels to the end of his career. In most of them Tarzan has unashamedly fantastic adventures, some of which – discovering lost cities and live Dinosaurs, being reduced to 18 in (46 cm) in height, visiting the Earth's core – evoke the adventure tropes of Pulp sf.

Burroughs's third major series, the Pellucidar novels based on the Hollow-Earth theory of John Cleves Symmes, began with *At the Earth's Core* (1922) and continued in *Pellucidar* (1923), *Tanar of Pellucidar* (1930), *Tarzan at the Earth's Core* (1930) – a notable 'overlap' volume – *Back to the Stone Age* (1937), *Land of Terror* (1944) and *Savage Pellucidar* (1963). Pellucidar is perhaps the best of Burroughs's locales – a world without time where Dinosaurs and beast-men roam circularly forever – and is a perfect setting for bloodthirsty romantic adventure. The first of the series was filmed disappointingly as At the Earth's Core (*1976*).

After Pellucidar came Burroughs's last completed sequence, the Venus tales (see below). A posthumous story, 'The Wizard of Venus', was published in *Tales of Three Planets* (1964) and subsequently as the title story of a separate paperback, *The Wizard of Venus* (1970). Two of the stories from *Tales of Three Planets*, 'Beyond the Farthest Star' (January 1942 *Blue Book*) and the posthumous 'Tangor Returns' (in *Tales of Three Planets* 1964), form the opening of a fifth series which Burroughs abandoned. They are of particular sf interest because they are his only tales with an interstellar setting. The two stories were subsequently republished as a paperback entitled *Beyond the Farthest Star* (1965).

Of Burroughs's non-series tales, perhaps the finest is *The Land that Time Forgot* (1924; revised in three volumes under the original magazine titles: *The Land that Time Forgot* 1962, *The People that Time Forgot* 1962 and *Out of Time's Abyss* 1962), set in the lost world of Caspak near the South Pole, and cunningly presenting in literal form – for animals here metamorphose through evolutionary stages – the dictum that ontogeny recapitulates phylogeny. The book was loosely adapted into two films, *The Land That Time Forgot* (*1975*) and *The People That Time Forgot* (*1977*). Also of interest is *The Moon Maid* 1926), which describes a civilization in the hollow interior of the Moon and a future Invasion of the Earth.

Among Burroughs's other books, those which can be claimed as sf include: *The Eternal Lover* (1925), a prehistoric adventure involving Time Travel featuring a character, Barney Custer, who reappears in the Ruritanian *The Mad King* (1926); *The Monster Men* (1929), a reworking of the Frankenstein theme, which should not be confused with *The Man without a Soul* (1922), which is not fantasy or sf; *The Cave Girl* (1925), another prehistoric romance; *Jungle Girl* (1932), about a lost civilization in Cambodia; and *Beyond Thirty* (1956), a story set in the twenty-second century after the collapse of European civilization.

It cannot be claimed that Burroughs's works aim at literary polish, or that their merits are intellectual. His lovers and his critics agree on this. Nevertheless, because of their efficient narrative style, and because Burroughs had a genius for highly-energized literalizations of dream-worlds, they have endured. Tarzan is a figure with the iconic density of Sherlock Holmes or Dracula. His "rediscovery" during the 1960s was an astonishing publishing phenomenon, with the majority of his books being reprinted regularly. He had never been forgotten, however. Burroughs has probably had more imitators than any other sf writer, ranging from Otis Adelbert Kline in the 1930s to Kenneth Bulmer (writing as Alan Burt Akers) in the 1970s, with homages from much later writers like Terry Bisson in *Voyage to the Red Planet* (1990) and Hitoshi Yoshioka in *Nangun Kihei Taii John Carter* ["Southern Cavalry Captain John Carter"] (2005). Serious sf writers who owe a debt to Burroughs include Leigh Brackett, Ray Bradbury, Michael Moorcock and, above all, Philip José Farmer, whose Lord Grandrith and Ancient Opar novels are among the most enjoyable of latter-day Burroughs-inflected romances. Burroughs was posthumously inducted into the Science Fiction Hall of Fame in 2003. It was clear he belonged there.

Burroughs's fourth series, created later in his career, was the Venus sequence, the first three volumes of which – here presented – are the strongest and most unified. *Pirates of Venus* (1934), *Lost on Venus* (1935) and *Carson of Venus* (1939) focus on the exploits of spaceman Carson Napier on Venus, after he has crash-landed. It is a complex world, full of high colours and a certain amount of sex, all of which Burroughs heightens, and at points satirizes. Carson has a chance to become immortal. We go along with him on the ride.

For a more detailed version of the above, see Edgar Rice Burroughs' author entry in *The Encyclopedia of Science Fiction*: http://sf-encyclopedia.com/entry/burroughs_edgar_rice

Some terms above are capitalised when they would not normally be so rendered; this indicates that the terms represent discrete entries in *The Encyclopedia of Science Fiction*.

PIRATES OF VENUS

I

Carson Napier

'If a female figure in a white shroud enters your bedchamber at midnight on the thirteenth day of this month, answer this letter; otherwise, do not.'

Having read this far in the letter, I was about to consign it to the wastebasket, where all my crank letters go; but for some reason I read on, 'If she speaks to you, please remember her words and repeat them to me when you write.' I might have read on to the end; but at this juncture the telephone bell rang, and I dropped the letter into one of the baskets on my desk. It chanced to be the 'out' basket; and had events followed their ordinary course, this would have been the last of the letter and the incident in so far as I was concerned, for from the 'out' basket the letter went to the files.

It was Jason Gridley on the telephone. He seemed excited and asked me to come to his laboratory at once. As Jason is seldom excited about anything, I hastened to accede to his request and satisfy my curiosity. Jumping into my roadster, I soon covered the few blocks that separate us, to learn that Jason had good grounds for excitement. He had just received a radio message from the inner world, from Pellucidar.

On the eve of the departure of the great dirigible, O-220, from the Earth's core, following the successful termination of that historic expedition, Jason had determined to remain and search for von Horst, the only missing member of the party; but Tarzan, David Innes, and Captain Zuppner persuaded him of the folly of such an undertaking, inasmuch as David had promised to dispatch an expedition of his own native Pellucidarian warriors to locate the young German lieutenant if he still lived and it were possible to discover any clue to his whereabouts.

Notwithstanding this, and though he had returned to the outer world with the ship, Jason had always been harassed by a sense of responsibility for the fate of von Horst, a young man who had been most popular with all the members of the expedition; and had insisted time and time again that he regretted having left Pellucidar until he had exhausted every means within his power of rescuing von Horst or learned definitely that he was dead.

Jason waved me to a chair and offered me a cigarette. 'I've just had a message from Abner Perry,' he announced, 'the first for months.'

'It must have been interesting,' I commented, 'to excite *you.*'

'It was,' he admitted. 'A rumor has reached Sari that von Horst has been found.'

Now as this pertains to a subject entirely foreign to the present volume, I might mention that I have alluded to it only for the purpose of explaining two facts which, while not vital, have some slight bearing on the remarkable sequence of events which followed. First, it caused me to forget the letter I just mentioned, and, second, it fixed the date in my mind – the tenth.

My principal reason for mentioning the first fact is to stress the thought that the matter of the letter, so quickly and absolutely forgotten, had no opportunity to impress itself upon my mind and therefore could not, at least objectively, influence my consideration of ensuing events. The letter was gone from my mind within five minutes of its reading as completely as though it had never been received.

The next three days were exceedingly busy ones for me, and when I retired on the night of the thirteenth my mind was so filled with the annoying details of a real estate transaction that was going wrong, that it was some time before I could sleep. I can truthfully affirm that my last thoughts were of trust deeds, receivers in equity, and deficiency judgments.

What awoke me, I do not know. I sat up with a start just in time to see a female figure, swathed in what appeared to be a white winding sheet, enter my room through the door. You will note that I say door rather than doorway, for such was the fact; the door was closed. It was a clear, moonlit night; the various homely objects in my room were plainly discernible, especially the ghostly figure now hovering near the foot of my bed.

I am not subject to hallucinations, I had never seen a ghost, I had never wished to, and I was totally ignorant of the ethics governing such a situation. Even had the lady not been so obviously supernatural, I should yet have been at a loss as to how to receive her at this hour in the intimacy of my bedchamber, for no strange lady had ever before invaded its privacy, and I am of Puritan stock.

'It is midnight of the thirteenth,' she said, in a low, musical voice.

'So it is,' I agreed, and then I recalled the letter that I had received on the tenth.

'He left Guadalupe today,' she continued; 'he will wait in Guaymas for your letter.'

That was all. She crossed the room and passed out of it, not through the window which was quite convenient, but through the solid wall. I sat there for a full minute, staring at the spot where I had last seen her and endeavoring to convince myself that I was dreaming, but I was not dreaming; I was wide awake. In fact I was so wide awake that it was fully an hour before I had successfully wooed Morpheus, as the Victorian writers so neatly expressed it, ignoring the fact that his sex must have made it rather embarrassing for gentlemen writers.

I reached my office a little earlier than usual the following morning, and it is needless to say that the first thing that I did was to search for that letter which I had received on the tenth. I could recall neither the name of the writer nor the point of origin of the letter, but my secretary recalled the latter, the letter having been sufficiently out of the ordinary to attract his attention.

'It was from somewhere in Mexico,' he said, and as letters of this nature are filed by states and countries, there was now no difficulty in locating it.

You may rest assured that this time I read the letter carefully. It was dated the third and postmarked Guaymas. Guaymas is a seaport in Sonora, on the Gulf of California.

Here is the letter:

My dear Sir:
Being engaged in a venture of great scientific importance, I find it necessary to solicit the assistance (not financial) of someone psychologically harmonious, who is at the same time of sufficient intelligence and culture to appreciate the vast possibilities of my project.

Why I have addressed you I shall be glad to explain in the happy event that a personal interview seems desirable. This can only be ascertained by a test which I shall now explain.

If a female figure in a white shroud enters your bedchamber at midnight on the thirteenth day of this month answer this letter; otherwise, do not. If she speaks to you, please remember her words and repeat them to me when you write.

Assuring you of my appreciation of your earnest consideration of this letter, which I realize is rather unusual, and begging that you hold its contents in strictest confidence until future events shall have warranted its publication, I am, Sir,
Very respectfully yours,

CARSON NAPIER

'It looks to me like another nut,' commented Rothmund.

'So it did to me on the tenth,' I agreed; 'but today is the fourteenth, and now it looks like another story.'

'What has the fourteenth got to do with it?' he demanded.

'Yesterday was the thirteenth,' I reminded him.

'You don't mean to tell me –' he started, skeptically.

'That is just what I do mean to tell you,' I interrupted. 'The lady came, I saw, she conquered.'

Ralph looked worried. 'Don't forget what your nurse told you after your last operation,' he reminded me.

'Which nurse? I had nine, and no two of them told me the same things.'

'Jerry. She said that narcotics often affected a patient's mind for months afterward.' His tone was solicitous.

'Well, at least Jerry admitted that I had a mind, which some of the others didn't. Anyway, it didn't affect my eyesight; I saw what I saw. Please take a letter to Mr Napier.'

A few days later I received a telegram from Napier dated Guaymas.

'LETTER RECEIVED STOP THANKS STOP SHALL CALL ON YOU TOMORROW,' it read.

'He must be flying,' I commented.

'Or coming in a white shroud,' suggested Ralph. 'I think I'll phone Captain Hodson to send a squad car around here; sometimes these nuts are dangerous.' He was still skeptical.

I must admit that we both awaited the arrival of Carson Napier with equal interest. I think Ralph expected to see a wild-eyed maniac. I could not visualize the man at all.

About eleven o'clock the following morning Ralph came into my study. 'Mr Napier is here,' he said.

'Does his hair grow straight out from his scalp, and do the whites of his eyes show all around the irises?' I inquired, smiling.

'No,' replied Ralph, returning the smile; 'he is a very fine looking man, but,' he added, 'I still think he's a nut.'

'Ask him to come in,' and a moment later Ralph ushered in an exceptionally handsome man whom I judged to be somewhere between twenty-five and thirty years old, though he might have been even younger.

He came forward with extended hand as I rose to greet him, a smile lighting his face; and after the usual exchange of banalities he came directly to the point of his visit.

'To get the whole picture clearly before you,' he commenced, 'I shall have to tell you something about myself. My father was a British army officer, my mother an American girl from Virginia. I was born in India while my father was stationed there, and brought up under the tutorage of an old Hindu who was much attached to my father and mother. This Chand Kabi was something of a mystic, and he taught me many things that are not in the curriculums of schools for boys under ten. Among them was telepathy, which he had cultivated to such a degree that he could converse with one in psychological harmony with himself quite as easily at great distances as when face to face. Not only that, but he could project mental images to great distances, so that the recipient of his thought waves could see what Chand Kabi was seeing, or whatever else Chand Kabi wished him to see. These things he taught me.'

'And it was thus you caused me to see my midnight visitor on the thirteenth?' I inquired.

He nodded. 'That test was necessary in order to ascertain if we were in psychological harmony. Your letter, quoting the exact words that I had caused the apparition to appear to speak, convinced me that I had at last found the person for whom I have been searching for some time.

'But to get on with my story. I hope I am not boring you, but I feel that it is absolutely necessary that you should have full knowledge of my antecedents and background in order that you may decide whether I am worthy of your confidence and assistance, or not.' I assured him that I was far from being bored, and he proceeded.

'I was not quite eleven when my father died and my mother brought me to America. We went to Virginia first and lived there for three years with my mother's grandfather, Judge John Carson, with whose name and reputation you are doubtless familiar, as who is not?

'After the grand old man died, mother and I came to California, where I attended public schools and later entered a small college at Claremont, which is noted for its high scholastic standing and the superior personnel of both its faculty and student body.

'Shortly after my graduation the third and greatest tragedy of my life occurred – my mother died. I was absolutely stunned by this blow. Life seemed to hold no further interest for me. I did not care to live, yet I would not take my own life. As an alternative I embarked upon a life of recklessness. With a certain goal in mind, I learned to fly. I changed my name and became a stunt man in pictures.

'I did not have to work. Through my mother I had inherited a considerable fortune from my great-grandfather, John Carson; so great a fortune that only a spendthrift could squander the income. I mention this only because the venture I am undertaking requires considerable capital, and I wish you to know that I am amply able to finance it without help.

'Not only did life in Hollywood bore me, but here in Southern California were too many reminders of the loved one I had lost. I determined to travel, and I did. I flew all over the world. In Germany I became interested in rocket cars and financed several. Here my idea was born. There was nothing original about it except that I intended to carry it to a definite conclusion. I would travel by rocket to another planet.

'My studies had convinced me that of all the planets Mars alone offered presumptive evidence of habitability for creatures similar to ourselves. I was at the same time convinced that if I succeeded in reaching Mars the probability of my being able to return to Earth was remote. Feeling that I must have some reason for embarking upon such a venture, other than selfishness, I determined to seek out someone with whom I could communicate in the event that I succeeded. Subsequently it occurred to me that this might also afford the means for launching a second expedition, equipped to make the return journey, for I had no doubt but that there would be many adventurous spirits ready to undertake such an excursion once I had proved it feasible.

'For over a year I have been engaged in the construction of a gigantic rocket on Guadalupe Island, off the west coast of Lower California. The Mexican government has given me every assistance, and today everything is complete to the last detail. I am ready to start at any moment.'

As he ceased speaking, he suddenly faded from view. The chair in which he had been sitting was empty. There was no one in the room but myself. I was stunned, almost terrified. I recalled what Rothmund had said about the effect of the narcotics upon my mentality. I also recalled that insane people seldom realize that they are insane. Was I insane! Cold sweat broke out upon my forehead and the backs of my hands. I reached toward the buzzer to summon Ralph. There is no question but that Ralph is sane. If he had seen Carson Napier and shown him into my study – what a relief that would be!

But before my finger touched the button Ralph entered the room. There was a puzzled expression on his face. 'Mr Napier is back again,' he said, and then he added, 'I didn't know he had left. I just heard him talking to you.'

I breathed a sigh of relief as I wiped the perspiration from my face and hands; if I was crazy, so was Ralph. 'Bring him in,' I said, 'and this time you stay here.'

When Napier entered there was a questioning look in his eyes. 'Do you fully grasp the situation as far as I have explained it?' he asked, as though he had not been out of the room at all.

'Yes, but –' I started.

'Wait, please,' he requested. 'I know what you are going to say, but let me apologize first and explain. I have not been here before. That was my final test. If you are confident that you saw me and talked to me and can recall what I said to you as I sat outside in my car, then you and I can communicate just as freely and easily when I am on Mars.'

'But,' interjected Rothmund, 'you were here. Didn't I shake hands with you when you came in, and talk to you?'

'You thought you did,' replied Napier.

'Who's loony now?' I inquired inelegantly, but to this day Rothmund insists that we played a trick on him.

'How do you know he's here now, then?' he asked.

'I don't,' I admitted.

'I am, this time,' laughed Napier. 'Let's see; how far had I gotten?'

'You were saying that you were all ready to start, had your rocket set up on Gaudalupe Island,' I reminded him.

'Right! I see you got it all. Now, as briefly as possible, I'll outline what I hope you will find it possible to do for me. I have come to you for several reasons, the more important of which are your interest in Mars, your profession (the results of my experiment must be recorded by an experienced writer), and your reputation for integrity – I have taken the liberty of investigating you most thoroughly. I wish you to record and publish the messages you receive from me and to administer my estate during my absence.'

'I shall be glad to do the former, but I hesitate to accept the responsibility of the latter assignment,' I demurred.

'I have already arranged a trust that will give you ample protection,' he replied, in a manner that precluded further argument. I saw that he was a young man who brooked no obstacles; in fact I think he never admitted the existence of an obstacle. 'As for your remuneration,' he continued, 'you may name your own figure.'

I waved a deprecatory hand. 'It will be a pleasure,' I assured him.

'It may take a great deal of your time,' interjected Ralph, 'and your time is valuable.'

'Precisely,' agreed Napier. 'Mr Rothmund and I will, with your permission, arrange the financial details later.'

'That suits me perfectly,' I said, for I detest business and everything connected with it.

'Now, to get back to the more important and far more interesting phases of our discussion; what is your reaction to the plan as a whole?'

'Mars is a long way from Earth,' I suggested; 'Venus is nine or ten million miles closer, and a million miles are a million miles.'

'Yes, and I would prefer going to Venus,' he replied. 'Enveloped in clouds, its surface forever invisible to man, it presents a mystery that intrigues the imagination; but recent astronomical research suggests conditions there inimical to the support of any such life as we know on Earth. It has been thought by some that, held in the grip of the Sun since the era of her pristine fluidity, she always presents the same face to him, as does the Moon to Earth. If such is the case, the extreme heat of one hemisphere and the extreme cold of the other would preclude life.

'Even if the suggestion of Sir James Jeans is borne out by fact, each of her days and nights is several times as long as ours on Earth, these long nights having a temperature of thirteen degrees below zero, Fahrenheit, and the long days a correspondingly high temperature.'

'Yet even so, life might have adapted itself to such conditions,' I contended; 'man exists in equatorial heat and arctic cold.'

'But not without oxygen,' said Napier. 'St John has estimated that the amount of oxygen above the cloud envelope that surrounds Venus is less than one tenth of one per cent of the terrestrial amount. After all, we have to bow to the superior judgment of such men as Sir James Jeans, who says, "The evidence, for what it is worth, goes to suggest that Venus, the only planet in the solar system outside Mars and the Earth on which life could possibly exist, possesses no vegetation and no oxygen for higher forms of life to breathe," which definitely limits my planetary exploration to Mars.'

We discussed his plans during the remainder of the day and well into the night, and early the following morning he left for Guadalupe Island in his Sikorsky amphibian. I have not seen him since, at least in person, yet, through the marvellous medium of telepathy, I have communicated with him continually and seen him amid strange, unearthly surroundings that have been graphically photographed upon the retina of my mind's eye. Thus I am the medium through which the remarkable adventures of Carson Napier are being recorded on Earth; but I am only that, like a typewriter or a Dictaphone – the story that follows is his.

II

Off For Mars

As I set my ship down in the sheltered cove along the shore of desolate Guadalupe a trifle over four hours after I left *Tarzana*, the little Mexican steamer I had chartered to transport my men, materials, and supplies from the mainland rode peacefully at anchor in the tiny harbor, while on the shore, waiting to welcome me, were grouped the laborers, mechanics, and assistants who had worked with such wholehearted loyalty for long months in preparation for this day. Towering head and shoulders above the others loomed Jimmy Welsh, the only American among them.

I taxied in close to shore and moored the ship to a buoy, while the men launched a dory and rowed out to get me. I had been absent less than a week, most of which had been spent in Guaymas awaiting the expected letter from Tarzana, but so exuberantly did they greet me, one might have thought me a long-lost brother returned from the dead, so dreary and desolate and isolated is Guadalupe to those who must remain upon her lonely shores for even a brief interval between contacts with the mainland.

Perhaps the warmth of their greeting may have been enhanced by a desire to conceal their true feelings. We had been together constantly for months, warm friendships had sprung up between us, and tonight we were to separate with little likelihood that they and I should ever meet again. This was to be my last day on Earth; after today I should be as dead to them as though three feet of Earth covered my inanimate corpse.

It is possible that my own sentiments colored my interpretation of theirs, for I am frank to confess that I had been apprehending this last moment as the most difficult of the whole adventure. I have come in contact with the peoples of many countries, but I recall none with more lovable qualities than Mexicans who have not been contaminated by too close contact with the intolerance and commercialism of Americans. And then there was Jimmy Welsh! It was going to be like parting with a brother when I said goodbye to him. For months he had been begging to go with me; and I knew that he would continue to beg up to the last minute, but I could not risk a single life unnecessarily.

We all piled into the trucks that we had used to transport supplies and materials from the shore to the camp, which lay inland a few miles, and bumped over our makeshift road to the little table-land where the giant torpedo lay upon its mile long track.

'Everything is ready,' said Jimmy. 'We polished off the last details this morning. Every roller on the track has been inspected by at least a dozen men, we towed the old crate back and forth over the full length of the track three times with the truck, and then repacked all the rollers with grease. Three of us have checked over every item of equipment and supplies individually; we've done about everything but fire the rockets; and now we're ready to go – you *are* going to take me along, aren't you, Car?'

I shook my head. 'Please don't, Jimmy,' I begged; 'I have a perfect right to gamble with my own life, but not with yours; so forget it. But I am going to do something for you,' I added, 'just as a token of my appreciation of the help you've given me and all that sort of rot. I'm going to give you my ship to remember me by.'

He was grateful, of course, but still he could not hide his disappointment in not being allowed to accompany me, which was evidenced by an invidious comparison he drew between the ceiling of the Sikorsky and that of the old crate, as he had affectionately dubbed the great torpedolike rocket that was to bear me out into space in a few hours.

'A thirty-five million mile ceiling,' he mourned dolefully; 'think of it! Mars for a ceiling!'

'And may I hit the ceiling!' I exclaimed, fervently.

The laying of the track upon which the torpedo was to take off had been the subject of a year of calculation and consultation. The day of departure had been planned far ahead and the exact point at which Mars would rise above the eastern horizon on that night calculated, as well as the time; then it was necessary to make allowances for the rotation of the Earth and the attraction of the nearer heavenly bodies. The track was then laid in accordance with these calculations. It was constructed with a very slight drop in the first three quarters of a mile and then rose gradually at an angle of two and one half degrees from horizontal.

A speed of four and one half miles per second at the take-off would be sufficient to neutralize gravity; to overcome it, I must attain a speed of 6.93 miles per second. To allow a sufficient factor of safety I had powered the torpedo to attain a speed of seven miles per second at the end of the runway, which I purposed stepping up to ten miles per second while passing through the Earth's atmosphere. What my speed would be through space was problematical, but I based all my calculations on the theory that it would not deviate much from the speed at which I left the Earth's atmosphere, until I came within the influence of the gravitational pull of Mars.

The exact instant at which to make the start had also caused me considerable anxiety. I had calculated it again and again, but there were so many factors to be taken into consideration that I had found it expedient to have my figures checked and rechecked by a well-known physicist and an equally prominent astronomer. Their deductions tallied perfectly with mine – the torpedo must start upon its journey toward Mars some time before the red planet rose above the eastern horizon. The trajectory would be along a constantly flattening arc, influenced considerably at first by the Earth's gravitational pull, which would decrease inversely as the square of the distance attained. As the torpedo left the Earth's surface on a curved tangent, its departure must be so nicely timed that when it eventually escaped the pull of the Earth its nose would be directed toward Mars.

On paper, these figures appeared most convincing; but, as the moment approached for my departure, I must confess to a sudden realization that they were based wholly upon theory, and I was struck with the utter folly of my mad venture.

For a moment I was aghast. The enormous torpedo, with its sixty tons, lying there at the end of its mile long track, loomed above me, the semblance of a gargantuan coffin – my coffin, in which I was presently to be dashed to Earth, or to the bottom of the Pacific, or cast out into space to wander there to the end of time. I was afraid. I admit it, but it was not so much the fear of death as the effect of the sudden realization of the stupendousness of the cosmic forces against which I had pitted my puny powers that temporarily unnerved me.

Then Jimmy spoke to me. 'Let's have a last look at things inside the old crate before you shove off,' he suggested, and my nervousness and my apprehensions vanished beneath the spell of his quiet tones and his matter-of-fact manner. I was myself again.

Together we inspected the cabin where are located the controls, a wide and comfortable berth, a table, a chair, writing materials, and a well-stocked bookshelf. Behind the cabin is a small galley and just behind the galley a storeroom containing canned and dehydrated foods sufficient to last me a year. Back of this is a small battery room containing storage batteries for lighting, heating, and cooking, a dynamo, and a gas engine. The extreme stern compartment is filled with rockets and the intricate mechanical device by which they are fed to the firing chambers by means of the controls in the cabin. Forward of the main cabin is a large compartment in which are located the water and oxygen tanks, as well as a quantity of odds and ends necessary either to my safety or comfort.

Everything, it is needless to say, is fastened securely against the sudden and terrific stress that must accompany the take-off. Once out in space, I anticipate no sense of motion, but the start is going to be rather jarring. To absorb, as much as possible, the shock of the take-off, the rocket consists of two torpedoes, a smaller torpedo within a larger one, the former considerably shorter than the latter and consisting of several sections, each one comprising one of the compartments I have described. Between the inner and outer shells and between each two compartments is installed a system of ingenious hydraulic shock absorbers designed to more or less gradually overcome the inertia of the inner torpedo during the take-off. I trust that it functions properly.

In addition to these precautions against disaster at the start, the chair in which I shall sit before the controls is not only heavily overstuffed but is secured to a track or framework that is equipped with shock absorbers. Furthermore, there are means whereby I may strap myself securely into the chair before taking off.

I have neglected nothing essential to my safety, upon which depends the success of my project.

Following our final inspection of the interior, Jimmy and I clambered to the top of the torpedo for a last inspection of the parachutes, which I hope will sufficiently retard the speed of the rocket after it enters the atmosphere of Mars to permit me to bail out with my own parachute in time to make a safe landing. The main parachutes are in a series of compartments running the full length of the top of the torpedo. To explain them more clearly, I may say that they are a continuous series of batteries of parachutes, each battery consisting of a number of parachutes of increasing diameter from the uppermost, which is the smallest. Each battery is in an individual compartment, and each compartment is covered at the will of the operator by controls in the cabin. Each parachute is anchored to the torpedo by a separate cable. I expect about one half of them to be torn loose while checking the speed of the torpedo sufficiently to permit the others to hold and further retard it to a point where I may safely open the doors and jump with my own parachute and oxygen tank.

The moment for departure was approaching. Jimmy and I had descended to the ground and the most difficult ordeal now faced me – that of saying goodbye to these loyal friends and co-workers. We did not say much, we were too filled with emotion, and there was not a dry eye among us. Without exception none of the Mexican laborers could understand why the nose of the torpedo was not pointed straight up in the air if my intended destination were *Marte*. Nothing could convince them that I would not shoot out a short distance and make a graceful nose dive into the Pacific – that is, if I started at all, which many of them doubted.

There was a handclasp all around, and then I mounted the ladder leaning against the side of the torpedo and entered it. As I closed the door of the outer shell, I saw my friends piling into the trucks and pulling away, for I had given orders that no one should be within a mile of the rocket when I took off, fearing, as I did, the effect upon them of the terrific explosions that must accompany the take-off. Securing the outer door with its great vaultlike bolts, I closed the inner door and fastened it; then I took my seat before the controls and buckled the straps that held me to the chair.

I glanced at my watch. It lacked nine minutes of the zero hour. In nine minutes I should be on my way out into the great void, or in nine minutes I should be dead. If all did not go well, the disaster would follow within a fraction of a split second after I touched the first firing control.

Seven minutes! My throat felt dry and parched; I wanted a drink of water, but there was no time.

Four minutes! Thirty-five million miles are a lot of miles, yet I planned on spanning them in between forty and forty-five days.

Two minutes! I inspected the oxygen gauge and opened the valve a trifle wider.

One minute! I thought of my mother and wondered if she were way out there somewhere waiting for me.

Thirty seconds! My hand was on the control. Fifteen seconds! Ten, five, four, three, two–one!

I turned the pointer! There was a muffled roar. The torpedo leaped forward. I was off!

I knew that the take-off was a success. I glanced through the port at my side at the instant that the torpedo started, but so terrific was its initial speed that I saw only a confused blur as the landscape rushed past. I was thrilled and delighted by the ease and perfection with which the take-off had been accomplished, and I must admit that I was not a little surprised by the almost negligible effects that were noticeable in the cabin. I had had the sensation as of a giant hand pressing me suddenly back against the upholstery of my chair, but that had passed almost at once, and now there was no sensation different from that which one might experience sitting in an easy chair in a comfortable drawing-room on terra firma.

There was no sensation of motion after the first few seconds that were required to pass through the Earth's atmosphere, and now that I had done all that lay within my power to do, I could only leave the rest to momentum, gravitation, and fate. Releasing the straps that held me to the chair, I moved about the cabin to look through the various ports, of which there were several in the sides, keel, and top of the torpedo. Space was a black void dotted with countless points of light. The Earth I could not see, for it lay directly astern; far ahead was Mars. All seemed well. I switched on the electric lights, and seating myself at the table, made the first entries in the log; then I checked over various computations of time and distances.

My calculations suggested that in about three hours from the take-off the torpedo would be moving almost directly toward Mars; and from time to time I took observations through the wide-angle telescopic periscope that is mounted flush with the upper surface of the torpedo's shell, but the results were not entirely reassuring. In two hours Mars was dead ahead – the arc of the trajectory was not flattening as it should. I became apprehensive. What was wrong? Where had our careful computations erred?

I left the periscope and gazed down through the main keel port. Below and ahead was the Moon, a gorgeous spectacle as viewed through the clear void of space from a distance some seventy-two thousand miles less than I had ever seen it before and with no Earthly atmosphere to reduce visibility. Tycho, Plato, and Copernicus stood out in bold relief upon the brazen disc of the great satellite, deepening by contrast the shadows of Mare Serenitatis and Mare Tranquilitatis. The rugged peaks of the Apennine and the Altai lay revealed as distinctly as I had ever seen them through the largest telescope. I was thrilled, but I was distinctly worried, too.

Three hours later I was less than fifty-nine thousand miles from the Moon; where its aspect had been gorgeous before, it now beggared description, but my apprehension had cause to increase in proportion; I might say, as the square of its increasing gorgeousness. Through the periscope I had watched the arc of my trajectory pass through the plane of Mars and drop below it. I knew quite definitely then that I could never reach my goal. I tried not to think of the fate that lay ahead of me; but, instead, sought to discover the error that had wrought this disaster.

For an hour I checked over various calculations, but could discover nothing that might shed light on the cause of my predicament; then I switched off the lights and looked down through the keel port to have a closer view of the Moon. It was not there! Stepping to the port side of the cabin, I looked through one of the heavy circular glasses out into the void of space. For an instant I was horror stricken; apparently just off the port bow loomed an enormous world. It was the Moon, less than twenty-three thousand miles away, and I was hurtling toward it at the rate of thirty-six thousand miles an hour!

I leaped to the periscope, and in the next few seconds I accomplished some lightning mental calculating that must constitute an all-time record. I watched the deflection of our course in the direction of the Moon, following it across the lens of the periscope, I computed the distance to the Moon and the speed of the torpedo, and I came to the conclusion that I had better than a fighting chance of missing the great orb. I had little fear of anything but a direct hit, since our speed was so great that the attraction of the Moon could not hold us if we missed her even by a matter of feet; but it was quite evident that it had affected our flight, and with this realization came the answer to the question that had been puzzling me.

To my mind flashed the printer's story of the first perfect book. It had been said that no book had ever before been published containing not a single error. A great publishing house undertook to publish such a book. The galley proofs were read and reread by a dozen different experts, the page proofs received the same careful scrutiny. At last the masterpiece was ready for the press – errorless! It was printed and bound and sent out to the public, and then it was discovered that the title had been misspelled on the title page. With all our careful calculation, with all our checking and rechecking, we had overlooked the obvious; we had not taken the Moon into consideration at all.

Explain it if you can; I cannot. It was just one of those things, as people say when a good team loses to a poor one; it was a *break*, and a bad one. How bad it was I did not even try to conjecture at the time; I just sat at the periscope watching the Moon racing toward us. As we neared it, it presented the most gorgeous spectacle that I have ever witnessed. Each mountain peak and crater stood out in vivid detail. Even the great height of summits over twenty-five thousand feet appeared distinguishable to me, though imagination must have played a major part in the illusion, since I was looking down upon them from above.

Suddenly I realized that the great sphere was passing rapidly from the field of the periscope, and I breathed a sigh of relief – we were not going to score a clean hit, we were going to pass by.

I returned then to the porthole. The Moon lay just ahead and a little to the left. It was no longer a great sphere; it was a world that filled my whole range of vision. Against its black horizon I saw titanic peaks; below me huge craters yawned. I stood with God on high and looked down upon a dead world.

Our transit of the Moon required a little less than four minutes; I timed it carefully that I might check our speed. How close we came I may only guess; perhaps five thousand feet above the tallest peaks, but it was close enough. The pull of the Moon's gravitation had definitely altered our course, but owing to our speed we had eluded her clutches. Now we were racing away from her, but to what?

The nearest star, Alpha Centauri, is twenty-five and a half million million miles from Earth. Write that on your type-writer – 25,500,000,000,000 miles. But why trifle with short distances like this? There was little likelihood that I should visit Alpha Centauri with all the wide range of space at my command and many more interesting places to go. I knew that I had ample room in which to wander, since science has calculated the diameter of space to be eighty-four thousand million light years, which, when one reflects that light travels at the rate of one hundred eighty-six thousand miles a second, should satisfy the wanderlust of the most inveterate roamer.

However, I was not greatly concerned with any of these distances, as I had food and water for only a year, during which time the torpedo might travel slightly more than three hundred fifteen million miles. Even if it reached our near neighbor, Alpha Centauri, I should not then be greatly interested in the event, as I should have been dead for over eighty thousand years. Such is the immensity of the universe!

During the next twenty-four hours the course of the torpedo nearly paralleled the Moon's orbit around the Earth. Not only had the pull of the Moon deflected its course, but now it seemed evident that the Earth had seized us and that we were doomed to race through eternity around her, a tiny, second satellite. But I did not wish to be a moon, certainly not an insignificant moon that in all probability might not be picked up by even the largest telescope.

The next month was the most trying of my life. It seems the height of egotism even to mention my life in the face of the stupendous cosmic forces that engulfed it; but it was the only life I had and I was fond of it, and the more imminent seemed the moment when it should be snuffed out, the better I liked it.

At the end of the second day it was quite apparent that we had eluded the grip of the Earth. I cannot say that I was elated at the discovery. My plan to visit Mars was ruined. I should have been glad to return to Earth. If I could have landed safely on Mars, I certainly could have landed safely on Earth. But there was another reason why I should have been glad to have returned to Earth, a reason that loomed, large and terrible, ahead – the Sun. We were heading straight for the Sun now. Once in the grip of that mighty power, nothing could affect our destiny; we were doomed. For three months I must await the inevitable end, before plunging into that fiery furnace. Furnace is an inadequate word by which to suggest the Sun's heat, which is reputedly from thirty to sixty million degrees at the center, a fact which should not have concerned me greatly, since I did not anticipate reaching the center.

The days dragged on, or, I should say, the long night – there were no days, other than the record that I kept of the passing hours. I read a great deal. I made no entries in the log. Why write something that was presently to be plunged into the Sun and consumed? I experimented in the galley, attempting fancy cooking. I ate a great deal; it helped to pass the time away, and I enjoyed my meals.

On the thirtieth day I was scanning space ahead when I saw a gorgeous, shimmering crescent far to the right of our course; but I must confess that I was not greatly interested in sights of any sort. In sixty days I should be in the Sun. Long before that, however, the increasing heat would have destroyed me. The end was approaching rapidly.

III

Rushing Toward Venus

The psychological effects of an experience such as that through which I had been passing must be considerable, and even though they could be neither weighed nor measured, I was yet conscious of changes that had taken place in me because of them. For thirty days I had been racing alone through space toward absolute annihilation, toward an end that would probably not leave a single nucleus of the atoms that compose me an electron to carry on with, I had experienced the ultimate in solitude, and the result had been to deaden my sensibilities; doubtless a wise provision of nature.

Even the realization that the splendid crescent, looming enormously off the starboard bow of the torpedo, was Venus failed to excite me greatly. What if I were to approach Venus more closely than any other human being of all time! It meant nothing. Were I to see God himself, even that would mean nothing. It became apparent that the value of what we see is measurable only by the size of our prospective audience. Whatever I saw, who might never have an audience, was without value.

Nevertheless, more to pass away the time than because I was particularly interested in the subject, I began to make some rough calculations. These indicated that I was about eight hundred sixty-five thousand miles from the orbit of Venus and that I should cross it in about twenty-four hours. I could not, however, compute my present distance from the planet accurately. I only knew that it appeared very close. When I say close, I mean relatively. The Earth was some twenty-five million miles away, the Sun about sixty-eight million, so that an object as large as Venus, at a distance of one or two million miles, appeared close.

As Venus travels in her orbit at the rate of nearly twenty-two miles per second, or over one million six hundred thousand miles in a terrestrial day, it appeared evident to me that she would cross my path some time within the next twenty-four hours.

It occurred to me that, passing closely, as was unavoidable, she might deflect the course of the torpedo and save me from the Sun; but I knew this to be a vain hope. Undoubtedly, the path of the torpedo would be bent, but the Sun would not relinquish his prey. With these thoughts, my apathy returned, and I lost interest in Venus.

Selecting a book, I lay down on my bed to read. The interior of the cabin was brightly illuminated. I am extravagant with electricity. I have the means of generating it for eleven more months; but I shall not need it after a few weeks, so why should I be parsimonious?

I read for a few hours, but as reading in bed always makes me sleepy, I eventually succumbed. When I awoke, I lay for a few minutes in luxurious ease. I might be racing toward extinction at the rate of thirty-six thousand miles an hour, but I, myself, was unhurried. I recalled the beautiful spectacle that Venus had presented when I had last observed her and decided to have another look at her. Stretching languorously, I arose and stepped to one of the starboard portholes.

The picture framed by the casing of that circular opening was gorgeous beyond description. Apparently less than half as far away as before, and twice as large, loomed the mass of Venus outlined by an aureole of light where the Sun, behind her, illuminated her cloudy envelope and lighted to burning brilliance a thin crescent along the edge nearest me.

I looked at my watch. Twelve hours had passed since I first discovered the planet, and now, at last, I became excited. Venus was apparently half as far away as it had been twelve hours ago, and I knew that the torpedo had covered half the distance that had separated us from her orbit at that time. A collision was possible, it even seemed within the range of probability that I should be dashed to the surface of this inhospitable, lifeless world.

Well, what of it? Am I not already doomed? What difference can it make to me if the end comes a few weeks sooner than I had anticipated? Yet I was excited. I cannot say that I felt fear. I have no fear of death – that left me when my mother died; but now that the great adventure loomed so close I was overwhelmed by contemplation of it and the great wonder that it induced. What would follow?

The long hours dragged on. It seemed incredible to me, accustomed though I am to thinking in units of terrific speed, that the torpedo and Venus were racing toward the same point in her orbit at such inconceivable velocities, the one at the rate of thirty-six thousand miles per hour, the other at over sixty-seven thousand.

It was now becoming difficult to view the planet through the side port, as she moved steadily closer and closer to our path. I went to the periscope – she was gliding majestically within its range. I knew that at that moment the torpedo was less than thirty-six thousand miles, less than an hour, from the path of the planet's orbit, and there could be no doubt now but that she had already seized us in her grasp. We were destined to make a clean hit. Even under the circumstances I could not restrain a smile at the thought of the marksmanship that this fact revealed. I had aimed at Mars and was about to hit Venus; unquestionably the all-time cosmic record for poor shots.

Even though I did not shrink from death, even though the world's best astronomers have assured us that Venus must be unfitted to support human life, that where her surface is not unutterably hot it is unutterably cold, even though she be oxygenless, as they aver, yet the urge to live that is born with each of us compelled me to make the same preparations to land that I should have had I successfully reached my original goal, Mars.

Slipping into a fleece-lined suit of coveralls, I donned goggles and a fleece-lined helmet; then I adjusted the oxygen tank that was designed to hang in front of me, lest it foul the parachute, and which can be automatically jettisoned in the event that I reach an atmosphere that will support life, for it would be an awkward and dangerous appendage to be cumbered with while landing. Finally, I adjusted my chute.

I glanced at my watch. If my calculations have been correct, we should strike in about fifteen minutes. Once more I returned to the periscope.

The sight that met my eyes was awe inspiring. We were plunging toward a billowing mass of black clouds. It was like chaos on the dawn of creation. The gravitation of the planet had seized us. The floor of the cabin was no longer beneath me – I was standing on the forward bulkhead now; but this condition I had anticipated when I designed the torpedo. We were diving nose on toward the planet. In space there had been neither up nor down, but now there was a very definite down.

From where I stood I could reach the controls, and beside me was the door in the side of the torpedo. I released three batteries of parachutes and opened the door in the wall of the inner torpedo. There was a noticeable jar, as though the parachutes had opened and temporarily checked the speed of the torpedo. This must mean that I had entered an atmosphere of some description and that there was not a second to waste.

With a single movement of a lever I loosed the remaining parachutes; then I turned to the outer door. Its bolts were controlled by a large wheel set in the center of the door and were geared to open quickly and with ease. I adjusted the mouthpiece of the oxygen line across my lips and quickly spun the wheel.

Simultaneously the door flew open and the air pressure within the torpedo shot me out into space. My right hand grasped the rip cord of my chute; but I waited. I looked about for the torpedo. It was racing almost parallel with me, all its parachutes distended above it. Just an instant's glimpse I had of it, and then it dove into the cloud mass and was lost to view; but what a weirdly magnificent spectacle it had presented in that brief instant!

Safe now from any danger of fouling with the torpedo, I jerked the rip cord of my parachute just as the clouds swallowed me. Through my fleece-lined suit I felt the bitter cold; like a dash of ice water the cold clouds slapped me in the face; then, to my relief, the chute opened, and I fell more slowly.

Down, down, down I dropped. I could not even guess the duration, nor the distance. It was very dark and very wet, like sinking into the depths of the ocean without feeling the pressure of the water. My thoughts during those long moments were such as to baffle description. Perhaps the oxygen made me a little drunk; I do not know. I felt exhilarated and intensely eager to solve the great mystery beneath me. The thought that I was about to die did not concern me so much as what I might see before I died. I was about to land on Venus – the first human being in all the world to see the face of the veiled planet.

Suddenly I emerged into a cloudless space; but far below me were what appeared in the darkness to be more clouds, recalling to my mind the often advanced theory of the two cloud envelopes of Venus. As I descended, the temperature rose gradually, but it was still cold.

As I entered the second cloud bank, there was a very noticeable rise in temperature the farther I fell. I shut off the oxygen supply and tried breathing through my nose. By inhaling deeply I discovered that I could take in sufficient oxygen to support life, and an astronomical theory was shattered. Hope flared within me like a beacon on a fog-hid landing field.

As I floated gently downward, I presently became aware of a faint luminosity far below. What could it be? There were many obvious reasons why it could not be sunlight; sunlight would not come from below, and, furthermore, it was night on this hemisphere of the planet. Naturally many weird conjectures raced through my mind. I wondered if this could be the light from an incandescent world, but immediately discarded that explanation as erroneous, knowing that the heat from an incandescent world would long since have consumed me. Then it occurred to me that it might be refracted light from that portion of the cloud envelope illuminated by the Sun, yet if such were the case, it seemed obvious that the clouds about me should be luminous, which they were not.

There seemed only one practical solution. It was the solution that an Earthman would naturally arrive at. Being what I am, a highly civilized creature from a world already far advanced by science and invention, I attributed the source of this light to these twin forces of superior intelligence. I could only account for that faint glow by attributing it to the reflection upon the under side of the cloud mass of artificial light produced by intelligent creatures upon the surface of this world toward which I was slowly settling.

I wondered what these beings would be like, and if my excitement grew as I anticipated the wonders that were soon to be revealed to my eyes, I believe that it was a pardonable excitement, under the circumstances. Upon the threshold of such an adventure who would not have been moved to excitement by contemplation of the experiences awaiting him?

Now I removed the mouthpiece of the oxygen tube entirely and found that I could breathe easily. The light beneath me was increasing gradually. About me I thought I saw vague, dark shapes among the cloud masses. Shadows, perhaps, but of what? I detached the oxygen tank and let it fall. I distinctly heard it strike something an instant after I had released it. Then a shadow loomed darkly beneath me, and an instant later my feet struck something that gave beneath them.

I dropped into a mass of foliage and grasped wildly for support. A moment later I began to fall more rapidly and guessed what had happened; the parachute had been up-tilted by contact with the foliage. I clutched at leaves and branches, fruitlessly, and then I was brought to a sudden stop; evidently the chute had fouled something. I hoped that it would hold until I found a secure resting place.

As I groped about in the dark, my hand finally located a sturdy branch, and a moment later I was astride it, my back to the bole of a large tree – another theory gone the ignoble path of countless predecessors; it was evident that there was vegetation on Venus. At least there was one tree; I could vouch for that, as I was sitting in it, and doubtless the black shadows I had passed were other, taller trees.

Having found secure lodgment, I divested myself of my parachute after salvaging some of its ropes and the straps from the harness, which I thought I might find helpful in descending the tree. Starting at the top of a tree, in darkness and among clouds, one may not be positive what the tree is like nearer the ground. I also removed my goggles. Then I commenced to descend. The girth of the tree was enormous, but the branches grew sufficiently close together to permit me to find safe footing.

I did not know how far I had fallen through the second cloud stratum before I lodged in the tree nor how far I had descended the tree, but all together it must have been close to two thousand feet; yet I was still in the clouds. Could the entire atmosphere of Venus be forever fog laden? I hoped not, for it was a dreary prospect.

The light from below had increased a little as I descended, but not much; it was still dark about me. I continued to descend. It was tiresome work and not without danger, this climbing down an unfamiliar tree in a fog, at night, toward an unknown world. But I could not remain where I was, and there was nothing above to entice me upward; so I continued to descend.

What a strange trick fate had played me. I had wanted to visit Venus, but had discarded the idea when assured by my astronomer friends that the planet could not support either animal or vegetable life. I had started for Mars, and now, fully ten days before I had hoped to reach the red planet, I was on Venus, breathing perfectly good air among the branches of a tree that evidently dwarfed the giant Sequoias.

The illumination was increasing rapidly now, the clouds were thinning; through breaks I caught glimpses far below, glimpses of what appeared to be an endless vista of foliage, softly moonlit – but Venus had no moon. In that, insofar as the seeming moonlight was concerned, I could fully concur with the astronomers. This illumination came from no moon, unless Venus's satellite lay beneath her inner envelope of clouds, which was preposterous.

A moment later I emerged entirely from the cloud bank, but though I searched in all directions, I saw nothing but foliage, above, around, below me, yet I could see far down into that abyss of leaves. In the soft light I could not determine the color of the foliage, but I was sure that it was not green; it was some light, delicate shade of another color.

I had descended another thousand feet since I had emerged from the clouds, and I was pretty well exhausted (the month of inactivity and overeating had softened me), when I saw just below me what appeared to be a causeway leading from the tree I was descending to another adjacent. I also discovered that from just below where I clung the limbs had been cut away from the tree to a point below the causeway. Here were two startling and unequivocal evidences of the presence of intelligent beings. Venus was inhabited! But by what? What strange, arboreal creatures built causeways high among these giant trees? Were they a species of monkey-man? Were they of a high or low order of intelligence? How would they receive me?

At this juncture in my vain speculations I was startled by a noise above me. Something was moving in the branches overhead. The sound was coming nearer, and it seemed to me that it was being made by something of considerable size and weight, but perhaps, I realized, that conjecture was the child of my imagination. However, I felt most uncomfortable. I was unarmed. I have never carried weapons. My friends had urged a perfect arsenal upon me before I embarked upon my adventure, but I had argued that if I arrived on Mars unarmed it would be *prima facie* evidence of my friendly intentions, and even if my reception were warlike, I should be no worse off, since I could not hope, single-handed, to conquer a world, no matter how well armed I were.

Suddenly, above me, to the crashing of some heavy body through the foliage were added hideous screams and snarls; and in the terrifying dissonance I recognized the presence of more than a single creature. Was I being pursued by all the fearsome denizens of this Venusan forest!

Perhaps my nerves were slightly unstrung; and who may blame them if they were, after what I had passed through so recently and during the long, preceding month? They were not entirely shattered, however, and I could still appreciate the fact that night noises often multiply themselves in a most disconcerting way. I have heard coyotes yapping and screaming around my camp on Arizona nights when, but for the actual knowledge that there were but one or two of them, I could have sworn that there were a hundred, had I trusted only to my sense of hearing.

But in this instance I was quite positive that the voices of more than a single beast were mingling to produce the horrid din that, together with the sound of their passage, was definitely and unquestionably drawing rapidly nearer me. Of course I did not know that the owners of those awesome voices were pursuing me, though a still, small voice within seemed to be assuring me that such was the fact.

I wished that I might reach the causeway below me (I should feel better standing squarely on two feet), but it was too far to drop and there were no more friendly branches to give me support; then I thought of the ropes I had salvaged from the abandoned parachute. Quickly uncoiling them from about my waist, I looped one of them over the branch upon which I sat, grasped both strands firmly in my hands, and prepared to swing from my porch. Suddenly the screams and snarling growls ceased; and then, close above me now, I heard the noise of something descending toward me and saw the branches shaking to its weight.

Lowering my body from the branch, I swung downward and slid the fifteen or more feet to the causeway, and as I alighted the silence of the great forest was again shattered by a hideous scream just above my head. Looking up quickly, I saw a creature launching itself toward me and just beyond it a snarling face of utter hideousness. I caught but the briefest glimpse of it – just enough to see that it was a face, with eyes and a mouth – then it was withdrawn amidst the foliage.

Perhaps I only sensed that hideous vision subconsciously at the time, for the whole scene was but a flash upon the retina of my eye, and the other beast was in mid-air above me at the instant; but it remained indelibly impressed upon my memory, and I was to recall it upon a later day under circumstances so harrowing that the mind of mortal Earthman may scarce conceive them.

As I leaped back to avoid the creature springing upon me, I still clung to one strand of the rope down which I had lowered myself to the causeway. My grasp upon the rope was unconscious and purely mechanical; it was in my hand, and my fist was clenched; and as I leaped away, I dragged the rope with me. A fortuitous circumstance, no doubt, but a most fortunate one.

The creature missed me, alighting on all fours a few feet from me, and there it crouched, apparently slightly bewildered, and, fortunately for me, it did not immediately charge, giving me the opportunity to collect my wits and back slowly away, at the same time mechanically coiling the rope in my right hand. The little, simple things one does in moments of stress or excitement often seem entirely beyond reason and incapable of explanation; but I have thought that they may be dictated by a subconscious mind reacting to the urge of self-preservation. Possibly they are not always well directed and may as often fail to be of service as not, but then it may be possible that subconscious minds are no less fallible than the objective mind, which is wrong far more often than it is right. I cannot but seek for some explanation of the urge that caused me to retain that rope, since, all unknown to me, it was to be the slender thread upon which my life was to hang.

Silence had again descended upon the weird scene. Since the final scream of the hideous creature that had retreated into the foliage after this thing had leaped for me, there had been no sound. The creature that crouched facing me seemed slightly bewildered. I am positive now that it had not been pursuing me, but that it itself had been the object of pursuit by the other beast that had retreated.

In the dim half-light of the Venusan night I saw confronting me a creature that might be conjured only in the half-delirium of some horrid nightmare. It was about as large as a full-grown puma, and stood upon four handlike feet that suggested that it might be almost wholly arboreal. The front legs were much longer than the hind, suggesting, in this respect, the hyena; but here the similarity ceased, for the creature's furry pelt was striped longitudinally with alternate bands of red and yellow, and its hideous head bore no resemblance to any Earthly animal. No external ears were visible, and in the low forehead was a single large, round eye at the end of a thick antenna about four inches long. The jaws were powerful and armed with long, sharp fangs, while from either side of the neck projected a powerful chela. Never have I seen a creature so fearsomely armed for offense as was this nameless beast of another world. With those powerful crablike pincers it could easily have held an opponent far stronger than a man and dragged it to those terrible jaws.

For a time it eyed me with that single, terrifying eye that moved to and fro at the end of its antenna, and all the time its chelae were waving slowly, opening and closing. In that brief moment of delay I looked about me, and the first thing that I discovered was that I stood directly in front of an opening cut in the bole of the tree; an opening about three feet wide and over six feet high. But the most remarkable thing about it was that it was closed by a door; not a solid door, but one suggesting a massive wooden grill.

As I stood contemplating it and wondering what to do, I thought that I saw something moving behind it. Then a voice spoke to me out of the darkness beyond the door. It sounded like a human voice, though it spoke in a language that I could not understand. The tones were peremptory. I could almost imagine that it said, 'Who are you, and what do you want here in the middle of the night?'

'I am a stranger,' I said. 'I come in peace and friendship.'

Of course I knew that whatever it was behind that door, it could not understand me; but I hoped that my tone would assure it of my peaceful designs. There was a moment's silence and then I heard other voices. Evidently the situation was being discussed; then I saw that the creature facing me upon the causeway was creeping toward me, and turned my attention from the doorway to the beast.

I had no weapons, nothing but a length of futile rope; but I knew that I must do something. I could not stand there supinely and let the creature seize and devour me without striking a blow in my own defense. I uncoiled a portion of the rope and, more in despair than with any hope that I could accomplish anything of a defensive nature, flicked the end of it in the face of the advancing beast. You have seen a boy snap a wet towel at a companion; perhaps you have been flicked in that way, and if you have, you know that it hurts.

Of course I did not expect to overcome my adversary by any such means as this; to be truthful, I did not know what I did expect to accomplish. Perhaps I just felt that I must do something, and this was the only thing that occurred to me. The result merely demonstrated the efficiency of that single eye and the quickness of the chelae. I snapped that rope as a ringmaster snaps a whip; but though the rope end travelled with great speed and the act must have been unexpected, the creature caught the rope in one of its chelae before it reached its face. Then it hung on and sought to drag me toward those frightful jaws.

I learned many a trick of roping from a cowboy friend of my motion picture days, and one of these I now put into use in an endeavor to entangle the crablike chelae. Suddenly giving the rope sufficient slack, I threw a half hitch around the chela that gripped it, immediately following it with a second, whereupon the creature commenced to pull desperately away. I think it was motivated solely by an instinctive urge to pull toward its jaws anything that was held in its chelae; but for how long it would continue to pull away before it decided to change its tactics and charge me, I could not even guess; and so I acted upon a sudden inspiration and hurriedly made fast the end of the rope that I held to one of the stout posts that supported the handrail of the causeway; then, of a sudden, the thing charged me, roaring furiously.

I turned and ran, hoping that I could get out of the reach of those terrible chelae before the creature was stopped by the rope; and this I but barely managed to do. I breathed a sigh of relief as I saw the great body flipped completely over on its back as the rope tautened, but the hideous scream of rage that followed left me cold. Nor was my relief of any great duration, for as soon as the creature had scrambled to its feet, it seized the rope in its other chela and severed it as neatly as one might with a pair of monstrous tinner's snips; and then it was after me again, but this time it did not creep.

It seemed evident that my stay upon Venus was to be brief, when suddenly the door in the tree swung open and three men leaped to the causeway just behind the charging terror that was swiftly driving down upon me. The leading man hurled a short, heavy spear that sank deep into the back of my infuriated pursuer. Instantly the creature stopped in its tracks and wheeled about to face these new and more dangerous tormentors; and as he did so two more spears, hurled by the companions of the first man, drove into his chest, and with a last frightful scream, the thing dropped in its tracks, dead.

Then the leading man came toward me. In the subdued light of the forest he appeared no different from an Earthman. He held the point of a straight, sharp sword pointed at my vitals. Close behind him were the other two men, each with a drawn sword.

The first man spoke to me in a stern, commanding voice, but I shook my head to indicate that I could not understand; then he pressed the point of his weapon against my coveralls, opposite the pit of my stomach, and jabbed. I backed away. He advanced and jabbed at me again, and again I backed along the caseway. Now the other two men advanced and the three of them fell to examining me, mean-while talking among themselves.

I could see them better now. They were about my own height and in every detail of their visible anatomy they appeared identical with terrestrial human beings, nor was a great deal left to my imagination – the men were almost naked. They wore loincloths and little else other than the belts that supported the scabbards of their swords. Their skins appeared to be much darker than mine, but not so dark as a negro's, and their faces were smooth and handsome.

Several times one or another of them addressed me and I always replied, but neither understood what the other said. Finally, after a lengthy discussion, one of them reentered the opening in the tree and a moment later I saw the interior of a chamber, just within the doorway, illuminated; then one of the two remaining men motioned me forward and pointed toward the doorway.

Understanding that he wished me to enter, I stepped forward, and, as I passed them, they kept their sword points against my body – they were tak-ing no chances with me. The other man awaited me in the center of a large room hewn from the interior of the great tree. Beyond him were other door-ways leading from this room, doubtless into other apartments. There were chairs and a table in the room; the walls were carved and painted; there was a large rug upon the floor; from a small vessel depending from the center of the ceiling a soft light illuminated the interior as brightly as might sunlight flooding through an open window, but there was no glare.

The other men had entered and closed the door, which they fastened by a device that was not apparent to me at the time; then one of them pointed to a chair and motioned me to be seated. Under the bright light they examined me intently, and I them. My clothing appeared to puzzle them most; they examined and discussed its material, texture, and weave, if I could judge cor-rectly by their gestures and inflections.

Finding the heat unendurable in my fleece-lined coveralls, I removed them and my leather coat and polo shirt. Each newly revealed article aroused their curiosity and comment. My light skin and blond hair also received their speculative attention.

Presently one of them left the chamber, and while he was absent another removed the various articles that had lain upon the table. These consisted of what I took to be books bound in wooden and in leather covers, several ornaments, and a dagger in a beautifully wrought sheath.

When the man who had left the room returned, he brought food and drink which he placed upon the table; and by signs the three indicated that I might eat. There were fruits and nuts in highly polished, carved wooden bowls; there was something I took to be bread, on a golden platter; and there was honey in a silver jug. A tall, slender goblet contained a whitish liquid that resembled milk. This last receptacle was a delicate, translucent ceramic of an exquisite blue shade. These things and the appointments of the room bespoke culture, refinement, and good taste, making the savage apparel of their owners appear incongruous.

The fruits and nuts were unlike any with which I was familiar, both in appearance and flavor; the bread was coarse but delicious; and the honey, if such it were, suggested candied violets to the taste. The milk (I can find no other Earthly word to describe it) was strong and almost pungent, yet far from unpleasant. I imagined at the time that one might grow to be quite fond of it.

The table utensils were similar to those with which we are familiar in civilized portions of the Earth; there were hollowed instruments with which to dip or scoop, sharp ones with which to cut, and others with tines with which to impale. There was also a handled pusher, which I recommend to Earthly hostesses. All these were of metal.

While I ate, the three men conversed earnestly, one or another of them occasionally offering me more food. They seemed hospitable and courteous, and I felt that if they were typical of the inhabitants of Venus I should find my life here a pleasant one. That it would not be a bed of roses, however, was attested by the weapons that the men constantly wore; one does not carry a sword and a dagger about with him unless he expects to have occasion to use them, except on dress parade.

When I had finished my meal, two of the men escorted me from the room by a rear doorway, up a flight of circular stairs, and ushered me into a small chamber. The stairway and corridor were illuminated by a small lamp similar to that which hung in the room where I had eaten, and light from this lamp shone through the heavy wooden grating of the door, into the room where I was now locked and where my captors left me to my own devices.

Upon the floor was a soft mattress over which were spread coverings of a silky texture. It being very warm, I removed all of my clothing except my undershorts and lay down to sleep. I was tired after my arduous descent of the giant tree and dozed almost immediately. I should have been asleep at once had I not been suddenly startled to wakefulness by a repetition of that hideous scream with which the beast that had pursued me through the tree had announced its rage and chagrin when I had eluded it.

However, it was not long before I fell asleep, my dozing mind filled with a chaos of fragmentary recollections of my stupendous adventure.

IV

To the House of the King

When I awoke, it was quite light in the room, and through a window I saw the foliage of trees, lavender and heliotrope and violet in the light of a new day. I arose and went to the window. I saw no sign of sunlight, yet a brightness equivalent to sunlight pervaded everything. The air was warm and sultry. Below me I could see sections of various causeways extending from tree to tree. On some of these I caught glimpses of people. All the men were naked, except for loincloths, nor did I wonder at their scant apparel, in the light of my experience of the temperatures on Venus. There were both men and women; and all the men were armed with swords and daggers, while the women carried daggers only. All those whom I saw seemed to be of the same age; there were neither children nor old people among them. All appeared comely.

From my barred window I sought a glimpse of the ground, but as far down as I could see there was only the amazing foliage of the trees, lavender, heliotrope and violet. And what trees! From my window I could see several enormous boles fully two hundred feet in diameter. I had thought the tree I descended a giant, but compared with these, it was only a sapling.

As I stood contemplating the scene before me, there was a noise at the door behind me. Turning, I saw one of my captors entering the room. He greeted me with a few words, which I could not understand, and a pleasant smile, that I could. I returned his smile and said, 'Good morning!'

He beckoned me to follow him from the room, but I made signs indicating that I wished to don my clothes first. I knew I should be hot and uncomfortable in them; I was aware that no one I had seen here wore any clothing, yet so powerful are the inhibitions of custom and habit that I shrank from doing the sensible thing and wearing only my undershorts.

At first, when he realized what I wished to do, he motioned me to leave my clothes where they were and come with him as I was; but eventually he gave in with another of his pleasant smiles. He was a man of fine physique, a little shorter than I; by daylight, I could see that his skin was about that shade of brown that a heavy sun tan imparts to people of my own race; his eyes were dark brown, his hair black. His appearance formed a marked contrast to my light skin, blue eyes, and blond hair.

When I had dressed, I followed him downstairs to a room adjoining the one I had first entered the previous night. Here the man's two companions and two women were seated at a table on which were a number of vessels containing food. As I entered the room the women's eyes were turned upon me curiously; the men smiled and greeted me as had their fellow, and one of them motioned me to a chair. The women appraised me frankly but without boldness, and it was evident that they were discussing me freely between themselves and with the men. They were both uncommonly good-looking, their skins being a shade lighter than those of the men, while their eyes and hair were of about the same color as those of their male companions. Each wore a single garment of a silken material similar to that of which my bed cover had been made and in the form of a long sash, which was wrapped tightly around the body below the armpits, confining the breasts. From this point it was carried half way around the body downward to the waist, where it circled the body again, the loose end then passing between the legs from behind and up through the sash in front, after the manner of a G string, the remainder falling in front to the knees.

In addition to these garments, which were beautifully embroidered in colors, the women wore girdles from which depended pocket pouches and sheathed daggers, and both were plentifully adorned with ornaments such as rings, bracelets, and hair ornaments. I could recognize gold and silver among the various materials of which these things were fabricated, and there were others that might have been ivory and coral; but what impressed me most was the exquisite workmanship they displayed, and I imagined that they were valued more for this than for the intrinsic worth of the materials that composed them. That this conjecture might be in accordance with fact was borne out by the presence among their ornaments of several of the finest workmanship, obviously carved from ordinary bone.

On the table was bread different from that which I had had the night before, a dish that I thought might be eggs and meat baked together, several which I could not recognize either by appearance or taste, and the familiar milk and honey that I had encountered before. The foods varied widely in range of flavor, so that it would have been a difficult palate indeed that would not have found something to its liking.

During the meal they engaged in serious discussion, and I was certain from their glances and gestures that I was the subject of their debate. The two girls enlivened the meal by attempting to carry on a conversation with me, which appeared to afford them a great deal of merriment, nor could I help joining in their laughter, so infectious was it. Finally one of them hit upon the happy idea of teaching me their language. She pointed to herself and said, 'Zuro,' and to the other girl and said, 'Alzo'; then the men became interested, and I soon learned that the name of him who seemed to be the head of the house, the man who had first challenged me the preceding night, was Duran, the other two Olthar and Kamlot.

But before I had mastered more than these few words and the names of some of the foods on the table, breakfast was over and the three men had conducted me from the house. As we proceeded along the causeway that passed in front of the house of Duran, the interest and curiosity of those we passed were instantly challenged as their eyes fell upon me; and it was at once evident to me that I was a type either entirely unknown on Venus or at least rare, for my blue eyes and blond hair caused quite as much comment as my clothing, as I could tell by their gestures and the direction of their gaze.

We were often stopped by curious friends of my captors, or hosts (I was not sure yet in which category they fell); but none offered me either harm or insult, and if I were the object of their curious scrutiny, so were they of mine. While no two of them were identical in appearance, they were all handsome and all apparently of about the same age. I saw no old people and no children.

Presently we approached a tree of such enormous diameter that I could scarcely believe the testimony of my eyes when I saw it. It was fully five hundred feet in diameter. Stripped of branches for a hundred feet above and below the causeway, its surface was dotted with windows and doors and encircled by wide balconies or verandas. Before a large and elaborately carved doorway was a group of armed men before whom we halted while Duran addressed one of their number.

I thought at the time that he called this man Tofar, and such I learned later was his name. He wore a necklace from which depended a metal disc bearing a hieroglyphic in relief; otherwise he was not accoutered differently from his companions. As he and Duran conversed, he appraised me carefully from head to feet. Presently he and Duran passed through the doorway into the interior of the tree, while the others continued to examine me and question Kamlot and Olthar.

While I waited there, I embraced the opportunity to study the elaborate carvings that surrounded the portal, forming a frame fully five feet wide. The *motif* appeared historical, and I could easily imagine that the various scenes depicted important events in the life of a dynasty or a nation. The workmanship was exquisite, and it required no stretch of the imagination to believe that each delicately carved face was the portrait of some dead or living celebrity. There was nothing grotesque in the delineation of the various figures, as is so often the case in work of a similar character on Earth, and only the borders that framed the whole and separated contiguous plaques were conventional.

I was still engrossed by these beautiful examples of the wood carver's art when Duran and Tofar returned and motioned Olthar and Kamlot and me to follow them into the interior of the great tree. We passed through several large chambers and along wide corridors, all carved from the wood of the living tree, to the head of a splendid stairway, which we descended to another level. The chambers near the periphery of the tree received their light through windows, while the interior chambers and corridors were illuminated by lamps similar to those I had already seen in the house of Duran.

Near the foot of the stairway we had descended we entered a spacious chamber, before the doorway to which stood two men armed with spears and swords, and before us, across the chamber, we saw a man seated at a table near a large window. Just inside the doorway we halted, my companions standing in respectful silence until the man at the table looked up and spoke to them; then they crossed the room, taking me with them, and halted before the table, upon the opposite side of which the man sat facing us.

He spoke pleasantly to my companions, calling each by name, and when they replied they addressed him as Jong. He was a fine-looking man with a strong face and a commanding presence. His attire was similar to that worn by all the other male Venusans I had seen, differing only in that he wore about his head a fillet that supported a circular metal disc in the center of his forehead. He appeared much interested in me and watched me intently while listening to Duran, who, I had no doubt, was narrating the story of my strange and sudden appearance the night before.

When Duran had concluded, the man called Jong addressed me. His manner was serious, his tones kindly. Out of courtesy, I replied, though I knew that he could understand me no better than I had understood him. He smiled and shook his head; then he fell into a discussion with the others. Finally he struck a metal gong that stood near him on the table; then he arose and came around the table to where I stood. He examined my clothing carefully, feeling its texture and apparently discussing the materials and the weave with the others. Then he examined the skin of my hands and face, felt of my hair, and made me open my mouth that he might examine my teeth. I was reminded of the horse market and the slave block. 'Perhaps,' I thought, 'the latter is more apropos.'

A man entered now whom I took to be a servant and, receiving instructions from the man called Jong, departed again, while I continued to be the object of minute investigation. My beard, which was now some twenty-four hours old, elicited considerable comment. It is not a beautiful beard at any age, being sparse and reddish, for which reason I am careful to shave daily when I have the necessary utensils.

I cannot say that I enjoyed this intimate appraisal, but the manner in which it was conducted was so entirely free from any suggestion of intentional rudeness or discourtesy, and my position here was so delicate that my better judgment prevented me from openly resenting the familiarities of the man called Jong. It is well that I did not.

Presently a man entered through a doorway at my right. I assumed that he had been summoned by the servant recently dispatched. As he came forward, I saw that he was much like the others; a handsome man of about thirty. There are those who declaim against monotony; but for me there can never be any monotony of beauty, not even if the beautiful things were all identical, which the Venusans I had so far seen were not. All were beautiful, but each in his own way.

The man called Jong spoke to the newcomer rapidly for about five minutes, evidently narrating all that they knew about me and giving instructions. When he had finished, the other motioned me to follow him; and a few moments later I found myself in another room on the same level. It had three large windows and was furnished with several desks, tables, and chairs. Most of the available wall space was taken up by shelves on which reposed what I could only assume to be books – thousands of them.

The ensuing three weeks were as delightful and interesting as any that I have ever experienced. During this time, Danus, in whose charge I had been placed, taught me the Venusan language and told me much concerning the planet, the people among whom I had fallen, and their history. I found the language easy to master, but I shall not at this time attempt to describe it fully. The alphabet consists of twenty-four characters, five of which represent vowel sounds, and these are the only vowel sounds that the Venusan vocal chords seem able to articulate. The characters of the alphabet all have the same value, there being no capital letters. Their system of punctuation differs from ours and is more practical; for example, before you start to read a sentence you know whether it is exclamatory, interrogative, a reply to an interrogation, or a simple statement. Characters having values similar to the comma and semicolon are used much as we use these two; they have no colon; their character that functions as does our period follows each sentence, their question mark and exclamation point preceding the sentences the nature of which they determine.

A peculiarity of their language that renders it easy to master is the absence of irregular verbs; the verb root is never altered for voice, mode, tense, number, or person, distinctions that are achieved by the use of several simple, auxiliary words.

While I was learning to speak the language of my hosts, I also learned to read and write it, and I spent many enjoyable hours delving into the large library of which Danus is the curator while my tutor was absent attending to his other duties, which are numerous. He is chief physician and surgeon of his country, physician and surgeon to the king, and head of a college of medicine and surgery.

One of the first questions that Danus had asked me when I had acquired a working knowledge of his language was where I came from, but when I told him I had come from another world more than twenty-six million miles from his familiar Amtor, which is the name by which the Venusans know their world, he shook his head skeptically.

'There is no life beyond Amtor,' he said. 'How can there be life where all is fire?'

'What is your theory of the –' I started, but I had to stop. There is no Amtorian word for universe, neither is there any for sun, moon, star, or planet. The gorgeous heavens that we see are never seen by the inhabitants of Venus, obscured as they perpetually are by the two great cloud envelopes that surround the planet. I started over again. 'What do you believe surrounds Amtor?' I asked.

He stepped to a shelf and returned with a large volume, which he opened at a beautifully executed map of Amtor. It showed three concentric circles. Between the two inner circles lay a circular belt designated as Trabol, which means warm country. Here the boundaries of seas, continents, and islands were traced to the edges of the two circles that bounded it, in some places crossing these boundaries as though marking the spots at which venturesome explorers had dared the perils of an unknown and inhospitable land.

'This is Trabol,' explained Danus, placing a finger upon that portion of the map I have briefly described. 'It entirely surrounds Strabol, which lies in the center of Amtor. Strabol is extremely hot, its land is covered with enormous forests and dense undergrowth, and is peopled by huge land animals, reptiles, and birds, its warm seas swarm with monsters of the deep. No man has ventured far into Strabol and lived to return.

'Beyond Trabol,' he continued, placing his finger on the outer band designated as Karbol (Cold Country), 'lies Karbol. Here it is as cold as Strabol is hot. There are strange animals there too, and adventurers have returned with tales of fierce human beings clothed in fur. But it is an inhospitable land into which there is no occasion to venture and which few dare penetrate far for fear of being precipitated over the rim into the molten sea.'

'Over what rim?' I asked.

He looked at me in astonishment. 'I can well believe that you come from another world when you ask me such questions as you do,' he remarked. 'Do you mean to tell me that you know nothing of the physical structure of Amtor?'

'I know nothing of your theory concerning it,' I replied.

'It is not a theory; it is a fact,' he corrected me gently. 'In no other way may the various phenomena of nature be explained. Amtor is a huge disc with an upturned rim, like a great saucer; it floats upon a sea of molten metal and rock, a fact that is incontrovertibly proved by the gushing forth of this liquid mass occasionally from the summits of mountains, when a hole has been burned in the bottom of Amtor. Karbol, the cold country, is a wise provision of nature that tempers the terrific heat that must constantly surge about the outer rim of Amtor.

'Above Amtor, and entirely surrounding her above the molten sea, is a chaos of fire and flame. From this our clouds protect us. Occasionally there have occurred rifts in the clouds, and at such times the heat from the fires above, when the rifts occurred in the daytime, has been so intense as to wither vegetation and destroy life, while the light that shone through was of blinding intensity. When these rifts occurred at night there was no heat, but we saw the sparks from the fire shining above us.'

I tried to explain the spherical shape of the planets and that Karbol was only the colder country surrounding one of Amtor's poles, while Strabol, the hot country, lay in the equatorial region; that Trabol was merely one of two temperate zones, the other one being beyond the equatorial region, which was a band around the middle of a globe and not, as he supposed, a circular area in the center of a disc. He listened to me politely, but only smiled and shook his head when I had finished.

At first I could not comprehend that a man of such evident intelligence, education, and culture should cling to such a belief as his, but when I stopped to consider the fact that neither he nor any of his progenitors had ever seen the heavens, I began to realize that there could not be much foundation for any other theory, and even theories must have foundations. I also realized, even more than I had before, something of what astronomy has meant to the human race of Earth in the advancement of science and civilization. Could there have been such advancement had the heavens been perpetually hidden from our view? I wonder.

But I did not give up. I drew his attention to the fact that if his theory were correct, the boundary between Trabol and Strabol (the temperate and the equatorial zones) should be much shorter than that separating Trabol from Karbol, the polar region, as was shown on the map, but could not have been proved by actual survey; while my theory would require that the exact oppos- ite be true, which was easily demonstrable and must have been demonstrated if surveys had ever been made, which I judged from the markings on the map to be the case.

He admitted that surveys had been made and that they had shown the apparent discrepancy that I had pointed out, but he explained this ingen- iously by a purely Amtorian theory of the relativity of distance, which he proceeded to elucidate.

'A degree is one thousandth part of the circumference of a circle,' he com- menced. (This is the Amtorian degree, her savants not having had the advantage of a visible sun to suggest another division of the circumference of a circle as did the Babylonians, who hit upon three hundred sixty as being close enough.) 'And no matter what the length of the circumference, it meas- ures just one thousand degrees. The circle which separates Strabol from Trabol is necessarily one thousand degrees in length. You will admit that?'

'Certainly,' I replied.

'Very good! Then, will you admit that the circle which separates Trabol from Karbol measures exactly one thousand degrees?'

I nodded my assent.

'Things which equal the same thing equal each other, do they not? Therefore, the inner and outer boundaries of Trabol are of equal length, and this is true because of the truth of the theory of relativity of distance. The degree is our unit of linear measure. It would be ridiculous to say that the farther one was removed from the center of Amtor the longer the unit of distance became; it only appears to become longer; in relation to the circumference of the circle and in relation to the distance from the center of Amtor it is precisely the same.

'I know,' he admitted, 'that on the map it does not appear to be the same, nor do actual surveys indicate that it is the same; but it must be the same, for if it were not, it is obvious that Amtor would be larger around the closer one approached the center and smallest of all at the perimeter, which is so obviously ridiculous as to require no refutation.

'This seeming discrepancy caused the ancients considerable perturbation until about three thousand years ago, when Klufar, the great scientist, expounded the theory of relativity of distance and demonstrated that the real and apparent measurements of distance could be reconciled by multiplying each by the square root of minus one.'

I saw that argument was useless and said no more; there is no use arguing with a man who can multiply anything by the square root of minus one.

V

The Girl in the Garden

For some time I had been aware that I was in the house of Mintep, the king, and that the country was called Vepaja. Jong, which I had originally thought to be his name, was his title; it is Amtorian for king. I learned that Duran was of the house of Zar and that Olthar and Kamlot were his sons; Zuro, one of the women I had met there, was attached to Duran; the other, Alzo, was attached to Olthar; Kamlot had no woman. I use the word attached partially because it is a reasonably close translation of the Amtorian word for the connection and partially because no other word seems exactly to explain the relationship between these men and women.

They were not married, because the institution of marriage is unknown here. One could not say that they belonged to the men, because they were in no sense slaves or servants, nor had they been acquired by purchase or feat of arms. They had come willingly, following a courtship, and they were free to depart whenever they chose, just as the men were free to depart and seek other connections; but, as I was to learn later, these connections are seldom broken, while infidelity is as rare here as it is prevalent on Earth.

Each day I took exercise on the broad veranda that encircled the tree at the level upon which my apartment was located; at least, I assumed that it encircled the tree, but I did not know, as that portion assigned to me was but a hundred feet long, a fifteenth part of the circumference of the great tree. At each end of my little segment was a fence. The section adjoining mine on the right appeared to be a garden, as it was a mass of flowers and shrubbery growing in soil that must have been brought up from that distant surface of the planet that I had as yet neither set foot upon nor seen. The section on my left extended in front of the quarters of several young officers attached to the household of the king. I call them young because Danus told me they were young, but they appear to be about the same age as all the other Amtorians I have seen. They were pleasant fellows, and after I learned to speak their language we occasionally had friendly chats together.

But in the section at my right I had never seen a human being; and then one day, when Danus was absent and I was walking alone, I saw a girl among the flowers there. She did not see me; and I only caught the briefest glimpse of her, but there was something about her that made me want to see her again, and thereafter I rather neglected the young officers on my left.

38

Though I haunted the end of my veranda next the garden for several days, I did not again see the girl during all that time. The place seemed utterly deserted until one day I saw the figure of a man among the shrubbery. He was moving with great caution, creeping stealthily; and presently, behind him, I saw another and another, until I had counted five of them all together.

They were similar to the Vepajans, yet there was a difference. They appeared coarser, more brutal, than any of the men I had as yet seen; and in other ways they were dissimilar to Danus, Duran, Kamlot, and my other Venusan acquaintances. There was something menacing and sinister, too, in their silent, stealthy movements.

I wondered what they were doing there; and then I thought of the girl, and for some reason the conclusion was forced upon me that the presence of these men here had something to do with her, and that it boded her harm. Just in what way I could not even surmise, knowing so little of the people among whom fate had thrown me; but the impression was quite definite, and it excited me. Perhaps it rather overcame my better judgment, too, if my next act is an index to the matter.

Without thought of the consequences and in total ignorance of the identity of the men or the purpose for which they were in the garden, I vaulted the low fence and followed them. I made no noise. They had not seen me originally because I had been hidden from their view by a larger shrub that grew close to the fence that separated the garden from my veranda. It was through the foliage of this shrub that I had observed them, myself unobserved.

Moving cautiously but swiftly, I soon overtook the hindmost man and saw that the five were moving toward an open doorway beyond which, in a richly furnished apartment, I saw the girl who had aroused my curiosity and whose beautiful face had led me into this mad adventure. Almost simultaneously, the girl glanced up and saw the leading man at the doorway. She screamed, and then I knew that I had not come in vain.

Instantly I leaped upon the man in front of me, and as I did so I gave a great shout, hoping by that means to distract the attention of the other four from the girl to me, and in that I was wholly successful. The other four turned instantly. I had taken my man so completely by surprise that I was able to snatch his sword from its scabbard before he could recover his wits; and as he drew his dagger and struck at me, I ran his own blade through his heart; then the others were upon me.

Their faces were contorted by rage, and I could see that they would give me no quarter.

The narrow spaces between the shrubbery reduced the advantage which four men would ordinarily have had over a single antagonist, for they could attack me only singly; but I knew what the outcome must eventually be if help did not reach me, and as my only goal was to keep the men from the girl, I backed slowly toward the fence and my own veranda as I saw that all four of the men were following me.

My shout and the girl's scream had attracted attention; and presently I heard men running in the apartment in which I had seen the girl, and her voice directing them toward the garden. I hoped they would come before the fellows had backed me against the wall, where I was confident that I must go down in defeat beneath four swords wielded by men more accustomed to them than I. I thanked the good fortune, however, that had led me to take up fencing seriously in Germany, for it was helping me now, though I could not long hold out against these men with the Venusan sword which was a new weapon to me.

I had reached the fence at last and was fighting with my back toward it. The fellow facing me was cutting viciously at me. I could hear the men coming from the apartment. Could I hold out? Then my opponent swung a terrific cut at my head, and, instead of parrying it, I leaped to one side and simultaneously stepped in and cut at him. His own swing had carried him off balance, and, of course, his guard was down. My blade cut deep into his neck, severing his jugular. From behind him another man was rushing upon me.

Relief was coming. The girl was safe. I could accomplish no more by remaining there and being cut to pieces, a fate I had only narrowly averted in the past few seconds. I hurled my sword, point first, at the oncoming Venusan; and as it tore into his breast I turned and vaulted the fence into my own veranda.

Then, as I looked back, I saw a dozen Vepajan warriors overwhelm the two remaining intruders, butchering them like cattle. There was no shouting and no sound other than the brief clash of swords as the two sought desperately but futilely to defend themselves. The Vepajans spoke no word. They seemed shocked and terrified, though their terror had most certainly not been the result of any fear of their late antagonists. There was something else which I did not understand, something mysterious in their manner, their silence, and their actions immediately following the encounter.

Quickly they seized the bodies of the five strange warriors that had been killed and carrying them to the outer garden wall, hurled them over into that bottomless abyss of the forest the terrific depths of which my eyes had never been able to plumb. Then, in equal silence, they departed from the garden by the same path by which they had entered it.

I realized that they had not seen me, and I knew that the girl had not. I wondered a little how they accounted for the deaths of the three men I had disposed of, but I never learned. The whole affair was a mystery to me and was only explained long after in the light of ensuing events.

I thought that Danus might mention it and thus give me an opportunity to question him; but he never did, and something kept me from broaching the subject to him, modesty perhaps. In other respects, however, my curiosity concerning these people was insatiable; and I fear that I bored Danus to the verge of distraction with my incessant questioning, but I excused myself on the plea that I could only learn the language by speaking it and hearing it spoken; and Danus, that most delightful of men, insisted that it was not only a pleasure to inform me but his duty as well, the jong having requested him to inform me fully concerning the life, customs, and history of the Vepajans.

One of the many things that puzzled me was why such an intelligent and cultured people should be living in trees, apparently without servants or slaves and with no intercourse, as far as I had been able to discover, with other peoples; so one evening I asked him.

'It is a long story,' replied Danus; 'much of it you will find in the histories here upon my shelves, but I can give you a brief outline that will at least answer your question.

'Hundreds of years ago the kings of Vepaja ruled a great country. It was not this forest island where you now find us, but a broad empire that embraced a thousand islands and extended from Strabol to Karbol; it included broad land masses and great oceans; it was graced by mighty cities and boasted a wealth and commerce unsurpassed through all the centuries before or since.

'The people of Vepaja in those days were numbered in the millions; there were millions of merchants and millions of wage earners and millions of slaves, and there was a smaller class of brain workers. This class included the learned professions of science, medicine, and law, of letters and the creative arts. The military leaders were selected from all classes. Over all was the hereditary jong.

'The lines between the classes were neither definitely nor strictly drawn; a slave might become a free man, a free man might become anything he chose within the limits of his ability, short of jong. In social intercourse the four principal classes did not intermingle with each other, due to the fact that members of one class had little in common with members of the other classes and not through any feeling of superiority of inferiority. When a member of a lower class had won by virtue of culture, learning, or genius to a position in a higher class, he was received upon an equal footing, and no thought was given to his antecedents.

'Vepaja was prosperous and happy, yet there were malcontents. These were the lazy and incompetent. Many of them were of the criminal class. They were envious of those who had won to positions which they were not mentally equipped to attain. Over a long period of time they were responsible for minor discord and dissension, but the people either paid no attention to them or laughed them down. Then they found a leader. He was a laborer named Thor, a man with a criminal record.

'This man founded a secret order known as Thorists and preached a gospel of class hatred called Thorism. By means of lying propaganda he gained a large following, and as all his energies were directed against a single class, he had all the vast millions of the other three classes to draw from, though naturally he found few converts among the merchants and employers which also included the agrarian class.

'The sole end of the Thorist leaders was personal power and aggrandizement; their aims were wholly selfish, yet, because they worked solely among the ignorant masses, they had little difficulty in deceiving their dupes, who finally rose under their false leaders in a bloody revolution that sounded the doom of the civilization and advancement of a world.

'Their purpose was the absolute destruction of the cultured class. Those of the other classes who opposed them were to be subjugated or destroyed; the jong and his family were to be killed. These things accomplished, the people would enjoy absolute freedom; there would be no masters, no taxes, no laws.

'They succeeded in killing most of us and a large proportion of the merchant class; then the people discovered what the agitators already knew, that someone must rule, and the leaders of Thorism were ready to take over the reins of government. The people had exchanged the beneficent rule of an experienced and cultured class for that of greedy incompetents and theorists.

'Now they are all reduced to virtual slavery. An army of spies watches over them, and an army of warriors keeps them from turning against their masters; they are miserable, helpless, and hopeless.

'Those of us who escaped with our jong sought out this distant, uninhabited island. Here we constructed tree cities, such as this, far above the ground, from which they cannot be seen. We brought our culture with us and little else; but our wants are few, and we are happy. We would not return to the old system if we might. We have learned our lesson, that a people divided amongst themselves cannot be happy. Where there are even slight class distinctions there are envy and jealousy. Here there are none; we are all of the same class. We have no servants; whatever there is to do we do better than servants ever did it. Even those who serve the jong are not servants in the sense that they are menials, for their positions are considered posts of honor, and the greatest among us take turns in filling them.'

'But I still do not understand why you choose to live in trees, far above the ground,' I said.

'For years the Thorists hunted us down to kill us,' he explained, 'and we were forced to live in hidden, inaccessible places; this type of city was the solution of our problem. The Thorists still hunt us; and there are still occasional raids, but now they are for a very different purpose. Instead of wishing to kill us, they now wish to capture as many of us as they can.

'Having killed or driven away the brains of the nation, their civilization has deteriorated, disease is making frightful inroads upon them which they are unable to check, old age has reappeared and is taking its toll; so they seek to capture the brains and the skill and the knowledge which they have been unable to produce and which we alone possess.'

'Old age is reappearing! What do you mean?' I asked.

'Have you not noticed that there are no signs of old age among us?' he inquired.

'Yes, of course,' I replied, 'nor any children. I have often meant to ask you for an explanation.'

'These are not natural phenomena,' he assured me; 'they are the crowning achievements of medical science. A thousand years ago the serum of longevity was perfected. It is injected every two years and not only provides immunity from all diseases but insures the complete restoration of all wasted tissue.

'But even in good there is evil. As none grew old and none died, except those who met with violent death, we were faced with the grave dangers of overpopulation. To combat this, birth control became obligatory. Children are permitted now only in sufficient numbers to replace actual losses in population. If a member of a house is killed, a woman of that house is permitted to bear a child, if she can; but after generations of childlessness there is a constantly decreasing number of women who are capable of bearing children. This situation we have met by anticipating it.

'Statistics compiled over a period of a thousand years indicate the average death rate expectancy per thousand people; they have also demonstrated that only fifty per cent of our women are capable of bearing children; therefore, fifty per cent of the required children are permitted yearly to those who wish them, in the order in which their applications are filed.'

'I have not seen a child since I arrived in Amtor,' I told him.

'There are children here,' he replied, 'but, of course, not many.'

'And no old people,' I mused. 'Could you administer that serum to me, Danus?'

He smiled. 'With Mintep's permission, which I imagine will not be difficult to obtain. Come,' he added, 'I'll take some blood tests now to determine the type and attenuation of serum best adapted to your requirements.' He motioned me into his laboratory.

When he had completed the tests, which he accomplished with ease and rapidity, he was shocked by the variety and nature of malignant bacteria they revealed.

'You are a menace to the continued existence of human life on Amtor,' he exclaimed with a laugh.

'I am considered a very healthy man in my own world,' I assured him.

'How old are you?' he asked.

'Twenty-seven.'

'You would not be so healthy two hundred years from now if all those bacteria were permitted to have their way with you.'

'How old might I live to be if they were eradicated?' I asked.

He shrugged. 'We do not know. The serum was perfected a thousand years ago. There are people among us today who were of the first to receive injections. I am over five hundred years old; Mintep is seven hundred. We believe that, barring accidents, we shall live forever; but, of course, we do not know. Theoretically, we should.'

He was called away at this juncture; and I went out on the veranda to take my exercise, of which I have found that I require a great deal, having always been athletically inclined. Swimming, boxing, and wrestling had strengthened and developed my muscles since I had returned to America with my mother when I was eleven, and I became interested in fencing while I was travelling in Europe after she died. During my college days I was amateur middleweight boxer of California, and I captured several medals for distance swimming; so the enforced inactivity of the past two months had galled me considerably. Toward the end of my college days I had grown into the heavyweight class, but that had been due to an increase of healthy bone and sinew; now I was at least twenty pounds heavier and that twenty pounds was all fat.

On my one hundred feet of veranda I did the best I could to reduce. I ran miles, I shadow boxed, I skipped rope, and I spent hours with the old seventeen setting-up exercises of drill regulations. Today I was shadow boxing near the right end of my veranda when I suddenly discovered the girl in the garden observing me. As our eyes met I halted in my tracks and smiled at her. A frightened look came into her eyes, and she turned and fled. I wondered why.

Puzzled, I walked slowly back toward my apartment, my exercises forgotten. This time I had seen the girl's full face, looked her squarely in the eyes, and I had been absolutely dumfounded by her beauty. Every man and woman I had seen since I had come to Venus had been beautiful; I had come to expect that. But I had not expected to see in this or any other world such indescribable perfection of coloring and features, combined with character and intelligence, as that which I had just seen in the garden beyond my little fence. But why had she run away when I smiled?

Possibly she had run away merely because she had been discovered watching me for, after all, human nature is about the same everywhere. Even twenty-six million miles from Earth there are human beings like ourselves and a girl, with quite human curiosity, who runs away when she is discovered. I wondered if she resembled Earthly girls in other respects, but she seemed too beautiful to be just like anything on Earth or in heaven. Was she young or old? Suppose she were seven hundred years old!

I went to my apartment and prepared to bathe and change my loincloth; I had long since adopted the apparel of Amtor. As I glanced in a mirror that hangs in my bathroom I suddenly understood why the girl may have looked frightened and run away – my beard! It was nearly a month old now and might easily have frightened anyone who had never before seen a beard.

When Danus returned I asked him what I could do about it. He stepped into another room and returned with a bottle of salve.

'Rub this into the roots of the hair on your face,' he directed, 'but be careful not to get it on your eyebrows, lashes, or the hair on your head. Leave it there a minute and then wash your face.'

I stepped into my bathroom and opened the jar; its contents looked like Vaseline and smelled like the devil, but I rubbed it into the roots of my beard as Danus had directed. When I washed my face a moment later my beard came off, leaving my face smooth and hairless. I hurried back to the room where I had left Danus.

'You are quite handsome after all,' he remarked. 'Do all the people of this fabulous world of which you have told me have hair growing on their faces?'

'Nearly all,' I replied, 'but in my country the majority of men keep it shaved off.'

'I should think the women would be the ones to shave,' he commented. 'A woman with hair on her face would be quite repulsive to an Amtorian.'

'But our women do not have hair on their faces,' I assured him.

'And the men do! A fabulous world indeed.'

'But if Amtorians do not grow beards, what was the need of this salve that you gave me?' I asked.

'It was perfected as an aid to surgery,' he explained. 'In treating scalp wounds and in craniectomies it is necessary to remove the hair from about the wound. This unguent serves the purpose better than shaving and also retards the growth of new hair for a longer time.'

'But the hair will grow out again?' I asked.

'Yes, if you do not apply the unguent too frequently,' he replied.

'How frequently?' I demanded.

'Use it every day for six days and the hair will never again grow on your face. We used to use it on the heads of confirmed criminals. Whenever one saw a bald-headed man or a man wearing a wig he watched his valuables.'

'In my country when one sees a bald-headed man,' I said, 'he watches his girls. And that reminds me; I have seen a beautiful girl in a garden just to the right of us here. Who is she?'

'She is one whom you are not supposed to see,' he replied. 'Were I you, I should not again mention the fact that you have seen her. Did she see you?'

'She saw me,' I replied.

'What did she do?' His tone was serious.

'She appeared frightened and ran.'

'Perhaps you had best keep away from that end of the veranda,' he suggested.

There was that in his manner which precluded questions, and I did not pursue the subject further. Here was a mystery, the first suggestion of mystery that I had encountered in the life of Vepaja, and naturally it piqued my curiosity. Why should I not look at the girl? I had looked at other women without incurring displeasure. Was it only this particular girl upon whom I must not look, or were there other girls equally sacrosanct? It occurred to me that she might be a priestess of some holy order, but I was forced to discard that theory because of my belief that these people had no religion, at least none that I could discover in my talks with Danus. I had attempted to describe some of our Earthly religious beliefs to him, but he simply could not perceive either their purpose or meaning any more than he could visualize the solar system of the universe.

Having once seen the girl, I was anxious to see her again; and now that the thing was proscribed, I was infinitely more desirous than ever to look upon her divine loveliness and to speak with her. I had not promised Danus that I would heed his suggestions, for I was determined to ignore them should the opportunity arise.

I was commencing to tire of the virtual imprisonment that had been my lot ever since my advent upon Amtor, for even a kindly jailer and a benign prison régime are not satisfactory substitutes for freedom. I had asked Danus what my status was and what they planned for me in the future, but he had evaded a more direct answer by saying that I was the guest of Mintep, the jong, and that my future would be a matter of discussion when Mintep granted me an audience.

Suddenly now I felt more than before the restrictions of my situation, and they galled me. I had committed no crime. I was a peaceful visitor to Vepaja. I had neither the desire nor the power to harm anyone. These considerations decided me. I determined to force the issue.

A few minutes ago I had been contented with my lot, willing to wait the pleasure of my hosts; now I was discontented. What had induced this sudden change? Could it be the mysterious alchemy of personality that had transmuted the lead of lethargy to the gold of ambitious desire? Had the aura of a vision of feminine loveliness thus instantly reversed my outlook upon life?

I turned toward Danus. 'You have been very kind to me,' I said, 'and my days here have been happy, but I am of a race of people who desire freedom above all things. As I have explained to you, I am here through no intentional fault of my own; but I am here, and being here I expect the same treatment that would be accorded you were you to visit my country under similar circumstances.'

'And what treatment would that be?' he asked.

'The right to life, liberty, and the pursuit of happiness – freedom,' I explained. I did not think it necessary to mention chambers of commerce dinners, Rotary and Kiwanis luncheons, triumphal parades and ticker tape, keys to cities, press representatives and photographers, nor news reel cameramen, the price that he would undoubtedly have had to pay for life, liberty, and the pursuit of happiness.

'But, my dear friend, one would think from your words that you are a prisoner here!' he exclaimed.

'I am, Danus,' I replied, 'and none knows it better than you.'

He shrugged. 'I am sorry that you feel that way about it, Carson.'

'How much longer is it going to last?' I demanded.

'The jong is the jong,' he replied. 'He will send for you in his own time; until then, let us continue the friendly relations that have marked our association up to now.'

'I hope they will never be changed, Danus,' I told him, 'but you may tell Mintep, if you will, that I cannot accept his hospitality much longer; if he does not send for me soon, I shall leave on my own accord.'

'Do not attempt that, my friend,' he warned me.

'And why not?'

'You would not live to take a dozen steps from the apartments that have been assigned you,' he assured me seriously.

'Who would stop me?'

'There are warriors posted in the corridors,' he explained; 'they have their orders from the jong.'

'And yet I am not a prisoner!' I exclaimed with a bitter laugh.

'I am sorry that you raised the question,' he said, 'as otherwise you might never have known.'

Here indeed was the iron hand in the velvet glove. I hoped it was not wielded by a wolf in sheep's clothing. My position was not an enviable one. Even had I the means to escape, there was no place that I could go. But I did not want to leave Vepaja – I had seen the girl in the garden.

VI

Gathering Tarel

A week passed, a week during which I permanently discarded my reddish whiskers and received an injection of the longevity serum. The latter event suggested that possibly Mintep would eventually liberate me, for why bestow immortality upon a potential enemy who is one's prisoner; but then I knew that the serum did not confer absolute immortality – Mintep could have me destroyed if he wished, by which thought was suggested the possibility that the serum had been administered for the purpose of lulling me into a sense of security which I did not, in reality, enjoy. I was becoming suspicious.

While Danus was injecting the serum, I asked him if there were many doctors in Vepaja. 'Not so many in proportion to the population as there were a thousand years ago,' he replied. 'All the people are now trained in the care of their bodies and taught the essentials of health and longevity. Even without the serums we use to maintain resistance to disease constantly in the human body, our people would live to great ages. Sanitation, diet, and exercise can accomplish wonders by themselves.

'But we must have some doctors. Their numbers are limited now to about one to each five thousand citizens, and in addition to administering the serum, the doctors attend those who are injured by the accidents of daily life, in the hunt, and in duels and war.

'Formerly there were many more doctors than could eke out an honest living, but now there are various agencies that restrict their numbers. Not only is there a law restricting these, but the ten years of study required, the long apprenticeship thereafter, and the difficult examinations that must be passed have all tended to reduce the numbers who seek to follow this profession; but another factor probably achieved more than all else to rapidly reduce the great number of doctors that threatened the continuance of human life on Amtor in the past.

'This was a regulation that compelled every physician and surgeon to file a complete history of each of his cases with the chief medical officer of his district. From diagnosis to complete recovery or death, each detail of the handling of each case had to be recorded and placed on record for the public to consult. When a citizen requires the services of a physician or surgeon now, he may easily determine those who have been successful and those who have not. Fortunately, today there are few of the latter. The law has proved a good one.'

This was interesting, for I had had experience with physicians and surgeons on Earth. 'How many doctors survived the operation of this new law?' I asked.

'About two per cent,' he replied.

'There must have been a larger proportion of good doctors on Amtor than on Earth,' I commented.

Time hung heavily upon my hands. I read a great deal, but an active young man cannot satisfy all his varied life interests with books alone. And then there was the garden at my right. I had been advised to avoid that end of my veranda, but I did not, at least not when Danus was absent. When he was away I haunted that end of the veranda, but it seemed deserted. And then one day I caught a glimpse of her; she was watching me from behind a flowering shrub.

I was close to the fence that separated my runway from her garden; it was not a high fence, perhaps slightly under five feet. She did not run this time, but stood looking straight at me, possibly thinking that I could not see her because of the intervening foliage. I could not see her plainly enough, that is true; and, God, how I wanted to see her!

What is that inexplicable, subtle attraction that some woman holds for every man? For some men there is only one woman in the world who exercises this influence upon him, or perhaps if there are more, the others do not cross his path; for other men there are several; for some none. For me there was this girl of an alien race, upon an alien planet. Perhaps there were others, but if there were, I had never met them. In all my life before I had never been moved by such an irresistible urge. What I did, I did upon the strength of an impulse as uncontrollable as a law of nature; perhaps it was a law of nature that motivated me. I vaulted the fence.

Before the girl could escape me, I stood before her. There were consternation and horror in her eyes. I thought that she was afraid of me.

'Do not be afraid,' I said; 'I have not come to harm you, only to speak to you.'

She drew herself up proudly. 'I am not afraid of you,' she said; 'I–' she hesitated and then started over. 'If you are seen here you will be destroyed. Go back to your quarters at once and never dare such a rash act again.'

I thrilled to the thought that the fear that I had seen so clearly reflected in her eyes was for my safety. 'How may I see you?' I asked.

'You may never see me,' she replied.

'But I have seen you, and I intend seeing you again. I am going to see a lot of you, or die in the attempt.'

'Either you do not know what you are doing or you are mad,' she said and turned her back on me as she started to walk away.

I seized her arm. 'Wait,' I begged.

She wheeled on me like a tigress and slapped my face, and then she whipped the dagger from the scabbard at her girdle. 'How dare you,' she cried, 'lay a hand upon me! I should kill you.'

'Why don't you?' I asked.

'I loathe you,' she said, and it sounded as though she meant it.

'I love you,' I replied, and I knew that I spoke the truth.

At that declaration her eyes did indeed reflect horror. She wheeled then so quickly that I could not stop her and was gone. I stood for a moment, debating whether I should follow her or not, and then a modicum of reason intervened to save me from such an asininity. An instant later I had vaulted the fence again. I did not know whether anyone had seen me or not, and I did not care.

When Danus returned a short time later, he told me that Mintep had sent him for me. I wondered if the summons was in any way related to my adventure in the garden at the right, but I did not inquire. If it were, I should know in due time. The attitude of Danus was unchanged, but that no longer reassured me. I was beginning to suspect that the Amtorians were masters of dissimulation.

Two young officers from the quarters adjoining mine accompanied us to the chamber where the jong was to question me. Whether or not they were acting as an escort to prevent my escape I could not tell. They chatted pleasantly with me during the short walk along the corridor and up the staircase to the level above; but then the guards usually chat pleasantly with the condemned man, if he feels like chatting. They accompanied me into the room where the jong sat. This time he was not alone; there were a number of men gathered about him, and among these I recognized Duran, Olthar, and Kamlot. For some reason the assemblage reminded me of a grand jury, and I could not help but wonder if they were going to return a true bill.

I bowed to the jong, who greeted me quite pleasantly enough, and smiled and nodded to the three men in whose home I had spent my first night on Venus. Mintep looked me over in silence for a moment or two; when he had seen me before I had been dressed in my Earthly clothes, now I was garbed (or ungarbed) like a Vepajan.

'Your skin is not as light in color as I thought it,' he commented.

'Exposure to light on the veranda has darkened it,' I replied. I could not say sunlight, because they have no word for sun, of the existence of which they do not dream. However, such was the case, the ultra violet rays of sunlight having penetrated the cloud envelopes surrounding the planet and tanned my body quite as effectively as would exposure to the direct rays of the sun have done.

'You have been quite happy here, I trust,' he said.

'I have been treated with kindness and consideration,' I replied, 'and have been quite as happy as any prisoner could reasonably be expected to be.'

The shadow of a smile touched his lips. 'You are candid,' he commented.

'Candor is a characteristic of the country from which I come,' I replied.

'However, I do not like the word prisoner,' he said.

'Neither do I, jong, but I like the truth. I have been a prisoner, and I have been awaiting this opportunity to ask you why I am a prisoner and to demand my freedom.'

He raised his eyebrows; then he smiled quite openly. 'I think that I am going to like you,' he said; 'you are honest and you are courageous, or I am no judge of men.'

I inclined my head in acknowledgment of the compliment. I had not expected that he would receive my blunt demand in a spirit of such generous understanding; but I was not entirely relieved, for experience had taught me that these people could be very suave while being most uncompromising.

'There are some things that I wish to tell you and some questions that I wish to ask you,' he continued. 'We are still beset by our enemies, who yet send occasional raiding parties against us, who upon numerous occasions have sought to introduce their spies among us. We have three things that they require if they are not to suffer extinction: scientific knowledge, and the brains and experience to apply it. Therefore they go to any lengths to abduct our men, whom they purpose holding in slavery and forcing to apply the knowledge that they themselves do not have. They also abduct our women in the hope of breeding children of greater mentality than those which are now born to them.

'The story that you told of crossing millions of miles of space from another world is, of course, preposterous and naturally aroused our suspicions. We saw in you another Thorist spy, cleverly disguised. For this reason you have been under the careful and intelligent observation of Danus for many days. He reports that there is no doubt but that you were totally ignorant of the Amtorian language when you came among us, and as this is the only language spoken by any of the known races of the world, we have come to the conclusion that your story may be, in part, true. The fact that your skin, hair, and eyes differ in color from those of any known race is further substantiation of this conclusion. Therefore, we are willing to admit that you are not a Thorist, but the questions remain: who are you, and from whence came you?'

'I have told only the truth,' I replied; 'I have nothing to add other than to suggest that you carefully consider the fact that the cloud masses surrounding Amtor completely obscure your view and therefore your knowledge of what lies beyond.'

He shook his head. 'Let us not discuss it; it is useless to attempt to

51

overthrow the accumulated scientific research and knowledge of thousands of years. We are willing to accept you as of another race, perhaps, as was suggested by the clothing you wore upon your arrival, from cold and dreary Karbol. You are free to come and go as you please. If you remain, you must abide by the laws and customs of Vepaja, and you must become self-supporting. What can you do?'

'I doubt that I can compete with Vepajans at their own trades or professions,' I admitted, 'but I can learn something if I am given time.'

'Perhaps we can find someone who will undertake your training,' said the jong, 'and in the meantime you may remain in my house, assisting Danus.'

'We will take him into our house and train him,' spoke up Duran, 'if he cares to help us collect tarel and hunt.'

Tarel is the strong, silky fiber from which their cloth and cordage are made. I imagined that collecting it would be tame and monotonous work, but the idea of hunting appealed to me. In no event, however, could I ignore Duran's well-meant invitation, as I did not wish to offend him, and, furthermore, anything would be acceptable that would provide the means whereby I might become self-supporting. I therefore accepted his offer, and, the audience being concluded, I bid goodbye to Danus, who invited me to visit him often, and withdrew with Duran, Olthar, and Kamlot.

As no mention had been made of the subject, I concluded that no one had witnessed my encounter with the girl in the garden, who was still uppermost in my thoughts and the principal cause of my regret that I was to leave the house of the jong.

Once more I was established in the house of Duran, but this time in a larger and more comfortable room. Kamlot took charge of me. He was the younger of the brothers, a quiet, reserved man with the muscular development of a trained athlete. After he had shown me my room, he took me to another apartment, a miniature armory, in which were many spears, swords, daggers, bows, shields, and almost countless arrows. Before a window was a long bench with racks in which were tools of various descriptions; above the bench were shelves upon which were stacked the raw materials for the manufacture of bows, arrows, and spear shafts. Near the bench were a forge and anvil, and there were sheets and rods and ingots of metal stored nearby.

'Have you ever used a sword?' he asked as he selected one for me.

'Yes, but for exercise only,' I replied; 'in my country we have perfected weapons that render a sword useless in combat.'

He asked me about these weapons and was much interested in my description of Earthly firearms. 'We have a similar weapon on Amtor,' he said. 'We of Vepaja do not possess them, because the sole supply of the material with which they are charged lies in the heart of the Thorist country. When the weapons are made they are charged with an element that emits a ray of extremely short wave length that is destructive of animal tissue, but the element only emits these rays when exposed to the radiation of another rare element. There are several metals that are impervious to these rays. Those shields that you see hanging on the walls, the ones that are metal covered, are ample protection from them. A small shutter of similar metal is used in the weapon to separate the two elements; when this shutter is raised and one element is exposed to the emanations of the other, the destructive R-ray is released and passes along the bore of the weapon toward the target at which the latter has been aimed.

'My people invented and perfected this weapon,' he added ruefully, 'and now it has been turned against us; but we get along very well with what we have, as long as we remain in our trees.

'In addition to a sword and dagger, you will need a bow, arrows, and a spear,' and as he enumerated them he selected the various articles for me, the last of which was really a short, heavy javelin. A swivelled ring was attached to the end of the shaft of this weapon, and attached to the ring was a long, slender cord with a hand loop at its extremity. This cord, which was no heavier than ordinary wrapping twine, Kamlot coiled in a peculiar way and tucked into a small opening in the side of the shaft.

'What is the purpose of that cord?' I asked, examining the weapon.

'We hunt high in the trees,' he replied, 'and if it were not for the cord we should lose many spears.'

'But that cord is not heavy enough for that, is it?' I asked.

'It is of tarel,' he replied, 'and could support the weight of ten men. You will learn much of the properties and value of tarel before you have been with us long. Tomorrow we shall go out together and gather some. It has been rather scarce of late.'

At the evening meal that day I met Zuro and Alzo again, and they were most gracious to me. In the evening they all joined in teaching me the favorite Vepajan game, tork, which is played with pieces that are much like those used in mah jong and bears a startling resemblance to poker.

I slept well that night in my new quarters and when daylight broke I arose, for Kamlot had warned me that we should start early upon our expedition. I cannot say that I looked forward with any considerable degree of enthusiasm to spending the day gathering tarel. The climate of Vepaja is warm and sultry, and I pictured the adventure as being about as monotonous and disagreeable as picking cotton in Imperial Valley.

After a light breakfast, which I helped Kamlot to prepare, he told me to get my weapons. 'You should always wear your sword and dagger,' he added.

'Even in the house?' I asked.

'Always, wherever you are,' he replied. 'It is not only a custom, but it is the law. We never know when we may be called upon to defend ourselves, our houses, or our jong.'

'Those are all that I need bring, I suppose,' I remarked as I was leaving the room.

'Bring your spear, of course; we are going to gather tarel,' he replied.

Why I should need a spear to gather tarel I could not imagine; but I brought all the weapons that he had mentioned, and when I returned he handed me a bag with a strap that went around my neck to support it at my back.

'Is this for the tarel?' I asked.

He replied that it was.

'You do not expect to gather much,' I remarked.

'We may not get any,' he replied. 'If we get a bagful between us we may do some tall boasting when we return.'

I said no more, thinking it best to learn by experience rather than to be continually revealing my lamentable ignorance. If tarel were as scarce as his statement suggested, I should not have much picking to do, and that suited me perfectly. I am not lazy, but I like work that keeps my mind on the alert.

When we were both ready, Kamlot led the way upstairs, a procedure which mystified me, but did not tempt me into asking any more questions. We passed the two upper levels of the house and entered a dark, spiral staircase that led still farther upward into the tree. We ascended this for about fifteen feet, when Kamlot halted and I heard him fumbling with something above me.

Presently the shaft was bathed with light, which I saw came through a small circular opening that had been closed with a stout door. Through this opening Kamlot crawled, and I followed him, to find myself on a limb of the tree. My companion closed and locked the door, using a small key. I now saw that the door was covered on the outside with bark, so that when it was closed it would have been difficult for anyone to have detected it.

With almost monkeylike agility, Kamlot ascended, while I, resembling anything but a monkey in this respect, followed, thankful for the lesser gravitational pull of Venus, however little less than that of Earth it might be, for I am not naturally arboreal.

After ascending about a hundred feet, Kamlot crossed to an adjacent tree, the branches of which interlocked with those of the one we had been ascending, and again the upward climb commenced. Occasionally the Vepajan stopped to listen as we passed from tree to tree or clambered to higher levels. After we had travelled for an hour or more, he stopped again and waited until I had overtaken him. A finger on his lips enjoined me to silence.

'Tarel,' he whispered, pointing through the foliage in the direction of an adjacent tree.

I wondered why he had to whisper it, as my eyes followed the direction of his index finger. Twenty feet away I saw what appeared to be a huge spider web, partially concealed by the intervening foliage.

'Be ready with your spear,' whispered Kamlot. 'Put your hand through the loop. Follow me, but not too closely; you may need room to cast your spear. Do you see him?'

'No,' I admitted. I saw nothing but the suggestion of a spider web; what else I was supposed to see I did not know.

'Neither do I, but he may be hiding. Look up occasionally so that he can't take you by surprise from above.'

This was more exciting than picking cotton in Imperial Valley, though as yet I did not know just what there was to be excited about. Kamlot did not appear excited; he was very cool, but he was cautious. Slowly he crept toward the great web, his javelin ready in his hand; and I followed. When we were in full sight of it we saw that it was empty. Kamlot drew his dagger.

'Start cutting it away,' he said. 'Cut close to the branches and follow the web around; I will cut in the other direction until we meet. Be careful that you do not get enmeshed in it, especially if he happens to return.'

'Can't we go around it?' I asked.

Kamlot looked puzzled. 'Why should we go around it?' he demanded, a little shortly I thought.

'To get the tarel,' I replied.

'What do you suppose this is?' he demanded.

'A spider's web.'

'It is tarel.'

I subsided. I had thought that the tarel he pointed at was beyond the web, although I had seen nothing; but then of course I had not known what tarel was or what it looked like. We had been cutting away for a few minutes when I heard a noise in a tree near us. Kamlot heard it at the same time.

'He is coming,' he said. 'Be ready!' He slipped his dagger into his sheath and grasped his spear. I followed his example.

The sound stopped, but I could see nothing through the foliage. Presently there was a rustling among the foliage, and a face appeared some fifteen yards from us. It was a hideous face – the face of a spider tremendously enlarged. When the thing saw that we had discovered it, it emitted the most frightful scream I had ever heard save once before. Then I recognized them – the voice and the face. It had been a creature such as this that had pursued my pursuer the night that I had dropped to the causeway in front of the house of Duran.

'Be ready,' cautioned Kamlot; 'he will charge.'

The words had scarcely crossed the lips of the Vepajan when the hideous creature rushed toward us. Its body and legs were covered with long, black hair, and there was a yellow spot the size of a saucer above each eye. It screamed horribly as it came, as though to paralyze us with terror.

Kamlot's spear hand flew back and forward, and the heavy javelin, rushing to meet the maddened creature, buried itself deeply in the repulsive carcass; but it did not stop the charge. The creature was making straight for Kamlot as I hurled my javelin, which struck it in the side; but even this did not stop it, and to my horror I saw it seize my companion as he fell back upon the great limb upon which he had stood, with the spider on top of him.

The footing was secure enough for Kamlot and the spider, for they were both accustomed to it, but to me it seemed very precarious. Of course the tree limbs were enormous and often the branches were laced together, yet I felt anything but secure. However, I had no time to think of that now. If not already dead, Kamlot was being killed. Drawing my sword, I leaped to the side of the huge arachnid and struck viciously at its head, whereupon it abandoned Kamlot and turned upon me; but it was badly wounded now and moved with difficulty.

As I struck at that hideous face, I was horrified to see that Kamlot lay as though dead. He did not move. But I had only time for that single brief glance. If I were not careful I, too, should soon be dead. The thing confronting me seemed endowed with unsappable vitality. It was oozing sticky blood from several wounds, at least two of which I thought should have been almost instantly lethal; yet still it struggled to reach me with the powerful claws that terminated its forelegs, that it might draw me to those hideous jaws.

The Vepajan blade is a keen, two-edged affair, a little wider and thicker near the point than at the haft, and, while not well balanced to my way of thinking, is a deadly cutting weapon. I found it so in this my first experience with it, for as a great claw reached out to seize me I severed it with a single blow. At this the creature screamed more horribly than ever, and with its last remaining vitality sprang upon me as you have seen spiders spring upon their prey. I cut at it again as I stepped back; and then thrust my point directly into that hideous visage, as the weight of the creature overbore me and I went down beneath it.

As it crashed upon me, my body toppled from the great branch upon which I had been standing, and I felt myself falling. Fortunately, the interlacing, smaller branches gave me some support; I caught at them and checked my fall, bringing up upon a broad, flat limb ten or fifteen feet below. I had clung to my sword, and being unhurt, clambered back as quickly as I could to save Kamlot from further attack, but he needed no protection – the great targo, as the creature is called, was dead.

Dead also was Kamlot; I could find no pulse nor detect any beating of the heart. My own sank within my breast. I had lost a friend, I who had so few here, and I was as utterly lost as one may be. I knew that I could not retrace our steps to the Vepajan city, even though my life depended upon my ability to do so, as it doubtless did. I could descend, but whether I was still over the city or not I did not know; I doubted it.

So this was gathering tarel; this was the occupation that I had feared would bore me with its monotony!

VII

By Kamlot's Grave

Having set out to gather tarel, I finished the work that Kamlot and I had nearly completed when the targo attacked us; if I succeeded in finding the city, I should at least bring something to show for our efforts. But what about Kamlot? The idea of leaving the body here was repugnant to me. Even in the brief association I had had with the man I had come to like him and to look upon him as my friend. His people had befriended me; the least that I could do would be to take his body back to them. I realized, of course, that that was going to be something of a job, but it must be done. Fortunately, I am extraordinarily muscular, and then, too, the gravitational pull of Venus favored me more than would that of Earth, giving me an advantage of over twenty pounds in the dead weight I should have to carry and even a little better than that in the amount of my own live weight, for I am heavier than Kamlot.

With less difficulty than I had anticipated I succeeded in getting Kamlot's body onto my back and trussed there with the cord attached to his javelin. I had previously strapped his weapons to him with strands of the tarel that half-filled my bag, for, being unfamiliar with all the customs of the country, I did not know precisely what would be expected of me in an emergency of this nature, and preferred to be on the safe side.

The experiences of the next ten or twelve hours are a nightmare that I should like to forget. Contact with the dead and naked body of my companion was sufficiently gruesome, but the sense of utter bewilderment and futility in this strange world was even more depressing. As the hours passed, during which I constantly descended, except for brief rests, the weight of the corpse seemed to increase. In life Kamlot would have weighed about one hundred eighty pounds on Earth, nearly one hundred sixty on Venus, but by the time darkness enveloped the gloomy forest I could have sworn that he weighed a ton.

So fatigued was I that I had to move very slowly, testing each new hand-and foothold before trusting my tired muscles to support the burden they were carrying, for a weak hold or a misstep would have plunged me into eternity. Death was ever at my elbow.

It seemed to me that I descended thousands of feet and yet I had seen no sign of the city. Several times I heard creatures moving through the trees at a distance, and twice I heard the hideous scream of a targo. Should one of these monstrous spiders attack me – well, I tried not to think about that. Instead I tried to occupy my mind with recollections of my Earthly friends; I visualized my childhood days in India as I studied under old Chand Kabi, I thought of dear old Jimmy Welsh, and I recalled a bevy of girls I had liked and with some of whom I had almost been serious. These recalled the gorgeous girl in the garden of the jong, and the visions of the others faded into oblivion. Who was she? What strange interdiction had forbidden her to see or to speak with me? She had said that she loathed me, but she had heard me tell her that I loved her. That sounded rather silly now that I gave it thought. How could I love a girl the first instant that I laid eyes upon her, a girl concerning whom I knew absolutely nothing, neither her age nor her name? It was preposterous, yet I knew that it was true. I loved the nameless beauty of the little garden.

Perhaps my preoccupation with these thoughts made me careless; I do not know, but my mind was filled with them when my foot slipped a little after night had fallen. I grasped for support, but the combined weights of myself and the corpse tore my hands loose, and with my dead companion I plunged downward into the darkness. I felt Death's cold breath upon my cheek.

We did not fall far, being brought up suddenly by something soft that gave to our combined weights, then bounced up again, vibrating like a safety net such as we have all seen used by aerial performers. In the faint but all pervading light of the Amtorian night I could see what I had already guessed – I had fallen into the web of one of Amtor's ferocious spiders!

I tried to crawl to an edge where I might seize hold of a branch and drag myself free, but each move but entangled me the more. The situation was horrible enough, but a moment later it became infinitely worse, as, glancing about me, I saw at the far edge of the web the huge, repulsive body of a targo.

I drew my sword and hacked at the entangling meshes of the web as the fierce arachnid crept slowly toward me. I recall wondering if a fly entangled in a spider's web suffered the hopelessness and the mental anguish that seized me as I realized the futility of my puny efforts to escape this lethal trap and the ferocious monster advancing to devour me. But at least I had some advantages that no fly enjoys. I had my sword and a reasoning brain; I was not so entirely helpless as the poor fly.

The targo crept closer and closer. It uttered no sound. I presume that it was satisfied that I could not escape and saw no reason why it should seek to paralyze me with fright. From a distance of about ten feet it charged, moving with incredible swiftness upon its eight hairy legs. I met it with the point of my sword.

There was no skill in my thrust; it was just pure luck that my point penetrated the creature's tiny brain. When it collapsed lifeless beside me, I could scarcely believe the testimony of my eyes. I was saved!

Instantly I fell to work severing the strands of tarel that enmeshed me, and in four or five minutes I was free and had lowered myself to a branch below. My heart was still pounding rapidly and I was weak from exhaustion. For a quarter of an hour I remained resting; then I continued the seemingly endless descent out of this hideous forest.

What other dangers confronted me I could not guess. I knew that there were other creatures in this gigantic wood; those powerful webs, capable of sustaining the weight of an ox, had not been built for man alone. During the preceding day I had caught occasional glimpses of huge birds, which might themselves, if carnivorous, prove as deadly menaces as the targo; but it was not them that I feared now, but the nocturnal prowlers that haunt every forest by night.

Down and down I descended, feeling that each next moment must witness the final collapse of my endurance. The encounter with the targo had taken terrific toll of my great strength, already sapped by the arduous experiences of the day, yet I could not stop, I dared not. Yet how much longer could I drive exhausted nature on toward the brink of utter collapse?

I had about reached the end of my endurance when my feet struck solid ground. At first I could not believe the truth, but glancing down and about me I saw that I had indeed reached the floor of the forest; after a month on Venus I had at last placed foot upon her surface. I could see little or nothing – just the enormous boles of great trees in whatever direction I looked. Beneath my feet lay a thick matting of fallen leaves, turned white in death.

I cut the cords that bound the corpse of Kamlot to my back and lowered my poor comrade to the ground; then I threw myself down beside him and was asleep almost immediately.

When I awoke, it was daylight again. I looked about me, but could see nothing but the counterpane of whitened leaves spread between the boles of trees of such gargantuan girth that I almost hesitate to suggest the size of some of them, lest I discredit the veracity of this entire story of my experiences on Venus. But indeed they must needs be huge to support their extraordinary height, for many of them towered over six thousand feet above the surface of the ground, their lofty pinnacles enshrouded forever in the eternal fog of the inner cloud envelope.

To suggest an idea of the size of some of these monsters of the forest, I may say that I walked around the bole of one, counting over a thousand paces in the circuit, which gives, roughly, a diameter of a thousand feet, and there were many such. A tree ten feet in diameter appeared a frail and slender sapling – and there can be no vegetation upon Venus!

What little knowledge of physics I had and a very slight acquaintance with botany argued that trees of such height could not exist, but there must be some special, adaptive forces operating on Venus that permit the seemingly impossible. I have attempted to figure it out in terms of Earthly conditions, and I have arrived at some conclusions that suggest possible explanations for the phenomenon. If vertical osmosis is affected by gravity, then the lesser gravity of Venus would favor the growth of taller trees, and the fact that their tops are forever in the clouds would permit them to build up an ample supply of carbohydrates from the abundant water vapor, provided there was the requisite amount of carbon dioxide in the atmosphere of Venus to promote this photosynthetic process.

I must admit, however, that at the time I was not greatly interested in these intriguing speculations; I had to think about myself and poor Kamlot. What was I to do with the corpse of my friend? I had done my best to return him to his people, and failed. I doubted now that I could ever find his people. There remained but a single alternative; I must bury him.

This decided, I started to scrape away the leaves beside him, that I might reach the ground beneath and dig a grave. There were about a foot of leaves and leaf mold and below that a soft, rich soil which I loosened easily with the point of my spear and scooped out with my hands. It did not take me long to excavate a nice grave; it was six feet long, two feet wide, and three feet deep. I gathered some freshly fallen leaves and carpeted its bottom with them, and then I gathered some more to place around and over Kamlot after I had lowered him to his final resting place.

While I worked I tried to recall the service for the dead; I wanted Kamlot to have as decent and orderly a burial as I could contrive. I wondered what God would think about it, but I had no doubt but that he would receive this first Amtorian soul to be launched into the unknown with a Christian burial and welcome him with open arms.

As I stooped and put my arms about the corpse to lower it into the grave, I was astounded to discover that it was quite warm. This put an entirely new aspect on the matter. A man dead for eighteen hours should be cold. Could it be that Kamlot was not dead? I pressed an ear to his chest; faintly I heard the beating of his heart. Never before had I experienced such an access of relief and joy. I felt as one reborn to new youth, to new hopes, to new aspirations. I had not realized until that instant the depth of my loneliness.

But why was Kamlot not dead? And how was I to resuscitate him? I felt that I should understand the former before I attempted the latter. I examined the wound again. There were two deep gashes on his chest just below the prest-ernum. They had bled but little, and they were discolored, as I now noticed, by a greenish tint. It was this, meaningless though it may be, that suggested an explanation, of Kamlot's condition. Something about that greenish tint suggested poison to my mind, and at once I recalled that there were varieties of spiders that paralyzed their victims by injecting a poison into them that preserved them in a state of suspended animation until they were ready to devour them. The targo had paralyzed Kamlot!

My first thought was to stimulate circulation and respiration, and to this end I alternately massaged his body and applied the first aid measures adapted to the resuscitation of the drowned. Which of these accomplished the result I do not know (perhaps each helped a little), but at any rate I was rewarded after a long period of effort with evidences of returning animation. Kamlot sighed and his eyelids fluttered. After another considerable period, during which I nearly exhausted myself, he opened his eyes and looked at me.

At first his gaze was expressionless and I thought that perhaps his mind had been affected by the poison; then a puzzled, questioning look entered his eyes and eventually recognition. I was witnessing a resurrection.

'What happened?' he asked in a whisper, and then, 'Oh, yes, I recall; the targo got me.' He sat up, with my assistance, and looked around. 'Where are we?' he demanded.

'On the ground,' I replied, 'but where on the ground I do not know.'

'You saved me from the targo,' he said. 'Did you kill it? But you must have, or you never could have gotten me away from it. Tell me about it.'

Briefly, I told him. 'I tried to get you back to the city, but I became lost and missed it. I have no idea where it lies.'

'What is this?' he asked, glancing at the excavation beside him.

'Your grave,' I replied. 'I thought that you were dead.'

'And you carried a corpse half a day and half a night! But why?'

'I do not know all the customs of your people,' I replied; 'but your family has been kind to me, and the least that I could do was to bring your body back to them, nor could I leave a friend up there to be devoured by birds and beasts.'

'I shall not forget,' he said quietly. He tried to rise then, but I had to assist him. 'I shall be all right presently,' he assured me, 'after I have exercised a little. The effects of the targo's poison wear off in about twenty-four hours even without treatment. What you have done for me has helped to dissipate them sooner, and a little exercise will quickly eradicate the last vestiges of them.' He stood looking about as though in an effort to orient himself, and as he did so his eyes fell upon his weapons, which I had intended burying with him and which lay on the ground beside the grave. 'You even brought these!' he exclaimed. 'You are a jong among friends!'

After he had buckled his sword belt about his hips, he picked up his spear, and together we walked through the forest, searching for some sign that would indicate that we had reached a point beneath the city, Kamlot having explained that trees along the important trails leading to the location of the city were marked in an inconspicuous and secret manner, as were certain trees leading upward to the hanging city.

'We come to the surface of Amtor but seldom,' he said, 'though occasionally trading parties descend and go to the coast to meet vessels from the few nations with which we carry on a surreptitious commerce. The curse of Thorism has spread far, however, and there are few nations of which we have knowledge that are not subject to its cruel and selfish domination. Once in a while we descend to hunt the basto for its hide and flesh.'

'What is a basto?' I inquired.

'It is a large, omnivorous animal with powerful jaws armed with four great fangs in addition to its other teeth. On its head grow two heavy horns. At the shoulder it is as tall as a tall man. I have killed them that weighed thirty-six hundred tob.'

A tob is the Amtorian unit of weight, and is the equivalent of one third of an English pound; all weights are computed in tobs or decimals thereof, as they use the decimal system exclusively in their tables of weights and measures. It seems to me much more practical than the confusing Earthly collection of grains, grams, ounces, pounds, tons, and the other designations in common use among the various nations of our planet.

From Kamlot's description I visualized the basto as an enormous boar with horns, or a buffalo with the jaws and teeth of a carnivore, and judged that its twelve hundred pounds of weight would render it a most formidable beast. I asked him with what weapons they hunted the animal.

'Some prefer arrows, others spears,' he explained, 'and it is always handy to have a low branched tree nearby,' he added with a grin.

'They are bellicose?' I asked.

'Very. When a basto appears upon the scene, man is as often the hunted as the hunter, but we are not hunting bastos now. What I should most like to find is a sign that would tell me where we are.'

We moved on through the forest, searching for the tiny road signs of the Vepajans, which Kamlot had described to me as well as explaining the location in which they are always placed. The sign consists of a long, sharp nail with a flat head bearing a number in relief. These nails are driven into trees at a uniform height from the ground. They are difficult to find, but it is necessary to have them so, lest the enemies of the Vepajans find and remove them, or utilize them in their search for the cities of the latter.

The method of the application of these signs to the requirements of the Vepajans is clever. They would really be of little value to any but a Vepajan as guide posts, yet each nail tells a remarkable story to the initiated; briefly it tells him precisely where he is on the island that comprises the kingdom of Mintep, the jong. Each nail is placed in position by a surveying party and its exact location is indicated on a map of the island, together with the number on the head of the nail. Before a Vepajan is permitted to descend to the ground alone, or to lead others there, he must memorize the location of every sign nail in Vepaja. Kamlot had done so. He told me that if we could find but a single nail he would immediately know the direction of and distance to those on either side of it, our exact position upon the island, and the location of the city; but he admitted that we might wander a long time before we discovered a single nail.

The forest was monotonously changeless. There were trees of several species, some with branches that trailed the ground, others bare of branches for hundreds of feet from their bases. There were boles as smooth as glass and as straight as a ship's mast, without a single branch as far up as the eye could see. Kamlot told me that the foliage of these grew in a single enormous tuft far up among the clouds.

I asked him if he had ever been up there, and he said he had climbed, he believed, to the top of the tallest tree, but that he had nearly frozen to death in the attempt. 'We get our water supply from these trees,' he remarked. 'They drink in the water vapor among the clouds and carry it down to their roots. They are unlike any other tree. A central, porous core carries the water from the clouds to the roots, from whence it rises again in the form of sap that carries the tree's food upward from the ground. By tapping one of these trees anywhere you may obtain a copious supply of clear, cool water – a fortunate provision of—'

'Something is coming, Kamlot,' I interrupted. 'Do you hear it?'

He listened intently for a moment. 'Yes,' he replied. 'We had better take to a tree, at least until we see what it is.'

As he climbed into the branches of a nearby tree, I followed him; and there we waited. Distinctly I could hear something moving through the forest as it approached us. The soft carpet of leaves beneath its feet gave forth but little sound – just a rustling of the dry leaves. Nearer and nearer it came, apparently moving leisurely; then, suddenly, its great head came into view from behind the bole of a tree a short distance from us.

'A basto,' whispered Kamlot, but from his previous description of the beast I had already guessed its identity.

It looked like a basto, only more so. From the eyes up its head resembled that of an American bison, with the same short, powerful horns. Its poll and forehead were covered with thick, curly hair, its eyes were small and red-rimmed. Its hide was blue and of about the same texture as that of an elephant, with sparsely growing hairs except upon the head and at the tip of the tail. It stood highest at the shoulders and sloped rapidly to its rump. Its front legs were short and stocky and ended in broad, three-toed feet; its hind legs were longer and the hind feet smaller, a difference necessitated by the fact that the forelegs and feet carried fully three quarters of the beast's weight. Its muzzle was similar to that of a boar, except that it was broader, and carried heavy, curved tusks.

'Here comes our next meal,' remarked Kamlot in an ordinary tone of voice. The basto stopped and looked about as he heard my companion's voice. 'They are mighty good eating,' added Kamlot, 'and we have not eaten for a long while. There is nothing like a basto steak grilled over a wood fire.'

My mouth commenced to water. 'Come on,' I said, and started to climb down from the tree, my spear ready in my hand.

'Come back!' called Kamlot. 'You don't know what you are doing.'

The basto had located us and was advancing, uttering a sound that would have put to shame the best efforts of a full-grown lion. I do not know whether to describe it as a bellow or a roar. It started with a series of grunts and then rose in volume until it shook the ground.

'He seems to be angry,' I remarked; 'but if we are going to eat him we must kill him first, and how are we to kill him if we remain in the tree?'

'I am not going to remain in the tree,' replied Kamlot, 'but you are. You know nothing about hunting these beasts, and you would probably not only get yourself killed but me into the bargain. You stay where you are. I will attend to the basto.'

This plan did not suit me at all, but I was forced to admit Kamlot's superior knowledge of things Amtorian and his greater experience and defer to his wishes; but nevertheless I held myself ready to go to his assistance should occasion require.

To my surprise, he dropped his spear to the ground and carried in its stead a slender leafy branch which he cut from the tree before descending to engage the bellowing basto. He did not come down to the floor of the forest directly in front of the beast, but made his way part way around the tree before descending, after asking me to keep the basto's attention diverted, which I did by shouting and shaking a branch of the tree.

Presently, to my horror, I saw Kamlot out in the open a dozen paces in rear of the animal, armed only with his sword and the leafy branch which he carried in his left hand. His spear lay on the ground not far from the enraged beast and his position appeared utterly hopeless should the basto discover him before he could reach the safety of another tree. Realizing this, I redoubled my efforts to engage the creature's attention, until Kamlot shouted to me to desist.

I thought that he must have gone crazy and should not have heeded him had not his voice attracted the attention of the basto and frustrated any attempt that I might have made to keep the beast's eyes upon me. The instant that Kamlot called to me the great head turned ponderously in his direction and the savage eyes discovered him. The creature wheeled and stood for a moment eyeing the rash but puny man-thing; then it trotted toward him.

I waited no longer but dropped to the ground with the intention of attacking the thing from the rear. What happened thereafter happened so quickly that it was over almost in the time it takes to tell it. As I started in pursuit, I saw the mighty basto lower its head and charge straight for my companion, who stood there motionless with his puny sword and the leafy branch grasped one in either hand. Suddenly, at the very instant that I thought the creature was about to impale him on those mighty horns, he waved the leaf covered branch in its face and leaped lightly to one side, simultaneously driving the keen point of his blade downward from a point in front of the left shoulder until the steel was buried to the hilt in the great carcass.

The basto stopped, its four legs spread wide; for an instant it swayed, and then it crashed to the ground at the feet of Kamlot. A shout of admiration was on my lips when I chanced to glance upward. What attracted my attention I do not know, perhaps the warning of that inaudible voice which we sometimes call a sixth sense. What I saw drove the basto and the feat of Kamlot from my thoughts.

'My God!' I cried in English, and then in Amtorian, 'Look, Kamlot! What are those?'

VIII

On Board the *Sofal*

Hovering just above us, I saw what at first appeared to be five enormous birds; but which I soon recognized, despite my incredulity, as winged men. They were armed with swords and daggers, and each carried a long rope at the end of which dangled a wire noose.

'Voo klangan!' shouted Kamlot. (The bird-men!)

Even as he spoke a couple of wire nooses settled around each of us. We struggled to free ourselves, striking at the snares with our swords, but our blades made no impression upon the wires, and the ropes to which they were attached were beyond our reach. As we battled futilely to disengage ourselves, the klangan settled to the ground, each pair upon opposite sides of the victim they had snared. Thus they held us so that we were helpless, as two cowboys hold a roped steer, while the fifth angan approached us with drawn sword and disarmed us. (Perhaps I should explain that angan is singular, klangan plural, plurals of Amtorian words being formed by prefixing kloo to words commencing with a consonant and kl to those commencing with a vowel.)

Our capture had been accomplished so quickly and so deftly that it was over, with little or no effort on the part of the birdmen, before I had had time to recover from the astonishment that their weird appearance induced. I now recalled having heard Danus speak of *voo klangan* upon one or two occasions, but I had thought that he referred to poultry breeders or something of that sort. How little could I have dreamed of the reality!

'I guess we are in for it,' remarked Kamlot gloomily.

'What will they do with us?' I inquired.

'Ask them,' he replied.

'Who are you?' demanded one of our captors.

For some reason I was astonished to hear him speak, although I do not know why anything should have astonished me now. 'I am a stranger from another world,' I told him. 'My friend and I have no quarrel with you. Let us go.'

'You are wasting your breath,' Kamlot advised me.

'Yes, he is wasting his breath,' agreed the angan. 'You are Vepajans, and we have orders to bring Vepajans to the ship. You do not look like a Vepajan,' he added, surveying me from head to feet, 'but the other does.'

'Anyway, you are not a Thorist, and therefore you must be an enemy,' interjected another.

They removed the nooses from about us and tied ropes around our necks and other ropes about our bodies beneath our arms; then two klangan seized the ropes attached to Kamlot and two more those attached to me, and, spreading their wings, rose into the air, carrying us with them. Our weight was supported by the ropes beneath our arms, but the other ropes were a constant suggestion to us of what might happen if we did not behave ourselves.

As they flew, winding their way among the trees, our bodies were suspended but a few feet above the ground, for the forest lanes were often low ceiled by overhanging branches. The klangan talked a great deal among themselves, shouting to one another and laughing and singing, seemingly well satisfied with themselves and their exploit. Their voices were soft and mellow, and their songs were vaguely reminiscent of Negro spirituals, a similarity which may have been enhanced by the color of their skins, which were very dark.

As Kamlot was carried in front of me, I had an opportunity to observe the physical characteristics of these strange creatures into whose hands we had fallen. They had low, receding foreheads, huge, beaklike noses, and undershot jaws; their eyes were small and close set, their ears flat and slightly pointed. Their chests were large and shaped like those of birds, and their arms were very long, ending in long-fingered, heavy-nailed hands. The lower part of the torso was small, the hips narrow, the legs very short and stocky, ending in three-toed feet equipped with long, curved talons. Feathers grew upon their heads instead of hair. When they were excited, as when they attacked us, these feathers stand erect, but ordinarily they lie flat. They are all alike; commencing near the root they are marked with a band of white, next comes a band of black, then another of white, and the tip is red. Similar feathers also grow at the lower extremity of the torso in front, and there is another, quite large bunch just above the buttocks – a gorgeous tail which they open into a huge pompon when they wish to show off.

Their wings, which consist of a very thin membrane supported on a light framework, are similar in shape to those of a bat and do not appear adequate to the support of the apparent weight of the creatures' bodies, but I was to learn later that this apparent weight is deceptive, since their bones, like the bones of true birds, are hollow.

The creatures carried us a considerable distance, though how far I do not know. We were in the air fully eight hours; and, where the forest permitted, they flew quite rapidly. They seemed utterly tireless, though Kamlot and I were all but exhausted long before they reached their destination. The ropes beneath our arms cut into our flesh, and this contributed to our exhaustion as did our efforts to relieve the agony by seizing the ropes above us and supporting the weight of our bodies with our hands.

But, as all things must, this hideous journey ended at last. Suddenly we broke from the forest and winged out across a magnificent land-locked harbor, and for the first time I looked upon the waters of a Venusan sea. Between two points that formed the harbor's entrance I could see it stretching away as far as the eye could reach – mysterious, intriguing, provocative. What strange lands and stranger people lay off there beyond the beyond? Would I ever know?

Suddenly now my attention and my thoughts were attracted to something in the left foreground that I had not before noticed; a ship lay at anchor on the quiet waters of the harbor and just beyond it a second ship. Toward one of them our captors were winging. As we approached the nearer and smaller, I saw a craft that differed but little in the lines of its hull from Earthly ships. It had a very high bow, its prow was sharp and sloped forward in a scimitar-like curve; the ship was long and narrow of beam. It looked as though it might have been built for speed. But what was its motive power? It had no masts, sails, stacks, nor funnels. Aft were two oval houses – a smaller one resting upon the top of a larger; on top of the upper house was an oval tower surmounted by a small crow's nest. There were doors and windows in the two houses and the tower. As we came closer, I could see a number of open hatches in the deck and people standing on the walkways that surrounded the tower and the upper house and also upon the main deck. They were watching our approach.

As our captors deposited us upon the deck, we were immediately surrounded by a horde of jabbering men. A man whom I took to be an officer ordered the ropes removed from us, and while this was being done he questioned the klangan who had brought us.

All the men that I saw were similar in color and physique to the Vepajans, but their countenances were heavy and unintelligent; very few of them were good-looking, and only one or two might have been called handsome. I saw evidences of age among them and of disease – the first I had seen on Amtor.

After the ropes had been removed, the officer ordered us to follow him, after detailing four villainous-looking fellows to guard us, and conducted us aft and up to the tower that surmounted the smaller house. Here he left us outside the tower, which he entered.

The four men guarding us eyed us with surly disfavor. 'Vepajans, eh!' sneered one. 'Think you're better than ordinary men, don't you? But you'll find out you ain't, not in The Free Land of Thora; there everybody's equal. I don't see no good in bringing your kind into the country anyway. If I had my way you'd get a dose of this,' and he tapped a weapon that hung in a holster at his belt.

The weapon, or the grip of it, suggested a pistol of some kind, and I supposed that it was one of those curious firearms discharging deadly rays, that Kamlot had described to me. I was about to ask the fellow to let me see it when the officer emerged from the tower and ordered the guard to bring us in.

We were escorted into a room in which sat a scowling man with a most unprepossessing countenance. There was a sneer on his face as he appraised us, the sneer of the inferior man for his superior, that tries to hide but only reveals the inferiority complex that prompts it. I knew that I was not going to like him.

'Two more klooganfal!' he exclaimed. (A ganfal is a criminal.) 'Two more of the beasts that tried to grind down the workers; but you didn't succeed, did you? Now we are the masters. You'll find that out even before we reach Thora. Is either of you a doctor?'

Kamlot shook his head. 'Not I,' he said.

The fellow, whom I took to be the captain of the ship, eyed me closely. 'You are no Vepajan,' he said. 'What are you, anyway? No one ever saw a man with yellow hair and blue eyes before.'

'As far as you are concerned,' I replied, 'I am a Vepajan. I have never been in any other country in Amtor.'

'What do you mean by saying as far as I am concerned?' he demanded.

'Because it doesn't make any difference what you think about it,' I snapped. I did not like the fellow, and when I do not like people I have difficulty in hiding the fact. In this case I did not try to hide it.

He flushed and half rose from his chair. 'It doesn't, eh?' he cried.

'Sit down,' I advised him. 'You're here under orders to bring back Vepajans. Nobody cares what you think about them, but you'll get into trouble if you don't bring them back.'

Diplomacy would have curbed my tongue, but I am not particularly diplomatic, especially when I am angry, and now I was both angry and disgusted, for there had been something in the attitude of all these people toward us that bespoke ignorant prejudice and bitterness. Furthermore, I surmised from scraps of information I had picked up from Danus, as well as from the remarks of the sailor who had announced that he would like to kill us, that I was not far wrong in my assumption that the officer I had thus addressed would be exceeding his authority if he harmed us. However, I realized that I was taking chances, and awaited with interest the effect of my words.

The fellow took them like a whipped cur and subsided after a single weakly blustering, 'We'll see about that.' He turned to a book that lay open before him. 'What is your name?' he asked, nodding in Kamlot's direction. Even his nod was obnoxious.

'Kamlot of Zar,' replied my companion.

'What is your profession?'

'Hunter and wood carver.'

'You are a Vepajan?'

'Yes.'

'From what city of Vepaja?'

'From Kooaad,' replied Kamlot.

'And you?' demanded the officer, addressing me.

'I am Carson of Napier,' I replied, using the Amtorian form; 'I am a Vepa-jan from Kooaad.'

'What is your profession?'

'I am an *aviator*,' I replied, using the English word and English pronunciation.

'A what?' he demanded. 'I never heard of such a thing.' He tried to write the word in his book and then he tried to pronounce it, but he could do nei-ther, as the Amtorians have no equivalents for many of our vowel sounds and seem unable even to pronounce them. Had I written the word for him in Amtorian he would have pronounced it ah-vy-ah-tore, as they cannot form the long *a* and short *o* sounds, and their *i* is always long.

Finally, to cover his ignorance, he wrote something in his book, but what it was I did not know; then he looked up at me again. 'Are you a doctor?'

'Yes,' I replied, and as the officer made the notation in his book, I glanced at Kamlot out of the corner of an eye and winked.

'Take them away,' the man now directed, 'and be careful of this one,' he added, indicating me; 'he is a doctor.'

We were taken to the main deck and led forward to the accompaniment of jeers and jibes from the sailors congregated on the deck. I saw the klangan strutting around, their tail feathers erect. When they saw us, they pointed at Kamlot, and I heard them telling some of the sailors that he was the one who had slain the basto with a single sword thrust, a feat which appeared to force their admiration, as well it might have.

We were escorted to an open hatch and ordered below into a dark, poorly ventilated hole, where we found several other prisoners. Some of them were Thorans undergoing punishment for infractions of discipline; others were Vepajan captives like ourselves, and among the latter was one who recog-nized Kamlot and hailed him as we descended into their midst.

'Jodades, Kamlot!' he cried, voicing the Amtorian greeting 'luck-to-you.'

'Ra jodades,' replied Kamlot; 'what ill fortune brings Honan here?'

'"Ill fortune" does not describe it,' replied Honan; 'catastrophe would be a better word. The klangan were seeking women as well as men; they saw Duare' (pronounced Doo-ah-ree) 'and pursued her; as I sought to protect her they captured me.'

'Your sacrifice was not in vain,' said Kamlot; 'had you died in the perform-ance of such a duty it would not have been in vain.'

'But it was in vain; that is the catastrophe.'

'What do you mean?' demanded Kamlot.

'I mean that they got her,' replied Honan dejectedly.

'They captured Duare!' exclaimed Kamlot in tones of horror. 'By the life of the jong, it cannot be.'

'I wish it were not,' said Honan.

'Where is she? On this ship?' demanded Kamlot.

'No; they took her to the other, the larger one.'

Kamlot appeared crushed, and I could only attribute his dejection to the hopelessness of a lover who has irretrievably lost his beloved. Our association had not been either sufficiently close nor long to promote confidences, and so I was not surprised that I had never heard him mention the girl, Duare, and, naturally, under the circumstances, I could not question him concerning her. I therefore respected his grief and his silence, and left him to his own sad thoughts.

Shortly after dawn the following morning the ship got under way. I wished that I might have been on deck to view the fascinating sights of this strange world, and my precarious situation as a prisoner of the hated Thorists engendered less regret than the fact that I, the first Earthman to sail the seas of Venus, was doomed to be cooped up in a stuffy hole below deck where I could see nothing. But if I had feared being kept below for the duration of the voyage, I was soon disillusioned, for shortly after the ship got under way we were all ordered on deck and set to scrubbing and polishing.

As we came up from below, the ship was just passing between the two headlands that formed the entrance to the harbor, in the wake of the larger vessel; and I obtained an excellent view of the adjacent land, the shore that we were leaving, and the wide expanse of ocean stretching away to the horizon.

The headlands were rocky promontories clothed with verdure of delicate hues and supporting comparatively few trees, which were of a smaller variety than the giants upon the mainland. These latter presented a truly awe inspiring spectacle from the open sea to the eyes of an Earthman, their mighty boles rearing their weirdly colored foliage straight up for five thousand feet, where they were lost to view among the clouds. But I was not permitted to gaze for long upon the wonders of the scene. I had not been ordered above for the purpose of satisfying the aesthetic longings of my soul.

Kamlot and I were set to cleaning and polishing guns. There were a number of these on either side of the deck, one at the stern, and two on the tower deck. I was surprised when I saw them, for there had been no sign of armament when I came on board the preceding day; but I was not long in discovering the explanation – the guns were mounted on disappearing carriages, and when lowered, a sliding hatch, flush with the deck, concealed them.

The barrels of these pieces were about eight inches in diameter, while the bore was scarcely larger than my little finger; the sights were ingenious and complicated, but there was no breech block in evidence nor any opening into a breech, unless there was one hidden beneath a hoop that encircled the breech, to which it was heavily bolted. The only thing that I could discover that might have been a firing device projected from the rear of the breech and resembled the rotating crank that is used to revolve the breech block in some types of Earthly guns.

The barrels of the guns were about fifteen feet long and of the same diameter from breech to muzzle. When in action they can be extended beyond the rail of the ship about two thirds of their length, thus affording a wider horizontal range and more deck room, which would be of value on a ship such as that on which I was a captive, which was of narrow beam.

'What do these guns fire?' I asked Kamlot, who was working at my side.

'T-rays,' he replied.

'Do those differ materially from the R-rays you described when you were telling me about the small arms used by the Thorans?'

'The R-ray destroys only animal tissue,' he replied, 'while there is nothing that the T-ray may not dissipate. It is a most dangerous ray to work with because even the material of the gun barrel itself is not wholly impervious to it, and the only reason that it can be used at all is that its greatest force is expended along the line of least resistance, which in this case naturally is the bore of the gun. But eventually it destroys the gun itself.'

'How is it fired?' I asked.

He touched the crank at the end of the breech. 'By turning this, a shutter is raised that permits radiations from element 93 to impinge on the charge, which consists of element 97, thus releasing the deadly T-ray.'

'Why couldn't we turn this gun about and rake the ship above deck,' I suggested, 'thus wiping out the Thorans and giving us our freedom?'

He pointed to a small, irregular hole in the end of the crank shaft. 'Because we haven't the key that fits this,' he replied.

'Who has the key?'

'The officers have keys to the guns they command,' he replied. 'In the captain's cabin are keys to all the guns, and he carries a master key that will unlock any of them. At least that was the system in the ancient Vepajan navy, and it is doubtless the same today in the Thoran navy.'

'I wish we could get hold of the master key,' I said.

'So do I,' he agreed, 'but that is impossible.'

'Nothing is impossible,' I retorted.

He made no answer, and I did not pursue the subject, but I certainly gave it a lot of thought.

As I worked, I noted the easy, noiseless propulsion of the ship and asked

Kamlot what drove it. His explanation was long and rather technical; suffice it to say that the very useful element 93 (vik-ro) is here again employed upon a substance called lor, which contains a considerable proportion of the element yor-san (105). The action of vik-ro upon yor-san results in absolute annihilation of the lor, releasing all its energy. When you consider that there is eighteen thousand million times as much energy liberated by the annihilation of a ton of coal than by its combustion you will appreciate the inherent possibilities of this marvellous Venusan scientific discovery. Fuel for the life of the ship could be carried in a pint jar.

I noticed as the day progressed that we cruised parallel to a coast line, after crossing one stretch of ocean where no land was in sight, and thereafter for several days I noted the same fact – land was almost always in sight. This suggested that the land area of Venus might be much greater in proportion to its seas; but I had no opportunity to satisfy my curiosity on that point, and of course I took no stock in the maps that Danus had shown me, since the Amtorians' conception of the shape of their world precluded the existence of any dependable maps.

Kamlot and I had been separated, he having been detailed to duty in the ship's galley, which was located in the forward part of the main deck house aft. I struck up a friendship with Honan; but we did not work together, and at night we were usually so tired that we conversed but little before falling asleep on the hard floor of our prison. One night, however, the sorrow of Kamlot having been brought to my mind by my own regretful recollections of the nameless girl of the garden, I asked Honan who Duare was.

'She is the hope of Vepaja,' he replied, 'perhaps the hope of a world.'

IX

Soldiers of Liberty

Constant association breeds a certain *camaraderie* even between enemies. As the days passed, the hatred and contempt which the common sailors appeared to have harbored for us when we first came aboard the ship were replaced by an almost friendly familiarity, as though they had discovered that we were not half bad fellows after all; and, for my part, I found much to like in these simple though ignorant men. That they were the dupes of unscrupulous leaders is about the worst that may be said of them. Most of them were kindly and generous; but their ignorance made them gullible, and their emotions were easily aroused by specious arguments that would have made no impression upon intelligent minds.

Naturally, I became better acquainted with my fellow prisoners than with my guards, and our relations were soon established upon a friendly basis. They were greatly impressed by my blond hair and blue eyes which elicited inquiries as to my genesis. As I answered their questions truthfully, they became deeply interested in my story, and every evening after the day's work was completed I was besieged for tales of the mysterious, far distant world from which I came. Unlike the highly intelligent Vepajans, they believed all that I told them, with the result that I was soon a hero in their eyes; I should have been a god had they had any conception of deities of any description.

In turn, I questioned them; and discovered, with no surprise, that they were not at all contented with their lots. The former free men among them had long since come to the realization that they had exchanged this freedom, and their status of wage earners, for slavery to the state, that could no longer be hidden by a nominal equality.

Among the prisoners were three to whom I was particularly attracted by certain individual characteristics in each. There was Gamfor, for instance, a huge, hulking fellow who had been a farmer in the old days under the jongs. He was unusually intelligent, and although he had taken part in the revolution, he was now bitter in his denunciation of the Thorists, though this he was careful to whisper to me in secrecy.

Another was Kiron, the soldier, a clean-limbed, handsome, athletic fellow who had served in the army of the jong, but mutinied with the others at the time of the revolution. He was being disciplined now for insubordination to an officer who had been a petty government clerk before his promotion.

75

The third had been a slave. His name was Zog. What he lacked in intelligence he made up in strength and good nature. He had killed an officer who had struck him and was being taken back to Thora for trial and execution. Zog was proud of the fact that he was a free man, though he admitted that the edge was taken off his enthusiasm by the fact that everyone else was free and the realization that he had enjoyed more freedom as a slave than he did now as a freeman.

'Then,' he explained, 'I had one master; now I have as many masters as there are government officials, spies, and soldiers, none of whom cares anything about me, while my old master was kind to me and looked after my welfare.'

'Would you like to be really free?' I asked him, for a plan had been slowly forming in my mind.

But to my surprise he said, 'No, I should rather be a slave.'

'But you'd like to choose your own master, wouldn't you?' I demanded.

'Certainly,' he replied, 'if I could find someone who would be kind to me and protect me from the Thorists.'

'And if you could escape from them now, you would like to do so?'

'Of course! But what do you mean? I cannot escape from them.'

'Not without help,' I agreed, 'but if others would join you, would you make the attempt?'

'Why not? They are taking me back to Thora to kill me. I could be no worse off, no matter what I did. But why do you ask all these questions?'

'If we could get enough to join us, there is no reason why we should not be free,' I told him. 'When you are free, you may remain free or choose a master to your liking.' I watched closely for his reaction.

'You mean another revolution?' he asked. 'It would fail. Others have tried, but they have always failed.'

'Not a revolution,' I assured him, 'just a break for liberty.'

'But how could we do it?'

'It would not be difficult for a few men to take this ship,' I suggested. 'The discipline is poor, the night watches consist of too few men; they are so sure of themselves that they would be taken completely by surprise.'

Zog's eyes lighted. 'If we were successful, many of the crew would join us,' he said. 'Few of them are happy; nearly all of them hate their officers. I think the prisoners would join us almost to a man, but you must be careful of spies – they are everywhere. That is the greatest danger you would have to face. There can be no doubt but there is at least one spy among us prisoners.'

'How about Gamfor,' I asked; 'is he all right?'

'You can depend upon Gamfor,' Zog assured me. 'He does not say much, but in his eyes I can read his hatred of them.'

'And Kiron?'

'Just the man!' exclaimed Zog. 'He despises them, and he does not care who knows it; that is the reason he is a prisoner. This is not his first offense, and it is rumored that he will be executed for high treason.'

'But I thought that he only talked back to an officer and refused to obey him,' I said.

'That is high treason – if they wish to get rid of a man,' explained Zog. 'You can depend on Kiron. Do you wish me to speak to him about the matter?'

'No,' I told him. 'I will speak to him and to Gamfor; then if anything goes wrong before we are ready to strike, if a spy gets wind of our plot, you will not be implicated.'

'I do not care about that,' he exclaimed. 'They can kill me for but one thing, and it makes no difference which thing it is they kill me for.'

'Nevertheless, I shall speak to them, and if they will join us, we can then decide together how to approach others.'

Zog and I had been working together scrubbing the deck at the time, and it was not until night that I had an opportunity to speak with Gamfor and Kiron. Both were enthusiastic about the plan, but neither thought that there was much likelihood that it would succeed. However, each assured me of his support; and then we found Zog, and the four of us discussed details through- out half the night. We had withdrawn to a far corner of the room in which we were confined and spoke in low whispers with our heads close together.

The next few days were spent in approaching recruits – a very ticklish business, since they all assured me that it was almost a foregone conclusion that there was a spy among us. Each man had to be sounded out by devious means, and it had been decided that this work should be left to Gamfor and Kiron. I was eliminated because of my lack of knowledge concerning the hopes, ambitions, and the grievances of these people, or their psychology; Zog was eliminated because the work required a much higher standard of intelligence than he possessed.

Gamfor warned Kiron not to divulge our plan to any prisoner who too openly avowed his hatred of the Thorists. 'This is a time-worn trick that all spies adopt to lull the suspicions of those they suspect of harboring treason- able thoughts, and to tempt them into avowing their apostasy. Select men whom you know to have a real grievance, and who are moody and silent,' he counselled.

I was a little concerned about our ability to navigate the ship in the event that we succeeded in capturing her, and I discussed this matter with both Gamfor and Kiron. What I learned from them was illuminating, if not par- ticularly helpful.

The Amtorians have developed a compass similar to ours. According to Kiron, it points always toward the center of Amtor – that is, toward the center of the mythical circular area called Strabol, or Hot Country. This statement assured me that I was in the southern hemisphere of the planet, the needle of the compass, of course, pointing north toward the north magnetic pole. Having no sun, moon, nor stars, their navigation is all done by dead reckoning; but they have developed instruments of extreme delicacy that locate land at great distances, accurately indicating this distance and the direction; others that determine speed, mileage, and drift, as well as a depth gauge wherewith they may record soundings anywhere within a radius of a mile from the ship.

All of their instruments for measuring distances utilize the radioactivity of the nuclei of various elements to accomplish their ends. The gamma ray, for which they have, of course, another name, being uninfluenced by the most powerful magnetic forces, is naturally the ideal medium for their purposes. It moves in a straight line and at uniform speed until it meets an obstruction, where, even though it may not be deflected, it is retarded, the instrument recording such retardation and the distance at which it occurs. The sounding device utilizes the same principle. The instrument records the distance from the ship at which the ray encounters the resistance of the ocean's bottom; by constructing a right triangle with this distance representing the hypotenuse it is simple to compute both the depth of the ocean and the distance from the ship at which bottom was found, for they have a triangle of which one side and all three angles are known.

Owing to their extremely faulty maps, however, the value of these instruments has been greatly reduced, for no matter what course they lay, other than due north, if they move in a straight line they are always approaching the Antarctic regions. They may know that land is ahead and its distance, but they are never sure what land it is, except where the journey is a short and familiar one. For this reason they cruise within sight of land wherever that is practical, with the result that journeys that might otherwise be short are greatly protracted. Another result is that the radius of Amtorian maritime exploration has been greatly circumscribed; so much so that I believe there are enormous areas in the south temperate zone that have never been discovered by the Vepajans or the Thorists, while the very existence of the northern hemisphere is even unguessed by them. On the maps that Danus showed me considerable areas contained nothing but the single word *ioram*, ocean.

However, notwithstanding all this (and possibly because of it), I was confident that we could manage to navigate the ship quite as satisfactorily as her present officers, and in this Kiron agreed.

'At least we know the general direction of Thora,' he argued; 'so all we have to do is sail in the other direction.'

As our plans matured, the feasibility of the undertaking appeared more and more certain. We had recruited twenty prisoners, five of whom were Vepajans, and this little band we organized into a secret order with passwords, which were changed daily, signs, and a grip, the last reminiscent of my fraternity days in college. We also adopted a name. We called ourselves Soldiers of Liberty. I was chosen vookor, or captain. Gamfor, Kiron, Zog, and Honan were my principal lieutenants, though I told them that Kamlot would be second in command if we were successful in taking the ship.

Our plan of action was worked out in detail; each man knew exactly what was expected of him. Certain men were to overpower the watch, others were to go to the officers' quarters and secure their weapons and keys; then we would confront the crew and offer those who chose an opportunity to join us. The others – well, there I was confronted with a problem. Almost to a man the Soldiers of Liberty wanted to destroy all those who would not join us, and really there seemed no alternative; but I still hoped that I could work out a more humane disposition of them.

There was one man among the prisoners of whom we were all suspicious. He had an evil face, but that was not his sole claim upon our suspicions – he was too loud in his denunciation of Thorism. We watched him carefully, avoiding him whenever we could, and each member of the band was warned to be careful when talking to him. It was evident to Gamfor first that this fellow, whose name was Anoos, was suspicious. He persisted in seeking out various members of our group and engaging them in conversation which he always led around to the subject of Thorism and his hatred of it, and he constantly questioned each of us about the others, always insinuating that he feared certain ones were spies. But of course we had expected something of this sort, and we felt that we had guarded against it. The fellow might be as suspicious of us as he wished; so long as he had no evidence against us I did not see how he could harm us.

One day Kiron came to me evidently laboring under suppressed excitement. It was at the end of the day, and our food had just been issued to us for the evening meal – dried fish and a hard, dark-colored bread made of coarse meal.

'I have news, Carson,' he whispered.

'Let us go off in a corner and eat,' I suggested, and we strolled away together, laughing and talking of the day's events in our normal voices. As we seated ourselves upon the floor to eat our poor food, Zog joined us.

'Sit close to us, Zog,' directed Kiron; 'I have something to say that no one but a Soldier of Liberty may hear.'

He did not say Soldier of Liberty, but 'kung, kung, kung,' which are the Amtorian initials of the order's title. Kung is the name of the Amtorian character that represents the *k* sound in our language, and when I first translated the initials I was compelled to smile at the similarity they bore to those of a well-known secret order in the United States of America.

'While I am talking,' Kiron admonished us, 'you must laugh often, as though I were telling a humorous tale; then, perhaps, no one will suspect that I am not.

'Today I was working in the ship's armory, cleaning pistols,' he commenced. 'The soldier who guarded me is an old friend of mine; we served together in the army of the jong. He is as a brother to me. For either the other would die. We talked of old times under the banners of the jong and compared those days with these, especially we compared the officers of the old régime with those of the present. Like me and like every old soldier, he hates his officers, so we had a pleasant time together.

'Finally he said to me, quite suddenly, "What is this I hear of a conspiracy among the prisoners?"

'That almost took me off my feet; but I showed no emotion, for there are times when one must not trust even a brother. "What have you heard?" I asked.

' "I overheard one of the officers speaking to another," he told me. "He said that a man named Anoos had reported the matter to the captain and that the captain had told Anoos to get the names of all the prisoners whom he knew to be involved in the conspiracy and to learn their plans if he possibly could."

' "And what did Anoos say?" I asked my friend.

' "He said that if the captain would give him a bottle of wine he believed that he could get one of the conspirators drunk and worm the story from him. So the captain gave him a bottle of wine. That was today."

'My friend looked at me very closely, and then he said, "Kiron, we are more than brothers. If I can help you, you have but to ask."

'I knew this, and knowing how close to discovery we already were, I decided to confide in him and enlist his aid; so I told him. I hope you do not feel that I did wrong, Carson.'

'By no means,' I assured him. 'We have been forced to tell others of our plans whom we knew and trusted less well than you know and trust your friend. What did he say when you had told him?'

'He said that he would help us, and that when we struck he would join us. He promised, too, that many others of the soldiers would do likewise; but the most important thing he did was to give me a key to the armory.'

'Good!' I exclaimed. 'There is no reason now why we should not strike at once.'

'Tonight?' asked Zog eagerly.

'Tonight!' I replied. 'Pass the word to Gamfor and Honan, and you four to the other Soldiers of Liberty.'

We all laughed heartily, as though someone had told a most amusing story, and then Kiron and Zog left me, to acquaint Gamfor and Honan with our plan.

But upon Venus as upon Earth, the best laid plans of mice and men 'gang aft a-gley,' which is slang for haywire. Every night since we had sailed from the harbor of Vepaja the hatch had been left off our ill-smelling prison to afford us ventilation, a single member of the watch patrolling near to see that none of us came out; but tonight the hatch was closed.

'This,' growled Kiron, 'is the result of Anoos's work.'

'We shall have to strike by daylight,' I whispered, 'but we cannot pass the word tonight. It is so dark down here that we should certainly be overheard by someone outside our own number if we attempted it.'

'Tomorrow then,' said Kiron.

I was a long time getting to sleep that night, for my mind was troubled by fears for our entire plan. It was obvious now that the captain was suspicious, and that while he might not know anything of the details of what we purposed, he did know that something was in the air, and he was taking no chances.

During the night, as I lay awake trying to plan for the morrow, I heard someone prowling around the room, and now and again a whisper. I could only wonder who it was and try to guess what he was about. I recalled the bottle of wine that Anoos was supposed to have, and it occurred to me that he might be giving a party, but the voices were too subdued to bear out that theory. Finally I heard a muffled cry, a noise that sounded like a brief scuffle, and then silence again fell upon the chamber.

'Someone had a bad dream,' I thought and fell asleep.

Morning came at last, and the hatch was removed, letting a little light in to dissipate the gloom of our prison. A sailor lowered a basket containing the food for our meager breakfast. We gathered about it and each took his share, and moved away to eat it, when suddenly there was a cry from the far side of the room.

'Look what's here!' the man shouted. 'Anoos has been murdered!'

X

Mutiny

Yes, Anoos had been murdered, and there was a great hue and cry, much more of a hue and cry, it seemed to me, than the death of an ordinary prisoner should have aroused. Officers and soldiers swarmed in our quarters. They found Anoos stretched out on his back, a bottle of wine at his side. His throat was discolored where powerful fingers had crushed it. Anoos had been choked to death.

Soon they herded us on deck, where we were searched for weapons following an order from the captain of the ship, who had come forward to conduct an investigation. He was angry and excited and, I believe, somewhat frightened. One by one, he questioned us. When it was my turn to be questioned, I did not tell him what I had heard during the night; I told him that I had slept all night on the far side of the room from where Anoos's body was discovered.

'Were you acquainted with the dead man?' he asked.

'No more so than with any of the other prisoners,' I replied.

'But you are very well acquainted with some of them,' he said rather pointedly, I thought. 'Have you ever spoken with the man?'

'Yes, he has talked to me on several occasions.'

'About what?' demanded the captain.

'Principally about his grievances against the Thorists.'

'But he was a Thorist,' exclaimed the captain.

I knew that he was trying to pump me to discover if I harbored any suspicions concerning the actual status of Anoos, but he was not clever enough to succeed. 'I certainly would never have suspected it from his conversation,' I replied. 'If he were a Thorist, he must have been a traitor to his country, for he continually sought to enlist my interest in a plan to seize the ship and murder all her officers. I think he approached others, also.' I spoke in a tone loud enough to be heard by all, for I wanted the Soldiers of Liberty to take the cue from me. If enough of us told the same story it might convince the officers that Anoos's tale of a conspiracy was hatched in his own brain and worked up by his own efforts in an attempt to reap commendation and reward from his superiors, a trick by no means foreign to the ethics of spies.

'Did he succeed in persuading any of the prisoners to join him?' asked the captain.

'I think not; they all laughed at him.'

'Have you any idea who murdered him?'

'Probably some patriot who resented his treason,' I lied glibly.

As he questioned the other men along similar lines, I was pleased to discover that nearly every one of the Soldiers of Liberty had been approached by the perfidious Anoos, whose traitorous overtures they had virtuously repulsed. Zog said that he had never talked with the man, which, to the best of my knowledge, was the truth.

When the captain finished his investigation, he was farther from the truth than when he commenced it, for I am certain that he went aft convinced that there had been no truth in the tales that Anoos had carried to him.

I had been considerably worried at the time we were being searched, for fear that the key to the armory would be discovered on Kiron, but it had not been, and later he told me that he had hidden it in his hair the night before as a precaution against just such an eventuality as had occurred.

The Amtorian day consists of 26 hours, 56 minutes, 4 seconds of Earth time, which the Amtorians divide into twenty equal periods called te, which, for clarity, I shall translate into its nearest Earthly equivalent, hour, although it contains 80.895 Earth minutes. On shipboard, the hours are sounded by a trumpeter, there being a distinguishing bar of music for each hour of the day. The first hour, or one o'clock, corresponds to mean sunrise. It is then that the prisoners are awakened and given food; forty minutes later they start work, which continues until the tenth hour, with a short recess for food in the middle of the day. Occasionally we were allowed to quit work at the ninth and even the eighth hour, according to the caprices of our masters.

On this day the Soldiers of Liberty congregated during the midday rest period, and, my mind being definitely determined on immediate action, I passed the word around that we would strike during the afternoon at the moment the trumpeter sounded the seventh hour. As many of us as were working aft near the armory were to make a dash for it with Kiron, who would unlock it in the event that it were locked. The remainder were to attack the soldiers nearest them with anything that they could use as weapons, or with their bare hands if they had no weapons, and take the soldiers' pistols and swords from them. Five of us were to account for the officers. Half of our number was to constantly shout our battle cry, 'For liberty!' The other half was instructed to urge the remaining prisoners and the soldiers to join us.

It was a mad scheme and one in which only desperate men could have found hope.

The seventh hour was chosen because at that time the officers were nearly all congregated in the wardroom, where a light meal and wine were served them daily. We should have preferred launching our plan at night, but we feared a continuation of the practice of locking us below deck would prevent, and our experience with Anoos had taught us that we might expect the whole conspiracy to be divulged by another spy at any time; therefore we dared not wait.

I must confess to a feeling of increasing excitement as the hour approached. As, from time to time, I glanced at the other members of our little band, I thought that I could note signs of nervousness in some of them, while others worked on as placidly as though nothing unusual was about to occur. Zog was one of these. He was working near me. He never glanced toward the tower deck from which the trumpeter would presently sound the fateful notes, though it was with difficulty that I kept my eyes from it at all. No one would have thought that Zog was planning to attack the soldier lolling near him, nor have imagined that the night before he had murdered a man. He was humming a tune, as he polished the barrel of the big gun on which he was working.

Gamfor and, fortunately, Kiron were working aft, scrubbing the deck, and I saw that Kiron kept scrubbing closer and closer to the door of the armory. How I wished for Kamlot as the crucial moment approached! He could have done so much to insure the success of our *coup*, and yet he did not even know that such a stroke was contemplated, much less that it was so soon to be launched.

As I glanced about, I met Zog's gaze. Very solemnly he closed his left eye. At last he had given a sign that he was alert and ready. It was a little thing, but it put new heart into me. For some reason, during the past half hour I had felt very much alone.

The time was approaching the zero hour. I moved closer to my guard, so that I stood directly in front of him with my back toward him. I knew precisely what I was going to do, and I knew that it would be successful. Little did the man behind me dream that in a minute, or perhaps a few seconds, he would be lying senseless on the deck, or that the man he guarded would be carrying his sword, his dagger, and his pistol as the last notes of the seventh hour floated sweetly out across the calm waters of this Amtorian sea.

My back was now toward the deck houses. I could not see the trumpeter when he emerged from the tower to sound the hour, but I knew that it could not be long now before he stepped out onto the tower deck. Yet when the first note sounded I was as startled as though I had expected it never to sound. I presume it was the reaction after the long period of nervous tension.

My nervousness, however, was all mental; it did not affect my physical reactions to the needs of the moment. As the first note came softly down to my awaiting ears, I pivoted on a heel and swung my right for the chin of my unsuspecting guard. It was one of those blows that is often described as a haymaker, and it made hay. The fellow dropped in his tracks. As I stooped to recover his arms, pandemonium broke loose upon the deck. There were shrieks and groans and curses, and above all rose the war cry of the Soldiers of Liberty – my band had struck, and it had struck hard.

For the first time now, I heard the weird staccato hiss of Amtorian fire-arms. You have heard an X-ray machine in operation? It was like that, but louder and more sinister. I had wrenched the sword and pistol from the scabbard and holster of my fallen guard, not taking the time to remove his belt. Now I faced the scene for which I had so long waited. I saw the powerful Zog wrest the weapons from a soldier, and then lift the man's body above his head and cast it overboard. Evidently Zog had no time for proselyting.

At the door to the armory a battle was being waged; men were trying to enter, and soldiers were shooting them down. I ran in that direction. A soldier leaped in front of me, and I heard the hiss of the death rays that must have passed close to my body, as he tried to stop me. He must have been either nervous or a very poor shot, for he missed me. I turned my own weapon upon him and pressed the lever. The man slumped to the deck with a hole in his chest, and I ran on.

The fight at the door of the armory was hand to hand with swords, daggers, and fists, for by now the members of the two factions were so intermingled that none dared use a firearm for fear of injuring a comrade. Into this mêlée I leaped. Tucking the pistol into the band of my G string, I ran my sword through a great brute who was about to knife Honan; then I grabbed another by the hair and dragged him from the door, shouting to Honan to finish him – it took too long to run a sword into a man and then pull it out again. What I wanted was to get into the armory to Kiron's side and help him.

All the time I could hear my men shouting, 'For liberty!' or urging the soldiers to join us – as far as I had been able to judge, all the prisoners had already done so. Now another soldier barred my way. His back was toward me, and I was about to seize him and hurl him back to Honan and the others who were fighting at his side, when I saw him slip his dagger into the heart of a soldier in front of him and, as he did so, cry, 'For liberty!' Here was one convert at least. I did not know it then, but at that time there were already many such.

When I finally got into the armory, I found Kiron issuing arms as fast as he could pass them out. Many of the mutineers were crawling through the windows of the room to get weapons, and to each of these Kiron passed several swords and pistols, directing the men to distribute them on deck.

Seeing that all was right here, I gathered a handful of men and started up the companionway to the upper decks, from which the officers were firing down upon the mutineers and, I may say, upon their own men as well. In fact, it was this heartless and stupid procedure that swung many of the soldiers to our side. Almost the first man I saw as I leaped to the level of the second deck was Kamlot. He had a sword in one hand and a pistol in the other, and he was firing rapidly at a group of officers who were evidently attempting to reach the main deck to take command of the loyal soldiers there.

You may be assured that it did my heart good to see my friend again, and as I ran to his side and opened fire on the officers, he flashed me a quick smile of recognition.

Three of the five officers opposing us had fallen, and now the remaining two turned and fled up the companionway to the top deck. Behind us were twenty or more mutineers eager to reach the highest deck, where all the surviving officers had now taken refuge, and I could see more mutineers crowding up the companionway from the main deck to join their fellows. Kamlot and I led the way to the next deck, but at the head of the companionway the surging mob of howling, cursing mutineers brushed past us to hurl themselves upon the officers.

The men were absolutely out of control, and as there were but few of my original little band of Soldiers of Liberty among them, the majority of them knew no leader, with the result that it was every man for himself. I wished to protect the officers, and it had been my intention to do so; but I was helpless to avert the bloody orgy that ensued with a resulting loss of life entirely disproportionate to the needs of the occasion.

The officers, fighting for their lives with their backs against a wall, took a heavy toll of the mutineers, but they were eventually overwhelmed by superior numbers. Each of the common soldiers and sailors appeared to have a special grudge to settle either with some individual officer or with them all as a class and for the time all were transformed into maniacal furies, as time and again they charged the last fortress of authority, the oval tower on the upper deck.

Each officer that fell, either killed or wounded, was hurled over the rail to the deck below, where willing hands cast the body to the main deck from which, in turn, it was thrown into the sea. And then, at last, the mutineers gained access to the tower, from which they dragged the remaining officers, butchering them on the upper deck or hurling them to their shrieking fellows below.

The captain was the last to be dragged out. They had found him hiding in a cupboard in his cabin. At sight of him arose such a scream of hate and rage as I hope never to hear again. Kamlot and I were standing at one side, helpless witnesses of this holocaust of hate. We saw them literally tear the captain to pieces and cast him into the sea.

With the death of the captain the battle was over, the ship was ours. My plan had succeeded, but the thought suddenly assailed me that I had created a terrible power that it might be beyond me to control. I touched Kamlot on the arm. 'Follow me,' I directed and started for the main deck.

'Who is at the bottom of this?' asked Kamlot as we forced our way among the excited mutineers.

'The mutiny was my plan, but not the massacre,' I replied. 'Now we must attempt to restore order out of chaos.'

'If we can,' he remarked dubiously.

As I made my way toward the main deck, I collected as many of the original band of Soldiers of Liberty as we passed, and when I finally reached my destination, I gathered most of them about me. Among the mutineers I had discovered the trumpeter who had unknowingly sounded the signal for the outbreak, and him I caused to sound the call that should assemble all hands on the main deck. Whether or not the notes of the trumpet would be obeyed, I did not know, but so strong is the habit of discipline among trained men that immediately the call sounded the men began to pour onto the deck from all parts of the vessel.

I mounted the breech of one of the guns, and, surrounded by my faithful band, I announced that the Soldiers of Liberty had taken over the ship, that those who wished to accompany us must obey the vookor of the band; the others would be put ashore.

'Who is vookor?' demanded a soldier whom I recognized as one of those who had been most violent in the attack upon the officers.

'I am,' I replied.

'The vookor should be one of us,' he growled.

'Carson planned the mutiny and carried it to success,' shouted Kiron. 'Carson is vookor.'

From the throats of all my original band and from a hundred new recruits rose a cheer of approval, but there were many who remained silent or spoke in grumbling undertones to those nearest them. Among these was Kodj, the soldier who had objected to my leadership, and I saw that already a faction was gathering about him.

'It is necessary,' I said, 'that all men return at once to their duties, for the ship must be handled, no matter who commands. If there is any question about leadership, that can be settled later. In the meantime, I am in command; Kamlot, Gamfor, Kiron, Zog, and Honan are my lieutenants; with me, they will officer the ship. All weapons must be turned over immediately to Kiron at the armory, except those carried by men regularly detailed by him for guard duty.'

'No one is going to disarm me,' blustered Kodj. 'I have as much right to carry weapons as anyone. We are all free men now. I take orders from no one.'

Zog, who had edged closer to him as he spoke, seized him by the throat with one of his huge hands and with the other tore the belt from about his hips. 'You take orders from the new vookor or you go overboard,' he growled, as he released the man and handed his weapons to Kiron.

For a moment there was silence, and there was a tenseness in the situation that boded ill; then someone laughed and cried, 'No one is going to disarm me,' mimicking Kodj. That brought a general laugh, and I knew that for the time being the danger was over. Kiron, sensing that the moment was ripe, ordered the men to come to the armory and turn in their weapons, and the remainder of the original band herded them aft in his wake.

It was an hour before even a semblance of order or routine had been reestablished. Kamlot, Gamfor, and I were gathered in the chart room in the tower. Our consort was hull down below the horizon, and we were discussing the means that should be adopted to capture her without bloodshed and rescue Duare and the other Vepajan prisoners aboard her. The idea had been in my mind from the very inception of the plan to seize our own ship, and it had been the first subject that Kamlot had broached after we had succeeded in quieting the men and restoring order; but Gamfor was frankly dubious concerning the feasibility of the project.

'The men are not interested in the welfare of Vepajans,' he reminded us, 'and they may resent the idea of endangering their lives and risking their new-found liberty in a venture that means nothing whatever to them.'

'How do you feel about it, personally?' I asked him.

'I am under your orders,' he replied; 'I will do anything that you command, but I am only one – you have two hundred whose wishes you must consult.'

'I shall consult only my officers,' I replied; 'to the others, I shall issue orders.'

'That is the only way,' said Kamlot in a tone of relief.

'Inform the other officers that we shall attack the *Sovong* at daybreak,' I instructed them.

'But we dare not fire on her,' protested Kamlot, 'lest we endanger the life of Duare.'

'I intend boarding her,' I replied. 'There will be no one but the watch on deck at that hour. On two other occasions the ships have been brought close together on a calm sea; so our approach will arouse no suspicion. The boarding party will consist of a hundred men who will remain concealed until the command to board is given when the ships are alongside one another. At that hour in the morning the sea is usually calm; if it is not calm tomorrow morning we shall have to postpone the attack until another morning.

'Issue strict orders that there is to be no slaughter; no one is to be killed who does not resist. We shall remove all of the *Sovong*'s small arms and the bulk of her provisions, as well as the Vepajan prisoners, to the *Sofal*.'

'And then what do you propose doing?' asked Gamfor.

'I am coming to that,' I replied, 'but first I wish to ascertain the temper of the men aboard the *Sofal*. You and Kamlot will inform the other officers of my plans insofar as I have explained them; then assemble the original members of the Soldiers of Liberty and explain my intentions to them. When this has been done, instruct them to disseminate the information among the remainder of the ship's company, reporting to you the names of all those who do not receive the plan with favor. These we shall leave aboard the *Sovong* with any others who may elect to transfer to her. At the eleventh hour muster the men on the main deck. At that time I will explain my plans in detail.'

After Kamlot and Gamfor had departed to carry out my orders, I returned to the chart room. The *Sofal*, moving ahead at increased speed, was slowly overhauling the *Sovong*, though not at a rate that might suggest pursuit. I was certain that the *Sovong* knew nothing of what had transpired upon her sister ship, for the Amtorians are unacquainted with wireless communication, and there had been no time for the officers of the *Sofal* to signal their fellows aboard the *Sovong*, so suddenly had the mutiny broken and so quickly had it been carried to a conclusion.

As the eleventh hour approached, I noticed little groups of men congregated in different parts of the ship, evidently discussing the information that the Soldiers of Liberty had spread among them. One group, larger than the others, was being violently harangued by a loud-mouthed orator whom I recognized as Kodj. It had been apparent from the first that the fellow was a trouble maker. Just how much influence he had, I did not know; but I felt that whatever it was, it would be used against me. I hoped to be rid of him after we had taken the *Sovong*.

The men congregated rapidly as the trumpeter sounded the hour, and I came down the companionway to address them. I stood just above them, on one of the lower steps, where I could overlook them and be seen by all. Most of them were quiet and appeared attentive. There was one small group muttering and whispering – Kodj was its center.

'At daybreak we shall board and take the *Sovong*,' I commenced. 'You will receive your orders from your immediate officers, but I wish to emphasize one in particular – there is to be no unnecessary killing. After we have taken the ship we shall transfer to the *Sofal* such provisions, weapons, and prisoners as we wish to take with us. At this time, also, we shall transfer from the *Sofal* to the *Sovong* all of you who do not wish to remain on this ship under my command, as well as those whom I do not care to take with me,' and as I said this, I looked straight at Kodj and the malcontents surrounding him.

'I shall explain what I have in mind for the future, so that each of you may be able to determine between now and daybreak whether he cares to become a member of my company. Those who do will be required to obey orders; but they will share in the profits of the cruise, if there are profits. The purposes of the expedition are twofold: To prey on Thorist shipping and to explore the unknown portions of Amtor after we have returned the Vepajan prisoners to their own country.

'There will be excitement and adventure; there will be danger, too; and I want no cowards along, nor any trouble makers. There should be profits, for I am assured that richly laden Thorist ships constantly ply the known seas of Amtor; and I am informed that we can always find a ready market for such spoils of war as fall into our hands – and war it shall be, with the Soldiers of Liberty fighting the oppression and tyranny of Thorism.

'Return to your quarters now, and be prepared to give a good account of yourselves at daybreak.'

XI

Duare

I got little sleep that night. My officers were constantly coming to me with reports. From these I learned, what was of the greatest importance to me, the temper of the crew. None was averse to taking the *Sovong*, but there was a divergence of opinion as to what we should do thereafter. A few wanted to be landed on Thoran soil, so that they could make their way back to their homes; the majority was enthusiastic about plundering merchant ships; the idea of exploring the unknown waters of Amtor filled most of them with fear; some were averse to restoring the Vepajan prisoners to their own country; and there was an active and extremely vocal minority that insisted that the command of the vessel should be placed in the hands of Thorans. In this I could see the hand of Kodj even before they told me that the suggestion had come from the coterie that formed his following.

'But there are fully a hundred,' said Gamfor, 'upon whose loyalty you may depend. These have accepted you as their leader, and they will follow you and obey your commands.'

'Arm these,' I directed, 'and place all others below deck until after we have taken the *Sovong*. How about the klangan? They took no part in the mutiny. Are they for us or against us?'

Kiron laughed. 'They received no orders one way or the other,' he explained. 'They have no initiative. Unless they are motivated by such primitive instincts as hunger, love, or hate, they do nothing without orders from a superior.'

'And they don't care who their master is,' interjected Zog. 'They serve loyally enough until their master dies, or sells them, or gives them away, or is overthrown; then they transfer the same loyalty to a new master.'

'They have been told that you are their new master,' said Kamlot, 'and they will obey you.'

As there were only five of the birdmen aboard the *Sofal*, I had not been greatly exercised about their stand; but I was glad to learn that they would not be antagonistic.

At the twentieth hour I ordered the hundred upon whom we could depend assembled and held in the lower deck house, the others having all been confined below earlier in the night, in the accomplishment of which a second mutiny was averted only by the fact that all the men had been previously disarmed except the loyal Soldiers of Liberty.

All during the night we had been gradually gaining upon the unsuspecting *Sovong* until now we were scarcely a hundred yards astern of her, slightly aport. Across our starboard bow I could see her looming darkly in the mysterious nocturnal glow of the moonless Amtorian night, her lanterns white and colored points of light, her watch dimly visible upon her decks.

Closer and closer the *Sofal* crept toward her prey. A Soldier of Liberty, who had once been an officer in the Thoran navy, was at the wheel; no one was on deck but the members of the watch; in the lower deck house a hundred men were huddled waiting for the command to board; I stood beside Honan in the chart room (he was to command the *Sofal* while I led the boarding party), my eyes upon the strange Amtorian chronometer. I spoke a word to him and he moved a lever. The *Sofal* crept a little closer to the *Sovong*. Then Honan whispered an order to the helmsman and we closed in upon our prey.

I hastened down the companionway to the main deck and gave the signal to Kamlot standing in the doorway of the deck house. The two ships were close now and almost abreast. The sea was calm; only a gentle swell raised and lowered the softly gliding ships. Now we were so close that a man could step across the intervening space from the deck of one ship to that of the other.

The officer of the watch aboard the *Sovong* hailed us. 'What are you about?' he demanded. 'Sheer off, there!'

For answer I ran across the deck of the *Sofal* and leaped aboard the other ship, a hundred silent men following in my wake. There was no shouting and little noise – only the shuffling of sandalled feet and the subdued clank of arms.

Behind us the grappling hooks were thrown over the rail of the *Sovong*. Every man had been instructed as to the part he was to play. Leaving Kamlot in command on the main deck, I ran to the tower deck with a dozen men, while Kiron led a score of fighting men to the second deck where most of the officers were quartered.

Before the officer of the watch could gather his scattered wits, I had him covered with a pistol. 'Keep quiet,' I whispered, 'and you will not be harmed.' My plan was to take as many of them as possible before a general alarm could be sounded and thus minimize the necessity for bloodshed; therefore, the need for silence. I turned him over to one of my men after disarming him; and then I sought the captain, while two of my detachment attended to the helmsman.

I found the officer for whom I sought reaching for his weapons. He had been awakened by the unavoidable noise of the boarding party, and, suspecting that something was amiss, had seized his weapons as he arose and uncovered the lights in his cabin.

I was upon him as he raised his pistol, and struck it from his hand before he could fire; but he stepped back with his sword on guard, and thus we stood facing one another for a moment.

'Surrender,' I told him, 'and you will not be harmed.'

'Who are you?' he demanded, 'and where did you come from?'

'I was a prisoner on board the *Sofal*,' I replied, 'but now I command her. If you wish to avoid bloodshed, come out on deck with me and give the command to surrender.'

'And then what?' he demanded. 'Why have you boarded us if not to kill?'

'To take off provisions, weapons, and the Vepajan prisoners,' I explained.

Suddenly the hissing staccato of pistol fire came up to us from the deck below.

'I thought there was to be no killing!' he snapped.

'If you want to stop it, get out there and give the command to surrender,' I replied.

'I don't believe you,' he cried. 'It's a trick,' and he came at me with his sword.

I did not wish to shoot him down in cold blood, and so I met his attack with my own blade. The advantage was on his side in the matter of skill, for I had not yet fully accustomed myself to the use of the Amtorian sword; but I had an advantage in strength and reach and in some tricks of German sword-play that I had learned while I was in Germany.

The Amtorian sword is primarily a cutting weapon, its weight near the tip making it particularly effective for this method of attack, though it lessens its effectiveness in parrying thrusts, rendering it a rather sluggish defensive weapon. I therefore found myself facing a savage cutting attack against which I had difficulty in defending myself. The officer was an active man and skillful with the sword. Being experienced, it did not take him long to discover I was a novice, with the result that he pressed his advantage viciously, so that I soon regretted my magnanimity in not resorting to my pistol before the encounter began; but it was too late now – the fellow kept me so busy that I had no opportunity to draw the weapon.

He forced me back and around the room until he stood between me and the doorway, and then, having me where no chance for escape remained, he set to work to finish me with dispatch. The duel, as far as I was concerned, was fought wholly on the defensive. So swift and persistent was his attack that I could only defend myself, and not once in the first two minutes of the encounter did I aim a single blow at him.

I wondered what had become of the men who had accompanied me; but pride would not permit me to call upon them for help nor did I learn until later that it would have availed me nothing, since they were having all that they could attend to in repelling the attack of several officers who had run up from below immediately behind them.

The teeth of my antagonist were bared in a grim and ferocious smile, as he battered relentlessly at my guard, as though he already sensed victory and was gloating in anticipation. The clanging of steel on steel now drowned all sounds from beyond the four walls of the cabin where we fought; I could not tell if fighting were continuing in other parts of the ship, nor, if it were, whether it were going in our favor or against us. I realized that I *must* know these things, that I was responsible for whatever took place aboard the *Sovong*, and that I must get out of that cabin and lead my men either in victory or defeat.

Such thoughts made my position even more impossible than as though only my life were at stake and drove me to attempt heroic measures for releasing myself from my predicament and my peril. I must destroy my adversary, and I must do so at once!

He had me now with my back almost against the wall. Already his point had touched me upon the cheek once and twice upon the body, and though the wounds were but scratches, I was covered with blood. Now he leaped upon me in a frenzy of determination to have done with me instantly, but this time I did not fall back. I parried his cut, so that his sword passed to the right of my body which was now close to his; and then I drew back my point, and, before he could recover himself, drove it through his heart.

As he sagged to the floor, I jerked my sword from his body and ran from his cabin. The entire episode had required but a few minutes, though it had seemed much longer to me, yet in that brief time much had occurred on the decks and in the cabins of the *Sovong*. The upper decks were cleared of living enemies; one of my own men was at the wheel, another at the controls; there was still fighting on the main deck where some of the *Sovong*'s officers were making a desperate last stand with a handful of their men. But by the time I reached the scene of the battle, it was over; the officers, assured by Kamlot that their lives would be spared, had surrendered – the *Sovong* was ours. The *Sofal* had taken her first prize!

As I sprang into the midst of the excited warriors on the main deck, I must have presented a sorry spectacle, bleeding, as I was, from my three wounds; but my men greeted me with loud cheers. I learned later that my absence from the fighting on the main deck had been noticed and had made a poor impression on my men, but when they saw me return bearing the scars of combat, my place in their esteem was secured. Those three little scratches proved of great value to me, but they were as nothing in comparison with the psychological effect produced by the wholly disproportionate amount of blood they had spilled upon my naked hide.

We now quickly rounded up our prisoners and disarmed them. Kamlot took a detachment of men and released the Vepajan captives whom he transferred at once to the *Sofal*. They were nearly all women, but I did not see them as they were taken from the ship, being engaged with other matters.

I could imagine, though, the joy in the hearts of Kamlot and Duare at this reunion, which the latter at least had probably never even dared to hope for.

Rapidly we transferred all of the small arms of the *Sovong* to the *Sofal*, leaving only sufficient to equip the officers of the ill-starred vessel. This work was entrusted to Kiron and was carried out by our own men, while Gamfor, with a contingent of our new-made prisoners, carried all of the *Sovong*'s surplus provisions aboard our own ship. This done, I ordered all the *Sovong*'s guns thrown overboard – by that much at least I would cripple the power of Thora. The last act in this drama of the sea was to march our one hundred imprisoned malcontents from the *Sofal* to the *Sovong* and present them to the latters' new commander with my compliments. He did not seem greatly pleased, however, nor could I blame him. Neither were the prisoners pleased. Many of them begged me to take them back aboard the *Sofal*; but I already had more men than I felt were needed to navigate and defend the ship; and each of the prisoners had been reported as having expressed disapproval of some part or all of our plan; so that I, who must have absolute loyalty and cooperation, considered them valueless to me.

Kodj, strange to say, was the most persistent. He almost went on his knees as he pleaded with me to permit him to remain with the *Sofal*, and he promised me such loyalty as man had never known before; but I had had enough of Kodj and told him so. Then, when he found that I could not be moved, he turned upon me, swearing by all his ancestors that he would get even with me yet, even though it took a thousand years.

Returning to the deck of the *Sofal*, I ordered the grappling hooks cast off; and presently the two ships were under way again, the *Sovong* proceeding toward the Thoran port that was her destination, the *Sofal* back toward Vepaja. Now, for the first time, I had opportunity to inquire into our losses and found that we had suffered four killed and twenty-one wounded, the casualties among the crew of the *Sovong* having been much higher.

For the greater part of the remainder of the day I was busy with my officers organizing the personnel of the *Sofal* and systematizing the activities of this new and unfamiliar venture, in which work Kiron and Gamfor were of inestimable value; and it was not until late in the afternoon that I had an opportunity to inquire into the welfare of the rescued Vepajan captives. When I asked Kamlot about them, he said that they were none the worse for their captivity aboard the *Sovong*.

'You see, these raiding parties have orders to bring the women to Thora unharmed and in good condition,' he explained. 'They are destined for more important persons than ships' officers, and that is their safeguard.

'However, Duare said that notwithstanding this, the captain made advances to her. I wish I might have known it while I was still aboard the

Sovong, that I might have killed him for his presumption.' Kamlot's tone was bitter and he showed signs of unusual excitement.

'Let your mind rest at ease,' I begged him; 'Duare has been avenged.'

'What do you mean?'

'I killed the captain myself,' I explained.

He clapped a hand upon my shoulder, his eyes alight with pleasure. 'Again you have won the undying gratitude of Vepaja,' he cried. 'I wish that it might have been my good fortune to have killed the beast and thus wiped out the insult upon Vepaja, but if I could not be the one, then I am glad that it was you, Carson, rather than another.'

I thought that he took the matter rather seriously and was placing too much importance upon the action of the *Sovong*'s captain, since it had resulted in no harm to the girl; but then, of course, I realized that love plays strange tricks upon a man's mental processes, so that an affront to a mistress might be magnified to the proportions of a national calamity.

'Well, it is all over now,' I said, 'and your sweetheart has been returned to you safe and sound.'

At that he looked horrified. 'My sweetheart!' he exclaimed. 'In the name of the ancestors of all the jongs! Do you mean to tell me that you do not know who Duare is?'

'I thought of course that she was the girl you loved,' I confessed. 'Who is she?'

'Of course I love her,' he explained; 'all Vepaja loves her – she is the virgin daughter of a Vepajan jong!'

Had he been announcing the presence of a goddess on shipboard, his tone could have been no more reverential and awed. I endeavored to appear more impressed than I was, lest I offend him.

'Had she been the woman of your choice,' I said, 'I should have been even more pleased to have had a part in her rescue than had she been the daughter of a dozen jongs.'

'That is nice of you,' he replied, 'but do not let other Vepajans hear you say such things. You have told me of the divinities of that strange world from which you come; the persons of the jong and his children are similarly sacred to us.'

'Then, of course, they shall be sacred to me,' I assured him.

'By the way, I have word for you that should please you – a Vepajan would consider it a high honor. Duare desires to see you, that she may thank you personally. It is irregular, of course; but then circumstances have rendered strict adherence to the etiquette and customs of our country impracticable, if not impossible. Several hundred men already have looked upon her, many have spoken to her, and nearly all of them were enemies; so it can do no harm if she sees and speaks with her defenders and her friends.'

I did not understand what he was driving at, but I assented to what he had said and told him that I would pay my respects to the princess before the day was over.

I was very busy; and, if the truth must be told, I was not particularly excited about visiting the princess. In fact, I rather dreaded it, for I am not particularly keen about fawning and kotowing to royalty or anything else; but I decided that out of respect for Kamlot's feelings I must get the thing over as soon as possible, and after he had left to attend to some duty, I made my way to the quarters allotted to Duare on the second deck.

The Amtorians do not knock on a door – they whistle. It is rather an improvement, I think, upon our custom. One has one's own distinctive whistle. Some of them are quite elaborate airs. One soon learns to recognize the signals of one's friends. A knock merely informs you that some one wishes to enter; a whistle tells you the same thing and also reveals the identity of your caller.

My signal, which is very simple, consists of two short low notes followed by a higher longer note; and as I stood before the door of Duare and sounded this, my mind was not upon the princess within but upon another girl far away in the tree city of Kooaad, in Vepaja. She was often in my mind – the girl whom I had glimpsed but twice, to whom I had spoken but once and that time to avow a love that had enveloped me as completely, spontaneously, and irrevocably as would death upon some future day.

In response to my signal a soft, feminine voice bade me enter. I stepped into the room and faced Duare. At sight of me her eyes went wide and a quick flush mounted her cheeks. 'You!' she exclaimed.

I was equally dumfounded – she was the girl from the garden of the jong!

XII

'A Ship!'

What a strange *contretemps!* Its suddenness left me temporarily speechless; the embarrassment of Duare was only too obvious. Yet it was that unusual paradox, a happy *contretemps* – for me at least.

I advanced toward her, and there must have been a great deal more in my eyes than I realized, for she shrank back, flushing even more deeply than before.

'Don't touch me!' she whispered. 'Don't dare!'

'Have I ever harmed you?' I asked.

That question seemed to bring her confidence. She shook her head. 'No,' she admitted, 'you never have – physically. I sent for you to thank you for the service you have already rendered me; but I did not know it was *you*. I did not know that the Carson they spoke of was the man who –' She stopped there and looked at me appealingly.

'The man who told you in the garden of the jong that he loved you,' I prompted her.

'Don't!' she cried. 'Can it be that you do not realize the offensiveness, the criminality of such a declaration?'

'Is it a crime to love you?' I asked.

'It is a crime to tell me so,' she replied with something of haughtiness.

'Then I am a confirmed criminal,' I replied, 'for I cannot help telling you that I love you, whenever I see you.'

'If that is the case, you must not see me again, for you must never again speak those words to me,' she said decisively. 'Because of the service you have rendered me, I forgive you your past offenses; but do not repeat them.'

'What if I can't help it?' I inquired.

'You must help it,' she stated seriously; 'it is a matter of life and death to you.'

Her words puzzled me. 'I do not understand what you mean,' I admitted.

'Kamlot, Honan, any of the Vepajans aboard this ship would kill you if they knew,' she replied. 'The jong, my father, would have you destroyed upon our return to Vepaja – it would all depend upon whom I told first.'

I came a little closer to her and looked straight into her eyes. 'You would never tell,' I whispered.

'Why not? What makes you think that?' she demanded, but her voice quavered a little.

'Because you want me to love you,' I challenged her.

She stamped her foot angrily. 'You are beyond reason or forbearance or decency!' she exclaimed. 'Leave my cabin at once; I do not wish ever to see you again.'

Her bosom was heaving, her beautiful eyes were flashing, she was very close to me, and an impulse seized me to take her in my arms. I wanted to crush her body to mine, I wanted to cover her lips with kisses; but more than all else I wanted her love, and so I restrained myself, for fear that I might go too far and lose the chance to win the love that I felt was hovering just below the threshold of her consciousness. I do not know why I was so sure of that, but I was. I could not have brought myself to force my attentions upon a woman to whom they were repugnant, but from the first moment that I had seen this girl watching me from the garden in Vepaja, I had been impressed by an inner consciousness of her interest in me, her more than simple interest. It was just one of those things that are the children of old Chand Kabi's training, a training that has made me infinitely more intuitive than a woman.

'I am sorry that you are sending me away into virtual exile,' I said. 'I do not feel that I deserve that, but of course the standards of your world are not the standards of mine. There, a woman is not dishonored by the love of a man, or by its avowal, unless she is already married to another,' and then of a sudden a thought occurred to me that should have occurred before. 'Do you already belong to some man?' I demanded, chilled by the thought.

'Of course not!' she snapped. 'I am not yet nineteen.' I wondered that it had never before occurred to me that the girl in the garden of the jong might be already married.

I did not know what that had to do with it, but I was glad to learn that she was not seven hundred years old. I had often wondered about her age, though after all it could have made no difference, since on Venus, if anywhere in the universe, people are really no older than they look – I mean, as far as their attractiveness is concerned.

'Are you going?' she demanded, 'or shall I have to call one of the Vepajans and tell them that you have affronted me?'

'And have me killed?' I asked. 'No, you cannot make me believe that you would ever do that.'

'Then I shall leave,' she stated, 'and remember that you are never to see me or speak to me again.'

With that parting and far from cheering ultimatum she quit the room, going into another of her suite. That appeared to end the interview; I could not very well follow her, and so I turned and made my way disconsolately to the captain's cabin in the tower.

As I thought the matter over, it became obvious to me that I not only had not made much progress in my suit, but that there was little likelihood that I ever should. There seemed to be some insuperable barrier between us, though what it was I could not imagine. I could not believe that she was entirely indifferent to me; but perhaps that was just a reflection of my egotism, for I had to admit that she had certainly made it plain enough both by words and acts that she wished to have nothing to do with me. I was unquestionably *persona non grata*.

Notwithstanding all this, or maybe because of it, I realized that this second and longer interview had but served to raise my passion to still greater heat, leaving me in a fine state of despair. Her near presence on board the *Sofal* was constantly provocative, while her interdiction of any relations between us only tended to make me more anxious to be with her. I was most unhappy, and the monotony of the now uneventful voyage back toward Vepaja offered no means of distraction. I wished that we might sight another vessel, for any ship that we sighted would be an enemy ship. We were outlaws, we of the *Sofal* – pirates, buccaneers, privateers. I rather leaned toward the last and most polite definition of our status. Of course we had not as yet been commissioned by Mintep to raid shipping for Vepaja, but we were striking at Vepaja's enemies, and so I felt that we had some claim upon the dubious respectability of privateerism. However, either of the other two titles would not have greatly depressed me. Buccaneer has a devil-may-care ring to it that appeals to my fancy; it has a trifle more *haut ton* than pirate.

There is much in a name. I had liked the name of the *Sofal* from the first. Perhaps it was the psychology of that name that suggested the career upon which I was now launched. It means killer. The verb meaning kill is *fal*. The prefix *so* has the same value as the suffix *er* in English; so sofal means killer. *Vong* is the Amtorian word for defend; therefore, *Sovong*, the name of our first prize, means defender; but the *Sovong* had not lived up to her name.

I was still meditating on names in an effort to forget Duare, when Kamlot joined me, and I decided to take the opportunity to ask him some questions concerning certain Amtorian customs that regulated the social intercourse between men and maids. He opened a way to the subject by asking me if I had seen Duare since she sent for me.

'I saw her,' I replied, 'but I do not understand her attitude, which suggested that it was almost a crime for me to look at her.'

'It would be under ordinary circumstances,' he told me, 'but of course, as I explained to you before, what she and we have passed through has temporarily at least minimized the importance of certain time-honored Vepajan laws and customs.

'Vepajan girls attain their majority at the age of twenty; prior to that they may not form a union with a man. The custom, which has almost the force of a law, places even greater restrictions upon the daughters of a jong. They may not even see or speak to any man other than their blood relatives and a few well-chosen retainers until after they have reached their twentieth birthday. Should they transgress, it would mean disgrace for them and death for the man.'

'What a fool law!' I ejaculated, but I realized at last how heinous my transgression must have appeared in the eyes of Duare.

Kamlot shrugged. 'It may be a fool law,' he said, 'but it is still the law; and in the case of Duare its enforcement means much to Vepaja, for she is the hope of Vepaja.'

I had heard that title conferred upon her before, but it was meaningless to me. 'Just what do you mean by saying that she is the hope of Vepaja?' I asked.

'She is Mintep's only child. He has never had a son, though a hundred women have sought to bear him one. The life of the dynasty ends if Duare bears no son; and if she is to bear a son, then it is essential that the father of that son be one fitted to be the father of a jong.'

'Have they selected the father of her children yet?' I asked.

'Of course not,' replied Kamlot. 'The matter will not even be broached until after Duare has passed her twentieth birthday.'

'And she is not even nineteen yet,' I remarked with a sigh.

'No,' agreed Kamlot, eyeing me closely, 'but you act as though that fact were of importance to you.'

'It is,' I admitted.

'What do you mean?' he demanded.

'I intend to marry Duare!'

Kamlot leaped to his feet and whipped out his sword. It was the first time that I had ever seen him show marked excitement. I thought he was going to kill me on the spot.

'Defend yourself!' he cried. 'I cannot kill you until you draw.'

'Just why do you wish to kill me at all?' I demanded. 'Have you gone crazy?'

The point of Kamlot's sword dropped slowly toward the floor. 'I do not wish to kill you,' he said rather sadly, all the nervous excitement gone from his manner. 'You are my friend, you have saved my life – no, I would rather die myself than kill you, but the thing you have just said demands it.'

I shrugged my shoulders; the thing was inexplicable to me. 'What did I say that demands death?' I demanded.

'That you intend to marry Duare.'

'In my world,' I told him, 'men are killed for saying that they do *not* intend marrying some girl.' I had been sitting at the desk in my cabin at the time that Kamlot had threatened me, and I had not arisen; now I stood up and faced him. 'You had better kill me, Kamlot,' I said, 'for I spoke the truth.'

He hesitated for a moment, standing there looking at me; then he returned his sword to its scabbard. 'I cannot,' he said huskily. 'May my ancestors forgive me! I cannot kill my friend.

'Perhaps,' he added, seeking some extenuating circumstance, 'you should not be held accountable to customs of which you had no knowledge. I often forget that you are of another world than ours. But tell me, now that I have made myself a party to your crime by excusing it, what leads you to believe that you will marry Duare? I can incriminate myself no more by listening to you further.'

'I intend to marry her, because I know that I love her and believe that she already half loves me.'

At this Kamlot appeared shocked and horrified again. 'That is impossible,' he cried. 'She never saw you before; she cannot dream what is in your heart or your mad brain.'

'On the contrary, she has seen me before; and she knows quite well what is in my "mad brain,"' I assured him. 'I told her in Kooaad; I told her again today.'

'And she listened?'

'She was shocked,' I admitted, 'but she listened; then she upbraided me and ordered me from her presence.'

Kamlot breathed a sigh of relief. 'At least *she* has not gone mad. I cannot understand on what you base your belief that she may return your love.'

'Her eyes betrayed her; and, what may be more convincing, she did not expose my perfidy and thus send me to my death.'

He pondered that and shook his head. 'It is all madness,' he said; 'I can make nothing of it. You say that you talked with her in Kooaad, but that would have been impossible. But if you had ever even seen her before, why did you show so little interest in her fate when you knew that she was a prisoner aboard the *Sovong*? Why did you say that you thought that she was my sweetheart?'

'I did not know until a few minutes ago,' I explained, 'that the girl I saw and talked with in the garden at Kooaad was Duare, the daughter of the jong.'

A few days later I was again talking with Kamlot in my cabin when we were interrupted by a whistle at the door; and when I bade him do so, one of the Vepajan prisoners that we had rescued from the *Sovong* entered. He was not from Kooaad but from another city of Vepaja, and therefore none of the other Vepajans aboard knew anything concerning him. His name was Vilor, and he appeared to be a decent sort of fellow, though rather inclined to taciturnity. He had manifested considerable interest in the klangans and was with them often, but had explained this idiosyncrasy on the grounds that he was a scholar and wished to study the birdmen, specimens of which he had never before seen.

'I have come,' he explained in response to my inquiry, 'to ask you to appoint me an officer. I should like to join your company and share in the work and responsibilities of the expedition.'

'We are well officered now,' I explained, 'and have all the men we need. Furthermore,' I added frankly, 'I do not know you well enough to be sure of your qualifications. By the time we reach Vejapa, we shall be better acquainted; and if I need you then, I will tell you.'

'Well, I should like to do something,' he insisted. 'May I guard the janjong until we reach Vepaja?'

He referred to Duare, whose title, compounded of the two words daughter and king, is synonymous to princess. I thought that I noticed just a trace of excitement in his voice as he made the request.

'She is well guarded now,' I explained.

'But I should like to do it,' he insisted. 'It would be a service of love and loyalty for my jong. I could stand the night guard; no one likes that detail ordinarily.'

'It will not be necessary,' I said shortly; 'the guard is already sufficient.'

'She is in the after cabins of the second deck house, is she not?' he asked. I told him that she was.

'And she has a special guard?'

'A man is always before her door at night,' I assured him.

'Only one?' he demanded, as though he thought the guard insufficient.

'In addition to the regular watch, we consider one man enough; she has no enemies aboard the *Sofal*.' These people were certainly solicitous of the welfare and safety of their royalty, I thought; and, it seemed to me, unnecessarily so. But finally Vilor gave up and departed, after begging me to give his request further thought.

'He seems even more concerned about the welfare of Duare than you,' I remarked to Kamlot after Vilor had gone.

'Yes, I noticed that,' replied my lieutenant thoughtfully.

'There is no one more concerned about her than I,' I said, 'but I cannot see that any further precautions are necessary.'

'Nor I,' agreed Kamlot; 'she is quite well protected now.'

We had dropped Vilor from our minds and were discussing other matters, when we heard the voice of the lookout in the crow's nest shouting, 'Voo notar!' ('A ship!') Running to the tower deck, we got the bearings of the stranger as the lookout announced them the second time, and, sure enough, almost directly abeam on the starboard side we discerned the superstructure of a ship on the horizon.

For some reason which I do not clearly understand, the visibility on Venus is usually exceptionally good. Low fogs and haze are rare, notwithstanding the humidity of the atmosphere. This condition may be due to the mysterious radiation from that strange element in the planet's structure which illuminates her moonless nights; I do not know.

At any rate, we could see a ship, and almost immediately all was excitement aboard the *Sofal*. Here was another prize, and the men were eager to be at her. As we changed our course and headed for our victim, a cheer rose from the men on deck. Weapons were issued, the bow gun and the two tower guns were elevated to firing positions. The *Sofal* forged ahead at full speed.

As we approached our quarry, we saw that it was a ship of about the same size as the *Sofal* and bearing the insignia of Thora. Closer inspection revealed it to be an armed merchantman.

I now ordered all but the gunners into the lower deck house, as I planned on boarding this vessel as I had the *Sovong* and did not wish her to see our deck filled with armed men before we came alongside. As before, explicit orders were issued; every man knew what was expected of him; all were cautioned against needless killing. If I were to be a pirate, I was going to be as humane a pirate as possible. I would not spill blood needlessly.

I had questioned Kiron, Gamfor, and many another Thoran in my company relative to the customs and practices of Thoran ships of war until I felt reasonably familiar with them. I knew for instance that a warship might search a merchantman. It was upon this that I based my hope of getting our grappling hooks over the side of our victim before he could suspect our true design.

When we were within hailing distance of the ship, I directed Kiron to order her to shut down her engines, as we wished to board and search her; and right then we ran into our first obstacle. It came in the form of a pennant suddenly hoisted at the bow of our intended victim. It meant nothing to me, but it did to Kiron and the other Thorans aboard the *Sofal*.

'We'll not board her so easily after all,' said Kiron. 'She has an ongyan on board, and that exempts her from search. It probably also indicates that she carries a larger complement of soldiers than a merchantman ordinarily does.'

'Whose friend?' I asked, 'Yours?' for ongyan means great friend, in the sense of eminent or exalted.

Kiron smiled. 'It is a title. There are a hundred klongyan in the oligarchy; one of them is aboard that ship. They are great friends unquestionably, great friends of themselves; they rule Thora more tyrannically than any jong and for themselves alone.'

'How will the men feel about attacking a ship bearing so exalted a personage?' I inquired.

'They will fight among themselves to be the first aboard and to run a sword through him.'

'They must not kill him,' I replied. 'I have a better plan.'

'They will be hard to control once they are in the thick of a fight,' Kiron assured me; 'I have yet to see the officer who can do it. In the old days, in the days of the jongs, there were order and discipline; but not now.'

'There will be aboard the *Sofal*,' I averred. 'Come with me; I am going to speak to the men.'

Together we entered the lower deck house where the majority of the ship's company was massed, waiting for the command to attack. There were nearly a hundred rough and burly fighting men, nearly all of whom were ignorant and brutal. We had been together as commander and crew for too short a time for me to gauge their sentiments toward me; but I realized that there must be no question in any mind as to who was captain of the ship, no matter what they thought of me.

Kiron had called them to attention as we entered, and now every eye was on me as I started to speak. 'We are about to take another ship,' I began, 'on board which is one whom Kiron tells me you will want to kill. He is an ong-yan. I have come here to tell you that he must not be killed.' Growls of disapproval greeted this statement, but, ignoring them, I continued, 'I have come here to tell you something else, because I have been informed that no officer can control you after you enter battle. There are reasons why it will be better for us to hold this man prisoner than to kill him, but these have nothing to do with the question; what you must understand is that my orders and the orders of your other officers must be obeyed.

'We are embarked upon an enterprise that can succeed only if discipline be enforced. I expect the enterprise to succeed. I will enforce discipline. Insubordination or disobedience will be punishable by death. That is all.'

As I left the room, I left behind me nearly a hundred silent men. There was nothing to indicate what their reaction had been. Purposely, I took Kiron out with me; I wanted the men to have an opportunity to discuss the matter among themselves without interference by an officer. I knew that I had no real authority over them, and that eventually they must decide for themselves whether they would obey me; the sooner that decision was reached the better for all of us.

Amtorian ships employ only the most primitive means of intercommunication. There is a crude and cumbersome hand signalling system in which flags are employed; then there is a standardized system of trumpet calls which covers a fairly wide range of conventional messages, but the most satisfactory medium and the one most used is the human voice.

Since our quarry had displayed the pennant of the ongyan, we had held a course parallel to hers and a little distance astern. On her main deck a company of armed men was congregated. She mounted four guns, which had been elevated into firing position. She was ready, but I think that as yet she suspected nothing wrong in our intentions.

Now I gave orders that caused the *Sofal* to close in upon the other ship, and as the distance between them lessened I saw indications of increasing excitement on the decks of our intended victim.

'What are you about?' shouted an officer from her tower deck. 'Stand off there! There is an ongyan aboard us.'

As no reply was made him, and as the *Sofal* continued to draw nearer, his excitement waxed. He gesticulated rapidly as he conversed with a fat man standing at his side; then he screamed, 'Stand off! Or someone will suffer for this'; but the *Sofal* only moved steadily closer. 'Stand off, or I'll fire!' shouted the captain.

For answer I caused all our starboard guns to be elevated into firing position. I knew he would not dare fire now, for a single broadside from the *Sofal* would have sunk him in less than a minute, a contingency which I wished to avoid as much as he.

'What do you want of us?' he demanded.

'We want to board you,' I replied, 'without bloodshed if possible.'

'This is revolution! This is treason!' shouted the fat man at the captain's side. 'I order you to stand off and leave us alone. I am the ongyan, Moosko,' and then to the soldiers on the main deck he screamed, 'Repel them! Kill any man who sets foot upon that deck!'

XIII

Catastrophe

At the same moment that the ongyan, Moosko, ordered his soldiers to repel any attempt to board his ship, her captain ordered full speed ahead and threw her helm to starboard. She veered away from us and leaped ahead in an effort to escape. Of course I could have sunk her, but her loot would have been of no value to me at the bottom of the sea; instead I directed the trumpeter at my side to sound full speed ahead to the officer in the tower, and the chase was on.

The *Yan*, whose name was now discernible across her stern, was much faster than Kiron had led me to believe; but the *Sofal* was exceptionally speedy, and it soon became obvious to all that the other ship could not escape her. Slowly we regained the distance that we had lost in the first, unexpected spurt of the *Yan*; slowly but surely we were closing up on her. Then the captain of the *Yan* did just what I should have done had I been in his place; he kept the *Sofal* always directly astern of him and opened fire on us with his after tower gun and with a gun similarly placed in the stern on the lower deck. The maneuver was tactically faultless, since it greatly reduced the number of guns that we could bring into play without changing our course, and was the only one that might offer him any hope of escape.

There was something eerie in the sound of that first heavy Amtorian gun that I had heard. I saw nothing, neither smoke nor flame; there was only a loud staccato roar more reminiscent of machine gun fire than of any other sound. At first there was no other effect; then I saw a piece of our starboard rail go and two of my men fall to the deck.

By this time our bow gun was in action. We were in the swell of the *Yan*'s wake, which made accurate firing difficult. The two ships were racing ahead at full speed; the prow of the *Sofal* was throwing white water and spume far to either side; the sea in the wake of the *Yan* was boiling, and a heavy swell that we were quartering kept the ships rolling. The thrill of the chase and of battle was in our blood, and above all was the venomous rattle of the big guns.

I ran to the bow to direct the fire of the gun there, and a moment later we had the satisfaction of seeing the crew of one of the *Yan*'s guns crumple to the deck man by man, as our gunner got his sights on them and mowed them down.

The *Sofal* was gaining rapidly upon the *Yan*, and our guns were concentrating on the tower gun and the tower of the enemy. The ongyan had long since disappeared from the upper deck, having doubtlessly sought safety in a less exposed part of the ship, and in fact there were only two men left alive upon the tower deck where he had stood beside the captain; these were two of the crew of the gun that was giving us most trouble.

I did not understand at the time why the guns of neither ship were more effective. I knew that the T-ray was supposedly highly destructive, and so I could not understand why neither ship had been demolished or sunk; but that was because I had not yet learned that all the vital parts of the ships were protected by a thin armor of the same metal of which the large guns were composed, the only substance at all impervious to the T-ray. Had this not been true, our fire would have long since put the *Yan* out of commission, as our T-rays, directed upon her after tower gun, would have passed on through the tower, killing the men at the controls and destroying the controls themselves. Eventually this would have happened, but it would have been necessary first to have destroyed the protective armor of the tower.

At last we succeeded in silencing the remaining gun, but if we were to draw up alongside the *Yan* we must expose ourselves to the fire of other guns located on her main deck and the forward end of the tower. We had already suffered some losses, and I knew that we must certainly expect a great many more if we put ourselves in range of those other guns; but there seemed no other alternative than to abandon the chase entirely, and that I had no mind to do.

Giving orders to draw up along her port side, I directed the fire of the bow gun along her rail where it would rake her port guns one by one as we moved up on her, and gave orders that each of our starboard guns in succession should open fire similarly as they came within range of the *Yan*'s guns. Thus we kept a steady and continuous fire streaming upon the unhappy craft as we drew alongside her and closed up the distance between us.

We had suffered a number of casualties, but our losses were nothing compared to those of the *Yan*, whose decks were now strewn with dead and dying men. Her plight was hopeless, and her commander must at last have realized it, for now he gave the signal of surrender and stopped his engines. A few minutes later we were alongside and our boarding party had clambered over her rail.

As Kamlot and I stood watching these men who were being led by Kiron to take possession of the prize and bring certain prisoners aboard the *Sofal*, I could not but speculate upon what their answer was to be to my challenge for leadership. I knew that their freedom from the constant menace of their tyrannical masters was so new to them that they might well be expected to commit excesses, and I dreaded the result, for I had determined to make an example of any men who disobeyed me, though I fell in the attempt. I saw the majority of them spread over the deck under the command of the great Zog, while Kiron led a smaller detachment to the upper decks in search of the captain and the ongyan.

Fully five minutes must have elapsed before I saw my lieutenant emerge from the tower of the *Yan* with his two prisoners. He conducted them down the companionway and across the main deck toward the *Sofal*, while a hundred members of my pirate band watched them in silence. Not a hand was raised against them as they passed.

Kamlot breathed a sigh of relief as the two men clambered over the rail of the *Sofal* and approached us. 'I think that our lives hung in the balance then, quite as much as theirs,' he said, and I agreed with him, for if my men had started killing aboard the *Yan* in defiance of my orders, they would have had to kill me and those loyal to me to protect their own lives.

The ongyan was still blustering when they were halted in front of me, but the captain was awed. There was something about the whole incident that mystified him, and when he got close enough to me to see the color of my hair and eyes, I could see that he was dumfounded.

'This is an outrage,' shouted Moosko, the ongyan. 'I will see that every last man of you is destroyed for this.' He was trembling, and purple with rage.

'See that he does not speak again unless he is spoken to,' I instructed Kiron, and then I turned to the captain. 'As soon as we have taken what we wish from your ship,' I told him, 'you will be free to continue your voyage. I am sorry that you did not see fit to obey me when I ordered you to stop for boarding; it would have saved many lives. The next time you are ordered to lay to by the *Sofal*, do so; and when you return to your country, advise other shipmasters that the *Sofal* is abroad and that she is to be obeyed.'

'Do you mind telling me,' he asked, 'who you are and under what flag you sail?'

'For the moment I am a Vepajan,' I replied, 'but we sail under our own flag. No country is responsible for what we do, nor are we responsible to any country.'

Pressing the crew of the *Yan* into service, Kamlot, Kiron, Gamfor, and Zog had all her weapons, such of her provisions as we wished, and the most valuable and least bulky portion of her cargo transferred to the *Sofal* before dark. We then threw her guns overboard and let her proceed upon her way.

Moosko I retained as a hostage in the event that we should ever need one; he was being held under guard on the main deck until I could determine just what to do with him. The Vepajan women captives we had rescued from the *Sovong*, together with our own officers who were also quartered on the second deck, left me no vacant cabin in which to put Moosko, and I did not wish to confine him below deck in the hole reserved for common prisoners.

I chanced to mention the matter to Kamlot in the presence of Vilor, when the latter immediately suggested that he would share his own small cabin with Moosko and be responsible for him. As this seemed an easy solution of the problem, I ordered Moosko turned over to Vilor, who took him at once to his cabin.

The pursuit of the *Yan* had taken us off our course, and now, as we headed once more toward Vepaja, a dark land mass was dimly visible to starboard. I could not but wonder what mysteries lay beyond that shadowy coast line, what strange beasts and men inhabited that *terra incognita* that stretched away into Strabol and the unexplored equatorial regions of Venus. To partially satisfy my curiosity, I went to the chart room, and after determining our position as accurately as I could by dead reckoning, I discovered that we were off the shore of Noobol. I remembered having heard Danus mention this country, but I could not recall what he had told me about it.

Lured by imaginings, I went out onto the tower deck and stood alone, looking out across the faintly illuminated nocturnal waters of Amtor toward mysterious Noobol. The wind had risen to almost the proportions of a gale, the first that I had encountered since my coming to the Shepherd's Star; heavy seas were commencing to run, but I had every confidence in the ship and in the ability of my officers to navigate her under any circumstances; so I was not perturbed by the increasing violence of the storm. It occurred to me though that the women aboard might be frightened, and my thoughts, which were seldom absent from her for long, returned to Duare. Perhaps she was frightened!

Even no excuse is a good excuse to the man who wishes to see the object of his infatuation; but now I prided myself that I had a real reason for seeing her and one that she herself must appreciate, since it was prompted by solicitude for her welfare. And so I went down the companionway to the second deck with the intention of whistling before the door of Duare; but as I had to pass directly by Vilor's cabin, I thought that I would take the opportunity to look in on my prisoner.

There was a moment's silence following my signal, and then Vilor bade me enter. As I stepped into the cabin, I was surprised to see an angan sitting there with Moosko and Vilor. Vilor's embarrassment was obvious; Moosko appeared ill at ease and the birdman frightened. That they were disconcerted did not surprise me, for it is not customary for members of the superior race to fraternize with klangan socially. But if they were embarrassed, I was not. I was more inclined to be angry. The position of the Vepajans aboard the *Sofal* was a delicate one. We were few in numbers, and our ascendency depended wholly upon the respect we engendered and maintained in the minds of the Thorans, who constituted the majority of our company, and who looked up to the Vepajans as their superiors despite the efforts of their leaders to convince them of the equality of all men.

'Your quarters are forward,' I said to the angan; 'you do not belong here.'

'It is not his fault,' said Vilor, as the birdman rose to leave the cabin. 'Moosko, strange as it may seem, had never seen an angan; and I fetched this fellow here merely to satisfy his curiosity. I am sorry if I did wrong.'

'Of course,' I said, 'that puts a slightly different aspect on the matter, but I think it will be better if the prisoner inspects the klangan on deck where they belong. He has my permission to do so tomorrow.'

The angan departed, I exchanged a few more words with Vilor, and then I left him with his prisoner and turned toward the after cabin where Duare was quartered, the episode that had just occurred fading from my mind almost immediately, to be replaced by far more pleasant thoughts.

There was a light in Duare's cabin as I whistled before her door, wondering if she would invite me in or ignore my presence. For a time there was no response to my signal, and had about determined that she would not see me, when I heard her soft, low voice inviting me to enter.

'You are persistent,' she said, but there was less anger in her voice than when last she had spoken to me.

'I came to ask if the storm has frightened you and to assure you that there is no danger.'

'I am not afraid,' she replied. 'Was that all that you wished to say?'

It sounded very much like a dismissal. 'No,' I assured her, 'nor did I come solely for the purpose of saying it.'

She raised her eyebrows. 'What else could you have to say to me – that you have not already said?'

'Perhaps I wished to repeat,' I suggested.

'You must not!' she cried.

I came closer to her. 'Look at me, Duare; look me in the eyes and tell me that you do not like to hear me tell you that I love you!'

Her eyes fell. 'I must not listen!' she whispered and rose as though to leave the room.

I was mad with love for her; her near presence sent the hot blood boiling through my veins; I seized her in my arms and drew her to me; before she could prevent it, I covered her lips with mine. Then she partially tore away from me, and I saw a dagger gleaming in her hand.

'You are right,' I said. 'Strike! I have done an unforgivable thing. My only excuse is my great love for you; it swept away reason and honor.'

Her dagger hand dropped to her side. 'I cannot,' she sobbed, and, turning, fled from the room.

I went back to my own cabin, cursing myself for a beast and a cad. I could not understand how it had been possible for me to have committed such an unpardonable act. I reviled myself, and at the same time the memory of that soft body crushed against mine and those perfect lips against my lips suffused me with a warm glow of contentment that seemed far removed from repentance.

I lay awake for a long time after I went to bed, thinking of Duare, recalling all that had ever passed between us. I found a hidden meaning in her cry, 'I must not listen!' I rejoiced in the facts that once she had refused to consign me to death at the hands of others and that again she had refused to kill me herself. Her 'I cannot' rang in my ears almost like an avowal of love. My better judgment told that I was quite mad, but I found joy in hugging my madness to me.

The storm increased to such terrific fury during the night that the screeching of the wind and the wild plunging of the *Sofal* awakened me just before dawn. Arising immediately, I went on deck, where the wind almost carried me away. Great waves lifted the *Sofal* on high, only to plunge her the next moment into watery abysses. The ship was pitching violently; occasionally a huge wave broke across her bow and flooded the main deck; across her starboard quarter loomed a great land mass that seemed perilously close. The situation appeared fraught with danger.

I entered the control room and found both Honan and Gamfor with the helmsman. They were worried because of our proximity to land. Should either the engines or the steering device fail, we must inevitably be driven ashore. I told them to remain where they were, and then I went down to the second deck house to arouse Kiron, Kamlot, and Zog.

As I turned aft from the foot of the companionway on the second deck, I noticed that the door of Vilor's cabin was swinging open and closing again with each roll of the vessel; but I gave the matter no particular thought at the time and passed on to awaken my other lieutenants. Having done so, I kept on to Duare's cabin, fearing that, if awake, she might be frightened by the rolling of the ship and the shrieking of the wind. To my surprise, I found her door swinging on its hinges.

Something, I do not know what, aroused my suspicion that all was not right far more definitely than the rather unimportant fact that the door to her outer cabin was unlatched. Stepping quickly inside, I uncovered the light and glanced quickly about the room. There was nothing amiss except, perhaps, the fact that the door to the inner cabin where she slept was also open and swinging on its hinges. I was sure that no one could be sleeping in there while both those doors were swinging and banging. It was possible, of course, that Duare was too frightened to get up and close them.

I stepped to the inner doorway and called her name aloud. There was no reply. I called again, louder; again, silence was my only answer. Now I was definitely perturbed. Stepping into the room, I uncovered the light and looked at the bed. It was empty – Duare was not there! But in the far corner of the cabin lay the body of the man who had stood guard outside her door.

Throwing conventions overboard, I hastened to each of the adjoining cabins where the rest of the Vepajan women were quartered. All were there except Duare. They had not seen her; they did not know where she was. Frantic from apprehension, I ran back to Kamlot's cabin and acquainted him with my tragic discovery. He was stunned.

'She must be on board,' he cried. 'Where else can she be?'

'I know she *must* be,' I replied, 'but something tells me she is not. We must search the ship at once – from stem to stern.'

Zog and Kiron were emerging from their cabins as I came from Kamlot's. I told them of my discovery and ordered the search commenced; then I hailed a member of the watch and sent him to the crow's nest to question the lookout. I wanted to know whether he had seen anything unusual transpiring on the ship during his watch, for from his lofty perch he could overlook the entire vessel.

'Muster every man,' I told Kamlot; 'account for every human being on board; search every inch of the ship.'

As the men left to obey my instructions, I recalled the coincidence of the two cabin doors swinging wide – Duare's and Vilor's. I could not imagine what relation either fact had to the other, but I was investigating everything, whether it was of a suspicious nature or not; so I ran quickly to Vilor's cabin, and the moment that I uncovered the light I saw that both Vilor and Moosko were missing. But where were they? No man could have left the *Sofal* in that storm and lived, even could he have launched a boat, which would have been impossible of accomplishment, even in fair weather, without detection.

Coming from Vilor's cabin, I summoned a sailor and dispatched him to inform Kamlot that Vilor and Moosko were missing from their cabin and direct him to send them to me as soon as he located them; then I returned to the quarters of the Vepajan women for the purpose of questioning them more carefully.

I was puzzled by the disappearance of Moosko and Vilor, which, taken in conjunction with the absence of Duare from her cabin, constituted a mystery of major proportions; and I was trying to discover some link of circumstance that might point a connection between the two occurrences, when I suddenly recalled Vilor's insistence that he be permitted to guard Duare. Here was the first, faint suggestion of a connecting link. However, it seemed to lead nowhere. These three people had disappeared from their cabins, yet reason assured me that they would be found in a short time, since it was impossible for them to leave the ship, unless—

It was that little word 'unless' that terrified me most of all. Since I had discovered that Duare was not in her cabin, a numbing fear had assailed me that, considering herself dishonored by my avowal of love, she had hurled herself overboard. Of what value now the fact that I constantly upbraided myself for my lack of consideration and control? Of what weight my vain regrets?

Yet now I saw a tiny ray of hope. If the absence of Vilor and Moosko from their cabin and Duare from hers were more than a coincidence, then it were safe to assume that they were together and ridiculous to believe that all three had leaped overboard.

With these conflicting fears and hopes whirling through my brain, I came to the quarters of the Vepajan women, which I was about to enter when the sailor I had sent to question the lookout in the crow's nest came running toward me in a state of evident excitement.

'Well,' I demanded, as, breathless, he halted before me, 'what did the lookout have to say?'

'Nothing, my captain,' replied the man, his speech retarded by excitement and exertion.

'Nothing! And why not?' I snapped.

'The lookout is dead, my captain,' gasped the sailor.

'Dead!'

'Murdered.'

'How?' I asked.

'A sword had been run through his body – from behind, I think. He lay upon his face.'

'Go at once and inform Kamlot; tell him to replace the lookout and investigate his death, then to report to me.'

Shaken by this ominous news, I entered the quarters of the women. They were huddled together in one cabin, pale and frightened, but outwardly calm.

'Have you found Duare?' one of them asked immediately.

'No,' I replied, 'but I have discovered another mystery – the ongyan, Moosko, is missing and with him the Vepajan, Vilor.'

'Vepajan!' exclaimed Byea, the woman who had questioned me concerning Duare. 'Vilor is no Vepajan.'

'What do you mean?' I demanded. 'If he is not a Vepajan, what is he?'

'He is a Thoran spy,' she replied. 'He was sent to Vepaja long ago to steal the secret of the longevity serum, and when we were captured the klangan took him, also, by mistake. We learned this, little by little, aboard the *Sovong*.'

'But why was I not informed when he was brought aboard?' I demanded.

'We supposed that everyone knew it,' explained Byea, 'and thought that Vilor was transferred to the *Sofal* as a prisoner.'

Another link in the chain of accumulating evidence! Yet I was as far as ever from knowing where either end of the chain lay.

XIV

Storm

After questioning the women, I went to the main deck, too impatient to await the reports of my lieutenants in the tower where I belonged. I found that they had searched the ship and were just coming to me with their report. None of those previously discovered missing had been found, but the search had revealed another astounding fact – the five klangan also were missing!

Searching certain portions of the ship had been rather dangerous work, as she was rolling heavily, and the deck was still occasionally swept by the larger seas; but it had been accomplished without mishap, and the men were now congregated in a large room in the main deck house. Kamlot, Gamfor, Kiron, Zog, and I had also entered this same room, where we were discussing the whole mysterious affair. Honan was in the control room of the tower.

I told them that I had just discovered that Vilor was not Vepajan but a Thoran spy, and had reminded Kamlot of the man's request that he be allowed to guard the janjong. 'I learned something else from Byea while I was questioning the women,' I added. 'During their captivity aboard the *Sovong*, Vilor persisted in annoying Duare with his attentions; he was infatuated with her.

'I think that gives us the last bit of evidence we need to enable us to reconstruct the hitherto seemingly inexplicable happenings of the past night,' said Gamfor. 'Vilor wished to possess Duare; Moosko wished to escape from captivity. The former had fraternized with the klangan and made friends of them; that was known to everyone aboard the *Sofal*. Moosko was an ongyan; during all their lives, doubtless, the klangan have looked upon the klongyan as the fountain heads of supreme authority. They would believe his promises, and they would obey his commands.

'Doubtless Vilor and Moosko worked out the details of the plot together. They dispatched an angan to kill the lookout, lest their movements arouse suspicion and be reported before they could carry their plan to a successful conclusion. The lookout disposed of, the other klangan congregated in Vilor's cabin; then Vilor, probably accompanied by Moosko, went to the cabin of Duare, where they killed the guard and seized her in her sleep, silenced her with a gag, and carried her to the gangway outside, where the klangan were waiting.

'A gale was blowing, it is true, but it was blowing toward land which lay but a short distance to starboard; and the klangan are powerful fliers.

'There you have what I believe to be a true picture of what happened aboard the *Sofal* while we slept.'

'And you believe that the klangan carried these three people to the shores of Noobol?' I asked.

'I think there can be no question but that such is the fact,' replied Gamfor.

'I quite agree with him,' interjected Kamlot.

'Then there is but one thing to do,' I announced. 'We must turn back and land a searching party on Noobol.'

'No boat could live in this sea,' objected Kiron.

'The storm will not last forever,' I reminded him. 'We shall lie off the shore until it abates. I am going up to the tower; I wish you men would remain here and question the crew; it is possible that there may be someone among them who has overheard something that will cast new light on the subject. The klangan are great talkers, and they may have dropped some remark that will suggest the ultimate destination Vilor and Moosko had in mind.'

As I stepped out onto the main deck, the *Sofal* rose upon the crest of a great wave and then plunged nose downward into the watery abyss beyond, tilting the deck forward at an angle of almost forty-five degrees. The wet and slippery boards beneath my feet gave them no hold, and I slid helplessly forward almost fifty feet before I could check my descent. Then the ship buried her nose in a mountainous wave and a great wall of water swept the deck from stem to stern, picking me up and whirling me helplessly upon its crest.

For a moment I was submerged, and then a vagary of the Titan that had seized me brought my head above the water, and I saw the *Sofal* rolling and pitching fifty feet away.

Even in the immensity of interstellar space I had never felt more helpless nor more hopeless than I did at that moment on the storm-lashed sea of an unknown world, surrounded by darkness and chaos and what terrible creatures of this mysterious deep I could not even guess. I was lost! Even if my comrades knew of the disaster that had overwhelmed me, they were helpless to give me aid. No boat could live in that sea, as Kiron had truly reminded us, and no swimmer could breast the terrific onslaught of those racing, wind-driven mountains of water that might no longer be described by so puny a word as wave.

Hopeless! I should not have said that; I am never without hope. If I could not swim against the sea, perhaps I might swim with it; and at no great distance lay land. I am an experienced distance swimmer and a powerful man. If any man could survive in such a sea, I knew that I could; but if I could not, I was determined that I should at least have the satisfaction of dying fighting.

I was hampered by no clothes, as one could scarcely dignify the Amtorian loincloth with the name of clothing; my only impediment was my weapons; and these I hesitated to discard, knowing that my chances for survival on that unfriendly shore would be slight were I unarmed. Neither the belt, nor the pistol, nor the dagger inconvenienced me, and their weight was negligible; but the sword was a different matter. If you have never tried swimming with a sword dangling from your middle, do not attempt it in a heavy sea. You might think that it would hang straight down and not get in the way, but mine did not. The great waves hurled me about mercilessly, twisting and turning me; and now my sword was buffeting me in some tender spot, and now it was getting between my legs, and once, when a wave turned me completely over, it came down on top of me and struck me on the head; yet I would not discard it.

After the first few minutes of battling with the sea, I concluded that I was in no immediate danger of being drowned. I could keep my head above the waves often enough and long enough to insure sufficient air for my lungs; and, the water being warm, I was in no danger of being chilled to exhaustion, as so often occurs when men are thrown into cold seas. Therefore, as closely as I could anticipate any contingency in this unfamiliar world, there remained but two major and immediate threats against my life. The first lay in the possibility of attack by some ferocious monster of the Amtorian deeps; the second, and by far the more serious, the storm-lashed shore upon which I must presently attempt to make a safe landing.

This in itself should have been sufficient to dishearten me, for I had seen seas breaking upon too many shores to lightly ignore the menace of those incalculable tons of hurtling waters pounding, crashing, crushing, tearing their way even into the rocky heart of the eternal hills.

I swam slowly in the direction of the shore, which, fortunately for me, was in the direction that the storm was carrying me. I had no mind to sap my strength by unnecessarily overexerting myself; and so, as I took it easily, content to keep afloat as I moved slowly shoreward, daylight came; and as each succeeding wave lifted me to its summit, I saw the shore with increasing clearness. It lay about a mile from me, and its aspect was most forbidding. Huge combers were breaking upon a rocky coast line, throwing boiling fountains of white spume high in air; above the howling of the tempest, the thunder of the surf rolled menacingly across that mile of angry sea to warn me that death lay waiting to embrace me at the threshold of safety.

I was in a quandary. Death lay all about me; it remained but for me to choose the place and manner of the assignation; I could drown where I was, or I could permit myself to be dashed to pieces on the rocks. Neither eventuality aroused any considerable enthusiasm in my breast. As a mistress, death seemed sadly lacking in many essentials. Therefore, I decided not to die.

Thoughts may be, as has been said, things; but they are not everything. No matter how favorably I thought of living, I knew that I must also do something about it. My present situation offered me no chance of salvation; the shore alone could give me life; so I struck out for the shore. As I drew nearer it, many things, some of them quite irrelevant, passed through my mind; but some were relevant, among them the Burial Service. It was not a nice time to think of this, but then we cannot always control our thoughts; however, 'In the midst of life we are in death' seemed wholly appropriate to my situation. By twisting it a bit, I achieved something that contained the germ of hope – in the midst of death there is life. Perhaps—

The tall waves, lifting me high, afforded me for brief instants vantage points from which I could view the death ahead in the midst of which I sought for life. The shore line was becoming, at closer range, something more than an unbroken line of jagged rocks and white water; but details were yet lacking, for each time I was allowed but a brief glimpse before being dropped once more to the bottom of a watery chasm.

My own efforts, coupled with the fury of the gale driving me shoreward, brought me rapidly to the point where I should presently be seized by the infuriated seas and hurled upon the bombarded rocks that reared their jagged heads bleakly above the swirling waters of each receding comber.

A great wave lifted me upon its crest and carried me forward – the end had come! With the speed of a racehorse it swept me toward my doom; a welter of spume engulfed my head; I was twisted and turned as a cork in a whirlpool; yet I struggled to lift my mouth above the surface for an occasional gasp of air; I fought to live for a brief moment longer, that I might not be dead when I was dashed by the merciless sea against the merciless rocks – thus dominating is the urge to live.

I was carried on; moments seemed an eternity! Where were the rocks? I almost yearned for them now to end the bitterness of my futile struggle. I thought of my mother and of Duare. I even contemplated, with something akin to philosophic calm, the strangeness of my end. In that other world that I had left forever no creature would ever have knowledge of my fate. Thus spoke the eternal egotism of man, who, even in death, desires an audience.

Now I caught a brief glimpse of rocks. They were upon my left when they should have been in front of me. It was incomprehensible. The wave tore on, carrying me with it; and still I lived, and there was only water against my naked flesh.

Now the fury of the sea abated, I rose to the crest of a diminishing comber to look with astonishment upon the comparatively still waters of an inlet. I had been carried through the rocky gateway of a landlocked cove, and before me I saw a sandy crescent beach. I had escaped the black fingers of death; I had been the beneficiary of a miracle!

The sea gave me a final flip that rolled me high upon the sands to mingle with the wrack and flotsam she had discarded. I stood up and looked about me. A more devout man would have given thanks, but I felt that as yet I had been spared temporarily, but Duare was still in peril.

The cove into which I had been swept was formed by the mouth of a canyon that ran inland between low hills, the sides and summits of which were dotted with small trees. Nowhere did I see any such giants as grow in Vepaja; but perhaps, I mused, what I see here are not trees on Venus but only underbrush. However, I shall call them trees, since many of them were from fifty to eighty feet in height.

A little river tumbled down the canyon's bottom to empty into the cove; pale violet grass, starred with blue and purple flowers, bordered it and clothed the hills. There were trees with red boles, smooth and glossy as lacquer. There were trees with azure boles. Whipping in the gale was the same weird foliage of heliotrope and lavender and violet that had rendered the forests of Vepaja so unearthly to my eyes. But beautiful and unusual as was the scene, it could not claim my undivided attention. A strange freak of fate had thrown me upon this shore to which, I had reason to believe, Duare must undoubtedly have been carried; and now my only thought was to take advantage of this fortunate circumstance and attempt to find and succor her.

I could only assume that in the event her abductors had brought her to this shore their landing must have been made farther along the coast to my right, which was the direction from which the *Sofal* had been moving. With only this slight and unsatisfactory clue, I started immediately to scale the side of the canyon and commence my search.

At the summit I paused a moment to survey the surrounding country and get my bearings. Before me stretched a rolling tableland, tree-dotted and lush with grass, and beyond that, inland, rose a range of mountains, vague and mysterious along the distant horizon. My course lay to the east, along the coast (I shall use the Earthly references to points of compass); the mountains were northward, toward the equator. I am assuming of course that I am in the southern hemisphere of the planet. The sea was south of me. I glanced in that direction, looking for the *Sofal*; there she was, far out and moving toward the east. Evidently my orders were being carried out, and the *Sofal* was lying off shore waiting for calm weather that would permit a landing.

Now I turned my steps toward the east. At each elevation I stopped and scanned the tableland in all directions, searching for some sign of those I sought. I saw signs of life, but not of human life. Herbivorous animals grazed in large numbers upon the flower-starred violet plain. Many that were close enough to be seen plainly appeared similar in form to Earthly animals, but there was none exactly like anything I had ever seen on Earth. Their extreme wariness and the suggestion of speed and agility in their conformations suggested that they had enemies; the wariness, that among these enemies was man; the speed and agility, that swift and ferocious carnivores preyed upon them.

These observations served to warn me that I must be constantly on the alert for similar dangers that might threaten me, and I was glad that the table-land was well supplied with trees growing at convenient intervals. I had not forgotten the ferocious basto that Kamlot and I had encountered in Vepaja, and, though I had seen nothing quite so formidable as yet among the nearer beasts, there were some creatures grazing at a considerable distance from me whose lines suggested a too great similarity to those bisonlike omnivores to insure ease of mind.

I moved rather rapidly, as I was beset by fears for Duare's safety and felt that if I did not come upon some clue this first day my search might prove fruitless. The klangan, I believed, must have alighted near the coast, where they would have remained at least until daylight, and my hope was that they might have tarried longer. If they had winged away immediately, my chances of locating them were slight; and now my only hope lay in the slender possibility that I might come across them before they took up their flight for the day.

The table-land was cut by gullies and ravines running down to the sea. Nearly all of these carried streams varying in size from tiny rivulets to those which might be dignified by the appellation of river, but none that I encountered offered any serious obstacle to my advance, though upon one or two occasions I was forced to swim the deeper channels. If these rivers were inhabited by dangerous reptiles, I saw nothing of them, though I admit that they were constantly on my mind as I made my way from bank to bank.

Once, upon the table-land, I saw a large, cat-like creature at a distance, apparently stalking a herd of what appeared to be a species of antelope; but either it did not see me or was more interested in its natural prey, for although I was in plain sight, it paid no attention to me.

Shortly thereafter I dropped into a small gully, and when I had regained the higher ground upon the opposite side the beast was no longer in sight; but even had it been, it would have been driven from my thoughts by faint sounds that came to me out of the distance far ahead. There were what sounded like the shouts of men and the unmistakable hum of Amtorian pistol fire.

Though I searched diligently with my eyes to the far horizon, I could see no sign of the authors of these noises; but it was enough for me to know that there were human beings ahead and that there was fighting there. Being only human, I naturally pictured the woman I loved in the center of overwhelming dangers, even though my better judgment told me that the encounter reverberating in the distance might have no connection with her or her abductors.

Reason aside, however, I broke into a run; and as I advanced the sounds waxed louder. They led me finally to the rim of a considerable canyon, the bottom of which formed a level valley of entrancing loveliness, through which wound a river far larger than any I had yet encountered.

But neither the beauty of the valley nor the magnitude of the river held my attention for but an instant. Down there upon the floor of that nameless canyon was a scene that gripped my undivided interest and left me cold with apprehension. Partially protected by an outcropping of rock at the river's edge, six figures crouched or lay. Five of them were klangan, the sixth a woman. It was Duare!

Facing them, hiding behind trees and rocks, were a dozen hairy, manlike creatures hurling rocks from slings at the beleaguered six or loosing crude arrows from still cruder bows. The savages and the klangan were hurling taunts and insults at one another, as well as missiles; it was these sounds that I had heard from a distance blending with the staccato hum of the klangan's pistols.

Three of the klangan lay motionless upon the turf behind their barrier, apparently dead. The remaining klangan and Duare crouched with pistols in their hands, defending their position and their lives. The savages cast their stone missiles directly at the three whenever one of them showed any part of his body above the rocky breastwork, but the arrows they discharged into the air so that they fell behind the barrier.

Scattered about among the trees and behind rocks were the bodies of fully a dozen hairy savages who had fallen before the fire of the klangan, but, while Duare's defenders had taken heavy toll of the enemy, the outcome of the unequal battle could have been only the total destruction of the klangan and Duare had it lasted much longer.

The details which have taken long in the telling I took in at a single glance, nor did I waste precious time in pondering the best course of action. At any moment one of those crude arrows might pierce the girl I loved; and so my first thought was to divert the attention of the savages, and perhaps their fire, from their intended victims to me.

I was slightly behind their position, which gave me an advantage, as also did the fact that I was above them. Yelling like a Comanche, I leaped down the steep side of the canyon, firing my pistol as I charged. Instantly the scene below me changed. The savages, taken partially from the rear and unexpectedly menaced by a new enemy, leaped to their feet in momentary bewilderment; and simultaneously the two remaining klangan, recognizing me and realizing that succor was at hand, sprang from the shelter of their barrier and ran forward to complete the demoralization of the savages.

Together we shot down six of the enemy before the rest finally turned and fled, but they were not routed before one of the klangan was struck full between the eyes by a jagged bit of rock. I saw him fall, and when we were no longer menaced by a foe I went to him, thinking that he was only stunned; but at that time I had no conception of the force with which these primitive, apelike men cast the missiles from their slings. The fellow's skull was crushed, and a portion of the missile had punctured his brain. He was quite dead when I reached him.

Then I hastened to Duare. She was standing with a pistol in her hand, tired and dishevelled, but otherwise apparently little worse for the harrowing experiences through which she had passed. I think that she was glad to see me, for she certainly must have preferred me to the hairy apemen from which I had been instrumental in rescuing her; yet a trace of fear was reflected in her eyes, as though she were not quite sure of the nature of the treatment she might expect from me. To my shame, her fears were justified by my past behavior; but I was determined that she should never again have cause to complain of me. I would win her confidence and trust, hoping that love might follow in their wake.

There was no light of welcome in her eyes as I approached her, and that hurt me more than I can express. Her countenance reflected more a pathetic resignation to whatever new trials my presence might portend.

'You have not been harmed?' I asked. 'You are all right?'

'Quite,' she replied. Her eyes passed beyond me, searching the summit of the canyon wall down which I had charged upon the savages. 'Where are the others?' she asked in puzzled and slightly troubled tones.

'What others?' I inquired.

'Those who came with you from the *Sofal* to search for me.'

'There were no others; I am quite alone.'

Her countenance assumed an even deeper gloom at this announcement. 'Why did you come alone?' she asked fearfully.

'To be honest with you, it was through no fault of my own that I came at all at this time,' I explained. 'After we missed you from the *Sofal*, I gave orders to stand by off the coast until the storm abated and we could land a searching party. Immediately thereafter I was swept overboard, a most fortunate circumstance as it turned out; and naturally when I found myself safely ashore my first thought was of you. I was searching for you when I heard the shouts of the savages and the sound of pistol fire.'

'You came in time to save me from them,' she said, 'but for what? What are you going to do with me now?'

'I am going to take you to the coast as quickly as possible,' I replied, 'and there we will signal the *Sofal*. She will send a boat to take us off.'

Duare appeared slightly relieved at this recital of my plans. 'You will win the undying gratitude of the jong, my father, if you return me to Vepaja unharmed,' she said.

'To have served his daughter shall be reward enough for me,' I replied, 'even though I succeed in winning not even her gratitude.'

'That you already have for what you have just done at the risk of your life,' she assured me, and there was more graciousness in her voice than before.

'What became of Vilor and Moosko?' I asked.

Her lip curled in scorn. 'When the kloonobargan attacked us, they fled.'

'Where did they go?' I asked.

'They swam the river and ran away in that direction.' She pointed toward the east.

'Why did the klangan not desert you also?'

'They were told to protect me. They know little else than to obey their superiors, and, too, they like to fight. Having little intelligence and no imagination, they are splendid fighters.'

'I cannot understand why they did not fly away from danger and take you with them when they saw that defeat was certain. That would have insured the safety of all.'

'By the time they were assured of that, it was too late,' she explained. 'They could not have risen from behind our protection without being destroyed by the missiles of the kloonobargan.'

This word, by way of parenthesis, is an interesting example of the derivation of an Amtorian substantive. Broadly, it means savages; literally, it means hairy men. In the singular, it is nobargan. *Gan* is man; *bar* is hair. *No* is a contraction of *not* (with), and is used as a prefix with the same value that the suffix *y* has in English; therefore *nobar* means hairy, *nobargan*, hairy man. The prefix *kloo* forms the plural, and we have *kloonobargan* (hairy men), savages.

After determining that the four klangan were dead, Duare, the remaining angan, and I started down the river toward the ocean. On the way Duare told me what had occurred on board the *Sofal* the preceding night, and I discovered that it had been almost precisely as Gamfor had pictured it.

'What was their object in taking you with them?' I asked.

'Vilor wanted me,' she replied.

'And Moosko merely wished to escape?'

'Yes. He thought that he would be killed when the ship reached Vepaja.'

'How did they expect to survive in a wild country like this?' I asked. 'Did they know where they were?'

'They said that they thought that the country was Noobol,' she replied, 'but they were not positive. The Thorans have agents in Noobol who are fomenting discord in an attempt to overthrow the government. There are several of these in a city on the coast, and it was Moosko's intention to search for this city, where he was certain that he would find friends who would be able to arrange transportation for himself, Vilor, and me to Thora.'

We walked on in silence for some time. I was just ahead of Duare, and the angan brought up the rear. He was crestfallen and dejected. His head and tail feathers drooped. The klangan are ordinarily so vociferous that this preternatural silence attracted my attention, and, thinking that he might have been injured in the fight, I questioned him.

'I was not wounded, my captain,' he replied.

'Then what is the matter with you? Are you sad because of the deaths of your comrades?'

'It is not that,' he replied; 'there are plenty more where they came from. It is because of my own death that I am sad.'

'But you are not dead!'

'I shall be soon,' he averred.

'What makes you think so?' I demanded.

'When I return to the ship, they will kill me for what I did last night. If I do not return, I shall be killed here. No one could live alone for long in such a country as this.'

'If you serve me well and obey me, you will not be killed if we succeed in the reaching the *Sofal* again,' I assured him.

At that he brightened perceptibly. 'I shall serve you well and obey you, my captain,' he promised, and presently he was smiling and singing again as though he had not a single care in the world and there was no such thing as death.

On several occasions, when I had glanced back at my companions, I had discovered Duare's eyes upon me, and in each instance she had turned them away quickly, as though I had surprised and embarrassed her in some questionable act. I had spoken to her only when necessary, for I had determined to atone for my previous conduct by maintaining a purely official attitude toward her that would reassure her and give her no cause for apprehension as to my intentions.

This was a difficult role for me to play while I yearned to take her into my arms and tell her again of the great love that was consuming me; but I had succeeded so far in controlling myself and saw no reason to believe that I should not be able to continue to do so, at least as long as Duare continued to give me no encouragement. The very idea that she might give me encouragement caused me to smile in spite of myself.

Presently, much to my surprise, she said, 'You are very quiet. What is the matter?'

It was the first time that Duare had ever opened a conversation with me or given me any reason to believe that I existed for her as a personality; I might have been a clod of earth or a piece of furniture, for all the interest she had seemed to take in me since those two occasions upon which I had surprised her as she watched me from the concealing foliage of her garden.

'There is nothing the matter with me,' I assured her. 'I am only concerned with your welfare and the necessity for getting you back to the *Sofal* as quickly as possible.'

'You do not talk any more,' she complained. 'Formerly, when I saw you, you used to talk a great deal.'

'Probably altogether too much,' I admitted, 'but you see, now I am trying not to annoy you.'

Her eyes fell to the ground. 'It would not annoy me,' she said almost inaudibly, but now that I was invited to do the very thing that I had been longing to do, I became dumb; I could think of nothing to say. 'You see,' she continued in her normal voice, 'conditions are very different now from any that I have ever before encountered. The rules and restrictions under which I have lived among my own people cannot, I now realize, be expected to apply to situations so unusual or to people and places so foreign to those whose lives they were intended to govern.

'I have been thinking a great deal about many things – and you. I commenced to think these strange thoughts after I saw you the first time in the garden at Kooaad. I have thought that perhaps it might be nice to talk to other men than those I am permitted to see in the house of my father, the jong. I became tired of talking to these same men and to my women, but custom had made a slave and a coward of me. I did not dare do the things I most wished to do. I always wanted to talk to you, and now for the brief time before we shall be again aboard the *Sofal*, where I must again be governed by the laws of Vepaja, I am going to be free; I am going to do what I wish; I am going to talk to you.'

This naïve declaration revealed a new Duare, one in the presence of whom it was going to be most difficult to maintain an austere platonicism; yet I continued to steel myself to the carrying out of my resolve.

'Why do you not talk to me?' she demanded when I made no immediate comment on her confession.

'I do not know what to talk about,' I admitted, 'unless I talk about the one thing that is uppermost in my mind.'

She was silent for a moment, her brows knit in thought, and then she asked with seeming innocence, 'What is that?'

'Love,' I said, looking into her eyes.

Her lids dropped and her lips trembled. 'No!' she exclaimed. 'We must not talk of that; it is wrong; it is wicked.

'Is love wicked on Amtor?' I asked.

'No, no; I do not mean that,' she hastened to deny; 'but it is wrong to speak to me of love until after I am twenty.'

'May I then, Duare?' I asked.

She shook her head, a little sadly I thought. 'No, not even then,' she answered. 'You may never speak to me of love, without sinning, nor may I listen without sinning, for I am the daughter of a jong.'

'Perhaps it would be safer were we not to talk at all,' I said glumly.

'Oh, yes, let us talk,' she begged. 'Tell me about the strange world you are supposed to come from.'

To amuse her, I did as she requested; and walking beside her I devoured her with my eyes until at last we came to the ocean. Far out I saw the *Sofal*, and now came the necessity for devising a scheme by which we might signal her.

On either side of the canyon, through which the river emptied into the ocean, were lofty cliffs. That on the west side, and nearer us, was the higher, and to this I made my way, accompanied by Duare and the angan. The ascent was steep, and most of the way I found it, or made it, necessary to assist Duare, so that often I had my arm about her as I half carried her upward.

At first I feared that she might object to this close contact; but she did not, and in some places where it was quite level and she needed no help, though I still kept my arm about her, she did not draw away nor seem to resent the familiarity.

At the summit of the cliff I hastily gathered dead wood and leaves with the assistance of the angan, and presently we had a signal fire sending a smoke column into the air. The wind had abated, and the smoke rose far above the cliff before it was dissipated. I was positive that it would be seen aboard the *Sofal*, but whether it would be correctly interpreted, I could not know.

A high sea was still running that would have precluded the landing of a small boat, but we had the angan, and if the *Sofal* were to draw in more closely to shore, he could easily transport us to her deck one at a time. However, I hesitated to risk Duare in the attempt while the ship was at its present considerable distance from shore, as what wind there was would have been directly in the face of the angan.

From the summit of this cliff we could overlook the cliff on the east side of the canyon, and presently the angan called my attention to something in that direction. 'Men are coming,' he said.

I saw them immediately, but they were still too far away for me to be able to identify them, though even at a distance I was sure that they were not of the same race as the savages which had attacked Duare and the klangan.

Now indeed it became imperative that we attract the attention of the *Sofal* immediately, and to that end I built two more fires at intervals from the first, so that it might be obvious to anyone aboard the ship that this was in fact a signal rather than an accidental fire or a camp fire.

Whether or not the *Sofal* had seen our signal, it was evident that the party of men approaching must have; and I could not but believe that, attracted by it, they were coming to investigate. Constantly they were drawing nearer, and as the minutes passed we saw that they were armed men of the same race as the Vepajans.

They were still some distance away when we saw the *Sofal* change her course and point her bow toward shore. Our signal had been seen, and our comrades were coming to investigate; but would they be in time? For us it was a thrilling race. The wind had sprung up again and the sea was rising once more. I asked the angan if he could breast the gale, for I had determined to send Duare off at once if I received a favorable reply.

'I could alone,' he said, 'but I doubt that I could if I were carrying another.'

We watched the *Sofal* plunging and wallowing in the rising sea as it forged steadily closer, and we watched the men drawing near with equal certainty. There was no doubt in my mind as to which would reach us first; my only hope now was that the *Sofal* could lessen the distance in the meantime sufficiently so that it would be safe for the angan to attempt to carry Duare to her.

Now the men had reached the summit of the cliff on the opposite side of the canyon, and here they halted and observed us while carrying on a discussion of some nature.

'Vilor is with them!' exclaimed Duare suddenly.

'And Moosko,' I added. 'I see them both now.'

'What shall we do?' cried Duare. 'Oh, they must not get me again!'

'They shall not,' I promised her.

Down the canyon side they came now. We watched them swim the river and cross to the foot of the cliff where we were standing. We watched the *Sofal* creeping slowly shoreward. I went to the edge of the cliff and looked down upon the ascending men. They were half way up now. Then I returned to Duare and the angan.

'We can wait no longer,' I said, and then to the angan, 'Take the janjong and fly to the ship. She is closer now; you can make it; you *must* make it!'

He started to obey, but Duare drew away from him. 'I will not go,' she said quietly. 'I will not leave you here alone!'

For those words I would gladly have laid down my life. Here again was still another Duare. I had expected nothing like this, for I did not feel that she owed me any such loyalty. It was not as though she had loved me; one might expect such self-sacrifice on the part of a woman for the man she loves. I was swept completely from my feet, but only for an instant. The enemy, if such it were, must by now be almost to the summit of the cliff, in a moment they would be upon us, and even as the thought touched my mind, I saw the first of them running toward us.

'Take her!' I cried to the angan. 'There is no time to waste now.'

He reached for her, but she attempted to elude him; and then I caught her, and as I touched her, all my good resolutions were swept away, as I felt her in my arms. I pressed her to me for an instant; I kissed her, and then I gave her over to the birdman.

'Hurry!' I cried. 'They come!'

Spreading his powerful wings, he rose from the ground, while Duare stretched her hands toward me. 'Do not send me away from you, Carson! Do not send me away! I love you!'

But it was too late; I would not have called her back could I have done so, for the armed men were upon me.

Thus I went into captivity in the land of Noobol, an adventure that is no part of this story; but I went with the knowledge that the woman I loved, loved me, and I was happy.

LOST ON VENUS

FOREWORD

When Carson Napier left my office to fly to Guadalupe Island and take off for Mars in the giant rocket that he had constructed there for that purpose, I was positive that I should never see him again in the flesh. That his highly developed telepathic powers, through the medium of which he hoped to communicate with me, might permit me to envisage him and communicate with him I had no doubts; but I expected no messages after he had detonated the first rocket. I thought that Carson Napier would die within a few seconds of the initiation of his mad scheme.

But my fears were not realized. I followed him through his mad, month-long journey through space, trembling with him as the gravitation of the Moon drew the great rocket from its course and sent it hurtling toward the Sun, holding my breath as he was gripped by the power of Venus, and thrilling to his initial adventures upon that mysterious, cloud-enwrapped planet – Amtor, as it is known to its human inhabitants.

His love for the unattainable Duare, daughter of a king, their capture by the cruel Thorians, his self-sacrificing rescue of the girl, held me enthralled.

I saw the strange, unearthly bird-man bearing Duare from the rockbound shore of Noobol to the ship that was to bear her back to her native land just as Carson Napier was overwhelmed and made prisoner by a strong band of Thorians.

I saw – but now let Carson Napier tell his own story in his own words while I retire again to the impersonality of my rôle of scribe.

I

The Seven Doors

Leading my captors, but taking no part in the capture, were Moosko, the Ongyan, and Vilor, the Thorist spy, who had together conceived and carried out the abduction of Duare from aboard the *Sofal*.

They had reached the mainland, carried there by the flying angans, those strange winged humans of Venus. (To make the story simpler to understand, I am abandoning the Amtorian plural prefix, 'kl' or 'kloo,' and am forming the plural of nouns in the regular Earth fashion – by adding 's.') The pair had left Duare to her fate when the party was attacked by the hairy wild men from whom I had fortunately been able to rescue her with the aid of the angan who had so heroically defended her.

But now, though they had abandoned her to almost certain death, they were furious with me for having caused her to be carried from their clutches back to the deck of the *Sofal* by the last survivor of the angans; and having me within their power, after some one else had disarmed me, they became courageous again and attacked me violently.

I think they would have killed me on the spot had not a better idea suggested itself to another member of the Thorist party that had captured me.

Vilor, who had been unarmed, seized a sword from one of his fellows and set upon me with the evident intention of hacking me to pieces, when this man intervened.

'Wait!' he cried. 'What has this man done that he should be killed swiftly and without suffering?'

'What do you mean?' demanded Vilor, lowering the point of his weapon.

This country in which we were was almost as strange to Vilor as to me, for he was from the distant mainland of Thora proper, while the party who had assisted in my capture were natives of this land of Noobol who had been induced to join the Thorists in their world-wide attempt to foment discord and overthrow all established forms of government and replace them with their own oligarchy of ignorance.

As Vilor hesitated, the other explained. 'In Kapdor,' he said, 'we have far more interesting ways of disposing of enemies than spitting them on a sword.'

'Explain,' commanded the Ongyan, Moosko. 'This man does not deserve the mercy of a quick death. A prisoner aboard the *Sofal*, with other Vepajans, he led a mutiny in which all the ship's officers were murdered; then he seized the Sovong, liberated her prisoners, looted her, threw her big guns into the sea, and sailed away upon a piratical expedition.

'In the *Sofal*, he overhauled the *Yan*, a merchant ship on which I, an ong-yan, was a passenger. Ignoring my authority, he opened fire upon the *Yan* and then boarded her. After looting her and destroying her armament, he took me prisoner aboard the *Sofal*. He treated me with the utmost disrespect, threatening my life and destroying my liberty.

'For these things he must die, and if you have a death commensurate with his crimes you shall not go unrewarded by those who rule Thora.'

'Let us take him back to Kapdor with us,' said the man. 'There we have the room with seven doors, and I promise you that if he be an intelligent being he will suffer more agony within its circular walls than any prick of a sword point might inflict upon him.'

'Good!' exclaimed Vilor, handing his sword back to the man from whom he had borrowed it. 'The creature deserves the worst.'

They led me back along the coast in the direction from which they had come, and during the march I discovered from their conversation to what unfortunate chance I could attribute the ill fortune that had befallen me at the very moment when it seemed possible that Duare and I might easily return to the *Sofal* and our loyal friends.

This armed party from Kapdor had been searching for an escaped prisoner when their attention had been attracted by the fight between the hairy wild men and the angans who were defending Duare, just as I had similarly been attracted to the scene while searching for the beautiful daughter of Mintep, the jong of Vepaja.

As they were coming to investigate, they met Moosko and Vilor fleeing from the engagement, and these two had accompanied them back to the scene just as Duare, the remaining angan, and I had sighted the *Sofal* off shore and were planning on signaling to her.

As the birdman could transport but one of us at a time, I had commanded him, much against his will, to carry Duare to the ship. She refused to desert me, and the angan feared to return to the *Sofal*, from which he had aided in the abduction of the princess; but I at length compelled him to seize Duare and fly away with her just as the party of Thorists were upon us.

There had been a stiff gale blowing from the sea; and I was much worried for fear that the angan might not have been able to beat his way against it to the deck of the *Sofal*, but I had known that death beneath the waters of the sea would be far less horrible to Duare than captivity among the Thorists and especially in the power of Moosko.

My captors had watched the birdman battling his way against the gale with his burden, but only for a few minutes; then they had started upon the return march to Kapdor when Moosko had suggested that Kamlot, who was now in command of the *Sofal*, would doubtless land a force and pursue them as soon as Duare acquainted him with the fact of my capture. And so, as our path dropped behind the rocky pinnacles of the shore line, the angan and Duare were lost to our view; and I felt that I was doomed to go through whatever brief hours of life remained to me without knowledge of the fate of the gorgeous Venusan girl whom fate had decreed to be my first love.

The fact that I should have chanced to fall in love with this particular girl, in the land of Vepaja where there were so many beautiful girls, was in itself a tragedy. She was the virgin daughter of a jong, or king, whom custom rendered sacrosanct.

During the eighteen years of her life she had been permitted neither to see nor to speak to any man other than members of the royal family and a few trusted servitors until I had invaded her garden and forced my unwelcome attentions upon her. And then, shortly thereafter, the worst had befallen her. A raiding party of Thorists had succeeded in abducting her, members of the same party that had captured Kamlot and me.

She had been shocked and terrified at my avowal of my love, but she had not informed against me. She had seemed to despise me up until the last moment upon the summit of the rocky cliffs overlooking the raging Venusan sea, when I had ordered the angan to carry her to the *Sofal*; then, with outstretched hands, she had implored, 'Do not send me away from you, Carson! Do not send me away! I love you!'

Those words, those unbelievable words, still rang in my ears, leaving me elated even in the face of the nameless death that I knew awaited me in the mysterious chamber of seven doors.

The Thorists from Kapdor who formed my escort were much intrigued by my blond hair and blue eyes, for such were unknown to any of the Venusans I had yet encountered. They questioned Vilor concerning me; but he insisted that I was a Vepajan, and as the Vepajans are the deadliest enemies of the Thorists he could not more effectually have sealed my doom even had I not been guilty of the offenses charged against me by Moosko.

'He says that he comes from another world far from Amtor; but he was captured in Vepaja in company with another Vepajan, and he was well known to Duare, the daughter of Mintep, the jong of Vepaja.'

'What other world could there be but Amtor?' scoffed one of the soldiers.

'None, of course,' assented another; 'beyond Amtor lie only boiling rocks and fire.'

The cosmic theory of the Amtorians is as wrapped in impenetrable fog as is their world by the two great cloud envelopes that surround it. From the spouting lava of their volcanoes they visualize a sea of molten rock upon which floats Amtor, a vast disk; the occasional rents in the enveloping clouds, through which they glimpse the fiery sun and feel his consuming heat assure them that all is fire above; and when these rents occur at night they believe the myriad stars to be sparks from the eternal, fiery furnace that fuses the molten sea beneath their world.

I was almost exhausted by what I had passed through since the screeching of the hurricane and the plunging of the *Sofal* had awakened me the preceding night. After the great wave had swept me overboard I had had a battle with the great waves that would have wholly sapped the strength of a less powerful man than I; and then, after I had reached shore, I had walked far in search of Duare and her abductors only to have my strength further sapped by a strenuous battle with the savage nobargans, the hairy beast-men, who had attacked her abductors.

And now I was about all in as, topping a rise, there burst upon my view a walled city lying close to the sea at the mouth of a little valley. I guessed that this was Kapdor, our destination; and though I knew that death awaited me there I could not but look forward to the city with anticipation, since I guessed that food and drink might also await me behind those substantial walls.

The city gate through which we entered was well guarded, suggesting that Kapdor had many enemies; and all the citizens were armed – with swords, or daggers, or pistols, the last similar to those I had first become acquainted with in the house of Duran, the father of Kamlot, in the tree-city of Kooaad, which is the capitol of Mintep's island kingdom, Vepaja.

These weapons discharge the lethal R-ray, which destroys animal tissue, and are far more deadly than the .45 automatics with which we are familiar, since they discharge a continuous stream of the destructive rays as long as the mechanism which generates them is kept in action by the pressure of a finger.

There were many people on the streets of Kapdor, but they seemed dull and apathetic. Even the sight of a blond haired, blue eyed prisoner aroused no interest within their sodden brains. To me they appeared like beasts of burden, performing their dull tasks without the stimulus of imagination or of hope. It was these that were armed with daggers, and there was another class that I took to be the soldier class who carried swords and pistols. These seemed more alert and cheerful, for evidently they were more favored, but had no appearance of being more intelligent than the others.

The buildings for the most part were mean hovels of a single story, but there were others that were more pretentious – two and even three story buildings. Many were of lumber, for forests are plentiful in this portion of Amtor, though I had seen none of the enormous trees such as grow upon the island of Vepaja and which afforded me my first introduction to Venus.

There were a number of stone buildings facing the streets along which I

136

was conducted; but they were all box-like, unprepossessing structures with no hint of artistic or imaginative genius.

Presently my captors led me into an open square surrounded by larger if not more beautiful buildings than we had previously passed. Yet even here were squalor and indications of inefficiency and incompetence.

I was led into a building the entrance to which was guarded by soldiers. Vilor, Moosko, and the leader of the party that had captured me accompanied me into the interior, where, in a bare room, a large, gross appearing man was asleep in a chair with his feet on a table that evidently served him both as desk and dining table, for its top was littered with papers and the remains of a meal.

Disturbed by our entrance, the sleeper opened his eyes and blinked dully at us for a moment.

'Greetings, Friend Sov!' exclaimed the officer who accompanied me.

'Oh, it is you, Friend Hokal?' mumbled Sov, sleepily. 'And who are these others?'

'The Ongyan Moosko from Thora, Vilor, another friend, and a Vepajan prisoner I captured.'

At the mention of Moosko's title, Sov arose, for an ongyan is one of the oligarchy and a great man. 'Greetings, Ongyan Moosko!' he cried. 'So you have brought us a Vepajan? Is he a doctor, by chance?'

'I do not know and I do not care,' snapped Moosko. 'He is a cutthroat and a scoundrel; and, doctor or no doctor, he dies.'

'But we need doctors badly,' insisted Sov. 'We are dying of disease and old age. If we do not have a doctor soon, we shall all be dead.'

'You heard what I said, did you not, Friend Sov?' demanded Moosko testily.

'Yes, Ongyan,' replied the officer, meekly; 'he shall die. Shall I have him destroyed at once?'

'Friend Hokal tells me that you have a slower and pleasanter way of dispatching villains than by gun or sword. I am interested. Tell me about it.'

'I referred to the room of the seven doors,' explained Hokal. 'You see, this man's offenses were great; he made the great Ongyan a prisoner and even threatened his life.'

'We have no death adequate to such a crime,' cried the horrified Sov; 'but the room of the seven doors, which is the best that we have to offer, shall be made ready.'

'Describe it, describe it,' snapped Moosko. 'What is it like? What will happen to him? How will he die?'

'Let us not explain it in the presence of the prisoner,' said Hokal, 'if you would reap the full pleasure of the room of the seven doors.'

'Yes, lock him up; lock him up!' ordered Moosko. 'Put him in a cell.'

Sov summoned a couple of soldiers, who conducted me to a rear room and shoved me down into a dark, windowless cellar. They slammed down and locked the heavy trap door above me and left me to my gloomy thoughts.

The room of the seven doors. The title fascinated me. I wondered what awaited me there, what strange form of horrible death. Perhaps it might not be so terrible after all; perhaps they were attempting to make my end more terrible by suggestion.

So this was to be the termination of my mad attempt to reach Mars! I was to die alone in this far-flung outpost of the Thorists in the land of Noobol that was scarcely more than a name to me. And there was so much to see upon Venus, and I had seen so little.

I recalled all that Danus had told me, the things concerning Venus that had so stimulated my imagination – sketchy tales, little more than fables, of Karbol, the cold country, where roamed strange and savage beasts and even more strange and more savage men; and Trabol, the warm country, where lay the island of Vepaja toward which chance had guided the rocket in which I had journeyed from Earth. Most of all had I been interested in Strabol, the hot country, for I was positive that this corresponded with the equatorial regions of the planet and that beyond it lay a vast, unexplored region entirely unguessed of by the inhabitants of the southern hemisphere – the north temperate zone.

One of my hopes when I seized the *Sofal* and set myself up as a pirate chieftain was that I might find an ocean passage north to this *terra incognita*. What strange races, what new civilizations might I not discover there! But now I had reached the end, not only of hope, but of life as well.

I determined to stop thinking about it. It was going to be too easy to feel sorry for myself if I were to keep on in that vein, and that would never do; it unnerves a man.

I had enough pleasant memories stored away inside my head, and these I called to my aid. The happy days that I had spent in India before my English father died were food for glorious recollection. I thought of old Chand Kabi, my tutor, and of all that I had learned from him outside of school books; not the least of which was that satisfying philosophy which I found it expedient to summon to my aid in this, my last extremity. It was Chand Kabi who had taught me to use my mind to the fullest extent of its resources and to project it across illimitable space to another mind attuned to receive its message, without which power the fruits of my strange adventure must die with me in the room of the seven doors.

I had other pleasant recollections to dissolve the gloom that shrouded my immediate future; they were of the good and loyal friends I had made during my brief sojourn on this distant planet: Kamlot, my best friend on Venus, and those 'three musketeers' of the *Sofal*, Gamfor, the farmer; Kiron, the soldier; and Zog, the slave. These had been friends indeed!

And then, pleasantest memory of all, there was Duare. She was worth all that I had risked; her last words to me compensated even for death. She had told me that she loved me – she, the incomparable, the unattainable – she, the hope of a world, the daughter of a king. I could scarcely believe that my ears had not tricked me, for always before, in the few words she had deigned to fling me, she had sought to impress upon me the fact that not only was she not for such as I, but that she abhorred me. Women are peculiar.

How long I remained in that dark hole, I do not know. It must have been several hours; but at last I heard footsteps in the room above, and then the trap door was raised and I was ordered to come up.

Several soldiers escorted me back to the filthy office of Sov, where I found that officer seated in conversation with Moosko, Vilor, and Hokal. A jug and glasses, together with the fumes of strong drink, attested the manner in which they had enlivened their converence.

'Take him to the room of the seven doors,' Sov directed the soldiers who guarded me; and as I was escorted into the open square, the four who had condemned me to death followed.

A short distance from Sov's office the soldiers turned into a narrow, crooked alley; and presently we came to a large open space in the center of which were several buildings, one a circular tower rising above the others from the center of a large inclosure that was surrouded by a high stone wall.

Through a small gate we passed into a covered passageway, a gloomy tunnel, at the end of which was a stout door which one of the soldiers opened with a great key that Hokal passed to him; then the soldiers stood aside and I entered the room, followed by Sov, Moosko, Vilor, and Hokal.

I found myself in a circular apartment in the walls of which were seven identical doors placed at regular intervals about the circumference; so that there was no way of distinguishing one door from another.

In the center of the room was a circular table upon which were seven vessels containing seven varieties of food and seven cups containing liquids. Depending above the center of the table was a rope with a noose in the end of it, the upper end of the rope being lost in the shadows of the high ceiling, for the chamber was but dimly lighted.

Suffering with thirst, as I was, and being half famished for food, the sight of that laden table aroused my flagging spirits. It was evident that even if I were about to die I should not die hungry. The Thorists might be cruel and heartless in some respects, but it was clear that there was some kindliness in them, else they would never furnish such an abundance of food to a condemned man.

'Attend!' snapped Sov, addressing me. 'Listen well to what I shall say to you.' Moosko was inspecting the room with a gloating smile on his thick lips. 'We shall leave you here alone presently,' continued Sov. 'If you can escape from this building your life will be spared.

'As you see, there are seven doors leading from this room; none of them has bolt or bar. Beyond each is a corridor identical to that through which we just approached the chamber. You are free to open any of the doors and enter any of these corridors. After you pass through a door, a spring will close it; and you cannot open it again from the opposite side, the doors being so constructed that from the corridor there is nothing to lay hold upon wherewith to open them, with the exception of the secret mechanism of that one which let us into the room; through that one door lies life; beyond the others, death.

'In the corridor of the second door you will step upon a hidden spring that will cause long, sharp spikes to be released upon you from all directions; and upon these you will be impaled and die.

'In the third corridor a similar spring will ignite a gas that will consume you in flames. In the fourth, R-rays will be loosed upon you, and you will die instantly. In the fifth, another door will open at the far end and admit a tharban.'

'What is a tharban?' I asked.

Sov looked at me in astonishment. 'You know as well as I,' he growled.

'I have told you that I am from another world,' I snapped. 'I do not know what the word means.'

'It will do no harm to tell him,' suggested Vilor; 'for if, by chance, he does not know, some of the horror of the room of the seven doors may be lost upon him.'

'Not a bad thought,' interjected Moosko. 'Describe the tharban, Friend Sov.'

'It is a terrible beast,' explained Sov, 'a huge and terrible beast. It is covered with stiff hair, like bristles, and is of a reddish color with white stripes running lengthwise of its body, its belly being of a bluish tinge. It has great jaws and terrible talons, and it eats naught but flesh.'

At that instant a terrific roar that seemed to shake the building broke upon our ears.

'That is the tharban,' said Hokal with a grin. 'He has not eaten for three days, and he is not only very hungry, but he is very angry.'

'And what lies beyond the sixth door?' I demanded.

'In the corridor beyond the sixth door hidden jets will deluge you with a corrosive acid. It will fill your eyes and burn them out; and it will consume your flesh slowly, but you will not die too quickly. You will have ample time in which to repent the crimes that brought you to the room of the seven doors. The sixth door, I think, is the most terrible of all.'

'To my mind the seventh is worse,' remarked Hokal.

'Perhaps,' admitted Sov. 'In the seventh, death is longer in coming, and the mental agony is protracted. When you step upon the concealed spring in the corridor beyond the seventh door the walls commence to move slowly toward you. Their movement is so slow as to be almost imperceptible, but eventually they will reach you and slowly crush you between them.'

'And what is the purpose of the noose above the table?' I asked.

'In the agony of indecision as to which door is the door to life,' explained Sov, 'you will be tempted to destroy yourself, and the noose is there for that purpose. But it is cunningly arranged at such a distance above the table that you cannot utilize it to break your neck and bring death quickly; you can only strangle to death.'

'It appears to me that you have gone to considerable pains to destroy your enemies,' I suggested.

'The room of the seven doors was not designed primarily to inflict death,' explained Sov. 'It is used as a means for converting unbelievers to Thorism, and you would be surprised to know how efficacious it has been.'

'I can imagine,' I replied. 'And now that you have told me the worst, may I be permitted to satisfy my hunger and thirst before I die?'

'All within this room is yours to do with as you please during your last hours on Earth, but before you eat let me explain that of the seven varieties of food upon this table all but one are poisoned. Before you satisfy your thirst, you may be interested in knowing that of the seven delicious beverages sparkling in those seven containers, six are poisoned. And now, murderer, we leave you. For the last time in life you are looking upon fellow human beings.'

'If life held only the hope of continuing to look upon you, I would gladly embrace death.'

In single file they left the room by that door to life. I kept my eyes upon that door to mark it well; and then the dim light went out.

Quickly I crossed the chamber in a straight line toward the exact spot where I knew the door to be, for I had been standing facing it squarely. I smiled to myself to think how simple they were to imagine that I should instantly lose my bearings because the light had been extinguished. If they had not been lying to me, I should be out of that room almost as soon as they to claim the life they had promised me.

With outstretched hands I approached the door. I felt unaccountably dizzy. I was having difficulty in keeping my balance. My fingers came in contact with a moving surface; it was the wall, passing across my hands toward the left. I felt a door brush past them and then another and another; then I guessed the truth – the floor upon which I stood was revolving. I had lost the door to life.

II

Coiled Fury

As I stood there, plunged for the moment into despondency, the light came on again; and I saw the wall and the procession of doors passing slowly before me. Which was the door to life? Which was the door to choose?

I felt very tired and rather hopeless; the pangs of hunger and thirst assailed me. I walked to the table in the center of the room. Wines and milk mocked me from the seven cups. One of the seven was harmless and would quickly satisfy the gnawing craving for drink that was become almost a torture. I examined the contents of each receptacle, testing each with my nose. There were two cups of water, the contents of one of which had a cloudy appearance; I was positive that the other was the one unpoisoned liquid.

I lifted it in my hands. My parched throat begged for one little drink. I raised the cup to my lips, and then doubts assailed me. While there was a single remote chance for life I must not risk death. Resolutely I replaced the cup upon the table.

Glancing about the room, I saw a chair and a couch in the shadows against the wall beyond the table; at least, if I could not eat nor drink, I could rest and, perhaps, sleep. I would rob my captors of the fulfillment of their expectations as long as possible, and with this idea in mind I approached the couch.

The light in the room was poor, but as I was about to throw myself upon the couch it was sufficient to enable me to discern that its bed was composed of needle-sharp metal spikes, and my vision of restful sleep was dispelled. An examination of the chair revealed the fact that it was similarly barbed.

What ingenious fiendishness the Thorists had displayed in the conception of this room and its appurtenances! There was nothing about it that I might use that was not feral, with the single exception of the floor; and I was so tired as I stretched myself at full length upon it that for the moment it seemed a luxurious couch.

It is true that the discomfort of its hardness became more and more appreciable; yet, so exhausted was I, I was upon the verge of sleep, half dozing, when I felt something touch my naked back – something cold and clammy.

Instantly apprehending some new and devilish form of torture, I sprang to my feet. Upon the floor, wriggling and writhing toward me, were snakes of all kinds and sizes, many of them unearthly reptiles of horrifying appearance –

snakes with saber-like fangs, snakes with horns, snakes with ears, snakes of blue, of red, of green, of white, of purple. They were coming from holes near the bottom of the wall, spreading out across the floor as though they were seeking what they might devour – seeking me.

Now even the floor, that I had considered my sole remaining hope, was denied me. I sprang to the table top amidst the poisoned food and drink, and there I squatted watching the hideous reptiles squirming about.

Suddenly the food began to tempt me, but now for a reason apart from hunger. I saw in it escape from the hopelessness and torture of my situation. What chance had I for life? My captors had known, when they put me in here, that I would never come out alive. What a vain and foolish thing was hope under such circumstances!

I thought of Duare; and I asked myself, what of her? Even were I to escape through some miracle, what chance had I of ever seeing Duare again? I, who could not even guess the direction in which lay Vepaja, the land of her people, the land to which Kamlot was most assuredly returning her even now.

I had harbored a half, faint-hearted hope immediately after my capture that Kamlot would land the fighting crew of the *Sofal* in an attempt to rescue me; but I had long since abandoned it, for I knew that his first duty was to Duare, the daughter of his king; and that no consideration would tempt him to delay an instant the return voyage to Vepaja.

As, immersed in thought, I watched the snakes, there came faintly to my ears what sounded like a woman's scream; and I wondered, indifferently, what new horror was occurring in this hateful city. Whatever it was, I could neither know nor prevent; and so it made little impression upon me, especially in view of a sudden, new interest in the snakes.

One of the larger of them, a great, hideous creature some twenty feet in length, had raised his head to the level of the table and was watching me with its lidless, staring eyes. It seemed to me that I could almost read that dim, reptilian brain reacting to the presence of food.

It laid its head flat upon the table; and, its body undulating slowly, it glided toward me across the table top.

I glanced quickly about the room, vainly seeking some avenue of escape. There, evenly spaced in the periphery of the chamber, were the seven doors, stationary now; for the floor had ceased to revolve shortly after the light had come on again. Behind one of those identical doors lay life; behind each of the other six, death. Upon the floor, between them and me, were the snakes. They had not distributed themselves evenly over the entire area of the flagging. There were spaces across which one might run swiftly without encountering more than an occasional reptile; yet a single one, were it venomous, would be as fatal as a score of them; and I was harassed by knowledge

143

of my ignorance of the nature of a single one of the numerous species represented.

The hideous head of the serpent that had raised itself to the table top was gliding slowly toward me; the greater part of its length extended along the floor, moved in undulating waves as it crept after the head. As yet it had given no indication of the method of its attack. I did not know if it might be expected to strike first with poison fangs, to crush within its constricting folds, or merely to seize in widespread jaws and swallow as I had seen snakes, in my boyhood, swallowing frogs and birds. In any event the outlook was far from pleasing.

I shot a quick glance toward the doors. Should I risk all on a single cast of the die with fate?

The repulsive head was moving closer and closer to me; I turned away from it, determined to run for the door the way to which was clearest of snakes. As I glanced quickly about the room I saw a comparatively open avenue leading toward a door just beyond the spiked couch and chair.

One door was as good as another – I had one chance in seven! And there was no way to differentiate one door from another. Life might lie behind this door, or death. Here was, at least, a chance. To remain where I was, the certain prey of that hideous reptile, offered no chance whatever.

I have always enjoyed more than my share of the lucky 'breaks' of life, and now something seemed to tell me that fate was driving me toward the one door beyond which lay life and liberty. So it was with the optimism of almost assured success that I leaped from the table and the yawning jaws of the great snake and ran toward that fateful door.

Yet I was not unmindful of that sound advice, 'Put your trust in God, my boys; and keep your powder dry!' In this event I might have paraphrased it to read, 'Put your trust in fate, but keep an avenue of retreat open!'

I knew that the doors swung outward from the circular room and that once I had passed through one of them and it had closed behind me there could be no returning. But how could I circumvent this?

All this that I take so long to tell occupied but a few seconds. I ran swiftly across the room, eluding the one or two snakes that were in my path; but I could not be unaware of the hissing and screaming that arose about me nor fail to see the snakes writhing and wriggling forward to intercept or pursue me.

What prompted me to seize the spiked chair as I passed it I do not know – the idea seemed to come to me like an inspiration. Perhaps, subconsciously, I hoped to use it as a weapon of defense; but it was not thus that it was to serve me.

As the nearer snakes were closing upon me I reached the door. There was no time now for further deliberation. I pushed the door open and stepped into the gloomy corridor beyond! It was exactly like the corridor through which I had been brought to the room of the seven doors. Hope sprang high within my breast, but I braced the door open with the spiked chair – I was keeping my powder dry!

I had taken but a few steps beyond the doorway when my blood was frozen by the most terrifying roar that I have ever heard, and in the gloom ahead I saw two blazing balls of fire. I had opened the door of the fifth corridor that led to the lair of the tharban!

I did not hesitate. I *knew* that death awaited me in the darkness of that gloomy hole. No, it was not awaiting me; it was coming charging toward me. I turned and fled for the temporary safety that the light and space of the larger room would give me, and as I passed through the doorway I sought to snatch the chair away and let the door close in the face of the savage beast that was pursuing me. But something went wrong. The door, impelled by a powerful spring, closed too quickly – before I could drag the chair out of the way, wedging it tightly so that I could not free it; and there it stuck, holding the door half open.

I had been in tight places before, but nothing like this. Before me were the snakes and, dominating them, the huge creature that had sought me on the table; behind me was the roaring tharban. And now the only haven that I could think of was that very table top from which I had so thankfully escaped a few seconds before.

To the right of the doorway was a small open space in which there were no snakes; and, hurdling those hissing and striking at me from the threshold, I leaped to it at the very instant that the tharban sprang into the room.

For the instant I was held in the power of a single urge – to reach the top of the table. How futile and foolish the idea may have been did not occur to me; my mind clung to it to the effacement of all other thoughts. And perhaps because of my very singleness of purpose I would have reached my goal in any event, but when I stood again among the dishes and cups of poisoned food and drink and turned to face my fate I saw that another factor had intervened to save me for the moment and permit me to attain the questionable sanctuary of the table top.

Halfway between the door and the table the tharban, a fighting, rearing, roaring monster, was being set upon by the snakes. He snapped and struck and clawed, ripping them to pices, tearing them in halves; but still they came for him, hissing, striking, entwining. Bodies cut in two, heads severed still sought to reach him; and from all parts of the room came ten to replace each that he disposed of.

Immense and threatening, standing out above them all, rose the huge reptile that had sought to devour me; and the tharban seemed to realize that in this creature lay a foe worthy of its mettle, for while he brushed away the lesser snakes with irritable contempt, he always faced the great one and launched his most vicious attacks against it. But of what avail! With lightning-like movements the sinuous coils darted hither and thither, eluding every blow like some practiced boxer and striking with terrific force at every opening, burying its fangs deep in the bloody flesh of the tharban.

The roars and screams of the carnivore mingled with the hisses of the reptiles to produce the most horrid din that the mind of man might imagine, or at least so it seemed to me, cooped up in this awful room filled with implacable engines of death.

Which would win this struggle of the Titans? What difference could it make to me other than the difference as to which belly I should eventually fill? Yet I could not help watch the encounter with the excited interest of a disinterested spectator at some test of strength and skill.

It was a bloody encounter, but the blood was all that of the tharban and the lesser snakes. The huge creature that was championing my cause that it might later devour me was so far unscathed. How it manipulated its huge body with sufficient quickness to avoid the savage rushes of the tharban is quite beyond me, though perhaps an explanation lies in the fact that it usually met a charge with a terrific blow of its head that sent the tharban reeling back half stunned and with a new wound.

Presently the tharban ceased its offensive and began to back away. I watched the weaving, undulating head of the great snake following every move of its antagonist. The lesser snakes swarmed over the body of the tharban; it seemed not to notice them. Then, suddenly, it wheeled and sprang for the entrance to the corridor that led to its lair.

This, evidently, was the very thing for which the snake had been waiting. It lay half coiled where it had been fighting; and now like a giant spring suddenly released it shot through the air; and, so quickly that I could scarcely perceive the action, it wrapped a dozen coils about the body of the tharban, raised its gaping jaws above the back of the beast's neck, and struck!

A horrible scream burst from the distended jaws of the stricken carnivore as the coils tightened suddenly about it, then it was limp.

I breathed a sigh of relief as I thought for how long an entire tharban might satisfy the hunger of this twenty foot snake and distract its mind from other sources of food supply, and as I anticipated this respite the mighty victor unwound its coils from about the body of its victim and turned its head slowly in my direction.

I gazed spellbound for a moment into those cold, lidless eyes, then I was horror-stricken as I saw the creature gliding slowly toward the table. It did not move swiftly as in battle, but very slowly. There was a seemingly predetermined finality, an inevitableness, in that undulating approach that was almost paralyzing in its frightfulness.

I saw it raise its head to the level of the table top; I saw the head glide among the dishes toward me. I could stand it no longer. I turned to run – where, made no difference – anywhere, if only the length of the room, to get away even for a moment from the cold glitter of those baleful eyes.

III

The Noose

As I turned, two things happened: I heard again, faintly, the screams of a woman; and my face struck the noose dangling from the dense shadows of the rafters.

The screams made little impression upon me, but the noose gave birth to a new thought – not the thought that it was placed there to arouse, but another. It suggested an avenue of momentary escape from the snakes; nor was I long in availing myself of it.

I felt the snout of the snake touch my bare leg as I sprang upward and seized the rope above the noose; I heard a loud hiss of rage as I clambered, hand over hand, toward the gloomy shadows where I hoped to find at least temporary refuge.

The upper end of the rope was fastened to a metal eye-bolt set in a great beam. Onto this beam I clambered and looked down. The mighty serpent was hissing and writhing below me. He had raised a third of his body upward and was endeavoring to coil about the dangling rope and follow me upward, but it swung away and eluded his efforts.

I doubted that a snake of his great girth could ascend this relatively tiny strand; but, not caring to take the chance, I drew the rope up and looped it over the beam. For the moment, at least, I was safe, and I breathed a deep sigh of relief. Then I looked about me.

The shadows were dense and almost impenetrable, yet it appeared that the ceiling of the room was still far above me; about me was a maze of beams and braces and trusses. I determined to explore this upper region of the room of the seven doors.

Standing upright upon the beam, I moved cautiously toward the wall. At the end of the beam I discovered a narrow walkway that, clinging to the wall, apparently encircled the room. It was two feet wide and had no handrail. It seemed to be something in the nature of a scaffolding left by the workmen who had constructed the building.

As I took my exploratory way along it, feeling each step carefully and brushing the wall with my hand, I again heard the agonized scream that had twice before attracted my attention if not my keenest interest; for I was still more interested in my troubles than in those of some unknown female of this alien race.

And a moment later my fingers came in contact with something that drove all thoughts of screaming women from my mind. By feel, it was the frame of a door or of a window. With both hands I examined my find. Yes, it was a door! It was a narrow door about six feet in height.

I felt the hinges; I searched for a latch – and at last I found it. Cautiously I manipulated it and presently I felt the door move toward me.

What lay beyond? Some new and fiendishly conceived form of death or torture, perhaps; perhaps freedom. I could not know without opening that portal of mystery.

I hesitated, but not for long. Slowly I drew the door toward me, an eye close to the widening crack. A breath of night air blew in upon me; I saw the faint luminosity of a Venusan night.

Could it be possible that with all their cunning the Thorists had inadvertently left this avenue of escape from this lethal chamber? I could scarcely credit it, yet there was naught that I could do but go on and chance whatever lay beyond.

I opened the door and stepped out upon a balcony which extended in both directions until it passed from the range of my vision beyond the curve of the circular wall to which it clung.

At the outer edge of the balcony was a low parapet behind which I now crouched while I reconnoitered my new situation. No new danger seemed to threaten me, yet I was still suspicious. I moved cautiously forward upon a tour of investigation, and again an agonized scream rent the silence of the night. This time it seemed quite close; previously, the walls of the building in which I had been imprisoned had muffled it.

I was already moving in the direction of the sound, and I continued to do so. I was searching for an avenue of descent to the ground below, not for a damsel in distress. I am afraid that at that moment I was callous and selfish and far from chivalric; but, if the truth be known, I would not have cared had I known that every inhabitant of Kapdor, male and female, was being destroyed.

Rounding the curve of the tower, I came in sight of another building standing but a few yards distant; and at the same instant I saw something that greatly aroused my interest and even my hope. It was a narrow causeway leading from the balcony on which I stood to a similar balcony on the adjoining structure.

Simultaneously the screams were renewed; they seemed to be coming from the interior of the building I had just discovered. It was not the screams, however, that lured me across the causeway, but the hope that I might find there the means of descent to the ground.

Crossing quickly to the other balcony, I followed it to the nearest corner;

and as I rounded it I saw a light apparently shining from windows on a level with it.

At first I was of a mind to turn back lest, in passing the windows, I be discovered; but once again that scream burst upon my ears, and this time it was so close that I knew it must come from the apartment from which the light shone.

There was such a note of hopelessness and fear in it that I could no longer ignore the demand it made upon my sympathies; and, setting discretion aside, I approached the window nearest me.

It was wide open, and in the room beyond I saw a woman in the clutches of a man. The fellow was holding her down upon a couch and with a sharp dagger was pricking her. Whether he had it in his mind to kill her eventually or not was not apparent, his sole purpose at the moment seeming to be torture.

The fellow's back was toward me, and his body hid the features of the woman; but when he pricked her and she screamed, he laughed – a hideous, gloating laugh. I guessed at once the psychopathic type he represented, deriving pleasure from the infliction of pain upon the object of his maniacal passion.

I saw him stoop to kiss her, and then she struck him in the face; and as she did so he half turned his head to avoid the blow, revealing his profile to me; and I saw that it was Moosko, the Ongyan.

He must have partially released his hold upon her as he shrank aside, for the girl half rose from the couch in an effort to escape him. As she did so her face was revealed to me, and my blood froze in rage and horror. It was Duare!

With a single bound I cleared the sill and was upon him. Grasping him by the shoulder, I whirled him about; and when he saw my face he voiced a cry of terror and shrank back, drawing his pistol from its holster. Instantly I closed with him, grasping the weapon and turning its muzzle toward the ceiling. He toppled backward across the couch, carrying me with him, both of us falling on top of Duare.

Moosko had dropped his dagger as he reached for his pistol, and now I tore the latter from his grasp and hurled it aside; then my fingers sought his throat.

He was a large, gross man, not without strength; and the fear of death seemed to increase the might of his muscles. He fought with the desperation of the doomed.

I dragged him from the couch, lest Duare be injured, and we rolled upon the floor, each intent upon winning a death hold upon the other. He was screaming for help now, and I redoubled my efforts to shut off his wind before his cries attracted the aid of any of his fellows.

He was snapping at me like a savage beast as he screamed, alternately striking at my face and seeking to close upon my throat. I was exhausted from all that I had passed through and from loss of sleep and lack of food. I realized that I was weakening rapidly, while Moosko seemed to my frenzied imagination to be growing stronger.

I knew that if I were not to be vanquished and Duare lost, I must overcome my antagonist without further loss of time; and so, drawing away from him to get greater distance for a blow, I drove my fist full into his face with all my remaining strength.

For an instant he wilted, and in that instant my fingers closed upon his throat. He struggled and writhed and struck me terrific blows; but, dizzy and half stunned though I was, I clung to him until at last he shuddered convulsively, relaxed, and sank to the floor.

If ever a man were dead, Moosko appeared so as I arose and faced Duare, who, half sitting, had crouched upon the cot where she had been a silent witness to this brief duel for possession of her.

'You!' she cried. 'It cannot be!'

'It is,' I assured her.

Slowly she arose from the couch as I approached it and stood facing me as I opened my arms to press her to me. She took a step forward; her hands went up; then she stopped in confusion.

'No!' she cried. 'It is all a mistake.'

'But you told me that you loved me, and you know that I love you,' I said, bewildered.

'That is the mistake,' she said. 'I do not love you. Fear, gratitude, sympathy, nerves distraught by all that I had passed through, brought strange words to my lips that I might not – not have meant.'

I felt suddenly cold and weary and forlorn. All hope of happiness was crushed in my breast. I turned away from her. I no longer cared what happened to me. But only for an instant did this mood possess me. No matter whether she loved me or not, my duty remained plain before me; I must get her out of Kapdor, out of the clutches of the Thorists and, if possible, return her to her father, Mintep, king of Vepaja.

I stepped to the window and listened. Moosko's cries had not attracted succor in so far as I could perceive; no one seemed to be coming. And if they had not come in response to Duare's screams, why should they be attracted by Moosko's? I realized that there was now little likelihood that anyone would investigate.

I returned to the body of Moosko and removed his harness to which was attached a sword that he had had no opportunity to draw against me; then I retrieved his dagger and pistol. I now felt much better, far more efficient. It is strange what the possession of weapons will do even for one not accustomed to bearing them, and until I had come to Venus I had seldom if ever carried a lethal weapon.

I took the time now to investigate the room, on the chance that it might contain something else of use or value to us in our bid for liberty. It was a rather large room. An attempt had been made to furnish it ornately, but the result was a monument to bad taste. It was atrocious.

At one end, however, was something that attracted my keenest interest and unqualified approval; it was a table laden with food.

I turned to Duare. 'I am going to try to take you away from Noobol,' I told her. 'I shall try also to return you to Vepaja. I may not succeed, but I shall do my best. Will you trust me and come with me?'

'How can you doubt it?' she replied. 'If you succeed in returning me to Vepaja you will be well repaid by the honors and rewards that will be heaped upon you if my wishes prevail.'

That speech angered me, and I turned upon her with bitter words on my lips; but I did not utter them. What was the use? I once more focused my attention upon the table. 'What I started to say,' I continued, 'is that I shall try to save you, but I can't do it on an empty stomach. I am going to eat before we leave this room. Do you care to join me?'

'We shall need strength,' she replied. 'I am not hungry, but it is wiser that we both eat. Moosko ordered the food for me, but I could not eat it while he was present.'

I turned away and approached the table where she joined me presently, and we ate in silence.

I was curious to know how Duare had come to the Thorist city of Kapdor, but her cruel and incomprehensible treatment of me made me hesitate to evince any further interest in her. Yet presently I realized how childish was my attitude – how foolish it was of me not to realize that the strictness and seclusion of her previous life probably accounted for her frightened and distant manner now – and I asked her to tell me all that had happened since I had despatched the angan with her toward the *Sofal* and the moment that I had discovered her in the clutches of Moosko.

'There is not much to tell,' she replied. 'You will recall how fearful the angan was of returning to the ship lest he be punished for the part he had taken in my abduction? They are very low creatures, with illy developed minds that react only to the most primitive forces of nature – self preservation, hunger, fear.

'When we were almost above the deck of the *Sofal*, the angan hesitated and then turned back toward the shore. I asked him what he was doing, why he did not continue on and place me aboard the ship; and he replied that he was afraid. He said they would kill him because he had helped to steal me.

'I promised him that I would protect him and that no harm would befall him, but he would not believe me. He replied that the Thorists, who had been his original masters, would reward him if he brought me back to them. That much he knew, but he had only my word that Kamlot would not have him killed. He doubted my authority with Kamlot.

'I pleaded and threatened but all to no purpose. The creature flew directly to this hideous city and delivered me to the Thorists. When Moosko learned that I had been brought here he exercised his authority and claimed me as his own. The rest you know.'

'And now,' I said, 'we must find a way out of Kapdor and back to the coast. Perhaps the *Sofal* has not departed. It is possible that Kamlot has landed a party to search for us.'

'It will not be easy to escape from Kapdor,' Duare reminded me. 'As the angan brought me here, I saw high walls and hundreds of sentries. There is not much hope for us.'

IV

'Open the Gates!'

'First we must get out of this building,' I said. 'Do you recall any of its details as you were brought through it?'

'Yes. There is a long hallway from the front of the building on the ground floor leading directly to stairs that lie at the back of the first floor. There are several rooms opening from each side of the hall. There were people in the two front rooms, but I could not see into the others as the doors were closed.'

'We shall have to investigate, and if there are sounds of life below we must wait until all are asleep. In the meantime I am going out on the balcony and see if I can discover some safer way to the ground.'

When I went to the window I found that it had started to rain. I crept around the building until I could look down onto the street that passed before it. There was no sign of life there; it was likely that the rain had driven all within doors. In the distance I could dimly make out the outlines of the city wall at the end of the street. Everything was faintly illumined by the strange night light that is so peculiar a feature of the Amtorian scene. There was no stairway or ladder leading from the balcony to the ground. Our only avenue of descent was by way of the interior stairs.

I returned to Duare. 'Come,' I said. 'We might as well try it now as later.'

'Wait!' she exclaimed. 'I have a thought. It just occurred to me from something I overheard on board the *Sofal* relative to the customs of the Thorists. Moosko is an ongyan.'

'Was,' I corrected her, for I thought him dead.

'That is immaterial. The point is that he was one of the rulers of the so-called Free Land of Thora. His authority, especially here, where there is no other member of the oligarchy, would be absolute. Yet he was unknown to any of the natives of Kapdor. What proof did he bring of his identity or his high position?'

'I do not know,' I admitted.

'I believe that you will find upon the index finger of his right hand a great ring that is the badge of his office.'

'And you think that we could use this ring as authority to pass the sentries?'

'It is possible,' replied Duare.

'But not probable,' I demurred. 'Not by the wildest flight of fancy could any one mistake me for Moosko – unless my conceit flatters me.'

A faint smile touched Duare's lips. 'I am believing that it will not be necessary for you to look like him,' she explained. 'These people are very ignorant. Probably only a few of the common warriors saw Moosko when he arrived. Those same men would not be on watch now. Furthermore, it is night, and with the darkness and the rain the danger that your imposture will be discovered is minimized.'

'It is worth trying,' I agreed; and, going to the body of Moosko, I found the ring and removed it from his finger. It was too large for me, as the ongyan had gross, fat hands; but if any one was stupid enough to accept me as the ongyan he would not notice so minor a discrepancy as an ill-fitting ring.

Now Duare and I crept silently out of the chamber to the head of the stairs, where we paused, listening. All was dark below, but we heard the sound of voices, muffled, as though coming from behind a closed door. Slowly, stealthily, we descended the stairs. I felt the warmth of the girl's body as it brushed mine, and a great longing seized me to take her in my arms and crush her to me; but I only continued on down the stairway as outwardly cool and possessed as though no internal fire consumed me.

We had reached the long hallway and had groped our way about half the distance to the door that opened upon the street, a feeling of optimism enveloping me, when suddenly a door at the front end of the corridor opened and the passageway was illuminated by the light from the room beyond.

I saw a portion of the figure of a man standing in the open doorway. He had paused and was conversing with some one in the room he was about to quit. In another moment he might step into the corridor.

At my elbow was a door. Gingerly I tripped the latch and pushed the door open; the room beyond was in darkness, but whether or not it was occupied I could not tell. Stepping through the doorway I drew Duare in after me and partially closed the door again, standing close to the aperture, watching and listening.

Presently I heard the man who had been standing in the other doorway say, 'Until tomorrow, friends, and may you sleep in peace,' then the door slammed and the hallway was plunged into darkness again.

Now I heard footsteps; they were coming in our direction. Very gingerly I drew the sword of Moosko, the ongyan. On came the footsteps; they seemed to hesitate before the door behind which I waited; but perhaps it was only my imagination. They passed on; I heard them ascending the stairway.

Now a new fear assailed me. What if this man should enter the room in which lay the dead body of Moosko! He would spread the alarm. Instantly I recognized the necessity for immediate action.

'Now, Duare!' I whispered, and together we stepped into the corridor and almost ran to the front door of the building.

A moment later we were in the street. The drizzle had become a down-pour. Objects were undiscernable a few yards distant, and for this I was thankful.

We hastened along the street in the direction of the wall and the gate, passing no one, seeing no one. The rain increased in violence.

'What are you going to say to the sentry?' asked Duare.

'I do not know,' I replied candidly.

'He will be suspicious, for you can have no possible excuse for wishing to leave the safety of a walled city on a night like this and go out without an escort into a dangerous country where savage beasts and savage men roam.'

'I shall find a way,' I said, 'because I must.'

She made no reply, and we continued on toward the gate. It was not at a great distance from the house from which we had escaped and presently we came upon it looming large before us through the falling rain.

A sentry, standing in the shelter of a niche in the wall, discovered us and demanded what we were doing abroad at this hour of such a night. He was not greatly concerned, since he did not know that it was in our minds to pass through the gateway; he merely assumed, I presume, that we were a couple of citizens passing by on our way to our home.

'Is Sov here?' I demanded.

'Sov here!' he exclaimed in astonishment. 'What would Sov be doing here on a night like this?'

'He was to meet me here at this hour,' I said. 'I instructed him to be here.'

'You instructed Sov to be here!' The fellow laughed. 'Who are you to give instructions to Sov?'

'I am the ongyan, Moosko,' I replied.

The man looked at me in astonishment. 'I do not know where Sov is,' he said, a little sullenly, I thought.

'Well, never mind,' I told him; 'he will be here presently; and in the meantime, open up the gate, for we shall want to hurry on as soon as he arrives.'

'I cannot open the gate without orders from Sov,' replied the sentry.

'You refuse to obey an ongyan?' I demanded in the most ferocious tones I could command.

'I have never seen you before,' he parried. 'How do I know you are an ongyan?'

I held out my hand with the ring of Moosko on the index finger. 'Do you know what that is?' I demanded.

He examined it closely. 'Yes, ongyan,' he said fearfully, 'I know.'

'Then open the gate, and be quick about it,' I snapped.

'Let us wait until Sov comes,' he suggested. 'There will be time enough then.'

'There is no time to be lost, fellow. Open up, as I command. The Vepajan prisoner has just escaped, and Sov and I are going out with a party of warriors to search for him.'

Still the obstinate fellow hesitated; and then we heard a great shouting from the direction from which we had come, and I guessed that the fellow who had passed us in the corridor had discovered the dead body of Moosko and given the alarm.

We could hear men running. There was no more time to be lost.

'Here comes Sov with the searching party,' I cried. 'Throw open the gates, you fool, or it will go ill with you.' I drew my sword, intending to run him through if he did not obey.

As, finally, he turned to do my bidding, I heard the excited voices of the approaching men grow louder as they neared us. I could not see them yet for the rain, but as the gate swung open I glimpsed the oncoming figures through the murk.

Taking Duare by the arm I started through the gate. The sentry was still suspicious and wanted to stop us, but he was not sure of himself.

'Tell Sov to hurry,' I said, and before the man could bolster his courage to do his duty, Duare and I hastened into the outer darkness and were lost to his view in the rain.

It was my intention to reach the coast and follow along it until daylight, when, I hoped and prayed, we should sight the *Sofal* off shore and be able to contrive a means of signaling to her.

We groped our way through the darkness and the rain during all that terrible night. No sound of pursuit reached our ears, nor did we come upon the ocean.

The rain ceased about dawn, and when full daylight came we looked eagerly for the sea, but only low hills and rolling country dotted with trees and a distant forest where we had thought the sea to be rewarded our straining eyes.

'Where is the sea?' asked Duare.

'I do not know,' I admitted.

Only at sunrise and at sunset, for a few minutes, is it possible to differentiate between the points of the compass on Venus; then the direction of the sun is faintly indicated by a slightly intensified light along the eastern or the western horizon.

And now the sun was rising at our left, when it should have been upon our right were we going in the direction that I believed the ocean to be.

My heart sank in my breast, for I knew that we were lost.

V

Cannibals

Duare, who had been watching my face intently, must have read the truth in the despair of my expression.

'You do not know where the sea lies?' she asked.

I shook my head. 'No.'

'Then we are lost?'

'I am afraid so. I am sorry, Duare; I was so sure that we would find the *Sofal* and that you would soon be out of danger. It is all my fault, the fault of my stupidity and ignorance.'

'Do not say that; no one could have known the direction he was going during the darkness of last night. Perhaps we shall find the sea yet.'

'Even if we could, I am afraid that it will be too late to insure your safety.'

'What do you mean – that the *Sofal* will be gone?' she asked.

'There is that danger, of course; but what I most fear is that we may be recaptured by the Thorists. They will certainly search along the coast for us in the locality where they found us yesterday. They are not so stupid as not to guess that we will try to reach the *Sofal*.'

'If we can find the ocean, we might hide from them,' she suggested, 'until they tire of the search and return to Kapdor; then, if the *Sofal* is still there, we may yet be saved.'

'And if not, what?' I asked. 'Do you know anything about Noobol? Is there not some likelihood that we may find a friendly people somewhere in this land who will aid us to reach Vepaja again?'

She shook her head. 'I know little about Noobol,' she replied, 'but what little I have heard is not good. It is a sparsely settled land reaching, it is supposed, far into Strabol, the hot country, where no man may live. It is filled with wild beasts and savage tribes. There are scattered settlements along the coast, but most of these have been captured or reduced by the Thorists; the others, of course, would be equally dangerous, for the inhabitants would consider all strangers as enemies.'

'The outlook is not bright,' I admitted, 'but we will not give up; we will find a way.'

'If any man can, I am sure that it is you,' she said.

Praise from Duare was sweet. In all the time that I had known her she had said only one other kind thing to me, and later she had retracted that.

'I could work miracles if only you loved me, Duare.'

She straightened haughtily. 'You will not speak of that,' she said.

'Why do you hate me, Duare, who have given you only love?' I demanded.

'I do not hate you,' she replied, 'but you must not speak of love to the daughter of a jong. We may be together for a long time, and you must remember that I may not listen to love from the lips of any man. Our very speaking together is a sin, but circumstances have made it impossible to do otherwise.

'Before I was stolen from the house of the jong no man had ever addressed me other than the members of my own family, except a few loyal and privileged members of my father's household, and until I should be twenty it were a sin in me and a crime in any man who should disregard this ancient law of the royal families of Amtor.'

'You forget,' I reminded her, 'that one man did address you in the house of your father.'

'An impudent knave,' she said, 'who should have died for his temerity.'

'Yet you did not inform on me.'

'Which made me equally guilty with you,' she replied, flushing. 'It is a shameful secret that will abide with me until my death.'

'A glorious memory that will always sustain my hope,' I told her.

'A false hope that you would do well to kill,' she said, and then, 'Why did you remind me of that day?' she demanded. 'When I think of it, I hate you; and I do not want to hate you.'

'That is something,' I suggested.

'Your effrontery and your hope feed on meager fare.'

'Which reminds me that it might be well for me to see if I can find something in the way of food for our bodies, too.'

'There may be game in that forest,' she suggested, indicating the wood toward which we had been moving.

'We'll have a look,' I said, 'and then turn back and search for the elusive sea.'

A Venusan forest is a gorgeous sight. The foliage itself is rather pale – orchid, heliotrope and violet predominate – but the boles of the trees are gorgeous. They are of brilliant colors and often so glossy as to give the impression of having been lacquered.

The wood we were approaching was of the smaller varieties of trees, ranging in height from two hundred to three hundred feet, and in diameter from twenty to thirty feet. There were none of the colossi of the island of Vepaja that reared their heads upward five thousand feet to penetrate the eternal inner cloud envelope of the planet.

The interior of the forest was illuminated by the mysterious Venusan ground glow, so that, unlike an Earthly forest of similar magnitude upon a cloudy day, it was far from dark or gloomy. Yet there was something sinister about it. I cannot explain just what, nor why it should have been.

'I do not like this place,' said Duare, with a little shudder; 'there is no sight of animal, no sound of bird.'

'Perhaps we frightened them away,' I suggested.

'I do not think so; it is more likely that there is something else in the forest that has frightened them.'

I shrugged. 'Nevertheless, we must have food,' I reminded her, and I continued on into the forbidding, and at the same time gorgeous, wood that reminded me of a beautiful but wicked woman.

Several times I thought I saw a suggestion of movement among the boles of distant trees, but when I reached them there was nothing there. And so I pressed on, deeper and deeper; and constantly a sense of impending evil grew stronger as I advanced.

'There!' whispered Duare suddenly, pointing. 'There is something there, behind that tree. I saw it move.'

Something, just glimpsed from the corner of my eye, caught my attention to the left of us; and as I turned quickly in that direction something else dodged behind the bole of a large tree.

Duare wheeled about. 'There are things all around us!'

'Can you make out what they are?' I asked.

'I thought that I saw a hairy hand, but I am not sure. They move quickly and keep always out of sight. Oh, let us go back! This is an evil place, and I am afraid.'

'Very well,' I agreed. 'Anyway, this doesn't seem to be a particularly good hunting ground; and after all that is all that we are looking for.'

As we turned to retrace our steps a chorus of hoarse shouts arose upon all sides of us – half human, half bestial, like the growls and roars of animals blending with the voices of men; and then, suddenly, from behind the boles of trees a score of hairy, manlike creatures sprang toward us.

Instantly I recognized them – nobargans – the same hairy, manlike creatures that had attacked the abductors of Duare, whom I had rescued from them. They were armed with crude bows and arrows and with slings from which they hurled rocks; but, as they closed upon us, it appeared that they wished to take us alive, for they launched no missiles at us.

But I had no mind to be thus taken so easily, nor to permit Duare to fall into the hands of these savage beast-men. Raising my pistol, I loosed the deadly R-ray upon them; and as some fell others leaped behind the boles of the trees.

'Do not let them take me,' said Duare in a level voice unshaken by emotion. 'When you see there is no further hope of escape, shoot me.'

The very thought of it turned me cold, but I knew that I should do it before permitting her to fall into the hands of these degraded creatures.

A nobargan showed himself, and I dropped him with my pistol; then they commenced to hurl rocks at me from behind. I wheeled and fired, and in the same instant a rock felled me to the ground unconscious.

When I regained consciousness I was aware first of an incredible stench, and then of something rough rubbing against my skin, and of a rhythmic jouncing of my body. These sensations were vaguely appreciable in the first dim light of returning reason. With the return of full control of my faculties they were accounted for; I was being carried across the shoulder of a powerful nobargan.

The odor from his body was almost suffocating in its intensity, and the rough hair abrading my skin was only a trifle more annoying than the motion that his stride imparted to my body.

I sought to push myself from his shoulder; and, realizing that I was no longer unconscious, he dropped me to the ground. All about me were the hideous faces and hairy bodies of the nobargans and permeating the air the horrid stench that emanated from them.

They are, I am sure, the filthiest and most repulsive creatures I have ever seen. Presumably they are one of evolution's first steps from beast to man; but they are no improvement upon the beast. For the privilege of walking upright upon two feet, thus releasing their hands from the mean servitude of ages, and for the gift of speech they have sacrificed all that is fine and noble in the beast.

It is true, I believe, that man *descended* from the beasts; and it took him countless ages to rise to the level of his progenitors. In some respects he has not succeeded yet, even at the height of his vaunted civilization.

As I looked about, I saw Duare being dragged along by her hair by a huge nobargan. It was then that I discovered that my weapons had been taken from me. So low in the scale of intelligence are the nobargans, they cannot use the weapons of civilized man that fall into their hands, and so they had simply thrown mine aside.

But even though I was disarmed, I could not see Duare suffering this ignominy and abuse without making an effort to aid her.

I sprang forward before the beasts at my side could prevent and hurled myself upon the creature that dared to maltreat this daughter of a jong, this incomparable creature who had aroused within my breast the first exquisite tortures of love.

I seized him by one hairy arm and swung him around until he faced me, and then I struck him a terrific blow upon the chin that felled him. Instantly his fellows broke into loud laughter at his discomfiture; but that did not prevent them from falling upon me and subduing me, and you may be assured that their methods were none too gentle.

*

As the brute that I had knocked down staggered to his feet his eyes fell upon me, and with a roar of rage he charged me. It might have fared badly with me had not another of them interfered. He was a burly creature, and when he interposed himself between me and my antagonist the latter paused.

'Stop!' commanded my ally, and had I heard a gorilla speak I could not have been more surprised. It was my introduction to a remarkable ethnological fact: all the races of mankind on Venus (at least those that I have come in contact with) speak the same tongue. Perhaps you can explain it; I cannot. When I have questioned Amtorian savants on the matter, they were merely dumfounded by the question; they could not conceive of any other condition; therefore there had never been any occasion to explain it.

Of course the languages differ in accordance with the culture of the nations; those with the fewest wants and the fewest experiences have the fewest words. The language of the nobargans is probably the most limited; a vocabulary of a hundred words may suffice them. But the basic root-words are the same everywhere.

The creature that had protected me, it presently developed, was the jong, or king, of this tribe; and I later learned that his act was not prompted by humanitarian considerations but by a desire to save me for another fate.

My act had not been entirely without good results, for during the balance of the march Duare was no longer dragged along by her hair. She thanked me for championing her; and that in itself was something worth being manhandled for, but she cautioned me against antagonizing them further.

Having discovered that at least one of these creatures could speak at least one word of the Amtorian language with which I was familiar, I sought to delve farther in the hope that I might ascertain the purpose for which they had captured us.

'Why have you seized us?' I inquired of the brute that had spoken that single word.

He looked at me in surprise, and those near enough to have overheard my question commenced to laugh and repeat it. Their laugh is far from light, airy, or reassuring. They bare their teeth in a grimace and emit a sound that is for all the world like the retching of *mal de mer*, and there is no laughter in their eyes. It took quite a stretch of my imagination to identify this as laughter.

'Albargan not know?' asked the jong. Albargan is, literally, no-hair-man, or without-hair-man, otherwise, hairless man.

'I do not know,' I replied. 'We were not harming you. We were searching for the sea coast where our people are.'

'Albargan find out soon,' and then he laughed again.

I tried to think of some way to bribe him into letting us go; but inasmuch as he had thrown away as useless the only things of value that we possessed, it seemed rather hopeless.

'Tell me what you want most,' I suggested, 'and perhaps I can get it for you if you will take us to the coast.'

'We have what we want,' he replied, and that answer made them all laugh.

I was walking close to Duare now, and she looked up at me with a hopeless expression. 'I am afraid we are in for it,' she said.

'It is all my fault. If I had had brains enough to find the ocean this would never have happened.'

'Don't blame yourself. No one could have done more to protect and save me than you have. Please do not think that I do not appreciate it.'

That was a lot for Duare to say, and it was like a ray of sunshine in the gloom of my despondency. That is a simile entirely Earthly, for there is no sunshine upon Venus. The relative proximity of the sun lights up the inner cloud envelope brilliantly, but it is a diffused light that casts no well defined shadows nor produces contrasting highlights. There is an all pervading glow from above that blends with the perpetual light emanations from the soil, and the resultant scene is that of a soft and beautiful pastel.

Our captors conducted us into the forest for a considerable distance; we marched practically all day. They spoke but seldom and then usually in monosyllables. They did not laugh again, and for that I was thankful. One can scarcely imagine a more disagreeable sound.

We had an opportunity to study them during this long march, and there is a question if either of us was quite sure in his own mind as to whether they were beast-like men or man-like beasts. Their bodies were entirely covered with hair; their feet were large and flat, and their toes were armed; like the fingers, with thick, heavy, pointed nails that resembled talons. They were large and heavy, with tremendous shoulders and necks.

Their eyes were extremely close set in a baboon-like face; so that in some respects their heads bore a more striking similarity to the heads of dogs than of men. There was no remarkable dissimilarity between the males and the females, several of which were in the party; and the latter deported themselves the same as the bulls and appeared to be upon a plane of equality with these, carrying bows and arrows and slings for hurling rocks, a small supply of which they carried in skin pouches slung across their shoulders.

At last we reached an open space beside a small river where there stood a collection of the rudest and most primitive of shelters. These were constructed of branches of all sizes and shapes thrown together without symmetry and covered with a thatch of leaves and grasses. At the bottom of each was a single aperture through which one might crawl on hands and knees. They reminded me of the nests of pack rats built upon a gargantuan scale.

Here were other members of the tribe, including several young, and at sight of us they rushed forward with excited cries. It was with difficulty that the jong and other members of the returning party kept them from tearing us to pieces.

The former hustled us into one of their evil smelling nests and placed a guard before the entrance, more to protect us from his fellows, I suspect, than to prevent our escape.

The hut in which we were was filthy beyond words, but in the dim light of the interior I found a short stick with which I scraped aside the foul litter that covered the floor until I had uncovered a space large enough for us to lie down on the relatively clean earth.

We lay with our heads close to the entrance that we might get the benefit of whatever fresh air should find its way within. Beyond the entrance we could see a number of the savages digging two parallel trenches in the soft earth; each was about seven feet long and two feet wide.

'Why are they doing that, do you suppose?' asked Duare.

'I do not know,' I replied, although I had my suspicions; they looked remarkably like graves.

'Perhaps we can escape after they have gone to sleep tonight,' suggested Duare.

'We shall certainly take advantage of the first opportunity,' I replied, but there was no hope within me. I had a premonition that we should not be alive when the nobargans slept next.

'Look what they're doing now,' said Duare, presently; 'they're filling the trenches with wood and dry leaves. You don't suppose –?' she exclaimed, and caught her breath with a little gasp.

I placed a hand on one of hers and pressed it. 'We must not conjure unnecessary horrors in our imaginations,' but I feared that she had guessed what I had already surmised – that my graves had become pits for cooking fires.

In silence we watched the creatures working about the two trenches. They built up walls of stone and earth about a foot high along each of the long sides of each pit; then they laid poles at intervals of a few inches across the tops of each pair of walls. Slowly before our eyes we saw two grilles take shape.

'It is horrible,' whispered Duare.

Night came before the preparations were completed; then the savage jong came to our prison and commanded us to come forth. As we did so we were seized by several shes and bulls who carried the long stems of tough jungle vines.

They threw us down and wound the vines about us. They were very clumsy and inept, not having sufficient intelligence to tie knots; but they accomplished their purpose in binding us by wrapping these fiber ropes around and around us until it seemed that it would be impossible to extricate ourselves even were we given the opportunity.

They bound me more securely than they did Duare, but even so the job was a clumsy one. Yet I guessed that it would be adequate to their purpose as they lifted us and laid us on the two parallel grilles.

This done, they commenced to move slowly about us in a rude circle, while near us, and also inside the circle, squatted a bull that was engaged in the business of making fire in the most primitive manner, twirling the end of a sharpened stick in a tinder-filled hole in a log.

From the throats of the circling tribesmen issued strange sounds that were neither speech nor song, yet I guessed that they were groping blindly after song just as in their awkward circling they were seeking self-expression in the rhythm of the dance.

The gloomy wood, feebly illumined by the mysterious ground glow, brooded darkly above and about the weird and savage scene. In the distance the roar of a beast rumbled menacingly.

As the hairy men-things circled about us the bull beside the log at last achieved fire. A slow wisp of smoke rose lazily from the tinder. The bull added a few dry leaves and blew upon the feeble spark. A tiny flame burst forth, and a savage cry arose from the circling dancers. It was answered from the forest by the roar of the beast we had heard a short time before. Now it was closer, and was followed by the thundering voices of others of its kind.

The nobargans paused in their dancing to look apprehensively into the dark wood, voicing their displeasure in grumblings and low growls; then the bull beside the fire commenced to light torches, a quantity of which lay prepared beside him; and as he passed them out the others resumed their dancing.

The circle contracted, and occasionally a dancer would leap in and pretend to light the faggots beneath us. The blazing torches illumined the weird scene, casting grotesque shadows that leaped and played like gigantic demons.

The truth of our predicament was now all too obvious, though I knew that we both suspected it since long before we had been laid upon the grilles – we were to be barbecued to furnish the flesh for a cannibal feast.

Duare turned her head toward me. 'Goodbye, Carson Napier!' she whispered. 'Before I go, I want you to know that I appreciate the sacrifice you have made for me. But for me you would be aboard the *Sofal* now, safe among loyal friends.'

'I would rather be here with you, Duare,' I replied, 'than to be anywhere else in the universe without you.'

I saw that her eyes were wet as she turned her face from me, but she did not reply, and then a huge, shaggy bull leaped in with a flaming torch and ignited the faggots at the lower end of the trench beneath her.

VI

Fire

From the surrounding forest came the roars of hungry beasts; but the sounds affected me none, so horrified was I by the hideous fate that had overtaken Duare.

I saw her struggling with her bonds, as I struggled with mine; but in the clumsily wound coils of the tough lianas we were helpless. Little flames below her feet were licking the larger faggots. Duare had managed to wriggle toward the head of the grille, so that the flames were not as yet directly beneath her, and she was still struggling with her bonds.

I had been paying little attention to the nobargans, but suddenly I realized that they had ceased their crude dancing and singing. Glancing toward them, I saw that they were standing looking off into the forest, the torches dangling in their hands, nor had they as yet lighted the faggots beneath me. Now I took note again of the thunderous roars of the beasts; they sounded very close. I saw dim figures slinking amidst the shadows of the trees and blazing eyes gleaming in the half light.

Presently a huge beast slunk out of the forest into the clearing, and I recognized it. I saw the stiff hair, like bristles. It was standing erect along the shoulders, neck, and spine. I saw the white, longitudinal stripes marking the reddish coat, and the bluish belly and the great, snarling jaws. The creature was a tharban.

The nobargans were also watching it. Presently they commenced to cry out against it and cast rocks at it from their slings in an obvious effort to frighten it away; but it did not retreat. Instead it came closer slowly, roaring horribly; and behind it came others – two, three, a dozen, two score – slinking from the concealing shadows of the forest. All were roaring, and the hideous volume of those mighty voices shook the ground.

And now the nobargans fell back. The great beasts invading the village increased their speed, and suddenly the hairy savages turned and fled. After them, roaring and growling, sprang the tharbans.

The speed of the clumsy appearing nobargans was a revelation to me, and as they disappeared into the dark mazes of the forest it was not apparent that the tharbans were gaining on them, though as the latter raced past me they seemed to be moving as swiftly as a charging lion.

The beasts paid no attention to Duare or me. I doubt that they even saw us, their whole attention being fixed upon the fleeing savages.

Now I turned again toward Duare, just in time to see her roll herself from the grille to the ground as the licking flames were about to reach her feet. For the moment she was safe, and I breathed a little prayer of thanksgiving. But what of the future? Must we lie here until inevitably the nobargans returned?

Duare looked up at me. She was struggling steadily with her bonds. 'I believe that I can free myself,' she said. 'I am not bound so tightly as you. If only I can do it before they return!'

I watched her in silence. After what seemed an eternity, she got one arm free. After that the rest was comparatively easy, and when she was free she quickly released me.

Like two phantoms in the eerie light of the Amtorian night we faded into the shadows of the mysterious forest; and you may rest assured that we took a direction opposite to that in which the lions and the cannibals had disappeared.

The momentary elation that escape from the clutches of the nobargans had given me passed quickly as I considered our situation. We two were alone, unarmed, and lost in a strange country that brief experience had already demonstrated to be filled with dangers and that imagination peopled with a hundred menaces even more frightful than those we had encountered.

Raised in the carefully guarded seclusion of the house of a jong, Duare was quite as ignorant of the flora, the fauna, and the conditions existing in the land of Noobol as was I, an inhabitant of a far distant planet; and notwithstanding our culture, our natural intelligence, and my considerable physical strength we were still little better than babes in the woods.

We had been walking in silence, listening and looking for some new menace to our recently won respite from death, when Duare spoke in low tones, as one might who is addressing a question to himself.

'And should I ever return to the house of my father, the jong, who will believe the story that I shall tell? Who will believe that I, Duare, the daughter of the jong, passed through such incredible dangers alive?' She turned and looked up into my face. 'Do you believe, Carson Napier, that I ever shall return to Vepaja?'

'I do not know, Duare,' I replied honestly. 'To be perfectly frank, it seems rather hopeless inasmuch as neither of us knows where we are or where Vepaja is, or what further dangers may confront us in this land.

'And what if we never find Vepaja, Duare? What if you and I go on for many years together? Must it always be as strangers, as enemies? Is there no hope for me, Duare? No hope to win your love?'

'Have I not told you that you must not speak to me of love? It is wicked for a girl under twenty to speak or even think of love; and for me, the daughter of a jong, it is even worse. If you persist, I will not talk to you at all.'

After this we walked on in silence for a long time. We were both very tired and hungry and thirsty, but for the time we subordinated all other desires to that of escaping the clutches of the nobargans; but at last I realized that Duare had about reached the limit of her endurance and I called a halt.

Selecting a tree, and lower branches of which were within easy reach, we climbed upward until I chanced upon a rude nest-like platform that might have been built by some arboreal creature or formed by debris falling from above during a storm. It lay upon two almost horizontal branches that extended from the bole of the tree in about the same plane, and was amply large enough to accommodate both of us.

As we stretched our tired bodies upon this mean yet none the less welcome couch, the growl of some great beast arose from the ground beneath to assure us that we had found sanctuary none too soon. What other dangers menaced us from arboreal creatures I did not know, but any thought of keeping wakeful vigil was dissipated by the utter exhaustion of both my mind and my body. I doubt that I could have kept awake much longer even in the act of walking.

As I was dozing off, I heard Duare's voice. It sounded sleepy and far away. 'Tell me, Carson Napier,' she said, 'what is this thing called love?'

When I awoke, another day had come. I looked up at the mass of foliage lying motionless in the air above me, and for a moment I had difficulty in recalling my surroundings and the events that had led me to this place. I turned my head and saw Duare lying beside me, and then it all came back to me. I smiled a little as I recalled that last, sleepy question she had asked me – a question that I realized now I had not answered. I must have fallen asleep as it was propounded.

For two days we moved steadily in what we thought was the direction of the ocean. We subsisted on eggs and fruit, which we found in abundance. There was a great deal of life in the forest – strange birds such as no Earthly eye had ever gazed upon before, monkey-like creatures that raced, chattering, through the trees, reptiles, herbivorous and carnivorous animals. Many of the latter were large and predacious. The worst of these that we encountered were the tharbans; but their habit of senseless roaring and growling preserved us from them by warning us of their proximity.

Another creature that caused us some bad moments was the basto. I had met this animal once before, that time that Kamlot and I had gone out upon our disastrous tarel gathering excursion; and so I was prepared to take to the trees with Duare the instant that we sighted one of these beasts.

Above the eyes, the head of a basto resembles the American bison, having the same short powerful horns and the thick hair upon its poll and forehead. Its eyes are small and red rimmed. The hide is blue and about the same texture as that of an elephant, with sparsely growing hairs except upon the head and tip of the tail, where the hair is thicker and longer. The beast stands very high at the shoulders but slopes downward rapidly to the rump. It has a tremendous depth of shoulder and exceedingly short, stocky fore legs, which are supplied with three toed feet. The fore legs carry fully three-quarters of the beast's weight. The muzzle is similar to that of a boar, except that it is broader, with heavy, curved tusks.

The basto is an ill tempered, omnivorous brute, always looking for trouble. Between him and the tharban, Duare and I became most proficient tree climbers during the first few days that we wandered through the forest.

My two greatest handicaps in this encounter with the primitive were lack of weapons and my inability to make fire. The latter was probably the worse, since, without a knife, fire was indispensable to the fashioning of weapons.

At every rest I experimented. Duare became inoculated with the virus of the quest, and fire became our sole aim. We talked about little else and were forever experimenting with different combinations of wood and with bits of rock that we picked up along the way.

All my life I had read of primitive men making fire in various ways, and I tried them all. I blistered my hands twirling firesticks. I knocked bits of flesh off my fingers striking pieces of stone together. At last I was on the point of giving up in disgust.

'I don't believe any one ever made fire,' I grumbled.

'You saw the nobargan make it,' Duare reminded me.

'There's a catch in it somewhere,' I insisted.

'Are you going to give up?' she asked.

'Of course not. It's like golf. Most people never learn to play it, but very few give up trying. I shall probably continue my search for fire until death overtakes me or Prometheus descends to Venus as he did to Earth.'

'What is golf and who is Prometheus?' demanded Duare.

'Golf is a mental disorder and Prometheus a fable.'

'I don't see how they can help you.'

I was squatting over a little pile of tinder laboriously knocking together various bits of rock that we had collected during the day.

'Neither do I,' I replied, viciously striking two new specimens together. A string of sparks shot from the two rocks and ignited the tinder! 'I apologize to Prometheus,' I cried; 'he is no fable.'

With the aid of this fire I was able to fashion a bow and to make and sharpen a spear and arrows. I strung the bow with a fiber from a tough liana, and I feathered my arrows gayly with the plumage of birds.

*

Duare was much interested in this work. She gathered feathers, split them, and bound them to the arrows with the long blades of a very tough grass that grew in profusion throughout the forest. Our work was facilitated by the use of bits of stone we had found so shaped that they made excellent scrapers.

I cannot express the change that came over me with the possession of weapons. I had come to feel like a hunted beast whose only defense is flight, and that is a most unhappy situation for the man who wishes to impress the object of his love with his heroic qualities.

I really cannot say that I had any such intention in my mind at any time, yet with the growing realization of my futility I really did come to wish that I might cut a better figure before Duare.

Now I stepped out with a new stride. I was the hunter rather than the hunted. My pitiful, inadequate little weapons swept all doubts from my mind. I was now equal to any emergency.

'Duare,' I exclaimed, 'I am going to find Vepaja; I am going to take you home!'

She looked at me questioningly. 'The last time we spoke of that,' she reminded me, 'you said that you hadn't the remotest idea where Vepaja was and that if you had, you couldn't hope to get there.'

'That,' I said, 'was several days ago. Things are different now. Now, Duare, we are going hunting; we are going to have meat for dinner. You walk behind me so as not to frighten the game.'

I moved forward with my old assurance and, perhaps, a little incautiously. Duare followed a few paces in the rear. There was considerable undergrowth in this portion of the forest, more than I had encountered before, and I could not see very far in any direction. We were following what appeared to be a game trail, along which I advanced boldly but silently.

Presently I saw a movement in the foliage ahead and then what appeared to be the outlines of some large animal. Almost instantly the silence of the forest was broken by the thunderous bellow of a basto, and there was a great crashing in the undergrowth.

'Take to the trees, Duare!' I cried, and at the same time I turned and ran back to assist her in climbing out of danger; and then Duare stumbled and fell.

Again the basto bellowed, and a quick backward glance revealed the mighty creature in the trail only a few paces in my rear. He was not charging, but he was advancing, and I could see that he would be upon us before we could possibly climb to safety, because of the slight delay occasioned by Duare's fall.

There appeared to be but one course of action open to me – I must delay the beast until Duare had gained a place of safety. I recalled how Kamlot had slain one of the creatures by distracting its attention from himself to a leafy branch held in his left hand and then plunged his keen sword behind the shoulder down into the heart. But I had no leafy branch and only a crude wooden spear.

He was almost upon me, his red rimmed eyes blazing, his white tusks gleaming. He loomed as large as an elephant to my excited imagination. He put his head down, another thunderous roar rumbled from his cavernous chest, and then he charged.

As the basto bore down upon me my only thought was to divert his attention from Duare until she should be safely out of his reach. It all happened so quickly that I imagine I had no time to think of my own almost certain fate.

The brute was so close to me when he started his charge that he attained no great speed. He came straight toward me with his head lowered, and so mighty and awe inspiring was he that I did not even consider attempting to stop him with my puny weapons.

Instead, all my thoughts centered upon one objective – to save myself from being impaled upon those horns.

I grasped them, one with each hand, as the basto struck me, and, thanks to my unusual strength, I succeeded in breaking the force of the impact as well as diverting the horns from my vitals.

The instant that he felt my weight the brute ripped upward with his head in an effort to gore and toss me, and in the latter he succeeded beyond anything that I might have expected and, I imagine, beyond what he intended.

With almost the force of an explosion I was hurtled upward to crash through the foliage and the branches of the tree above, dropping my weapons as I went. Fortunately my head came in contact with no large limb, and so I retained consciousness through it all. I also retained my presence of mind and, clutching frantically, I succeeded in grasping a branch across which my body had fallen. From there I dragged myself to the safety of a larger limb.

My first thought was of Duare. Was she safe? Had she been able to climb out of danger before the basto disposed of me and was upon her, or had he reached and gored her?

My fears were almost immediately allayed by the sound of her voice. 'Oh, Carson, Carson! Are you hurt?' she cried. The anguish of her tones was ample reward for any hurts I might have sustained.

'I think not,' I replied; 'just shaken up a bit. Are you all right? Where are you?'

'Here, in the next tree. Oh, I thought he had killed you!'

I was testing out my joints and feeling of myself for possible injuries; but I discovered nothing more serious than bruises, and scratches, and of these I had plenty.

As I was examining myself, Duare made her way along interlocking branches and presently she was at my side. 'You're bleeding,' she exclaimed. 'You *are* hurt.'

'These are nothing but scratches,' I assured her; 'only my pride is hurt.'

'You have nothing to be ashamed of; you should be very proud of what you did. I saw. I glanced behind me as I got to my feet, and I saw you standing right in the path of that terrible beast so that it would not reach me.'

'Perhaps,' I suggested, 'I was too terrified to run – just paralyzed by fear.'

She smiled and shook her head. 'I know better than that; I know you too well.'

'Any risk would be worth taking if it won your approval.'

She was silent for a moment, looking down at the basto. The brute was pawing the ground and bellowing. Occasionally it would pause and look up at us.

'We could get away from it by going through the trees,' suggested Duare. 'They grow very close together here.'

'And abandon my new weapons?' I demanded.

'He'll probably go away in a few minutes, as soon as he realizes we are not coming down.'

But he didn't go away in a few minutes. He bellowed and pawed and gored the ground for half an hour, and then he lay down beneath the tree.

'That fellow's an optimist,' I remarked. 'He thinks that if he waits long enough we'll probably come down of our own volition.'

Duare laughed. 'Maybe he thinks we'll die of old age and fall down.'

'That's a joke on him; he doesn't know that we have been inoculated with the serum of longevity.'

'In the meantime, the joke is on us; and I am getting hungry.'

'Look, Duare!' I whispered, as I caught sight of something dimly visible through the tangled undergrowth beyond the basto.

'What is it?' she asked.

'I don't know, but it's something large.'

'It is creeping silently through the brush, Carson. Do you suppose it is something that has caught our scent, some other terrible beast of prey?'

'Well, we are up a tree,' I reassured her.

'Yes, and many of these creatures climb trees. I wish you had your weapons.'

'If that basto would look the other way for a minute, I'd go down and get them.'

'No, you mustn't do that – one or the other of them would get you.'

'Here it comes now, Duare! Look!'

'It's a tharban,' she whispered.

VII

Bull Against Lion

The evil face of the fierce carnivore was protruding from the underbrush a short distance beyond and behind the basto. The latter did not see it, nor did his nostrils catch the scent of the great cat-like creature.

'It's not looking at us,' I said; 'it's watching the basto.'

'Do you suppose –' commenced Duare, and then her words were drowned by the most blood-curdling scream I have ever heard.

It came from the savage throat of the tharban at the instant it sprang toward the basto. The latter beast, lumbering to its feet, was caught at a disadvantage. The tharban leaped full upon its back, sinking talons and fangs deep into the tough flesh.

The bellowing of the basto mingled with the roars and growls of the tharban in a hideous diapason of bestial rage that seemed to rock the forest.

The huge bull wheeled in a frenzy of pain and sought to sink its horn in the thing upon its back. The tharban struck viciously at the savage face, raking downward from poll to muzzle, tearing hide and flesh to the bone, one great talon ripping an eye from its socket.

Its head a bloody mass of torn flesh, the basto threw itself upon its back with almost cat-like agility, seeking to crush the life from its tormentor; but the tharban leaped to one side and, as the bull scrambled to its feet, sprang in again.

This time the basto, wheeling with lowered head and incredible swiftness, caught the tharban full upon its horns and tossed it high into the foliage of the tree above.

A screaming, clawing hellion of unrestrained primitive rage and hate, the great carnivore hurtled upward within a few feet of Duare and me; and then, still clawing and screaming, it fell back.

Like a huge cat, that it most closely resembled, it came down feet first. With ready horns and tail stiffly erect, the basto waited to catch it and toss it again. Full on those powerful horns the tharban fell; but when the basto surged upward with all the strength of that mighty, bulging neck, the tharban did not soar upward into the tree again. With powerful claws and mighty jaws it clung to the head and neck of its antagonist. It raked shoulder and throat as the basto attempted to shake it loose. With fearful strokes of its talons it was tearing the basto to shreds.

In a bloody welter of gore, the stricken creature, now totally blinded by the loss of its remaining eye, wheeled in a grotesque and futile pirouette of death; but still its screaming nemesis clung to it, tearing, striking in mad, blind rage, its hideous cries mingling with the now shrill death bellowings of the stricken bull.

Suddenly the basto stopped in its tracks, its feet spread, swaying weakly. Blood was gushing from its neck in such a torrent that I was positive its jugular must have been severed; I knew that the end must be near and only wondered at the unbelievable tenacity with which the creature clung to life.

Nor was the tharban in an enviable state. Once badly gored and now impaled upon those two mighty horns, the blood of his terrible wounds mingling with the blood of his intended victim, his chances of survival were as negligible as those of the weaving bull, already seemingly dead upon its feet.

But how could I guess the inconceivable vitality of these mighty creatures?

With a sudden shake of his horns the bull stiffened; then he lowered his head and charged blindly, apparently with all the strength and vigor of unimpaired vitality.

It was to be a short charge. With terrific impact he struck the bole of the tree in which we were crouching. The branch upon which we sat swayed and snapped like a loose spar in a gale, and Duare and I were toppled from our perch.

Clutching futilely for support, we shot downward on top of the tharban and the basto. For an instant I was terrified for Duare's safety, but there was no need for apprehension. Neither of these mighty engines of destruction turned upon us; neither moved. Except for a few convulsive shudders they lay still in death.

The tharban had been caught between the bole of the tree and massive poll of the basto and crushed to pulp; the basto had died as it wreaked its final, fearful vengeance on the tharban.

Duare and I had rolled to the ground beside the bodies of these mighty Titans; and now, uninjured, we sprang to our feet. Duare was pale and a trifle shaken, but she smiled bravely up into my face.

'Our hunting was more successful than we dreamed,' she said. 'Here is meat enough for many men.'

'Kamlot told me that there was nothing like a basto steak grilled over a wood fire.'

'They are delicious. My mouth is watering already.'

'And mine, too, Duare; but without a knife we are still a long way from the steak. Look at that thick hide.'

Duare looked crestfallen. 'Did ever two people have such continuous bad luck?' she exclaimed. 'But never mind,' she added. 'Get your weapons, and perhaps we shall find something small enough to tear to pieces or cook whole.'

'Wait!' I exclaimed, opening the pocket pouch that hung over my shoulder by a stout cord. 'I have a piece of stone with a sharp edge that I use for scraping my bow and arrows. I may be able to hack out a meal with it.'

It was a laborious job but I finally succeeded, and while I was engaged upon this crude and ragged butchery Duare gathered tinder and wood and surprised us both by starting a fire. She was very happy and excited over her success, and proud, too. In all her pampered life at home she had never been required to do a practical thing, and the reward of even this small accomplishment filled her with joy.

That meal was a memorable one; it was epochal. It marked the emergence of primitive man from the lower orders of life. He had achieved fire; he had fashioned weapons; he had made his kill (figuratively, in this case); and now for the first time he was eating cooked food. And I liked to carry the metaphor a little further in this instance and think of the partner of his achievements as his mate. I sighed as I thought of the happiness that might be ours did Duare but return my love.

'What's the matter?' demanded Duare. 'Why do you sigh?'

'I am sighing because I am not really a primitive man instead of a poor, weak imitation of one.'

'Why do you want to be a primitive man?' she inquired.

'Because primitive man was not bound by silly conventions,' I replied. 'If he wanted a woman and she did not want him, he grabbed her by the hair and dragged her to his lair.'

'I am glad that I did not live in those times,' said Duare.

For several days we wandered on through the forest. I knew that we were hopelessly lost, but I was anxious to get out of that gloomy wood. It was getting on our nerves. I managed to kill small game with my spear and my arrows; there was an abundance of fruit and nuts; and water was plentiful. In the matter of food we lived like kings, and we were fortunate in our encounters with the more formidable creatures we met. Luckily for us we saw none that were arboreal, though I am positive that this was merely by the luckiest chance, for the woods of Amtor harbor many terrible creatures that live wholly in the trees.

Duare, notwithstanding all the hardships and dangers she was constantly undergoing, seldom complained. She remained remarkably cheerful in the face of what was now palpably the absolute certainty that we could never hope to find the distant island where her father was king. Sometimes she was sober and silent for long periods, and I guessed that at these times she was sorrowing; but she did not share her sorrows with me. I wished that she would; we often share our sorrows with those we love.

But one day she suddenly sat down and began to cry. I was so surprised that I just stood there for several minutes staring at her before I could think of anything to say, and then I didn't think of anything very brilliant.

'Why, Duare!' I cried. 'What's the matter? Are you ill?'

She shook her head and sought to stifle her sobs. 'I'm sorry,' she managed to say at last. 'I didn't mean to; I've tried not to; but this forest! Oh, Carson, it's on my nerves; it haunts me even in my sleep. It is endless; it goes on and on forever – gloomy, forbidding, filled with terrible dangers. There!' she exclaimed, and rising she shook her head as though to dispel unwelcome visions. 'I'm all right now; I won't do it again.' She smiled through her tears.

I wanted to take her in my arms and comfort her – oh, how badly I wanted to! But I only laid a hand upon her shoulder. 'I know just how you feel,' I told her. 'I've felt the same way for days. I have to take it out by swearing to myself. But it can't last forever, Duare. There must be an end to it pretty soon; and, anyway, you must remember that the forest has fed us and sheltered us and protected us.'

'As a jailer feeds and shelters and protects the criminal condemned to die,' she responded dully. 'Come! Let's not speak of it any more.'

Once again the underbrush was thick, and we were following a game trail that was as erratic as most game trails. I think it was this thick brush that depressed Duare even more than the forest itself. I know it always depressed me. The trail was wide and we were walking abreast when suddenly at a turning the forest seemed to disappear in front of us. There was a void staring us in the face, and beyond that, far, far away, the outlines of distant mountains.

VIII

Down the Escarpment

Wonderingly we advanced until we stood upon the brink of a lofty escarpment. Far below, at least five thousand feet, a great valley spread before our eyes. Far, far away, across it, we saw the outlines of the distant mountains that hemmed it upon that side; but to the right and left its extent was shrouded in the mists of distance.

During the days that we had been wandering in the forest we must have been climbing steadily, but the ascent had been so gradual that we had scarcely noticed it. Now, the effect of coming suddenly upon this mighty depression was startling. It was as though I were looking into a deep pit that lay far below sea level. This impression, however, was soon dispelled, for in the distance I saw a great river winding along the bed of the valley; and I knew that it must run downward to some sea.

'A new world!' breathed Duare. 'How beautiful by contrast with this frightful forest!'

'Let us hope that it will be no less kind to us than the forest has been.'

'How could it be otherwise than kind? It is so beautiful,' she replied. 'There must be people living there, generous, kindly people as lovely as their lovely valley. There could be no evil where there is so much beauty. Perhaps they will help us to return to my Vepaja. I am sure they will.'

'I hope so, Duare,' I said.

'See!' she exclaimed. 'There are little rivers running into the big river, and there are level plains dotted with trees, and there are forests, too, but no terrible forest that stretches on and on seemingly without end as this that we are escaping. Do you see any cities or signs of man, Carson?'

I shook my head. 'I cannot be positive. We are very high above the valley; and the large river, where it is probable the cities would be, is far away. Only a very great city with tall buildings would be visible from here, and the haze that hangs over the valley might even hide a large city from us. We shall have to go down into the valley to find out.'

'I can scarcely wait,' exclaimed Duare.

The trail on which we had approached the edge of the escarpment turned sharply to the left and skirted the brink, but from it a smaller trail branched and dropped over the edge.

This trail was little better than a faintly marked foot path, and it zigzagged down the almost vertical face of the escarpment in a manner calculated to send the cold chills up one's back if he happened to be affected by such things.

'Few creatures go up and down here,' remarked Duare, as she looked over the edge of the escarpment at the dizzy trail.

'Perhaps we had better go on farther; there may be an easier way down,' I suggested, thinking that she might be fearful.

'No,' she demurred. 'I wanted to get out of the forest, and here is my chance. Something has gone up and down here; and if something else has, we can.'

'Take my hand, then; it is very steep.'

She did as I bid, and I also handed her my spear to use as a staff. Thus we started the perilous descent. Even now I hate to recall it. It was not only fraught with danger but it was exceedingly exhausting. A dozen times I thought that we were doomed; seemingly it was impossible to descend farther, and certainly it would have been impossible to retrace our steps to the summit, for there had been places where we had lowered ourselves over ledges that we could not have again scaled.

Duare was very brave. She amazed me. Not only was her courage remarkable, but her endurance was almost unbelievable in one so delicately moulded. And she kept cheerful and good-natured. Often she laughed when she would slip and almost fall, where a fall meant death.

'I said,' she recalled, once while we were resting, 'that something must have come up and down this trail. Now I wonder what manner of creature it may be.'

'Perhaps it is a mountain goat,' I suggested. 'I can think of nothing else that might do it.'

She did not know what a mountain goat was, and I knew of no Venusan animal with which to compare it. She thought that a mistal might easily go up and down such a trail. I had never heard of this animal, but from her description I judged it to be a rat-like animal about the size of a house cat.

As we were starting down again after a rest, I heard a noise below us and looked over the edge of the ledge on which we stood to see what had caused it.

'We are about to have our curiosity satisfied,' I whispered to Duare. 'Here comes the trail maker.'

'Is it a mistal?' she asked.

'No, nor a mountain goat; but it is just the sort of a creature that might most easily cling to this vertical pathway. I don't know what you Amtorians call it. Take a look; perhaps you will recognize it.'

It was a huge, hideous lizard about twenty feet in length that was climbing sluggishly upward toward our position.

Leaning on my shoulder, Duare glanced downward over the ledge. She voiced a low gasp of terror.

'I think it is a vere,' she said, 'and if it is we are in for it. I have never seen one, but I have read of them in books and seen their pictures; this one looks like the pictures I have seen.'

'Are they dangerous?' I asked.

'They are deadly,' she replied. 'We wouldn't have a chance against a vere.'

'See if you can climb back out of the way,' I said to Duare. 'I will try to hold it here until you are safe.' Then I turned toward the creature crawling slowly upward.

It was covered with scales of red, black, and yellow arranged in intricate designs. Its coloration and ornamentation were beautiful, but right there its beauty stopped. It had a head not unlike that of a crocodile, and along each side of its upper jaw was a row of gleaming white horns. Across the top and down the sides of its head sprawled a single huge eye of myriad facets.

It had not discovered us yet, but in another half minute it would be upon us. I loosened a bit of rock near my hand and hurled it down, thinking I might turn the creature back. The missile struck it on the snout, and with a grunt it raised its head and saw me.

Its great jaws opened and out shot the most prodigious tongue I had ever seen. Like lightning it curled about me and snapped me toward those gaping jaws from which was issuing a harsh screaming whistle.

All that saved me from being instantly engulfed was the fact that I was a little too large a mouthful for the creature to negotiate with ease. I wedged crosswise of his snout and there I fought with all my strength to keep from being dragged into that rapacious maw.

It was a great slimy, toothless, sucking gullet that I struggled to escape. Evidently the creature swallowed its prey whole, its horns being probably solely for defense. From that repulsive throat issued a fetid odor that almost overpowered me. I think that it may have been a poisonous exhalation that was intended to anaesthetize its victims. I felt myself growing weak and dizzy, and then I saw Duare at my side.

She was grasping my spear in both hands and lunging viciously at the horrid face of the vere. All the time she was moaning, 'Carson! Carson!'

How small and frail and inadequate she looked to be pitting herself against this fearsome creature! – and how magnificent!

She was risking her life to save mine, and yet she did not love me. Still, it was not incredible – there are noble qualities far more unselfish than love. Loyalty is of these. But I could not permit her to sacrifice her life for loyalty.

'Run, Duare!' I cried. 'You can't save me – I am done for. Run while you can, or it will kill us both.'

She paid no attention to me, but thrust again. This time the spear tore into the many-faceted eye. With a shrill whistle of pain, the reptile turned upon Duare and sought to strike her with its gleaming horns; but she stood her ground and, thrusting again, drove the weapon between the distended jaws, drove it deep and far into the pink flesh of that repulsive maw.

The spear point must have pierced the tongue, for it suddenly went limp; and I rolled from its encircling grasp to the ground.

Instantly I was on my feet again, and seizing Duare's arm dragged her to one side as the vere charged blindly. It brushed past us, whistling and screaming, and then turned, but in the wrong direction.

It was then that I realized that the creature had been totally blinded by the wound in its eye. Taking a perilous risk, I threw an arm about Duare and slid over the edge of the ledge upon which the brute had encountered us, for to have remained even an instant where we were would have meant being maimed or hurled to our doom by the viciously lashing tail of the frenzied lizard.

Fortune favored us, and we came safely to rest upon another ledge at a slightly lower level. Above us we could hear the whistling scream of the vere and the thudding of his tail against the rocky escarpment.

Fearing that the creature might descend upon us, we hurried on, taking even greater risks than we had before; nor did we stop until we had reached comparatively level ground near the foot of the escarpment. Then we sat down to rest. We were both panting from our exertions.

'You were wonderful,' I said to Duare. 'You risked your life to save mine.'

'Perhaps I was just afraid to be left alone,' she said with some embarrassment. 'I may have been entirely selfish.'

'I don't believe that,' I remonstrated.

The truth was that I didn't want to believe it. Another implication was far sweeter to me.

'Anyhow,' remarked Duare, 'we found out what made the trail up the escarpment.'

'And that our beautiful valley may not be as secure as it looks,' I added.

'But the creature was going out of the valley up into the forest,' she argued. 'That is probably where it lived.'

'However, we had best be on our guard constantly.'

'And now you have no spear; and that is a real loss, for it is because of the spear that you are alive.'

'Down there a little way,' I indicated, pointing, 'is a winding strip of wood that seems to be following the meanderings of a stream. There we can find material for another spear and also water – I am as dry as a bone.'

'So am I,' said Duare, 'and hungry too. Perhaps you can kill another basto.'

I laughed. 'This time I shall make you a spear and a bow and arrows, too.

From what you have already done, you seem to be better able to kill bastos than I.'

Leisurely we walked toward the wood, which was about a mile away, through soft grass of a pale violet hue. Flowers grew in profusion on every hand. There were purple flowers and blue and pale yellow; and their foliage, like the blossoms, was strange and unearthly. There were flowers and leaves of colors that have no name, colors such as no Earthly eye had ever seen before.

Such things bear in upon me the strange isolation of our senses. Each sense lives in a world of its own, and though it lives a lifetime with its fellow senses it knows nothing of their worlds.

My eyes see a color; but my fingers, my ears, my nose, my palate may never know that color. I cannot even describe it so that any of your senses may perceive it as I perceive it, if it is a new color that you have never seen. Even less well might I describe an odor or a flavor or the feel of some strange substance.

Only by comparison might I make you see the landscape that stretched before our eyes, and there is nothing in your world with which I may compare it – the glowing fog bank overhead, the pale, soft pastels of field and forest and distant misty mountains – no dense shadows and no high lights – strange and beautiful and weird – intriguing, provocative, compelling, always beckoning one on to further investigation, to new adventure.

All about us the plain between the escarpment and the forest was dotted with trees; and, lying beneath them or grazing in the open, were animals that were entirely new to my experience either here or on Earth. That several distinct families and numerous genera were represented was apparent to even a cursory survey.

Some were large and cumbersome, others were small and dainty. All were too far away for me to note them in detail; and for that I was glad, for I guessed that among that array of wild beasts there must be some at least which might prove dangerous to man. But, like all animals except hungry carnivores and men, they showed no disposition to attack us so long as we did not interfere with them or approach them too closely.

'I see that we shall not go hungry here,' remarked Duare.

'I hope some of those little fellows are good to eat,' I laughed.

'I am sure that big one under the tree is delicious; the one looking at us,' and she pointed to an enormous, shaggy creature as large as an elephant. Duare had a sense of humor.

'Possibly it entertains the same idea concerning us,' I suggested; 'here it comes!'

The huge beast was walking toward us. The forest was still a hundred yards away.

'Shall we run?' asked Duare.

'I am afraid that would be fatal. You know, it is almost instinctive for a beast to pursue any creature that runs away from it. I think the best course for us to follow is to continue steadily toward the forest without seeming haste. If the thing does not increase its speed we shall reach the trees ahead of it; if we run for it the chances are that it will overtake us, for of all created things mankind seems to be about the slowest.'

As we proceeded, we constantly cast backward glances at the shaggy menace trailing us. He lumbered along, exhibiting no signs of excitement; but his long strides were eating up the distance between us. I saw that he would overtake us before we reached the forest. I felt utterly helpless, with my puny bow and my tiny arrows, before this towering mountain of muscle.

'Quicken your pace a little, Duare,' I directed.

She did as I bid, but after a few steps she glanced back. 'Why don't you come, too?' she demanded.

'Don't argue,' I snapped a little shortly. 'Do as I bid you.'

She stopped and waited for me. 'I shall do as I please,' she informed me, 'and it does not please me to let you make this sacrifice for me. If you are to be killed, I shall be killed with you. Furthermore, Carson Napier, please remember that I am the daughter of a jong and am not accusoomed to being ordered about.'

'If there were not more pressing matters to occupy me I would spank you,' I growled.

She looked at me, horrified; then she stamped one little foot in rage and commenced to cry. 'You take advantage of me because there is no one to protect me,' she sputtered. 'I hate you, you – you—'

'But I am trying to protect you, Duare; and you are only making it harder for me.'

'I don't want any of your protection; I would rather be dead. It is more honorable to be dead than to be talked to like that – I am the daughter of a jong.'

'I think you have mentioned that several times before,' I said, coldly.

She threw up her head and walked stiffly on without looking back at me. Even her little shoulders and back radiated offended dignity and stifled rage.

I glanced behind me. The mighty beast was scarce fifty feet away; ahead of us the forest was about the same distance. Duare could not see me. I stopped and faced the colossus. By the time it had dispatched me Duare would probably be close to the safety of the branches of the nearest tree.

I held my bow in one hand, but my arrows remained in the crude quiver. I had fashioned to hold them behind my right shoulder. I had sense enough to realize that the only effect they might have upon this mountain of hairy sinew would be to enrage it.

After I stopped, the beast approached more slowly, almost warily. Two little eyes, set far apart, regarded me intently; two large, mulish ears pricked forward; quivering nostrils dilated.

On it came, very gradually now. A bony protuberance extending from its snout to its forehead commenced to rise until it revealed itself to my astonished gaze as a sharp-pointed horn. The horn rose until it pointed fiercely at me, a terrible weapon of offense.

I did not move. My experience of Earthly animals had taught me that few will attack without provocation, and I staked my life on the chance that the same rule prevailed on Venus. But there are other provocations besides those that arouse fear or anger; a most potent one is hunger. However, this creature looked herbivorous; and I hoped that it *was* a vegetarian. But I could not forget the basto; that somewhat resembled an American bison, yet would eat meat.

Closer and closer came the remarkable beast, very, very slowly, as though its mind were assailed by doubts. It towered above me like a living mountain. I could feel its warm breath upon my almost naked body; but, better still, I could smell its breath – the sweet, inoffensive breath of a grass eater. My hopes rose.

The creature stuck out its muzzle toward me; a low rumbling issued from its cavernous chest; that terrible horn touched me; then the cool, moist muzzle. The beast sniffed at me. Slowly the horn subsided.

Suddenly, with a snort, the animal wheeled about and went galloping off, bucking and jumping as I have seen a playful steer buck and jump, its little tail stiffly erect. It presented a most ludicrous appearance – as would a steam locomotive skipping rope. I laughed, possibly a little hysterically, for my knees were suddenly weak and wobbly. If I had not been near death, I had at least thought that I was.

As I turned back toward the forest I saw Duare standing there looking at me, and as I approached her I perceived that she was wide-eyed and trembling.

'You are very brave, Carson,' she said with a little catch in her throat. Her anger seemed to have departed. 'I know that you remained there so that I might escape.'

'There really wasn't much else that I could do,' I assured her. 'And now that that's over, let's see if we can't find something to eat – something a few sizes smaller than that mountain of steaks and roasts. I think we'll go on until we strike the stream that flows through this forest. We may find a drinking place or a ford that the animals are accustomed to coming to.'

'There are many animals out there on the plain that are small,' suggested Duare. 'Why don't you hunt there?'

'There are plenty of animals, but there are not enough trees,' I replied with a laugh. 'We may need some trees in our hunting. I don't know enough about these Amtorian beasts as yet to warrant me in taking unnecessary risks.'

We moved on into the wood beneath the delicate foliage and among the strangely beautiful boles with their lacquer-like bark of white and red and yellow and blue.

Presently we came in sight of a little river winding leisurely between its violet banks, and at the same instant I saw a small creature drinking. It was about the size of a goat, but it didn't look like a goat. Its sharply pointed ears were constantly moving, as though on the alert for the slightest sound of danger; its tufted tail switched nervously. A collar of short horns encircled its neck just where it joined the head. They pointed slightly forward. There must have been a dozen of them. I could not but wonder what their specific purpose might be until I recalled the vere from whose horrible maw I had so recently escaped. That necklace of short horns would most certainly have discouraged any creature that was in the habit of swallowing its prey whole.

Very gently, I pushed Duare behind a tree and crept forward, fitting an arrow to my bow. As I was preparing to shoot, the creature threw up its head and turned half around. Probably it had heard me. I had been creeping on it from behind, but its change of position revealed its left side to me, and I planted my first arrow squarely in its heart.

So we made our camp beside the river and dined on juicy chops, delicious fruits, and the clear water from the little stream. Our surroundings were idyllic. Strange birds sang to us, arboreal quadrupeds swung through the trees jabbering melodiously in soft sing-song voices.

'It is very lovely here,' said Duare, dreamily. 'Carson – I wish that I were not the daughter of a jong.'

IX

The Gloomy Castle

We were both loath to leave this lovely spot, and so we tarried there for two days while I made weapons for Duare and a new spear for myself.

I had constructed a little platform in a tree that overhung the river; and there at night we were comparatively safe from predatory animals while the soft music of the purling water lulled us to sleep, a sleep that might be suddenly broken by the savage roars of hunting beasts or the screams of their victims, to which the distant lowing and bellowing of the vast herds upon the plain furnished a harmonious undertone in this raw aria of life.

It was our last night in this pleasant camp. We were sitting on our little platform watching the fish leaping and jumping in the river below.

'I could be happy here forever – with you, Duare,' I said.

'One may not think of happiness alone,' she replied; 'there is duty also.'

'But what if circumstances make us helpless to perform our duties? Aren't we warranted in making the best of our fate and making the most of the chance for happiness where we find it?'

'What do you mean?' she asked.

'I mean that there is practically no possibility that we can ever reach Vepaja. We do not know where it is, and if we did it seems to me that there is not even the remotest chance that we should survive the dangers that must lie along that unknown trail that leads back to the house of Mintep, your father.'

'I know that you are right,' she replied a little wearily, 'but it is my duty to try; and I may never cease to seek to return, to the end of my life, no matter how remote I may know the chance of success may be.'

'Isn't that being a little unreasonable, Duare?'

'You do not understand, Carson Napier. If I had a brother or sister it might make a difference; but I have neither, and my father and I are the last of our line. It is not for myself nor for my father that I must return but for my country – the royal line of the jongs of Vepaja must not be broken, and there is none to perpetuate it but myself.'

'And if we do return – what then?'

'When I am twenty I shall marry a noble selected by my father, and after my father dies I shall be vadjong, or queen, until my oldest son is twenty; then he will be jong.'

'But with the longevity serum that your scientists have perfected your father will never die; so why return?'

'I hope he will not die, but there are accidents and battles and assassins. Oh, why discuss it! The royal line must be preserved!'

'And what of me, if we reach Vepaja?' I asked.

'What do you mean?'

'Will there be a chance for me?'

'I do not understand.'

'If your father consents, will you marry me?' I blurted.

Duare flushed. 'How many times must I tell you that you may not speak of such serious things to me?'

'I can't help it, Duare; I love you. I care nothing for customs nor jongs nor dynasties. I shall tell your father that I love you, and I shall tell him that you love me.'

'I do not love you; you have no right to say that. It is sinful and wicked. Because once I was weak and lost my head and said a thing I did not mean you have no right to constantly throw it in my face.'

Now that was just like a woman. I had been fighting every impulse to keep from speaking of love during all the time we had been together. I couldn't recall but one other instance when I had lost control of myself, yet she accused me of constantly throwing in her face the one admission of love that she had made.

'Well,' I said, sullenly, 'I shall do what I said I'd do, if I ever see your father again.'

'And do you know what he will do?'

'If he's the right kind of a father he'll say, "Bless you, my children." '

'He is a jong before he is a father, and he will have you destroyed. Even if you do not make any such mad admission to him, I shall have to use all of my powers of persuasion to save you from death.'

'Why should he kill me?'

'No man who has spoken, without royal permission, to a janjong, or princess, is ordinarily permitted to live. That you may be with me alone for months and possibly years before we return to Vepaja will but tend to exaggerate the seriousness of the situation. I shall plead your service to me; that you risked your life innumerable times to preserve mine; and that I think will have sufficient weight to save you from death; but, of course, you will be banished from Vepaja.'

'That is a pleasant outlook. I may lose my life, and I am certain to lose you. Under such circumstances, do you think that I will prosecute the search for Vepaja with much enthusiasm or diligence?'

'Perhaps not with enthusiasm; but with diligence, yes. You will do it for me, because of that thing which you call love.'

'Possibly you are right,' I said, and I knew that she was.

The next day we started, in accordance with a plan we had formulated, to follow the little river down toward the big river along which we would continue to the sea. Where we should go from there was problematical. We decided to wait until we reached the sea before making any further plans. What lay before us we could not guess; had we been able to we might have fled back to the comparative safety of the gloomy forest we had so recently quitted with delight.

Late in the afternoon we were taking a short cut across open ground where the river made a great bend. It was rather rough going, for there were many rocks and bowlders and the surface of the land was cut by gullies.

As we clambered up the bank of a particularly deep gully I chanced to glance back and saw a strange animal standing on the opposite rim watching us. It was about the size of a German police dog, but there the similarity ceased. It had a massive, curved beak remarkably similar to that of a parrot; and its body was covered with feathers; but it was no bird, for it went on four legs and had no wings. Forward of its two short ears were three horns, one in front of either ear and the third growing midway between the others. As it turned part way around to look back at something we could not see, I saw that it had no tail. At a distance its legs and feet appeared bird-like.

'Do you see what I see, Duare?' I asked, nodding in the direction of the weird creature; 'or am I suffering from a touch of fever?'

'Of course I see it,' she replied, 'but I don't know what it is. I am sure that there is no such creature on the island of Vepaja.'

'There's another of them, and another, and another!' I exclaimed. 'Lord! There must be a dozen of them.'

They were standing in a little knot surveying us when suddenly the one we had first seen raised its grotesque head and voiced a hoarse, wailing scream; then it started down into the gully and headed for us at a rapid gallop, and behind it came its fellows, all now voicing that hideous cry.

'What are we going to do?' asked Duare. 'Do you suppose they are dangerous?'

'I don't know whether they are dangerous or not,' I replied, 'but I wish that there were a tree handy.'

'A forest does have its advantages,' admitted Duare. 'What are we going to do?'

'It would do no good to run; so we might as well stand here and have it out with them. We'll have some advantage as they come up the bank of the gully.'

I fitted an arrow to my bow and Duare did likewise; then we stood waiting for them to come within range. They loped easily across the bottom of the gully and started the ascent. They didn't seem to be in much of a hurry; that is, they didn't seem to be extending themselves to their full speed, probably because we were not running away from them.

Perhaps this surprised them, for they presently slowed down to a walk and advanced warily. They had ceased their baying. The feathers along their backs rose stiffly erect as they slunk toward us.

Aiming carefully at the foremost, I loosed an arrow. It struck the beast full in the chest, and with a scream it stopped and tore at the feathered shaft protruding from its body. The others halted and surrounded it. They made a strange cackling sound.

The wounded creature staggered and sank to the ground, and instantly its fellows were upon it, tearing and rending. For a moment it fought fiercely to defend itself, but futilely.

As the others commenced to devour their fallen comrade I motioned Duare to follow me, and we turned and ran toward the trees we could see about a mile away where the river turned back across our line of march. But we hadn't gone far before we heard again the infernal screaming that told us that the pack was on our trail.

This time they overtook us while we were at the bottom of a depression, and once again we made a stand. Instead of attacking us directly, the beasts slunk about just out of range, as though they knew the danger line beyond which they would be safe; then slowly they circled us until we were surrounded.

'If they charge now, all at once,' said Duare. 'we are sure to be finished.'

'Perhaps if we succeed in killing a couple of them the others will stop to devour them, thus giving us another chance to get closer to the wood,' I argued with an assumed optimism.

As we waited for the next move of our antagonists, we heard a loud shout in the direction from which we had come. Looking quickly up, I saw a man seated upon the back of a four footed animal at the rim of the depression in which we stood.

At the sound of the human voice, the beasts surrounding us looked in the direction of the interruption and immediately commenced to cackle. The man on the beast rode slowly down toward us, and as he came to the ring of beasts they moved aside and let him pass through their savage ranks.

'It is fortunate for you that I came when I did,' said the stranger, as the beast he rode stopped in front of us; 'these kazars of mine are a ferocious lot.' He was eying us intently, especially Duare. 'Who are you, and where are you from?' he demanded.

'We are strangers, and we are lost,' I replied. 'I am from California.' I did not wish to tell him that we were from Vepaja until we knew more of him. If he was a Thorist he was an enemy; and the less he knew about us the better, especially that we were from the country of Mintep, the jong, than whom the Thorists have no more bitter enemy.

'California,' he repeated. 'I never heard of such a country. Where is it?'

'In North America,' I replied, but he only shook his head. 'And who are you,' I asked, 'and what country is this?'

'This is Noobol, but that of course you already know. This part of it is known as Morov. I am Skor, the jong of Morov. But you have not told me your names.'

'This is Duare,' I replied, 'and I am Carson.' I did not give my surname as they are seldom used on Venus.

'And where were you going?'

'We were trying to find our way to the sea.'

'From where did you come?'

'Recently we were in Kapdor,' I explained.

I saw his eyes narrow ominously. 'So you are Thorists!' he snapped.

'No,' I assured him, 'we are not. We were prisoners of the Thorists.' I hoped that my guess had been a good one and that he was not kindly disposed toward the Thorists. The slender thread upon which I hung my hopes was no more substantial than the frown that had clouded his brow at my admission that we had just come from Kapdor.

To my relief his expression changed. 'I am glad that you are not Thorists; otherwise I would not help you. I have no use for the breed.'

'You will help us, then?' I asked.

'With pleasure,' he replied. He was looking at Duare as he spoke, and I did not exactly relish the tone of his voice nor the expression on his face.

The kazars were circling around us, cackling and whistling. When one of them approached us too close, Skor would flick it with the lash of a long whip he carried; and the creature would retreat, screaming and cackling the louder.

'Come,' he said presently, 'I will take you to my house; then we may discuss plans for the future. The woman may ride behind me on my zorat.'

'I prefer to walk,' said Duare. 'I am accustomed to it now.'

Skor's eyes narrowed a bit. He started to speak, and then he checked himself. Finally he shrugged. 'As you will,' he said, and turned the head of his mount back in the direction from which he had come.

The creature he rode, which he called a zorat, was unlike any beast that I had ever seen before. It was about the size of a small horse. Its long, slender legs suggested great speed. Its feet were round and nailless and heavily calloused on the bottoms. Its almost vertical pasterns suggested that it might be a hard gaited beast, but this was not so. Later I learned that almost horizontal femurs

190

and humeri absorbed the jolts and rendered the zorat an easy riding saddle animal.

Above its withers and just forward of its kidneys were soft pads or miniature humps which formed a perfect saddle with natural pommel and cantle. Its head was short and broad, with two large, saucer-like eyes and pendulous ears. Its teeth were those of a grass-eater. Its only means of defense seemed to lie in its fleetness, although, as I afterward had occasion to discover, it could use its jaws and teeth most effectively when its short temper was aroused.

We walked beside Skor on the journey toward his house, the grotesque kazars following docilely behind at the command of their master. The way led toward the great bend of the river, that we had sought to avoid by taking a short cut, and a forest that lined its banks. The proximity of the kazars made me nervous, for occasionally one of them would trot close at our heels; and I was fearful that Duare might be injured by one of the fierce beasts before I could prevent it. I asked Skor what purpose the creatures served.

'I use them for hunting,' he replied, 'but principally for protection. I have enemies; and then, too, there are many savage beasts roaming at large in Morov. The kazars are quite fearless and very savage fighters. Their greatest weakness is their predilection for cannibalism; they will abandon a fight to devour one of their own number that has fallen.'

Shortly after we entered the forest we came upon a large, gloomy, fortress-like building of stone. It was built upon a low rise of ground at the water's edge, the river lapping the masonry upon that side. A stone wall connecting with the river wall of the building inclosed several acres of clear land in front of the structure. A heavy gate closed the only aperture that was visible in this wall.

As we approached, Skor shouted, 'Open! It is the jong,' and the gates swung slowly outward.

As we entered, several armed men, who had been sitting beneath one of the several trees that had been left standing when the ground was cleared, arose and stood with bowed heads. They were a hard and also a sad looking lot. The feature that struck me most forcibly was the strange hue of their skin, a repulsive, unhealthy pallor, a seeming bloodlessness. I caught the eyes of one that chanced to raise his head as we passed, and I shivered. They were glazed, clammy eyes; without light, without fire. I would have thought the fellow stone blind but for the fact that the instant that my eyes caught his they dropped swiftly. Another had an ugly, open wound across his cheek from temple to chin; it gaped wide, but it did not bleed.

Skor snapped a brief order; and two of the men herded the pack of cackling kazars into a strong inclosure built beside the gateway, as we proceeded on toward the house. Perhaps I should call it castle.

The inclosure across which we passed was barren except for the few trees that had been left standing. It was littered with refuse of all descriptions and was unspeakably disorderly and untidy. Old sandals, rags, broken pottery, and the garbage from the castle kitchens were strewn promiscuously about. The only spot from which any effort had been made to remove the litter was a few hundred square feet of stone flagging before the main entrance to the building.

Here Skor dismounted as three more men similar to those at the gate came lifelessly from the interior of the building. One of these took Skor's mount and led it away, the others stood one on either side of the entrance as we passed in.

The doorway was small, the door that closed it thick and heavy. It seemed to be the only opening on the first floor on this side of the castle. Along the second and third floor levels I had seen small windows heavily barred. At one corner of the building I had noticed a tower rising two more stories above the main part of the castle. This, too, had small windows, some of which were barred.

The interior of the building was dark and gloomy. Coupled with the appearance of the inmates I had already seen it engendered within me a feeling of depression that I could not throw off.

'You must be hungry,' suggested Skor. 'Come out into the inner court – it is pleasanter there – and I will have food served.'

We followed him down a short corridor and through a doorway into a courtyard around which the castle was built. The inclosure reminded me of a prison yard. It was flagged with stone. No living thing grew there. The gray stone walls, cut with their small windows, rose upon four sides. There had been no effort toward architectural ornamentation in the design of the structure, nor any to beautify the courtyard in any way. Here, too, was litter and trash that it had evidently been easier to throw into the inner court than carry to the outer.

I was oppressed by forebodings of ill. I wished that we had never entered the place, but I tried to brush my fears aside. I argued that Skor had given no indications of being other than a kindly and solicitous host. He had seemed anxious to befriend us. That he was a jong I had commenced to doubt, for there was no suggestion of royalty in his mode of living.

In the center of the court a plank table was flanked by grimy, well worn benches. On the table were the remains of a meal. Skor graciously waved us toward the benches; then he clapped his hands together three times before he seated himself at the head of the table.

'I seldom have guests here,' he said. 'It is quite a pleasant treat for me. I hope that you will enjoy your stay. I am sure that I shall,' and as he spoke he looked at Duare in that way that I did not like.

'I am sure that we might enjoy it could we remain,' replied Duare quickly, 'but that is not possible. I must return to the house of my father.'

'Where is that?' asked Skor.

'In Vepaja,' explained Duare.

'I never heard of that country,' said Skor. 'Where is it?'

'You never heard of Vepaja!' exclaimed Duare incredulously. 'Why, all the present country of Thora was called Vepaja until the Thorists rose and took it and drove the remnants of the ruling class to the island that is now all that remains of ancient Vepaja.'

'Oh, yes, I had heard of that,' admitted Skor; 'but it was a long time ago and in distant Trabol.'

'Is this not Trabol?' asked Duare.

'No,' replied Skor; 'this is Strabol.'

'But Strabol is the hot country,' argued Duare. 'No one can live in Strabol.'

'You are in Strabol now. It is hot here during a portion of the year, but not so hot as to be unendurable.'

I was interested. If what Skor said were true, we had crossed the equator and were now in the northern hemisphere of Venus. The Vepajans had told me that Strabol was uninhabitable – a steaming jungle reeking with heat and moisture and inhabited only by fierce and terrible beasts and reptiles. The entire northern hemisphere was a *terra incognita* to the men of the southern hemisphere, and for that reason I had been anxious to explore it.

With the responsibility of Duare on my shoulders I could not do much exploring, but I might learn something from Skor; so I asked him of the country farther north.

'It is no good,' he snapped. 'It is the land of fools. They frown upon true science and progress. They drove me out; they would have killed me. I came here and established the kingdom of Morov. That was many years ago – perhaps a hundred years. I have never returned since to the country of my birth; but sometimes their people come here,' and he laughed unpleasantly.

Just then a woman came from the building, evidently in response to Skor's summons. She was middle aged. Her skin was the same repulsive hue as that of the men I had seen, and it was very dirty. Her mouth hung open and her tongue protruded; it was dry and swollen. Her eyes were glazed and staring. She moved with a slow, awkward shuffle. And now, behind her, came two men. They were much as she; there was something indescribably revolting about all three.

'Take these away!' snapped Skor with a wave of the hand toward the soiled dishes. 'And bring food.'

The three gathered up the dishes and shuffled away. None of them spoke. The look of horror in Duare's eyes could not have gone unnoticed by Skor.

'You do not like my retainers?' demanded Skor testily.

'But I said nothing,' objected Duare.

'I saw it in your face.' Suddenly Skor broke into laughter. There was no mirth in it, nor was there laughter in his eyes but another expression, a terrible glint that passed as quickly as it had come. 'They are excellent servants,' he said in normal tones; 'they do not talk too much, and *they do whatever I tell them to do.*'

Presently the three returned carrying vessels of food. There was meat, partially raw, partially burned, and wholly unpalatable; there were fruits and vegetables, none of which appeared to have been washed; there was wine. It was the only thing there fit for human consumption.

The meal was not a success. Duare could not eat. I sipped my wine and watched Skor eat ravenously.

Darkness was falling as Skor arose from the table. 'I will show you to your rooms,' he said. 'You must be tired.' His tone and manner were those of the perfect host. 'Tomorrow you shall set out again upon your journey.'

Relieved by this promise we followed him into the house. It was a dark and gloomy abode, chill and cheerless. We followed him up a stairway to the second floor and into a long, dark corridor. Presently he stopped before a door and threw it open.

'May you sleep well,' he said to Duare, bowing and motioning her to enter.

Silently Duare crossed the threshold and Skor closed the door behind her; then he conducted me to the end of the corridor, up two flights of stairs and ushered me into a circular room that I guessed was in the tower I had seen when we entered the castle.

'I hope you awaken refreshed,' he said politely and withdrew, closing the door behind him.

I heard his footsteps descending the stairs until they were lost in the distance. I thought of Duare down there alone in this gloomy and mysterious pile. I had no reason to believe that she was not safe, but nevertheless I was apprehensive. Anyway, I had no intention of leaving her alone.

I waited until he had had plenty of time to go to his own quarters wherever they might be; then I stepped to the door, determined to go to Duare. I laid my hand upon the latch and sought to open it. It was locked from the outside. Quickly I went to the several windows. Each was heavily barred. Faintly from the distant recesses of that forbidding pile I thought I heard a mocking laugh.

X

The Girl in the Tower

The tower room in which I found myself imprisoned was lighted only by the mysterious night glow that relieves the nocturnal darkness of Venus, which would otherwise have been impenetrable. Dimly I saw the furnishings of the room – they were meager. The place had more the aspect of a prison cell than a guest chamber.

I crossed to a chest of drawers and investigated it. It was filled with odds and ends of worn and useless apparel, bits of string, a few lengths of rope which, I had an ugly suspicion, might once have served as bonds. I paced the floor worrying about Duare. I was helpless. I could do nothing. It would be vain to pound upon the door or call for release. The will that had incarcerated me was supreme here. Only by the voluntary act of that will could I be released.

Seating myself on a rude bench before a small table I tried to plan; I sought to discover some loophole for escape. Apparently there was none. I arose and once again examined the window bars and the sturdy door; they were impregnable.

Finally I crossed to a rickety couch that stood against the wall and lay down upon the worn and odorous hide that covered it. Absolute silence reigned – the silence of the tomb. For a long time it was unbroken; then I heard a sound above me. I listened, trying to interpret it. It was like the slow padding of naked feet – back and forth, to and fro above my head.

I had thought that I was on the top floor of the tower, but now I realized that there must be another room above the one in which I had been placed – if the sound I heard was that of human feet.

Listening to that monotonous padding had a soporific effect upon my jaded nerves. I caught myself dozing a couple of times. I did not wish to go to sleep; something seemed to warn me that I must remain awake, but at last I must have succumbed.

How long I slept I do not know. I awoke with a start, conscious that something touched me. A dim figure was leaning over me. I started to rise. Instantly strong fingers clutched my throat – cold, clammy fingers – the fingers of Death they seemed.

Struggling, I sought the throat of my antagonist. I closed upon it – it, too, was cold and clammy. I am a strong man, but the Thing upon my chest was stronger. I struck at it with closed fists. From the doorway came a low, hideous laugh. I felt my scalp stiffen to the horror of it all.

I sensed that death was close, and a multitude of thoughts raced through my mind. But uppermost among them were thoughts of Duare, and harrowing regret that I must leave her here in the clutches of the fiend I was now certain was the instigator of this attack upon me. I guessed that its purpose was to dispose of me and thus remove the only possible obstacle that might stand between himself and Duare.

I was still struggling when something struck me on the head; then came oblivion.

It was daylight when I regained consciousness. I still lay upon the couch, sprawled upon my back. Staring up at the ceiling, trying to collect my thoughts and memories, I perceived a crack just above me such as might have been made by a trap door partially raised; and through the crack two eyes were peering down at me.

Some new horror? I did not move. I lay there fascinated, watching the trap door slowly open. Presently a face was revealed. It was the face of a girl, a very beautiful girl; but it was strained and drawn and the eyes were terrified, frightened eyes.

In a whisper, the girl spoke. 'You are alive?' she asked.

I raised myself on an elbow. 'Who are you?' I demanded. 'Is this some new trick to torture me?'

'No. I am a prisoner, too. He has gone away. Perhaps we can escape.'

'How?' I asked. I was still skeptical, believing her a confederate of Skor.

'Can you get up here? There are no bars on my windows; that is because they are so high that no one could jump from them without being killed or badly injured. If we only had a rope!'

I considered the matter for a moment before I replied. What if it was a trick? Could I be any worse off in one room in this accursed castle than in another?

'There is rope down here,' I said. 'I will get it and come up. Perhaps there is not enough to be of any use to us, but I will bring what there is.'

'How will you get up?' she asked.

'That will not be difficult. Wait until I get the rope.'

I went to the chest of drawers and took out all the rope and string that I had discovered there the previous night; then I shoved the chest across the floor until it was directly beneath the trap door.

From the top of the chest I could easily reach the edge of the floor above. Handing the rope up to the girl, I quickly drew myself up into the room with her; then she closed the trap and we stood facing each other.

Despite her disheveled and frightened appearance, I found her even more beautiful than I had at first thought her; and as her fine eyes met mine in mutual appraisal my fears of treachery vanished. I was sure that no duplicity lurked behind that lovely countenance.

'You need not doubt me,' she said as though she had read my thoughts, 'though I cannot wonder that you doubt every one in this terrible place.'

'Then how can you trust me?' I asked. 'You know nothing of me.'

'I know enough,' she replied. 'From that window I saw you when you and your companion came yesterday with Skor, and I knew that he had two more victims. I heard them bring you to the room below last night. I did not know which one of you it was. I wanted to warn you then, but I was afraid of Skor. I walked the floor for a long time trying to decide what to do.'

'Then it was you I heard walking?'

'Yes. Then I heard them come again; I heard sounds of a scuffle and Skor's awful laugh. Oh, how I hate and fear that laugh! After that it was quiet. I thought they had killed you, if it was you, or taken the girl away, if it was she they had imprisoned in the room below. Oh, the poor thing! And she is so beautiful. I hope she got away safely, but I am afraid there can be little hope of that.'

'Got away? What do you mean?' I demanded.

'She escaped very early this morning. I do not know how she got out of her room, but from the window I saw her cross the outer courtyard. She climbed the wall on the river side, and she must have dropped into the river. I did not see her again.'

'Duare has escaped! You are sure it was she?'

'It was the beautiful girl who came here with you yesterday. About an hour after she got away Skor must have discovered that she was gone. He came out of the castle in a terrible rage. He took with him all of the miserable creatures that watch the gate, and all his fierce kazars, and set out in pursuit. Possibly never again may we have such an opportunity to escape.'

'Let's get busy, then!' I exclaimed. 'Have you a plan?'

'Yes,' she replied. 'With the rope we can lower ourselves to the castle roof and from there to the courtyard. There is no one watching the gate; the kazars are gone. If we are discovered we shall have to trust to our legs, but there are only three or four of Skor's retainers left in the castle and they are not very alert when he is not here.'

'I have my weapons,' I reminded her. 'Skor did not take them from me, and if any of his people try to stop us I will kill them.'

She shook her head. 'You cannot kill them,' she whispered, shuddering.

'What do you mean?' I demanded. 'Why can I not kill them?'

'Because they are already dead.'

*

I looked at her in astonishment as the meaning of her words slowly filtered to my shocked brain to explain the pitiful creatures that had filled me with such disgust on the previous day.

'But,' I exclaimed, 'how can they be dead? I saw them move about and obey the commands of Skor.'

'I do not know,' she replied; 'it is Skor's terrible secret. Presently you will be as they, if we do not escape; and the girl who came with you, and I – after a while. He will keep us a little longer in the flseh for the purpose of his experiments. Every day he takes a little blood from me. He is seeking the secret of life. He says that he can reproduce body cells, and with these he has instilled synthetic life into the poor creatures that he has resurrected from the grave. But it is only a parody on life; no blood flows in those dead veins, and the dead minds are animated only by the thoughts that Skor transmits to them by some occult, telepathic means.

'But what he most desires is the power to reproduce germ cells and thus propagate a new race of beings fashioned according to his own specifications. That is why he takes blood from me; that is why he wanted the girl you call Duare. When our blood has become so depleted that death is near, he will kill us and we will be like these others. But he would not keep us here; he would take us to the city where he rules as jong. Here he keeps only a few poor, degraded specimens; but he says that in Kormor he has many fine ones.'

'So he *is* a jong? I doubted it.'

'He made himself a jong and created his own subjects,' she said.

'And he kept you only to draw blood from you?'

'Yes. He is not like other men; he is not human.'

'How long have you been here?'

'A long time; but I am still alive because Skor has been away most of the time in Kormor.'

'Well, we must get away, too, before he returns. I want to search for Duare.'

I went to one of the windows, none of which was barred, and looked down on the castle roof below, a distance of about twenty feet. Then I got the rope and examined it carefully. There were several pieces, in all about forty feet – more than enough; also it was stout rope. I tied the pieces together and then returned to the window. The girl was at my elbow.

'Can anyone see us from here?' I asked.

'The creatures are not very alert,' she replied. 'Those that Skor left here are the servants. They remain in a room on the first floor on the other side of the castle. When he is away they just sit. After a while two of them will bring food for us; and we should get away before they come, for sometimes they forget to go back to their quarters; then they sit around outside my door for hours. You will notice that there is a grille in the door; they would see us if we attempted to escape while they were there.'

'We'll start now,' I said. Then I made a loop in one end of the rope and passed it around the girl's body so that she could sit in it while I lowered her to the roof.

Without an instant's hesitation she stepped to the sill of the window and lowered herself over the edge until she was seated securely in the loop. Bracing my feet against the wall, I let her down rapidly until I felt the rope go slack in my hands.

I then dragged her cot close beneath the window, passed the free end of the rope beneath it and out the window, letting it fall toward the roof below. This gave me two strands of rope reaching to the roof with the middle part of the rope passing around the cot which was too large to be dragged through the window by my weight as I descended.

Grasping both strands firmly in my two hands, I slipped through the window and slid quickly to the side of the waiting girl; then I pulled in rapidly on one end of the rope, dragging the free end around the cot until it fell to the roof. Thus I retrieved the rope for use in descending the remainder of the way to the ground.

We crossed the roof quickly to the edge overlooking the outer courtyard into which we expected to descend. There was no one in sight, and I was just about to lower the girl over the edge when a loud shout from behind us startled us both.

Turning, we saw three of Skor's creatures looking at us from an upper window of the castle on the opposite side of the inner court. Almost as we turned, the three left the window and we could hear them shouting through the castle.

'What shall we do?' cried the girl. 'We are lost! They will come to the roof by the tower door, and they will have us trapped. They were not the servants; they were three of his armed men. I thought they had all accompanied him, but I was wrong.'

I said nothing, but I seized her hand and started toward the far end of the castle roof. A sudden hope had flared within me, born of an idea suggested by what the girl had told me of Duare's escape.

We ran as fast as we could, and when we reached the edge we looked down upon the river lapping the castle wall two stories below. I passed the rope about the girl's waist. She asked no question; she made no comment. Quickly she climbed over the low parapet, and I commenced lowering her toward the river below.

Hideous mouthings arose behind me. I turned and saw three dead men running toward me across the roof. Then I lowered away so rapidly that the rope burned my fingers, but there was no time to lose. I feared that they would be upon me before I could lower the girl to the dubious safety of the swirling waters.

Nearer and nearer sounded the hurrying footsteps and the incoherent yammerings of the corpses. I heard a splash, and the rope went slack in my fingers. I glanced behind. The nearest of the creatures was already extending his hands to seize me. It was one of those that I had noticed at the gate the day before; I recognized it by the bloodless gash across its cheek. Its dead eyes were expressionless – glazed and staring – but its mouth was contorted in a ghastly snarl.

Immediate recapture faced me; there was but a single alternative. I sprang to the top of the parapet and leaped. I have always been a good diver, but I doubt that I ever made a prettier swan dive in my life than I did that day from the parapet of the gloomy castle of Skor, the jong of Morov.

As I rose to the surface of the river, shaking the water from my eyes, I looked about for the girl; she was nowhere to be seen. I knew that she could not have reached the river bank in the short time that had elapsed since I had lowered her into the water, for the masonry of the castle and the walls which extended it both above and below the building offered not even a hand-hold for hundreds of feet in both directions, and the opposite shore was too far away.

I cast about me in all directions as the current carried me down stream, and I saw her head rise above the surface of the water a short distance below me. Swiftly I struck out for her. She went down again just before I reached her, but I dived for her and brought her to the surface. She was still conscious but almost out.

Glancing back at the castle, I saw that my would-be captors had disappeared from the roof; and I guessed that they would shortly appear on the bank of the river ready to seize us when we emerged. But I had no intention of emerging on their side.

Dragging the girl with me, I struck out for the opposite shore. The river here was considerably deeper and broader than at the point we had first encountered it farther up stream. Now it was quite a river. What strange creatures inhabited its depths I had no means of knowing. I could only hope that none would discover us.

The girl lay very quiet; she did not struggle at all. I began to fear that she was dead and I exerted myself still more to reach the bank quickly. The current bore us down stream, and I was glad of that, for it was taking us farther away from the castle and retainers of Skor.

At last I reached the bank and dragged the girl out onto a little patch of pale violet grass and set to work to resuscitate her, but even as I commenced she opened her eyes and looked up at me. A shadow of a smile touched her lips.

'I shall be all right in a minute,' she said weakly. 'I was so frightened.'

'Don't you know how to swim?' I asked.

She shook her head. 'No.'

'And you let me lower you into the river without telling me!' I was amazed by the sheer bravery of her act.

'There was nothing else to do,' she said simply. 'Had I told you, you would not have lowered me, and we both should have been recaptured. I do not see even now how you got down before they seized you.'

'I dived,' I explained.

'You jumped from the top of that castle? It is incredible!'

'You do not come from a land where there is much water,' I commented with a laugh.

'What makes you think so?'

'If you did you would have seen enough diving to know that mine was nothing extraordinary.'

'My country is in a mountainous district,' she admitted, 'where the streams are torrents and there is little swimming.'

'And where is that?' I asked.

'Oh, it is very far,' she replied. 'I do not even know where.'

'How did you happen to get into Skor's country?'

'During a war in my country I was captured with others by the enemy. They carried us down out of the mountains into a great plain. One night two of us escaped. My companion was a soldier who had been long in the service of my father. He was very loyal. He tried to return me to my country, but we became lost. I do not know how long we wandered, but at last we came to a great river.

'Here were people who went in boats upon the river. They lived in the boats always, fighing. They sought to capture us, and my companion was killed defending me; then they took me. But I was not with them long. The first night several men were quarreling over me; each of them claimed me as his own. And while they quarreled, I slipped into a small boat tied to the larger one and floated away down the great river.

'I drifted for many days and nearly starved to death, although I saw fruits and nuts growing along the banks of the river. But the boat was without oars and was so heavy that I could not bring it in to shore.

'Finally it ran aground by itself on a sand bar where the river ran slowly about a great bend, and it chanced that Skor was hunting near and saw me. That is all. I have been here a long time.'

XI

The Pygmies

As the girl finished her story I saw the three dead men standing upon the opposite bank. For a moment they hesitated, then they plunged into the river.

I seized the girl by the hand and raised her to her feet. Our only defense lay in flight. Although I had had to abandon my spear, I had saved my bow and arrows, the latter being tied securely in my quiver while the former I had looped across one shoulder before leaving the tower; but of what use were arrows against dead men?

Casting another glance toward our pursuers I saw them floundering in the deep water of the channel, and it became immediately evident that none of them could swim. They were bobbing around helplessly as the current swept them down stream. Sometimes they floated on their backs, sometimes on their faces.

'We haven't much to fear from them,' I said; 'they will all drown.'

'They cannot drown,' replied the girl with a shudder.

'I hadn't thought of that,' I admitted. 'But at least there is little likelihood that they will reach this shore; certainly not before they have been carried a long distance down stream. We shall have plenty of time to escape them.'

'Then let's be going. I hate this place. I want to get away from it.'

'I cannot go away until I have found Duare,' I told her. 'I must search for her.'

'Yes, that is right; we must try to find her. But where shall we look?'

'She would try to reach the big river and follow it to the sea,' I explained, 'and I think that she would reason much as we would, that it would be safer to follow this stream down to the larger one inasmuch as then she would have the concealing protection of the forest.'

'We shall have to keep careful watch for the dead men,' cautioned the girl. 'If they wash ashore on this side we shall be sure to meet them.'

'Yes; and I want to make sure where they do come ashore, because I intend crossing over and hunting for Duare on the other side.'

For some time we moved cautiously down stream in silence, both constantly alert for any sound that might portend danger. My mind was filled with thoughts of Duare and apprehension for her safety, yet occasionally it reverted to the girl at my side; and I could not but recall her courage during our escape and her generous willingness to delay her own flight that we might search for Duare. It was apparent that her character formed a trinity of loveliness with her form and her face. And I did not even know her name!

That fact struck me as being as remarkable as that I had only known her for an hour. So intimate are the bonds of mutual adversity and danger that it seemed I had known her always, that that hour was indeed an eternity.

'Do you realize,' I asked, turning toward her, 'that neither of us knows the other's name?' And then I told her mine.

'Carson Napier!' she repeated. 'That is a strange name.'

'And what is yours?'

'Nalte voo jan kum Baltoo,' she replied, which means Nalte, the daughter of Baltoo. 'The people call me Voo Jan, but my friends call me Nalte.'

'And what am I to call you?' I asked.

She looked at me in surprise. 'Why, Nalte, of course.'

'I am honored by being included among your friends.'

'But are you not my best, my only friend now in all Amtor?'

I had to admit that her reasoning was sound, since as far as all the rest of Amtor was concerned we were the only two people on that cloud-girt planet, and we were certainly not enemies.

We were moving cautiously along within sight of the river when Nalte suddenly touched my arm and pointed toward the opposite bank, at the same time dragging me down behind a shrub.

Just opposite us a corpse had washed ashore; and a short distance below, two others. They were our pursuers. As we watched, they slowly crawled to their feet; then the one we had first seen called to the others, who presently joined him. The three corpses talked together, pointing and gesticulating. It was horrible. I felt my skin creep.

What would they do? Would they continue the search or would they return to the castle? If the former, they would have to cross the river; and they must already have learned that there was little likelihood of their being able to do that. But that was attributing to dead brains the power to reason! It seemed incredible. I asked Nalte what she thought about it.

'It is a mystery to me,' she replied. 'They converse, and they appear to reason. At first I thought they were motivated through the hypnotic influence of Skor's mind solely – that they thought his thoughts, as it were; but they take independent action when Skor is away, as you have seen them do today, which refutes that theory. Skor says that they do reason. He has stimulated their nervous systems into the semblance of life, though no blood flows in their veins; but the past experiences of their lives before they died are less potent in influencing their judgments than the new system of conduct and ethics that Skor has instilled into their dead brains. He admits that the specimens he has at the castle are very dull; but that, he insists, is because they were dull people in life.'

The dead men conversed for some time and then started slowly up river in the direction of the castle, and it was with a sigh of relief that we saw them disappear.

'Now we must try to find a good place to cross,' I said. 'I wish to search the other side for some sign of Duare. She must have left footprints in the soft earth.'

'There is a ford somewhere down river,' said Nalte. 'When Skor captured me we crossed it on our way to the castle. I do not know just where it is, but it cannot be far.'

We had descended the river some two miles from the point at which we had seen the dead man emerge upon the opposite bank, without seeing any sign of a crossing, when I heard faintly a familiar cackling that seemed to come from across the river and farther down.

'Do you hear that?' I asked Nalte.

She listened intently for a moment as the cackling grew louder. 'Yes,' she replied – 'the kazars. We had better hide.'

Acting upon Nalte's suggestion we concealed ourselves behind a clump of underbrush and waited. The cackling grew in volume, and we knew that the kazars were approaching.

'Do you suppose that it is Skor's pack?' I asked.

'It must be,' she replied. 'There is no other pack in this vicinity, according to Skor.'

'Nor any wild kazars?'

'No. He says that there are no wild ones on this side of the big river. They range on the opposite side. These must be Skor's!'

We waited in silence as the sounds approached, and presently we saw the new leader of the pack trot into view on the opposite bank. Behind him strung several more of the grotesque beasts, and then came Skor, mounted on his zorat, with the dead men that formed his retinue surrounding him.

'Duare is not there!' whispered Nalte. 'Skor did not recapture her.'

We watched Skor and his party until they had passed out of sight among the trees of the forest on the other side of the river, and it was with a sigh of relief that I saw what I hoped would be the last of the jong of Morov.

While I was relieved to know that Duare had not been recaptured, I was still but little less apprehensive concerning her fate. Many dangers might beset her, alone and unprotected in this savage land; and I had only the vaguest conception of where to search for her.

After the passing of Skor we had continued on down the river, and presently Nalte pointed ahead to a line of ripples that stretched from bank to bank where the river widened.

'There is the ford,' she said, 'but there is no use crossing it to look for Duare's trail. If she had escaped on that side of the river the kazars would have found her before now. The fact that they didn't find her is fairly good proof that she was never over there.'

I was not so sure of that. I did not know that Duare could swim nor that she could not, but the chances were highly in favor of the latter possibility, since Duare had been born and reared in the tree city of Kooaad.

'Perhaps they found her and killed her,' I suggested, horrified at the very thought of such a tragedy.

'No,' dissented Nalte. 'Skor would have prevented that; he wanted her.'

'But something else might have killed her; they might have found her dead body.'

'Skor would have brought it back with him and invested it with the synthetic life that animates his retinue of dead,' argued Nalte.

Still I was not convinced. 'How do the kazars trail?' I asked. 'Do they follow the spoor of their quarry by scent?'

Nalte shook her head. 'Their sense of smell is extremely poor, but their vision is acute. In trailing, they depend wholly upon their eyes.'

'Then it is possible that they might not have crossed Duare's trail at all and so missed her.'

'Possible, but not probable,' replied Nalte. 'What is more probable is that she was killed and devoured by some beast before Skor was able to recapture her.'

That explanation had already occurred to me, but I did not wish to even think about it. 'Nevertheless,' I said, 'we might as well cross over to the other bank. If we are going to follow the big river down stream we shall have to cross this affluent sooner or later, and we may not find another ford as it grows broader and deeper toward its mouth.'

The ford was broad and well marked by ripples, so we had no difficulty in following it toward the opposite bank. However, we were compelled to keep our eyes on the water most of the time as the ford took two curves that formed a flattened S, and it would have been quite easy to have stepped off into deep water and been swept down stream had we not been careful.

The result of our constant watchfulness approached disaster as we neared the left bank of the stream. The merest chance caused me to look up. I was slightly in advance of Nalte as we walked hand in hand for greater safety. I stopped so suddenly at what I saw that the girl bumped into me. Then she looked up, and a little, involuntary cry of alarm burst from her lips.

'What are they?' she asked.

'I don't know,' I replied. 'Don't you?'

'No; I never saw such creatures before.'

At the edge of the water, awaiting us, were half a dozen manlike creatures, while others like them were coming from the forest, dropping from the trees to shuffle awkwardly toward the ford. They were about three feet tall and entirely covered with long hair. At first I thought that they were monkeys, although they bore a startling resemblance to human beings, but when they saw that we had discovered them one of them spoke, and the simian theory was exploded.

'I am Ul,' said the speaker. 'Go away from the land of Ul. I am Ul; I kill!'

'We will not harm you,' I replied. 'We only want to pass through your country.'

'Go away!' growled Ul, baring sharp fighting fangs.

By now, fifty of the fierce little men were gathered at the water's edge, growling, menacing. They were without clothing or ornaments and carried no weapons, but their sharp fangs and the bulging muscles of their shoulders and arms bespoke their ability to carry out Ul's threats.

'What are we going to do?' demanded Nalte. 'They will tear us to pieces the moment we step out of the water.'

'Perhaps I can persuade them to let us pass,' I said, but after five minutes of fruitless effort I had to admit defeat. Ul's only reply to my arguments was, 'Go away! I kill! I kill!'

I hated to turn back, for I knew that we must cross the river eventually and we might not find such another crossing, but at last, reluctantly, I retraced my steps to the right bank hand in hand with Nalte.

All the remainder of the day I searched for traces of Duare as we followed the course of the river downward, but my efforts were without success. I was disheartened. I felt that I should never see her again. Nalte tried to cheer me up, but inasmuch as she believed that Duare was dead she was not very successful.

Late in the afternoon I succeeded in killing a small animal. As we had eaten nothing all that day we were both famished, so we soon had a fire going and were grilling cuts of the tender meat.

After we had eaten I built a rude platform among the branches of a large tree and gathered a number of huge leaves to serve as mattress and covering, and as darkness fell Nalte and I settled ourselves, not uncomfortably, in our lofty sanctuary.

For a while we were silent, wrapped in our own thoughts. I do not know about Nalte's, but mine were gloomy enough. I cursed the day that I had conceived the idea to build the huge torpedo that had carried me from Earth to Venus, and in the next thought I blessed it because it had made it possible for me to know and to love Duare.

It was Nalte who broke the silence. As though she had read my thoughts, she said, 'You loved Duare very much?'

'Yes,' I replied.

Nalte sighed. 'It must be sad to lose one's mate.'

'She was not my mate.'

'Not your mate!' Nalte's tone expressed her surprise. 'But you loved one another?'

'Duare did not love me,' I replied. 'At least she said she didn't. You see, she was the daughter of a jong and she couldn't love any one until after she was twenty.'

Nalte laughed. 'Love does not come or go in accordance with any laws or customs,' she said.

'But even if Duare had loved me, which she didn't, she couldn't have said so; she couldn't even talk of love because she was the daughter of a jong and too young. I don't understand it, of course, but that is because I am from another world and know nothing of your customs.'

'I am nineteen,' said Nalte, 'and the daughter of a jong, but if I loved a man I should say so.'

'Perhaps the customs of your country and those of Duare's are not the same,' I suggested.

'They must be very different,' agreed Nalte, 'for in my country a man does not speak to a girl of love until she has told him that she loves him; and the daughter of the jong chooses her own mate whenever she pleases.'

'That custom may have its advantages,' I admitted, 'but if I loved a girl I should want the right to tell her so.'

'Oh, the men find ways of letting a girl know without putting it into words. I could tell if a man loved me, but if I loved him very much I wouldn't wait for that.'

'And what if he didn't love you?' I asked.

Nalte tossed her head. 'I'd make him.'

I could readily understand that Nalte might be a very difficult young person not to love. She was slender and dark, with an olive skin and a mass of black hair in lovely disorder. Her eyes sparkled with health and intelligence. Her features were regular and almost boyish, and over all was the suggestion of a veil of dignity that bespoke her blood. I could not doubt but that she was the daughter of a jong.

It seemed to be my fate to encounter daughters of jongs. I said as much to Nalte.

'How many have you met?' she asked.

'Two,' I replied, 'you and Duare.'

'That is not very many when you consider how many jongs there must be in Amtor and how many daughters they must have. My father has seven.'

'Are they all as lovely as you?' I asked.

'Do you think me lovely?'

'You know you are.'

'But I like to hear people say so. I like to hear you say it,' she added softly.

The roars of hunting beasts came up to us from the dim forest aisles, the screams of stricken prey; then the silence of the night broken only by the murmuring of the river rolling down to some unknown sea.

I was considering a tactful reply to Nalte's ingenuous observation when I dozed and fell asleep.

I felt some one shaking me by the shoulder. I opened my eyes to look up into Nalte's. 'Are you going to sleep all day?' she demanded.

It was broad daylight. I sat up and looked around. 'We have survived another night,' I said.

I gathered some fruit, and we cooked some more of the meat left from my kill of the previous day. We had a splendid breakfast, and then we set off again down stream in our quest for – what?

'If we do not find Duare today,' I said, 'I shall have to admit that she is irrevocably lost to me.'

'And then what?' asked Nalte.

'You would like to return to your own country?'

'Of course.'

'Then we shall start up the big river toward your home.'

'We shall never reach it,' said Nalte, 'but—'

'But what?' I demanded.

'I was thinking that we might be very happy while we were trying to reach Andoo,' she said.

'Andoo?' I queried.

'That is my country,' she explained. 'The mountains of Andoo are very beautiful.'

There was a note of wistfulness in her voice; her eyes were contemplating a scene that mine could not see. Suddenly I realized how brave the girl had been, how cheerful she had remained through the hardships and menacing dangers of our flight, all despite the probably hopelessness of her situation. I touched her hand gently.

'We shall do our best to return you to the beautiful mountains of Andoo,' I assured her.

Nalte shook her head. 'I shall never see them again, Carson. A great company of warriors might not survive the dangers that lie between here and Andoo – a thousand kobs of fierce and hostile country.'

'A thousand kobs is a long way,' I agreed. 'It does seem hopeless, but we'll not give up.'

The Amtorians divide the circumference of a circle into a thousand parts to arrive at their hita, or degree; and the kob is one tenth of a degree of longitude at the equator (or what the Amtorians call The Small Circle), roughly about two and a half Earth miles; therefore a thousand kobs would be about two thousand five hundred miles.

A little mental arithmetic convinced me that Nalte could not have drifted down the big river two thousand five hundred miles without food, and I asked her if she was sure that Andoo was that far away.

'No,' she admitted, 'but it seems that far. We wandered a long time before we reached the river, and then I drifted for so long that I lost track of time.'

Nevertheless, if we found Duare, I was going to be faced by a problem. One girl must go down the valley in search of her own country, the other up the valley! And only one of them had even a hazy idea of where her country lay!

XII

The Last Second

During the afternoon of the second day of our search for Duare, Nalte and I came to the big river that Duare and I had seen from the summit of the escarpment, the same river down which Nalte had drifted into the clutches of Skor.

And it was a big river, comparable to the Mississippi. It ran between low cliffs of gleaming white limestone, flowing silently out of the mystery above, flowing silently toward the mystery below. Upon its broad expanse, from where it swept majestically into sight around a low promontory to where it disappeared again beyond a curve down stream, there was no sign of life, nor on either bank – only the girl, Nalte, and I. I felt the awe of its grandeur and my own insignificance.

I had no words to express my thoughts; and I was glad that Nalte stood in silence that was almost reverential as we viewed the majesty and the desolation of the scene.

Presently the girl sighed. It awoke me to the need of the moment. I could not stand mooning there in the face of the immediate necessity that confronted us.

'Well,' I said, 'this is not crossing the river.' I referred to the affluent that we had followed down from the castle of Skor.

'I am glad that we do not have to cross the big river,' remarked Nalte.

'We may have enough trouble crossing this other,' I suggested.

It flowed at our left, making a sudden turn before it emptied into the larger stream. Below us was a great eddy that had strewn the nearer bank with flotsam – leaves, twigs, branches of all sizes, and even the boles of great trees. These things appeared to have been deposited during a period of high water.

'How are we going to cross?' asked Nalte. 'There is no ford, and it seems too wide and swift to swim even if I were a good swimmer.' She looked up at me quickly then as a new thought seemed to strike her. 'I am a burden to you,' she said. 'If you were alone you would doubtless be able to cross easily. Pay no attention to me; I shall remain on this side and start up the river on my journey toward Andoo.'

I looked down at her and smiled. 'You really do not believe or hope that I will do anything of the sort.'

'It would be the sensible thing to do,' she said.

'The sensible thing to do is to build a raft with some of that stuff down there and float across the river.' I pointed to the débris pilled up on the bank.

'Why, we could do that, couldn't we?' she cried.

She was all eagerness and excitement now, and a moment later she pitched in and helped me drag out such pieces as I thought we could use in the construction of a raft.

It was hard work, but at last we had enough material to float us in safety. The next job was to fasten the elements of our prospective raft together so securely that the river could not tear it to pieces before we had gained the opposite bank.

We gathered lianas for that purpose, and though we worked as rapidly as we could it was almost dark before we had completed our rude ferry.

As I contemplated the fruit of our labor, I saw Nalte surveying the swirling waters of the eddy with a dubious eye.

'Are we going to cross now,' she asked, 'or wait until morning?'

'It is almost dark now,' I replied. 'I think we had better wait until tomorrow.'

She brightened visibly and drew a deep sigh of relief. 'Then we had better think about eating now,' she said. I had found the girls of Venus not unlike their Earthly sisters in this respect.

The meal that night was a matter of fruit and tubers, but it was sufficient. Once more I constructed a platform among the branches of a tree and prayed that no prowling arboreal carnivore would discover us.

Each morning that I awoke on Venus it was with a sense of surprise that I still lived, and this first morning on the big river was no exception.

As soon as we had eaten we went to our raft, and after some difficulty succeeded in launching it. I had equipped it with several long branches for poling and some shorter ones that we might use as oars after we got into the deep channel, but they were most inadequate makeshifts. I was depending almost exclusively on the eddy to carry us within striking distance of the opposite shore, where I hoped that we would then be able to pole the raft to the bank.

Our craft floated much better than I had anticipated. I had feared that it would be almost awash and most uncomfortable; but the wood was evidently light, with the result that the top of the raft was several inches above the water.

No sooner had we shoved off than the eddy seized us and commenced to bear us up stream and out toward the center. Our only concern now was to keep from being drawn into the vortex, and by poling frantically we managed to keep near the periphery of the whirlpool until the water deepened to such a degree that our poles would no longer touch bottom; then we seized the shorter branches and paddled desperately. It was gruelling work, yet Nalte never faltered.

At last we swung in toward the left bank, and once more we seized our poles, but, to my astonishment and chagrin, I discovered that the water here was still too deep. The current, too, was much stronger on this side than on the other; and our futile oars were almost useless.

Remorselessly the river held us in its grip and dragged us back toward the vortex. We paddled furiously, and held our own; we were keeping away from the center of the eddy, but we were being carried farther from the left bank.

Presently we were in mid-channel. We seemed to be hanging on the very edge of the eddy. Both of us were almost exhausted by this time, yet we might not pause for an instant. With a last, supreme effort we tore the raft from the clutches of the current that would have drawn us back into the embrace of the swirling Titan; then the main current of the mid-channel seized us – a fierce, relentless force. Our craft swirled and bobbed about absolutely beyond control, and we were swept down toward the great river.

I laid aside my inadequate paddle. 'We have done our best, Nalte,' I said, 'but it wasn't good enough. Now all that we can do is to hope that this thing will hang together until we drift to one shore or the other somewhere along the big river.'

'It will have to be soon,' said Nalte.

'Why?' I asked.

'When Skor found me he said that I was fortunate to have come to shore where I did, as farther down the river tumbles over falls.'

I looked at the low cliffs that lined the river on both sides. 'There isn't any chance of making a landing here,' I said.

'Perhaps we shall have better luck lower down,' suggested Nalte.

Down we drifted with the current, sometimes borne close to one shore, sometimes close to the other as the channel meandered from bank to bank; or again we rode far out on the center of the flood. Sometimes we saw little breaks in the cliffs where we might have made a landing; but we always saw them too late, and were carried past before we could maneuver our clumsy craft within reach.

As we approached each bend we looked expectantly for some change in the shore line that would offer us some hope of landing, but always we were disappointed. And then, at last, as we swung around a headland, we saw two cities. One lay upon the left bank of the river, the other on the right directly opposite. The former appeared gray and drab even at a distance, while that upon the right bank shone white and beautiful and gay with its limestone walls and towers and its roofs of many colors.

Nalte nodded toward the city on the left bank. 'That must be Kormor; this is about the location that Skor told me his city occupied.'

'And the other?' I asked.

She shook her head. 'Skor never mentioned another city.'

'Perhaps it is all one city built upon both banks of the river,' I suggested.

'No; I do not think so. Skor told me that the people who dwelt across the river from Kormor were his enemies, but he never said anything about a city. I thought it was just some savage tribe. Why, that is a splendid city – far larger and handsomer than Kormor.'

We could not, of course, see the entire expanse of either city, but as we drifted closer it was apparent that the city on our right extended along the river front for several miles. This we could see because at this point the river ran almost as straight as a canal for a greater distance than I could see. But the city on our left, which was Kormor, was much smaller, extending but about a mile along the water front. As far as we could see both cities were walled, a high wall extending along the river side of each. Kormor had a short quay in front of a gate about the center of this wall, while the quay of the other city appeared to be a long avenue extending as far as I could see.

We had been drifting for some time opposite the right hand city before we came close to Kormor. There were a few fishermen on the long quay of the former city, and others, possibly sentries, on top of the wall behind them. Many of these saw us and pointed at us and seemed to be discussing us, but at no time did we drift close enough to that side of the river so that we could obtain a close view of them.

As we came down toward the quay of Kormor, a small boat pushed out into the river. It contained three men, two of whom were rowing while the third stood in the bow. That they were pulling out to intercept us appeared quite evident.

'They are Skor's men,' said Nalte.

'What do you suppose they want of us?' I asked.

'To capture us, of course, for Skor; but they will never capture me!' She stepped toward the edge of the raft.

'What do you mean?' I demanded. 'What are you going to do?'

'I am going to jump into the river.'

'But you can't swim,' I objected. 'You will be sure to drown.'

'That is what I wish to do. I shall never let Skor take me again.'

'Wait, Nalte,' I begged. 'They haven't taken us yet. Perhaps they won't.'

'Yes, they will,' she said hopelessly.

'We must never give up hope, Nalte. Promise me that you will wait. Even in the last second you can still carry out your plan.'

'I will wait,' she promised, 'but in the last second you had better follow my example and join me in death rather than fall into the hands of Skor and become one of those hopeless creatures that you saw at his castle, for then you will be denied even the final escape of death.'

The boat was now approaching closer, and I hailed its occupants. 'What do you want of us?' I demanded.

'You must come ashore with us,' said the man in the bow.

I was close enough now so that I could get a good look at the fellow. I had thought at first that they were some more of Skor's living dead, but now I saw that this fellow's cheeks had the hue of health and blood.

'We will not come with you,' I called back to him. 'Leave us alone; we are not harming you. Let us go our way in peace.'

'You will come ashore with us,' said the man, as his boat drew closer.

'Keep away, or I'll kill you!' I cried, fitting an arrow to my bow.

The fellow laughed – a dry, mirthless laugh. Then it was that I saw his eyes, and a cold chill swept over me. They were the dead eyes of a corpse!

I loosed an arrow. It drove straight through the creature's chest, but he only laughed again and left the arrow sticking there.

'Do you not know,' cried Nalte, 'that you cannot kill the dead?' She stepped to the far side of the raft. 'Goodbye, Carson,' she said quietly; 'the last second is here!'

'No! No, Nalte!' I cried. 'Wait! It is not the last second.'

I turned again toward the approaching boat. Its bow was already within a foot of the raft. Before the fellow standing in it could grasp my intention I leaped upon him. He struck at me with his dead hands; his dead fingers clutched for my throat. But my attack had been too quick and unexpected. I had carried him off his balance, and in the same instant I seized him and threw him overboard.

The two other creatures had been rowing with their backs toward the bow and were unaware that any danger threatened them until I crashed upon their leader. As he went overboard the nearer of the others rose and turned upon me. His skin, too, was painted in the semblance of life, but those dead eyes could not be changed.

With a horrid, inarticulate scream he leaped for me. I met his rush with a right to the jaw that would have knocked a living man down for a long count; and while, of course, I couldn't knock the thing out, I did knock it overboard.

A quick glance at the two in the water convinced me that my guess had not been amiss – like their fellows at the castle, the two could not swim and were floating helplessly down stream with the current. But there was still another, and it was stepping across the thwarts toward me.

I sprang forward to meet it, ripping in a blow toward the side of the jaw that would have sent it after the other two had it connected; but it did not.

Our movements caused the boat to rock and threw me off my balance, and before I could regain my equilibrium the creature seized me.

It was very powerful, but it fought without fire or enthusiasm – just the cold, deadly application of force. It reached for my throat; to reach for its throat was useless. I could not choke the life from something that had no life. The best that I could do was to try to evade its clutches and wait for an opening that might never come.

I am rather muscular myself; and I did manage to push the thing from me for a moment, but it came right back. It didn't say anything; it didn't make any sound at all. There was no expression in its glazed eyes, but its dry lips were drawn back over yellow teeth in a snarling grimace. The sight of it and the touch of those cold, clammy fingers almost unnerved me – these and the strange odor that emanated from it, the strange odor that is the odor of death.

As it came toward me the second time it came with lowered head and outstretched arms. I leaped for it, and locked my right arm about its head from above. The back of its neck was snug against my armpit as I seized my own right wrist with my left hand and locked my hold tighter. Then I swung quickly around, straightening up as I did so and, incidentally, nearly capsizing the boat. The creature lost its footing as I swung it about; its arms flailed wildly, as with a last mighty surge I released my hold and sent it stumbling over the gunwale into the river. Like the others, it floated away.

A few yards away, the raft was drifting with Nalte wide-eyed and tense with excitement. Seizing an oar I brought the boat alongside and extending a hand assisted Nalte over the side. I noticed that she was trembling.

'Were you frightened, Nalte?' I asked.

'For you, yes. I didn't think that you had a chance against three of them. Even now I can't believe what I saw. It is incredible that one man could have done what you did.'

'Luck had a lot to do with it,' I replied, 'and the fact that I took them by surprise. They weren't expecting anything of the sort.'

'How strangely things happen,' mused Nalte. 'A moment ago I was about to drown myself in sheer desperation, and now everything is changed. The danger is over, and instead of an inadequate raft we have a comfortable boat.'

'Which proves that one should never give up hope.'

'I shan't again – while you are with me.'

I had been keeping an eye on the Kormor quay rather expecting to see another boat put out in pursuit of us, but none did.

The fishermen and the sentries on the waterfront of the other city had all stopped what they were doing and were watching us.

'Shall we row over there and see if they will take us in?' I asked.

'I am afraid,' replied Nalte. 'We have a saying in Andoo that the farther strangers are away the better friends they are.'

'You think that they would harm us?' I asked.

Nalte shrugged. 'I do not know, but the chances are that they would kill you and keep me.'

'Then we won't take the chance, but I would like to remain near here for a while and search for Duare.'

'You can't land on the left bank until we are out of sight of Kormor,' said Nalte, 'or they would be after us in no time.'

'And if we land in sight of this other city these people would take after us, if what you fear be true.'

'Let's go down stream until we are out of sight of both cities,' suggested the girl, 'and then wait until night before coming back near Kormor to search, for that is where you will have to search for Duare.'

Following Nalte's suggestion we drifted slowly down stream. We soon passed Kormor, but the white city on the right bank extended on for a couple of miles farther. I should say that its full length along the river front was fully five miles, and along all that length was the broad quay backed by a gleaming white wall pierced by an occasional gate – I counted six or seven along the full length of the water front.

Just below the city the river turned to the right, and almost immediately the cliffs shut off our view of both cities. Simultaneously the aspect of the country changed. The limestone cliffs ended abruptly, the river running between low banks. Here it spread out to considerable width, but farther ahead I could see where it narrowed again and entered a gorge between cliffs much higher than any that we had passed. They were wooded cliffs, and even from a distance I could see that they were not of the white limestone that formed those with which we had now become familiar.

There came to my ears faintly an insistent sound that was at first little more than a murmur, but as we drifted down the river it seemed to grow constantly in volume.

'Do you hear what I hear?' I demanded, 'or am I the victim of head noises?'

'That distant roaring?'

'Yes; it has become a roar now. What do you suppose it can be?'

'It must be the falls that Skor told me of,' said Nalte.

'By Jove! That's just what it is,' I exclaimed. 'And the best thing that we can do is to get to shore while we can.'

The current had carried us closer to the right bank at this point, and just ahead of us I saw a small stream emptying into the river. There was an open forest on the farther side of the stream and scattered trees on the nearer.

It appeared an ideal location for a camp.

We made the shore easily, for the current here was not swift. I ran the boat into the mouth of the small stream, but there was not water enough to float it. However, I managed to drag it up far enough to tie it to an overhanging limb of a tree where it was out of sight of any possible pursuers from Kormor who might come down the river in search of Nalte and myself.

'Now,' I said, 'the thing that interests me most at present is securing food.'

'That is something that always interests me,' admitted Nalte, with a laugh. 'Where are you going to hunt? That forest on the other side of this little stream looks as though it should be filled with game.'

She was facing the forest as she spoke, while my back was toward it. Suddenly the expression on her face changed, and she seized my arm with a little cry of alarm. 'Look, Carson! What is that?'

XIII

To Live or Die

As I turned at Nalte's warning cry, I thought that I saw something dodge behind low bushes on the opposite bank.

'What was it, Nalte?' I demanded.

'Oh, it couldn't be what I thought I saw,' she whispered excitedly. 'I must be mistaken.'

'What did you think you saw?'

'There's another – there – look!' she cried.

And then I saw it. It stepped from behind the bole of a large tree and stood eying us, its fangs bared in a snarl. It was a man that went on four feet like a beast. Its hind legs were short, and it walked on its hind toes, the heels corresponding to the hocks of animals. Its hands were more human, and it walked flat on the palms of them in front. Its nose was flat, its mouth broad, and its heavy, undershot jaws were armed with powerful teeth. Its eyes were small and close set and extremely savage. Its skin was white and almost hairless except upon its head and jowls. Another one appeared suddenly beside it.

'You don't know what they are?' I asked Nalte.

'We have heard of them in Andoo, but no one ever believed that they existed. They are called zangans. If the stories I have heard are true they are terribly ferocious. They hunt in packs and devour men as well as beasts.'

Zangan means beast-man, and no better word could have been coined to describe the creature that faced us across that little stream in far Noobol. And now others came slinking into view from the shelter of bushes and from behind the boles of trees.

'I think we had better hunt elsewhere,' I said in a weak effort to be jocose.

'Let's take to the boat again,' suggested Nalte.

We had already walked a little distance from the spot where I had moored our craft, and as we turned to retrace our steps I saw several of the zangans enter the water on the opposite side and approach the boat. They were much closer to it than we, and long before I could untie it and drag it into deeper water they could be upon us.

'It is too late!' cried Nalte.

'Let's fall back slowly to that little rise of ground behind us,' I said. 'Perhaps I can hold them off there.'

We retreated slowly, watching the zangans as they crossed the stream toward us. When they came out on shore they shook themselves as dogs do, and then they came slinking after us again. They reminded me of tigers – human tigers – and their gait was much that of a stalking tiger as they approached with flattened heads and snarling lips.

They growled and snapped at one another, revealing a viciousness greater than that of beasts. Momentarily I expected a charge, and I knew that when it came Nalte's troubles and mine would be over forever. We wouldn't have even a fighting chance against that savage pack.

There were about twenty of them, mostly males; but there were a couple of females and two or three half grown cubs. On the back of one of the females rode a baby, its arms tightly hugging the neck of its mother.

Savage as they appeared, they followed us warily as though they were half afraid of us; but their long, easy strides were constantly cutting down the distance between us.

When we reached the little mound toward which we had been retreating they were still fifty yards behind us. As we started to ascend the rise a large male trotted forward, voicing a low roar. It was as though it had just occurred to him that we might be trying to escape and that he ought to try to prevent it.

I stopped and faced him, fitting an arrow to my bow. Drawing the shaft back to the very tip I let him have it squarely in the chest. He stopped in his tracks, roared horribly, and clawed at the feathered end protruding from his body; then he came on again; but he was staggering, and presently he sank to the ground, struggled for a moment, and lay still.

The others had stopped and were watching him. Suddenly a young male ran up to him and bit him savagely about the head and neck; then raised his head and voiced a hideous roar. I guessed that it was a challenge as I saw him look about him at the other members of the pack. Here, perhaps, was a new leader usurping the powers of the one who had fallen.

Apparently no one was prepared to question his authority, and now he turned his attention again to us. He did not advance directly toward us, but slunk off to one side. As he did so he turned and growled at his fellows. That he was communicating orders to them at once became evident, for immediately they spread out as though to surround us.

I loosed another arrow then, this time at the new leader. I struck him in the side and elicited such a roar of pain and rage as I hope I may never hear again – at least not under such circumstances.

Reaching back with one hand the beast man seized the shaft and tore it from his body, inflicting a far more serious hurt than the arrow had made in entering; and now his roars and screams fairly shook the ground.

The others paused to watch him, and I saw one large male slink slowly toward the wounded leader. The latter saw him, too; and with bared fangs and ferocious growls charged him. The ambitious one, evidently realizing that his hopes had been premature, wheeled and fled; and the new chief let him go and turned again toward us.

By this time we were three-quarters surrounded. There were nearly twenty ferocious beasts confronting us, and I had less than a dozen arrows.

Nalte touched me on the arm. 'Goodbye, Carson,' she said. 'Now, surely, the last second is upon us.'

I shook my head. 'I am saving the last second in which to die,' I replied. 'Until then I shall not admit that there is ever to be a last second for me, and then it will be too late to matter.'

'I admire your courage if not your reasoning,' said Nalte, the ghost of a smile on her lips. 'But at least it will be a quick death – did you see how that fellow tore at the throat of the first one you shot? It is better than what Skor would have done to us.'

'At least we shall be dead,' I observed.

'Here they come!' cried Nalte.

They were closing in on us now from three sides. Arrow after arrow I drove into them, nor once did I miss my mark; but they only stopped those that I hit – the others slunk steadily forward.

They were almost upon us as I loosed my last arrow. Nalte was standing close beside me. I put an arm about her.

'Hold me close,' she said. 'I am not afraid to die, but I do not want to be alone – even for an instant.'

'You are not dead yet, Nalte.' I couldn't think of anything else to say. It must have sounded foolish at such a time, but Nalte ignored it.

'You have been very good to me, Carson,' she said.

'And you have been a regular brick, Nalte, if you know what that means – which you don't.'

'Goodbye, Carson! It *is* the last second.'

'I guess it is, Nalte.' I stooped and kissed her. 'Goodbye!'

From above us and behind us on the mound came a sudden crackling hum that was like the noise that an X-ray machine makes, but I knew that it was not an X-ray machine. I knew what it was even without the evidence of the crumpling bodies of the zangans dropping to the ground before us – it was the hum of the R-ray rifle of Amtor!

I wheeled and looked up toward the summit of the mound. There stood a dozen men pouring streams of the destructive rays upon the pack. It lasted for but a few seconds, but not one of the ferocious beasts escaped death. Then one of our rescuers (or were they our captors) came toward us.

He, like his companions, was a man of almost perfect physique, with a handsome, intelligent face. My first impression was that if these were fair examples of the citizens of that white city from which I assumed they had come, we must have stumbled upon an Olympus inhabited solely by gods.

In every company of men we are accustomed to seeing some whose proportions or features are ungainly or uncouth; but here, though no two men exactly resembled one another, all were singularly handsome and symmetrically proportioned.

He who approached us wore the customary gee-string and military harness of the men of Amtor. His trappings were handsome without being ornate, and I guessed from the insigne on the fillet that encircled his brow that he was an officer.

'You had a close call,' he said pleasantly.

'Rather too close for comfort,' I replied. 'We have you to thank for our lives.'

'I am glad that I arrived in time. I happened to be on the river wall as you drifted past, and saw your encounter with the men from Kormor. My interest was aroused; and, knowing that you were headed for trouble down river on account of the falls, I hurried down to try to warn you.'

'A rather unusual interest in strangers for a man of Amtor,' I commented, 'but I can assure you that I appreciate it even if I do not understand it.'

He laughed shortly. 'It was the way you handled those three creatures of Skor,' he explained. 'I saw possibilities in such a man, and we are always looking for better qualities to infuse into the blood of Havatoo. But come, let me introduce myself. I am Ero Shan.'

'And this is Nalte of Andoo,' I replied, 'and I am Carson Napier of California.'

'I have heard of Andoo,' he acknowledged. 'They raise an exceptionally fine breed of people there, but I never heard of your country. In fact I have never seen a man before with blue eyes and yellow hair. Are all the people of Cal—'

'California,' I prompted.

'– of California like you?'

'Oh, no! There are all colors among us, of hair and eyes and skin.'

'But how can you breed true to type, then?' he demanded.

'We don't,' I had to admit.

'Rather shocking,' he said, half to himself. 'Immoral – racially immoral. Well, be that as it may, your system seems to have produced a rather fine type at that; and now, if you will come with me, we shall return to Havatoo.'

'May I ask,' I inquired, 'if we return as guests or as prisoners?'

He smiled, just the shadow of a smile. 'Will that make any difference – as to whether you return with me or not?'

221

I glanced up at the armed men behind him and grinned. 'None,' I replied.

'Let us be friends,' he said. 'You will find justice in Havatoo. If you deserve to remain as a guest, you will be treated as a guest – if not –' he shrugged.

As we reached the top of the little hillock we saw, just behind it, a long, low car with transverse seats and no top. It was the first motor car that I had seen on Venus. The severity of its streamlines and its lack of ornamentation suggested that it was a military car.

As we entered the rear seat with Ero Shan his men took their places in the forward seats. Ero Shan spoke a word of command and the car moved forward. The driver was too far from me, and hidden by the men between us, to permit me to see how he controlled the car, which moved forward over the uneven ground smoothly and swiftly.

Presently as we topped a rise of ground we saw the city of Havatoo lying white and beautiful before us. From our elevation I could see that it was built in the shape of a half circle with the flat side lying along the water front, and it was entirely walled.

The river curves to the right below the city, and the direct route that we followed returning to it brought us to a gate several miles from the river. The gate itself was of magnificent proportions and an architectural gem, bespeaking a high order of civilization and culture. The city wall, of white limestone, was beautifully carved with scenes that I took to portray the history of the city or of the race that inhabited it, the work having apparently been conceived and executed with the rarest taste; and these carvings extended as far as I could see.

When one considers the fact that the wall on the land side is about eight miles long and on the river side about five miles, and that all of it is elaborately carved, one may understand the vast labor and the time required to complete such an undertaking along both faces of a twenty foot wall.

As we were halted at the gate by the soldiers on guard I saw emblazoned above the portal, in the characters of the universal Amtorian language, 'TAG KUM VOO KLAMBAD,' Gate of the Psychologists.

Beyond the gate we entered a broad, straight avenue that ran directly toward the center of the water front. It was filled with traffic – cars of various sizes and shapes, running swiftly and quietly in both directions. There was nothing but vehicular traffic on this level, pedestrians being accommodated on walkways at the level of the second stories of the buildings, which were connected by viaducts at all intersections.

There was practically no noise – no tooting of horns, no screeching of brakes – traffic seemed to regulate itself. I asked Ero Shan about it.

'It is very simple,' he said. 'All vehicles are energized from a central power station from which power emanates in three frequencies; on the control

222

board of each vehicle is a dial that permits the operator to pick up any frequency he desires. One is for avenues running from the outer wall to the center of the city, another is for transverse avenues, and the third for all traffic outside the city. The first two are cut off and on alternately; when one is on all traffic moving in the opposite direction is stopped at intersections automatically.'

'But why doesn't the traffic between intersections stop at the same time?' I asked.

'That is regulated by the third frequency, which is always operative,' he explained. 'A hundred feet before a vehicle reaches an intersection a photoelectric current moves the dial on the control board to the proper frequency for that lane.'

Nalte was thrilled by all that she saw. She was a mountain girl from a small kingdom, and this was the first large city that she had ever seen.

'It is marvelous,' she said. 'And how beautiful the people are!'

I had noticed that fact myself. Both the men and the women in the cars that passed us were of extraordinary perfection of form and feature.

Ambad Lat, Psychologist Avenue, led us directly to a semicircular civic center at the water front, from which the principal avenues radiated toward the outer wall like the spokes of a wheel from the hub toward the felloe.

Here were magnificent buildings set in a gorgeous park, and here Ero Shan escorted us from the car toward a splendid palace. There were many people in the park, going to or coming from the various buildings. There was no hurry, no bustle, no confusion; nor was there idling or loitering. All suggested well considered, unhurried efficiency. The voices of those who conversed were pleasant, well modulated. Like the people I had seen elsewhere in the city, these were all handsome and well formed.

We followed Ero Shan through an entrance into a wide corridor. Many of those we passed spoke pleasant greetings to our companion, and all of them looked at us with seemingly friendly interest, but without rudeness.

'Beautiful people in a beautiful city,' murmured Nalte.

Ero Shan turned toward her with a quick smile. 'I am glad that you like us and Havatoo,' he said. 'I hope that nothing will ever alter this first impression.'

'You think that something may?' asked Nalte.

Ero Shan shrugged. 'That all depends upon you,' he replied, 'or rather upon your ancestors.'

'I do not understand,' said Nalte.

'You will presently.'

He stopped before a door and, swinging it open, bade us enter. We were in a small anteroom in which several clerks were employed.

'Please inform Korgan Kantum Mohar that I wish to see him,' said Ero Shan to one of the clerks.

The man pressed one of several buttons on his desk and said, 'Korgan Sentar Ero Shan wishes to see you.'

Apparently from the desk top a deep voice replied, 'Send him in.'

'Come with me,' directed Ero Shan, and we crossed the anteroom to another door which a clerk opened. In the room beyond a man faced us from a desk behind which he was seated. He looked up at us with the same friendly interest that had been manifested by the people we had passed in the park and the corridor.

As we were introduced to Korgan Kantum Mohar he arose and acknowledged the introduction with a bow; then he invited us to be seated.

'You are strangers in Havatoo,' he remarked. 'It is not often that strangers enter our gates.' He turned to Ero Shan. 'Tell me, how did it happen?'

Ero Shan told of witnessing my encounter with the three men from Kormor. 'I hated to see a man like this go over the falls,' he continued, 'and I felt that it was worthwhile bringing them into Havatoo for an examination. Therefore I have brought them directly to you, hoping that you will agree with me.'

'It can do no harm,' admitted Mohar. 'The examining board is in session now. Take them over. I will advise the board that I have authorized the examination.'

'What is the examination, and what is its purpose?' I asked. 'Perhaps we do not care to take it.'

Korgan Kantum Mohar smiled. 'It is not for you to say,' he said.

'You mean that we are prisoners?'

'Let us say rather guests by command.'

'Do you mind telling me the purpose of this examination?' I asked.

'Not at all. It is to determine whether or not you shall be permitted to live.'

XIV

Havatoo

They were all very polite and pleasant, very professional and efficient. First we were bathed; then blood tests were made, our hearts examined, our blood pressure taken, our reflexes checked. After that we were ushered into a large room where five men sat behind a long table.

Ero Shan accompanied us throughout the examination. Like the others, he was always pleasant and friendly. He encouraged us to hope that we would pass the examination successfully. Even yet I did not understand what it was all about. I asked Ero Shan.

'Your companion remarked upon the beauty of Havatoo and its people,' he replied. 'This examination is the explanation of that beauty – and of many other things here which you do not yet know of.'

The five men seated behind the long table were quite as pleasant as any of the others we had met. They questioned us rapidly for fully an hour and then dismissed us. From the questions propounded I judged that one of them was a biologist, another a psychologist, one a chemist, the fourth a physicist, and the fifth a soldier.

'Korgan Sentar Ero Shan,' said he who appeared to be the head of the examining board, 'you will take custody of the man until the result of the examination is announced. Hara Es will take charge of the girl.' He indicated a woman who had entered the room with us and had been standing beside Nalte.

The latter pressed closer to me. 'Oh, Carson! They are going to separate us,' she whispered.

I turned toward Ero Shan to expostulate, but he motioned me to be silent. 'You will have to obey,' he said, 'but I think you have no reason to worry.'

Then Nalte was led away by Hara Es, and Ero Shan took me with him. A car was waiting for Ero Shan, and in it we were driven into a district of beautiful homes. Presently the car drew up in front of one of these and stopped.

'This is my home,' said my companion. 'You will be my guest here until the result of the examination is announced. I wish you to enjoy yourself while you are with me. Do not worry; it will do no good. Nalte is safe. She will be well cared for.'

'At least, they have provided me with a beautiful prison and a pleasant jailer,' I remarked.

'Please do not think of yourself as a prisoner,' begged Ero Shan. 'It will make us both unhappy, and unhappiness is not to be tolerated in Havatoo.'

'I am far from unhappy,' I assured him. 'On the contrary, I am greatly enjoying the experience, but I still cannot understand what crime is charged against Nalte and me that we should have been put on trial for our lives.'

'It was not you who were on trial; it was your heredity,' he explained.

'An answer,' I assured him, 'that leaves me as much at sea as I was before.'

We had entered the house as we were conversing, and I found myself amid as lovely surroundings as I have ever seen. Good taste and good judgment had evidently dictated not only the design of the house, but its appointments as well. From the entrance there was a vista of shrubbery and flowers and trees in a beautiful garden at the end of a wide hall.

It was to this garden that Ero Shan led me and then to an apartment that opened upon it.

'You will find everything here for your convenience and comfort,' he said. 'I shall detail a man to wait upon you; he will be courteous and efficient. But he will also be responsible for your presence when it is again required at the Central Laboratories.

'And now,' he said, seating himself in a chair near a window, 'let me try to answer your last question more explicitly.'

'Havatoo and the race that inhabits it are the result of generations of scientific culture. Originally we were a people ruled by hereditary jongs that various factions sought to dominate for their own enrichment and without consideration for the welfare of the remainder of the people.

'If we had a good jong who was also a strong character we were well ruled; otherwise the politicians misruled us. Half of our people lived in direst poverty, in vice, in filth; and they bred like flies. The better classes, refusing to bring children into such a world, dwindled rapidly. Ignorance and mediocrity ruled.

'Then a great jong came to the throne. He abrogated all existing laws and government and vested both in himself. Two titles have been conferred upon him – one while he lived, the other after his death. The first was Mankar the Bloody; the second, Mankar the Savior.

'He was a great warrior, and he had the warrior class behind him. With what seemed utter ruthlessness he wiped out the politicians, and to the positions many of them had filled he appointed the greatest minds of Havatoo – physicists, biologists, chemists, and psychologists.

'He encouraged the raising of children by people whom these scientists passed as fit to raise children, and he forbade all others to bear children. He saw to it that the physically, morally, or mentally defective were rendered incapable of bringing their like into the world; and no defective infant was allowed to live.

'Then, before his death, he created a new form of government – a government without laws and without a king. He abdicated his throne and relinquished the destinies of Havatoo to a quintumvirate that but guides and judges.

'Of these five men one is a sentar (biologist), one an ambad (psychologist), one a kalto (chemist), one a kantum (physicist), and one a korgan (soldier). This quintumvirate is called Sanjong (literally, five-king), and the fitness of its members to serve is determined by examinations similar to that which was given you. These examinations are held every two years. Any citizen may take them; any citizen may become one of the Sanjong. It is the highest honor to which a citizen of Havatoo may win, and he may only achieve it through actual merit.'

'And these men make the laws and administer justice,' I remarked.

Ero Shan shook his head. 'There are no laws in Havatoo,' he replied. 'During the many generations since Mankar we have bred a race of rational people who know the difference between right and wrong, and for such no rules of behavior are necessary. The Sanjong merely guides.'

'Do you have any difficulty in finding the proper men to form the Sanjong?' I asked.

'None whatever. There are thousands of men in Havatoo capable of serving with honor and distinction. There is a tendency to breed Sanjongs among five of the six classes into which the people of Havatoo are naturally divided.

'When you become more familiar with the city you will discover that the semicircular area facing the Central Laboratories is divided into five sections. The section next to the river and above the Central Laboratories is called Kantum. Here reside the physicists. There are no caste distinctions between the physicists and any of the other five classes, but because they all live in the same district and because their interests are alike there is a greater tendency for them to associate with one another than with members of other classes. The result is that they more often mate with their own kind – the laws of heredity do the rest, and the breed of physicists in Havatoo is constantly improving.

'The next district is Kalto; here live the chemists. The center district is Korgan, the district in which I dwell. It is reserved for the warrior class. Next comes Ambad, the section where the psychologists live; and, last, Sentar, for the biologists, lies along the water front and down the river from the Central Laboratories.

'Havatoo is laid out like the half of a wagon wheel, with the Central

Laboratories at the hub. The main sections of the city are bounded by four concentric semicircles. Inside the first is the civic center, where the Central Laboratories are situated; this I have called the hub. Between this and the next semicircle lie the five sub districts I have just described. Between this and the third semicircle lies the largest district, called Yorgan; here dwell the common people. And in the fourth section, a narrow strip just inside the outer wall, are the shops, markets, and factories.'

'It is all most interesting,' I said, 'and to me the most interesting part of it is that the city is governed without laws.'

'Without man-made laws,' Ero Shan corrected me. 'We are governed by natural laws with which all intelligent people are conversant. Of course occasionally a citizen commits an act that is harmful to another or to the peace of the city, for the genes of vicious and nonconformist characteristics have not all been eradicated from the germ cells of all of the citizens of Havatoo.

'If one commits an act that is subversive of the rights of others or of the general welfare of the community he is tried by a court that is not hampered by technicalities nor precedent, and which, taking into consideration all of the facts in the case, including the heredity of the defendant, reaches a decision that is final and without appeal.'

'It seems rather drastic to punish a man for the acts of his ancestors,' I remarked.

'But let me remind you that we do not punish,' explained Ero Shan. 'We only seek to improve the race to the end that we shall attain the greatest measure of happiness and contentment.'

'Havatoo, with no bad people in it, must be an ideal city in which to live,' I said.

'Oh, there are some bad people,' replied Ero Shan, 'for there are bad genes in all of us; but we are a very intelligent race, and the more intelligent people are the better able are they to control their bad impulses. Occasionally strangers enter Havatoo, bad men from the city across the river. How they accomplish it is a mystery that has never been solved, but we know that they come and steal a man or a woman occasionally. Sometimes we catch them, and when we do we destroy them. Rarely, our own people commit crimes, usually crimes of passion; but occasionally one commits a premeditated crime. The latter are a menace to the race and are not permitted to survive and transmit their characteristics to future generations or influence the present by their bad examples.'

As he ceased speaking a very powerfully built man came to the door of the room. 'You sent for me, Korgan Sentar Ero Shan?' he asked.

'Come in, Herlak,' said Ero Shan. Then he turned to me. 'Herlak will serve and guard you until the result of the examination is announced. You will find him an efficient and pleasant companion.

'Herlak,' he continued, addressing my guard, 'this man is a stranger in Havatoo. He has just been before the examining board. You will be responsible for him until the board's decision has been announced. His name is Carson Napier.'

The man inclined his head. 'I understand,' he said.

'You will both dine with me in an hour,' Ero Shan announced as he took his departure.

'If you would like to rest before dinner,' said Herlak, 'there is a couch in the next room.'

I went in and lay down, and Herlak came and sat in a chair in the same room. It was evident that he was not going to let me get out of his sight. I was tired, but not sleepy; so I started a conversation with Herlak.

'Are you employed in Ero Shan's house?' I asked.

'I am a soldier in the unit he commands,' he explained.

'An officer?'

'No, a common soldier.'

'But he asked you to dine with him. In my world officers do not mingle socially with common soldiers.'

Herlak laughed. 'Similar social conditions prevailed in Havatoo ages ago,' he said, 'but not now. There are no social distinctions. We are all far too intelligent, too cultured, and too sure of ourselves to need artificial conventions to determine our importance. Whether a man cleans a street or is a member of the Sanjong is not so important as is how he performs the duties of his position, his civic morality, and his culture.

'In a city where all are intelligent and cultured all men must be more or less companionable, and an officer suffers no loss of authority by mingling with his men socially.'

'But don't the soldiers take advantage of this familiarity to impose upon their officers?' I asked.

Herlak looked his surprise. 'Why should they?' he demanded. 'They know their duties as well as the officer knows his; and it is the aim in life of every good citizen to do his duty, not to evade it.'

I shook my head as I thought of the mess that Earthmen have made of government and civilization by neglecting to apply to the human race the simple rules which they observe to improve the breeds of dogs and cows and swine.

'Do the various classes mingle to the extent of intermarrying?' I asked.

'Of course,' replied Herlak. 'It is thus that we maintain the high moral and mental standards of the people. Were it otherwise, the yorgans must deteriorate while the several other classes diverged so greatly from one another that eventually they would have nothing in common and no basis for mutual understanding and regard.'

We talked of many things during that hour while we awaited dinner, and this common soldier of Havatoo discussed the sciences and the arts with far greater understanding and appreciation than I myself possessed. I asked him if he was particularly well educated, and he said that he was not – that all the men and women of Havatoo were schooled alike to a certain point, when a series of elaborate examinations determined the calling for which they were best fitted and in which they would find the greatest happiness.

'But where do you find your street cleaners?' I asked.

'You speak as though some reproach might attach to that calling,' he remonstrated.

'But it is work that many might find distasteful,' I argued.

'Necessary and useful work is never distasteful to the man best fitted to do it. Of course, highly intelligent people prefer creative work, and so these necessary but more or less mechanical duties, which, by the way, are usually done by means of mechanical contrivances in Havatoo, never become the permanent calling of any man. Any one can do them; so every one takes his turn – that is, every one in the yorgan class. It is his contribution to the public welfare – a tax paid in useful labor.'

And now a girl came to summon us to dinner. She was a very lovely girl; her saronglike garment was of fine material, her ornaments of great beauty.

'A member of Ero Shan's family?' I asked Herlak after she had left.

'She is employed in his house,' replied Herlak. 'Korgan Sentar Ero Shan has no family.'

I had heard this Korgan Sentar title attached to Ero Shan's name previously, and had wondered relative to its significance. The two words mean warrior biologist, but they made no sense to me as a title. I questioned Herlak concerning them as we crossed the garden in response to the summons to dinner.

'The title means that he is both a warrior and a biologist; he has passed examinations admitting him to both classes. The fact that he is a member of one of the other four classes as well as a Korgan makes him an officer and eligible to the title. We common soldiers would not care to serve under any but a brilliant man; and believe me it takes a brilliant man to pass the entrance examination to any of the scientific classes, for he has to pass creditably even in the three to which he is not seeking elevation.'

Herlak led me to a large apartment where I saw Ero Shan, three other men, and six women laughing and talking together. There was a suggestion of a lull in the conversation as we entered the room, and interested glances were cast in my direction. Ero Shan came forward to meet me and then introduced me to the others.

I should have enjoyed that dinner, with its marvelous food and sparkling conversation, and the kindness showed me by the other guests, but I could not rid my mind of a suspicion that their kindness might be prompted by pity – that they might share my doubt as to my ability to pass the hereditary test.

They knew, as well as I did, that the shadow of death was hovering over me. I thought of Duare, and hoped she was safe.

XV

The Judgment

Herlak slept on a couch near me that night. I called him the death watch, and he was polite enough to seem to enjoy my little joke.

Ero Shan, Herlak and I breakfasted together the next morning. The girl who had summoned us to dinner the night before waited on us. She was so radiantly beautiful that it was almost embarrassing; I felt that I should be waiting on her. She was young, but then every one I had seen in Havatoo appeared young.

Of course I was not greatly surprised by this, for I knew of the longevity serum developed by the scientists of Amtor. I myself had been inoculated against old age, but I remarked on it casually to Ero Shan.

'Yes,' he said, 'we could live forever if the Sanjong so decreed. At least we would never die of old age or disease, but they have decreed otherwise. Our serum gives immunity for two or three hundred years, depending upon the natural constitution of the individual. When it ceases to be effective death comes quickly. As a rule we anticipate it when we see that the end is coming.'

'But why not live forever if you can?' I asked.

'It was quite apparent that if we lived forever the number of children that could be permitted would be too small to result in any considerable improvement of the race, and so we have refused immortality in the interest of future generations and of all Amtor.'

As we were finishing breakfast word was brought to Ero Shan directing him to bring me before the examining board immediately; and a short time later, with Herlak accompanying us, we entered Ero Shan's car and drove down the Korgan Lat, or Avenue of Warriors, toward the Central Laboratories that stand in the civic center of Havatoo.

Both Ero Shan and Herlak were unusually quiet and grave during the drive, and I sensed that they anticipated that the worst was about to befall me. Nor can I say that I was particularly blithe though the least of my worries was occasioned by what lay in store for me; it was Duare I was thinking of, Duare and Nalte.

The stately government buildings, the Sera Tartum or Central Laboratories as they call them, looked very beautiful in the gorgeous setting of Mankar Pol, the park that is named for the great last jong of Havatoo, as we drove in and stopped before the building in which I had been examined the day before.

We did not have to wait after we entered the building, but were immediately ushered into the presence of the examining board. Their grave faces portended bad news, and I prepared myself for the worst. Through my mind raced plans for escape, but something told me that these people did things so well and were so efficient that there would be no escape from whatever fate they decreed for me.

Kantum Shogan, chief of the board, invited me to be seated; and I took a chair facing the august five. Ero Shan sat at my right, Herlak at my left.

'Carson Napier,' commenced Kantum Shogan, 'our examination of you shows that you are not without merit. Physically you approach that perfection toward which our race is constantly striving; intellectually you are alert but ill trained – you have no culture. While that might be remedied, I regret to advise you that you possess inherent psychological faults that, if transmitted to progeny or allowed to contaminate others through association with you, would work inestimable wrong on future generations.

'You are the unfortunate victim of inherited repressions, complexes and fears. To a great extent you have risen above these destructive characteristics but the chromosomes of your germ cells are replete with these vicious genes, constituting a potential menace to generations yet unborn.

'With deep regret, therefore, we could but conclude that it would best serve the interests of humanity were you destroyed.'

'May I ask,' I inquired, 'by what right you elect to say whether or not I shall live? I am not a citizen of Havatoo. I did not come to Havatoo of my own free will. If—'

Kantum Shogan raised his hand in a gesture that enjoined silence. 'I repeat,' he said, 'that we regret the necessity, but there is nothing more to be said upon the subject. Your accomplishments are not such as to outweigh your inherited defects. This is unfortunate, but of course Havatoo cannot be expected to suffer because of it.'

So I was to die! After all that I had passed through it verged upon the ridiculous that I should die thus tamely simply because one of my ancestors failed to exercise a little intelligence in the selection of his bride. And to come all this long way just to die! It made me smile.

'Why do you smile?' inquired a member of the board. 'Does death seem an amusing thing to you? Or do you smile because you expect to escape death through some ruse?'

'I smile,' I replied, 'when perhaps I should weep – weep at the thought of all the toil and knowledge and energy that were wasted to transport me twenty-six million miles just to die because five men of another world believe that I have inherited some bad genes.'

'Twenty-six million miles!' exclaimed a member of the board; and a second:

'Another world! What do you mean?'

'I mean that I came here from another world twenty-six million miles from Amtor,' I replied. 'A world much further advanced in some respects than yours.'

The members of the board stared at each other. I heard one of them remark to another: 'This bears out the theory that many of us have long held.'

'Most interesting, and not improbable,' said another.

'You say that Amtor is not the only world?' demanded Kantum Shogan; 'that there is another?'

'The heavens are filled with countless worlds,' I replied. 'Your world and mine and at least eight other worlds revolve around a great ball of flaming gases that we call a sun, and this sun with its worlds or planets is called a solar system. The illimitable void of the heavens is starred with countless other suns, many of which are the centers of other solar systems; and no man knows how many worlds there are.'

'Wait!' said Kantum Shogan. 'You have said enough to suggest that our examination of you may have been faulty in that it presumed that we possessed the sum total of available human knowledge. Now it appears that you may possess knowledge of such vast importance as to outweigh the biological inadequacies inherent in you.

'We shall question you further upon the subject of this theory which you have propounded, and in the meantime the execution of our sentence is postponed. Our final decision as to your future will depend upon the outcome of this further questioning. Science may ignore no possible source of knowledge, and if your theory is sound and opens a new field to science, you shall be free to enjoy Havatoo for life; nor shall you go unhonored.'

Although I had graduated with honors from a college of high scholastic standing I realized as I stood in the presence of these supermen of science that what Kantum Shogan had said of me was true. By comparison with them I was poorly trained and uncultured – my degrees meaningless, my diploma a mere scrap of paper. Yet in one field of science I surpassed them, and as I explained the solar system and drew diagrams of it for them I saw the keen interest and the ready understanding with which they grasped all I said.

Now, for the first time, they were listening to an explanation of the phenomena of the transition from day to night and from night to day, of the seasons, of the tides. Their vision restricted by the cloud envelopes that constantly enshroud Venus, they had been able to see nothing upon which to base a planetary theory; and so it is not strange that astronomy was an unknown science to them, that the sun and the stars did not exist insofar as they were concerned.

For four hours they listened to me and questioned me; then they instructed Ero Shan and Herlak to withdraw to an anteroom with me and wait there until we were again summoned.

We did not have long to wait. In less than fifteen minutes we were recalled before the board.

'It is our unanimous opinion,' announced Kantum Shogan, 'that your value to humanity far outweighs the danger that it incurs from your inherited defects. You are to live and enjoy the freedom of Havatoo. Your duties will consist of instructing others in that new science which you call astronomy and in applying it for the welfare of humanity.

'As you are now the only member of your class you may live in any section of the city you choose. Your requisitions for all that you require for your personal needs and the advancement of your department will be honored by the Sera Tartum.

'For the time being I recommend you to the guidance of Korgan Sentar Ero Shan as you are a stranger to Havatoo and will wish to become familiar with our customs and our manners.'

With that he dismissed us.

'Before I go may I ask what is to become of the girl, Nalte, who was taken with me yesterday?' I inquired.

'She was considered fit to remain in the yorgan section of Havatoo,' he replied. 'When her duties have been definitely determined and her living quarters assigned her I will let you know where you may find her.'

It was with a feeling of relief that I left the Sera Tartum with Ero Shan and Herlak. Nalte was safe, and so was I. Now if I could only find Duare!

I spent the following several days familiarizing myself with the city and purchasing such things as I required, all of which were suggested by Ero Shan. Among them was a car. It was very easy – all I had to do was sign a voucher.

'But what check have they on my expenditures?' I asked my friend. 'I do not even know how much has been placed to my credit.'

'Why should they check what you spend?' he asked.

'But I might be dishonest. I might buy things for which I had no need and resell them.'

Ero Shan laughed. 'They know you will not do that,' he assured me. 'If the psychologist who examined you had not known that you are an honorable man, not even your knowledge of astronomy would have saved you; that is one vice we will not tolerate in Havatoo. When Mankar destroyed the corrupt and the vicious he almost completely eradicated the breeds in Havatoo, and during the many generations of men that have followed him we have succeeded in completing the work he inaugurated. There are no dishonest men in Havatoo.'

I often talked with Ero Shan about Duare. I wanted to cross the river to Kormor and search for her, but he convinced me that it would be suicidal to attempt it. And in view of the fact that I had no reason to believe that she was there I reluctantly put the idea away from me.

'If I had an airplane,' I said, 'I would find a way to search Kormor.'

'What is an airplane?' asked Ero Shan, and when I explained it he became very much interested, as flying has never been developed in Amtor, at least in those portions with which I am familiar.

The idea intrigued my companion to such an extent that he could scarcely talk of anything else. I explained the various types of both heavier and lighter than air ships and described the rocket in which I had traversed space from Earth to Venus. In the evening he had me sketch the several types I had explained. His interest seemed to be becoming an obsession.

One evening when I returned to the house I now shared with Ero Shan I found a message awaiting me. It was from an under-clerk of the board of examiners and it gave the address of the house in which Nalte lived.

As I was now familiar with the city I started out in my car after the evening meal to visit Nalte. I went alone as Ero Shan had another engagement.

I found the house in which Nalte lived in the yorgan section on a quiet street not far from the Korgan Lat, the Avenue of Warriors. The house was occupied by women who cleaned the preparatory schools on the Korgan Lat nearby. One of their number admitted me and said that she would call Nalte; then she conducted me to a living room in which were eight or ten women. One of them was playing a musical instrument, the others were painting, embroidering, or reading.

As I entered, they stopped what they were doing and greeted me pleasantly. There was not one among them that was not beautiful, and all were intelligent and cultured. These were the scrub women of Havatoo! Breeding had done for the people of Havatoo what it has done for our prize-winning dairy herds; it has advanced them all toward perfection.

Nalte was glad to see me, and as I wished to visit with her alone I asked her to come for a ride with me.

'I am glad that you passed your examination successfully,' I said as we started toward the Korgan Lat.

Nalte laughed joyously. 'I just squeezed through,' she admitted. 'I wonder what they would say back in Andoo if they knew that I, the daughter of their jong, was considered fit only to scrub floors in Havatoo!' and again she laughed happily. It was plain to be seen that her pride had not suffered by reason of her assignment. 'But after all,' she continued, 'it is a high honor to be considered fit to remain on any footing among such a race of supermen.

'And you! I am very proud of you, Carson Napier, for I have been told that you were elevated to a high place among them.'

It was my turn to laugh now. 'I did not pass the examination at all,' I admitted. 'I would have been destroyed but for my knowledge of a science that is unknown to Amtor. It was rather a jolt to my self esteem.'

We drove along the Korgan Lat, through the great public park and parade ground in the center of which stands a magnificent stadium, and thus to the Avenue of the Gates which forms a great arc nearly eight miles long just inside the outer wall on the land side of Havatoo.

Here are the factories and the shops in the district included between the Avenue of Gates and the Yorgan Lat, a wide avenue a third of a mile inside the wall, all the principal shops being located along the Avenue of Gates. The avenue and the shops were brilliantly lighted, the street swarmed with vehicles, and the walkways at the level of the second stories were crowded with pedestrians.

We drove twice the full length of the avenue, enjoying the life and beauty of the scene; then we drove into one of the parking places, to which all of the ground floors on the main arteries are devoted, and were lifted by an escalator to the walkway on the level above.

Here shops displayed their wares in show windows, much as is the custom in American cities, though many of the displays aimed solely to please the eye rather than to call attention to the goods for sale within.

The scientists of Havatoo have developed a light that is brilliant and at the same time soft with which they attain effects impossible of achievement by our relatively crude lighting methods. At no place is the source of the light apparent; it casts soft shadows and gives forth no heat. Ordinarily it resembles sunlight, but it can also produce soft, pastel shades of various hues.

After we had enjoyed the spectacle for an hour, mingling with the happy crowd upon the walkway, I made a few small purchases, including a gift for Nalte; then we returned to my car, and I took my companion home.

The next morning I was busy organizing my classes in astronomy, and so numerous were those wishing to enroll that I had to organize several large classes, and as only four hours a day are ordinarily devoted to work of any nature it was evident that I should have to devote my time at first to the training of instructors if the new science was to be expounded to all the inhabitants who were interested.

I was greatly flattered by the personnel of the first matriculants. Not only were there scientists and soldiers from the first five classes of Havatoo, but every member of the Sanjong, the ruling quintumvirate of Havatoo, enrolled. The thirst of these people for useful knowledge is insatiable.

Shortly after noon, my work for the day having been completed, I received a summons to call upon Korgan Kantum Mohar, the warrior physicist who had arranged for the examination of Nalte and myself the day Ero Shan brought us to the city.

I could not but wonder what he wanted of me. Could it be that I must undergo another examination? Always, I presume, I shall connect Mohar's name with examinations.

As I entered his office on the Sera Tartum he greeted me with the same pleasant demeanor that had marked his attidue the day he had told me I was to be examined to ascertain whether or not I should be permitted to live; so his graciousness was not entirely reassuring.

'Come over here and sit down near me,' he said. 'I have something here that I should like to discuss with you.'

As I took a chair beside him I saw spread on his desk the sketches of airships that I had made for Ero Shan.

'These,' he said, pointing to the sketches, 'were brought to me by Ero Shan who explained them as best he could. He was quite excited and enthusiastic about them, and I must confess that he imparted some of his enthusiasm to me. I am much interested, and would know more concerning these ships that sail through the air.'

For an hour I talked to him and answered his questions. I dwelt principally on the practical achievements of aeronautics – the long flights, the great speed, the uses to which ships had been put in times of peace and in times of war.

Korgan Kantum Mohar was deeply interested. The questions that he asked revealed the trained, scientific mind; and the last one that of the soldier, the man of action.

'Can you build one of these ships for me?' he demanded.

I told him that I could but that it might require long experimentation to adapt their motors and materials to the requirements of a successful airplane.

'You have two or three hundred years,' he said with a smile, 'and the resources of a race of scientists. Materials that we do not now possess we can produce; nothing is impossible to science.'

XVI

Attack in the Night

I was given a factory close to the Gate of the Physicists, at the end of Kantum Lat. I chose this location because there was a level plain beyond this gate that would make an excellent flying field, and also so that I would have my finished plane finally assembled where it could easily be wheeled out of the city without interfering with traffic to any great extent.

On the advice of the Sanjong, which took a deep interest in both this new venture into aeronautics and the, to them, new science of astronomy, I divided my time between the two.

My time was fully occupied, and I worked far more than the usual four hours a day. But I enjoyed the work, especially the building of a plane; and engrossing were the day dreams in which I indulged of exploring Venus in a ship of my own.

The necessity for relaxation and entertainment is stressed by the people of Havatoo, and Ero Shan was constantly dragging me away from my drawing board or my conferences with the corps of assistants that had been placed at my disposal by Mohar to take me to this thing or that.

There were theaters, art exhibits, lectures, musicales, concerts, and games of various descriptions in gymnasiums and the great stadium. Many of their games are extremely dangerous, and injury and death often accompany them. In the great stadium at least once a month men fight with wild beasts or with one another to the death, and once a year the great war game is played. Ero Shan, Gara Lo, Ero Shan's friend, Nalte, and I attended this year's game together. To Nalte and I it was all new; we did not know what to expect.

'Probably we shall witness an exhibition of such scientific wonders as only the men of Havatoo are capable,' I suggested to her.

'I haven't the faintest conception of what it will be,' she replied. 'No one will tell me anything about it. They say, "Wait and see. You will be thrilled as you have never been before."'

'The game doubtless hinges on the use of the most modern, scientific instruments of war and strategy,' I ventured.

'Well,' she remarked, 'we shall soon know. It is about time for the games to begin.'

The great stadium, seating two hundred thousand people, was crammed to capacity. It was gorgeous with the costumes and the jewels of the women and the handsome trappings of the men, for the intelligence of Havatoo concedes their full value to beauty and to art. But of all that went to make up this splendid spectacle there was nothing more outstanding than the divine beauty of the people themselves.

Suddenly a cry arose, a roar of welcome. 'They come! The warriors!'

Onto the field at each end marched two hundred men; a hundred men naked but for white gee-strings at one end of the field, a hundred men with red gee-strings at the other end of the field.

They carried short swords and shields. For a while they stood inactive, waiting; then two small cars were driven onto the field. Each contained a driver and a young woman.

One of the cars was red, the other white. The red car attached itself to the contingent wearing the red gee-strings, the white car to the whites.

When they were in position the two factions paraded entirely around the field clockwise. As they passed the stands the people cheered and shouted words of encouragement and praise, and when the warriors had completed the circuit they took their places again.

Presently a trumpet sounded, and the reds and the whites approached each other. Now their formations were changed. There was an advance party and a rear guard, there were flankers on either side. The cars remained in the rear, just in front of the rear guard. On running-boards that encircled the cars were a number of warriors.

I leaned toward Ero Shan. 'Tell us something of the idea of the game,' I begged, 'so that we may understand and enjoy it better.'

'It is simple,' he replied. 'They contend for fifteen vir (the equivalent of sixty minutes of Earth time), and the side that captures the opponent's queen oftenest is the winner.'

I do not know what I expected, but certainly not that which followed. The reds formed a wedge with its apex toward the whites, then charged. In the mêleé that ensued I saw three men killed and more than a dozen wounded, but the whites held their queen.

When a queen was pressed too closely her car turned and fled, the rear guard coming up to repel the enemy. The tide of battle moved up and down the field. Sometimes the whites seemed about to capture the red queen, again their own was in danger. There were many individual duels and a display of marvelous swordsmanship throughout.

But the whole thing seemed so out of harmony with all that I had heretofore seen in Havatoo that I could find no explanation for it. Here was the highest type of culture and civilization that man might imagine suddenly reverting to barbarism. It was inexplicable. And the strangest part of all of it to me was the almost savage enjoyment with which the people viewed the bloody spectacle.

I must admit that I found it thrilling, but I was glad when it was over. Only one queen was captured during the entire game. At the very last the white queen fell into the hands of the reds, but only after the last of her defenders had fallen.

Of the two hundred men who took part in the game, not one came through unwounded; fifty were killed on the field, and I afterward learned that ten more died of their wounds later.

As we drove from the stadium toward our house I asked Ero Shan how such a savage and brutal exhibition could be tolerated, much less enjoyed, by the refined and cultured inhabitants of Havatoo.

'We have few wars,' he replied. 'For ages war was man's natural state. It gave expression to the spirit of adventure which is a part of his inheritance. Our psychologists discovered that man must have some outlet for this age-old urge. If it be not given him by wars or dangerous games he will seek it in the commission of crimes or in quarrels with his fellows. It is better that it is so. Without it man would stagnate, he would die of ennui.'

I was now working on my plane with the keenest enthusiasm, for I now saw rapidly taking form such a ship as, I truly believe, might be built nowhere in the universe other than in Havatoo. Here I had at my disposal materials that only the chemists of Havatoo might produce, synthetic wood and steel and fabric that offered incalculable strength and durability combined with negligible weight.

I had also the element, vik-ro, undiscovered on Earth, and the substance, lor, to furnish fuel for my engine. The action of the element, vik-ro, upon the element, yor-san, which is contained in the substance, lor, results in absolute annihilation of the lor. Some conception of the amount of energy thus released may be obtained by considering the fact that there is eighteen thousand million times as much energy liberated by the annihilation of a ton of coal as by its combustion. Fuel for the life of my ship could be held in the palm of my hand, and with the materials that entered into its construction the probable life of the ship was computed by the physicists working on it to be in the neighborhood of fifty years. Can you wonder that I looked forward with impatience to the completion of such a marvel ship! With it I would be sure to find Duare.

At last it was finished! I spent the final afternoon checking it over carefully with my large corps of assistants. On the morrow it was to be wheeled out for my trial flight. I knew that it would be successful. All my assistants knew that it would be; it was a scientific certainty that it must fly.

That evening I determined to indulge in a little relaxation; and I called

Nalte on the wireless, transmitterless, receiverless communicating system that is one of the wonders of Havatoo. I asked her if she would take dinner with me, and she accepted with an alacrity and display of pleasure that warmed my heart.

We dined in a little public garden on the roof of a building at the corner of Yorgan Lat and Havatoo Lat, just inside the river wall.

'It seems good to see you again,' said Nalte. 'It has been a long time – not since the war games. I thought you had forgotten me.'

'Far from it,' I assured her, 'but I have been working day and night on my airship.'

'I have heard some mention of it,' she said, 'but no one that I have talked with seemed to understand very much about it. Just what is it and what will it do?'

'It is a ship that flies through the air faster than a bird can wing,' I replied.

'But what good will that be?' she demanded.

'It will carry people quickly and safely from one place to another,' I explained.

'You don't mean to say that people will ride in it!' she exclaimed.

'Why, certainly; why else should I build it?'

'But what will keep it in the air? Will it flap its wings like a bird?'

'No; it will soar like a bird on stationary wings.'

'But how will you get through the forests where the trees grow close together?'

'I shall fly over the forests.'

'So high? Oh, it will be dangerous,' she cried. 'Please do not go up in it, Carson.'

'It will be very safe,' I assured her, 'much safer than incurring the dangers of the forests on foot. No savage beasts or men can harm the voyager in an airship.'

'But think of being way up above the trees!' she said with a little shudder.

'I shall fly even higher than that,' I told her. 'I shall fly over the loftiest mountains.'

'But you will never fly over the great trees of Amtor; I know that.'

She referred to the gigantic trees that raise their tips five thousand feet above the surface of Amtor to drink the moisture from the inner cloud envelope.

'Yes; possibly I shall fly even above those,' I replied, 'though I will admit that flying blind in that solid bank of clouds does not appeal to me.'

She shook her head. 'I shall be afraid every time I know that you are up in the thing.'

'Oh, no you won't, not after you are familiar with it. Some day soon I am going to take you up with me.'

'Not me!'

'We could fly to Andoo,' I said. 'I have been thinking of that ever since I started to build the ship.'

'To Andoo!' she exclaimed. 'Home! Oh, Carson, if we only could!'

'But we can – that is if we can find Andoo. This ship will take us anywhere. If we could carry enough food and water we could stay in the air for fifty years, and it certainly wouldn't take that long to find Andoo.'

'I love it here in Havatoo,' she said, musingly, 'but after all, home is home. I want to see my own people, but I would like to come back to Havatoo again. That is, if—'

'If what?' I asked.

'If you are going to be here.'

I reached across the table and pressed her hand. 'We *have* been pretty good friends, haven't we, Nalte? I should miss you terribly if I thought that I were not to see you again.'

'I think that you are the best friend I ever had,' she said, and then she looked up at me quickly and laughed. 'Do you know,' she continued; but stopped suddenly and looked down, as a slight flush suffused her cheeks.

'Do I know what?' I asked.

'Well, I might as well confess. There was a long time that I thought that I loved you.'

'That would have been a great honor, Nalte.'

'I tried to hide it because I knew that you loved Duare; and now recently Ero Shan has been coming to see me, and I know that I did not know before what love was.'

'You love Ero Shan?'

'Yes.'

'I am glad. He is a splendid fellow. I know you will both be happy.'

'That might be true but for one thing,' she said.

'And what is that?'

'Ero Shan does not love me.'

'How do you know that he doesn't? I don't see how he could help it. If I had never known Duare—'

'If he loved me he would tell me,' she interrupted. 'Sometimes I think that he believes that I belong to you. We came here together, you know, and we have been much together since. But what's the good in speculating! If he loved me he would not be able to hide it.'

We had finished our dinner, and I suggested that we drive about the city for a while and then go to a concert.

'Let's take a little walk instead of driving,' suggested Nalte, and as we rose from our table, 'How beautiful the view is from here!'

In the strange glow of the Amtorian night the expanse of the great river stretched into the vanishing visibility above and below the city, while on the opposite shore gloomy Kormor was but a darker blotch against the darkness of the night, with here and there a few dim lights showing feebly in contrast to brilliant Havatoo lying at our feet.

We followed the walkway along Havatoo Lat to a narrow side street that extended away from the river.

'Let's turn here,' said Nalte. 'I feel like quiet and dim lights tonight, not the brilliance and the crowds of Havatoo Lat.'

The street that we turned into was in the yorgan section of the city; it was but dimly lighted, and the walkway was deserted. It was a quiet and restful street even by comparison with the far from noisy main avenues of Havatoo, where raucous noises are unknown.

We had proceeded but a short distance from Havatoo Lat when I heard a door open behind us and footsteps on the walkway. I gave the matter no thought; in fact I scarcely had time to give it thought when some one seized me roughly from behind and as I wheeled about I saw another man grab Nalte, clap a hand over her mouth and drag her into the doorway from which the two had come.

XVII

City of the Dead

I tried to break away from the man who held me, but he was very strong. I did succeed in turning about so that I could strike him; and this I did repeatedly, hitting him in the face as he sought to reach my throat with his fingers.

We must have made quite a lot of noise in that quiet street although neither of us spoke, for soon a head was put out of a window, and presently men and women came running from their houses. But before any of them reached us I had tripped my assailant and was on top of him clutching his throat. I would have choked the life out of him had not several men dragged me from him.

They were shocked and angry because of this unseemly disturbance and brawl on a street in Havatoo, and they placed us under arrest, nor would they listen to what I tried to tell them. All they would say was: 'The judges will listen to you;' 'it is not our province to judge.'

As every citizen of Havatoo has police powers and there is no other police force, there was no delay as there would have been in an Earthly city while waiting for the police to answer a summons.

We were bundled into a large car belonging to one of the citizens, and with an adequate guard we were whisked away toward the Sera Tartum.

They do things with celerity in Havatoo. They may have a jail; I presume they have, but they didn't waste any time or cause the state any expense by putting us in to be boarded and lodged by the taxpayers.

Five men were hastily summoned, one from each of the five upper classes; they were judge, jury, and court of last resort. They sat in a large room that resembled a huge library; they were served by a dozen clerks.

One of the judges asked us our names, and when we had given them two clerks went quickly to the shelves and brought forth books in which they began to search.

Then the judges asked those who had arrested us to explain why they brought us in. During the recital of our violation of the peace of Havatoo one of the clerks, evidently having found what he sought, laid his book open before the judges; the other was still searching.

From the open book one of the judges read aloud my official record since

I had come to Havatoo, including the result of the examination that I had undergone and its embarrassing finding.

A judge asked me to state my case. In a few brief words I told of the unprovoked attack upon us and the abduction of Nalte, and in conclusion I said, 'Instead of wasting time trying me for being the victim of this unwarranted attack and defending myself against my assailant you should be helping me search for the girl who has been stolen.'

'The peace of Havatoo is of more importance than the life of any individual,' replied a judge. 'When we have fixed the responsibility for this breach of the peace the other matter will be investigated.'

The second clerk now approached the judges. 'The name of the prisoner who calls himself Mal Un does not appear in the records of Havatoo.'

All eyes turned toward my assailant, Mal Un, and for the first time I had a good look at him under a bright light. I saw his eyes! Instantly I recalled what I had evidently noticed only subconsciously before – the chill of the flesh of his hands and his throat when I had fought with him. And now those eyes. They were the eyes of a dead man!

I wheeled toward the judges. 'I understand it all now,' I cried. 'When I first came to Havatoo I was told that there were few bad men in the city; but that occasionally, none knew how, bad men came from the city of Kormor across the river and stole men and women from Havatoo. This man is from Kormor. He is not a living man; he is a corpse. He and his companion sought to steal Nalte and me for Skor!'

With calm efficiency the judges made a few brief and simple, but none the less effective, tests upon Mal Un; then they whispered together for a few seconds without leaving the bench. Following this, the one who acted as spokesman for the tribunal cleared his throat.

'Mal Un,' he announced, 'you will be decapitated and cremated forthwith. Carson Napier, you are exonerated with honor. You are free. You may conduct a search for your companion and call upon any citizen of Havatoo to assist you in any way that you desire assistance.'

As I was leaving the room I heard a mirthless laugh burst from the dead mouth of Mal Un. Horribly it rang in my ears as I hastened out into the night. The dead man laughing because he was sentenced to death!

Naturally, the first person I thought of in my extremity was Ero Shan, who had rescued me from the ape-men. My own car was parked where I had left it at the corner of Yorgan Lat and Havatoo Lat; so I hailed a public conveyance and was driven rapidly to the house at which Ero Shan was being entertained that evening.

I did not go in but sent word that I wished to speak to him upon a matter of great urgency, and a moment later I saw him coming from the house toward me.

'What brings you here, Carson?' he asked. 'I thought you were spending the evening with Nalte.'

When I told him what had happened he went very white. 'There is no time to be lost!' he cried. 'Can you find that house again?'

I told him that I could. 'That doorway is indelibly burned into my memory.'

'Dismiss your car; we will go in mine,' he said, and a moment later we were speeding toward the place where I had lost Nalte.

'You have all my sympathy, my friend,' said Ero Shan. 'To have lost the woman you love, and such a woman! is a calamity beyond any feeble words to express.'

'Yes,' I replied, 'and even if I had loved Nalte I could scarcely be more grieved than I now am.'

' "Even if you had loved Nalte"!' he repeated incredulously. 'But, man, you do love her, do you not?'

'We were only the best of friends,' I replied. 'Nalte did not love me.'

Ero Shan made no reply; he drove swiftly on in silence. Presently we reached our destination. Ero Shan stopped his car beside the stairway, nearest the house, that led up to the walkway; and a moment later we were before the door.

Repeated summons elicited no response, and then I tried the door and found it unlocked.

Together we entered the dark interior, and I regretted that we had brought no weapons; but in peaceful Havatoo men do not ordinarily go armed. Ero Shan soon located a light switch, and as the room in which we stood was illuminated, we saw that it was entirely unfurnished.

The building rose two stories above the walkway, and of course there was a lower floor on a level with the street. We searched the upper stories first, and then the roof, for in this part of Havatoo most of the roofs are developed as gardens; but we found no sign of recent habitation. Then we went to the ground floor, but with no better results. Here was space for the parking of cars, and in rear of that a number of dark storerooms.

'There is no living creature in this house except ourselves,' said Ero Shan. 'They must have taken Nalte to some other house. It will be necessary to make a search, and only under the authority of the Sanjong itself may the home of a citizen be searched. Come! We will go and get that authority.'

'You go,' I said. 'I will remain here. We should keep a careful watch on this house.'

'You are right,' he replied. 'I shall not be gone long.'

*

After Ero Shan's departure I commenced another careful investigation of the premises. Once again I went through every room searching for some secret place where a person might be hidden.

I had covered the upper stories of the house thus, and was searching the first floor. The dust of neglect lay heavy upon everything, but I noticed that in one of the back rooms it had been disturbed upon the floor at a point where Ero Shan and I had not walked. Previously this had escaped my notice. It seemed to me that it might be fraught with importance.

I examined the floor carefully. I saw footprints. They approached a wall; and there they stopped; there seemed to be a path worn in the dust to this point in the wall. I examined the wall. It was covered with a form of synthetic wood common in Havatoo, and when I rapped upon it it sounded hollow.

The wall covering was applied in panels about three feet wide, and at the top of the panel I was examining was a small round hole about an inch in diameter. Inserting a forefinger in this hole I discovered just what I had imagined I would discover – a latch. I tripped it; and with a slight pressure the panel swung toward me, revealing a dark aperture beyond it.

At my feet I dimly discerned the top of a flight of steps. I listened intently; no sound came up to me from the gloom into which the stairs disappeared. Naturally, I was convinced that Nalte's abductor had carried her down that stairway.

I should have waited for the return of Ero Shan, but I thought that Nalte might be in danger. I could not think of wasting a single precious instant in delay.

I placed a foot upon the stairs and started to descend; and as I did so the panel closed softly behind me, actuated by a spring. I heard the latch click. I was now in utter darkness. I had to feel my way. At any moment I might come upon Nalte's abductor waiting to dispatch me. It was a most uncomfortable sensation, I can assure you.

The stairway, which was apparently cut from the living limestone that underlies Havatoo, ran straight down to a great depth. From the bottom of the stairway I felt my way along a narrow corridor. Occasionally I stopped and listened. At first I heard not a sound; the silence was the silence of the grave.

Presently the walls commenced to feel moist; and then, occasionally, a drop of water fell upon my head. Now a low, muffled sound like the shadow of a roar seemed to fill the subterranean corridor like a vague, oppressive menace.

On and on I groped my way. I could not advance rapidly, for I was compelled to feel every forward footstep before taking it; I could not know what lay beyond the last.

Thus I continued on for a long distance until finally my extended foot felt an obstruction. Investigating, I found that it was the lowest step of a flight of stairs.

Cautiously I ascended, and at the top I came against a blank wall. But experience had taught me where to search for a latch, for I was confident that what barred my progress was a door.

Presently my fingers found what they sought; a door gave to the pressure of my hand.

I pushed it slowly and cautiously until a narrow crack permitted me to look beyond it.

I saw a portion of a room dimly illuminated by the night light of Amtor. I opened the door a little farther; there was no one in the room. I stepped into it, but before I permitted the door to close I located the opening through which the latch could be tripped from that side.

The room in which I found myself was filthy and littered with débris. It was filled with a revolting, musty odor that suggested death and decay.

In the wall opposite me were three openings, a doorway and two windows; but there was no window sash and no door. Beyond the door, to which I now crossed, was a yard inclosed by one side of the building and a high wall.

There were three rooms on the ground floor of the building, and these I searched rapidly; they contained only broken furniture, old rags, and dirt. I went upstairs. Here were three more rooms; they revealed nothing more of interest than those downstairs.

Than these six rooms there was nothing more to the house, and so I was soon aware that I must search farther for Nalte. Neither she nor any one else was in this house.

From an upper window I looked out over the yard. Beyond the wall I saw a street. It was a dingy, gloomy street. The houses that fronted it were drab and dilapidated, but I did not have to look out upon this scene to know where I was. Long before this I had guessed that I was in Kormor, the city of the cruel jong of Morov. The tunnel through which I had passed from Havatoo had carried me beneath the great river that is called Gerlat kum Rov, River of Death. Now I knew that Nalte had been abducted by the agents of Skor.

From the window I saw an occasional pedestrian on the street that passed the house. They moved with slow, shuffling steps. Somewhere in this city of the dead was Nalte in danger so great that I turned cold at the mere thought of it. I must find her! But how?

Descending to the yard, I passed through a gateway in the wall and out into the street. Only the natural, nocturnal light of Amtor illuminated the scene. I did not know which way to go, yet I knew that I must keep moving if I were not to attract attention to myself.

My judgment and my knowledge of Skor suggested that where Skor was there I would find Nalte, and so I knew that I must find the jong's palace. If I might only stop one of the pedestrians and ask him; but that I did not dare do, for to reveal my ignorance of the location of the jong's palace would be to brand me a stranger and therefore an emeny.

I was approaching two men who were walking in the opposite direction to that which I had chosen. As I passed them I noted their somber garb, and I saw them half stop as we came abreast and eye me intently. But they did not accost me, and it was with relief that I realized that they had gone on their way.

Now I understood that with my handsome trappings and my brisk, alert step and carriage I would be a marked man in Kormor. It became absolutely imperative, therefore, that I disguise myself; but that was going to be more easily thought of than accomplished. However, it must be done. I could never hope to find and rescue Nalte if I were constantly subject to detection and arrest.

Turning, I retraced my steps to the mean hovel I had just quitted, for there I remembered having seen odds and ends of rags and discarded clothing from among which I hoped that I might select sufficient to cover my naked-ness and replace the fine apparel I had purchased in Havatoo.

Nor was I disappointed, and a few moments later I emerged again upon the streets clothed in the cleanest of the foul garments I had had to select from. And now, to carry out my disguise to the fullest, I shuffled slowly along like some carrion from a forgotten grave.

Again I met pedestrians; but this time they gave me no second look, and I knew that my disguise was ample. To all outward appearances, in this unlighted city of the dead, I was just another corpse.

In a few houses dim lights burned; but I heard no noises – no singing, no laughter. Somewhere in this city of horror was Nalte. That so sweet and lovely a creature was breathing this fetid air was sufficiently appalling, but of far greater import was the fact that her life hung in the balance.

If Skor was in the city he might kill her quickly in a fit of mad revenge because she had escaped him once. My sustaining hope was that Skor was at his castle and that his minions would hold Nalte unharmed until he returned to Kormor. But how to learn these things!

I knew that it would be dangerous to question any of the inhabitants; but finally I realized that in no other way might I quickly find the house of Skor, and haste was essential if I were to find Nalte before it was too late.

As I wandered without plan I saw nothing to indicate that I was approach-ing a better section such as I felt might contain the palace of a jong. The houses were all low and grimy and unlovely in design.

I saw a man standing at the intersection of two streets, and as I came close to him I stopped. He looked at me with his glassy eyes.

'I am lost,' I said.

'We are all lost,' he replied, his dead tongue thick in his dead mouth.

'I cannot find the house where I live.'

'Go into any house; what difference does it make?'

'I want to find my own house,' I insisted.

'Go and find it then. How should I know where it is if you do not?'

'It is near the house of the jong,' I told him.

'Then go to the house of the jong,' he suggested surlily.

'Where is it?' I demanded in the same thick tones.

He pointed down the street that I had been following; and then he turned and shuffled away in the opposite direction, while I continued on in the direction he had indicated. I wished to reach my destination quickly; but I dared not accelerate my speed for fear of attracting attention, and so I shuffled along in the lifeless manner of the other wayfarers.

Somewhere ahead of me lay the palace of Skor, Jong of Morov; there I was certain I would find Nalte. But after I found her – what?

XVIII

A Surprise

The palace of Skor was a three-storied building of gray stone similar in its ugliness to his castle by the river in the forest, but it was considerably larger. It stood in no spacious plaza. Mean hovels were its near neighbors. All about it was a high wall, and before heavy gates stood a dozen warriors. It looked impregnable.

I shuffled slowly past the gates, observing from the corners of my eyes. It seemed useless to attempt to enter there. The guards were posted for a purpose, and that purpose must be to keep out those who had no business within.

What reason could I give for wishing to enter? – what reason that they would accept?

It was evident that I must seek some other means of ingress. If I failed to find any then I might return to the gates as a last resort, but I can tell you that the outlook seemed most hopeless.

I followed the high wall that inclosed the palace grounds, but nowhere did I find any place to scale it. It was about twelve feet high, just too high for me to reach the top with my fingers by a running jump.

I reached the rear of the palace without discovering any place where I might scale the wall, and I was convinced that there was no place. There was plenty of litter and rubbish in the filthy street that encircled the wall but nothing that I could make use of as a ladder.

Upon the opposite side of the street were mean hovels, many of which appeared deserted. In only a few, dim lights revealed a sign of – life, I was going to say – of occupancy. Directly across from me an open door sagged on a single hinge.

It gave me an idea.

I crossed the street. There were no lights in any of the nearby houses. That before which I stood appeared tenantless. Stealthily I crept to the doorway and listened. There was no sound from the gloom of the interior, but I must make sure that no one was there.

Scarcely breathing, I entered the house. It was a one-story hovel of two rooms. I searched them both. The house was unoccupied. Then I returned to the door and examined the remaining hinge. To my delight I discovered that I could easily remove the door, and this I did.

I looked up and down the street. There was no one in sight. Lifting the door, I crossed to the wall and leaned the door against it.

Again I searched the street with my eyes. All was clear.

Cautiously I crawled up the door. From its top, precariously gained, I could reach the top of the wall. Then I threw caution to the winds, drew myself up, and dropped to the ground on the opposite side. I could not take the chance of remaining even for an instant on the summit of the wall in plain view of the palace windows on one side and the street on the other.

I recalled the vicious kazars that Skor kept at his castle, and I prayed that he kept none here. But no kazar attacked me, nor did any evidence suggest that my entry had been noted.

Before me loomed the palace, dark and forbidding even though some lights shone within it. The courtyard was flagged, and as barren as that of the castle in the wood.

Crossing quickly to the building I walked along it seeking an entrance. It was three stories high. I saw at least two towers. Many of the windows were barred, but not all. Behind one of those barred windows, perhaps, was Nalte. The task before me was to discover which.

I dared not go to the front of the palace lest I be questioned by the guard. Presently I discovered a small door; it was the only door on this side of the building, but it was securely locked. Carrying my investigation further, I came to an open window. The room beyond was unlighted. I listened but heard no sound; then I vaulted quietly to the sill and dropped within. At last I was inside the palace of the Jong of Morov.

Crossing the room, I found a door on the opposite side; and when I drew it open I saw a dimly lighted corridor beyond. And with the opening of the door sounds from the interior of the palace reached my ears.

The corridor was deserted as I stepped into it and made my way in the direction of the sounds I had heard. At a turning I came to a broader and better lighted corridor, but here dead men and women passed to and fro. Some were carrying dishes laden with food in one direction, others were bearing empty dishes in the opposite direction.

I knew that I risked detection and exposure, but I also knew that it was a risk I must take sooner or later. As well now, I thought, as any time. I noticed that these corpses were painted in the semblance of life and health; only their eyes and their shuffling gait revealed the truth. My eyes I could not change, but I kept them lowered as I shuffled into the corridor behind a man carrying a large platter of food.

I followed him to a large room in which two score men and women were seated at a banquet table. Here at last, I thought, were living people – the masters of Kormor. They did not seem a very gay company, but that I could understand in surroundings such as theirs. The men were handsome, the women beautiful. I wondered what had brought them and what kept them in this horrid city of death.

A remarkable feature of the assemblage was the audience that packed the room, leaving only sufficient space for the servants to pass around the table. These people were so well painted that at first I thought them alive too.

Seeing an opportunity to lose my identity in the crowd, I wormed my way behind the rear rank and then gradually worked my way around the room and toward the front rank of the spectators until I stood directly in rear of a large, thronelike chair that stood at the head of the table and which I assumed to be Skor's chair.

Close contact with the men and women watching the banqueters soon disclosed the fact that I was doubtless the only living creature among them, for no make-up, however marvelous, could alter the expressionlessness of those dead eyes or call back the fire of life or the light of soul. Poor creatures! How I pitied them.

And now, from the lower end of the chamber, came a blare of trumpets; and all the banqueters arose and faced in that direction. Four trumpeters marching abreast entered the banquet hall, and behind them came eight warriors in splendid harness. Following these were a man and a woman, partially hidden from my sight by the warriors and the trumpeters marching in front of them. These two were followed by eight more warriors.

And now the trumpeters and the warriors separated and formed an aisle down which the man and the woman walked. Then I saw them, and my heart stood still. Skor and – Duare!

Duare's head was still high – it would be difficult to break that proud spirit – but the loathing, the anguish, the hopelessness in her eyes, struck me like dagger to the heart. Yet, even so, hope bounded in my breast as I saw them, for they *were* expressions; and they told me that Skor had not yet worked his worst upon her.

They seated themselves, Skor at the head of the table, Duare at his right, scarce three paces from me; and the guests resumed their seats.

I had come for Nalte, and I had found Duare. How was I to rescue her now that I had found her? I realized that I must do nothing precipitate. Here, faced by overwhelming odds in the stronghold of an enemy, I knew that I might accomplish nothing by force.

I looked about the room. On one side were windows, in the center of the opposite wall was a small door, at the far end the large doors through which all seemed to be entering or leaving; and behind me was another small doorway. I had no plan, but it was well to note the things that I had noted.

I saw Skor pound on the table with his fist. All the guests looked up. Skor raised a goblet, and the guests did likewise.

'To the jong!' he cried.

'To the jong!' repeated the guests.

'Drink!' commanded Skor, and the guests drank.

Then Skor addressed them. It was not a speech; it was a monologue to which all listened. In it occurred what Skor evidently considered an amusing anecdote. When he had narrated it he paused, waiting. There was only silence. Skor scowled. 'Laugh!' he snapped, and the guests laughed – hollow, mirthless laughs. It was then, with those laughs, that my suspicions were aroused.

When Skor finished his monologue there was another silence until he commanded, 'Applaud!' Skor smiled and bowed in acknowledgment of the ensuing applause just as though it had been spontaneous and genuine.

'Eat!' he commanded, and the guests ate; then he said, 'Talk!' and they commenced to converse.

'Let us be gay!' cried Skor. 'This is a happy moment for Morov. I bring you your future queen!' He pointed to Duare. There was only silence. 'Applaud!' growled Skor, and when they had done his bidding he urged them again to be gay. 'Let us have laughter,' he bid them. 'Starting at my left you will take turns laughing, and when the laughter has passed around the table to the future queen you will start over again.'

The laughter commenced. It rose and fell as it passed around the table. God, what a travesty on gayety it was!

I had passed closer until I stood directly behind Skor's chair. Had Duare turned her eyes in my direction she must have seen me, but she did not. She sat staring straight before her.

Skor leaned toward her and spoke. 'Are they not fine specimens?' he demanded. 'You see I am coming closer and closer to the fulfillment of my dream. Do you not see how different are all the people of Kormor from the mean creatures at my castle? And look at these, the guests at my table. Even their eyes have the semblance of real life. Soon I shall have it – I shall be able to breathe full life into the dead. Then think what a nation I can create! And I shall be jong, and you shall be vadjong.'

'I do not wish to be vadjong,' replied Duare. 'I only wish my liberty.'

A dead man sitting across the table from her said, 'That is all that any of us wishes, but we shall never get it.' It was then his turn to laugh, and he laughed. It was incongruous, horrible. I saw Duare shudder.

Skor's sallow face paled. He glowered at the speaker. 'I am about to give you life,' cried the jong angrily, 'and you do not appreciate it.'

'We do not wish to live,' replied the corpse. 'We wish death. Let us have death and oblivion again – let us return to our graves in peace.'

At these words, Skor flew into a fit of rage. He half rose, and drawing a sword struck at the face of the speaker. The keen blade laid open an ugly wound from temple to chin. The edges of the wound gaped wide, but no blood flowed.

The dead man laughed. 'You cannot hurt the dead,' he mocked.

Skor was livid. He sought words, but his rage choked him. Flecks of foam whitened his lips. If ever I have looked upon a madman it was then. Suddenly he turned upon Duare.

'You are the cause of this!' he screamed. 'Never say such things again before my subjects. You shall be queen! I will make you queen of Morov, a living queen, or I will make you one of these. Which do you choose?'

'Give me death,' replied Duare.

'That you shall never have – not real death, only the counterfeit that you see before you – neither life nor death.'

At last the ghastly meal drew to a close. Skor arose and motioned Duare to accompany him. He did not leave the room as he had entered it; no trumpeters nor warriors accompanied him. He walked toward the small doorway at the rear of the room, the spectators giving way before him and Duare as they advanced.

So suddenly had Skor risen and turned that I thought he must surely see me; but if he did he did not recognize me, and a moment later he had passed me, and the danger was over. And as he and Duare moved toward the doorway I fell in behind and followed. Each instant I expected to feel a hand upon my shoulder stopping me, but no one seemed to pay any attention to me. I passed through the doorway behind Skor and Duare without a challenge. Even Skor did not turn as he raised the hangings at the doorway and let them fall again behind him.

I moved softly, making no noise. The corridor in which we were was deserted. It was a very short corridor, ending at a heavy door. As Skor threw this door open I saw a room beyond that at first I thought must be a storeroom. It was large and almost completely filled with a heterogeneous collection of odds and ends of furniture, vases, clothing, arms, and pictures. Everything was confusion and disorder, and everything was covered with dust and dirt.

Skor paused for a moment on the threshold, seemingly viewing the room with pride. 'What do you think of it?' he demanded.

'Think of what?' asked Duare.

'This beautiful room,' he said. 'In all Amtor there cannot be a more beautiful room; nowhere else can there be another such collection of beautiful objects; and now to them I am adding the most beautiful of all – you! This, Duare, is to be your room – the private apartment of the queen of Morov.'

I stepped in and closed the door behind me, for I had seen that but for us three there was no one else in the apartment; and now seemed as good a time to act as any.

I had not meant to make any noise as I entered. Skor was armed and I was not, and it had been my intention to throw myself upon him from the rear and overpower him before he could have an opportunity to use his weapons against me. But the lock of the door clicked as I closed it, and Skor wheeled and faced me.

XIX

In Hiding

As the eyes of the Jong of Morov fell upon me he recognized me, and he voiced a sardonic laugh as he whipped out his sword and brought my charge to a sudden, ignominious stop – one does not finish a charge with the point of a sword in one's belly.

'So!' he exclaimed; 'It is you? Well, well. It is good to see you again. I did not expect to be so honored. I thought Fortune had been very kind to me when she returned the two young women. And now you have come! What a merry party we shall have!'

With the last words his tone, which had been sarcastically bantering, changed; he fairly hissed that gay sentence. And the expression on his face changed too. It became suddenly malevolent, and his eyes glittered with the same mad fire of insanity that I had seen there before.

Behind him stood Duare, her wide eyes fixed upon me with incredulity mixed with terror. 'Oh, why did you come, Carson?' she cried. 'Now he will kill you.'

'I will tell you why he came,' said Skor. 'He came for the other girl, for Nalte, not for you. You have been here a long time, but he did not come. To-night one of my people seized the girl, Nalte, in Havatoo; and he came immediately to try to rescue her, the fool. I have known for a long time that they were in Havatoo. My spies have seen them there together. I do not know how he got here, but here he is – and here he stays, forever.'

He poked me in the belly with the point of his sword. 'How would you like to die, fool?' he snarled. 'A quick thrust through the heart, perhaps. That would mutilate you least. You will make a fine specimen. Come, now, what have you to say? Remember this will be the last chance you will have to think with your own brain; hereafter I shall do your thinking for you. You will sit in my banquet hall, and you will laugh when I tell you to laugh. You will see the two women who loved you, but they will shrink from the touch of your clammy hands, from your cold, dead lips. And whenever you see them they will be with Skor in whose veins flows the bright blood of life.'

My plight seemed quite hopeless. The sword at my belly was long, keen, and two-edged. I might have grasped it, but its edges were so sharp that it would have slipped through my fingers, severing them as it plunged into my body. Yet that I intended doing. I would not wait like a sheep the lethal blow of the butcher.

'You do not reply,' said Skor. 'Very well, we will have it over quickly!' He drew back his sword hand for the thrust.

Duare was standing just behind him beside a table littered with the sort of junk to which Skor seemed partial – his crazy *objects d'art*. I was waiting to seize the blade when he thrust. Skor hesitated a moment, I presume to better enjoy my final agony; but in that he was disappointed. I would not give him that satisfaction; and so, to rob him of most of his pleasure, I laughed in his face.

At that moment Duare raised a heavy vase from the table, held it high above her, and crashed it down on Skor's head. Without a sound he sank to the floor.

I leaped across his body to take Duare into my arms, but with a palm against my breast she pushed me away.

'Do not touch me!' she snapped. 'If you want to get out of Kormor there is no time to be wasted. Come with me! I know where the girl you came to rescue is imprisoned.'

Her whole attitude toward me seemed to have changed, and my pride was piqued. In silence I followed her from the room. She led me into the corridor along which we had approached the room to which I had followed her and Skor. Opening a door at one side, she hurried along another corridor and stopped before a heavily bolted door.

'She is in here,' she said.

I drew the bolts and opened the door. Standing in the middle of the room beyond, looking straight at me, was Nalte. As she recognized me she gave a little cry of joy and, running toward me, threw her arms about me.

'Oh, Carson! Carson!' she cried. 'I knew that you would come; something told me that you would surely come.'

'We must hurry,' I told her. 'We must get out of here.'

I turned toward the door. Duare stood there, her chin in the air, her eyes flashing; but she said nothing. Nalte saw her then and recognized her. 'Oh, it is you!' she exclaimed. 'You are alive! I am so glad. We thought that you had been killed.'

Duare seemed puzzled by the evident sincerity of Nalte's manner, as though she had not expected that Nalte would be glad that she was alive. She softened a little. 'If we are to escape from Kormor, though I doubt that we can, we must not remain here,' she said. 'I think that I know a way out of the castle – a secret way that Skor uses. He showed me the door once during some strange mood of his insanity; but he has the key to the door on his person, and we must get that before we can do anything else.'

We returned to the room where we had left Skor's body, and as I entered it

I saw the Jong of Morov stir and try to rise. He was not dead, though how he had survived that shattering blow I do not know.

I ran toward him and threw him down. He was still only half conscious and made little or no resistance. I suppose I should have killed him, but I shrank from killing a defenseless man – even a fiend like Skor. Instead I bound and gagged him; then I searched him and found his keys.

After that Duare led us to the second floor of the palace and to a large room furnished in the bizarre taste that was Skor's. She crossed the apartment and drew aside a grotesque hanging, revealing a small door behind it.

'Here is the door,' she said; 'see if you can find a key to fit the lock.'

I tried several keys, and at last found the right one. The opened door revealed a narrow corridor which we entered after rearranging the hangings, and then closed the door behind us. A few steps brought us to the top of a spiral staircase. I went first, carrying Skor's sword which I had taken from him with his keys. The two girls followed closely behind me.

The stairway was lighted, for which I was glad, since it permitted us to move more rapidly and with greater safety. At the bottom was another corridor. I waited there until both girls stood beside me.

'Do you know where this corridor leads?' I asked Duare.

'No,' she replied. 'All that Skor said was that he could get out of the castle this way without any one seeing him – he always came and went this way. Practically everything that he did, the most commonplace things in life, he veiled with mystery and secrecy.'

'From the height of that stairway,' I said, 'I believe that we are below the ground level of the palace. I wish that we knew where this corridor ends, but there is only one way to find out. Come on!'

This corridor was but dimly illuminated by the light from the stairway, and the farther we went from the stairway the darker it became. It ran straight for a considerable distance, ending at the foot of a wooden stairway. Up this I groped my way only a few steps, when my head came in contact with a solid substance above me. I reached up and felt of the obstruction. It consisted of planking and was obviously a trap door. I tried to raise it, but could not. Then I searched around its edges with my fingers, and at last I found that which I sought – a latch. Tripping it, I pushed again; and the door gave. I opened it only an inch or two, but no light showed in the crack. Then I opened it wider and raised my head through the aperture.

Now I could see more, but not much more – only the dark interior of a room with a single small window through which the night light of Amtor showed dimly. Grasping the sword of the Jong of Morov more tightly, I ascended the stairway and entered the room. I heard no sound.

The girls had followed me and now stood just behind me. I could hear them breathing. We stood waiting, listening. Slowly my eyes became accustomed to the darkness, and I made out what I thought was a door beside the single window. I crossed to it and felt; it was a door.

Cautiously I opened it and looked out into one of the sordid streets of Kormor. I peered about in an effort to orient myself and saw that the street was one of those that extended directly away from the palace which I could see looming darkly behind its wall at my right.

'Come!' I whispered, and with the girls behind me I stepped out into the street and turned to the left. 'If we meet any one,' I cautioned, 'remember to walk like the dead, shuffle along as you will see me do. Keep your eyes on the ground; it is our eyes that will most surely betray us.'

'Where are we going?' asked Duare in a whisper.

'I am going to try to find the house through which I came into the city,' I replied; 'but I don't know that I can do so.'

'And if you can't?'

'Then we shall have to make an attempt to scale the city wall; but we shall find a way, Duare.'

'What difference will it make?' she murmured, half to herself. 'If we escape from here there will only be something else. I think I would rather be dead than go on any more.'

The note of hopelessness in her voice was so unlike Duare that it shocked me. 'You mustn't feel like that, Duare,' I expostulated. 'If we can get back to Havatoo you will be safe and happy, and I have a surprise there for you that will give you new hope.' I was thinking of the plane in which we might hope to find Vepaja, the country that I could see she had about despaired of ever seeing again.

She shook her head. 'There is no hope, no hope of happiness, ever, for Duare.'

Some figures approaching us along the dusty street put an end to our conversation. With lowered eyes and shuffling feet we neared them.

They passed, and I breathed again in relief.

It would be useless to recount our futile search for the house I could not find. All the remainder of the night we searched, and with the coming of dawn I realized that we must find a place to hide until night came again.

I saw a house with a broken door, no unusual sight in dismal Kormor; and investigation indicated that it was tenantless. We entered and ascended to the second floor. Here, in a back room, we prepared to await the ending of the long day that lay ahead of us.

We were all tired, almost exhausted; and so we lay down on the rough planks and sought to sleep. We did not talk; each seemed occupied with their own dismal thoughts. Presently, from their regular breathing, I realized that the girls were both asleep; and very shortly thereafter I must have fallen asleep myself.

How long I slept I do not know. I was awakened by footsteps in an adjoining room. Some one was moving about, and I heard mutterings as of a person talking to himself.

Slowly I rose to my feet, holding Skor's sword in readiness. Its uselessness against the dead did not occur to me, yet had it, I still would have felt safer with the sword in my hand.

The footsteps approached the door to the room in which we had sought sanctuary, and a moment later an old woman stopped upon the threshold and looked at me in astonishment.

'What are you doing here?' she demanded.

If she was surprised, no less was I; for old age was something I had never before seen in Amtor. Her voice awakened the girls, and I heard them rising to their feet behind me.

'What are you doing here?' repeated the old woman querulously. 'Get out of my house, accursed corpses! I'll have none of the spawn of Skor's evil brain in my house!'

I looked at her in astonishment. 'Aren't you dead?' I demanded.

'Of course I'm not dead!' she snapped.

'Neither are we,' I told her.

'Eh? Not dead?' She came closer. 'Let me see your eyes. No, they do not look like dead eyes; but they say that Skor has found some foul way in which to put a false light of life into dead eyes.'

'We are not dead,' I insisted.

'Then what are you doing in Kormor? I thought that I knew all of the living men and women here, and I do not know you. Are the women alive too?'

'Yes, we are all alive.' I thought quickly. I wondered if I might trust her with our secret and seek her aid. She evidently hated Skor, and we were already in her power if she wished to denounce us. I felt that we could not be much worse off in any event. 'We were prisoners of Skor. We escaped. We want to get out of the city. We are at your mercy. Will you help us? – or will you turn us over to Skor?'

'I won't turn you over to Skor,' she snapped. 'I wouldn't turn a dead mistal over to that fiend; but I don't know how I can help you. You can't get out of Kormor. The dead sentries along the wall never sleep.'

'I got into Kormor without being seen by a sentry,' I said. 'If I could only find the house I could get out again.'

'What house?' she demanded.

'The house at the end of the tunnel that runs under Gerlat kum Rov to Havatoo.'

'A tunnel to Havatoo! I never heard of such a thing. Are you sure?'

'I came through it last night.'

She shook her head. 'None of us ever heard of it – and if we who live here cannot find it, how could you, a stranger, hope to? But I'll help as much as I can. At least I can hide you and give you food. We always help one another here in Kormor, we who are alive.'

'There are other living people in Kormor?' I asked.

'A few,' she replied. 'Skor has not succeeded in hunting us all down yet. We live a mean life, always hiding; but it is life. If he found us he would make us like those others.'

The old woman came closer. 'I cannot believe that you are alive,' she said. 'Perhaps you are tricking me.' She touched my face, and then ran her palms over the upper part of my body. 'You are warm,' she said, and then she felt my pulse. 'Yes, you are alive.'

Similarly she examined Duare and Nalte, and at last she was convinced that we had told her the truth. 'Come,' she said, 'I will take you to a better place than this. You will be more comfortable. I do not use this house very often.'

She led us down stairs and out into a yard at the rear of which stood another house. It was a mean house, poorly furnished. She took us into a back room and told us to remain there.

'I suppose you want food,' she said.

'And water,' added Nalte. 'I have had none since yesterday evening.'

'You poor thing,' said the old woman. 'I'll get it for you. How young and pretty you are. Once I was young and pretty too.'

'Why have you aged?' I asked. 'I thought that all the people of Amtor held the secret of longevity.'

'Aye, but how may one obtain the serum in Kormor? We had it once, before Skor came; but he took it away from us. He said that he would create a new race that would not require it, for they would never grow old. The effects of my last innoculation have worn off, and now I am growing old and shall die. It is not so bad to die – if Skor does not find one's corpse. We of the living here bury our dead in secret beneath the floors of our houses. My mate and our two children lie beneath this floor. But I must go and fetch food and water for you. I shall not be gone long.' And with that, she left us.

'Poor old creature,' said Nalte. 'She has nothing to look forward to except the grave, with the chance that Skor may rob her of even that poor future.'

'How strange she looked!' There was a shocked expression in Duare's eyes as she spoke. 'So that is old age! I never saw it before. That is the way I should look some day, were it not for the serum! How ghastly! Oh, I should rather die than be like that. Old age! Oh, how terrible!'

Here was a unique experience. I was witnessing the reactions of a nineteen-year-old girl who had never before seen the ravages of old age, and I could not but wonder if the subconscious effect of old age on youth accustomed to seeing it was not similar. But these meditations were interrupted by the return of the old woman, and I caught a new insight into the character of Duare.

As the old woman entered the room, her arms laden, Duare ran forward and took the things from her. 'You should have let me come with you and help you,' she said. 'I am younger and stronger.'

Then she placed the food and water upon a table, and with a sweet smile she put an arm about the withered shoulders of the old crone and drew her toward a bench. 'Sit down,' she said. 'Nalte and I will prepare the food. You just sit here and rest until it is ready, and then we shall all eat together.'

The old woman looked at her in astonishment for a moment and then burst into tears. Duare dropped to the bench beside her and put her arms about her.

'Why do you cry?' she asked.

'I don't know why I cry,' sobbed the old creature. 'I feel like singing, but I cry. It has been so long since I have heard kind words, since any one has cared whether I was happy or sad, tired or rested.'

I saw the tears come to Duare's eyes and to Nalte's, and they had to busy themselves with the preparation of the food to hide their emotions.

That night a dozen of the living of Kormor came to the house of Kroona, the old woman who had befriended us. They were all very old, some of them older than Kroona. They laughed at Kroona's fears that Skor wanted them; and pointed out, as evidently they had many times before, that if it was old bodies Skor wanted he long since could have found them, for their old age was ample evidence that they were of the living. But Kroona insisted that they were all in danger; and I soon realized that it was her pet obsession, without which she would probably be more miserable than she was with it. She got a great thrill out of leading a life of constant danger and hiding first in one house and then in another.

But they were all of one opinion that we were in great danger, and the dear old things pledged themselves to help us in every way they could – to bring us food and water and hide us from our enemies. That was all that they could do, for none of them believed that it was possible to escape from Kormor.

Early the following morning a very old man, one of the visitors of the previous evening, hobbled into the house. He was perturbed and greatly excited. His palsied hands were trembling. 'They are searching the city for you,' he whispered. 'There is a terrible story of what you did to Skor and of what Skor will do to you when he finds you. All night and all day last night he lay bound and helpless where you left him; then one of his creatures found and released him. Now the whole city is being scoured for you. They may be here any minute.'

'What can we do?' asked Duare, 'Where can we hide?'

'You can do nothing,' said the old man, 'but wait until they come. There is no place in all Kormor that they will not search.'

'We can do something,' said Nalte; then she turned to our informant. 'Can you get us paints such as the corpses use to make themselves appear like living men?'

'Yes,' said the old man.

'Well, go quickly and fetch them,' urged Nalte.

The old man hobbled out of the room, mumbling to himself.

'It is the only way, Nalte,' I cried. 'I believe that if he returns in time we can fool them; dead men are not very bright.'

It seemed a long time before the old man came back; but he came finally, and he brought a large box of make-up with him. It was quite an elaborate affair which he said that he had obtained from a friend of his, a living man, whose craft was applying the make-up to corpses.

Quickly Nalte went to work on Duare and soon had transformed her into an old woman with lines and wrinkles and hollows. The hair was the most difficult problem to solve, but we finally succeeded in approximating the results we desired, though we used up all of the cosmetician's white pigment, rubbing it into our hair.

Duare and I together worked on Nalte, for we knew that we had no time to spare, the old man having brought word when he returned with the make-up that the searchers were working in the next block and coming our way; then Nalte and Duare transformed me into a very sad looking old man.

Kroona said that we should each have some task that we could be performing when the searchers arrived, so that we might appear natural. She gave Duare and Nalte some old rags which they might pretend to be fashioning into garments, and she sent me out into the yard to dig a hole. It was fortunate that she did so, because the association of ideas resulting reminded me that I must hide Skor's sword. Were that found we were doomed.

I wrapped it up in a piece of cloth and carried it out into the yard with me, and you may take my word for it that I dug one hole there in record time. When I had covered the sword with dirt I started digging another hole beside it and threw that dirt also on the spot above the weapon.

I had just finished when the yard gate was thrown open and a score of dead men came shuffling in. 'We are looking for the strangers who escaped from the palace,' said one. 'Are they here?'

I cupped my hand behind my ear and said, 'Eh?'

The fellow repeated his question, shouting very loud, and again I did the same thing and said, 'Eh?' Then he gave up and went on into the house, followed by the others.

I heard them searching in there, and every instant I expected to hear cries of excitement when one of them discovered and pierced the thin disguises of Duare and Nalte.

XX

Under Suspicion

Skor's creatures searched Kroona's house far more carefully than they would have searched that of one of their own kind, for Skor must have assumed that of all the people in Kormor the living would be most likely to aid the living; but at last they came out and went away. And I sat down on the pile of dirt I had dug and mopped the perspiration from my forehead, nor was it the sweat of toil. I think that for fifteen minutes I had come as near to sweating blood as a man can.

When I went into the house I found Duare, Nalte, and Kroona just sitting there in dazed silence. They couldn't seem to realize that we had passed through the ordeal successfully.

'Well,' I said, 'that's over.'

My voice seemed to break the spell.

'Do you know what saved us?' demanded Nalte.

'Why, our disguises, of course,' I replied.

'Yes,' she admitted, 'they helped, but our real salvation was the stupidity of the searchers. They scarcely looked at us. They were hunting for somebody who was *hidden*, and because we were not hiding they didn't give us a second thought.'

'Do you think we might remove the paint now?' asked Duare. 'It is very uncomfortable.'

'I think we should not remove it at all,' I replied. 'As we know, they won't find us in this search; so Skor may order another search, and next time we may not have time to disguise ourselves even if we are lucky enough to get the materials again.'

'I suppose you are right,' said Duare, 'and after all the discomfort is not much by comparison to what we have already gone through.'

'The disguises have one advantage,' said Nalte. 'We can move about more freely without danger of detection. We won't have to sit in this stuffy little back room all the time, and I for one am going to the front of the house and get a breath of fresh air.'

It was not a bad suggestion, and Duare and I joined Nalte while Kroona went about some household duties. The front room on the second floor, to which we went, overlooked the street. We could hear the searchers ransacking the house next door, and we could see the pedestrians shuffling along the dusty street.

Suddenly Nalte seized my arm and pointed. 'See that man?' she exclaimed in an excited whisper.

Shuffling along the street was a large corpse painted in the semblance of life. His trappings were finer than those ordinarily seen in Kormor. Only his peculiar gait revealed to the initiated eye the fact that he was not as alive as we.

'Yes, I see him,' I replied. 'What about him?'

'He is the man that abducted me from Havatoo!'

'Are you sure?' I demanded.

'Absolutely,' replied Nalte. 'As long as I live I shall never forget that face.'

A plan, perhaps I had better call it an inspiration, shot into my mind. 'I am going to follow him,' I said. 'I shall be back soon; hope for the best.' I turned and hurried from the room.

A moment later I was in the street. The fellow was only a short distance ahead of me. If my guess was correct he would lead me eventually to the entrance to the tunnel that leads to Havatoo. Perhaps not today, but if I learned where he lived today; then some other day.

His gait was more rapid than that of the average Kormoran, and he walked as though with a definite purpose in view. I judged that he was one of Skor's more successful experiments and that for this reason he had been chosen as one of the jong's agents in Havatoo, where the ordinary run of Kormoran corpses could not long have passed themselves off as living men.

As I followed him I noted carefully every detail of the street in which we were; so that I would not again be unable to return to my starting point. When presently he turned into a street leading toward the river my hopes rose, and I noted carefully the buildings at the intersection.

Near the river the fellow turned into a small alley, followed it to the next street, and then turned again toward the river. Directly ahead of us, even before he turned into it, I saw and recognized the building beneath which lay the Kormor end of the tunnel.

At the gateway leading into the yard before the house the man turned for the first time and looked behind him, I presume to see if he was being observed. Then he saw me.

There was nothing for me to do but keep on toward him. I kept my eyes on the ground and paid no attention to him as I approached him, though I could almost feel his gaze upon me. It seemed an eternity before I reached him. I was about to breathe a sigh of relief as I passed him, then he spoke to me.

'Who are you and what are you doing here?' he demanded.

'I am looking for another house to live in,' I cackled. 'The doors and the windows have all fallen off mine.'

'There are no houses here for you,' he snapped. 'Your kind is not allowed in this district. Get out of here and never let me see you here again.'

'Yes,' I replied meekly, and turned back.

To my great joy he let me go, and a moment later I had turned into the alley and was hidden from his view. But I had learned what I wanted to know, and my blood was tingling with happiness. Now only the worst of ill fortune could prevent me guiding Duare and Nalte back to the safety of Havatoo.

As I made my way through the streets of Kormor toward the house of Kroona my mind was filled with thoughts and plans for escape. I was determined to leave as soon as darkness fell, and already I was looking forward to and planning on what I should do upon my return to Havatoo.

As I entered Kroona's house I saw immediately, even before any one had a chance to speak, that something was amiss. Duare and Nalte both rushed toward me, and it was evident that both were perturbed. Kroona and the old man who had brought us the pigments with which we had disguised ourselves were cackling together excitedly.

'At last you are back!' cried Nalte. 'We thought that you would never come.'

'Perhaps it is not too late even now,' said Duare.

'I wanted them to come with me and let me hide them,' croaked Kroona, 'but neither one of them would leave without you. They said that if you were to be taken then they would be taken too.'

'What in the world are you all talking about?' I demanded. 'What has happened?'

'It is soon told,' said the old man who had brought us the make-up. 'The cosmetician from whom I borrowed the materials to change you into old people has betrayed us in order to curry favor with Skor. A man heard him tell his servant to go to the palace and inform Skor that he would lead Skor's men to this hiding place of yours. The man was a friend of mine and came and told me. Skor's men may be here at any minute now.'

I thought rapidly; then I turned to Duare and Nalte. 'Get your make-up off as quickly as you can,' I directed, 'and I will do the same.'

'But then we shall be lost for certain,' exclaimed Duare.

'On the contrary,' I replied as I commenced to remove the pigment from my blond head.

'They will know us at once without our disguises,' insisted Duare, but I was glad to see that both she and Nalte were following my example and removing the paint from their hair and faces.

'Our own youth will be the best disguise we can adopt in this emergency,' I explained. 'These creatures of Skor are none too intelligent, and having been sent to find three fugitives who have disguised themselves as very old people they will be looking only for those who appear very old. If we can get out of the house before they come I think we have a good chance to avoid detection.'

We worked rapidly and soon had the last vestiges of our disguises removed; then we thanked Kroona and the old man, bid them goodbye, and left the house. As we entered the street we saw a body of warriors approaching from the direction of the palace.

'We were not quite in time,' said Nalte. 'Shall we turn and run for it?'

'No,' I replied. 'That would only arouse their suspicions immediately and they would pursue and most certainly overtake us. Come! We shall go and meet them.'

'What!' demanded Duare in astonishment. 'Are we going to give ourselves up?'

'By no means,' I replied. 'We are going to take a great chance, but there is no alternative. If they see three people walking away from them they will investigate, and if they do that we may be recognized; but if they see us approaching them they will believe that we do not fear anything from them and will be convinced therefore that we are not those whom they seek. Walk with the shuffling gait of the dead, and keep your eyes on the ground. Duare, you walk ahead, Nalte a few paces behind you; I shall cross to the other side of the street. By separating we shall attract less attention; they are looking for three people whom they expect to find together.'

'I hope your reasoning is correct,' said Duare, but it was evident that she was skeptical. I was none too enthusiastic about the plan myself.

I crossed the street to the side along which the warriors were approaching, knowing that there was less likelihood that any of them would recognize me than that they would know Duare, who had been in Skor's palace for some time.

I must admit that I felt none too comfortable as the distance between me and the warriors steadily lessened, but I kept my eyes on the ground and shuffled slowly along.

As I came abreast of them their leader halted and addressed me. My heart stood still. 'Where is the house of Kroona?' he asked.

'I do not know,' I replied and shuffled on my way. Momentarily I expected to be seized, but the warriors went on their way and let me go on mine. My ruse had been successful!

As soon as I felt that it was safe I crossed to the opposite side of the street, and as I caught up with the two girls I told them to follow behind me but not too closely.

It still lacked an hour until sunset, and I did not dare risk approaching the entrance to the tunnel until after dark. In the meantime we must find a place to hide and keep off the streets where every moment we were in danger of arousing suspicion.

Turning into a side street I soon found a deserted house, of which there are many in Kormor; and presently we were in hiding again.

Both girls were dejected. I could tell by their silence and listlessness. The future must have seemed hopeless to them, yet they voiced no complaints.

'I have some good news for you,' I said.

Duare looked at me with scarcely any indication of interest, as though there never could be any good news for her again. She had been unusually silent since our escape from the palace. She seldom spoke unless directly addressed; and she avoided speech with Nalte as much as possible, although her manner toward her was not definitely unfriendly.

'What is the good news?' demanded Nalte.

'I have found the entrance to the tunnel to Havatoo,' I replied.

The effect of that statement upon Nalte was electrical, but it seemed to arouse only passive interest in Duare. 'In Havatoo,' she said, 'I shall be as far as ever from Vepaja.'

'But your life will not be in danger,' I reminded her.

She shrugged. 'I do not know that I care to live,' she replied.

'Don't be discouraged, Duare,' I begged. 'Once we are in Havatoo I am confident that I shall discover a way to find Vepaja and return you to your people.' I was thinking of the plane ready and waiting in its hangar on Kantum Lat, but I didn't say anything about it. I wanted to save it as a surprise for her; and, anyway, we were not yet in Havatoo.

The two hours that we waited until complete darkness enveloped the city were as long a two hours as I have ever spent; but at last it seemed safe to attempt to reach the silent, deserted house near the river front, where all our hopes were centered.

The street was deserted when we left the building where we had been hiding; I was certain of my way to our destination, and without delay or adventure we at last came in sight of the decaying structure that hid the entrance to our avenue of escape.

I led the girls into the buildings, and there we huddled in the dark, listening. I regretted then that I had been unable to retrieve the sword I had taken from Skor and buried in the yard of Kroona's home. It would have given me a feeling of far greater security than I now enjoyed.

Satisfied at last that we were the sole occupants of the building and that no one had followed us, I crossed to the doorway that hid the entrance to the tunnel, Duare and Nalte close behind me.

I had no difficulty in finding the latch, and a moment later we were descending into the dark corridor with liberty and safety almost in our grasp.

There was a chance that we might meet one of Skor's creatures returning from Havatoo; but I felt that everything was in our favor inasmuch as one of them had just crossed in the opposite direction, and there had never been any evidence that they were in Havatoo in great numbers. It was my opinion that the two that set upon Nalte and me were alone in that venture, and if that were true it was also doubtless true that Skor never had more than a couple of his retainers in Havatoo at the same time. I certainly hoped that I was right.

In silence, through the utter darkness, we groped our way along the cold, moist corridor beneath the River of Death. I moved more rapidly than I had when I had come through it to Kormor, for I knew now that no pitfalls lay in my path.

At last I felt the stairs leading upward at the tunnel's end, and a moment later I stopped behind the door that would let us into Havatoo. I did not wait; I did not listen. Nothing could have stopped me then. I would have grappled a dozen of the gruesome corpses of Kormor had they stood in my way, and I believe that I should have overcome them, so desperate was my mood.

But we met neither dead nor living as we stepped out onto the lower floor of the dismal building off the Havatoo Lat. Quickly we crossed to the front of the building and out through the door there to the street beyond, and a moment later we stood in the Havatoo Lat with its brilliant lights and its two streams of traffic.

We were a conspicuous trio in our mean garments of rags with which we had sought to disguise ourselves in Kormor, and many were the suspicious glances cast in our direction.

As quickly as I could I hailed a public conveyance and instructed the driver to take us to the home of Ero Shan, and as we settled down upon the cushions we relaxed for the first time in many a day.

We talked a great deal during the drive, particularly Nalte and I. Duare was very quiet. She spoke of the beauty of Havatoo and the wonders that surrounded us, all strange and new to her, but only briefly and then lapsed into silence again.

Our driver had eyed us suspiciously when we entered his car, and when he deposited us in front of the house of Ero Shan he behaved peculiarly.

But Ero Shan was delighted to see us. He ordered food and drink, and plied us with questions until he had had the whole story from us several times. He congratulated me upon finding Duare, but I could see that his greatest happiness lay in the return of Nalte.

The girls were tired and needed rest, and we were preparing to take them to Nalte's home when the first blow fell that was to put the lives of two of us in jeopardy and plunge us all from the heights of happiness to the depths of despair.

There was a summons at the main entrance, and presently a servant entered the room. Behind him was a file of warriors commanded by an officer.

Ero Shan looked up in surprise. He knew the officer and called him by name, asking him what brought him here with armed men.

'I am sorry, Ero Shan,' the man replied, 'but I have orders from the Sanjong itself to arrest three suspicious appearing people who were seen to enter your house earlier in the evening.'

'But,' exclaimed Ero Shan, 'no one has entered my house but Carson Napier, whom you know, and these two young women. They are all my friends.'

The officer was eyeing our mean apparel and evidently not without suspicion. 'These must be those I was sent to arrest if no one else has entered your house this evening,' he said.

There was nothing to do but accompany the warriors, and this we did. Ero Shan came with us, and a short time later we were before an investigating board of three men.

The complaining witness was the driver who had brought us from the house that hid the entrance to the tunnel to Ero Shan's. He said that he lived in the neighborhood, and having known of the abduction of Nalte he was immediately suspicious when he saw three people, garbed as we were, in the vicinity of the place.

He accused us of being spies from Kormor and insisted that we were but painted corpses like the man I had grappled with at the time of the abduction of Nalte.

The examining board listened to my story; then they examined Nalte and Duare briefly. They questioned Ero Shan concerning us, and without leaving the room they discharged Nalte and myself and ordered Duare back for a further examination by the official examining board the following day.

I thought that they seemed a little suspicious of Duare; and so did Ero Shan, though he only admitted this after we had returned the girls to Nalte's home and were alone.

'Justice sometimes miscarries in Havatoo,' he said gravely. 'The loathing that we feel for Kormor and everything connected with it colors all our decisions in matters concerning it. Duare admits having been in Kormor for some time. She admits having resided in the palace of Skor, the jong. The examining board knows nothing about her other than what she claims and what you tell them, but they do not know that they can believe either of you. You will recall that the result of your examination was not such as to create considerable confidence in you.'

'And you think that Duare may be in danger?' I asked.

'I cannot tell,' he replied. 'Everything may come out all right; but, on the other hand, if the board has the slightest suspicion concerning Duare it will order her destroyed, for our theory of justice is that it is better to do an injustice to a single individual than to risk the safety and welfare of many. Sometimes that policy is a cruel one, but results have demonstrated that it is better for the race than a policy of weak sentimentalism.'

I did not sleep well that night. The weight of a great fear for the outcome of tomorrow's trial oppressed me.

XXI

Flight

I was not permitted to accompany Duare to her examination. She was placed in charge of the same woman who had guarded Nalte at the time of her examination, Hara Es.

To pass the hours until the result should be made known, I went to the hangar to inspect my plane. It was in perfect condition. The motor hummed almost noiselessly. I could not, under ordinary circumstances, have withstood the urge to have the ship wheeled out onto the plain before the city for a trial flight; but my mind was so distraught with apprehension concerning the fate of Duare that I had no heart for anything.

I spent an hour alone in the hangar. None of my assistants was there, they having all returned to their ordinary duties after the completion of the plane. Then I returned to the house that I shared with Ero Shan.

He was not there. I tried to read, but I could not concentrate long enough to know what I was reading about. My eyes followed the strange Amtorian characters, but my thoughts were with Duare. At last I gave it up and walked in the garden. An unreasoning terror enveloped me like a shroud, numbing my faculties.

How long I walked I do not know, but at last my sad reveries were interrupted by the approach of footsteps through the house. I knew that Ero Shan must be coming to the garden. I stood waiting, looking toward the doorway through which he must come; and the instant that I saw him my heart turned cold. I read the confirmation of my worst fears in the expression on his face.

He came and laid a hand upon my shoulder. 'I have bad news for you, my friend,' he said.

'I know,' I replied; 'I read it in your eyes. They have ordered her destroyed?'

'It is a miscarriage of justice,' he said, 'but there is no appeal. We must accept the decision as the board's honest conviction that they are thus serving the best interests of the city.'

'Is there nothing I can do?' I asked.

'Nothing,' he replied.

'Won't they let me take her away from Havatoo?'

'No; they are so afraid of the contaminating influence of Skor and his creatures that they will never permit one to live that falls into their hands.'

'But she is not one of Skor's creatures!' I insisted.

'I am quite sure that they had their doubts, but the benefit of the doubt is given to the city and not to the accused. There is nothing more to be done.'

'Do you think they would let me see her?' I asked.

'It is possible,' he replied. 'For some reason she is not to be destroyed until tomorrow.'

'Will you try to arrange it for me, Ero Shan?'

'Certainly,' he replied. 'Wait here, and I will see what I can do.'

I have never spent such long and bitter hours as those while I was awaiting the return of Ero Shan. Never before had I felt so helpless and hopeless in the face of an emergency. Had these been ordinary men with whom I had to deal, I might have seen somewhere a ray of hope, but there was none here. Their uprightness precluded the possibility that I might influence even a minor guard by bribery; they could not be moved by an appeal to sentiment; the cold, hard logic of their reasoning left their minds impregnable fortresses of conviction that it was useless to assail.

I have said that I was hopeless, but that was not entirely true. Upon what my hope fed I do not know, but it seemed so impossible to believe that Duare was to be destroyed that my mind must in some slight measure have been stunned.

It was dark before Ero Shan returned. I could read neither hope nor despair in his expression as he entered the room where I had finally gone to await him. He appeared very serious and very tired.

'Well?' I demanded. 'What is the verdict?'

'I had a hard time of it,' he said. 'I had to go all the way up to the Sanjong, but at last I got permission for you to visit her.'

'Where is she? When may I see her?'

'I will take you to her now,' he replied.

After we entered his car I asked him how he had accomplished it.

'I finally took Nalte with me,' he replied. 'She knew more about you and all that you and Duare have passed through together than any one else in Havatoo. For a while I almost thought that she was going to persuade the Sanjong to reverse the verdict against Duare, and it was solely through her appeal that they at last gave their consent to this last meeting.

'I learned a great deal about you and Duare from Nalte, much more than you have ever told me; and I learned something else.'

'What was that?' I asked as he paused.

'I learned that I love Nalte,' he replied.

'And did you learn that she loves you?'

'Yes. Were it not for your unhappiness I should be quite the happiest man in Havatoo tonight. But what made you think that Nalte loved me?'

'She told me so.'

'And you did not tell me?' he asked reproachfully.

'I could not,' I replied, 'until after I knew that you loved her.'

'I suppose not. She told me that you were planning on taking her back to Andoo; but now that won't be necessary – she seems quite content to remain in Havatoo.'

We had been driving along the Korgan Lat toward the stadium, and now Ero Shan turned into a side street and stopped before a small house.

'Here we are,' he said. 'This is the house of Hara Es, in whose charge Duare has been placed. Hara Es is expecting you. I shall wait out here. You are to be allowed to remain with Duare for five vir.'

Five vir are a little over twenty minutes of Earth time. It seemed all too short, but it was better than nothing. I went to the door of the house, and in answer to my summons Hara Es admitted me.

'I have been expecting you,' she said. 'Come with me.'

She led me up to the second floor and, unlocking a door, pushed it open. 'Go in,' she directed. 'In five vir I shall come for you.'

As I entered the room Duare rose from a couch and faced me. Hara Es closed the door and locked it. I heard her footsteps as she descended the stairs. We were alone, Duare and I, for the first time in what seemed an eternity to me.

'Why did you come here?' asked Duare in a tired voice.

'You ask me that!' I exclaimed. 'You know why I came.'

She shook her head. 'You cannot do anything for me; no one can. I supposed you would come if you could help me, but as you can't I do not know why you came.'

'If for no other reason, because I love you. Is not that reason enough?'

'Do not speak to me of love,' she said, looking at me queerly.

I determined not to make her last moments more unhappy by pressing unwelcome attention upon her. I sought to cheer her, but she said that she was not unhappy.

'I am not afraid to die, Carson Napier,' she said. 'As it seems impossible that, living, I should ever return to Vepaja, I prefer to die. I am not happy. I can never be happy.'

'Why could you never be happy?' I demanded.

'That is my secret; I shall take it to the grave with me. Let us not speak of it any more.'

'I don't wish you to die, Duare. You must not die!' I exclaimed.

'I know that you feel that way, Carson, but what are we to do about it?'

'There must be something we can do. How many are there in this house besides Hara Es and yourself?'

'There is no one.'

Suddenly a mad hope possessed me. I searched the room with my eyes. It was bare of all except absolute necessities. I saw nothing with which I might carry out my plan. Time was flying. Hara Es would soon return. My eyes fell upon the saronglike scarf that Duare wore, the common outer garment of Amtorian women.

'Let me take this,' I said, stepping to her side.

'What for?' she demanded.

'Never mind. Do as I say! We have no time to argue.'

Duare had long since learned to submerge her pride when my tone told her that an emergency confronted us and to obey me promptly. She did so now. Quickly she unwound the scarf from about her and handed it to me.

'Here it is,' she said. 'What are you going to do with it?'

'Wait and see. Stand over there on the right side of the room. Here comes Hara Es now; I hear her on the stairs.'

I stepped quickly to one side of the door so that I should be behind it and hidden from Hara Es as she entered. Then I waited. More than my own life lay in the balance, yet I was not nervous. My heart beat as quietly as though I were contemplating nothing more exciting than a pleasant social visit.

I heard Hara Es stop before the door. I heard the key turn in the lock. Then the door swung open and Hara Es stepped into the room. As she did so I seized her by the throat from behind and pushed the door shut with my foot.

'Don't make a sound,' I warned, 'or I shall have to kill you.'

She did not lose, her poise for an instant. 'You are very foolish,' she said. 'This will not save Duare, and it will mean your death. You cannot escape from Havatoo.'

I made no reply, but worked quickly and in silence. I bound her securely with the scarf and then gagged her. When I had finished I raised her from the floor and placed her on the couch.

'I am sorry, Hara Es, for what I was compelled to do. I am going now to get rid of Ero Shan. He will know nothing of what I have done. Please be sure to inform the Sanjong that Ero Shan is in no way responsible for what has happened – or what is going to happen. I shall leave you here until I can get away from Ero Shan without arousing his suspicions.

'In the meantime, Duare, watch Hara Es closely until I return. See that she does not loosen her bonds.'

I stooped and picked the key from the floor where Hara Es had dropped it; then I quit the room, locking the door after me. A moment later I was in the car with Ero Shan.

'Let's get home as quickly as possible,' I said; then I lapsed into silence, a silence which Ero Shan, respecting what he thought to be my sorrow, did not break.

He drove rapidly, but it seemed an eternity before he steered the car into the garage at the house. There being no thieves in Havatoo, locks are unnecessary; so our garage doors stood wide open as they always were except in inclement weather. My car, facing toward the street, stood there.

'You have eaten scarcely anything all day,' said Ero Shan as we entered the house; 'suppose we have something now.'

'No, thanks,' I replied. 'I am going to my room. I could not eat now.'

He laid a hand upon my arm and pressed it gently, but he did not say anything; then he turned and left me. A wonderful friend was Ero Shan. I hated to deceive him, but I would have deceived any one to save Duare.

I went to my room, but only long enough to procure weapons; then I returned to the garage. As I stepped into my car I offered a prayer of thanks that the motors of Havatoo are silent. Like a wraith the car slipped out of the garage into the night, and as I passed the house I whispered a silent goodbye to Ero Shan.

Approaching the house of Hara Es I felt the first qualm of nervousness that had assailed me during this adventure, but the house seemed quite deserted as I entered it and ran up the stairs to the second floor.

Unlocking the door of the room in which I had left Duare and Hara Es I breathed a sigh of relief as I saw them both there. I crossed quickly to the couch and examined Hara Es's bonds. They appeared quite secure.

'Come!' I said to Duare. 'We have no time to waste.'

She followed me out of the room. I locked the door on Hara Es, found another sarong for Duare in a room on the first floor, and a moment later Duare and I were in my car.

'Where are we going?' she asked. 'We cannot hide in Havatoo. They will find us.'

'We are going to leave Havatoo forever,' I replied, and just then I saw a car pass us and draw up in front of the house we had just left. Two men were in it; one of them jumped out and ran to the door; then I opened the throttle. I had seen enough to turn me cold with apprehension.

Duare had seen, too. 'Now they will discover everything,' she said, 'and you will be killed. I knew that it would end in disaster. Oh, why didn't you let me die alone? I want to die.'

'But I won't let you!'

She said nothing more, and we sped through the now almost deserted streets of Havatoo toward the Kantum Lat and the Gate of the Physicists.

We had gone about two miles of the three that we must cover before we reached our destination when I heard an ominous sound such as I had never before heard in Havatoo. It sounded like the wailing of sirens such as are used on police cars in the large cities of America. Instantly I knew that it was an alarm, and I guessed that the man who had entered the house of Hara Es had discovered her and that our escape was known.

Closer and closer came the sounds of the wailing sirens as I drew up before the hangar where my plane stood; they seemed to be converging upon us from all directions. I was not surprised that they should have guessed where they would find us, for it would have been obvious to even duller minds than those of Havatoo that here lay my only chance to escape.

Fairly dragging Duare with me, I leaped from the car and ran into the hangar. The great doors, operated by mechanical means, rolled open at the touch of a button. I lifted Duare into the cockpit. She asked no questions; there was no time for questions.

Then I took my place at her side. I had designed the plane for training purposes; and it had two seats, each accommodating two people. I started the motor – and such a motor! Silent, vibrationless, and it required no warming up.

I taxied out into the Kantum Lat. The sirens were very close now. I saw the lights of cars bearing down upon us. As I started toward the Gate of the Physicists I heard the staccato hum of Amtorian rifles behind us. They were firing at us!

I nosed up; the wheels left the ground; the great gate loomed directly ahead. Up! Faster! Faster! I held my breath. Would we make it? Responding perfectly, the light ship climbed almost vertically in the last few seconds; she sped over the top of the lofty gate with only inches to spare. We were safe!

Far below, the lights of Havatoo lay behind us as I turned the ship's nose toward the shimmering ribbon that was the River of Death – the River of Life to us – that was to guide us down to that unknown sea where, I was confident, we would find Vepaja.

Duare had not spoken. I felt her arm against mine trembling. I reached over and laid a hand upon it. 'Why are you trembling?' I asked. 'You are quite safe now.'

'What is this thing we are in?' she asked. 'Why does it not fall to the ground and kill us? What keeps it up?'

I explained as best I could, telling her that there was no danger that it would fall; and then she drew a deep, long sigh of relief.

'If you say that we are safe; then I am afraid no longer,' she said. 'But tell me, why are you making this sacrifice for me?'

'What sacrifice?' I asked.

'You can never return to Havatoo now; they would kill you.'

'I do not want to return to Havatoo if you cannot live there in safety,' I replied.

'But what of Nalte?' she asked. 'You love one another, and now you can never see her again.'

'I do not love Nalte, nor does she love me. I love only you, Duare; and Nalte and Ero Shan love one another. We are on our way to Vepaja; I would rather take my chances of winning you there than live a Sanjong in Havatoo without you.'

She sat in silence for a long time; then, presently, she turned and looked up into my face. 'Carson!' she said in a low voice.

'Yes, Duare, what is it?'

'I love you!'

I could not believe that I had heard aright. 'But, Duare, you are the daughter of a jong of Vepaja!' I exclaimed.

'That I have known always,' she said, 'but I have just learned that above all things else I am a woman.'

I took her in my arms then. I could have held her thus forever, as our marvelous plane raced onwards toward Vepaja and home.

CARSON OF VENUS

To Florence Gilbert Burroughs

FOREWORD

India is a world unto itself, apart in manners, customs, occultism from the world and life with which we are familiar. Even upon far Barsoom or Amtor might be found no more baffling mysteries than those which lie hidden in the secret places of the brains and lives of her people. We sometimes feel that what we do not understand must be bad; that is our heritage from the ignorance and superstition of the painted savages from which we are descended. Of the many good things that have come to us out of India I am concerned at present with but one – the power which old Chand Kabi transmitted to the son of an English officer and his American wife to transmit his thoughts and visualizations to the mind of another at distances even as great as those which separated the planets. It is to this power we owe the fact that Carson Napier has been able to record, through me, the story of his adventures upon the planet Venus.

When he took off from Guadalupe Island in his giant rocket ship for Mars, I listened to the story of that epochal flight that ended, through an error in calculation, upon Venus. I followed his adventures there that started in the island kingdom of Vepaja where he fell desperately in love with Duare, the unattainable daughter of the king. I followed their wanderings across seas and land masses into the hostile city of Kapdor, and Kormor, the city of the dead, to glorious Havatoo, where Duare was condemned to death through a strange miscarriage of justice. I thrilled with excitement during their perilous escape in the aeroplane that Carson Napier had built at the request of the rulers of Havatoo. And always I suffered with Napier because of Duare's unalterable determination to look upon his love as an insult to the virgin daughter of the king of Vepaja. She repulsed him constantly because she was a princess, but in the end I rejoiced with him when she realized the truth and acknowledged that though she could not forget that she was a princess she had discovered that she was a woman first. That was immediately after they had escaped from Havatoo and were winging their way above the River of Death toward an unknown sea in seemingly hopeless search for Vepaja, where Duare's father, Mintep, ruled.

Months passed. I commenced to fear that Napier had crashed in his new ship, and then I began to have messages from him again which I shall record for the benefit of posterity as nearly in his own words as I can recall them.

I

Disaster

Everyone who has ever flown will recall the thrill of his first flight over familiar terrain; viewing the old scenes from a new angle that imparted a strangeness and a mystery to them as of a new world; but always there was the comforting knowledge that the airport was not too far away and that even in the event of a forced landing one would know pretty well where he was and how to get home.

But that dawn that Duare and I took off from Havatoo to the accompaniment of the staccato hum of Amtorian rifles, I was actually flying over an unknown world; and there was no landing field and no home. I believe that this was the happiest and most thrilling moment of my life. The woman I loved had just told me that she loved me, I was once again at the controls of a ship, I was free, I was flying in safety above the innumerable menaces that haunt the Amtorian scene. Undoubtedly, other dangers lay ahead of us in our seemingly hopeless quest for Vepaja, but for the moment there was nothing to mar our happiness or arouse forebodings. At least, not in me. With Duare it may have been a little different. She may have had forebodings of disaster. It would not be strange if she had, for up until the very instant that we rose to top the walls of Havatoo she had had no conception that there might exist any contrivance in which man might leave the ground and fly through the air. It was naturally something of a shock to her; but she was very brave, and content, too, to accept my word that we were safe.

The ship was a model of perfection, such a ship as will one day be common along the airways of old Earth when science has progressed there as far as it has in Havatoo. Synthetic materials of extreme strength and lightness entered into her construction. The scientists of Havatoo assured me that she would have a life of at least fifty years without overhaul or repairs other than what might be required because of accident. The engine was noiseless and efficient beyond the dreams of Earthmen. Fuel for the life of the ship was aboard; and it took up very little space, for it could all be held in the palm of one hand. This apparent miracle is scientifically simple of explanation. Our own scientists are aware of the fact that the energy released by combustion is only an infinitesimal fraction of that which might be generated by the total annihilation of a substance. In the case of coal it is as eighteen thousand millions are to one. The fuel for my engine consists of a substance known as *lor*, which contains an element called *yor-san*, as yet unknown to Earthmen, and another element, *vik-ro*, the action of which upon *yor-san* results in absolute annihilation of the *lor*.

Insofar as the operation of the ship was concerned, we might have flown on for fifty years, barring adverse weather conditions; but our weakness lay in the fact that we had no provisions. The precipitancy of our departure had precluded any possibility of provisioning the ship. We had escaped with our lives and what we had on, and that was all; but we were very happy. I didn't want to spoil it by questioning the future. But, really, we had a great many questions to ask of the future; and Duare presently raised one quite innocently enough.

'Where are we going?' she asked.

'To look for Vepaja,' I told her. 'I am going to try to take you home.'

She shook her head. 'No, we can't go there.'

'But that is the one place you have been longing to go ever since you were kidnapped by the klangan,' I reminded her.

'But not now, Carson. My father, the jong, would have you destroyed. We have spoken of love to one another, and no man may speak of love to the daughter of the jong of Vepaja before she is twenty. You know that well enough.'

'I certainly should,' I teased her; 'you have told me often enough.'

'I did it for your own safety, but nevertheless I always liked to hear you say it,' she admitted.

'From the first,' I asked.

'From the first. I have loved you from the first, Carson.'

'You are an adept at dissimulation. I thought you hated me; and yet, sometimes I wondered.'

'And because I love you, you must never fall into the hands of my father.'

'But where can we go, Duare? Do you know a single spot in all this world where we should be safe? There is none; and in Vepaja you, at least, will be safe. I shall have to take the chance of winning your father over.'

'It could never be done,' she declared. 'The unwritten law that decrees this thing is as old as the ancient empire of Vepaja. You have told me of the gods and goddesses of the religions of your world. In Vepaja the royal family occupies a similar position in the minds and hearts of the people, and this is especially true of the virgin daughter of a jong – she is absolutely sacrosanct. To look at her is an offense; to speak to her is a crime punishable by death.'

'It's a crazy law,' I snapped. 'Where would you be now, had I abided by its dictates? Dead. I should think your father would feel some obligation toward me.'

'As a father, he would; but not as a jong.'

'And I suppose he is a jong first,' I said, a little bitterly.

'Yes, he is a jong first; and so we may not return to Vepaja,' she said with finality.

What an ironical trick Fate had played upon me. With many opportunities in two worlds to pick a girl for me to fall in love with, she had ended up by choosing a goddess. It was tough, yet I wouldn't have had it otherwise. To have loved Duare, and to know that she loved me, was better than a lifetime with any other woman.

Duare's decision that we must not return to Vepaja had left me in something of a quandary. Of course I didn't know that I could have found Vepaja anyway, but as least it was something to aim at. Now I had nothing. Havatoo was the grandest city I had ever seen; but the unbelievable decision of the judges who had examined Duare after I had rescued her from the City of the Dead, and our escape, made it impossible for us ever to return. To hunt for a hospitable city in this strange world seemed useless and hopeless. Venus is a world of contradictions, anomalies, and paradoxes. In the midst of scenes of peace and beauty, one meets the most fearsome beasts; among a friendly, cultured people exist senseless and barbarous customs; in a city peopled by men and women of super-intelligence and sweetness the quality of mercy is utterly unknown to its tribunals. What hope had I, then, of finding a safe retreat for Duare and myself? I determined then to return Duare to Vepaja, that she, at least, might be saved.

We were flying south along the course of Gerlat kum Rov, The River of Death, toward the sea to which I knew the waters must eventually guide me. I was flying low, as both Duare and I wished to see the country rolling majestically beneath us. There were forests and hills and plains and, in the distance, mountains; while overall, like the roof of a colossal tent, stretched the inner cloud envelope that entirely surrounds the planet; and which, with the outer cloud bank, tempers the heat of the sun and makes life possible on Venus. We saw herds of animals grazing on the plains, but we saw no cities and no men. It was a vast wilderness that stretched below us, beautiful but deadly – typically Amtorian.

Our course was due south, and I believed that when we reached the sea we would but have to continue on across it to find Vepaja. Knowing that Vepaja was an island, and always having in mind that some day I might wish to return to it, I had designed my ship with retractable pontoons as well as ordinary landing gear.

The sight of the herds below us suggested food and stimulated my appetite. I asked Duare if she were hungry. She said she was – very – but asked what good it would do her.

'There's our dinner down there,' I said, pointing.

'Yes, but by the time we get down there it will be gone,' she said. 'Wait till they catch a glimpse of this thing. There won't be one of them within miles by the time you get this thing on the ground – unless it scares some of them to death.'

She didn't say miles, of course; she said *klookob, kob* being a unit of distance equivalent to 2.5 Earth miles, the prefix *kloo* denoting the plural. But she did say 'this thing' in Amtorian.

'Please don't call my beautiful ship "this thing,"' I begged.

'But it is not a ship,' she demurred. 'A ship goes on water. I have a name for it, Carson – it is an *anotar.*'

'Splendid!' I applauded. '*Anotar* it shall be.'

It was a good name, too; for *notar* means ship, and *an* is the Amtorian word for bird – birdship. I thought this better than airship, possibly because Duare had coined it.

I had an elevation of about a thousand feet; but as my motor was absolutely noiseless, none of the animals beneath us was yet aware of the strange thing hovering above them. As I started to spiral downward, Duare gave a little gasp and touched my arm. She didn't seize it, as some women might have; she just touched it, as though the contact gave her assurance. It must have been rather a terrifying experience for one who had never even seen an airship before that morning.

'What are you going to do?' she asked.

'I'm going down after our dinner. Don't be frightened.'

She said no more, but she still kept her hand on my arm. We were dropping rapidly when suddenly one of the grazing animals looked up; and, at sight of us, gave a loud snort of warning and went careering off across the plain. Then they all stampeded. I straightened out and went after them, dropping down until I was just above their backs. At the altitude at which we had been flying, the ground speed had probably seemed slow to her; so that now that we were but a few feet above ground it surprised her to find that we could easily outdistance the fleetest of the racing beasts.

I do not consider that it is very sporting to shoot animals from an airplane, but I was not indulging in sport – I was after food, and this was about the only way that I could get it without endangering our lives by stalking on foot; so it was without compunction that I drew my pistol and brought down a fat young yearling of some strange herbivorous species unknown to our world; at least, I guess it was a yearling – it looked as though it should be. The chase had brought us quite close to a fringe of forest that grew along the banks of a tributary of The River of Death; so that I had to bank quite sharply to avoid piling up among the trees. When I glanced at Duare she was quite white; but she was keeping a stiff upper lip. By the time I landed beside my kill, the plain was deserted.

Leaving Duare in the cockpit, I got out to bleed and butcher the animal. It was my intention to cut off as much meat as I thought would remain fresh until we could use it and then take off and fly to a more suitable temporary campsite.

I was working close beside the plane, and neither Duare nor I faced the forest which lay but a short distance behind us. Of course, we were careless in not maintaining a better watch; but I suppose we were both intent on my butchering operations, which, I must admit, were doubtless strange and wonderful to behold.

The first intimation I had of impending danger was a frightened cry of 'Carson!' from Duare. As I wheeled toward her, I saw fully a dozen warriors coming for me. Three of them were right on top of me with raised swords. I saw no chance of defending myself; and went down beneath those swords like a felled ox, but not before the brief glimpse I had of my attackers revealed the astonishing fact that they were all women.

I must have lain there unconscious for more than an hour, and when I regained consciousness I found myself alone – the warriors and Duare were gone.

II

Warrior Women

I came at that moment to being as nearly spiritually crushed as I ever had been before in my life. To have Duare and happiness snatched from me after a few brief hours, at the very threshold of comparative security, completely unnerved me for the moment. It was the more serious aspect of the situation that gave me control of myself once more – the fate of Duare.

I was pretty badly mussed up. My head and the upper part of my body were caked with dried blood from several nasty sword cuts. Why I had not been killed I shall never understand, and I am certain that my attackers had left me for dead. My wounds were quite severe, but none of them was lethal. My skull was intact; but my head ached frightfully, and I was weak from shock and loss of blood.

An examination of the ship showed that it had not been damaged or tampered with; and as I glanced around the plain I saw that which convinced me that its presence there had doubtless saved my life, for there were several savage-appearing beasts pacing to and fro some hundred yards away eyeing me hungrily. It must have been the, to them, strange monster standing guard over me that kept them at bay.

The brief glimpse I had had of the warrior women suggested that they were not mere savages but had attained at least some degree of civilization – their apparel and arms bespoke that. From this I assumed that they must live in a village; and as they were on foot, it was reasonable to suppose that their village was at no great distance. I was sure that they must have come out of the forest behind the ship and therefore it was in this direction I must search for Duare first.

We had seen no village before landing, as it seemed almost certain that we should have had one of any size existed within a few miles of our position, for both of us had been constantly on the lookout for signs of the presence of human beings. To prosecute my search on foot, especially in view of the presence of the savage carnivores hungrily anticipating me, would have been the height of foolishness; and if the village of the warrior women were in the open I could find it more quickly and more easily from the plane.

I was rather weak and dizzy as I took my place at the controls, and only such an emergency as now confronted me could have forced me into the air in the condition in which I was. However, I made a satisfactory take-off; and once in the air my mind was so occupied by my search that I almost forgot my hurts. I flew low over the forest and as silently as a bird on the wing. If there were a village and if it were built in the forest, it might be difficult or even impossible to locate it from the air, but because of the noiselessness of my ship it might be possible to locate a village by sound could I fly low enough.

The forest was not of great extent and I soon spanned it, but I saw no village nor any sign of one. Beyond the forest was a range of hills, and through a pass in them I saw a well-worn trail. This I followed; but I saw no village, though the landscape lay spread before me for miles around. The hills were cut with little canyons and valleys. It was rough country where one would least expect to find a village; and so I gave up the search in this direction and turned the nose of my ship back toward the plain where Duare had been captured, intending to start my search from there in another direction.

I was still flying very low, covering once more the ground I had just been over, when my attention was attracted by the figure of a human being walking rapidly across a level mesa. Dropping still lower, I saw that it was a man. He was walking very rapidly and constantly casting glances behind. He had not discovered the ship. Evidently he was too much concerned with whatever was behind him, and presently I saw what it was – one of those ferocious lion-like creatures of Amtor, a tharban. The beast was stalking him; but I knew that it would soon charge, and so I dropped quickly in a steep dive. Nor was I a moment too soon.

As the beast charged, the man turned to face it with his pitifully inadequate spear, for he must have known that flight was futile. I had drawn my Amtorian pistol, charged with its deadly R-ray; and as I flattened out just above the tharban, narrowly missing a crack-up, I let him have it. I think it was more luck than skill that permitted me to hit him at all; and as he rolled over and over on the ground, I banked, circled the man and made a landing behind him. He was the first human being I had seen since the capture of Duare, and I wanted to question him. He was alone, armed only with primitive weapons; and, so, absolutely in my power.

I don't know why he didn't run away; for that airship must have been an appalling thing to him; but he stood his ground even as I taxied up and stopped near him. It may have been that he was just paralyzed by fright. He was a small, rather insignificant looking fellow wearing a loincloth so voluminous as to appear almost a short skirt. About his throat were several necklaces of colored stones and beads, while armlets, bracelets and anklets similarly fabricated adorned his limbs. His long black hair was coiled in two knots, one upon either temple; and these were ornamented with tiny, colored feathers stuck into them like arrows in a target. He carried a sword, a spear, and a hunting knife.

As I descended from the ship and approached him, he backed away; and his spear arm started back menacingly. 'Who are you?' he asked. 'I don't want to kill you, but if you come any closer I'll have to. What do you want?'

'I don't want to harm you,' I assured him; 'I just want to talk to you.' We spoke in the universal language of Amtor.

'What do you want to talk to me about? But first tell me why you killed the tharban that was about to kill and eat me?'

'So that it wouldn't kill and eat you.'

He shook his head. 'That is strange. You do not know me; we are not friends; so why should you wish to save my life?'

'Because we are both men,' I told him.

'That is a good idea,' he admitted. 'If all men felt that way we would be treated better than we are. But even then, many of us would be afraid. What is that thing you were riding in? I can see now that it is not alive. Why does it not fall to the ground and kill you?'

I had neither the time nor inclination to explain the science of aerodromics to him; so I told him it stayed up because I made it stay up.

'You must be a very wonderful man,' he said admiringly. 'What is your name?'

'Carson – and yours?'

'Lula,' he replied, and then, 'Carson is a strange name for a man. It sounds more like a woman's name.'

'More so than Lula?' I asked, restraining a smile.

'Oh, my, yes; Lula is a very masculine name. I think it is a very sweet name, too; don't you?'

'Very,' I assured him. 'Where do you live, Lula?'

He pointed in the direction from which I had just come after abandoning hope of finding a village there. 'I live in the village of Houtomai that is in The Narrow Canyon.'

'How far is it?'

'About two *klookob*,' he estimated.

Two *klookob!* That would be five miles of our system of linear measurement, and I had flown back and forth over that area repeatedly and hadn't seen any sign of a village.

'A little while ago I saw a band of warrior women with swords and spears,' I said. 'Do you know where they live?'

'They might live in Houtomai,' he said, 'or in one of several other villages. Oh, we Samary have many villages; we are very powerful. Was one of the women large and powerful and with a deep scar on the left side of her face?'

'I really didn't have much opportunity to observe them closely,' I told him.

'Well, perhaps not. If you'd gotten too close to them you'd be dead now, but

I thought maybe Bund might have been with them; then I would have known that they were from Houtomai. Bund, you see, is my mate. She is very strong, and really should be chief.' He said *jong*, which means king; but chief seems a better title for the leader of a savage tribe, and from my brief intercourse with the ladies of the Samary I could vouch for their savagery.

'Will you take me to Houtomai?' I asked.

'Oh, mercy, no,' he cried. 'They'd kill you, and after your having saved my life I couldn't think of exposing you to danger.'

'Why would they want to kill me?' I demanded. 'I never did anything to them and don't intend to.'

'That doesn't mean anything to the women of the Samary,' he assured me. 'They don't like men very well, and they kill every strange man they find in our country. They'd kill us, too, if they weren't afraid the tribe would become extinct. They do kill some of us occasionally, if they get mad enough. Bund tried to kill me yesterday, but I could run too fast for her. I got away, and I've been hiding out since. I think perhaps she's gotten over her anger by now; so I'm going to sneak back and see.'

'Suppose they captured a strange woman,' I asked, 'what would they do with her?'

'They'd make a slave of her and make her work for them.'

'Would they treat her well?'

'They don't treat anyone well – except themselves; they live on the fat of the land,' he said, resentfully.

'But they wouldn't kill her?' I asked. 'You don't think they'd do that, do you?'

He shrugged. 'They might. Their tempers are very short; and if a slave makes a mistake, she'd certainly be beaten. Often they beat them to death.'

'Are you very fond of Bund?' I asked him.

'Fond of Bund! Who ever heard of a man being fond of a woman? I hate her. I hate them all. But what can I do about it? I must live. If I went to another country, I'd be killed. If I stay here and try to please Bund, I am fed and protected and have a place to sleep. And then, too, we men do have a little fun once in a while. We can sit around and talk while we're making sandals and loincloths, and sometimes we play games – that is, when the women are out hunting or raiding. Oh, it's better than being dead, anyhow.'

'I'm in trouble, Lula; and I'm wondering if you won't help me. You know we men should stick together.'

'What do you want me to do?' he demanded.

'I want you to lead me to the village of Houtomai.'

He looked at me suspiciously, and hesitated.

'Don't forget that I saved your life,' I reminded him.

'That's right,' he said. 'I do owe you something – a debt of gratitude, at least. But why do you want to go to Houtomai?'

'I want to see if my mate is there. She was stolen by some warrior woman this morning.'

'Well, why do you want to get her back? I wish someone would steal Bund.'

'You wouldn't understand, Lula,' I told him; 'but I certainly do want to get her back. Will you help me?'

'I could take you as far as the mouth of The Narrow Canyon,' he said; 'but I couldn't take you into the village. They'd kill us both. They'll kill you when you get there, anyway. If you had black hair you might escape notice, but that funny yellow hair of yours would give you away the very first thing. Now, if you had black hair, you could sneak in after dark and come into one of the men's caves. That way you might escape notice for a long time. Even if some of the women saw you, they wouldn't know the difference. They don't pay much attention to any but their own men.'

'But wouldn't the men give me away?'

'No; they'd think it was a great joke – fooling the women. If you were found out, we'd just say you fooled us, too. My, I wish you had black hair.'

I, too, wished then that I had black hair, if that would help me get into the village of Houtomai. Presently, a plan occurred to me.

'Lula,' I asked. 'Did you ever see an anotar before?' nodding toward the ship.

He shook his head. 'Never.'

'Want to have a look at it?'

He said he'd like to; so I climbed into the cockpit, inviting him to follow me. When he had seated himself beside me, I buckled the safety belt across him to demonstrate it as I was explaining its purpose.

'Would you like to take a ride?' I asked.

'Up in the air?' he demanded. 'Mercy, I should say not.'

'Well, just along the ground?'

'Just a little way along the ground?'

'Yes,' I promised, 'just a little way along the ground,' and I wasn't lying to him. I taxied around until we were headed into the wind; then I gave her the gun.

'Not so fast!' he screamed; and he tried to jump out, but he didn't know how to unfasten the safety belt. He was so busy with it that he didn't look for several seconds. When he did, we were a hundred feet off the ground and climbing rapidly. He gave one look, screamed, and closed his eyes. 'You lied to me,' he cried. 'You said we'd go just a little way along the ground.'

'We ran only a little way along the ground,' I insisted. 'I didn't promise that I wouldn't go into the air.' It was a cheap trick, I'll admit; but there was more than life at stake for me, and I knew that the fellow was perfectly safe. 'You needn't be afraid,' I reassured him. 'It's perfectly safe. I've flown millions of *klookob* in perfect safety. Open your eyes and look around. You'll get used to it in a minute of two, and then you'll like it.'

He did as I bid, and though he gasped a bit at first he soon became interested and was craning his neck in all directions looking for familiar landmarks.

'You're safer here than you would be on the ground,' I told him; 'neither the women nor the tharbans can get you.'

'That's right,' he admitted.

'And you should be very proud, too, Lula.'

'Why?' he demanded.

'As far as I know, you're the third human being ever to fly in the air in Amtor, excepting the klangan; and I don't count them as human, anyway.'

'No,' he said, 'they're not – they're birds that can talk. Where are you taking me?'

'We're there. I'm coming down now.' I was circling above the plain where I had made the kill before Duare was stolen. A couple of beasts were feeding on the carcass, but they took fright and ran away as the ship dropped near them for a landing. Jumping out, I cut strips of fat from the carcass, threw them into the cockpit, climbed in and took off. By this time, Lula was an enthusiastic aeronaut, and if it hadn't been for the safety belt he would have fallen out in one of his enthusiastic attempts to see everything in all directions at one and the same time. Suddenly, he realized that we were not flying in the direction of Houtomai.

'Hey!' he cried. 'You're going in the wrong direction – Houtomai is over there. Where are you going?'

'I'm going to get black hair,' I told him.

He gave me a frightened look. I guess he thought he was up in the air with a maniac; then he subsided, but he kept watching me out of the corner of an eye.

I flew back to The River of Death, where I recalled having seen a low, flat island; and, dropping my pontoons, landed on the water and taxied into a little cove that indented the island. I managed, after a little maneuvering, to get ashore with a rope and tie the ship to a small tree; then I got Lula to come ashore and build me a fire. I could have done it myself, but these primitive men accomplish it with far greater celerity than I ever could acquire. From a bush I gathered a number of large, wax-like leaves. When the fire was burning well, I took most of the fat and dropped it in piece by piece and very laboriously and slowly accumulated soot on the waxy faces of the leaves. It took much longer that I had hoped it would, but at last I had enough for my purpose. Mixing the soot with a small quantity of the remaining fat I rubbed it thoroughly into my hair, while Lula watched me with a broadening grin.

From time to time I used the still surface of the cove for a mirror, and when I had completed the transformation I washed the soot from my hands and face, using the ashes of the fire to furnish the necessary lye to cut the greasy mess. At the same time, I washed the blood from my face and body. Now I not only looked, but felt, like a new man. I was rather amazed to realize that during all the excitement of the day I had almost forgotten my wounds.

'Now, Lula,' I said, 'climb aboard and we'll see if we can find Houtomai.'

The take-off from the river was rather exciting for the Amtorian, as I had to make a very long run of it because of the smoothness of the water, throwing spray in all directions; but at last we were in the air and headed for Houtomai. We had a little difficulty in locating The Narrow Canyon because from this new vantage point the ordinary familiar terrain took on a new aspect for Lula, but at last he gave a yell and pointed down. I looked and saw a narrow canyon with steep walls, but I saw no village.

'Where's the village?' I asked.

'Right there,' replied Lula, but still I could not see it; 'but you can't see the caves very well from here.'

Then I understood – Houtomai was a village of cave dwellers. No wonder I had flown over it many times without recognizing it. I circled several times studying the terrain carefully, and also watching the time. I knew that it must be quite close to sundown, and I had a plan. I wanted Lula to go into the canyon with me and show me the cave in which he dwelt. Alone, I could never have found it. I was afraid that if I brought him to the ground too soon he might take it into his head to leave for home at once; then there would have been trouble, and I might have lost his help and co-operation.

I had found what I considered a relatively safe place to leave the ship, and as night was falling I brought her into a beautiful landing. Taxiing to a group of trees, I tied her down as best I could; but I certainly hated to go off and leave that beautiful thing alone in this savage country. I was not much concerned for fear that any beast would damage it. I was sure they would be too much afraid of it to go near it for a long while, but I didn't know what some ignorant human savages might do to it if they found it there. However, there was nothing else to be done.

Lula and I reached The Narrow Canyon well after dark. It was not a very pleasant trip, what with savage hunting beasts roaring and growling in all directions and Lula trying to elude me. He was commencing to regret his rash promises of help and think of what would certainly happen to him if it were discovered that he had brought a strange man into the village. I had to keep constantly reassuring him that I would protect him and swear by all that an Amtorian holds holy that I had never seen him, in the event that I should be questioned by the women.

We reached the foot of the cliff, in which the caves of the Houtomaians were carved, without exciting incident. Some fires were burning on the ground – two fires, a large one and a small one. Around the large fire were grouped a number of strapping women, squatting, lying, standing. They shouted and laughed in loud tones as they tore at pieces of some animal that had been cooking over the fire. Around the smaller fire sat a few little men. They were very quiet; and when they spoke, it was in low tones. Occasionally, one of them would giggle, and then they would all look apprehensively in the direction of the women, but the latter paid no more attention to them than as though they had been so many guinea pigs.

To this group of men, Lula led me. 'Say, nothing,' he warned his unwelcome guest, 'and try not to call attention to yourself.'

I kept to the rear of those gathered about the fire, seeking always to keep my face in shadow. I heard the men greet Lula, and from their manner I judged that a bond of friendship, welded from their common misery and degradation, united them. I looked about in search of Duare, but saw nothing of her.

'How is Bund's humor?' I heard Lula inquire.

'As bad as ever,' replied one of the men.

'Were the raids and the hunting good today? Did you hear any of the women say?' continued Lula.

'They were good,' came the reply. 'There is plenty of meat now, and Bund brought in a woman slave that she captured. There was a man with her, whom they killed, and the strangest contraption that anyone ever beheld. I think even the women were a little afraid of it from what they said. At any rate, they evidently got away from it as quickly as they could.'

'Oh, I know what that was,' said Lula; 'It was an anotar.'

'How do you know what it was?' demanded one of the men.

'Why – er – can't you take a joke?' demanded Lula in a weak voice.

I smiled as I realized how nearly Lula's vanity had caused him to betray himself. It was evident that while he may have trusted his friends, he did not therefore trust them implicitly. And I smiled also from relief, for I knew now that I had come to the right village and that Duare was here – but where? I wanted to question these men, but if Lula could not trust them, how might I? I wanted to stand up and shout Duare's name. I wanted her to know that I was here, eager to serve her. She must think me dead; and, knowing Duare as I did, I knew that she might take her own life because of hopelessness and despair. I must get word to her somehow. I edged toward Lula, and when I was close to him whispered in his ear.

'Come away. I want to talk to you,' I said.

'Go away. I don't know you,' whispered Lula.

'You bet you know me; and if you don't come with me, I'll tell 'em all where you've been all afternoon and that you brought me here.'

'Oh, you wouldn't do that!' Lula was trembling.

'Then come with me.'

'All right,' said Lula, and rising walked off into the shadows beyond the fire.

I pointed toward the women. 'Is Bund there?' I asked.

'Yes, the big brute with her back toward us,' replied Lula.

'Would her new slave be in Bund's cave?'

'Probably.'

'Alone?' I asked.

'No, another slave whom Bund could trust would be watching her, so that she couldn't escape.'

'Where is Bund's cave?'

'High up, on the third terrace.'

'Take me to it,' I directed.

'Are you crazy, or do you think I am?' demanded Lula.

'You are allowed on the cliff, aren't you?'

'Yes, but I wouldn't go to Bund's cave unless she sent for me.'

'You don't have to go there; just come with me far enough to point it out to me.'

He hesitated, scratching his head. 'Well,' he said, finally, 'that's as good a way as any to get rid of you; but don't forget that you promised not to tell that it was I who brought you to the village.'

I followed him up a rickety ladder to the first and then to the second level, but as we were about to ascend to the third two women started down from above. Lula became panicky.

'Come!' he whispered nervously and took me by the arm.

He led me along a precarious footwalk that ran in front of the caves and to the far end of it. Trembling, he halted here.

'That was a narrow escape,' he whispered. 'Even with your black hair you don't look much like a Samaryan man – you're as big and strong as a woman; and that thing hanging at your side – that would give you away. No one else has one. You'd better throw it away.'

He referred to my pistol, the only weapon I had brought, with the exception of a good hunting knife. The suggestion was as bizarre as Lula was naïve. He was right in saying that its possession might reveal my imposture, but on the other hand its absence might insure my early demise. I did manage to arrange it, however, so that it was pretty well covered by my loincloth.

As we were standing on the runway waiting for the two women to get safely out of the way, I looked down upon the scene below, my interest centering principally upon the group of women surrounding the larger fire. They were strapping specimens, broad shouldered, deep chested, with the sturdy limbs of gladiators. Their hoarse voices rose in laughter, profanity, and coarse jokes. The firelight played upon their almost naked bodies and their rugged, masculine faces, revealing them distinctly to me. They were not unhandsome, with their short hair and bronzed skins; but even though their figures were, in a modified way, those of women, there seemed not even a trace of femininity among them. One just could not think of them as women, and that was all there was to it. As I watched them, two of them got into an altercation. They started by calling each other by vile names; then they went at it hammer and tongs, and they didn't fight like women. There was no hair pulling or scratching there. They fought like a couple of icemen.

How different the other group around the smaller fire. With mouse-like timidity they furtively watched the fight – from a distance. Compared with their women, their bodies were small and frail, their voices soft, their manner apologetic.

Lula and I didn't wait to ascertain the outcome of the fight. The two women who had interrupted our ascent passed down to a lower level leaving us free to climb to the next runway where Bund's cave was located. When we stood upon the catwalk of the third level, Lula told me that Bund's cave was the third to my left. That done, he was ready to leave me.

'Where are the men's caves?' I asked him before he could get away.

'On the highest level.'

'And yours?'

'The last cave to the left of the ladder,' he said. 'I'm going there now. I hope I never see you again.' His voice was shaking and he was trembling like a leaf. It didn't seem possible that a man could be reduced to such a pitiable state of abject terror, and by a woman. Yet he had faced the tharban with a real show of courage. With a shake of my head I turned toward the cave of Bund, the warrior woman of Houtomai.

III

Caves of Houtomai

The catwalks before the caves of the cliff dwellers of Houtomai seemed almost inadequate; but they served their purpose, and I suppose the dwellers there, being accustomed to nothing different, were content with them. Their construction was simple but practical. Into holes bored in the face of the sandstone cliff, straight tree limbs had been driven projecting about two feet from the cliff. These were braced by other pieces, the lower ends of which rested in notches cut about two feet below the holes. Along the tops of these brackets, poles had been laid and lashed down with rawhide. The runways seemed rather narrow when one glanced down the face of the precipitous cliff, and there were no handrails. I couldn't help but think how embarrassing it might be to get into a fight on one of these catwalks. As these thoughts passed through my mind, I made my way to the mouth of the third cave to my left. All was quiet and the interior as dark as a pocket.

'Hey! in there,' I called.

Presently a sleepy feminine voice answered. 'Who's that? What do you want?'

'Bund wants her new slave sent down,' I said.

I heard someone moving inside the cave, and almost immediately a woman with dishevelled hair crawled to the entrance. I knew that it was too dark for her to recognize features. All that I could hope for was that she would be too sleepy to have her suspicions aroused by my voice, which I didn't think sounded like the voices of the men I had heard talking. I hoped not, anyway. However, I tried to change it as much as I could, a ping Lula's soft tones.

'What does Bund want of her?' she asked.

'How should I know?' I demanded.

'It's very funny,' she said. 'Bund told me distinctly that I was not to let her out of the cave under any circumstances. Oh, here comes Bund now.'

I glanced down. The fight was over, and the women were ascending to their caves. To me that catwalk in front of Bund's cave looked like a most unhealthy place to loiter, and I knew that it would be impossible at this time to do anything for Duare; so I made my exit as gracefully and as quickly as I could.

'I guess Bund changed her mind,' I told the woman, as I turned back toward the ladder that led to the upper catwalk. Fortunately the slave woman was still half asleep, and doubtless her principal concern at the moment was to get back to her slumbers. She mumbled something about its being very odd, but before she could go deeper into the matter with me I was on my way.

It didn't take me long to clamber the rickety ladder to the catwalk in front of the men's caves and make my way to the last one to the left of the ladder. The interior was as dark as a pocket and smelled as though it needed airing and had needed it for several generations.

'Lula!' I whispered.

I heard a groan. 'You again?' asked a querulous voice.

'Your old friend, Carson himself,' I replied. 'You don't seem glad to see me.'

'I'm not. I hoped I'd never see you again. I hoped you'd be killed. Why weren't you killed? You didn't stay there long enough. Why did you come away?'

'I had to come up and see my old friend, Lula,' I said.

'And then you will go right away again?'

'Not tonight. Maybe tomorrow. I certainly hope tomorrow.'

He groaned again. 'Don't let them see you coming out of this cave tomorrow,' he begged. 'Oh, why did I tell you where my cave was!'

'That was very stupid of you, Lula; but don't worry. I won't get you in any trouble if you help me.'

'Help you! Help you get your mate away from Bund? Why, Bund would kill me.'

'Well, let's not worry about it until tomorrow. We both need sleep. But say, Lula, don't betray me. If you do, I'll tell Bund the whole story. One more thing. Do you occupy this cave alone?'

'No. Two other men are with me. They'll probably be up soon. Don't talk to me any more after they come.'

'You think they'd give us away?'

'I don't know,' he admitted; 'but I'm not going to take any chances.'

After this we relapsed into silence. It wasn't long before we heard footsteps outside, and a moment later the other two men entered the cave. They had been carrying on a conversation, and they brought the tail end of it in with them.

'– beat me; so I didn't say any more about it; but just before we came up I heard the women talking about it. Nearly all were in their caves at the time. It was just before we went down to build the fires for the last meal, just before darkness came. I had come out of the cave to go down when I happened to look up and see it.'

'Why did your woman beat you?'

'She said I was lying and that she didn't like liars, that she couldn't abide them and that if I'd tell a silly lie like that I'd lie about anything; but now two of the women said they saw it.'

'What did your woman say to that?'

'She said I probably had a beating coming to me anyway.'

'What did the thing look like?'

'Like a big bird, only it didn't flap its wings. It flew right over the canyon. The women who saw it said it was the same thing they saw sitting on the ground when they captured the new slave today and killed the yellow-haired man.'

'That thing must have been the anotar that Lula spoke of.'

'But he said he was only joking.'

'How could he joke about something he'd never seen? There's something funny about this. Hey, Lula!' There was no response. 'Hey, you, Lula!' the man called again.

'I'm asleep,' said Lula.

'Then you'd better wake up. We want to know about this anotar,' insisted the man.

'I don't know anything about it; I never saw it; I never went up in it.'

'Who ever said you went up in it? How could a man go up in the air in anything? It can't be done.'

'Oh, yes it can,' exclaimed Lula. 'Two men can ride in it, maybe four. It flies all around wherever you want it to go.'

'I thought you didn't know anything about it.'

'I am going to sleep,' announced Lula.

'You're going to tell us all about that anotar, or I'll tell Bund on you.'

'Oh, Vyla! You wouldn't do that?' cried Lula.

'Yes, I would so,' insisted Vyla. 'You'd better tell us everything.'

'If I do, will you promise not to tell *anyone?*'

'I promise.'

'And you, Ellie? Will you promise?' asked Lula.

'I wouldn't tell anyone on *you*, Lula; you ought to know *that*,' Ellie assured him. 'Now, go on and tell us.'

'Well, I have seen it; and I've ridden in it – way up in the sky.'

'Now you *are* lying, Lula,' chided Vyla.

'Honest to gracious, I'm not,' insisted Lula, 'and if you don't believe *me*, ask Carson.'

I had been expecting the nit-wit to spill the beans so I wasn't greatly surprised. I think that if Lula had had an I.Q. rating it would have been about decimal two.

'And who is Carson?' demanded Vyla.

'He makes the anotar go in the air,' explained Lula.

'Well, how can we ask *him?* I think you are lying again, Lula. You are getting into a bad habit of lying lately.'

'I am not lying, and if you don't believe me you can ask Carson. He's right here in this cave.'

'What?' demanded the two, in unison.

'Lula is not lying,' I said. 'I am here; also, Lula rode in the anotar with me. If you would like to ride, I'll take you up tomorrow – if you can get me out of here without the women seeing me.'

For a while there was silence; then Ellie spoke in a rather frightened voice. 'What would Jad say if she knew about this?' he asked. Jad was the chief.

'You promised not to tell,' Lula reminded him.

'Jad needn't know, unless one of you tells her,' I said; 'and if you do, I'll say that all three of you knew it and that you were trying to get me to kill her.'

'Oh, you wouldn't say that, would you?' cried Ellie.

'I certainly would. But if you'll help me, no one need ever know; and you can get a ride in the anotar to boot.'

'I'd be afraid,' said Ellie.

'It's nothing to be afraid of,' said Lula in a voice that swaggered. 'I wasn't afraid. You see the whole world all at once, and nothing can get at you. I'd like to stay up there all the time. I wouldn't be afraid of the tharbans then; I wouldn't even be afraid of Bund.'

'I'd like to go up,' said Vyla. 'If Lula wasn't afraid, nobody would be.'

'If you go up, I will,' promised Ellie.

'I'll go,' said Vyla.

Well, we talked a little longer; then, before going to sleep, I asked some questions about the habits of the women, and found that the hunting and raiding parties went out the first thing in the morning and that they left a small guard of warrior women to protect the village. I also learned that the slaves came down in the morning and while the hunting and raiding parties were out, gathered wood for the fires and brought water to the caves in clay jugs. They also helped the men with the making of sandals, loincloths, ornaments, and pottery.

The next morning I stayed in the cave until after the hunters and raiders had left; then I descended the ladders to the ground. I had learned enough about the women to be reasonably certain that I would not arouse their suspicions, as their men are so self-effacing and the women ignore them so completely that a woman might recognize scarcely any of the men other than her mate; but I was not so sure about the men. They all knew one another. What they might do when they recognized a stranger among them was impossible to foresee.

Half a dozen warrior women were loitering in a group near the middle of the canyon while the men and slaves busied themselves with their allotted duties. I saw some of them eyeing me as I reached the ground and walked toward a group down canyon from them where a number of female slaves were working, but they did not accost me.

I kept away from the men as much as possible and approached the female slaves. I was looking for Duare. My heart sank as I saw no sign of her, and I wished that I had gone first to Bund's cave to look for her. Some of the slaves looked at me questioningly; then one of them spoke to me.

'Who are you?' she demanded.

'*You* ought to know,' I told her and while she was puzzling that one out, I walked on.

Presently I saw some slaves emerging from a little side gully with armfuls of wood, and among them I recognized Duare. My heart leaped at sight of her. I sauntered to a point at which she would have to pass me, waiting for the expression in those dear eyes when she should recognize me. Closer and closer she came, and the nearer she got the harder my heart pounded. When she was a couple of steps away, she glanced up into my face; then she passed on without a sign of recognition. For an instant I was crushed; then I was angry, and I turned and overtook her.

'Duare!' I whispered.

She stopped and wheeled toward me. 'Carson!' she exclaimed. 'Oh, Carson. What has happened to you?'

I had forgotten the black hair and the ugly wounds on my forehead and cheek, the latter an ugly gash from temple to chin. She actually had not known me.

'Oh, but you are not dead; you are not dead! I thought that they had killed you. Tell me—'

'Not now, dear,' I said. 'We're going to get out of here first.'

'But how? What chance have we to escape while they are watching?'

'Simply run away. I don't think we'll ever have a better chance.' I glanced quickly about. The warriors were still unconcerned, paying no attention to us or anyone else. They were superior beings who looked with contempt upon men and slaves. Most of the slaves and men were farther up canyon than we, but there were a few that we would have to pass. 'Are you going back for more wood?' I asked.

'Yes, we are,' she told me.

'Good. When you come back, try to walk at the very rear of the others. I'll follow you into the canyon, if I can; unless a better plan occurs to me. You'd better go on now.'

After she left me, I boldly sought out Lula. The men who looked at me eyed me suspiciously, but they are so stupid that they were at first merely puzzled. They didn't think of doing anything about it. I hoped that when they did, it would be too late to interfere with my plans. When I found Lula and he saw who it was, he looked about as happy as he would had he suddenly been confronted by a ghost.

'Get Vyla and Ellie,' I told him, 'and come with me.'

'What for?' he demanded.

'Never mind. Do as I tell you, and do it quickly; or I'll tell those women.' He was too dumb to realize immediately that I wouldn't dare do that; so he went and got Ellie and Vyla.

'What do you want of us?' demanded the latter.

'I'm going to take you for that ride in the anotar, just as I promised you last night,' I said.

They looked at each other questioningly. I could see that they were afraid – probably frightened by the thought of flying, but more frightened of the women.

Ellie choked. 'I can't go today,' he said.

'You are coming with me whether you go up in the anotar or not,' I told them in no uncertain tones.

'What do you want of us?' asked Vyla.

'Come with me, and I'll show you. And don't forget that if you don't do as I tell you I'll tell the women about that plan of yours to have me kill Jad. Now, come!'

'You're a mean old thing,' whined Vyla.

They had been kicked around so much all their lives and had developed such colossal inferiority complexes that they were afraid of everybody; and, if they weren't given too much time to think, would obey anyone's commands; so they came with me.

The wood carriers had laid down their loads and were on their way back to the side gully for more as I herded my unwilling accomplices toward a point the slaves would have to pass; and as they approached, I saw, to my vast relief, that Duare was trailing the others. As she came opposite us, I gathered my three around her to hide her, if possible, from the sight of the warrior women; then I directed them at a loitering gait downward toward the mouth of The Narrow Canyon. Right then I would have given a lot for a rear-sight mirror; for I wanted to see what was going on behind us, but didn't dare look back for fear of suggesting that we were doing something we shouldn't be – it was a case of nonchalance or nothing, and not a cigarette of any brand among us. I never knew minutes to be so long; but finally we approached the lower end of the canyon, and then I heard the hoarse voice of a woman shouting at us.

'Hi, there! Where are you going? Come back here!'

With that, the three men stopped in their tracks; and I knew that the jig was up as far as secrecy was concerned. I took Duare's hand, and we kept on down the canyon. Now I could look back. Lula, Vyla and Ellie were marching back to their masters; and three of the women were coming down the canyon toward us. When they saw that two of us had ignored their command and were walking on, they commenced to shout again; and when we didn't pay any attention to them they broke into a trot; then we took to our heels. I didn't doubt but that we could outdistance them, for they were not built for speed. However, we would have to get to the ship far enough ahead of them to give us time to untie her before they overtook us.

As we turned out of the mouth of The Narrow Canyon into the wide canyon of which it is a branch, we came on fairly level ground sloping gently in the direction we were going. Groups of splendid trees dotted the landscape, and off there somewhere in the near beyond was the ship and safety; then, squarely across our path and a couple of hundred yards away, I saw three tharbans.

IV

A New Land

The sight of those three great beasts barring our way was just about as discouraging as anything I have ever encountered. Of course I had my pistol; but the rays don't always kill immediately any more than bullets do, and even if I should succeed in killing them the delay would permit the women to overtake us. I could hear them shouting, and I was afraid their voices might reach one of the hunting parties; so, all in all, I was in a tough spot. Fortunately, they hadn't come out of The Narrow Canyon yet; and I thought I saw a possible chance of eluding them and the tharbans. We were close to a group of trees the dense foliage of which would form an excellent hiding place; so I hoisted Duare to a lower branch and swung up after her. Climbing well up, we waited. Through the foliage we could look out, though I doubted that anyone could see us.

The three tharbans had witnessed our ruse and were coming toward the tree, but when the running warrior women hove into sight out of the mouth of The Narrow Canyon the beasts paid no more attention to us, but turned their attention to the women instead. The sight of the tharbans brought the women to a sudden stop. I saw them looking around for us; and then, as the tharbans advanced, they retreated into The Narrow Canyon. The three beasts followed them, and the moment that all were out of sight Duare and I dropped to the ground and continued on toward the ship.

We could hear the roars and growls of the tharbans and the shouts of the women growing fainter in the distance as we almost ran in our eagerness to reach the anotar. What had appeared a few moments before almost a catastrophe had really proved our salvation, for now we had no need to fear pursuit from the village. My only immediate concern now was the ship, and I can tell you that I breathed a sigh of relief when we came in sight of it and I saw that it was intact. Five minutes later we were in the air, and the adventure of Houtomai was a thing of the past. Yet, how near it had come to meaning death for me and a life of slavery for Duare! If the warrior women had taken but an extra moment to make sure that I was dead how very different the outcome would have been. I shall always think that fear of the ship, a thing so strange to them, caused them to hurry away. Duare says that they talked much about the ship on the way back to the village and that it was evident that they were troubled by it, not being quite sure that it was not some strange beast that might pursue them.

We had much to talk about as I circled in search of game, that I might make another kill; for I had not eaten for two days, and Duare only a few mean scraps while she was the slave of Bund. Duare kept looking at me and touching me to make sure that I was alive, so certain had she been that the Samaryans had killed me.

'I should not have lived long, Carson, if you hadn't come,' she said. 'With you dead, I didn't care to live – certainly not in slavery. I was only waiting for an opportunity to destroy myself.'

I located a herd of antelope-like animals and made my kill much as I had the previous day, but this time Duare kept vigilant lookout while I attended to the butchering; then we flew to the island where Lula and I had stopped while I transformed myself into a brunette. This time I reversed the operation, after we had cooked and eaten some of our meat. Once again we were happy and contended. Our recent troubles now seemed very remote, so quickly does the spirit of man rebound from depression and push black despair into the limbo of forgetfulness.

Duare was much concerned about my wounds and insisted on bathing them herself. The only danger, of course, was from infection; and we had no means of disinfecting them. Naturally there was much less danger than there would have been on Earth, where overpopulation and increased means of transportation have greatly spread and increased the numbers of malignant bacteria. Also, the longevity serum with which I had been inoculated by Danus shortly after my arrival upon Amtor gave me considerable immunity. All in all, I was not much concerned; but Duare was like a hen with one chicken. She had finally given in to her natural inclinations; and, having admitted her love, she was lavishing on its object the devotion and solicitude which raise love to its purest and most divine heights.

We were both of us pretty well done in by all that we had been through, and so we decided to remain at the island until the following day at least. I was quite sure that there were no men and no dangerous beasts there, and for the first time in many months we could utterly relax without concern about the safety of ourself or that of the other. Those were the most perfect twenty-four hours I had ever spent.

The next day we took off from our little island with real regret and flew south along the valley of The River of Death down toward the ocean into which we knew it must empty. But what ocean? What lay beyond it? Where in all this vast world could we go?

'Perhaps we can find another little island somewhere,' Duare suggested, 'and live there always, just you and I alone.'

I didn't have the heart to tell her that in a few months we'd probably be wanting to knife one another. I was really in a quandary. It was impossible that we return to Vepaja. I knew now definitely that Duare would rather die than be separated from me; and there was no question but that I should be executed the moment Mintep, her father, got his hands on me. My only reason for planning to take Duare back to Vepaja had been my sincere belief that, no matter what became of me, she would be happier there eventually and certainly much safer than roaming around this savage world with a man absolutely without a country; but now I knew differently. I knew that either of us would rather be dead than permanently separated from the other.

'We'll make a go of it some way,' I told her, 'and if there's a spot on Amtor where we can find peace and safety we'll locate it.'

'We have fifty years before the anotar falls to pieces,' said Duare, with a laugh.

We had flown but a short time before I saw what appeared to be a large body of water dead ahead, and such it soon proved to be. We had come to the ocean at last.

'Let's go out over it and look for our island,' said Duare.

'We'd better stock up with food and water first,' I suggested.

I had wrapped the remainder of our meat in the large waxy leaves I had found growing on the little island; and was sure that it would keep for several days, but of course we didn't want to eat it raw; and as we couldn't cook it while flying, there was nothing to do but land and cook the meat. I also wanted to gather some fruits and nuts and a tuber that grows almost everywhere on Amtor and is quite palatable and nutritious – palatable even when eaten raw.

I found an open flat that extended back from The River of Death for several miles. It was forest bordered on one side, and a little river ran through it down to the larger stream from mountains to the east. I made a landing near the forest in the hope that I would find such fruits and nuts as I desired, nor was I disappointed. After gathering them, I loaded some firewood into the rear cockpit and taxied over beside the small stream. Here we were in the open where we could see the surrounding country in all directions and therefore in no danger of being surprised by either man or beast. I built a fire and cooked our meat while Duare kept watch. I also filled the water tank with which I had equipped the ship at the time it was built. We now had food and water sufficient for several days, and filled with the spirit of exploration we took off and headed out to sea, passing over the great delta of The River of Death, a river that must rival the Amazon.

From the first, Duare had been keenly interested in the navigation of the ship. I had explained the purpose and operation of the controls, but she had not actually flown the anotar herself. Now I let her try it, for I knew that she must learn to fly against the possibility of our being in the air for long periods such as might be necessitated by a trans-oceanic flight. I would have to have sleep, and this would not be possible in the air unless Duare could fly the ship. Now, flying a ship in the air under ordinary weather conditions is not even so difficult as walking; so it required only a few minutes to establish her confidence and give her something of the feel of the ship. I knew that practice would give her smoothness, and I had her fly at an altitude that would permit me to come to the rescue if she got in any trouble.

We flew all that night with Duare at the controls about a third of the time, and when morning broke I sighted land. As far as I could see to the east and west the boles and foliage of great trees rose thousands of feet to disappear in the inner cloud envelope which floats forever over the entire expanse of Amtor, a second defense to the outer cloud envelope against the intense heat of the sun that would otherwise burn the surface of the planet to a crisp.

'That aspect looks familiar,' I said to Duare when she awoke.

'What do you mean?' she asked.

'I think it is Vepaja. We'll skirt the coast, and if I'm right we will see the natural harbor where the *Sofal* and the *Sovong* lay at anchor the day that you were kidnapped and Kamlot and I were captured by the klangan. I'm sure I shall recognize it.'

Duare said nothing. She was silent for a long time as we flew along the coast. Presently I saw the harbor.

'There it is,' I said. 'This is Vepaja, Duare.'

'Vepaja,' she breathed.

'We are here, Duare. Do you want to stay?'

She shook her head. 'Not without you.' I leaned toward her and kissed her.

'Oh, let's just keep on going. One direction's as good as another.'

The ship, at the time, was flying perhaps a couple of points north of west; so I simply maintained that course. The world ahead of us was absolutely unknown, as far as we were concerned; and as this course would keep us away from the antarctic regions and well into the northern part of the south temperate zone, it seemed as good a course to hold as any. In the opposite direction lay the stronghold of the Thorists, where we could hope to find only captivity and death.

As the long day wore away, nothing but illimitable ocean stretched monotonously before us. The ship functioned beautifully. It could not function otherwise, since into its construction had gone the best that the finest scientific minds of Havatoo could give. The design had been mine, as aircraft were absolutely undreamed of in Havatoo prior to my coming; but the materials, the motor, the fuel were exclusively Amtorian. For strength, durability, and lightness the first would be impossible of duplication on Earth; the motor was a marvel of ingenuity, compactness, power and durability combined with lightness of weight; the fuel I have already described. In design the ship was more or less of a composite of those with which I was familiar or had myself flown on Earth. It seated four, two abreast in an open front cockpit and two in a streamlined cabin aft; there were controls in both cockpits, and the ship could be flown from any of the four seats. As I have before stated, it was an amphibian.

During the long day I varied the monotony by instructing Duare in landings and take-offs, there being a gentle westerly breeze. We had to keep a sharp lookout at these times for the larger denizens of the sea, some of which might easily have wrecked the ship had their dispositions been as fearsome as their appearance.

As night fell, the vast Amtorian scene was bathed in the soft, mysterious, nocturnal light that beneficent Nature has vouchsafed a moonless planet. Seemingly as limitless as interstellar space, the endless sea rolled to the outer rim of our universe, glowing wanly. No land, no ship, no living thing impinged upon the awful serenity of the scene – only our silent plane and we two infinitesimal atoms wandering aimlessly through space. Duare moved a little closer to me. Companionship was good in this infinite loneliness.

During the night the wind veered and blew from the south, and at dawn I saw cloud banks rolling in ahead of us. The air was much cooler. It was evident that we were getting the tail end of a south polar storm. I didn't like the looks of that fog. I had blind flying instruments on the instrument board; but, even so, who would care to fly blind in a world concerning the topography of which he knew nothing? Nor was I particularly keen to chance waiting the fog out on the surface of the sea. The chances are it would have been safe enough, but I had seen far too many leviathans cavorting about in the waters beneath us to incline me toward spending any more time on the surface of the water than was absolutely necessary. I determined to change our course and fly north ahead of the fog. It was then that Duare pointed ahead.

'Isn't that land?' she asked.

'It certainly has all the appearances of land,' I said after taking a long look.

'Maybe it is our island,' she suggested laughingly.

'We'll go and have a look at it before the fog rolls over it. We can always beat that fog if it gets too thick.'

'Land will look pretty good again,' said Duare.

'Yes,' I agreed. 'We've been looking at an awful lot of water.'

As we approached the coast line we saw mountains in the distance and far to the northwest what appeared to be one of those giant tree forests such as cover almost the entire area of the island of Vepaja.

'Oh, there's a city!' exclaimed Duare.

'So it is – a seaport. Quite a good-sized city, too. I wonder what kind of people live there.'

Duare shook her head. 'I don't know. There is a land northwest of Vepaja that is called Anlap. I have seen it on the map. It lies partially in Trabol and partially in Strabol. The maps show it as an island, a very large island; but of course nobody knows. Strabol has never been thoroughly explored.'

It seemed to me that none of Venus had ever been thoroughly explored, nor could I wonder. The most able men I had met here clung to the belief that it was a saucer-shaped world floating on a molten sea. They thought that its greatest circumference lay at what I knew to be the south pole, and on their maps the equator was not even a dot. They never dreamed of the existence of another hemisphere. With maps based on such erroneous reasoning, everything was distorted; and because their maps were therefore useless, no navigator dared go far from familiar waters and seldom out of sight of land.

As we approached the city I saw that it was walled and heavily fortified, and closer inspection revealed the fact that it was being beleaguered by a large force. The hum of Amtorian guns came faintly to our ears. We saw the defenders on the walls; and, beyond the walls, we saw the enemy – long lines of men encircling the city, each lying behind his shield. These shields are composed of metal more or less impervious to both R-rays and T-rays; and their use must result in far more mobile attacking forces than could have been possible were the men facing Earthly bullets; it practically amounted to each man carrying his own trench. The troops could be maneuvered almost anywhere on the field of battle while under fire, with a minimum of casualties.

As we passed over the city, firing practically ceased on both sides. We could see thousands of faces upturned toward us, and I could imagine the wonder and amazement that the ship must have engendered in the minds of those thousands of soldiers and civilians, not one of whom could possibly have conceived the nature of this giant, birdlike thing speeding silently above them. As every portion of the ship, whether wood, metal, or fabric, had been sprayed with a solution of this ray-resisting substance I felt quite safe in flying low above the contending forces; and so I spiralled downward and, circling, flew close above the city's wall. Then I leaned out and waved my hand. A great shout rose from the men within the city, but the attackers were silent for a moment; then a volley of shots were directed at us.

The ship might have been coated with ray-resisting material; but Duare and I were not, and so I zoomed to a safer altitude and turned the ship's nose inland to reconnoiter farther. Beyond the lines of the investing forces we flew over their main camp, beyond which a broad highway led toward the southwest, from which direction troops were marching toward the camp; and there were long trains of wagons drawn by huge, elephantine animals, and men mounted on strange beasts, and big T-ray guns, and all the other impediments of a great army on the march.

Turning toward the north, I reconnoitered in search of information. I wanted to know something about this country and the disposition of its inhabitants. From what I had already seen, their dispositions seemed unequivocally warlike; but somewhere there might be a peaceful, hospitable city where strangers would be treated with consideration. What I was looking for was a single individual whom I might question without risking injury to Duare or myself, for to have made a landing among those fighting men would probably have been fatal – especially among comrades of the contingent that had fired on us. The attitude of the defenders of the city had been more friendly; but still I couldn't risk a landing there without knowing something about them, nor did it seem the part of wisdom to land in a beleaguered city that, from the number of its attackers, might be taken any day. Duare and I were looking for peace, not war.

I covered a considerable area of territory without seeing a human being, but at last I discovered a lone man coming out of a canyon in the hills several miles north of the big camp I have mentioned. As I dropped toward him, he turned and looked up. He did not run; but stood his ground, and I saw him draw the pistol at his hip.

'Don't fire!' I called to him as I glided past. 'We are friends.'

'What do you want?' he shouted back.

I circled and flew back, landing a couple of hundred yards from him. 'I am a stranger here,' I shouted to him. 'I want to ask for information.'

He approached the ship quite boldly, but he kept his weapon in readiness for any eventuality. I dropped down from the cockpit and went forward to meet him, raising my right hand to show that it held no weapon. He raised his left – he wasn't taking any chances; but the gesture signified a friendly attitude, or at least not a belligerent one.

A half smile touched his lips as I descended from the ship. 'So you *are* a human being, after all,' he said. 'At first I didn't know but that you were a part of that thing, whatever it is. Where are you from? What do you want of me?'

'We are strangers here,' I told him. 'We do not even know in what country we are. We want to know the disposition of the people here toward strangers, and if there is a city where we might be received hospitably.'

'This is the land of Anlap,' he said, 'and we are in the kingdom of Korva.'

'What city is that back by the sea? There was fighting going on there.'

'You saw fighting?' he demanded. 'How was it going? Had the city fallen?' He seemed eager for news.

'The city had not fallen,' I said, 'and the defenders seemed in good spirits.'

He breathed a sigh of relief. Suddenly his brow clouded. 'How do I know you're not a Zani spy?' he demanded.

I shrugged. 'You don't,' I said, 'but I'm not. I don't even know what a Zani is.'

'No, you couldn't be,' he said presently. 'With that yellow hair of yours I don't know what you could be – certainly not of our race.'

'Well, how about answering some of my questions?' I inquired with a smile.

He smiled in return. 'That's right. You wanted to know the disposition of the people of Korva to strangers and the name of the city by the sea. Well, before the Zanis seized the government, you would have been treated well in any Korvan city. But now it is different. Sanara, the city you asked about, would welcome you; it has not yet fallen under the domination of the Zanis. They are trying to reduce it now, and if it capitulates the last stronghold of freedom in Korva will have fallen.'

'You are from Sanara?' I asked.

'Yes, at present. I had always lived in Amlot, the capital, until the Zanis came into power; then I couldn't go back, because I had been fighting them.'

'I just flew over a big camp south of here,' I said; 'was that a Zani camp?'

'Yes. I'd give anything to see it. How many men have they?'

'I don't know; but it's a large camp, and more soldiers and supplies are coming in from the southwest.'

'From Amlot,' he said. 'Oh, if I could but see that!'

'You can,' I told him.

'How?' he demanded.

I pointed toward the ship. He looked just a little bit taken aback, but only for a second.

'All right,' he said. 'You will not regret your kindness. May I ask your name? Mine is Taman.'

'And mine is Carson.'

He looked at me curiously. 'What country are you from? I have never before seen an Amtorian with yellow hair.'

'It is a long story,' I said. 'Suffice it to say that I am not an Amtorian; I am from another world.'

We walked toward the ship together, he, in the meantime, having returned his pistol to its holster. When we reached it, he saw Duare for the first time. I could just note a faint expression of surprise, which he hid admirably. He was evidently a man of refinement. I introduced them, and then showed him how to enter the rear cockpit and fasten his lifebelt.

Of course I couldn't see him when we took off, but he afterward told me that he believed his end had come. I flew him directly back to the Zani camp and along the highway toward Amlot.

'This is wonderful!' he exclaimed time and again. 'I can see everything. I can even count the battalions and the guns and the wagons.'

'Tell me when you've seen enough,' I said.

'I think I've seen all that's necessary. Poor Sanara! How can it withstand such a horde? And I may not even be able to get back and make my report. The city must be surrounded by troops by now. I just barely got out an *ax* ago.' An *ax* is equivalent to twenty days of Amtorian time, or slightly over twenty-two days, eleven hours of Earth time.

'The city is entirely surrounded,' I told him, 'I doubt that you could possibly pass through the lines even at night.'

'Would you –' he hesitated.

'Would I what?' I asked, though I guessed what he wished to ask me.

'But no,' he said; 'it would be too much to ask of a stranger. You would be risking your life and that of your companion.'

'Is there any place large enough for me to land inside the walls of Sanara?' I asked.

He laughed. 'You guessed well,' he said. 'How much space do you require?' I told him.

'Yes,' he said; 'there is a large field near the center of town where races were held. You could land there easily.'

'A couple more questions,' I suggested.

'Certainly! Ask as many as you please.'

'Have you sufficient influence with the military authorities to insure our safety? I am, of course, thinking of my mate. I cannot risk harm befalling her.'

'I give you the word of a nobleman that you will both be safe under my protection,' he assured me.

'And that we shall be permitted to leave the city whenever we choose, and that our ship will not be molested or detained?'

'Again you have my word for all that you have asked,' he said; 'but still I think it is too much to ask of you – too much to permit you to do for a stranger.'

I turned to Duare. 'What is your answer, Duare?' I asked.

'I think that I shall like Sanara,' she said.

I turned the ship's nose in the direction of the Korvan seaport.

V

Sanara

Taman was profuse in his gratitude, but not too profuse. I felt from the first that he was going to prove a likeable fellow; and I know that Duare liked him, too. She ordinarily seldom enters into conversation with strangers. The old taboos of the jong's daughter are not to be easily dispelled, but she talked with Taman on the flight to Sanara, asking him many questions.

'You will like our people,' he told her. 'Of course, now, under the strain of a long siege, conditions are not normal nor are the people; but they will welcome you and treat you well. I shall take you both into my own home, where I know that my wife can make you comfortable even under the present conditions.'

As we passed over the Zanis' lines they commenced to take pot shots at us, but I was flying too high for their fire to have been effective even against an unprotected ship. Taman and I had discussed the matter of landing. I was a little fearful that the defenders might become frightened at this strange craft were it to attempt a landing in the city, especially as this time we would be approaching from enemy country. I suggested a plan which he thought might work out satisfactorily; so he wrote a note on a piece of paper which he had and tied it to one of the large nuts we had brought with us. In fact he wrote several notes, tying each one to a different nut. Each note stated that he was in the anotar they saw flying above the city and asked the commander to have the racing field cleared so that we could make a safe landing. If the note were received and permission to land was granted, they were to send several men with flags to the windward end of the field with instructions to wave them until they saw us come in for a landing. This would accomplish two purposes – show us that we would not be fired on and also give me the direction of the wind at the field.

I dropped the notes at intervals over the city, and then circled at a safe distance awaiting the outcome of our plan. I could see the field quite distinctly, and that there were quite a few people on it – far too many to make a landing safe. Anyway, there was nothing to do but wait for the signal. While we were waiting, Taman pointed out places of interest in the city – parks, public buildings, barracks, the governor's palace. He said that the jong's nephew lived there now and ruled as jong, his uncle being a prisoner of the Zanis at Amlot. There were even rumors that the jong had been executed. It was that

that the defenders of Sanara feared as much as they feared the Zanis, because they didn't trust the jong's nephew and didn't want him as permanent jong.

It seemed as though we'd circled over the city for an hour before we received any indication that our notes had been received; then I saw soldiers clearing the people out of the racing field. That was a good omen; then a dozen soldiers with flags went to one end of the field and commenced to wave them. At that I commenced to drop in a tight spiral – you see I didn't want to go too near the city walls for fear of attracting the fire of the Zanis.

Looking down, I saw people converging upon that field from all directions. The word that we were going to land must have spread like wildfire. They were coming in droves, blocking the avenues. I hoped that a sufficient detail of soldiers had been sent to keep them from swarming over the field and tearing us and the plane to pieces. I was so worried that I zoomed upward again and told Taman to write another note asking for a large military guard to keep the people away from the ship. This he did, and then I dropped down again and tossed the note out on the field near a group of men that Taman told me were officers. Five minutes later we saw a whole battalion marched onto the field and posted around the edges; then I came in for a landing.

Say, but weren't those people thrilled! They were absolutely breathless and silent until the ship rolled almost to a stop; then they burst into loud cheering. It certainly made me feel pretty good to realize that we were welcome somewhere in the world, for our situation had previously seemed utterly hopeless, realizing, as we did from past experience, that strangers are seldom welcome in any Amtorian city. My own experience on the occasion of my landing in Vepaja from my rocket ship had borne this out; for, though I was finally accepted, I had been a virtual prisoner in the palace of the jong for a long period of time.

After Taman alighted from the ship, I started to help Duare out; and as she stepped onto the wing in full view of the crowd the cheering stopped and there was a moment of breathless silence; then they burst forth again. It was a wonderful ovation they gave Duare. I think they hadn't realized that the third member of the party was a woman until she stepped into full view. The realization that it was a woman, coupled with her startling beauty, just simply took their breath away. You may be sure that I loved the people of Sanara from that moment.

Several officers had approached the ship, and there were greetings and introductions of course. I noted the deference they accorded Taman, and I realized my good fortune in having placed a really important man under obligations to me. Just how important a personage he really was, I was not to learn until later.

While we had been circling the field I had noticed a number of the huge animals, such as I had seen drawing the gun carriages and army wagons of the Zanis, standing at one side of the field behind the crowd. Several of the beasts were now brought onto the field and up to the ship, or as close as their drivers could urge them; for they were quite evidently afraid of this strange thing. I now got my first close view of a gantor. The animal was larger than an African elephant and had legs very similar to those of that animal, but here the likeness ceased. The head was bull-like and armed with a stout horn about a foot long that grew out of the center of the forehead; the mouth was large, and the powerful jaws were armed with very large teeth; the coat, back of the shoulders, was short and a light tawny yellow marked with white splotches like a pinto horse; while covering the shoulders and short neck was a heavy dark mane; the tail was like that of a bull; three enormous horny toes covered the entire bottoms of the feet, forming hoofs. The driver of each animal sat on the mane above the shoulders; and behind him, on the creature's long, broad back was an open howdah capable of seating a dozen people. That, at least, describes the howdah of the first beast I noted closely. I saw later that there are many forms of howdahs, and in fact the one on the animal that was brought to carry Duare, Taman, and me from the field was a very ornate howdah seating four. Along the left side of each gantor a ladder was lashed, and when the drivers had coaxed their mounts as close as they could to the ship each driver dropped to the ground and set his ladder up against his beast's side. Up these ladders the passengers climbed to the howdahs. I watched the whole procedure with interest, wondering how the driver was going to regain his seat if he lashed the ladder back to the gantor's side or what he would do with the ladder if he used it to climb back onto the gantor.

Well, I soon had my curiosity satisfied. Each driver lashed his ladder back in place against the gantor's side; then he walked around in front of the gantor and gave a command. Instantly the animal lowered its head until its nose almost touched the ground, which brought its horn into a horizontal position about three feet above the ground. The driver climbed onto the horn and gave another command, the gantor raised its head, and the driver stepped to its poll and from there to his seat above the shoulders.

The howdahs of the other gantors were filled with officers and soldiers who acted as our escort from the field, some preceding and some following us off the field and along a broad avenue. As we passed, the people raised their hands in salute, the arms extended at an angle of about forty-five degrees, their palms crossed. I noticed that they did this only as our gantor approached; and I soon realized that they were saluting Taman, as he acknowledged the salutes by bowing to the right and left. So once again I had evidence that he was a man of importance.

The people on the street wore the scant apparel that is common on Amtor, where it is usually warm and sultry; and they also wore, according to what seems to be a universal custom, daggers and swords, the women the former, the men both. The soldiers among them also carried pistols slung in holsters at their hips. They were a very nice, clean looking people with pleasant faces. The buildings facing the avenue were stuccoed; but of what materials they were built, I did not know. The architectural lines were simple but most effective; and notwithstanding the simpleness of the designs, the builders had achieved a diversity that gave pleasing contrasts.

As we proceeded and turned into another avenue the buildings became larger and more beautiful, but still the same simplicity of line was apparent. As we were approaching a rather large building, Taman told me it was the palace of the governor, where the nephew of the jong lived and ruled in the absence of his uncle. We stopped in front of another large home directly across the street from the governor's palace. A guard of soldiers stood before an enormous gate built in the center of the front wall, which was flush with the sidewalk. They saluted Taman, and swung the gate open. Our escort had previously moved back across the avenue, and now our driver guided his huge mount through the gateway along a wide corridor into an enormous courtyard where there were trees and flowers and fountains. This was the palace of Taman.

A small army of people poured from the building, whom, of course, I could not identify but whom I learned later were officers and officials of the palace, retainers, and slaves. They greeted Taman with the utmost deference, but their manner indicated real affection.

'Inform the janjong that I have returned and am bringing guests to her apartments,' Taman directed one of the officers.

Now janjong means, literally, daughter of a jong; in other words, a princess. It is the official title of the daughter of a living jong, but it is often used through life as a courtesy title after a jong dies. A tanjong, son of a jong, is a prince.

Taman himself showed us our apartments, knowing that we would wish to freshen ourselves up before being presented to the janjong. Women slaves took Duare in hand and a man slave showed me my bath and brought me fresh apparel.

Our apartments, consisting of three rooms and two baths, were beautifully decorated and furnished. It must have been like heaven to Duare who had known nothing of either beauty or comfort since she had been stolen from her father's palace over a year before.

When we were ready an officer came and conducted us to a small reception room on the same floor but at the opposite end of the palace. Here Taman was awaiting us. He asked me how we should be introduced to the janjong, and when I told him Duare's title I could see that he was both pleased and surprised. As for myself, I asked him to introduce me as Carson of Venus.

Of course the word Venus meant nothing to him, as the planet is known to the inhabitants as Amtor. We were then ushered into the presence of the janjong. The formality of introductions on Amtor are both simple and direct; there is no circumlocution. We were led into the presence of a most beautiful woman, who arose and smiled as we approached her.

'This is my wife, Jahara, janjong of Korva,' announced Taman; then he turned to Duare. 'This is Duare, janjong of Vepaja, wife of Carson of Venus,' and, indicating me, 'this is Carson of Venus.' It was all very simple. Of course Taman didn't say wife – there is no marriage among any of the peoples I have known on Amtor. A couple merely agree between themselves to live together, and they are ordinarily as faithful to one another as married couples on Earth are supposed to be. They may separate and take other mates if they choose, but they rarely do. Since the serum of longevity was discovered many couples have lived together for a thousand years in perfect harmony – possibly because the tie that bound them was not a fetter. The word that Taman used instead of wife was ooliaganja – lovewoman. I like it.

During our visit with Taman and Jahara we learned many things concerning them and Korva. Following a disastrous war, in which the resources of the nation had been depleted, a strange cult had arisen conceived and led by a common soldier named Mephis. He had usurped all the powers of government, seized Amlot, the capital, and reduced the principal cities of Korva with the exception of Sanara, to which many of the nobility had flocked with their loyal retainers. Mephis had imprisoned Jahara's father, Kord, hereditary jong of Korva, because he would not accede to the demand of the Zanis and rule as a figurehead dominated by Mephis. Recently rumors had reached Sanara that Kord had been assassinated, that Mephis would offer the jong-ship to some member of the royal family, that he would assume the title himself; but no one really knew anything about it.

We also inferred, though no direct statement to that effect was made, that the jong's nephew, Muso, acting jong, was none too popular. What we didn't learn until much later was that Taman, who was of royal blood, was directly in line for the throne after Muso and that Muso was intensely jealous of Taman's popularity with all classes of people. When we had picked Taman up behind the enemy lines he had been returning from a most hazardous assignment upon which Muso had sent him, possibly in the hope that he would never return.

Food was served in the apartments of Jahara; and while we were eating, an officer of the jong was announced. He brought a gracefully worded intimation that Muso would be glad to receive us immediately if Taman and Jahara would bring us to the palace and present us. It was, of course, a command.

We found Muso and his consort, Illana, in the audience room of the palace surrounded by a considerable retinue. They were seated on impressive thrones, and it was evident that Muso was taking his jongship very seriously. So great was his dignity that he did not condescend to smile, though he was courteous enough. The closest his equilibrium came to being upset was when his eyes fell on Duare. I could see that her beauty impressed him, but I was accustomed to that – it usually startled people.

He kept us in the audience chamber only long enough to conclude the formalities; then he led us into a smaller room.

'I saw the strange thing in which you fly as it circled above the city,' he said. 'What do you call it and what keeps it in the air?'

I told him that Duare had christened it an anotar, and then I explained briefly the principle of heavier-than-air craft flight.

'Has it any practical value?' he asked.

'In the world from which I come airlines have been established that transport passengers, mail, and express between all the large cities and to every portion of the world; civilized governments retain great fleets of planes for military purposes.'

'But how could an anotar be used for military purposes?' he asked.

'For reconnaissance, for one thing,' I told him. 'I flew Taman over the enemy camp and along its line of communication. They can be used for destroying supply bases, for disabling batteries, even for direct attack upon enemy troops.'

'How could your ship be used against the Zanis?' he asked.

'By bombing their lines, their camp, and their supply depots and trains we might lower their morale. Of course with but a single ship we could not accomplish much.'

'I am not so sure of that,' said Taman. 'The psychological effect of this new engine of destruction might be far more effective than you imagine.'

'I agree with Taman,' said Muso.

'I shall be glad to serve the jong of Korva in any way,' I said.

'Will you accept a commission under me?' he asked. 'It will mean that you must swear allegiance to the jong of Korva.'

'Why not?' I asked. 'I have no country on Amtor, and the ruler and people of Sanara have accorded us courtesy and hospitality,' and so I took the oath of allegiance to Korva and was commissioned a captain in the army of the jong. Now, at last, I had a country; but I also had a boss. That part of it I didn't like so well, for, if I am nothing else, I am a rugged individualist.

VI

A Spy

The next few weeks were filled with interest and excitement. The Sanarans manufactured both R-ray and T-ray bombs as well as incendiary bombs, and I made almost daily flights over the enemy lines and camp. In the latter and along their line of communication I wrought the most havoc, but a single ship could not win a war. On several occasions I so demoralized their front line that successful sorties were made by the Sanarans during which prisoners were taken. From these we learned the repeated bombings had had their effect on the morale of the enemy and that an enormous reward had been offered by the Zani chief, Mephis, for the destruction of the ship or for my capture dead or alive.

During these weeks we remained the guests of Taman and Jahara, and were entertained frequently by Muso, the acting jong, and his wife, Illana. The latter was a quiet, self-effacing woman of high lineage but of no great beauty. Muso usually ignored her; and when he didn't, his manner toward her was often brusque and almost offensive; but she was uniformly sweet and unresentful. He was far more attentive to Duare than he was to his own wife, but that is oftentimes a natural reaction of a host in his endeavor to please a guest. While we did not admire it, we could understand it.

The siege of Sanara was almost a stalemate. The city had enormous reserve supplies of synthetic foods; and its water supply was assured by artesian wells, nor was there any dearth of ammunition. The besiegers could not get into the city, and the besieged could not get out. So matters stood one day a month after my arrival in Sanara when Muso sent for me. He was pacing back and forth the width of a small, audience chamber when I was ushered into his presence. He appeared nervous and ill at ease. I supposed at the time that he was worried over the seeming hopelessness of raising the siege, for it was of that he spoke first. Later he came to the point.

'I have a commission for you, Captain,' he said. 'I want to get a message through to one of my secret agents in Amlot. With your ship you can easily cross the enemy lines and reach the vicinity of Amlot without the slightest danger of being captured. I can direct you to a spot where you can make contact with persons who can get you into the city. After that it will be up to you. This must be a secret expedition on your part – no one but you and I must know of it, not even Taman, not even your wife. You will leave the first thing in the morning ostensibly on a bombing expedition, and you will not come back – at least not until you have fulfilled your mission. After that there will be no need for secrecy. If you succeed, I shall create you a noble – specifically an ongvoo – and when the war is over and peace restored I shall see that you receive lands and a palace.'

Now, the title ongvoo means, literally, exalted one and is hereditary in the collateral branches of the royal family, though occasionally conferred on members of the nobility for highly meritorious service to the jong. It seemed to me at the time that the service I was commissioned to perform did not merit any such award, but I gave the matter little thought. It would have been better had I done so.

Muso stepped to a desk and took two thin leather containers, like envelopes, from a drawer. 'These contain the messages you are to deliver,' he said. 'Taman tells me that as you are from another world you probably do not read Amtorian; so you will write in your own language on the outside of each the names and location of those to whom you are to deliver these.' He handed me a pen and one of the containers. 'This one you will deliver to Lodas at his farm five klookob northwest of Amlot. I shall give you a map with the location marked on it. Lodas will see that you get into Amlot. There you will deliver this other message to a man named Spehon from whom you will receive further instructions.'

From another drawer in the desk he took a map and spread it on the table. 'Here,' he said, making a mark on the map a little northwest of Amlot, 'is a flat-topped hill that you will easily be able to locate from the air. It rises between two streams that join one another just southeast of it. In the fork of these two streams lies the farm of Lodas. You will not divulge to Lodas the purpose of your mission or the name of the man you are to meet in Amlot.'

'But how am I to find Spehon?' I asked.

'I am coming to that. He is posing as a Zani, and stands high in the councils of Mephis. His office is in the palace formerly occupied by my uncle, Kord, the jong of Korva. You will have no difficulty in locating him. Now, of course you can't be safe in Amlot with that yellow hair of yours. It would arouse immediate suspicion. With black hair you will be safe enough if you do not talk too much, for, while they will know that you are not a member of the Zani party, that will arouse no suspicion as not all the citizens of Amlot are members of the party, even though they may be loyal to Mephis.'

'How will they know that I'm not a member of the party?' I asked.

'Zanis distinguish themselves by a peculiar form of haircut,' he explained. 'They shave their heads except for a ridge of hair about two inches wide that runs from the forehead to the nape of the neck. I think you understand your instructions, do you not?'

I told him that I did.

'Then here are the envelopes and the map; and here, also, is a bottle of dye to color your hair after you leave Sanara.'

'You have thought of everything.' I said.

'I usually do,' he remarked with a smile. 'Now is there anything you'd like to ask before you leave?'

'Yes,' I said. 'I should like to ask your permission to tell my wife that I shall be away for some time. I do not wish to cause her unnecessary worry.'

He shook his head. 'That is impossible,' he said. 'No one must know. There are spies everywhere. If I find that she is unduly alarmed, I promise you that I shall reassure her. You will leave early tomorrow morning. I wish you luck.'

That seemed to close the audience; so I saluted and turned to leave. Before I reached the door he spoke again. 'You are sure you cannot read Amtorian?' he asked.

I thought the question a little strange and his tone a little too eager. Perhaps it was this, I don't know what else it could have been, that impelled me to reply as I did.

'If that is necessary,' I said, 'perhaps you had better send someone else. I could fly him to Lodas's farm and bring him back when his mission is completed.'

'Oh, no,' he hastened to assure me. 'It will not be necessary for you to read Amtorian.' Then he dismissed me. Of course, having studied under Danus in the palace of the jong of Vepaja, I could read Amtorian quite as well as Muso himself.

All that evening I felt like a traitor to Duare; but I had sworn allegiance to Muso, and while I served him I must obey his orders. The next morning, as I kissed her goodbye, I suddenly had a premonition that it might be for the last time. I held her close, dreading to leave her; and she must have sensed in the tenseness of my body that something was amiss.

She looked up at me questioningly. 'There is something wrong, Carson,' she said. 'What is it?'

'It is just that this morning I hate to leave you even more than usual.' Then I kissed her and left.

Following a plan of my own to deceive the enemy as to my possible destination, I flew east out over the ocean, turning north when I had passed beyond the range of their vision; then I circled to the west far north of their camp and finally came to the ocean again west of Amlot. Flying back parallel with the coast and a few miles inland I had no difficulty in locating the flat-topped hill that was my principal landmark. During the flight I had dyed my hair black and removed the insignia of my office and service from the scant trappings that, with my loincloth, constituted my apparel. Now I could pass as an ordinary citizen of Amlot, providing no one noticed the color of my eyes.

I easily located the farm of Lodas in the fork of the rivers, and circled low looking for a suitable landing place. As I did so, a number of men working in the fields dropped their tools and ran toward the house, from which several other persons came to observe the ship. Evidently we aroused much excitement, and when I finally landed several men came cautiously toward me with weapons ready for any eventuality. I climbed down from the cockpit and advanced to meet them, holding my hands above my head to assure them that my intentions were friendly. When we were within speaking distance, I hailed them.

'Which of you is Lodas?' I asked.

They all halted and looked at one big fellow who was in the lead.

'I am Lodas,' he replied. 'Who are you and what do you want of Lodas?'

'I have a message for you,' I said, holding out the leather envelope.

He came forward rather hesitantly and took it from me. The others waited while he opened and read it.

'All right,' he said finally, 'come to the house with me.'

'First I'd like to make my ship fast in a safe place,' I told him. 'Where would you suggest? It should be protected from the wind and be somewhere where it can be watched at all times.'

He looked at it rather dubiously for a moment; then he shook his head. 'I haven't a building large enough to hold it,' he said, 'but you can put it between those two buildings over there. It will be protected from the wind there.'

I looked in the direction he indicated and saw two large buildings, probably barns, and saw that they would answer as well as anything he had to offer; so I taxied the ship between them, and with the help of Lodas and his fellows fastened it down securely.

'Let no one ever touch it or go near it,' I cautioned Lodas.

'I think no one will wish to go near it,' he said feelingly.

It must have looked like some monster from another world to those simple Amtorian rustics.

The ship tied down, the hands returned to the fields; and Lodas led me to the house, two women who had run out to enjoy the excitement accompanying us. The house, a long narrow building running east and west, had a verandah extending its full length on the south side and was windowless on the north, the side from which the prevailing warm winds came and the occasional hot blasts from the equatorial regions. Lodas led me into a large central room that was a combination living room, dining room, and kitchen. In addition to a huge fireplace there was a large clay oven, the former necessitated during the winter months when the colder winds came from the antarctic.

At the door of the room Lodas sent the women away, saying that he wished to speak with me alone. He seemed nervous and fearful; and when we were alone he drew me to a bench in a far corner of the room and sat close to me, whispering in my ear.

'This is bad business,' he said. 'There are spies everywhere. Perhaps some of the men working for me were sent by Mephis. He has spies spying upon everyone and spies spying on spies. Already rumors have come from Amlot of a strange thing that flies through the air dropping death and fire upon the forces of Mephis. At once my workers will know that it is this thing that you came in. They will be suspicious; they will talk; if there is a spy among them he will get word to Mephis, and that will be the end of me. What am I to do?'

'What did the message tell you to do?' I asked.

'It told me to get you into Amlot; that was all.'

'Are you going to do it?'

'I would do anything for Kord, my jong,' he said simply. 'Yes, I shall do it, but I shall probably die for it.'

'Perhaps we can work out a plan,' I suggested. 'If there is a spy here or if your men talk too much, it will be as bad for me as for you. Is there any place near here where I could bide my ship – some place that it would be reasonably safe?'

'If Mephis hears of it, it will not be safe here,' said Lodas, and I appreciated the truth of his statement. He thought for a moment; then he shook his head. 'The only place that I can think of is an island off the coast just south of us.'

'What sort of island?' I asked. 'Any clear, level land on it?'

'Oh, yes; it is a very flat island. It is covered with grass. No one lives there. It is seldom that anyone goes there – never since the revolution.'

'How far off shore is it?'

'It lies very close. I row to it in a few minutes.'

'You row to it? You have a boat?'

'Yes, once a year we row over to pick the berries that grow there. The women make jam of them that lasts all the rest of the year.'

'Fine!' I exclaimed. 'Now I have a plan that will remove all suspicion from you. Listen.' For ten minutes I talked, explaining every detail of my scheme. Occasionally Lodas slapped his knee and laughed. He was hugely pleased and relieved. Lodas was a big, simple, good natured fellow. One couldn't help but like and trust him. I didn't want to get him in any trouble, on his own account; and too, I knew that any trouble I got him into I would have to share.

We decided to put my plan into execution immediately; so we left the house; and as we passed the women, Lodas spoke to me angrily.

'Get off my farm!' he cried. 'I'll have nothing to do with you.'

We went at once to the ship and cast off the ropes; then I taxied it out toward the field where I had landed. Lodas followed on foot, and when we were within earshot of some of the men, he shouted at me loudly. 'Get out of here! I'll have nothing to do with you. Don't ever let me see you on my farm again.' The farm hands looked on in wide-eyed amazement, that grew wider eyed as I took off.

As I had done when I took off from Sanara I flew in a direction opposite that I intended going; and when I was out of sight circled back toward the ocean. I found the island Lodas had described and landed easily. Some high bushes grew on the windward side, and behind these I made the ship fast. I worked on it until dark, and had it so securely fastened down that I didn't believe that anything short of a hurricane could blow it away.

I had brought a little food with me from Sanara; and after eating, I crawled into the cabin and settled myself for the night. It was very lonely out there with only the wind soughing through the bushes and the surf pounding on the shore of that unknown sea. But I slept and dreamed of Duare. I knew that she must be worrying about me already, and I felt like a dog to have treated her so. I hoped that Muso would soon tell her that I had but gone on a mission for him. At the worst, I hoped to be home by the second day.

I awoke early and crossed the island to the shoreward side; and about half an hour later I saw a huge gantor approaching, drawing a wagon behind him. As he came nearer I recognized Lodas perched upon the animal's back. I waved to him, and he waved back. Leaving his conveyance near the shore, Lodas climbed down to a little cove, and presently I saw him pushing a crude boat into the water. Soon I was in it with him, and he was rowing back to the mainland.

'How did our little scheme work?' I asked him.

'Oh, fine,' he said, with a broad grin. 'I wouldn't tell them what you wanted me to do, but I told them that it was something wrong and that I was going to Amlot to tell the authorities about it. That satisfied them all; so if there was a spy among them I don't think he will give us any trouble. You are a very smart man to have thought of this plan.'

Once in the cove, we pulled the boat up onto a little ledge and climbed up to the waiting conveyance, a four wheeled, boxlike cart loaded with hay and vegetables. Lodas forked some of the hay to one side and told me to lie down in the depression he had made; then he forked the hay back on top of me.

It was about ten miles to Amlot, and of all the uncomfortable ten miles I ever rode those took first prize. The hay was soft enough to lie on; but the seeds got in my ears and nose and mouth and under my harness and loin-cloth, and I almost suffocated beneath the pile of hay on top of me. The motion of the cart was eccentric, to say the least. It pitched and wobbled and bumped over a road that must have been new when longevity serum was invented, but never had a shot of it. The gait of the gantor was much faster than I had anticipated. He evidently had a long, swinging walk; and we must have made at least six miles an hour, which is somewhere between the speed of a horse's walk and trot.

But at last we got to Amlot. I knew that, when we came to a stop and I heard men's voices questioning Lodas. Finally I heard one say, 'Oh, I know this farmer. He brings stuff into the city often. He's all right.' They let us go on then, and I could tell by the sound of the wheels that we were rolling over a pavement. I was inside the walls of Amlot! I hoped the remainder of my mission would prove as readily fulfilled as this first part of it, and there was no reason to believe that it would not. If it did, I should be back with Duare by the following day.

We must have driven a considerable distance into the city before we stopped again. There was a short wait during which I heard voices; but they were low, and I could not overhear what was being said; then there was a creaking sound as of the hinges of a heavy gate, and immediately we moved forward a short distance and stopped again. Once more the hinges groaned, and then I heard Lodas's voice telling me to come out. I didn't need a second invitation. Throwing the hay aside, I stood up. We were in the courtyard of a one story house. A man was standing with Lodas looking up at me. He didn't seem very glad to see me.

'This is my brother, Horjan,' said Lodas, 'and, Horjan, this is – say, what is your name, my friend?'

'Wasn't it in the message I brought?' I asked, pretending surprise.

'No, it wasn't.'

Perhaps it would be as well, I thought, if I didn't publicize my true name too widely. 'Where I come from,' I said. 'I would be called Homo Sapiens. Call me Homo;' so Homo I became.

'This is bad business,' said Horjan. 'If we are found out, the Zani Guard will come and take us off to prison; and there we shall be tortured and killed. No, I do not like it.'

'But it is for the jong,' said Lodas, as though that were ample reason for any sacrifice.

'What did the jong ever do for us?' demanded Horjan.

'He is our jong,' said Lodas simply. 'Horjan, I am ashamed of you.'

'Well, let it pass. I will keep him this night, but tomorrow he must go on about his business. Come into the house now where I can hide you. I do not like it. I do not like it at all. I am afraid. The Zani Guard do terrible things to one whom they suspect.'

And so I went into the house of Horjan in Amlot, a most unwelcome guest. I sympathized with the two brothers, but I could do nothing about it. I was merely obeying the orders of Muso.

VII

Zerka

Horjan gave me a little room on the court and told me to stay there so that no one would see me; then he and Lodas left me. It was not long before Lodas returned to say that he was going to take his produce to market and then start home. He wanted to say goodbye to me and wish me luck. He was a fine, loyal fellow.

The hours dragged heavily in that stuffy little room. At dusk Horjan brought me food and water. He tried to find out what I had come to Amlot for, but I evaded all his questions. He kept repeating that he would be glad to get rid of me, but at last he went away. After I had eaten I tried to sleep, but sleep didn't seem to want to come. I had just finally started to doze when I heard voices. They came from the adjoining room, and the partition was so thin that I could hear what was said. I recognized Horjan's voice, and there was the voice of another man. It was not Lodas.

'I tell you it is bad business,' Horjan was saying. 'Here is this man about whom I know nothing. If it is known that he is hiding here I shall get the blame, even though I don't know why he is hiding.'

'You are a fool to keep him,' said the other.

'What shall I do with him?' demanded Horjan.

'Turn him over to the Zani Guard.'

'But still they will say that I had been hiding him,' groaned Horjan.

'No; say that you don't know how he got into your house – that you had been away, and when you came back you found him hiding in one of your rooms. They will not harm you for that. They may even give you a reward.'

'Do you think so?' asked Horjan.

'Certainly. A man who lives next to me informed on a neighbor, and they gave him a reward for that.'

'Is that so? It is worth thinking about. He may be a dangerous man. Maybe he has come to assassinate Mephis.'

'You could say that that was what he came for,' encouraged the other.

'They would give a very big reward for that, wouldn't they?' asked Horjan.

'Yes, I should think a very big reward.'

There was silence for several minutes; then I heard a bench pushed back. 'Where are you going?' demanded Horjan's visitor.

'I am going to tell the Zanis,' said Horjan.

'I shall go with you,' announced his companion. 'Don't forget that the idea was mine – I should have half the reward. Maybe two-thirds of it.'

'But he is my prisoner,' insisted Horjan. 'It is I who am going to notify the Zani Guard. You stay here.'

'I rather guess not. If I told them what I know, they would arrest you both; and I'd get a great big reward.'

'Oh, you wouldn't do that!' cried Horjan.

'Well, I certainly shall if you keep on trying to rob me of the reward.'

'Oh, I wouldn't rob you of it. I'll give you ten per cent.'

The other laughed. 'Ten per cent nothing. *I'll* give *you* ten per cent – and that's much more than you deserve – plotting against Mephis and Spehon and the rest of them.'

'You can't put that over on me,' shouted Horjan. 'Nobody'll believe you anyhow. Everybody knows what a liar you are. Hey, where are you going? Come back here! I'm the one that's going to tell them.'

I heard the sound of running feet, the slamming of a door, and then silence. That was my cue to get out of there, and I can tell you that I didn't waste any time acting on it. I didn't know how far they'd have to go to find a member of the Zani Guard. There might be one at the next corner for all that I knew. I found my way out of the house in short order, and when I reached the avenue my two worthy friends were still in sight, quarrelling as they ran. I turned and melted into the shadows of the night that fell in the opposite direction.

There was no use running. I didn't even hurry, but sauntered along as though I were an old resident of Amlot going to call on my mother-in-law. The avenue I was in was dark and gloomy, but I could see a better lighted one ahead; so I made for that. I passed a few people, but no one paid any attention to me. Presently I found myself in an avenue of small shops. They were all open and lighted, and customers were coming and going. There were lots of soldiers on the street, and here I caught my first sight of a member of the Zani Guard.

There were three of them together, and they were swaggering down the sidewalk elbowing men, women and children into the gutter. I felt a little nervous as I approached them, but they paid no attention to me.

I had been doing a great deal of thinking since I had overheard the conversation between Horjan and his accomplice. I couldn't forget that the latter had linked Spehon's name with that of Mephis. The message that I carried in my pocket was addressed to Spehon. What could Muso be communicating secretly with a leader of the Zanis for? It didn't make sense and it didn't sound good. It worried me. Then I recalled the inexplicable secrecy of my departure and the fact that Muso had warned me against telling Lodas the name of the person I was bearing a message to. Why was he afraid to have that known? And why had he been so relieved when he assured himself that I could not read Amtorian? It was a puzzle that was commencing to clear itself up in my mind, or at least I was beginning to suspect something of the solution. Whether I were right or not, I might never know; or I might learn it tomorrow. That depended largely upon whether or not I delivered the message to Spehon. I was almost minded to try to get out of the city and back to my ship; then fly to Sanara and lay the whole matter before Taman, whom I trusted. But my sometimes foolish sense of duty to a trust imposed in me soon put that idea out of my head. No, I would go on and carry out my orders – that was my duty as a soldier.

As I proceeded along the avenue the shops took on a more prosperous appearance, the trappings and jewels of the people on the street became richer. Gorgeously trapped gantors carried their loads of passengers to and fro or stopped before some shop while master or mistress entered to make a purchase. Before one brilliantly lighted building twenty or thirty huge gantors waited. When I came opposite the building, I looked in. It was a restaurant. The sight of the bright lights, the laughing people, the good food attracted me. The meager meal that Horjan had brought me had only served to whet my appetite. I entered the building, and as I did so I saw that it was apparently filled to capacity. I stood for a moment looking about for a vacant table, and was about to turn and walk out when an attendant came up to me and asked me if I wished to dine. I told him I did, and he led me to a small table for two where a woman was already seated.

'Sit here,' he said. It was a trifle embarrassing.

'But this table is occupied,' I said.

'That is all right,' said the woman. 'You are welcome to sit here.'

There was really nothing else for me to do but thank her and take the vacant chair. 'This is very generous of you,' I said.

'Not at all,' she assured me.

'I had no idea, of course, that the attendant was bringing me to someone else's table. It was very presumptuous of him.'

She smiled. She had a very lovely smile. In fact she was a very good-looking woman and, like all the civilized women of Amtor that I had seen, apparently quite young. She might have been seventeen or seven hundred years old. That is what the serum of longevity does for them.

'It was not so presumptuous as it might seem,' she said; 'at least not on the part of the attendant. I told him to fetch you.'

I must have looked my surprise. 'Well, of course, that was very nice of you,' was the only banality I could think of at the moment.

'You see,' she continued, 'I saw you looking for a table, there was a vacant chair here, I was alone and lonely. You don't mind, do you?'

'I'm delighted. You were not the only lonely person in Amlot. Have you ordered?'

'No; the service here is execrable. They never have enough attendants, but the food is the best in town. But of course you have eaten here often – everyone eats here.'

I didn't know just what position to take. Perhaps it would be better to admit that I was a stranger rather than pretend I was not and then reveal the fact by some egregious error that I would be certain to make in conversation with any person familiar with Amlot and the manners and customs of its people. I saw that she was appraising me closely. Perhaps it would be more correct to say inventorying me – my harness, my other apparel, my eyes. I caught her quizzical gaze upon my eyes several times. I determined to admit that I was a stranger when our attention was attracted to a slight commotion across the room. A squad of Zani Guards was questioning people at one of the tables. Their manner was officious and threatening. They acted like a bunch of gangsters.

'What's all that about?' I asked my companion.

'You don't know?'

'It is one of the many things I don't know,' I admitted.

'About Amlot,' she concluded for me. 'They are looking for traitors and for Atorians. It goes on constantly in Amlot nowadays. It is strange you have never noticed it. Here they come now.'

Sure enough, they were heading straight across the room for our table, and their leader seemed to have his eyes on me. I thought then that he was looking for me in particular. Later I learned that it is their custom to skip around a place, examining a few people in each. It is more for the moral effect on the citizens than for anything else. Of course they do make arrests, but that is largely a matter of the caprice of the leader unless a culprit has been pointed out by an informer.

The leader barged right up to me and stuck his face almost into mine. 'Who are you?' he demanded. 'Give an account of yourself.'

'He is a friend of mine,' said the woman across the table. 'He is all right, kordogan.'

The man looked at her, and then he wilted. 'Of course, Toganja,' he cried apologetically; then he marched his men away and out of the restaurant.

'Perhaps it was very well for me, in addition to having your company, that this was the only vacant chair in the restaurant; although I really had nothing to fear. It is just disconcerting for a stranger.'

'Then I guessed correctly? You are a stranger?'

'Yes, Toganja; I was about to explain when the kordogan pounced on me.'

'You have credentials though?'

'Credentials? Why, no.'

'Then it is very well for you that I was here. You would certainly have been on your way to prison now and probably shot tomorrow – unless you have friends here.'

'Only one,' I said.

'And may I ask who that one is?'

'You.' We both smiled.

'Tell me something about yourself,' she said. 'It doesn't seem possible that there is such an innocent abroad in Amlot today.'

'I just reached the city this afternoon,' I explained. 'You see, I am a soldier of fortune. I heard there was fighting here, and I came looking for a commission.'

'On which side?' she asked.

I shrugged. 'I know nothing about either side,' I said.

'How did you get into the city without being arrested?' she demanded.

'A company of soldiers, some workers, and a few farmers were coming through the gate. I just walked through with them. Nobody stopped me; nobody asked me any questions. Did I do wrong?'

She shook her head. 'Not if you could get away with it. Nothing is wrong that you can get away with. The crime is in getting caught. Tell me where you are from, if you don't mind.'

'Why should I mind? I have nothing to conceal. I am from Vodaro.' I remembered having seen a land mass called Vodaro on one of Danus's maps. It extended from the southern edge of the south temperate zone into the terra incognita of the antarctic. Danus said that little was known of it. I hoped that nothing was known of it. Nothing less than I knew of it could be known.

She nodded. 'I was sure you were from some far country,' she said. 'You are very different from the men of Korva. Do all your people have grey eyes?'

'Oh, yes, indeed,' I assured her. 'All Vodaroans have grey eyes, or nearly all.' It occurred to me that she might meet a Vodaroan some day who had black eyes. If she got to inquiring around right in this restaurant she might find one. I didn't know, and I wasn't taking any chances. She seemed to be quite an alert person who liked to seek after knowledge.

An attendant finally condescended to come and take our order, and after the dinner arrived I found that it was well worth waiting for. During the meal she explained many things about conditions in Amlot under the rule of the Zanis, but so, adroit was she that I couldn't tell whether she was a *phile* or a *phobe*. While we were in the midst of dinner another detachment of the Zani Guard entered. They went directly to a table next to us where a citizen who accompanied them pointed out one of the diners.

'That is he,' he cried accusingly. 'His great-grandmother was nursed by an Atorian woman.'

The accused rose and paled. 'Mistal!' cried the kordogan in charge of the detachment, and struck the accused man heavily in the face, knocking him down; then the others jumped on him and kicked and beat him. Finally they dragged him away, more dead than alive. (A *mistal* is a rodent about the size of a cat. The word is often used as a term of opprobrium, as one might say 'Pig!')

'Now what was all that about?' I asked my companion. 'Why should a man be beaten to death because his great-grandmother nursed at the breast of an Atorian woman?'

'The milk and therefore the blood of an Atorian entered the veins of an ancestor, thereby contaminating the pure blood of the super race of Korva,' she explained.

'But what is wrong with the blood of an Atorian?' I asked. 'Are Atorians diseased?'

'It is really rather difficult to explain,' she said. 'If I were you I should just accept it as fact while in Amlot – and not discuss it.'

I realized that that was excellent advice. From what I had seen in Amlot I was convinced that the less one discussed anything the better off he would be and the longer he would live.

'You haven't told me your name,' said the Toganja; 'mine is Zerka.'

I couldn't safely give her my own name, and I didn't dare use Homo any longer because I was sure I had been reported by Horjan and his good friend; so I had to think of another name quickly.

'Vodo,' I said quickly, thinking that Vodo of Vodaro sounded almost colossal.

'And in your own country you must be a very important man,' she said. I could see she was trying to pump me, and I saw no use in saying I was a street car conductor or an author or anything like that. They wouldn't sound important enough; and, anyway, as long as I was launched on, a career of deception I might as well make a good job of it.'

'I am the Tanjong of Vodaro,' I told her, 'but please don't tell anyone. I'm travelling incognito.' A tanjong is the son of a ruling jong – a prince.

'But how in the world did your government ever permit you to travel alone like this? Why, you might be killed.'

'From what I have seen of Amlot I can readily agree with you,' I said, laughing. 'As a matter of fact, I ran away. I got tired of all the pomp and cere-mony of the court. I wanted to live my life as a man.'

'That is very interesting,' she said. 'If you want to take service here, perhaps I can help you. I am not without influence. Come and see me tomorrow. The driver of any public gantor knows where my palace is. Now I must be going. This has been quite an adventure. You have kept me from utter boredom.'

I noticed that she said utter.

I walked to the door with her, where two warriors saluted her and followed us to the curb, one of them summoning the driver of a gantor – her private conveyance.

'Where do you stop?' she asked me, as she waited for her gantor.

'I haven't stopped yet,' I told her. 'You know I am a stranger here. Can you suggest a good place?'

'Yes, come with me; I'll take you there.'

The ornate howdah on the broad back of her gantor seated four in the front compartment – two and two, facing one another; behind this was another seat where the two armed guards rode.

As the great beast strode majestically along the avenue, I watched with interest the night life of this Amtorian city. Previously I had been in Kooaad, the tree city of Vepaja, in the Thorist city of Kapdor, in Kormor, the City of the Dead, and in lovely Havatoo. The latter and this city of Amlot were, of all of them, the only cities in the true sense of the word; and while Amlot could not compare with Havatoo, it was yet a city of life and activity. Though the hour was late, this main avenue was thronged with people; lines of gaily caparisoned gantors moved in both directions carrying their loads of passengers gay and laughing, grave and serious. Everywhere the Zani Guardsmen were in evidence, their strange headdress distinguishing them from all others – a two-inch ridge of hair from forehead to nape. Their apparel was distinctive too, because of its ornateness. Shops and restaurants, gambling houses and theaters, brilliantly lighted, lined the avenue. Amlot did not seem like a city at war. I mentioned this to Zerka.

'It is our way of keeping up the morale of the people,' she explained. 'As a matter of fact, the last war, which brought on the revolution, left us disillusioned, bitter, and impoverished. We were compelled to give up our entire navy and merchant marine. There was little life and less laughter on the avenues of Amlot; then, by decree of Kord, the jong, every public place was required to reopen and the people, in some instances, actually driven into the streets to patronize them. The effect was electrical, and after the revolution the Zanis encouraged the practice. It has been most helpful in maintaining the spirit of the people. Well, here we are at the travellers' house. Come and see me tomorrow.'

I thanked her for her courtesy to me and for the pleasant evening she had given me. The driver had placed the ladder against the gantor's side, and I was about to descend, when she laid a hand on my arm. 'If you are questioned,' she said, 'tell them what you told me; and if they do not believe you, or you get in any trouble, refer them to me. Tell them I have given you permission to do so. Here, take this and wear it,' and she slipped a ring from one of her fingers and handed it to me; 'it will substantiate your claim to my friendship. And now, one other thing. I would not mention again that you are a tanjong. Royalty is not so popular in Amlot as it once was; why, is immaterial. A very great jong came here recently in search of an only daughter who had been kidnapped. He is still imprisoned in the Gap kum Rov – if he is yet alive.'

A very great jong whose only daughter had been kidnapped! Could it be possible?

'What great jong is that?' I asked.

Her eyes narrowed a little as she replied, 'It is not well to be too inquisitive in Amlot during these times.'

'I am sorry,' I said; then I descended to the sidewalk, and her great gantor moved off down the avenue.

VIII

Muso's Message

The travellers' house, or hotel, to which Zerka had brought me was really quite magnificent, indicating that Amlot had been a city of considerable wealth and importance in this part of Amtor. The lobby served the same purpose that a lobby in an Earthly hotel does. The desk was a large, circular booth in the center. There were benches, chairs, divans, flowers; small shops opened from it. I felt almost at home. The lobby was crowded. The ubiquitous Zani Guard was well represented. As I stepped to the desk, two of them followed me and listened while the clerk questioned me, asking my name and address.

'Where are your credentials?' barked one of the Zanis.

'I have none,' I replied. 'I am a stranger from Vodaro, seeking military service here.'

'What! No credentials, you mistal? You are probably a dog of a spy from Sanara.' He bellowed so loud that the attention of everyone in the lobby was attracted, and all about us there fell silence that seemed to me the silence of terror. 'This is what you need,' he yelled, and struck at me. I am afraid I lost my temper, and I know I did a very foolish thing. I parried his blow and struck him heavily in the face – so heavily that he sprawled backward upon the floor fully ten feet from me; then his companion came for me with drawn sword.

'You had better be sure what you are doing,' I said, and held out the ring Zerka had given me so that he could see it.

He took one look at it and dropped the point of his weapon. 'Why didn't you say so?' he asked, and his tone was very different from that of his fellow had been. By this time the latter had staggered to his feet and was trying to draw his sword. He was quite groggy.

'Wait,' his companion cautioned him, and went and whispered in his ear, whereupon they both turned and left the lobby like a couple of whipped dogs. After that the clerk was the personification of courtesy. He inquired about my luggage, which I told him would arrive later; then he called a strapping porter who had a chair-like contraption strapped to his back. The fellow came and knelt before me and I took my seat in the chair, for it was obvious that that was what was expected of me; then he stood up, took a key from the clerk and ran up three flights of stairs with me – a human elevator, and the only sort of elevator known to Amlot. The fellow was a veritable composite of Hercules and Mercury. I tried to tip him after he had set me down in my room, but he couldn't understand my good intentions. He thought I was trying to bribe him to do something that he shouldn't do. I am sure he reported me as a suspicious character after he returned to the desk.

My room was large and well furnished; a bath opened from it. A balcony in front overlooked the city out to the ocean, and I went out there and stood for a long time thinking over all that had occurred to me, but mostly thinking of Duare. I also thought much on my strange encounter with the Toganja Zerka. I couldn't quite convince myself that her interest in me was wholly friendly, yet I really had no reason to doubt it; except, perhaps, that she seemed a woman of mystery. It is possible that I doubted her sincerity because of my own deceitfulness; yet what else could I have done. I was in an enemy city, where, if the truth about me were even suspected, I should have received short shrift. As I could not tell the truth, I had to lie; and while I was lying, I might as well make a good job of it, I reasoned. I was sure that I had completely deceived her. Had she also deceived me? I knew the city was full of spies. What better way to entice a stranger into unwary admissions than through a beautiful woman – it is as old as espionage itself.

The possibility that Duare's father, Mintep, might be a prisoner here gave me the most concern and resolved me to remain until I had definitely established the truth or falsity of my suspicions. The reference to Spehon, made by Horjan's companion, that linked closely with the leader of Zanism the name of the man to whom I bore a message from Muso was also good for considerable conjecture. I was frankly apprehensive that all was not as it should be. There was a way to discover, perhaps. I took the leather envelope containing Muso's message from my pocket pouch, broke the seals, and opened it. This is what I read:

Muso, the Jong,
    Addresses Spehon and Amlot.
    May success attend your ventures and old age never overtake you.
    Muso dispatches this message to Spehon by Carson of Venus, who
    cannot read Amtorian.
If Sanara were to fall into the hands of Mephis, this unfortunate civil
    war would be ended.
That would be well if Muso were to be jong of Korva after the fall of
    Sanara.
If Mephis wishes all this to happen, let three blue rockets be shot into
    the air before the main gate of Sanara on three successive nights.
On the fourth night let a strong force approach the main gate secretly,
    with stronger reserves held nearby; then Muso will cause the main

gates to be thrown open for the purpose of permitting a sortie. But there will be no sortie. The troops of Mephis may then enter the city in force. Muso will surrender, and the bloodshed may cease.

Muso will make a good jong, conferring always with Mephis.

The Zanis shall be rewarded.

It would be regrettable, but best, if Carson of Venus were destroyed in Amlot.

May success be yours.

MUSO

JONG

I turned a little cold at the thought of how near I had been to delivering that message without reading it. I hadn't realized that I had been carrying my death warrant around on me as innocently as a babe in the woods. I looked around for some means of destroying it, and found a fireplace in one corner of the room. That would answer the purpose nicely. I walked to it, carrying the document; and, taking my little pocket fire-maker from my pouch, was about to set fire to it when something caused me to hesitate. Here was a valuable document – a document that might mean much to Taman and to Korva if it were properly utilized. I felt that it should not be destroyed, yet I didn't like the idea of carrying it around with me. If I could but find a hiding place! But where? No place in this room would answer if I were even slightly under suspicion, and I knew that I already was. I was positive that the moment I left the room it would be thoroughly searched. I put the message back in its leather container and went to bed. Tomorrow I would have to solve this problem; tonight I was too tired.

I slept very soundly. I doubt that I moved all night. I awoke about the 2nd hour, which would be about 6:40 A.M. Earth time. The Amtorian day is 26 hours, 56 minutes, 4 seconds of Earth time. Here it is divided into thirty-six hours of forty minutes each, the hours being numbered from 1 to 36. The 1st hour corresponds roughly with mean sunrise, and is about 6 A.M. Earth time. As I rolled over and stretched for a moment before arising, I felt quite content with myself. I was to call on Zerka this very morning with the possibility of obtaining service of some nature with the Zanis that might make it possible for me to ascertain if Mintep were really in Amlot. I had read Muso's message to Spehon; so that that was no longer a menace to me. My only real problem now was to find a suitable hiding place for it, but I have so much confidence in myself that I did not apprehend any great difficulty in doing so.

Stepping out of bed, I walked to the balcony for a breath of fresh air and a look at the city by daylight. I saw that the travellers' house stood much closer to the waterfront than I had imagined. There was a beautiful landlocked harbor lying almost at my feet. Innumerable small boats lay at anchor or moored to quays. They were all that the enemy had left to the conquered nation.

A new day was before me. What would it bring forth? Well, I would bathe, dress, have breakfast, and see. As I crossed to the bath, I saw my apparel lying in disorder on the floor. I knew that I had not left it thus, and immediately I became apprehensive. My first thought, naturally, was of the message; and so the first thing that I examined was my pocket pouch. The message was gone! I went to the door. It was still locked as I had left it the night before. I immediately thought of the two Zani Guardsmen with whom I had had an altercation in the lobby. They would have their revenge now. I wondered when I would be arrested. Well, the worst they could do would be to take me before Spehon, unless he had already issued orders for my destruction. If I were not immediately arrested, I must try to escape from the city. I could not serve Mintep now by remaining. My only hope was to reach Sanara and warn Taman.

I performed my toilette rather perfunctorily and without interest; then I descended to the lobby. It was almost empty. The clerk on duty spoke to me quite civilly, for a hotel clerk. No one else paid any attention to me as I found the dining room and ordered my breakfast.

I had made up my mind that I was going to see Zerka. Maybe she could and would help me to escape from the city. I would give her a good reason for my wishing to do so. After finishing my breakfast, I returned to the lobby. The place was taking on an air of greater activity. Several members of the Zani Guard were loitering near the desk. I determined to bluff the whole thing through; so I walked boldly toward them and made some inquiry at the desk. As I turned away, I saw two more of the guardsmen enter the lobby from the avenue. They were coming directly toward me, and I at once recognized them as the two with whom I had had the encounter the preceding night. This, I thought, is the end. As they neared me both of them recognized me; but they passed on by me, and as they did so, both saluted me. After that I went out into the street and window shopped to kill time; then about the 8th hour (10:40 A.M.E.T.) I found a public gantor and directed the driver to take me to the palace of Toganja Zerka. A moment later I was in the cab of my amazing taxi and lumbering along a broad avenue that paralleled the ocean.

Shortly after we left the business portion of the city we commenced to pass magnificent private palaces set in beautiful grounds. Finally we stopped in front of a massive gate set in a wall that surrounded the grounds of one of these splendid residences. My driver shouted, and a warrior opened a small gate and came out. He looked up at me questioningly.

'What do you want?' he asked.

'I have come at the invitation of the Toganja Zerka,' I said.

'What is your name, please?' he asked.

'Vodo,' I replied; I almost said Homo.

'The Toganja is expecting you,' said the warrior as he threw open the gates.

The palace was a beautiful structure of white marble, or what looked like white marble to me. It was built on three sides of a large and beautiful garden, the fourth side being open to the ocean, down to the shore of which the flowers, shrubbery, and lawn ran. But just then I was not so much interested in scenic beauty as I was in saving my neck.

After a short wait, I was ushered into the presence of Zerka. Her reception room was almost a throne room, and she was sitting in a large chair on a raised dais which certainly carried the suggestion of sovereignty. She greeted me cordially and invited me to sit on cushions at her feet.

'You look quite rested this morning,' she observed. 'I hope you had a good night.'

'Very,' I assured her.

'Any adventure after I left you? You got along all right in the hotel?'

I had a feeling she was pumping me. I don't know why I should have, unless it was my guilty conscience; but I did.

'Well, I had a little altercation with a couple of the Zani Guardsmen,' I admitted; 'and I lost my temper and knocked one of them down – very foolishly.'

'Yes, that was foolish. Don't do such a thing again, no matter what the provocation. How did you get out of it?'

'I showed your ring. After that they left me alone. I saw them again this morning, and they saluted me.'

'And that was all that happened to you?' she persisted.

'All of any consequence.'

She looked at me for a long minute without speaking. She seemed either to be weighing something in her mind or trying to fathom my thoughts. Finally she spoke again. 'I have sent for a man to whom I am going to entrust your future. You may trust him implicitly. Do you understand? – implicitly!'

'Thank you,' I said. 'I don't know why you are doing these things for me, but I want you to know that I appreciate your kindness to a friendless stranger and that if I can serve you at any time – well, you know you have only to command me.'

'Oh, it is nothing,' she assured me. 'You saved me from a very bad evening with myself, and I am really doing very little in return.'

Just then a servant opened the door and announced: 'Maltu Mephis! Mantar!'

A tall man in the trappings and with the headdress of a Zani Guardsman entered the room. He came to the foot of the dais, saluted and said, 'Maltu Mephis!'

'Maltu Mephis!' replied Zerka. 'I am glad to see you, Mantar. This is Vodo,' and to me, 'this is Mantar.'

'Maltu Mephis! I am glad to know you, Vodo,' said Mantar.

'And I am glad to know you, Mantar,' I replied.

A questioning frown clouded Mantar's brow, and he glanced at Zerka. She smiled.

'Vodo is an utter stranger here,' she said. 'He does not yet understand our customs. It is you who will have to inform him.'

Mantar looked relieved. 'I shall start at once,' he said. 'You will forgive me, then, Vodo, if I correct you often?'

'Certainly. I shall probably need it.'

'To begin with, it is obligatory upon all loyal citizens to preface every greeting and introduction with the words Maltu Mephis. Please, never omit them. Never criticize the government or any official or any member of the Zani Party. Never fail to salute and cry Maltu Mephis whenever you see and hear others doing it. In fact, it will be well if you always do what you see everyone else doing, even though you may not understand.'

'I shall certainly follow your advice,' I told him; but what my mental reservations might be I wisely kept to myself, as he probably did also.

'Now, Mantar,' said Zerka, 'this ambitious young man is from far Vodaro, and he wishes to take service as a soldier of Amlot. Will you see what you can do for him? And now you must both be going, as I have many things to attend to. I shall expect you to call and report to me occasionally, Vodo.'

IX

I Become a Zani

Mantar took me immediately to the palace formerly occupied by the Jong, Kord, and now by Mephis and his lieutenants. 'We shall go directly to Spehon,' he said. 'No use wasting time on underlings.'

To Spehon! To the man whom Muso had advised to destroy me! I felt positive that the message must already be in his hands, as it must have been stolen by Zani spies who would have delivered it to him immediately.

'Why do we go to Spehon?' I asked.

'Because he is head of the Zani Guard, which also includes our secret police. Zerka suggested that I find you a berth in the Guard. You are fortunate indeed to have such a friend as the Toganja Zerka; otherwise, if you had been given service at all, it would have been at the front, which is not so good since Muso enlisted the services of this fellow called Carson of Venus with his diabolical contrivance that flies through the air and rains bombs on everyone.'

'Flies through the air,' I asked, in simulated surprise. 'Is there really such a thing? What can it be?'

'We really don't know much about it,' Mantar admitted. 'Of course everyone at the front has seen it, and we learned a little from some prisoners we took who were members of a Sanaran party making a sortie against our first line. They told us the name of the fellow who flies it and what little they knew of him and of the thing he calls an anotar, but that really was not much. Yes, you will be fortunate if you get into the Guard. If you are an officer, it is something of a sinecure; but you'll have to watch your step. You must hate everything we Zanis hate and applaud everything that we applaud, and under no circumstances must you ever even look critical of anything that is Zani. To demonstrate what I mean: we were listening to a speech by Our Beloved Mephis one evening, when a bright blue light shining in his eyes unexpectedly caused one of my fellow officers to knit his brows and half close his eyes in what appeared to be a frown of disapproval. He was taken out and shot.'

'I shall be very careful,' I assured him, and you may believe me that I meant it.

The palace of the former jong was, indeed, a magnificent structure; but I'm afraid I didn't fully appreciate it as I walked through its corridors toward the office of Spehon – my mind was on other things. We arrived at last at a waiting room just outside the office of the great man, and there we waited for about half an hour before we were summoned into the presence. Men were coming and going to and from the waiting room in a constant stream. It was a very busy place. Most of them wore the Zani uniform and sported the Zani coiffure, and as they came and went the air was filled with 'Maltu Mephises' and Zani salutes.

At last we were ushered into the presence of Spehon. Like nearly all civilized Amtorians, he was a handsome man; but his mouth was a shade too cruel and his eyes a little too shifty for perfection. Mantar and I each said 'Maltu Mephis' and saluted; Spehon said 'Maltu Mephis! Greetings, Mantar. What brings you here?' He barked the words like a human terrier.

'Maltu Mephis! This is Vodo,' announced Mantar. 'I bring him to you at the suggestion of the Toganja Zerka, his good friend. She recommends him for a commission in the Guard.'

'But he is not even a Zani,' expostulated Spehon.

'He is not even from Anlap,' said Mantar, 'but he wishes to be a Zani and serve Our Beloved Mephis.'

'From what country do you come?' demanded Spehon.

'From Vodaro,' I replied.

'Have you any Atorian blood in your veins?'

'Had I, I should have been killed in Vodaro,' I cried.

'And why?' he asked.

'And why, may I ask, Spehon, do *you* kill Atorians?' I demanded.

'Naturally, because they have large ears,' he replied. 'We must keep the blood of the Korvans pure.'

'You have answered your own question, Spehon,' I told him. 'We Vodaroans are very proud of our pure blood; so we, too, kill the Atorians because they have large ears.'

'Excellent!' he exclaimed. 'Will you swear to love, honor, and obey Our Beloved Mephis, give your life for him, if necessary, and hold him and the Zani Party above all else?'

'I swear!' I said, but I had my fingers crossed; then we all saluted and said, 'Maltu Mephis!'

'You are now a Zani,' he announced. He saluted me, and said, 'Maltu Mephis!'

'Maltu Mephis!' I said, and saluted him.

'I appoint you a tokordogan,' said Spehon, saluting, 'Maltu Mephis!'

'Maltu Mephis!' I replied, and saluted. A tokordogan is somewhat similar to a lieutenant. A kordogan is comparable to a sergeant and as the prefix *to* means either high or over, my title might be translated as oversergeant.

'You will be responsible for Vodo's training,' Spehon told Mantar, then we all Maltu Mephised and saluted.

I breathed a sigh of relief as I quitted the office of Spehon. Evidently he had not received the message as yet. I still had a little lease on life.

Mantar now took me to the officers' quarters adjoining the barracks of the Zani Guard, which are situated close to the palace; and here a barber gave me an approved Zani haircut, after which I went with Mantar to be outfitted with the regulation uniform and weapons of a tokordogan of the Zani Guard.

On the way back from the outfitters I heard a great commotion ahead of us on the broad avenue along which we were walking. People lining the curbs were shouting something that I could not understand at first, but presently recognized as the incessant chant of the Zanis – Maltu Mephis! As the sound approached I saw that the shouts were being directed at a procession of giant gantors.

'Our Beloved Mephis comes this way.' said Mantar. 'When he approaches, stand at salute and shout Maltu Mephis as loud as you can until he has passed.'

Presently I saw men standing on their heads in the street and along the curbs, and each of them was shouting Maltu Mephis at the top of his lungs. Only the women and the members of the Zani Guard did not stand on their heads; but everybody shouted, and everybody saluted who was not using his hands to keep him from falling down. They commenced when the first elephant came within a few yards of where they stood, and continued until the last elephant had passed them by the same distance. They all seemed absolutely devoid of any sense of humor.

When the procession came abreast of me I saw such ornately housed and trapped gantors as I had never before seen. In the gilded howdah of one of them sat a small, insignificant looking man in the uniform of a Zani kordogan. It was Mephis. He looked actually frightened; and his eyes were constantly darting from side to side, warily. I guessed, what I learned later, that he was in mortal fear of assassination – and with good reason.

After Mephis had passed I expressed a wish to Mantar to see something of the city. I told him that I would especially like to go down to the waterfront and look at the boats there. Immediately he was suspicious. I have never seen such suspicious people.

'Why do you want to go down to the waterfront?' he asked.

'We Vodaroans depend much on the sea for most of our food; therefore we are all familiar with boats and fond of them. I am naturally interested in seeing the design of the small boats of Anlap. As a matter of fact, I should like much to own one. I like to sail and fish.'

My explanation seemed to satisfy him, and he suggested that we hail a passing gantor and ride down to the quay, which we did. I saw innumerable boats, most of which had evidently not been in use for some considerable time. Mantar explained that they probably belonged to men who were serving at the front.

'Do you suppose I could buy or rent one of them?' I asked.

'You do not have to buy or rent anything,' he said. 'You are now a member of the Zani Guard and can take anything you please from anyone who is not a member of the Guard.' That was an excellent convention – for the Zani Guardsmen.

Having seen and learned what I had come to the waterfront for, I was ready to return into the city and commence my real training under Mantar. This lasted in an intensive form for about a week, during which time I did not visit Zerka nor receive any call from Spehon. Could it be that the message had not come into his hands? I could scarcely believe it. Perhaps, I thought, he is not going to accept Muso's offer and is not, therefore, interested in destroying me. But that line of reasoning was not wholly satisfactory. Knowing how suspicious they were and vindictive, I could not believe that Spehon would permit me to live or wear the uniform of a Zani Guardsman a day after he discovered how I had lied to him. I was compelled to consider the matter only as a wholly baffling mystery.

I cannot say that I enjoyed the companionship of my fellow officers, with the exception of Mantar. He was a gentleman. Most of the others were surly boors – an aggregation of ignorant thugs, bums, and gangsters. The men under us were of the same types. All seemed suspicious of one another, and I think especially of Mantar and me. They resented the fact that we were cultured; and the very fact that we were cultured seemed to feed their suspicions of us; and because they felt their inferiority, they hated us, too. Because of this atmosphere of suspicion it was difficult for me to learn anything about the one thing that kept me from escaping from Amlot at once – I refer to my belief that Mintep might be a prisoner in the city. I felt that I could easily escape by commandeering a small boat and sailing along the coast until I came to the island where my ship was hidden, but first I must assure myself of the truth or falsity of my suspicion. All that I might learn was what I overheard by accident. I could not ask direct questions nor reveal undue interest in any political or other controversial matter. As a result, my nerves were under constant strain, so watchful must I be of every word or act or even facial expression or tone of voice. But it was like that with everyone else – I think even with Spehon and perhaps with Mephis himself, for every man knew that a spy or an informer was watching to pounce upon him at his first mis-step. The result was not conducive to garrulity – conversation, as such, did not exist except between occasional intimates; and even then I doubt that men dared speak what was in their hearts.

Ten days had passed, and I was no nearer my goal than on the day I arrived in Amlot. I was worried and was grieving over Duare. What must she think?

Had Muso told her? Was she well? These unanswerable questions nearly drove me mad. They almost convinced me that I should abandon my self-imposed commission and return to Sanara, but when I thought of the happiness it would bring to Duare were she to be reunited with her father or her grief were she to know that he might be a prisoner in Amlot and in constant danger of being destroyed, I could only remain and do what I considered my duty. I was in such a mood when I received an invitation from Zerka to visit her. It was a welcome relief, and I went with pleasure.

We greeted each other with the usual 'Maltu Mephis!' which, for some reason, seemed wholly out of place and incongruous between us. I always had a feeling that Zerka was hiding a laugh about something, and especially so when we went through the silly flubdub of Zani ritual. Hers was a most engaging personality that seemed to me to be wholly out of harmony with the stupidities of Zanism.

'My!' she exclaimed with a little laugh, 'What a handsome Zani Guardsman we make.'

'With this haircut?' I demanded, making a wry face.

She put a finger to her lips. 'Ssh!' she cautioned. 'I thought that you would have learned better than that by this time.'

'Mayn't I even criticize myself?' I asked, laughing.

She shook her head. 'Were I you, I should criticize only Atorians and the enemy in Sanara.'

'I don't even do that,' I said. 'I am what would be called in my wor – country a rubber stamp.'

'That is a word I do not know,' she said. 'Can it be possible that the Vodaroans do not speak the same language as we?'

'Oh no; we speak the same language,' I assured her.

'And read it, too?' she inquired.

'Why, of course.'

'I thought so,' she mused.

I couldn't imagine why she had thought otherwise, or why the matter was of any importance. Before I could ask her she veered off onto another track. 'Do you like Mantar?' she asked.

'Very much,' I said. 'It is nice to have the companionship of one gentleman at least.'

'Be careful,' she cautioned again. 'That is indirect criticism, but I can assure you it may be just as fatal. You needn't worry about me, however; I caution you only because there are always spies. One never may know who may be listening intently to his conversation in addition to the one to whom it is addressed. Suppose we go for a ride; then we can talk, and you can say anything you wish to. My driver has been with my family all his life. He would never repeat anything he heard.'

It seemed a little strange that she should be encouraging me to talk openly, in view of the fact that she had previously warned me against it.

'I'm sure,' I said, 'that all the world might listen to what I have to say. I am most happy here.'

'I am glad of that,' she said.

'I have learned though that it is just as well not to talk too much. In fact, I am surprised that I have not forgotten how to talk.'

'But of course you talk freely with Mantar?' she asked. 'I do not talk at all about anything I am not supposed to talk about,' I said.

'But with Mantar, it is different,' she urged. 'You may trust him fully. Discuss anything you wish with him. Mantar would never betray you.'

'Why?' I asked bluntly.

'Because you are *my* friend,' she replied.

'I appreciate all that that implies,' I said, 'and am very grateful for your friendship. I wish that I might repay the obligation in some way.'

'Perhaps you may have the chance some day – when I know you better.'

A gantor was brought into the courtyard of the palace, and we mounted to the howdah. This time there were no armed guards – only ourselves and the driver.

'Where shall we go?' asked Zerka.

'Anywhere. I should like to see some more of the public buildings.' I hoped in this way to discover the location of the Gap kum Rov, where the mysterious jong was imprisoned. I hadn't dared ask anyone; and I didn't dare ask Zerka, for notwithstanding her assurances that I might speak freely to her, I was not so sure that it would be wise. As far as I knew she might be a spy herself. The sudden friendship that she had fostered between us gave some color to this suspicion. I didn't want to believe it, for she seemed very sincere in her liking for me; but I could take no chances. I must suspect everyone. In that, I was becoming a true Zani.

She gave some directions to the driver; and then she settled back. 'Now,' she said, 'that we are comfortable and alone let's have a good talk. You see we really know very little about one another.'

'I have wondered a great deal about you,' I said. 'You are such an important person, and yet you waste your time on a total stranger.'

'I do not feel that I am wasting my time,' she said. 'It is not a waste of time to make new friends. I really have very few, you know. The war and the revolution took most of them – the war took my man.' She said ooljagan – loveman. 'I have lived alone ever since – rather a useless life, I am afraid. Now tell me about yourself.'

'You know all there is to tell,' I assured her.

'Tell me of your life in Vodaro,' she insisted. 'I should like to know something of the customs and manners of the people of that far country.'

'Oh, I'm sure you wouldn't be interested. We are a simple people.' I couldn't very well tell her that she probably knew more about Vodaro than I.

'But I would be interested,' she insisted. 'Tell me how you got here.'

I was most uncomfortable. I feel that I am not a very convincing liar. This was really my first essay at really spectacular lying, and I was very much afraid that I might trip myself up. If I lied too much, I should have too many lies to remember. I already had enough to tax my memory as it was. My recollection of even the location of Vodaro was rather hazy. The country was shown on a map I had seen in the library of Danus at Kooaad. I remembered that fact concerning it; and that was about all, except that it was supposed to run far back into Karbol, the cold country.

I had to answer Zerka's question, and my explanation of how I got to Amlot would have to be uncheckable. It was necessary to do a lot of thinking in a split second.

'One of our merchants had chartered a small ship and had loaded it with furs with which he expected to trade for merchandise in foreign countries. We sailed north for a month without encountering land until we sighted Anlap. Here we were overtaken by a terrific storm which wrecked the ship. I was washed ashore, the sole survivor. A kindly farmer took me in, and from him I learned that I was in the Kingdom of Korva, on Anlap. He also told me about the war raging here, and brought me as far as the city gates with a load of farm produce. The rest I have told you.'

'And what was the name of this kindly farmer?' she asked. 'He should be rewarded.'

'I never learned his name,' I said.

She looked at me with the oddest expression that made me feel that she knew I was lying; but perhaps it was only my guilty conscience that suggested that fear. Anyway, she didn't say anything more about the matter, for which I was deeply grateful. As we approached one of the main avenues of the city, I saw men standing on their heads shouting 'Maltu Mephis!' and other saluting and shouting the same stereotyped mandatory laudative.

'Our Beloved Mephis must be abroad.' I said.

She shot me a quick glance, but I maintained a perfectly serious demeanor. 'Yes,' she said, 'and don't forget to stand up and salute and acclaim him. There is to be a review of troops outside the city. A new unit is going to the front. Our Beloved Mephis is on his way to review them now. Would you be interested in seeing it?'

I told her that I would; so after Mephis's cortege passed, we fell in behind and followed it out onto the plain beyond the city. After Mephis had taken his place and the shouting had died out and men had stopped standing on their heads, Zerka directed our driver to move to a point where we could watch the ceremonies advantageously. A large body of troops was massed at some distance to the left, and at a signal from Mephis, transmitted by trumpet to the waiting troops, they broke into column of companies and advanced toward the great man so that they would pass before him at the proper distance. It was so similar to the passing in review of troops in civilized countries on Earth that it was rather startling; but when I gave the matter thought, I could not conceive any more practical way of reviewing troops.

When the first company was at about a hundred yards from Mephis, the step was changed. The entire company, in unison, took three steps forward, hopped once on the left foot, took three more steps forward, leaped straight up to a height of about two feet, and then repeated. They continued in this way until they had passed a hundred yards beyond Mephis; and all the time they shouted 'Maltu Mephis!' in a sing-song chant.

'Is that not impressive?' demanded Zerka, at the same time watching me carefully as though to detect my exact reaction.

'Very,' I said.

'It is an innovation sponsored by Our Beloved Mephis,' explained Zerka.

'I could easily imagine that that might be so,' I replied.

X

The Prison of Death

I had enjoyed my long visit with Zerka. We had eaten again at the same restaurant in which we had met, we had gone to one of the amazing theaters at Amlot, and we had finally gotten home about the nineteenth hour, which would be about 2:00 A.M. Earth time; then Zerka had invited me in for a little supper. But during all that time neither one of us had learned anything of importance about the other, which I think was the uppermost desire in the mind of each of us; nor had I had the Gap kum Rov pointed out to me. However, I had had a rather enjoyable day, marred only by my constant and depressing worries concerning Duare.

The theaters of Amlot and the plays shown therein under the Zanis are, I believe, of sufficient interest to warrant a brief digression. The audiences in the theaters sit with their backs towards the stage. In front of them on the end wall of the theater is a huge mirror, so placed that everyone in the house may see it, just as a motion picture screen is placed in our cinemas. The action taking place on the stage behind the audience is reflected from the mirror, and by a system of very ingenious lighting stands out brilliantly. By manipulation of the lights the scenes may be blacked out completely to denote a lapse of time or permit a change of scenery. Of course the reflections of the actors are not life size, and therefore the result gives an illusion of unreality reminiscent of puppet shows or the old days of silent pictures. I asked Zerka why the audience didn't face the stage and look directly at the actors; and she explained that it was because the profession of acting had formerly been in disrepute, and it had been considered a disgrace to be seen upon a stage. They got around it in this ingenious way; and it was considered extremely poor form to turn around and look directly at the actors, even though the profession was now considered an honorable one.

But the thing that amused me most was the play. There are one hundred theaters in Amlot, and the same play was being shown in all of them. It was the life of Mephis! Zerka told me that it consisted of one hundred and one episodes, each episode constituting a night's performance, and that it was absolutely obligatory on all citizens to attend the theater at least once in every ten days. They were given certificates to attest that they had done so. The play had already been running for more than a year. Mephis's publicity agent should have been born in Hollywood.

The day following my visit with Zerka I was given a detachment of the Zani Guard and told to report to the Gap kum Rov. It was just as easy as that. Here I had been trying to locate the place for days, and without success; now I was being officially detailed to the prison. Just what my duties were to be and whether I was to remain there or not, I did not know. My orders were simply to report to one Torko, governor of the prison – the Prison of Death.

My detachment consisted of eleven men, one of whom was a kordogan, whom I ordered to march the detachment to the prison. I didn't wish them to know that I had no idea where it was. The prison stood on a small island in the bay, not more than a hundred yards off shore. I had seen it on several occasions, but had not guessed that it was the notorious Gap kum Rov. At the quay we entered a small launch belonging to the prison and were soon standing beneath its grim walls. The mere fact that we were members of the Zani Guard gave us immediate entrance, and I was presently in the office of Torko. He was a large man, heavy of feature and coarse, with one of the crudest human faces I have ever seen. Unlike most Amtorians, he was ill-favored. His manner was gruff and surly, and I sensed immediately that he did not like me. Well, our dislike was mutual.

'I never saw you before,' he growled, after I had reported. 'Why didn't they send someone I knew? What do *you* know about running a prison?'

'Nothing,' I assured him. 'I didn't ask for the assignment. If I can put up with it, I guess you can.'

He grunted something I couldn't understand, and then said, 'Come with me. Now that you're here, you've got to familiarize yourself with the prison and with my system of administration.'

A second door in his office, opposite the one through which I had entered, opened into a guardroom full of Zani Guardsmen, one of whom he ordered to go to the courtyard and fetch my men; then he crossed to another door, heavily bolted and barred. When this was opened it revealed a long corridor on either side of which were partitions of heavy iron bars back of which were huddled several hundred prisoners, many of whom were covered with wounds and sores.

'These mistals,' explained Torko, 'have been guilty of disrespect to Our Beloved Mephis or to the glorious heroes of the Zani Guard. Show them no mercy.'

Next he took me to the end of the corridor, through another door, and up a flight of stairs to the second floor, where there were two rows of individual cells, each cell containing from one to three prisoners, although each would have been cramped quarters for one.

'There are traitors,' said Torko. 'They are awaiting trial. We really haven't enough room here; so every day, when we receive a new batch, we take most of them out and shoot them. Of course, we give them a chance to confess first. If they do, why naturally a trial isn't necessary; and we shoot them. If they don't confess, we shoot them for impeding justice.'

'Very simple,' I commented.

'Very,' he agreed, 'and eminently fair, too. It was my idea.'

'Our Beloved Mephis knows how to choose his lieutenants, doesn't he?'

He looked very pleased at that, and really smiled. It was the first time I had seen him smile, and I hoped he wouldn't do it again – his smile seemed only to make his face appear more cruel and repulsive.

'Well,' he exclaimed, 'I guess I was wrong about you – you talk like a good man and an intelligent one. We shall get along splendidly. Are you very close to Our Beloved Mephis?'

'I'm sorry to say that I'm not,' I told him. 'I merely serve him.'

'Well, you must know someone who is,' he insisted.

I was about to reply, telling him that I was afraid I knew no one who had the ear of Mephis, when he caught sight of the ring hanging on a chain around my neck. It was too small to fit on any of my fingers; I wore it thus.

'I should say you do know someone close to Mephis,' he exclaimed. 'The Toganja Zerka! Man! But are you lucky!'

I did not reply, as I had no stomach to discuss Zerka with this beast; but he insisted. 'She was bright to come over to the Zanis,' he said. 'Most of her kind were killed; and those that did not come over are usually under suspicion, but not Toganja Zerka. They say Mephis has the utmost confidence in her and often consults her in matters of policy. It was her idea to have the Zani Guard patrol the city constantly looking for traitors and beating up citizens who couldn't give a good account of themselves. Playing the life of Our Beloved Mephis constantly in all the theaters was also her idea, as was that of having civilians stand on their heads and cheer whenever Our Beloved Mephis passed. Even the expression Our Beloved Mephis was coined by her. Oh, she's a brilliant one. Mephis owes her a lot.'

All this was most illuminating. I had always felt that Zerka applauded Mephis with her tongue in her cheek. I had even doubted her loyalty to him or to the Zani cause. Now I didn't know what to think, but I certainly congratulated myself upon the fact that I had not confided in her. Somehow, I felt a little sad and depressed, as one does when disillusioned, especially if the disillusionment concerns a friend he has admired.

'Now,' continued Torko, 'if you should put in a good word for me with the toganja, it would be sure to reach the ear of Our Beloved Mephis. How about it, my excellent friend?'

'Wait until I know you better,' I said; 'then I shall know what to report to the toganja.' This was almost blackmail, but I felt no compunction.

'You'll have nothing but the best to report of me,' he assured me; 'we shall get along splendidly. And now I'll take you down to the courtroom where the trials are conducted and show you the cells where Our Beloved Mephis keeps his favorite prisoners.'

He led me down into a dark basement and into a large room with a high bench running across one end. Behind the bench were a number of seats, the whole being raised a couple of feet above the floor level. Around the sides of the room were low benches which evidently served as seats for spectators. The rest of the room was devoted to an elaborate display of the most fiendish instruments of torture the mind of man might conceive. I shall not dwell upon them. It is enough to say that all were horrible and many of them absolutely unmentionable. All my life I shall be trying to forget them and the hideous things I was forced to see perpetrated there upon both men and women.

Torko made a wide, sweeping gesture, proudly. 'These are my pets,' he said. 'Many of them are my own invention. Believe me, just a look at them usually gets a confession; but we give them a taste of them anyway.'

'After they have confessed?' I asked.

'Why certainly. Is it not a treasonable thing to cheat the state of the usefulness of these ingenious contrivances that have cost so much in thought and money to produce?'

'Your logic is unimpeachable,' I told him. 'It is evident that you are a perfect Zani.'

'And you are a man of great intelligence, my friend, Vodo. And now, come with me – you shall see some more of this ideal plant.'

He led me into a dark corridor beyond the torture chamber. Here were small cells, feebly illuminated by a single dim light in the central corridor. A number of men were confined, each in a cell by himself. It was so dark that I could not distinguish the features of any of them, as all remained in the far corners of their cramped quarters; and many sat with their faces hidden in their hands, apparently oblivious of the fact that we were there. One was moaning; and another shrieked and gibbered, his mind gone.

'That one,' said Torko, 'was a famous physician. He enjoyed the confidence of everyone, including Our Beloved Mephis. But can you imagine how heinously he betrayed it?'

'No,' I admitted, 'I cannot. Did he attempt to poison Mephis?'

'What he did was almost as bad. He was actually apprehended in the act of alleviating the agony of an Atorian who was dying of an incurable disease. Can you imagine?'

'I am afraid,' I said, 'that my imagination is permanently incapacitated. There are things that transcend the limits of a normal imagination. Today you have shown me such things.'

'He should have been executed; but when he went mad, we felt that he would suffer far more if he lived. We were right. We Zanis are always right.'

'Yes,' I agreed, 'it is the indisputable privilege of all Zanis to be always right.'

He took me next down a dark corridor to another room at the far side of the building. There was nothing here but an enormous furnace and a foul odor.

'Here is where we burn the bodies,' Torko explained; then he pointed to a trap door in the floor. 'Be careful not to step on that,' he cautioned. 'It is not very substantial. We dump the ashes down there into the bay. The chute is quite large. If the door gave way with you, you'd land in the bay.'

I spent a week undergoing a sort of training in inhumanity; and then Torko obtained a leave of absence, and I was left in charge as acting governor of the Prison of Death. During the time that he was away I did what I could to alleviate the sufferings of the inmates of that hideous sink of misery and despair. I permitted them to clean up their foul cells and themselves, and I gave them quantities of good food. There were no 'trials' while I was in charge and only one execution, but that was ordered by a higher authority – in fact, by Mephis himself. I received word about the 11th hour one day that Mephis would visit the prison at the 13th hour – 2:00 P.M. E.T. As I had never met the great man and had no idea how to receive him or conduct myself, I was in something of a quandary; as I knew that a single error, however unintentional, would affront him and result in my execution. At last it occurred to me that my kordogan might help me out. He was more than anxious to display his knowledge; and so as the 13th hour approached, I anticipated the coming event with considerable assurance. With a number of warriors as an escort, I waited at the quay with the prison launch; and when Mephis hove in sight with his retinue, I lined up my men and we saluted and Maltu Mephised him in orthodox style. He was quite affable as he greeted me with condescending cordiality.

'I have heard of you,' he said. 'If you are a protégé of Toganja Zerka, you must be a good Zani.'

'There is only one good Zani,' I said.

He thought I meant him; and he was pleased. The kordogan had the remaining guardsmen lined up in the guard room; and as we passed through, every one saluted and shouted 'Maltu Mephis!' as the top of his voice. I wondered at the time how Mephis could listen to such forced acclaim without feeling like the ass he was; but I suppose an ass doesn't mind being an ass, or doesn't realize it.

The great man asked to be taken into the basement, where his own particular prisoners were incarcerated. He took only me and two of his aides with him, one of the latter being his present favorite – an effeminate looking man, bejeweled like a woman. When we reached the room where the prisoners' cells were located, Mephis directed me to show him the cell of Kord, the former jong of Korva.

'Torko has not told me the names of any of these prisoners,' I explained. 'He said it was your wish that they remain nameless.'

Mephis nodded. 'Quite right,' he said, 'but of course the acting governor of the prison should know who they are – and keep the knowledge to himself.'

'You wish to speak to me, Mephis?' asked a voice from a nearby cell.

'That is he,' said Mephis. 'Unlock his cell.'

I took the master key from my belt and did as Mephis bid me.

'Come out!' commanded he.

Kord was still a fine looking man, though wasted by confinement and starvation. 'What do you want of me?' he demanded. There was no 'Maltu Mephis!' here, no cringing. Kord was still the jong, and Mephis shrunk in his presence to the insignificant scum he had been born. I think he felt it; for he commenced to bluster and talk loud.

'Drag the prisoner to the courtroom!' he shouted to me, and turned back to that room himself, followed by his aides.

I took Kord gently by the arm. 'Come,' I said.

I think he had expected to be jerked or kicked, as he probably had been on former occasions, for he looked at me in something of surprise when I treated him with decent consideration. My heart certainly went out to him, for it must have been galling to a great jong such as he had been to be ordered about by scum like Mephis; and, too, there must have been the knowledge that he was probably going to be tortured. I expected it, and I didn't know how I was going to be able to stand and watch it without raising a hand in interference. Only my knowledge that it would have done him no good and resulted in my own death and, consequently, the defeat of all my own plans, convinced me that I must hide my indignation and accept whatever was forthcoming.

When we entered the courtroom, we saw that Mephis and his aides had already seated themselves at the judges' bench, before which Mephis directed me to bring the prisoner. For a full minute the dictator sat in silence, his shifty eyes roving about the room, never meeting those of Kord and myself but momentarily. At last he spoke.

'You have been a powerful jong, Kord,' he said. 'You may be jong once more. I have come here today to offer you your throne again.'

He waited, but Kord made no reply. He just stood there, erect and majestic, looking Mephis squarely in the face, every inch a king. His attitude naturally irritated the little man, who, though all-powerful, still felt his inferiority to the great man before him.

'I tell you, I will give you back your throne, Kord,' repeated Mephis, his voice rising. 'You have only to sign this,' and he held up a paper. 'It will end needless bloodshed and restore Korva the peace and prosperity she deserves.'

'What is written on the paper?' demanded Kord.

'It is an order to Muso,' replied Mephis, 'telling him to lay down his arms because you have been restored as jong and peace has been declared in Korva.'

'Is that all?' asked Kord.

'Practically all,' replied Mephis. 'There is another paper here that you will sign that will insure the peace and prosperity of Korva.'

'What is it?'

'It is an order appointing me advisor to the jong, with full power to act in his place in all emergencies. It also ratifies all laws promulgated by the Zani Party since it took control of Korva.'

'In other and more candid words, it betrays my few remaining loyal subjects into the hands of Mephis,' said Kord. 'I refuse, of course.'

'Just a moment,' snapped Mephis. 'There is another condition that may cause you to alter your decision.'

'And that?' inquired Kord.

'If you refuse, you will be considered a traitor to your country, and treated accordingly.'

'Assassinated?'

'Executed,' corrected Mephis.

'I still refuse,' said Kord.

Mephis rose from his seat. His face was livid with rage. 'Then die, you fool!' he almost screamed; and, drawing his Amtorian pistol, poured a stream of the deadly R-rays into the defenseless man standing before him. Without a sound, Kord, Jong of Korva, sank lifeless to the floor.

XI

The Net Draws Closer

The next day, as I was making my rounds of the prison, I took it upon myself to inquire of a number of the prisoners as to the nature of the offenses that had resulted in such drastic punishment, for to be imprisoned in Gap kum Rov was, indeed, real punishment. I found that many of them had expressed their opinions of Mephis and the Zanis too freely, and that supposed friends had informed upon them. Many did not know what the charges against them were, and quite a few were there because of old grudges held against them by members of the Zani Guard. One man was there because an officer of the Zani Guard desired his woman; another because he had sneezed while, standing upon his head, he should have been shouting Maltu Mephis. The only hope any of them had of release was through bribery or the influence of some member of the Zani Party, but this latter was difficult to obtain because of the fear the Zanis themselves felt of directing suspicion upon themselves. These inquiries I had made were of the prisoners in the big tanks on the main floor. My interest lay in the dim corridors below ground, where I thought that Mintep might be confined. I had not dared reveal any interest in these prisoners for fear of directing suspicion upon myself, for I knew that there were constantly informers among the prisoners, who won favors and sometimes freedom by informing upon their fellow prisoners. Torko had told me that I was not even to know the names of the prisoners on that lower level; but I was determined to learn if Mintep was among them, and finally I hit upon a plan that I hoped would serve my purpose. With difficulty, I wrote some very bad verse in Amtorian, which I sang to a tune that had been popular in America when I left the Earth. In two of the verses was the message I wished to use to elicit a sign from Mintep that he was a prisoner there, and thus to locate his cell.

To allay suspicion, I formed the habit of singing my song as I went about my daily duties; but I sang it at first only on the upper floors. My kordogan and some of the other members of the guard showed an interest in my song, and asked me questions about it. I told them that I didn't know the origin or significance of it, that the words meant nothing to me, and that I only sang it because I was fond of the tune.

In addition to my essay at poetry, I had been busy along another line of endeavor. The cell and door locks of the prison were not all alike, but there was a master key which opened any of them. In Torko's absence, I carried this master key; and one of the first things I did after it came into my possession was to take it into the city and have two duplicates made. I had no definite plan in mind at the time wherein they might figure; but though I took considerable risk in having them made, I felt that eventually they must be of the utmost value in releasing Mintep, if it developed that he was a prisoner in Gap kum Rov.

You can scarcely realize the caution I was forced to observe in everything that I did, in order not to arouse suspicion, to incur enmities, or engender envy, for every citizen of Amlot was a spy or a potential informer. Yet I had to make haste, for I knew that over my head hung constantly that Damoclean message from Muso. Who had it? Why had they not struck?

I was accustomed to wandering around the prison alone, inspecting the cells, the guardroom, the kitchen; so it would arouse no comment were I discovered anywhere; and the fact that I was almost constantly humming or singing my foolish song was, I felt, evidence that there was nothing irregular or surreptitious about my activities.

It was the day before Torko's return that I determined to try to ascertain definitely if Mintep were imprisoned at the lower level. With this idea in mind, I went singing through the prison, feeling, as usual, like a loony. Down to the basement I went, through the courtroom, and into the dim precincts of the forbidden cells. I went to the furnace and passed along the corridor where the cells were, and there I sang the two verses that I had written to arouse Mintep's interest and, perhaps, beguile an acknowledgement, if he were there. These are the verses to which I refer, roughly translated into English:

> 'Mourned by a nation,
> 'By her kinsman sought,
> 'Duare lives, and
> 'Of thy fate knows naught.

> 'A word, a sign, is
> 'All she asks of thee,
> 'If thou canst give it,
> 'Put thy trust in me.'

I kept right on singing other verses, or humming the air, as I passed along the cells; but there was no response. Clear to the end of the corridor I went, and then turned back. Once more I sang those two verses, and as I approached the last cells, I saw a man pressing close to the bars of one of them. In the dim light, I could not see his features plainly; but as I passed close to him, he whispered the single word, 'Here.' I noted the location of his cell and continued on my way.

With Torko, I occupied my office next to the guardroom; and when I arrived there, I found my kordogan waiting with some new prisoners. One of my duties was to receive all prisoners, question them, and assign them to cells. A clerk kept a record of all such matters. All I was supposed to do, according to Torko, was to insult and browbeat the prisoners.

There were three of them, and they lined them up in front of my desk. As I looked up at them, I immediately recognized one of them as Horjan, the brother of Lodas; and, to my horror I saw recognition slowly dawn in his eyes; or at least I thought I did.

'What is your name?' I asked.

'Horjan,' he replied.

'Why are you here?'

'Some time ago I reported a stranger hiding in my home,' he replied. 'When the guard came, they found no one – the man had escaped. They were very angry with me. A neighbor, whom I had told of my discovery of the man, became angry with me; and today he went to the Zani Guard and told them that he had seen the man and that I had been hiding him, and that I only reported the matter because I knew that he would. He told them that the man was a spy from Sanara and that he was still in the city.

'He says that he has seen him – that he could never forget his face or his *eyes* – he says that the man was wearing *the uniform of an officer of the Zani Guard.*'

I knew that Horjan's friend had not seen me, and that this was merely Horjan's way of communicating to me the fact that he recognized me.

'It would be too bad if your friend bore false witness against an officer of the Zani Guard,' I said. 'If anyone did that, it would be necessary to torture him before killing him. But perhaps it would be well to question your friend to learn if he ever did see this man in your house, and have him describe him.'

Horjan paled. He realized that he had committed an error; and he was terrified, for he knew that his friend had never seen me and could not describe me.

'I hope it does not get him into trouble,' I continued, 'It is deplorable that there should be so much loose talking in Amlot. It would be better if some people held their tongues.'

'Yes,' said Horjan, meekly, 'there is too much loose talk; but you rest assured that I shall never talk.'

I hoped that he meant it, but I was very much concerned. Now, indeed, must I take immediate steps to escape from Amlot. But how? My problem was now further complicated by my discovery of Mintep.

On the following day Torko returned and I was sent to make an arrest in the quarter occupied by scholars and scientists. There were many Atorians living in this quarter, for their minds incline toward scholarly pursuits and scientific investigation. Here the few who had not been killed were segregated, not being allowed to leave the quarter, which, because of them, was in bad repute with the Zanis, who wreaked mean little persecutions on the slightest pretext. The Zanis hated scholars and scientists, as they hated all who were superior to them in any way.

On my way to the quarter, I passed a field where hundreds of boys were being drilled by kordogans of the Zani Guard. There were little fellows of five and six and many older boys. This same thing was going on all over Amlot – this was the only schooling the Zani boys received. The only toys they were allowed to have were weapons. Babes in arms were given blunt daggers upon which to cut their teeth. I said that was all the schooling they received. I was wrong. They were taught to shout 'Maltu Mephis!' upon any pretext or upon none; and a chapter from *The Life of Our Beloved Mephis*, written by himself, was read to them daily. It was quite a comprehensive education – for a Zani.

The quarter where I was to make the arrest had formerly been a prosperous one, as, during the regime of the jongs, scholars and scientists were held in high esteem; but now it was run down, and the few people I saw on the streets looked shabby and half starved. Arrived at the home of my victim (I can think of nothing more suitable to call him) I walked in with a couple of my men, leaving the others outside. As I entered the main room, which might be called the living-room, I saw a woman step hurriedly between some hangings at the opposite side of the room; but not so quickly but that I recognized her. It was Zerka.

A man and woman sitting in the room rose and faced me. They both looked surprised; the woman, frightened. They were exceptionally fine looking, intelligent appearing people.

'You are Narvon?' I asked of the man.

He nodded. 'I am Narvon. What do you want of me?'

'I have orders to place you under arrest,' I said. 'You will come with me.'

'What is the charge against me?' he asked.

'I do not know,' I told him. 'I have orders to arrest you – that is all I know.'

He turned sadly to say goodbye to the woman; and as he took her in his arms and kissed her, she broke down. He choked a little as he tried to comfort her.

The kardogan who accompanied me stepped forward and seized him roughly by the arm. 'Come on!' he shouted gruffly. 'Do you think we are going to stand here all day while you two dirty traitors blubber?'

'Leave them alone!' I ordered. 'They may say goodbye.'

He shot me an angry look, and stepped back. He was not my own kardogan, who, while bad enough, had learned from me to temper his fanaticism a little with tolerance if not compassion.

'Well,' he said, 'while they're doing that, I'll search the house.'

'You'll do nothing of the kind,' I said. 'You'll stay here and keep still and take your orders from me.'

'Didn't you see that woman sneak into the back room when we entered?' he demanded.

'Of course I did,' I replied.

'Ain't you going to go after her?'

'No,' I told him. 'My orders were to arrest this man. I had no orders to search the house or question anyone else. I obey orders, and I advise you to do the same.'

He gave me a nasty look, and grumbled something I did not catch; then he sulked for the remainder of the day. On the way back to the prison I walked beside Narvon; and when I saw that the kardogan was out of earshot, I asked him a question in a whisper.

'Was the woman I saw in your house, the one who ran out of the room as I came in, a good friend of yours?'

He looked just a bit startled, and he hesitated a fraction of a second too long before he replied. 'No,' he said. 'I never saw her before. I do not know what she wanted. She came in just ahead of you. I think she must have made a mistake in the house, and been embarrassed and confused when you came in. You know it is often dangerous, nowadays, to make mistakes, however innocent they may be.'

He could have been tortured and executed for a statement such as that, and he should have known it. I cautioned him.

'You are a strange Zani,' he said. 'You act almost as though you were my friend.'

'Forget it,' I warned him.

'I shall,' he promised.

At the prison I took him at once to Torko's office.

'So you are the great scholar, Narvon,' snarled Torko. 'You should have stuck to your books instead of trying to foment a rebellion. Who were your accomplices?'

'I have done nothing wrong,' said Narvon; 'and so I had no accomplices in anything that was wrong.'

'Tomorrow your memory will be better,' snapped Torko. 'Our beloved Mephis himself will conduct your trial, and you will find that we have ways in which to make traitors tell the truth. Take him to the lower level, Vodo; and then report back here to me.'

As I passed through the courtroom with Narvon, I saw him pale as his eyes took in the instruments of torture there.

'You will not name your accomplices, will you?' I asked.

He shuddered and seemed to shrink suddenly. 'I do not know,' he admitted. 'I have never been able to endure pain. I do not know what I shall do. I only know that I am afraid – oh, so terribly afraid. Why can they not kill me without torturing me!'

I was very much afraid, myself – afraid for Zerka. I don't know why I should have been – she was supposed to be such a good Zani. Perhaps it was the fact that she had run away from men in the uniform of the Zani Guard that aroused my suspicions. Perhaps it was because I had never been able to reconcile my belief in her with the knowledge that she was a Zani. Quite a little, too, because Narvon had so palpably tried to protect her.

When I returned to Torko's office, the kardogan who had been with me when I made the arrest was just leaving. Torko was scowling ominously.

'I have heard bad reports of your conduct during my absence,' he said.

'That is strange,' I said – 'unless I have made an enemy here; then you might hear almost anything, as you know.'

'The information has come from different sources. I am told that you were very soft and lenient with the prisoners.'

'I was not cruel, if that is what you mean,' I replied. 'I had no orders to be cruel.'

'And today you did not search a house where you knew a woman to be hiding – the home of a traitor, too.'

'I had no orders to search the house or question anybody,' I retorted. 'I did not know the man was a traitor; I was not told what his offence had been.'

'Technically, you are right,' he admitted; 'but you must learn to have more initiative. We arrest no one who is not a menace to the state. Such people deserve no mercy. Then you whispered with the prisoner all the way to the prison.'

I laughed outright. 'The kardogan doesn't like me because I put him in his place. He became a little insubordinate. I will not stand for that. Of course I talked with the prisoner. Was there anything wrong in that?'

'The less one talks with anyone, the safer he is,' he said.

He dismissed me then; but I realized that suspicions were aroused; and there was that brother of Lodas just full of them, and of real knowledge concerning me, too; and primed to spill everything he knew or suspected at the first opportunity. Whatever I was going to do, I must do quickly if I were ever going to escape. There were too many fingers ready to point at me, and there was still the message from Muso. I asked permission to go fishing the next day; and as Torko loved fresh fish, he granted it.

'You'd better stay around until after Our Beloved Mephis has left the prison,' he said. 'We may want your help.'

The next day Narvon was tried before Mephis, and I was there with a detail of the guard – just ornamentally. We lined up at attention at each end of the bench where Mephis, Spehon, and Torko sat. The benches at the sides of the room were filled with other Zani bigwigs. When Narvon was brought in, Mephis asked him just one question.

'Who were your accomplices?'

'I have done nothing, and I had no accomplices,' said Narvon. He looked haggard and his voice was weak. Every time he looked at an instrument of torture he winced. I saw that he was in a state of absolute funk. I couldn't blame him.

Then they commenced to torture him. What I witnessed, I would not describe if I could. It beggars description. There are no words in any language to depict the fiendishly bestial cruelties they inflicted on his poor, quivering flesh. When he fainted, they resuscitated him; and went at it again. I think his screams might have been heard a mile away. At last he gave in.

'I'll tell! I'll tell!' he shrieked.

'Well?' demanded Mephis. 'Who are they?'

'There was only one,' whispered Narvon, in a weak voice that could scarcely be heard.

'Louder!' cried Mephis. 'Give him another turn of the screw! Then maybe he'll speak up.'

'It was the Toganja Z –' Then he fainted as they gave the screw another turn. They tried to revive him again, but it was too late – Narvon was dead.

XII

Hunted

I went fishing; and I caught some fish, but I couldn't forget how Narvon died. I shall never forget it. Nor could I forget his dying words. Coupled with what I had seen in his house, I knew the name that had died in his throat. I wondered if any of the Zanis there had guessed what I *knew*. Not only did I fish, but I did some reconnoitering and a great deal of thinking. I wondered what to do about Zerka. Should I risk Mintep's life to warn her, with considerable likelihood that I might be arrested with her? Really, there was but one answer. I must warn her, for she had befriended me. I sailed around close to the prison, for there were certain things I must know about the outside of the place. I knew all that was necessary about the inside. After satisfying myself on the points concerning which I had been in doubt, I came ashore, and went to my quarters in the barracks. Here I found an order relieving me of duty at the prison. I guess Torko had found me too soft for his purposes; or was there something else, something far more sinister behind it? I felt a net closing about me.

As I sat there in my quarters with this most unpleasant thought as my sole company, a guardsman came and announced that the commandant wished me to report to him at once. This, I thought, is the end. I am about to be arrested. I contemplated flight; but I knew how futile such an attempt would be, and so I went to the commandant's office and reported.

'A dozen prisoners have been brought from the front at Sanara,' he said. 'I am detailing twelve officers to question them. We can get more out of them if they are questioned separately. Be very kind to the man you question. Give him wine and food. Tell him what a pleasant life a soldier may have serving with the armies of the Zanis, but get all the information you can out of him. When they have all been questioned, we shall turn them over to some private soldiers to entertain for a few days; then we shall send two of them back to the front and let them escape to tell about the fine treatment they received in Amlot. That will mean many desertions. The other ten will be shot.'

The Zanis were full of cute little tricks like that. Well, I got my man and took him to my quarters. I plied him with food, wine, and questions. I wanted to know about Sanara on my own account, but I didn't dare let him know how much I knew about the city and conditions there. I had to draw him out without him suspecting me. It chanced that he was a young officer – a nice

367

chap, well connected. He knew everyone and all the gossip of the court and the important families.

There were certain questions that it would be quite natural for any Zani to ask. Those relative to the defenses of the city and other military matters he answered glibly – so glibly that I knew he was lying, and I admired him for it. When I asked him about Muso, he talked freely. It was evident that he didn't like Muso.

'He's turned his woman out,' he volunteered. 'Her name is Illana. She is a fine woman. Everyone is very much incensed over it, but what can anyone do? He is jong. The woman he has selected in Illana's place does not want to take it. It is common talk that she loathes Muso; but he is jong, and if he orders her to come, she will have to come, because she has no man. He was killed here in Amlot. Muso sent him here on a dangerous mission. Everyone believes that he sent him to his death purposely.'

I felt myself turning cold. The next question on my lips withered in my dry mouth. I made two attempts before I could utter an intelligible sound.

'Who was this man?' I asked.

'He was the man who used to fly over your lines and drop bombs on you,' he replied. 'His name was Carson of Venus – odd name.'

I had asked my last question of that man. I took him out and turned him over to the soldiers who were to entertain the prisoners; then I hastened towards the quay. It was already dark, and the street I chose was not well lighted. That was the reason I chose it. I had almost reached the quay, when I ran into a detachment of the Zani Guard in command of an officer. The latter hailed me from the opposite side of the street; then he crossed toward me, leaving his detachment behind.

'I thought I recognised you.' he said. It was Mantar. 'I have an order for your arrest. They are scouring the city for you.'

'I have been in my quarters. Why didn't they look there?'

'Torko said you had gone fishing.'

'Why am I being arrested?' I asked.

'They think you are a Sanaran spy. A prisoner named Horjan informed on you. He said he found you hiding in his house just the day before you applied for a commission in the Guard.'

'But Zerka?' I asked. 'Won't they suspect her? It was she who sponsored me.'

'I had thought of that,' he said.

'Well, what are you going to do with me?' I asked. 'Are you going to turn me in?'

'I wish you would tell me the truth,' he said. 'I am your friend; and if what Zerka and I have suspected for long is true, I will help you.'

I recalled that Zerka had told me I could trust this man implicitly. I was lost anyway. They had enough against me to torture and murder me. Here was a straw. I clutched it.

'I am Carson of Venus,' I said. 'I came here with a message for Spehon from Muso. It was stolen from me.'

'Where were you going when I stopped you?' he asked.

'I was going back to Sanara, where my friends and my heart are,' I told him.

'Can you get there?'

'I think I can.'

'Then go. It is fortunate for you that none of my detail knew Vodo by sight. Good luck!' He turned and crossed the street, and I went on toward the quay. I heard him say to his kardogan. 'He says that Vodo is in his quarters at the barracks. We shall go there.'

I reached the quay without further incident, and found the same boat I had used for fishing earlier in the day and on several other occasions. It was a small boat with a single sail, scarcely more than a canoe. As I put off, I heard the sound of running feet along the quay; and then I saw men approaching.

A voice cried, 'Stop! Come back here!' but I set my sail and got under way; then I heard the staccato br-r-r of R-rays, and a voice crying, 'Come back here, Vodo! You can't get away.'

For reply I drew my own pistol and fired back at them. I knew that I would disconcert their aim and give me a better chance to escape with my life. Long after I could no longer see them, they stood there firing out into the night.

I thought of Mintep with regret, but there was something far more precious at stake than his life or that of any man. I cursed Muso for his duplicity, and prayed that I might reach Sanara in time. If I did not, I could at least kill him; and that I promised to do.

Presently I heard the sound of a launch behind me, and knew that I was being pursued. Inside the harbor the breeze was light and fitful. If I couldn't reach the open sea ahead of my pursuers, I should have to depend on eluding them in the darkness. In this I might be successful, or I might not. I couldn't hope to outdistance a launch even with a good wind, and about my only hope was to escape detection until I was able to discern from the sound of the launch in which direction they were searching for me. I felt that they would naturally assume that I would head northeast up the coast in the direction of Sanara, whereas my destination lay southwest – the little island where I had grounded my ship. Nor was I mistaken, for presently I heard the sound of the launch receding to my left; and I knew that it was making for the open sea by way of the easterly side of the harbor's mouth. With a sigh of relief, I kept to my course; and presently rounded the headland at the west side of the harbor and turned into the open sea. The offshore breeze was no better than that which I had had in the harbor, but I continued to hug the shore because I had one last duty to perform in Amlot before I continued on my way.

I owed much to Zerka, and I could not leave without warning her of the danger which threatened her. I knew where her palace was situated on the shore of the ocean with its gardens running down to the water line. It would delay me no more than a few minutes to stop there and warn her. I felt that I could do no less. The conditions were ideal – low tide and an offshore wind.

Silently and smoothly my light craft skimmed the surface of the water, the faint luminosity of the Amtorian night revealing the shore line as a black mass dotted with occasional lights that shone from the windows of the palaces of the rich and powerful. Even in the semi-darkness, I had no difficulty in locating Zerka's palace. I ran in as close as I could on the tack I was holding; then dropped my sail and paddled for the shore. Beaching my craft, I drew it well up toward the sea wall, where only a very high tide could have reached it; then I made my way up to the palace.

I knew that I was undergoing considerable risk, for, if Zerka were under suspicion, as I feared might be the case, she would doubtless be under surveillance. There might be watchers in the palace grounds, or even in the palace itself. For all I knew, Zerka might already be under arrest, for Narvon's dying confession was not cut off quickly enough to hide from me the identity of the accomplice he had almost named. Of course, I had already been suspicious of the truth. I did not think that the Zanis were, and so there was a possibility that they had not connected Zerka's name with that which the dying man had almost spoken. In any event, I must take this chance.

I went directly to the great doors that opened onto the terrace overlooking the gardens and the sea. On Amtor there are no doorbells, nor do people knock on doors – they whistle. Each individual has his own distinctive notes, sometimes simple, sometimes elaborate. At entrance doorways there are speaking tubes into which one whistles, and it was with some perturbation that I now whistled into the mouthpiece of the tube at the great doors of the toganja's palace.

I waited for several minutes. I heard no sound within the building. The silence was ominous. I was, nevertheless, about to repeat my whistle when the door swung partly open, and Zerka stepped out onto the terrace. Without a word, she took my hand and hurried me down into the garden where trees and shrubbery cast black shadows. There was a bench there, and she drew me down on it.

'Are you mad?' she whispered 'They were just here looking for you. The doors on the avenue had scarcely closed behind them when I heard your whistle. How did you get here? If you can get away again, you must leave at once. There are probably spies among my servants. Oh, why did you come?'

'I came to warn you.'

'Warn me? Of what?'

'I saw Narvon tortured,' I said.

I felt her stiffen. 'And?'

'Mephis was trying to wring the names of his accomplices from him.'

'Did – did he speak?' she asked breathlessly.

'He said, "The Toganja"; and died with the beginning of her name on his lips. I do not know that Mephis suspected, for he had not seen what I had in the house of Narvon; but I feared that he might suspect, and so I came here to take you to Sanara with me.'

She pressed my hand. 'You are a good friend,' she said. 'I knew that you would be, and it was first proved to me when you prevented that kardogan from searching the back room of Narvon's house; now you have proved it again. Yes, you are a very good friend, Carson of Venus.'

That name on her lips startled me. 'How did you know?' I asked. 'When did you find out?'

'The morning after we dined together that first time in the evening of the day that you entered Amlot.'

'But how?' I insisted.

She laughed softly. 'We are all suspicious here in Amlot, suspicious of everyone. We are always searching for new friends, expecting new enemies. The instant that I saw you in that restaurant I knew that you were not of Amlot, probably not of Korva; but if you were of Korva, the chances were excellent that you were a spy from Sanara. I had to find out. Oh, how many times I have laughed when I recalled your stories of Vodaro. Why, you didn't know the first thing about that country.'

'But how did you find out about me?' I demanded.

'I sent an emissary to your room in the travellers' house to search your belongings while you slept. He brought me Muso's message to Spehon.'

'Oh, so that is why that was never used against me,' I exclaimed. 'It has had me worried ever since it disappeared, as you may well imagine.'

'I wanted to tell you, but I couldn't. You have no idea how careful we have to be.'

'You were very careless in going to the house of Narvon,' I said.

'We hadn't the slightest reason to believe that Narvon was suspected. Now that I know how loyal you are, I don't mind telling you that we are planning a counter-revolution that will overthrow the Zanis and restore Kord to the throne.'

'That can never be done,' I said.

'Why?' she demanded.

'Kord is dead.'

She was horrified. 'You are sure?' she asked.

'I saw Mephis assassinate him.' I told her the story briefly.

She shook her head sadly. 'There is so much less to fight for now,' she said. 'Muso might easily be as bad as Mephis.'

'Muso is a traitor to his own country,' I said. 'That message I brought you proves it clearly. I wish that I had it now to take back to Sanara with me. The army would rise against him; and with Kord dead, the people would rally around the man they love and make him jong.'

'Who is that?' she asked.

'Taman,' I said.

'Taman! But Taman is dead.'

'Taman dead? How do you know?' My heart sank at the thought. Duare and I would have no powerful friend in Sanara.

'We heard some time ago from a captured Sanarian officer that Muso had sent him to Amlot on a dangerous mission and that he had never returned to Sanara. It was a foregone conclusion that he must be dead.'

I breathed a sigh of relief. 'He was returned safely to Sanara before I left there; and unless he has been killed since I came to Amlot, he is still alive.'

'You shall have the message,' she said. 'I kept it. But how do you expect to escape from Amlot and get back through the Zani lines in safety?'

'Do you forget that Carson of Venus is the mistal that flies over Zani troops and drops bombs on them?' I asked.

'But the thing you fly in? You haven't that here?'

'It is not far away. I am praying that nothing has happened to it. That was the chance I had to take.'

'You are so lucky that I am sure you will find it just as you left it. And, speaking of luck, how in the world did you ever get out of the city, with the entire Zani Guard looking for you? They are absolutely turning the city inside out, I am told.'

'I was stopped by a detachment of the Guard on my way to the quay. Fortunately for me, it was commanded by Mantar. He is a good friend, thanks to you.'

'He is one of us,' she said.

'I suspected you both almost from the first, notwithstanding your Maltu Mephises and your Zani salutes.'

'I was so sure of you that I was a little freer than usual. Somehow, I knew you were all right – you just couldn't have been a Zani at heart.'

'We shouldn't be sitting here talking,' I told her. 'Go get Muso's message and a few of your belongings, and we'll be on our way to Sanara.'

She shook her head. 'I wish that I might,' she said, 'but I have a duty to perform before I leave Amlot.'

'There is nothing more important than saving your life,' I insisted.

'There is something more important to me than my life,' she replied. 'I am

going to tell you what it is and why I must stay and what I am going to do –
something that I have shared with only Mantar before. Mantar and my man
were the closest of friends. They were officers in the same regiment of The
Jong's Guard. When Mephis formed the Zani Party during the last disastrous
war, my man was one of his bitterest foes. It was in the last battle of the war
that my man was supposed to have been killed. His body was never found.
But he was not killed in battle. A private soldier, who had been closely
attached to Mantar, saw my man die; and he told Mantar the story of his end.
He was tortured and murdered by a band of Zanis under direction of Mephis.
When I learned this, I swore to kill Mephis; but I wished to wait until my act
would be of service to my country. We are preparing for a sudden stroke at
Zani power. When our forces are ready, the violent death of Mephis would
throw the Zanis into at least temporary demoralization. I must be here to see
that he dies a violent death at the proper time.'

'But suppose you are suspected now and arrested? You can't carry out your
plan then.'

'If I am arrested, I shall still carry out my plan to kill Mephis,' she said. 'I
shall certainly be taken before him for questioning and probably for torture;
then I shall kill him. You must go now. I'll fetch Muso's message. Just a
moment,' and she was gone.

I felt a wave of melancholy surge through me as I sat there waiting for her
to return. I knew that I should never see her again, for she was going to certain death, even if she succeeded in destroying Mephis. She was so beautiful
and fine, such a loyal friend – it was tragic that she must die.

Presently she came back with Muso's message. 'Here it is,' she said. 'I hope
it puts Taman on the throne. I wish that I were to live to see that day.'

Then she, too, knew that she would not! I think I loathed Mephis more
that instant than I ever had before – which is saying something which no
superlative can express.

'I am coming back, Zerka,' I said. 'Perhaps I can aid you in the overthrow
of the Zanis. A few bombs at the psychological moment might help your
cause. Or maybe you will have changed your mind and decided to come
away with me. Now listen carefully. Southwest of Amlot is a flat-topped
mountain.'

'Yes,' she said, 'it is called Borsan.'

'Two rivers join just this side of it, and in the fork of the rivers there is a
farm. It belongs to a man named Lodas.'

'I know him well,' she said. 'He is one of us – a loyal soul.'

'When I come back I shall circle over the farm of Lodas,' I explained. 'If I
see a smoke-fire lighted in one of his fields, I shall know that I am to land for
a message from you – or, better still, for you, I hope. If I see no smoke, I shall
fly on to Amlot and circle the city. That will throw the city into a turmoil, I

am sure. You will hear of it and see me. If you are alive, you will make one smoke-fire on your beach, here. If you would like to have me bomb the palace and the barracks, you will light two smoke-fires. If I see no smoke-fire, I shall know that you are dead; and then I shall bomb hell out of the Zanis.'

'What is *hell?*' she asked.

'That is something peculiar to Earthmen,' I laughed. 'And now I must be going. Goodbye, Zerka.' I touched her hand with my lips.

'Goodbye, Carson of Venus,' she said. 'I hope that you do come back and bomb hell out of the Zanis.'

XIII

Danger in Sanara

As I put out to sea from the beach in front of the palace of the Toganja Zerka, my mind was filled with such emotions as beggar description. My beloved Duare was in grave danger in Sanara – the greatest danger being that she might be forced to die by her own hand, which I knew she would do rather than mate with Muso. And in Amlot I was leaving behind a good friend who was in equal danger, and in the Prison of Death lay Duare's father. If ever a man's mind was beset by apprehension of dire import, it was mine that night.

Standing out from shore, I caught a brisker breeze, which finally veered into the northeast and drove me along at a spanking pace. As the wind rose, so did the seas, until I began to have doubts as to the ability of my frail craft to weather them. It was an almost following wind, and constantly I was expecting to be engulfed by the growing seas that pursued me. The lightness of my boat, however, kept me just out of danger from that cause; but there was always the possibility of striking a submerged rock or a reef in this sea of which I knew nothing. I was compelled to stay always too close to land for safety, lest I pass my little island without recognizing it as such; but at last I saw it; and, without a great deal of difficulty, made the little cove where I had previously been taken off by Lodas.

The fear that now assailed me was as to the safety of my ship. Would I find it where I left it? What if some prowling fisherman had discovered it? I thought of a dozen reasons why it should be missing or destroyed as I drew my canoe safely out of the water and hastened across the island toward the spot where I had fastened the anotar down. At last I saw it dimly through the night, and then I was beside it. The reaction and the relief left me weak for a moment, as I realized that the ship was just as I had left it.

Casting off the ropes and throwing them into the rear cockpit, I taxied out into open meadow that formed the greater part of the island. A moment later I was in the air and heading straight for Sanara. I saw lights in Lodas's cottage as I sped past, and a moment later the lights of Amlot shown on my right. After, that I saw no sign of life until the campfires of the Zani army flickered below me; and then, ahead, I could see the glow of the lights of Sanara. My Duare was there! In a few minutes I should be holding her in my arms again. I tried to open the throttle wider, only to find that it was open as far as it would go – I had been running the engine at maximum all the way from

Amlot without realizing it; but I had made good time. I had left the Zani barracks and started for the quay about the 20th hour, it was now approaching only the 26th hour. In six Amtorian hours, which are equivalent to four Earth hours, I had made my escape from Amlot, sailed about ten miles along the coast, and flown to Sanara. That little gale had helped me on my way, and my light craft had practically flown the distance.

I approached Sanara without lights and at a high altitude; then I spiraled down from directly above the landing field that I had previously used. I knew every bump and depression in it, so many times had I used it. With my noiseless motor, I came in as quietly as a falling leaf; and taxied to the hangar that Muso had had built for me. The field was deserted; and the hour being late and few people on the streets in this district, I believe that no one saw my ship or saw me land. That was as I wished it, for I wanted to see Duare and Taman before I talked with anyone else.

I kept my flying helmet on to hide my Zani haircut, hoped that no one would notice my Zani trappings, and set out on foot in the direction of Taman's palace. As I approached it, I saw Muso's palace across the avenue brilliant with a thousand lights. Many gorgeously trapped gantors were waiting patiently along both sides of the avenue. Strains of music floated out into the night from the interior of the palace. I could also hear the murmur of many voices. It was evident that Muso was entertaining.

One of the sentries in front of Taman's palace stepped up to me as I stopped at the entrance.

'What do *you* want?' he demanded. I guess putting a man in front of a door anywhere in the universe must do something to him. The tremendous responsibility implicit in such a cosmic assignment seems to remove all responsibility for good manners. I have seldom known it to fail. When it does, they must immediately transfer the man to some other form of activity.

'I want to go in,' I said; 'I am Carson of Venus.'

The fellow stepped back as though he had seen a ghost, as I imagine that he thought he had, for a moment.

'Carson of Venus!' he exclaimed. 'We thought you were dead. Muso issued a proclamation of mourning for you. You must be dead.'

'I am not, and I want to go in and see my wife and Taman.'

'They are not there,' he said.

'Where are they?'

'Across the street.' He looked a bit uncomfortable as he said it, or was it my imagination?

'Then I'll go over there,' I said.

'I do not think Muso will be glad to see you,' opined the sentry; but I had already started, and he did not attempt to detain me.

376

Once again, at Muso's palace, I was stopped by a sentry. He wouldn't believe that I was Carson of Venus, and was going to have me carted off to jail. But I finally prevailed on him, by means of a small bribe, to call an officer. He who came, I had known quite well and had liked. I had taken him up in my ship a number of times, and we were good friends. When he recognized me, he looked mighty uncomfortable. I laid a hand on his arm, reassuringly.

'Please don't be embarrassed,' I begged. 'I have heard. Am I in time?'

'Thank the good fates, you are,' he replied. 'It was to be announced at the 27th hour this night. It is almost that now.

'And may I go in?' I asked, out of courtesy; for I intended going in, if I had to kill someone doing it.

'I would be the last man to stop you,' he said, 'even if I lost my head for it.'

'Thanks,' I said, and ran up the broad stairway beyond the ornate portals.

I could see down the center corridor to the great throne-room. It was packed with the aristocracy of Sanara. I knew that whatever of interest was taking place in the palace was taking place there; so I hurried along the corridor toward the doorway. Over the heads of the assembly I could see Muso standing on a dais beside the throne. He was speaking.

'A jong,' he was saying, 'must take his woman before the eyes of all men; so that all may know whom to honor as their vadjong. Being without a woman, I have chosen to honor one whose man gave his life in the service of Korva and myself. It is the highest award of merit that I can confer upon his memory.'

I was elbowing my way through the crowd to the discomfiture of ribs and toes and to the accompaniment of scowls and muttered imprecations. Finally an officer seized me by the shoulder and swung me around facing him. When he saw who I was, his eyes went wide; and then a wry smile twisted his lips as he let me go and gave me a push forward. As I came in full view of the dais, I saw Duare sitting on a low bench, her eyes staring straight ahead, that noble little head of hers unbowed. A strapping warrior of the jong's guard sat on either side of her. That was the only reason she was there.

'And now,' said Muso, 'lives there any man who says I may not take Duare, Janjong of Vepaja, to be my queen?'

'There does,' I said in a loud voice, stepping forward. Duare looked quickly down at me; then, before the warriors could prevent, she had leaped to the floor and flung herself into my arms.

Muso stood there with his mouth open, his arms hanging limply at his side. If the saying about having the starch taken out of one was ever appropriate, it was then. Here was a situation with which it seemed impossible for him to cope. Here was a problem without a solution. Finally he forced a sickly smile.

'I thought you were dead,' he said. 'This is indeed a happy moment.'

I just looked at him, and made no reply. The silence in the room was death-like. It must have lasted for a full minute, which is a very long time under such circumstances; then someone started for the doorway, and like a funeral procession the guests passed out. I felt a hand on my arm, and turned to see whose it was. It was Taman's. Jahara was at his side. She looked both fright-ened and pleased.

'Come,' he said, 'you had better get out of here.'

As we reached the doorway, I turned and looked back. Muso was still standing there beside his throne like one in a trance. We left the jong's palace and crossed directly to Taman's, nor did any of us breathe freely until we were seated in Jahara's boudoir.

'You will have to leave Sanara at once,' said Taman – 'tonight, if possible.'

'I don't want to leave Sanara,' I said. 'At last Duare and I have found a place where we might live in peace and happiness. I shall not let one man drive me out.'

'But you cannot fight the jong,' he said; 'and until Kord is restored, Muso is jong.'

'I think I can,' I said, 'and I think I can create a new jong. Kord is dead.'

'Kord dead? How do you know?'

'I saw Mephis kill him,' and then I told them the story of the assassination of the Jong of Korva.

'And the new jong?' asked Jahara. 'Who is he to be?'

'Taman,' I said.

Taman shook his head. 'That cannot be. I owe allegiance to Muso, if Kord be dead.'

'Even if he were proved to be a traitor of his people?' I asked.

'No, not in that event, of course; but Muso is no traitor to the people of Korva.'

'How many high officers of the army and officials of the government would feel as you do?' I asked.

'All but a few who owe everything to Muso,' he replied.

'How many of them can you gather here tonight,' I asked.

'Twenty to thirty of the most important,' he said.

'Will you do it? I ask you to trust me. It will be for the best good of Korva – the country that I would wish to make my own.'

He summoned several aides and gave instructions; then Taman, Jahara, and Duare settled down to listen to the story of my adventures in Amlot while we awaited the coming of the invited guests. I did not tell Duare that I had found her father a prisoner in a Zani prison until after we were alone together the next morning after the guests had left. She was very brave about it, and was confident that I would rescue him eventually.

At last the great men commenced to arrive. There were generals and councillors of state and great nobles of the realm, the flower of Korvan aristocracy that had escaped the Zani massacres. We met in the large audience chamber and were seated at a great table that had been brought into the room for the occasion. Taman was seated at the head of the table; I, being without nobility or rank, sat at the lower end. When all were seated, Taman rose.

'You all know Carson of Venus and what he has done for Sanara,' he said. 'He has asked me to call you together at this late hour because a national emergency exists. I trust him, and have taken his word that such is the case. I feel that we should listen to him. Are you all agreed?'

Thirty heads nodded gravely then Taman turned to me. 'You may speak, Carson of Venus,' he said; 'but you must have proof of what you have insinuated to me, for though you are my friend, my first duty is to my jong. Do not forget that. Proceed.'

'Let me put a hypothetical question to you gentlemen before I lay my information before you,' I commenced. 'If it were proved beyond doubt that your jong had sought to conspire with the enemy to cause the defeat of the forces holding Sanara and turn the city over to the Zanis at a price, would you feel that you were relieved of your oaths of allegiance to him and be warranted in replacing him with one of royal blood in whom you had the utmost confidence?'

Many a face was clouded by a resentful scowl. 'You are suggesting a grievous charge,' said a great general.

'I am asking you a hypothetical question,' I replied. 'I have made no charge. Do you care to answer?'

'There is no question as to what I should do,' said the general, 'if such an emergency confronted me. I should be the first to turn against any jong who did such a traitorous thing as that, but that is something that no jong of Korva would do.'

'And you other gentlemen?' I asked.

Without exception they all concurred in the sentiments of the general.

'Then I may tell you that such an emergency exists,' I said. 'I shall shock you by my disclosures, but I must have your assurance that you will hear me through and consider impartially the evidence I have to offer.'

'I can assure you that we shall,' said Taman.

'Muso, swearing me to secrecy, sent me to Amlot with a message for Spehon, Mephis's chief lieutenant. He chose me for two reasons. One was that he thought I could not read Amtorian, and therefore could not know what was in the message; and the other you had proof of in his palace this night – he wanted my woman. But I can read Amtorian; and after I got to Amlot, I became suspicious and read Muso's message to Spehon. In it he offered to open the gates of Sanara to Zani troops in return for the throne of Korva, and he agreed to accept Mephis as his advisor and to reward the Zanis. He also suggested that it would be best if Carson of Venus were destroyed in Amlot.'

'This is preposterous!' cried a great noble. 'The man must be mad to make such charges. They are prompted by jealousy, because Muso desires his woman.'

'They cannot be true,' exclaimed another.

'Taman,' cried a third, 'I demand this man's arrest.'

'You are not keeping your promise to me,' I reminded them. 'Is this what I am to expect of Korvan nobility? And do you think I am such a fool as to make charges of this kind without ample evidence to substantiate them? What would I have to gain? I would be signing my own death warrant. I may be doing so anyway; but I am doing it for the only country on Amtor that I can call my own, the one country in which my princess and I feel that we have a chance to live happily among friends.'

'Go on,' said the great general. 'I apologize for my confreres.'

'Where are your proofs?' asked Taman.

'Here,' I said, and drew Muso's message from my pocket pouch. 'Here, in his own handwriting, Muso convicts himself.' I handed the envelope to Taman. He opened it and read it through carefully to himself; then he passed it to the man to his right. Thus it passed around the table, each man reading it carefully. It left them silent and sober-faced. Even after the last man had read it and passed it back to Taman, they sat in silence. It was the great general who spoke first.

'I do not doubt the integrity of this man or his belief in the duplicity of Muso,' he said. 'It is sufficient to shake the confidence of each of us. In addition, he knows that Muso sought his life. I cannot blame him for anything he may think; I should think as he does, were I he. But he is not a Korvan by birth. There is not bred in him the reverence and loyalty to our jongs that is part of every fiber of our beings. For him, this document is sufficient proof. As I have said, it would be for me, were I he; but I am not. I am a Korvan noble, the first general of the jong's armies; and so I must give Muso the benefit of every doubt. Perhaps this message was a ruse to lure the Zani troops from some part of the line, that Muso might order an attack upon that weakened part It would have been excellent strategy. Now I suggest that we prove conclusively whether such was his intent, or whether he did intend to open the gates to the enemy.'

'How may that be done?' asked Taman.

'We shall try to arrange to have the enemy shoot three blue rockets into the air before the main gates of Sanara on three successive nights, then wait and see what Muso does.'

'But how can we get the enemy to co-operate?' asked another.

'I shall commission Carson of Venus to drop a message behind their lines, telling them that I should like to hold a parley with them and asking them, if they are agreeable to the suggestion, to shoot the blue rockets.'

'An excellent suggestion,' said Taman.

'But,' I objected, 'seeing me returned alive, Muso may be suspicious; for he definitely asked Spehon to have me destroyed.'

'Write a report,' said the general, 'stating that after you delivered the message you became fearful and escaped.'

'That would certainly arouse Muso's suspicions,' said Taman.

'I might tell him the truth,' I suggested, 'and that is that the very night I arrived in Amlot the message was stolen from me. The very fact that I remained there so long should convince Muso that I had no suspicion of what the note contained.'

'I think your idea is the best one,' said the general; 'but why did you stay so long in Amlot – if you could have escaped?'

'I had several reasons,' I replied. 'I suspected that Mintep, Jong of Vepaja and father of my princess, was a prisoner there. I also wanted to gather what information I could for the Sanaran high command. Lastly, I had to establish myself before I could safely make an effort to escape. I became an officer in the Zani Guard and was, for a while, acting governor of the Gap kum Rov.'

'And you absorbed some information?'

'Much,' I replied. 'I have learned that a counter-revolution is about to be launched, the proponents of which hoped to restore Kord to his throne.'

'You say "hoped",' commented a noble. 'Have they now given up the idea?'

'Kord is dead,' I said.

I might as well have thrown a bomb among them. They leaped to their feet almost as one man. 'Kord dead?' It was the same stunned reaction that I had seen before.

'But,' cried one, 'we have heard that rumor often before, but it has never been substantiated.'

'I saw him die,' I told them; then I had to go all over that harrowing episode again.

Well, at last they prepared to go; but before they did I propounded another question. 'And now, gentlemen,' I said, 'just who is going to protect my princess and me from Muso? If I am not mistaken, I stand a good chance of being assassinated the first time I go on the streets.'

'He is right,' said the general.

'He should certainly be protected, General Varo,' agreed Taman.

'Well,' said Varo, 'I know of no safer place for them than where they are now, under the protection of the man who is next in line for the throne of Korva, after Muso.'

There was a subdued cheer at that, but I was not surprised. Taman was the most popular man in Sanara. He sat for a moment with his head bowed, and then looked up at Varo. His face showed traces of mental strain; his manner was tinged with embarrassment.

'I wish that I might agree with you in that,' he said; 'but, unfortunately, I cannot. As a matter of fact, I believe that my palace would be the least safe place for Carson of Venus and the Janjong of Vepaja. During the past ten days three attempts have been made upon my life – twice by poison, once by dagger.'

The disclosure so shocked the assembled nobles, that, for a moment, there was deep silence; then Varo spoke.

'Were the scoundrels apprehended?' he asked. 'Do you know who they were?'

'Yes,' replied Taman, 'but they were only the instruments of another.'

'And you know whom that may be?' asked a noble.

'I can only surmise,' replied Taman. 'Unfortunately, my retainers killed all three before I had an opportunity to question them.'

'Perhaps I had better remain here, then,' I said, 'as additional protection for the next jong of Korva.'

'No,' said Taman. 'I appreciate your generosity; but I am well protected by my own people, and there are more important things for you to do.'

'You may come to my palace,' said Varo. 'I swear no one shall take you from there, even if I have to protect you with the entire army of Sanara.'

I shook my head. 'Muso will unquestionably send for me,' I said. 'Should you refuse to give me up, his suspicions would be aroused; and our entire plan might come to nothing. I think I have a solution of the problem.'

'What is it?' asked Taman.

'Let Varo prepare his message to the enemy at once. At the same time I shall write my report to Muso. Get two officers to volunteer for extra hazard-ous duty. I shall want them to accompany me. As soon as Varo's message is ready, Varo can order me out on special duty. I shall take my princess and the two officers with me, drop the message behind the enemy lines, and remain away until you shall have had time to determine Muso's guilt or assure your-selves of his innocence. When I return above Sanara, liberate one balloon if it is unsafe for me ever to return to Sanara; liberate two if I am to return another day for further advice; liberate three if it is safe for me to land. In the event that I cannot land in safety to myself, I shall land the two officers the night that I get the message; and I must have your assurance now that I shall be permitted to do so and take off again in safety.'

'The entire plan is excellent,' said Taman. 'Please put it in writing; so that there shall be no misunderstanding of the signals.'

'May I ask why you wish to have two of our officers accompany you?' asked Varo.

'One of them will have to go with me into Amlot while I attempt to liberate the Jong of Vepaja from the Gap kum Rov; the other will remain with my princess and the ship while I am away in Amlot.'

'I shall have no difficulty in obtaining volunteers,' said Varo. 'Now, if we are to get you away before dawn, we must get to work.'

XIV

Back to Amlot

An hour before dawn we left the palace of Taman; Duare, the two officers who had volunteered to accompany us, and I. Because of Duare, I felt nervous and uneasy; for we had to leave the palace in full view of the guards before the palace of Muso, directly across the avenue; and while the fact that Varo had furnished us with a strong guard imparted a feeling of greater security, yet, at the same time, it certainly made us extremely conspicuous. There were ten military gantors loaded with soldiers, constituting what, to me, had taken on the proportions of a pageant; and I can tell you that I breathed a sigh of relief when I had my party aboard the ship and was taxiing out for the take-off; and as we soared above the walls of Sanara and out across open country, I was happier than I had been for many days. Once again I was free, and I had Duare with me.

I had put Ulan and Legan, the two officers, in the cabin. Duare sat beside me, and there was a basket of small bombs in each cockpit. The ship was more heavily laden than it had ever before been, but that had seemed to make no appreciable difference in the take-off, nor could I see that she handled differently in flight. We had determined in Havatoo, while designing her, that she would easily lift a load of fifteen hundred pounds; so I had little doubt that she would have no trouble with the approximately thousand-pound load that she was now carrying.

I flew slowly toward the enemy camp, killing time until daylight should have come. Ulan and Legan were thrilled beyond words, for this was the first flight either of them had taken; while Duare and I were just content to be together again, holding hands like a couple of kids.

I had hurriedly contrived a tiny parachute before leaving Taman's palace. It consisted of a square of very light fabric woven from the web of a small cousin of the targo, a giant spider that inhabits the mile-high trees that grow in many parts of Amtor; and which is so sheer as to be almost invisible, yet quite strong. To the four corners of this square piece I had tied strings, and to the ends of these strings I had attached the leather envelope which bore Varo's message to the enemy.

Dawn was just breaking as we flew over the Zani camp. An alert sentry must have sighted us, for I distinctly heard a shout; and almost immediately saw men running from the shelters which lined the streets of the camp. I continued to circle above them, well out of range of R-rays, until it was entirely light; then, estimating the velocity of the wind, I flew a little way beyond the windward side of the camp and tossed the message overboard. The little parachute opened immediately and floated gracefully down toward the camp. I could see thousands of men by now standing with upturned faces, watching it. They must have thought that it was some new engine of destruction, for when it came close to the ground near the center of the camp, they scattered like sheep. I continued to circle until I saw a brave soul advance to where the message lay and pick it up. Then I dipped a wing and flew away.

The trip to the island was uneventful. I circled Lodas's house for quite some time, but no smoke signal was lighted; then I dropped over to the island and landed. The country, except in the vicinity of the cities, is strangely deserted in every part of Amtor that I have visited. Between Sanara and the farm of Lodas we had not seen a sign of human life except that in the camp of the Zanis, which, of course, was no permanent habitation. Few farmers have the temerity that Lodas displayed in locating a farm so far from civilization, and open constantly to the danger of attack by some of the fearsome creatures which roam the plains and forests of Venus. It was, however, the very fact that few men traversed these interurban wildernesses that had rendered my little island so safe a place to hide the anotar and also the little craft that had brought me there from Amlot and which I hoped would bear me back to the Zani stronghold.

As we came in to land, I saw my boat lying where I had dragged it; and one more cause of anxiety was removed. Now I had only to wait for darkness and the proper moment to launch my attempt to rescue Mintep. I told Legan that he was to remain with Duare in the unlikely event that she should need protection, and I also instructed her to take to the air if any danger threatened them. Duare was by now an efficient pilot. I had taken her with me on many of my flights over the enemy lines, and had had her practice landings and take-offs on the surface of a dry lake I had discovered some fifty miles west of Sanara. I had also let her take off and land at the racing field in Sanara. She was quite competent to land anywhere that conditions were reasonably favorable. I drew a rough map of Amlot for her, marking the location of the palace and the barracks; and told her that if I had not returned to the island by dawn she and Legan were to fly along the coast toward Amlot, keeping a close lookout for my boat; and if they did not see me, they were to fly over the city and drop bombs on the palace and the barracks until they saw me put out into the harbor. I was sure they would be able to identify me from the air because of my flying helmet.

It had taken me about three Amtorian hours to sail from Amlot to the island. Allowing eight hours for the round trip, including the time it might take to get into the Gap kum Rov and take Mintep out, I estimated that I should leave the island about the 29th hour in order to get back by dawn. In the event that Ulan and I never returned, Duare was to take Legan back to Sanara; and if three balloons were sent up, indicating that it was safe to land, she should do so; for I felt that she would be safer there than anywhere else. If the signal were a discouraging one, she might try to reach Vepaja; but that would be almost suicidal, since she could not approach anywhere near Kooaad, her city, in the ship; and the dangers she would encounter on the ground were far too numerous and terrible to render it at all likely that she would survive.

'Do not even think of anything so terrible as that you may not return from Amlot,' she begged. 'If you do not, it will make no difference where I go, for I shall not live. I do not care to live unless I have you, Carson.'

Ulan and Legan were on the ground inspecting the boat; so I took her in my arms and kissed her, and told her that I would come back.

'For no one but your father would I go to Amlot and risk your life as well as my own,' I said.

'I wish you did not have to go, Carson. What a strange retribution it would be if, for the sake of the throne I gave up for you, I should lose you. It would not be just retribution, though – it would be wicked.'

'You'll not lose me, dear,' I assured her, 'unless your father takes you away from me.'

'He can't do that now. Even though he is my father and my jong, I should disobey him if he sought to.'

'I'm afraid he's going to be – well, disagreeable about the matter,' I suggested. 'You know how shocked you were at the very thought of even talking to me. When I told you I loved you, you wanted to knife me; and you really felt that I deserved death. How do you suppose he's going to feel about it when he finds that you are irrevocably mine? He'll want to kill me.'

'When are you going to tell him?' she asked.

'After I get him here on the island. I'm afraid he'd upset the boat if I told him at sea.'

She shook her head dubiously. 'I don't know,' she said – 'I can't imagine how he'll take it. He is a very proud jong, steeped in the traditions of a royal family that extends back into prehistoric times; and, Carson, he does not know you as I do. If he did, he would be glad that his daughter belonged to such as you. Do you know, Carson, he may even kill me. Even though you think you know, yet you have no conception of the taboos and interdictions that dictate the attitude of all toward the sacred person of the virgin daughter of a jong. There is nothing in your life with which I may compare it. There is nothing that you so reverence and hold so sacred.'

'Yes, there is, Duare,' I said.

'What?' she demanded.

'You.'

'Fool!' she said, laughing. 'But you're a dear fool, and I know that you believe what you said.'

The day drew to a close and the night wore on. Ulan and Legan amused themselves by fishing; and we built a fire and cooked what they caught, enjoying an unexpectedly excellent meal. I cut a slender sapling about twenty feet long and stowed it in the boat. As the 29th hour approached, I kissed Duare goodbye. She clung to me for a long time. I know she thought it was the last time she should ever see me. Then Ulan and I embarked. A good breeze was blowing; and we skimmed away into the darkness, bound for Amlot.

Did you ever reach into an inside pocket time after time to assure and reassure yourself that you had not forgotten the theater tickets that you knew were there? Well, that's the way I kept feeling in my pocket pouch for the duplicate master key to the cells of the Prison of Death I had had made just before I left Amlot. And not without reason was I thus solicitous – without that key, not even an act of God could have gotten Mintep's cell door unlocked without the co-operation of Torko; and somehow I couldn't see Torko co-operating.

We rounded the headland and drew into the harbor of Amlot just before the 3rd hour. Running before the wind, we approached the little island of horror where loomed the Gap kum Rov. As we came closer to shore I lowered the sail, lest its white expanse be seen by some watchful Zani eye, and paddled quietly in beneath those frowning walls. Feeling my way cautiously along the cold, damp stones, I came at last to that which I sought – the opening of the chute through which the ashes of burned men are discharged into the bay. Ulan and I spoke no word, as all the way from the island I had been coaching him on what he was to do; so that it would be unnecessary for us to speak in other than an emergency. Once more I felt to learn if I still had the key; then, as Ulan held the boat in position beneath the mouth of the chute, I carefully inserted the pole I had prepared and pushed it up its full length, letting the lower end rest on the bottom of the boat. This done, I proceeded to climb up the pole into the chute. Disturbed by the pole and my body brushing the sides of the chute, the ashes of a thousand dead men drifted gently down upon me.

When I reached the top of the pole, I raised one hand directly over my head. To my vast relief, it came in contact with the trap door just a few inches above me. I pushed up, and raised it far enough so that I could grasp the sill with my fingers; then remained quiet, listening. Only the moans and groans of the prisoners came to my ears. There was no alarm. So far, none had heard me. Pulling myself up, I raised the door with my head and shoulders until I could fall forward with the upper half of my body on the floor of the furnace room. A moment later I stood erect.

A few steps brought me to the dimly lighted corridor. I knew exactly where Mintep's cell lay, and walked directly it. Whatever I was to do must be done quickly and silently. Pressing my face to the bars, I looked in. I thought I saw a figure in the far corner, a figure huddled on the floor. I inserted the key in the lock and turned it. The door swung in. I crossed and kneeled beside the figure, listening. By the breathing, I knew that the man slept. I shook him lightly by the shoulder, and as he stirred I cautioned him to silence.

'Are you Mintep?' I asked, fearful that he might have been taken to his death and another placed in his cell since I had located it. I had not served in this prison without having learned how quickly changes might come, how unexpectedly one man might be rubbed out to make place for another. I held my breath waiting for his reply. At last he spoke.

'Who are you?' he demanded.

'Never mind that,' I snapped a little irritably. 'Are you Mintep?'

'Yes,' he said.

'Come with me quietly. Duare is waiting for you.'

That was enough. Like a new man, he came to his feet and followed me stealthily to the furnace room, though I could see that he staggered a little from weakness. It was no small job getting him down that pole. He was too weak to climb down himself; so I had practically to carry him. But at last we were in the boat. I lowered the pole into the water and pushed off. We paddled all the way to the mouth of the harbor, as otherwise we would have had to tack back and forth several times to have made it; and I was afraid the sail might attract attention from the shore. Had it, a launch must certainly have overhauled us before we could get out into the open sea. But at last we turned the headland, and Ulan hoisted the sail.

Then it was that I thought to do a very foolish thing. Once I had stopped and seen Zerka while I was escaping from Amlot. It had seemed very simple and quite safe. Conditions of tide and wind were again favorable. Why not do it again? I might obtain information that would be of value to my friends at Sanara. I told Ulan and Mintep what I intended doing. It was not for them to question my judgment; so they concurred. It was the first time that we had dared speak, so fearful had we been of discovery, knowing, as we did, how the sound of voices carries over water.

'Who are you?' asked Mintep

'Do you recall the prison officer who sang a song to you?' I asked.

'But he was a Zani,' said Mintep.

'Only posing as a Zani to find you,' I told him.

'But who are you?' he insisted.

'For some time I was a guest-prisoner in your palace at Kooaad,' I said. 'I am the stranger called Carson.'

'Carson!' he exclaimed. 'When Kamlot returned to Kooaad, he told me of all that you had done to serve my daughter, Duare. And now you say she is safe and waiting for me?'

'Yes; in two or three hours you shall see her.'

'And you have done all this for me?' he asked.

'For Duare,' I said simply.

He made no comment on the correction, and we sailed on in silence again until we came opposite the palace of Zerka; then I turned the boat's nose toward shore. Alas, what stupid things one does! The palace was lighted much as I had last seen it – all seemed quiet and peaceful. I hoped Zerka would be alone. I wanted only a few swift words with her.

'Stay in the boat,' I told Ulan, 'and be ready to push off on an instant's notice'; then I walked up the garden to the great doors that open onto the terrace. I paused and listened, but I could hear nothing; then I whistled – and waited. I did not have to wait long. I heard the sound of men running, but the sounds did not come from the house – they came from the garden behind me. I wheeled, and in the light from the palace windows I saw a dozen Zani Guardsmen running toward me.

'Shove off, Ulan!' I cried at the top of my voice. 'Shove off, and take Mintep to Duare! I command it!' Then they were upon me.

At the sound of my voice the great doors swung open, and I saw more Zani uniforms in the great hall of the palace of the Toganja Zerka. They dragged me in, and when I was recognized a sullen murmur filled the room.

XV

Tragic Error

There is nothing more annoying than to commit an egregious error of judgment and have no one but yourself upon whom to blame it. As I was dragged into that room, I was annoyed. I was more than annoyed – I was frightened; for I saw certain death staring me in the face. And not death alone – for I remembered Narvon. I wondered if I would go to pieces, too.

And there was some reason for my apprehension, for besides a company of Zani Guardsmen and officers, there were a number of the great men of Zanism – there were even Mephis and Spehon themselves. And to one side, their wrists manacled, stood Zerka and Mantar. There was an expression almost of anguish in Zerka's eyes as they met mine. Mantar shook his head sadly, as though to say, 'You poor fool, why did you stick your head into the noose again?'

'So you came back!' rasped Mephis. 'Don't you think that was a little unwise, a little stupid?'

'Let us say unfortunate, Mephis,' I replied. 'Unfortunate for you.'

'Why unfortunate for me?' he demanded, almost angrily. I could see that he was nervous. I knew that he was always fearful.

'Unfortunate, because you would like to kill me; but if you do – if you harm me in any way or harm the Toganja Zerka or Mantar – you will die shortly after dawn.'

'You dare threaten *me*?' he roared. 'You stinking mistal! You dare threaten the great Mephis? Off to the Gap kum Rov with him – with all of them! Let Torko do his worst with them. I want to see them writhe. I want to hear them scream.'

'Wait a minute, Mephis,' I advised him. 'I wasn't threatening you. I was merely stating facts. I know what I'm talking about, for I have given orders that I know will be carried out if I am not safely out of Amlot shortly after dawn.'

'You lie!' he almost screamed.

I shrugged. 'If I were you, though, I'd give instructions that none of us is to be tortured or harmed in any way until at least the third hour tomorrow – and be sure to have a boat ready that I and my friends can sail away in after you have released us.'

'I shall never release you,' he said; but nevertheless he gave instructions that we were not to be tortured or harmed until he gave further orders.

And so Zerka and Mantar and I were dragged away to the Gap kum Rov. They didn't abuse us, and they even took the manacles off Zerka and Mantar. They put us all together in a cell on the second floor, which surprised me; as the basement was reserved for Mephis's special hates as well as prisoners concerning whose incarceration he would rather not have too much known.

'Why did you do such a foolish thing as to come back?' asked Zerka, after we had been left alone.

'And right after I risked my life to get you out of here,' said Mantar, laughingly.

'Well,' I explained, 'I wanted to see Zerka and find out if there is any way in which the loyal forces at Sanara may cooperate with you.'

'They could,' she said, 'but now they'll never know. We need more weapons – you might have brought them in that flying boat you have told me about.'

'I may yet,' I assured her.

'Have you gone crazy?' she demanded, 'Don't you know, regardless of that courageous bluff you tried to pull, that we are all lost – that we shall be tortured and killed, probably today.'

'No,' I said. 'I know we may, but not that we shall. I was pulling no bluff. I meant what I said. But tell me, what caused them to arrest you and Mantar?'

'It was the culmination of growing suspicion on the part of Spehon,' explained Zerka. 'My friendship for you had something to do with it; and after Horjan informed on you and you escaped from the city, Spehon, in checking over all your connections, recalled this friendship and also the fact that Mantar and you were close friends and that Mantar was my friend. One of the soldiers in the detail that Mantar commanded the evening that he met you and let you proceed to the quay reported to Spehon that he thought your description, which he heard after he returned to the barracks, fitted the man with whom Mantar had talked. Then, these things having suggested my connection with you, Spehon recalled Narvon's last words – the same words that assured you that I was one of those who conspired with Narvon against the Zanis. So, all in all, they had a much clearer case against me than the Zanis ordinarily require, but Mephis would not believe that I had conspired against him. He is such an egotistical fool that he thought that my affection for him assured my loyalty.'

'I was, until recently, in a quandary as to your exact sentiments and your loyalties,' I said. 'I was told that you were high in the esteem of Mephis, that you were the author of the "Malta Mephis!" gesture of adulation, that it was you who suggested having citizens stand on their heads while they cheered Mephis, that it was your idea to have *The Life of Our Beloved Mephis* run continuously in all theatres, and to have Zani Guardsmen annoy and assault citizens continually.'

Zerka laughed. 'You were correctly informed,' she said. 'I was the instigator of those and other schemes for making Zanism obnoxious and ridiculous in the eyes of the citizens of Amlot; so that it might be easier to recruit members for our counter-revolution. So stupidly egotistical are the chief Zanis, they will swallow almost any form of flattery, however ridiculous and insincere it may be.'

While we were talking, Torko came stamping up the stairs to our cell. He had been absent from the prison when we were brought in. He wore one of his most fearsome frowns, but I could see he was delighted with the prospect of baiting and doubtless torturing such important prisoners as we. He stood and glowered at us a moment before he spoke. It was so evident that he was trying to impress and frighten us that I couldn't restrain a desire to laugh – well, perhaps I didn't try very hard. I knew how to bait such creatures as Torko. I also knew that no matter what attitude we assumed toward him he would give us the works, so to speak, the moment he was given the opportunity.

'What are you laughing at?' he demanded.

'I wasn't laughing before you came up, Torko; so I must be laughing at you.'

'Laughing at me, are you, you stinking mistal?' he bellowed. 'Well, you won't laugh when I get you in the courtroom tomorrow morning.'

'You won't get me into the courtroom tomorrow morning, Torko; and even if I am there, you won't be. You'll be in one of these cells; and then, later, you'll have an opportunity to discover how effective are the ingenious devices for torture you bragged of having invented.'

Zerka and Mantar looked their astonishment, the former smiling a little because she thought I was bluffing again. Torko stood there fairly boiling.

'I've a good mind to take you down there now,' he threatened, 'and get out of you what you mean by such talk.'

'You wouldn't dare do that, Torko,' I told him. 'You already have your orders about us. And, anyway, you don't have to – I'll tell you without being tortured. It's like this: Mephis is going to be angry with you when I tell him you offered to give me liberties while I was stationed here if I would speak a good word about you to the Toganja Zerka, that she might carry it to him. He won't like it when he learns that you let me go fishing whenever I wanted to and thus permitted me to pave the way for my escape by boat; and, Torko, there is another thing that is going to make him so furious that – well, I just don't know what he will do to you when he discovers it.'

Torko was commencing to look uncomfortable, but he came right through with the same argument that even great statesmen of our own Earth use when they're caught red-handed.

'They're a pack of lies!' he yelled.

'He won't think so when he learns about the other thing you have done – something that he can see with his own eyes,' I baited him.

'What's the other lie?' he demanded, his curiosity and fear getting the better of him.

'Oh, just that you unlocked the cell of Mintep, Jong of Vepaja, and let him escape,' I said.

'That is a lie,' he cried.

'Well, go and look for yourself,' I suggested. 'If he's gone, who else could have unlocked his cell? You have the only keys.'

'He's not gone,' he said; but he turned and ran down the stairs as fast as he could go.

'You seem to be having a good time,' said Mantar, 'and we might as well have all the fun we can while we may. It's not going to be so funny when morning comes – not for us.'

'On the contrary,' I objected, 'that may be the most amusing time of all.'

'I am amused now,' said Zerka. 'How furious Torko will be when he discovers that you have hoaxed him into running all the way down to the basement.'

'But it was not a hoax,' I said. 'He will find Mintep's cell door open and Mintep gone.'

'How can you possibly know that?' demanded Zerka.

'Because I released Mintep myself, and he is on his way to safety right now.'

'But how could you enter the Gap kum Rov and take a prisoner out under the noses of the Zani Guard?' demanded Zerka. 'Why, it is simply impossible. You couldn't have even unlocked his cell if you had managed to get into the prison, which, in itself, would have been impossible.'

I had to smile. 'But I did,' I said, 'and it was very easy.'

'Would you mind very much telling me how you did it?' she asked.

'Not at all,' I assured her. 'In the first place, I secured a duplicate master key to all the locks of Gap kum Rov while I was stationed here. Last night I came in a boat to the side of the prison and entered it through the chute that discharges the ashes from the furnace into the bay. I brought Mintep out the same way.'

Mantar and Zerka shook their heads in astonishment. It could not have seemed possible to many inhabitants of Amlot that a prisoner might escape from the Gap kum Rov, for few of them knew anything about the prison except that no prisoner had ever escaped from it.

'And you have a master key to the locks?' asked Mantar.

I took it from my pocket pouch. 'Here it is,' I said. 'If they had confined us in the basement, we might have escaped easily, at least as far as the waters of the bay; but with a guard watching constantly on the floor below there is no chance from here.'

'But aren't you afraid they'll find the key on you?' asked Zerka.

'Yes, of course; but what can I do about it? I have no place to hide it. I shall simply have to take the chance that they won't search me – they are so stupid. Anyway, unless they confine us in the basement, it cannot possibly be of any use to us. Furthermore, I have an idea that we'll walk out of here without any need of a key.'

'You are very optimistic,' said Mantar; 'but I can't see upon what food your optimism thrives.'

'Wait for dawn,' I counselled.

'Listen!' said Zerka.

From below we heard Torko's voice bellowing orders. Guards were running to and fro. They were searching the prison for Mintep. When they reached our floor they entered every cell and searched it carefully, although they could have seen the whole interior of each of them from the corridor. Torko's face was drawn and pale. He looked to me like a broken man. When he reached our cell he was trembling, as much, I think, from fright as from rage.

'What have you done with him?' he demanded.

'I?' I asked in feigned astonishment. 'Now, how could I have gotten into this impregnable prison, so ably guarded by the great Torko – unless with the connivance of Torko? Mephis will be sure to ask that very question.'

'Listen,' Torko said, coming close and whispering. 'I was good to you when you were here. Do not send me to my death. Do not tell Mephis that Mintep has escaped. If he is not told, he may never know it. The chances are he has forgotten all about Mintep by this time. If you do not tell him, I promise not to torture you and your accomplices unless I am forced to; and then I'll make it as easy as I can.'

'If you do torture us, I'll certainly tell him,' I replied. I certainly had Torko over a barrel.

Torko scratched his head in thought for a moment. 'Say,' he said at last, 'of course you couldn't have let him out; but how in the world did you know he was gone?'

'I'm psychic, Torko,' I told him. 'I even know things are going to happen before they do. What is the hour?'

He looked at me rather fearfully as he replied. 'It is the 1st hour,' he said. 'Why?'

'Presently you shall hear a great noise in the direction of the palace of Mephis,' I said, 'and then word will pass around that death and destruction are raining upon the Zanis from the sky because they hold me and my friends prisoners in Gap kum Rov. When Mephis sets us free, it shall stop.'

'Rubbish!' said Torko, and went on to search other cells for Mintep, Jong of Vepaja. He didn't find him.

Time dragged leadenly after dawn crept slowly out of the east and its light sought to penetrate the dirty windows of the Gap kum Rov. I was tense from waiting for the first detonation of a bomb. The second hour came and then the third, yet still nothing had happened. What could the reason be? Had disaster overtaken Duare? I imagined a hundred terrible things that might have happened. A crack-up at the take-off seemed the most likely. I was still worrying when Torko came with a detail of the guard and took us down to the courtroom. There were Mephis, Spehon, and a number of other high Zanis. We were lined up before them. They glowered at us like ogres out of a fairy tale.

'It is the third hour,' said Mephis. 'I have waited, and because you have made me wait it shall go the harder for you. If any of you expect any mercy you will name all your accomplices in the low plot you have fostered to over-throw the state. Torko, take the woman first. We'll make her talk, and I'll save you for the last. Take that thing off his head, Torko.' He pointed at me.

I looked at Torko, as he took of my flying helmet and threw it into a corner. The sweat was pouring down his face, although it was not hot. 'Do not forget, Torko,' I whispered.

'Mercy,' he pleaded. 'I must obey orders.'

They laid Zerka upon a hideous thing that would have crushed her slowly, inch by inch, starting at her toes; and they brought a brazier containing a pot of molten metal and set it down on a table beside her. It was not difficult to guess how they intended to use it. I turned my head, for I could not look at the frightful thing they contemplated.

'Do you wish to confess?' asked Mephis.

'No,' replied Zerka in a firm voice.

'Have you anything to say?' he inquired.

'Yes, this: I joined the Zani Party because I had learned that you tortured and murdered my man. I joined to undermine it; and for another, greater purpose – to kill you.'

Mephis laughed. 'And this is the way you kill me!' he taunted.

'No, not this way; nor the way I had hoped, but the only way I could find,' replied Zerka.

'What do you mean?' demanded Mephis.

'I mean that I have avenged my husband, but you did not know it. Know it now, then. Before another day has passed, you will be dead.'

'And how, please, am I to die at the hand of a dead woman?' jeered Mephis.

'You ate food in my home last night, Mephis. Do you recall? That food was poisoned. I have kept it there for a long time to cheat you of the pleasure of killing me, were I caught. Last night I had the opportunity I had never hoped for of letting you eat it instead. At any moment, now, you will die – certainly before another day has passed.'

The face of Mephis turned livid. He tried to speak, but no words came to his white lips. He rose and pointed at Torko. He was trying to order the torture to proceed. Torko looked at me and trembled. The other Zanis were staring at Mephis; then, close by, came a shattering detonation that shook the walls of Gap kum Rov. Duare had come! But she was bombing the prison instead of the palace – she must have mistaken the one for the other. It was possible.

'I warned you!' I shouted. 'The city will be destroyed if you don't set us free and give us a boat.'

'Never!' cried Mephis. 'Destroy them all!' Then he gasped, clutched his throat, and fell forward across the bench.

The Zanis rushed forward, surrounding him. Another bomb burst so close that I was certain that it had struck the building. It threw us all to the floor. Spehon was the first to his feet.

'Mephis is dead!' he cried. 'Spehon is ruler of Korva!'

'Maltu Spehon!' shouted the assembled Zanis; then a bomb exploded in the rear of the building, and again we were all thrown to the floor.

'Get them out of here!' screamed Spehon. 'Get them a boat! Hurry!'

Well, they got us out of there in short order; but we were far from safe. Bombs kept bursting all around us. In the sky above, I saw the anotar circling like a great bird of prey; yet it looked sweet to me. They hurried us to a safer part of the bay side and found us a boat – a fair size fishing boat with two sails; then they hustled us into it. We made sail quickly and started tacking for the harbor entrance; and as we moved slowly away from shore, I saw the anotar drop in graceful spiral toward us. Duare was coming to make sure that it was I. She didn't drop far enough to be in range of any R-ray or T-ray guns they might have trained on the ship, for I had warned her against this. She circled us a few times, and then flew back over the city. I wondered why she didn't follow us out to sea and pick us up. We were about the center of the harbor when I heard another bomb explode. In rapid succession five more fell. It was then that I guessed the truth – Duare had not recognized me! She must naturally have expected to see a man alone in a boat – a man wearing a flying helmet. Instead she had seen two men and a woman, and both men sported the Zani coiffure.

Briefly I explained our situation to Zerka and Mantar. It seemed almost hopeless. We could not return to shore because the Zanis would be furious at the continued bombing which I had promised them would stop if they set us free. If we waited around in the harbor on the chance that Duare might circle above us again and give me an opportunity to signal her, it was almost certain that the Zanis would send a launch out to recapture us.

'Perhaps,' I suggested, 'Duare may take another look, even out at sea. Suppose we round the headland and wait out of sight of the city?'

They both agreed that it would do no harm, and so I sailed the boat well out beyond the mouth of the harbor, where we would be hidden from the city by the headland. From that position we could see the anotar circling high over Amlot, and from time to time we heard the booming detonations of her bombs. Late in the afternoon we saw her turn her nose northeast in the direction of Sanara, and in a few minutes she was out of sight.

XVI

Despair

For a few minutes I plumbed the depths of despair, and then I thought of the torture chamber and how much worse things might have been for us, especially for Zerka and Mantar. Had I not stopped at her palace the night before, both of them would now be dead. They must have been thinking this same thing, too, for they were very gay and happy. Yet our position was far from being an enviable one. We were without food, water, or weapons, in a none too substantial boat, off an enemy shore; and Sanara was five hundred miles away and possibly in the hands of another enemy. But worst of all, for me, Duare was in equal danger. She would not dare return to Sanara until she knew that Muso had been deposed. If he were never deposed, what was she to do? Where could she go? And all the time she must be thinking that I was dead. I was that much better off, at least; I was sure she lived. Of course, she had her father; but I knew that that would scarcely compensate for the loss of the man she loved, nor would her father be able to protect her as well as I. He would have been all right as a protector back in his own kingdom, with his warriors and his other loyal subjects about him, but I had learned to take care of Duare under conditions far different. Of course, I hadn't always made such a good job of it; but in the end, I had come through all right.

As the anotar disappeared in the distance I made sail again and turned up the coast in the direction of Sanara.

'Where are we going?' asked Zerka.

I told her.

She nodded in approval. 'I only asked out of curiosity,' she said. 'Wherever you wish to go suits me. Thanks to you, we are alive. We can ask no more.'

'Perhaps we are as well off anyway,' I said. 'It might have been pretty nearly impossible to crowd seven people into the anotar.'

We sailed up the coast all that night under a fresh breeze, and in the morning I came in close and we watched for signs of fresh water. At last we saw a stream falling over a low cliff into the ocean, and I made for a strip of yellow sand where a long, low surf broke lazily.

We were all suffering from thirst, which is the only excuse I had for landing in such a spot. Fortunately the boat drew little water, and we were able to paddle it in to a point where we could wade. I held it there, while Zerka and Mantar slaked their thirst; then I went and drank my fill. We had nothing in which to carry water; so we put off again immediately, hoping we might find a more suitable spot where we might make a temporary camp and endeavor to improvise some sort of equipment. About the middle of the day, we found such a place – a little cove into which a stream of fresh water emptied, and about which grew a variety of trees and plants. Among the latter was a huge arborescent grass nearly a foot in diameter, with hard, smooth outer wood and a pithy core. We managed to break one of these down; and, after building a fire, we burned out one section. The sections were formed by well-marked joints or nodes, at which the inner cavity was closed by a strong diaphragm. Our efforts resulted in a receptacle about three feet high and a foot in diameter, in which we could carry fresh water. So successful was this first attempt that we made two more of them.

In the wood we found nuts and fruits; so that now all we lacked were weapons. If we had had a knife we might have fulfilled this want, as we could have made bows, arrows, and spears from the hard, outer wood of this bamboo-like plant. Mantar and I discussed this most important matter, for we knew that if we were ever compelled to remain on shore for any length of time we might need weapons sorely. We certainly should, if we were to have meat to eat. We searched the beach together, and finally found several pieces of sharp-edged stones and shells. With this meager encouragement, we decided to camp where we were until we had contrived some sort of weapons.

I shall not bore you with a recital of our methods. Suffice it to say that our technique was wholly primitive; but with fire and using our sharp-edged tools as wedges and scrapers, we managed to hack out spears, bows, arrows and sharp-pointed wooden knives. We also made two long harpoons for spearing fish; then, with a supply of fresh water and quantities of nuts and tubers, we set out again upon our long journey toward Sanara.

Fortune favored us, for the wind held; and though we had a few stiff blows, the seas were never such as we could not weather. This was fortunate for us, as we did not want to be forced ashore if we could avoid it. We often ran rather close in, and at such times it was not unusual for us to see savage beasts along the shore. No monsters of the sea attacked us. In fact, we saw but a couple that might have proved dangerous; and we left these strictly alone. With our harpoons we were able to vary our diet of nuts and tubers with excellent fish, which we ran ashore and cooked as quickly as we could find a suitable place after catching them.

Had I not had my mind filled almost entirely with thoughts of Duare and worries concerning her, I might have enjoyed this adventure exceedingly; but as it was I chafed at every delay, even to the point of begrudging the time it took to cook food or take on fresh water.

On the night of the sixth day out, we were sailing smoothly along a low coast, when I saw clearly in the night sky the flare of a blue rocket against the lower surface of the inner cloud envelope. It was followed in a moment by another and then another. The enemy were springing the trap that was to snare Muso! I wondered if this were the first, the second, or the third night. We might have been too far away before this to have seen them. It made no difference, as it might be two more days before we could hope to reach the coast near Sanara.

The next night we watched for a repetition of the rockets, the purpose of which I had explained to Zerka and Mantar; but nothing rewarded our vigil; and I was of the opinion that last night's rockets had completed the series of three nightly for three nights and that tonight Muso would walk into the trap that I had prepared for him. How I wished that I might be there to witness his undoing!

And now we encountered storms. The next day we were driven ashore by a wind of almost hurricane velocity. We managed to find a sheltered bay; and here we anchored, safe from the storm as well as from wild beasts and savage men. For three days we were storm-bound, and Sanara only one day's sail away! The delay was maddening, but there was nothing that we could do about it. Man-made obstacles we might overcome, but not those interposed by the elements. During our enforced wait, we speculated upon our chances of gaining entry into Sanara through the Zani lines which encircled the city; and we were all forced to admit that they seemed rather remote, as, by all means, we must avoid being recaptured by the Zanis; so here was a man-made obstacle quite as difficult of negotiation as any that the elements might raise. It appeared that we were stymied. However, we must go on, hoping for some fortuitous circumstance that would solve our difficulty.

In the evening of the third day, the storm suddenly abated; and, though the seas were still running high, we put out from our little harbor and set our course once more for Sanara. Perhaps it was a foolhardy thing to do, but the enforced delay and my anxiety to reach Sanara and be reunited with Duare had rendered me temerarious. The seas were like a great, grey army rushing, battalion after battalion, in their assault upon the shore; and we a tiny Argo between the Charybdis of the one and the Scylla of the other. Yet we came through without mishap, and dawn found us off the mouth of the river upon which Sanara lies a few miles from the coast.

'And now what are we to do?' asked Zerka.

I shook my head in despair. 'Pray to Lady Luck,' I said.

'The only plan that I can suggest that seems to contain even a germ of success,' said Mantar, 'is for me to get through the Zani lines at night and seek admission to the city. I am well known to many of the nobility and high officials. They would accept and believe me; and I should be safe even though Muso were still jong, which would not hold true with you, Carson. Once inside the city, it would be easy to arrange for your princess to fly out and pick up Zerka and you.'

'If she is there,' I amended. 'If Muso is still jong, she is not there.'

'That is what I must ascertain,' he replied.

'And what of Zerka?' I asked. 'If you are in the city and Muso is jong, I cannot come in; how then shall we get Zerka?'

'I shall be content to remain with you, Carson; so don't give me a thought,' said Zerka.

'Whatever we do can't be done until after dark,' I said; 'so we shall have to cruise around until then. Maybe in the meantime we shall have evolved a better plan than Mantar's, which I do not like because it subjects him to too much risk.'

It was very monotonous, cruising aimlessly about; and very tantalizing to be so near our goal and yet so far from reaching it. The seas had gone down, but enormous ground swells alternately lifted us to high crests and dropped us into deep hollows. Fishes swarmed about us – the sea was alive with them, and now and again some great monster of the deep passed close, like a giant submarine, as it voraciously gobbled the lesser creatures in its path. About the 8th hour Zerka voiced an exclamation of excitement and pointed toward the city; and as I looked, I saw the anotar above Sanara. It was evident that she had just risen from the city. That could mean but one thing to me; no, two – the first, that Duare lived; the second, that Muso no longer ruled as jong; for no one but Duare could fly the ship, and she would not have been in Sanara had Muso ruled the city.

As we watched, we saw that the plane was heading in our direction and we prepared to try to attract Duare's attention to us. I lowered the sails, lest it hide our efforts; and then I put one of our improvised water containers upside down over the end of the harpoon. As the ship approached, Mantar and I waved the crude signal back and forth.

From the time that she had left the city, Duare had been climbing; and had gained considerable altitude by the time she passed over us. We must have appeared very small to her. Perhaps she did not see us at all. She certainly gave no indication of it. I wondered why she was flying out over the ocean, and waited for her to circle back, hoping for better luck with our signalling next time. But she did not circle back – she continued straight upon her course into the southeast. In utter silence we watched until the ship became a little speck in the distance and finally disappeared.

My heart sank, for I knew the truth – Duare thought me dead and was flying back to Vepaja with her father! I should never see her again, for how could I reach Vepaja and what would it avail me were I to? Mintep would have me destroyed before I could even so much as see my Duare. I was utterly unnerved as I sat there staring out across that lonely ocean after my lost love.

I must have looked the picture of dejection that I felt. Zerka placed a hand upon mine. It was a gesture of sympathy and friendship which would have been negatived by words.

Presently I hoisted the sails again and headed in for shore. As we approached it, and it became evident that I was going to enter the mouth of the river, Mantar spoke.

'What are you going to do?' he asked.

'I am going through the Zani lines and up to the city,' I replied.

'Have you gone mad?' he demanded. 'At night you might stand a chance of getting through; but in broad daylight, none. You'll be arrested; and even if no one at the front recognizes you, there'll be plenty in Amlot, where you'll surely be sent.'

'I'll get through,' I said, 'or I won't; but I'll not go back to Amlot.'

'You're desperate now, Carson,' said Zerka. 'Don't throw your life away uselessly. There may be happiness for you yet; why, your princess may even return from Vepaja.'

'No,' I said; 'once she is there they will never permit her to leave again.'

I ran the boat close to the river bank and leaped ashore. 'Cruise around close by,' I called to Mantar. 'I'll get word to you, if it's humanly possible. Watch the city. If you see balloons go up by day or rockets by night, you'll know I've won through and that plans are being made to bring you and Zerka in. Goodbye!'

I had run the boat quite a distance up the river before landing; so the city was not far away as I set out on foot toward it. I made no effort to conceal myself, but walked boldly toward my goal. I should have been close behind the Zani lines, but I saw no sign of troops nor of any engines of war. Presently I came to where the Zanis had lain for so many months. The ground was littered with the rubbish of war. There were a few dead men lying where they had fallen, but no living thing was visible between me and the city. The siege had been raised, the Zanis were gone!

I turned and almost ran back to the river. Mantar and Zerka were drifting slowly down the stream toward the ocean. I shouted to them and beckoned them to return, and when they were within reach of my voice I told them that the Zanis had gone and that nothing lay between us and the city. They could scarcely believe the good news; and when they had taken me aboard, we sailed up the river toward Sanara. About a quarter of a mile from the city we came ashore and walked toward the nearest gate. From the city walls a number of warriors were watching us, and, I presume, with a great deal of suspicion, since Mantar and I still wore the Zani hairdress and apparel.

As we came closer to the gate, Mantar and I made the sign of peace; and as we stopped before it an officer hailed us.

'Ho, Zanis! What do you want at Sanara? To be shot as traitors?'

'We are not Zanis,' I replied. 'We want word with Taman.'

'So,' he laughed, 'you are not Zanis! Oh, no, not at all. Do you think we of Sanara do not know Zanis when we see them?'

'I am Carson of Venus,' I said. 'Tell that to Taman.'

At that he left the wall; and presently the gate swung open a little way, and he came out with a few warriors to have a closer look at us. As he did so, I recognized him; and he me. He was one of the officers who had flown with me on one of the occasions that I had bombed the Zani camp. I introduced him to Zerka and Mantar, for whom I vouched; and he told us to enter the city and that he would escort us personally to Taman.

'One question,' I said, 'before I come into Sanara.'

'And what is that?' he asked.

'Is Muso still jong?'

He smiled. 'I can understand that you might wish to know that,' he said, 'but I can assure you that Muso is no longer jong. The high council deposed him and created Taman jong.'

It was with a feeling of relief that I re-entered the city of Sanara after the trying weeks of danger and uncertainty through which I had passed, and during which I had never known of any place upon this strange planet where I might abide in safety – not in Kooaad, where even my best friends would have been in duty bound to have killed me because I had dared love their princess and she me; not in Kapdor, the Thorist city of Noobol, where they had placed me in the room of the seven doors from which no man before had escaped alive; not in Kormor, Skor's city of the dead, from which I had stolen Duare and Nalte from under Skor's nose in his own palace; not in Havatoo, that Utopian city on the banks of the River of Death, from which I had rescued Duare from an inexplicable miscarriage of justice; not in Amlot, where the followers of Spehon would have torn me limb from limb. There was only Sanara. Had Muso still been jong here I should have been doomed to wander on in hopeless loneliness.

At last I had a city I might call my own, where I might establish a home and live in peace and contentment; but there was only relief, not joy, in contemplation of the fact, because Duare was not there to share it with me. So I re-entered Sanara in sorrow, and in the howdah of a great military gantor we were escorted through the avenues toward the palace of Taman. It was well, too, that we had a strong military escort, for the people who saw us pass thought that we were Zani prisoners; and would have made quick work of us had it not been for the soldiers. Even to the very gates of the palace of the jong they followed us, booing and cursing and flinging insults at us. The officer who escorted us tried to tell them that we were not Zanis, but his voice was drowned in the tumult.

XVII

Forty Minutes!

When word was taken to Taman that I had returned to Sanara, he had us brought to him at once. He had known the Toganja Zerka well in Amlot, and after he had listened to her story he promised that both she and Mantar should be rewarded for the hazardous work they had performed in the stronghold of the Zanis. Upon me he conferred nobility, promising me palaces and land also as soon as the seat of government should have been re-established in Amlot. When he learned of the attitude of the Sanarans toward us because of our Zani appearance, he ordered black wigs for Mantar and me and new apparel for all of us; then he turned Zerka and Mantar over to members of his household staff and took me to see Jahara, his queen. I knew that he wanted to talk to me in private and tell me about Duare, the one subject uppermost in my mind but of which neither of us had spoken. The little Princess Nna was with her mother when we entered the apartments of the queen, and they both welcomed me with great cordiality and real friendship. Fortunately for Nna, she was not fettered by the ridiculous customs of Vepaja that had made of Duare a virtual prisoner in her own apartments in her father's palace; but could mingle as freely with the court as other members of the royal family. She was a sweet young girl and the pride of Taman and Jahara. Shortly after I was received by the latter, Nna was taken away by a lady-in-waiting; and I was not to see her again until after a harrowing episode and a dangerous adventure.

As soon as Taman, Jahara and I were alone I turned to the former. 'Tell me about Duare,' I begged. 'I saw the anotar leave Sanara this morning and head out over the ocean. No one but Duare could have been at the controls, for only she and I know how to fly the ship.'

'You are right,' he replied, 'it was Duare.'

'And she was flying her father back to Vepaja?' I asked.

'Yes. Mintep practically forced her to do so. She had not given up hope that you might be alive and she wanted to remain. She was planning on flying back to Amlot with more bombs and a message that she would continue to bomb the city until you were released, but Mintep would not let her do so. He swore that if you did live, he would kill you on sight, for while, as a father, he owed you a debt of gratitude for all that you had done for his daughter, as Jong of Vepaja he must destroy you for having dared to love his daughter and take her as your mate. Finally he commanded her to return to Vepaja with him and stand trial before the nobles of Kooaad for having broken one of the oldest taboos of Vepaja.'

'That may mean death for her,' I said.

'Yes, she realized that; and so did Mintep, but the dynastic customs and laws of Vepaja are so ingrained in every fiber of their beings that, to them, it was almost unthinkable to attempt to evade them. Duare would have had she known that you lived. She told me that, and she also told me that she would return to Vepaja willingly because she preferred death to life without you. I do not know what Mintep would have done had she refused to return to Kooaad; but I think he would have killed her with his own hands, notwithstanding the fact that he loved her. I was, however, prepared for such an eventually; and I should have protected Duare even to the extent of imprisoning Mintep. I can tell you that we were all in a most unhappy situation. I never before saw a man of such unquestioned intelligence so fanatical as Mintep, but on this one subject only. Otherwise he seemed perfectly normal and lavished upon Duare all the love of a devoted father. I have often wondered what he would have done if Duare had found you at Amlot. I can't imagine him in the anotar with you. But, tell me, what went wrong with your plans? Duare said that you did not put off from the city in a boat as you should have done were you released.'

'I put off just as had been planned; but I had Zerka and Mantar with me, and Duare would have been looking for a lone man in a boat. Also, my flying helmet had been taken from me in the courtroom of the prison; so there was nothing by which she could identify me. We must have looked like three Zanis to her.'

'Then she saw you,' said Taman. 'for she told me that she saw three Zanis put off into the harbor. When you did not come as she had hoped, she assumed that the Zanis had killed you; and she bombed the city until she had exhausted her supply of bombs. Then she flew back with Mintep, Ulan and Legan; and remained in the vicinity of Sanara for several days until we sent up three balloons to indicate that it was safe for you to enter Sanara – of course, at that time, we did not know that you were not in the ship.'

'And what of Muso? I was told at the gate that he had been deposed.'

'Yes, and imprisoned,' replied Taman; 'but he has a number of followers whose lives will not be safe in Korva now that Muso is no longer jong. They are desperate. Last night they succeeded in liberating Muso from prison, and he is hiding now somewhere in the city. We do not believe that he has been able to leave Sanara as yet, though that is his plan. He believes that if he can reach Amlot, the Zanis will make him jong; but he does not know what we know – that Mephis is dead and that after his death the counter-revolutionists struck and completely routed the Zani overlords, of whom the people, including the majority who claimed to be Zanis, were heartily sick. The word must have reached the troops before Sanara yesterday morning, for it was then that they evacuated their positions and started on the long march back toward Amlot.'

'Then the long civil war is over,' I said.

'Yes,' replied Taman, 'and I hope soon to re-establish the capital at Amlot. I have already sent word that I would extend amnesty to all except ringleaders and those whose acts have been definitely criminal. I expect to follow my messenger in person in a few days with a powerful army. And, my friend, I hope that you will accompany me and receive in my capital the honors that are your due.'

I shook my head. 'Do not think that I don't appreciate your generosity,' I said, 'but I think you will understand that they would be empty honors indeed without my princess to share them.'

'But why not?' he urged. 'You must live, and here you may live in comfort and in honor. What other plans may you have?'

'I am going to follow Duare to Vepaja.'

'Impossible!' he exclaimed. 'How can you hope to reach Vepaja? Every Korvan vessel was taken or destroyed by the enemy during the last war.'

'I have a boat that brought me safely from Amlot,' I reminded him.

'What is it? A fishing boat?' he demanded.

'Yes.'

'A mere cockleshell,' he cried. 'You would not last through the first storm.'

'Nevertheless, I shall make the attempt,' I said.

He shook his head sadly. 'I wish that I might dissuade you,' he said, 'not alone because of my friendship for you, but because you could be of such great value to Korva.'

'How?' I asked.

'By showing us how to build anotars and training my officers to fly them.'

'The temptation is great,' I admitted, 'but I shall never rest in peace until I know that I have done all that man can do to rescue Duare.'

'Well, you can't leave at once; so we shall make the most of the time that you are with us; and I shall not annoy you with further importunities.'

He called an aide then, and had me shown to the quarters he had assigned me. There I found new apparel and a black wig; and after a hot bath I felt like a new man; and looked like one, too, as my mirror revealed in a startling manner. I should not have known myself, so greatly did the wig change my appearance.

Zerka, Mantar, and I dined that night in the great banquet hall of the jong's palace with Taman and Jahara and a company of the great nobles of Korva. They had all known me, some of them quite well; but they all agreed that they would never have recognized me. This, I realized, was not entirely due to the black wig. I had lost considerable weight during my hazardous adventures in Amlot; and I had undergone considerable mental suffering, with the result that my face was haggard and lined, my cheeks sunken.

During the long dinner, we three from Amlot fairly monopolized the conversation, but not through any desire on our part. The other guests insisted upon hearing every detail of what we had observed there and what we had experienced. They were especially interested in Zerka's description of the devious methods whereby the counter-revolutionists had carried on their operations despite the highly organized Zani spy system and the ruthless extermination of all who became suspected. They were still listening to her, spellbound, when a highly agitated aide entered the banquet hall and approached Taman. As he whispered in the jong's ear, I saw the latter turn suddenly pale; then he rose and, taking Jahara's hand, led her from the hall. While the jong's departure left us free to depart if we wished, no one did so. We all felt that Taman was in trouble, and I think that as one man our only thought was to remain, in the event that we might be of service to our jong. We were right, for presently the aide returned and asked us to remain until Taman could speak with us. A few moments later he returned to the banquet hall; and, standing at the head of the long table, spoke to us.

'In this hall,' he said, 'are many of my most loyal subjects and trusted friends. I have come to you in a moment of great trouble to ask your aid. The Janjong Nna has been abducted from the palace.'

An involuntary exclamation of shock and sorrow filled the great room.

'She was taken with the connivance of someone in the palace,' continued Taman, 'but not before two loyal guardsmen had been killed attempting to defend her. That is all I know.'

A voice murmured, 'Muso!' It reflected the thought in every mind; and just then an officer hurried into the hall and up to Taman, handing him a message.

'This was just found in the janjong's apartment,' said the officer.

Taman read the message through; then he looked up at us. 'You were right,' he said. 'It was Muso. This is a threat to kill Nna unless I abdicate in favor of Muso and swear allegiance to him.'

We all stood there voiceless. What was there to say? Could we advise a father to sacrifice a loved daughter? Could we permit Muso to become jong of Korva? We were upon the horns of a dilemma.

'Does the message state any time when your decision must be reached?' asked Varo, the general.

Taman nodded. 'Between the first and second hours in the morning I must send up balloons from the palace roof – one if I refuse; two, if I accede.'

'It is now the 26th hour,' said Varo. 'We have eleven hours in which to work. In the meantime, Taman, I beg that you refrain from making any reply. Let us see what we can accomplish.'

'I shall leave the matter in your hands, Varo,' said Taman, 'until the 1st hour tomorrow. Keep me advised of any progress, but please do not jeopardize the life of my daughter.'

'Her safety shall be our first concern,' Varo assured the jong.

Taman sat with us while we discussed plans. There seemed nothing more practical than a thorough search of the city, and Varo issued orders that routed out every soldier in Sanara to prosecute such a search as few cities ever have been subjected to.

I asked permission to join the searchers, and when Varo granted it I went at once to my quarters and summoned the servant who had been detailed to attend me. When he came I asked him if he could quickly procure for me the apparel such as a poor man might wear, but one who might also reasonably carry a sword and pistol.

'That will be easy, sir,' he said. 'I have only to go to my own quarters and fetch the apparel that I wear when I am not in the livery of the jong's household.'

In ten minutes I was attired in the clothing of an ordinary citizen of the lower class, and was soon on the street. I had a plan – not a very brilliant one but the best I could think of. I knew some rather disreputable haunts of the underworld of Sanara where men might foregather who could be bribed to commit any crime however heinous, and it occurred to me that here I might overhear much discussion of a crime with which such men would be familiar and possibly a hint that would lead me on the right trail. I really didn't have much enthusiasm for the idea, but I had to do something. I liked little Nna, and I couldn't just sit still and do nothing while she was in danger.

I wandered down toward the lower end of the city where the fish markets had been and where the sailors had gathered to carouse and fight in the days before the war that had wiped out the merchant marine and most of the fishing industry of Sanara. Now it was almost deserted, but there were still many of the old drinking places eking out a mean existence by catering to the men and women of the underworld. I went from one to the other of them, buying drinks here, gambling there, and always listening for any chance scrap of conversation that might lead to a clue. There was much talk on the subject of the abduction of the princess, for the matter was uppermost in all minds; but nothing was said in any of the places I went right up to the 36th hour that would have indicated any knowledge of the whereabouts of Nna or of her abductors.

I was discouraged and about hopeless as the 36th hour saw me sitting in a dive near the river wall of Sanara, where I pretended to be slightly under the influence of the vile drink that is popular there and tastes something like a mixture of gin and kerosene oil, of neither of which am I very fond – as a beverage. I let myself be enticed into a gambling game that somewhat resembles fan-tan. I lost consistently and paid with great good humor.

'You must be a rich man,' said an ugly looking customer seated beside me.

'I know how to make money,' I said. 'I have made a lot this night. I may hang for it; so I might as well spend it.'

'That's the idea,' he applauded. 'But how did you make so much money so easily?'

'That I should tell – and get my neck twisted,' I said.

'I'll bet I know how he made it,' offered another man, 'and he will get his neck twisted for it, too – unless—'

'Unless what?' I demanded truculently.

'You know and so do Prunt and Skrag. They've gone for the rest of theirs now.'

'Oh, they have, have they?' I demanded. 'I haven't got the rest of mine. I don't know where to go to get it. They'll probably cheat me out of it. Oh, well, I've got plenty anyway.' I got up from the table and walked toward the door, staggering just a little. I hadn't the remotest idea that I was on a trap that would lead me where I wanted to go, but there was a chance. This was probably the biggest crime that had been committed in Sanara since it was founded; and when a great deal of money was exhibited under the conditions and in the manner that I had exhibited mine, it would naturally suggest connection of some kind with the criminals, for a man of my apparent walk of life would not have come suddenly upon great wealth honestly.

I had scarcely reached the door of the dive when I felt a hand on my arm. I turned to look into the cunning face of the man who had spoken to me last. 'Let us talk together, my friend,' he said.

'What about?' I asked.

'You have some money coming to you,' he commenced. 'What would you give me if I should show you where you could collect it?'

'If you can do that, I might give you half,' I said.

'Very well,' he said, 'for half I will do it. But this is a bad night to be about on work of this kind. Since they stole the jong's daughter the city is being searched and everyone being questioned. The boys got a lot of money for that. What you got for choking the old villain, Kurch, would be nothing beside what Muso paid to have the daughter of the jong brought to him.'

So I was off on a wrong trail! But how to get on the right one? The fellow was obviously drunk, which accounted for his loose tongue; and he knew something about the abduction of Nna, but how much? And how was I to switch him from one trail to another? I saw that I would have to take the bull by the horns.

'What made you think I had anything to do with murdering Kurch?' I demanded.

'Didn't you?' he asked.

'Of course not,' I assured him. 'I never said I did.'

'Then how did you come by so much money?' he demanded.

'Don't you suppose there were other jobs besides the Kurch job,' I demanded.

'There were only two big jobs in town tonight,' he said.

'If you were in on the other, you ought to know where to go.'

'Well, I don't,' I admitted. 'I think they're tryin' to beat me out of mine. They said they'd bring me the rest of mine down here, but they aren't here. They wouldn't tell me where they took the girl, either. I'd give anything to know. If I did, you can bet they'd come through, or –' I touched my sword significantly.

'How much would you give?' he asked.

'What difference does that make to you?' I demanded. 'You don't know where she is.'

'Oh, I don't, don't I? Just show me how high your money stacks. I know lots of things for a tall stack.'

Korvan money is all of the same metal, round pieces of different thicknesses, their centers punched out with different size circles, squares, ovals, and crosses; but all of the same outside diameter. Their value is determined by the weight of the metal each contains. They stack easily, and the thicker pieces of greatest value naturally stack higher, giving usage to the common expression 'a tall stack' meaning a considerable amount of money.

'Well, if you really showed me where she is,' I said. 'I might give you five hundred pandars.' A pandar has about the purchasing power in Korva that a dollar would have in America.

'You haven't got that much,' he said.

I shook my pocket pouch so that the money in it rattled. 'Doesn't that sound like it?' I asked.

'I like to feel money, not listen to it,' he said.

'Well, come outside where no one will see us; and I'll show it to you.'

I saw the cunning glint in his eyes as we passed out into the avenue. Finding a spot that was deserted and also dimly lighted by a lamp in a window, I counted out five hundred pandars into his cupped palms, definitely defeating for the moment any plan he had to murder me; then, before he could transfer the money to his pocket pouch, I drew my pistol and shoved it into his belly.

'If there's any shooting to be done, I'll do it,' I told him. 'Now take me to where the girl is, and no funny business. When you have done that, you may keep the money; but if you make a single break, or fail to show me the girl, I'll let you have it. Get going.'

He grinned a sickly grin, and turned away down the dark street. As he did so, I jerked his pistol from its holster; and shoved the muzzle of mine into the small of his back. I wasn't taking any chances.

'You're all right, fellow,' he said. 'When this job's over, I'd like to work with you. You work quick, and you know what you're doing. Nobody ain't going to fool you.'

'Thanks,' I said. 'Be at the same place tomorrow night, and we'll talk it over.' I thought this might keep him from trying to double-cross me, but I still kept my gun in his ribs.

He led me along the river wall to an old, abandoned building at one end of which was a huge incinerator within a firebox large enough to hold half a dozen men. He stopped here and listened, looking furtively in all directions.

'She's in here,' he whispered. 'This firebox opens into the inside of the building, too. Now give me back my pistol and let me go.'

'Not so fast,' I cautioned him. 'The agreement was that you were to show me the girl. Go on in!'

He hesitated, and I prodded him with my gun.

'They'll kill me,' he whimpered.

'If you don't show me the girl, they won't have to,' I threatened. 'Now don't talk any more – we may be overheard. If I have to go in alone, I'll leave you out here, dead.'

He said no more, but he was shaking as he crawled into the great incinerator. I laid his pistol on the ledge of the firebox and followed directly behind him. It was dark as a pocket in the firebox and not much better in the room into which we stepped – so dark that I had to hold onto my companion's trappings to keep him from eluding me entirely. We stood in silence, listening for a full minute. I thought I heard the murmur of voices. My guide moved forward cautiously, feeling his way step by step. It was evident that he had been here before. He crossed to the side of the room, where he found a bolted door.

'This is for our getaway,' he whispered, as he drew the bolt. I knew from the direction we had come that the door opened out onto the street.

He turned and moved diagonally across the room again to the opposite wall. Here he found another door which he opened with the utmost caution. When it was opened, the murmur of voices became more distinct. Ahead of us, I could see a tiny ray of dim light coming apparently from the floor of the room. My guide led me forward to it, and I saw that it came through a hole in the flooring – possibly a knothole.

'Look!' he whispered.

As I had to lie down on my stomach to look through the hole, I made him lie down, also. In the circumscribed range of my vision, I could not see much of the room below; but what I did see was almost enough. Two men were sitting at a table, talking – one of them was Muso. I could see no girl, but I knew that she might be there outside the little circle that was visible to me. I could hear the men talking.

'You don't really intend killing her, do you?' asked Muso's companion.

'If I don't get a favorable reply from Taman before the 2nd hour, I most certainly shall,' replied Muso. 'If she would write her father as I have asked her to, she would be free to go at once; for I know that Taman would not see his daughter die if she herself begged him to save her.'

'You'd better do it, Nna,' said the other man. 'The time is getting short.'

'Never!' said a girl's voice, and I knew that I had found Nna.

'You may go now,' I whispered to my companion. 'You will find your pistol on the ledge of the incinerator. But wait! How can I get into that room?'

'There is a trap door in the corner, to your right,' he replied. He moved away so silently that I did not hear him go, but I knew that he had. Only a fool would have remained with me.

Faintly into the darkness of the room came a suggestion of growing light. The sun was rising. The first hour had come. In forty minutes of Earth time the second hour would strike – strike the death knell of Nna, the daughter of Taman.

XVIII

A Tanjong

Forty minutes! What could I do in that time to insure the safety of the princess? Had I found her only a little sooner, I could have summoned soldiers and surrounded the building. They would not have killed her had they known they were going to be taken. But I must do something. The precious minutes were slipping by. There was nothing for it but to take the bull by the horns and do the best I could. I rose and felt my way to the corner of the room. On hands and knees I groped about in the darkness for the trap door, and at last I found it. Gingerly I tried it to learn if it were locked from below. It was not. I raised it quickly and jumped through, my pistol still in my hand. I heard it slam shut above my head as I touched the floor. Luckily I did not fall; and my advent had been so sudden and so unexpected that for an instant Muso and his companion seemed unable to move or speak. I backed to the wall and covered them.

'Don't move,' I warned, 'or I'll kill you both.'

It was then that I first saw two men in the far corner of the dimly lighted room as they leaped to their feet from a pile of rags upon which they had been lying asleep. As they reached for their pistols I opened fire on them. Muso dropped to the floor behind the table at which he had been sitting, but his companion now drew his own weapon and leveled it at me. I shot him first. How all three of them could have missed me in that small room I cannot understand. Perhaps the brains of two of them were dulled by sleep, and the other was unquestionably nervous. I had seen his hand shake as it held his weapon; but miss me they did, and the second and third went down before they could find me with the deadly stream of R-rays from their guns. Only Muso remained. I ordered him out from under the table and took his pistol from him; then I looked about for Nna. She was sitting on a bench at the far side of the room.

'Have they harmed you in any way, Nna?' I asked.

'No; but who are you? Do you come from my father, the jong? Are you a friend or another enemy?'

'I am your friend,' I said. 'I have come to take you away from here and back to the palace.' She did not recognize me in my black wig and mean apparel.

'Who are you?' demanded Muso, 'and what are you going to do to me?'

413

'I am going to kill you, Muso,' I said. 'I have hoped for this chance, but never expected to get it.'

'Why do you want to kill me? I haven't harmed the princess. I was only trying to frighten Taman into giving me back the throne that belongs to me.'

'You lie, Muso,' I said; 'but it is not this thing alone that I am going to kill you for – not something that you may say you did not intend doing, but something you did.'

'What did I ever do to you? I never saw you before.'

'Oh, yes you have. You sent me to Amlot to my death, as you hoped; and you tried to steal my woman from me.'

His eyes went wide and his jaw dropped. 'Carson of Venus!' he gasped.

'Yes, Carson of Venus – who took your throne away from you and is now going to take your life, but not because of what you did to him. I could forgive that, Muso; but I can't forgive the suffering you caused my princess. It is for that that you are about to die.'

'You wouldn't shoot me down in cold blood?' he cried.

'I should,' I said, 'but I am not going to. We'll fight with swords. Draw!'

I had laid his pistol on the bench beside Nna, and now I drew my own and placed it on the table at which Muso had been sitting; then we faced one another. Muso was no mean swordsman, and as our blades shattered the silence of that little room I commenced to suspect that I might have bitten off more than I could chew; so I fought warily and, I am free to admit, mostly on the defensive. That is no way to win any contest, but I knew that if I became too reckless in my attack he might easily slip cold steel through me. Yet something must be done. This could not go on like this forever. I redoubled my efforts; and because I had by now become accustomed to his mode of attack, which he seldom varied, I commenced to have the advantage. He realized it, too; and the yellow in him showed up immediately. Then I pressed my advantage. I backed him around the room, certain now that I could run him through almost at will. He stepped back against the table in what I took to be a last stand; then, suddenly, he hurled his sword directly in my face; and almost simultaneously I heard the br-r-r of an R-ray pistol. I had seen him reach for mine just as he hurled his sword at me. I expected to fall dead, but I did not. Instead, Muso slumped backward across the table and then rolled off onto the floor; and as I looked around, I saw Nna standing with Muso's pistol still leveled in her hand. She had robbed me of my revenge, but she had saved my life.

As I looked down at her, she sat down very suddenly and burst into tears. She was just a little girl, and she had been through too much in the past few hours. She soon regained control of herself, however; and looked up and smiled at me, rather wanly.

'I really didn't know you,' she said, 'until Muso called you by name; then I knew that I was safe – that is, safer. We are not safe yet. His men were to return here at the 2nd hour. It must be almost that now.'

'It is, and we must get out of here,' I said. 'Come!'

I slipped my pistol back into its holster; and we stepped to the ladder that led up to the trap door, and at the same moment we heard the heavy tramp of feet in the building above us. We were too late.

'They have come!' whispered Nna. 'What are we to do?'

'Go back to your bench and sit down,' I said. 'I think one man may hold this doorway against many.'

Stepping quickly to the sides of the dead men, I gathered their pistols and carried them all to a point from which I could command the ladder with the least danger to myself. The footsteps approached the room above us, they entered it and crossed to the trap door; and then a voice called down, 'Hello, there, Muso!'

'What do you want of Muso?' I asked.

'I have a message for him.'

'I will take it for him,' I said. 'Who are you? And what is your message?'

'I am Ulan, of the Jong's Guard. The message is from Taman. He agrees to your demands provided you will return Nna to him unharmed and guarantee the future safety of Taman and his family.'

I breathed a sigh of relief and sat down in a nearby chair. 'Muso scorns your offer,' I said. 'Come down, Ulan, and see for yourself why Muso is no longer interested.'

'No trickery!' he warned, as he raised the trap door and descended. When he turned at the foot of the ladder and saw the four corpses lying on the floor his eyes went wide as he recognized one of them as Muso; then he saw Nna and crossed to her.

'You are not harmed, Janjong?' he asked.

'No,' she replied. 'But if it had not been for this man I should have been dead by now.'

He turned to me. I could see that he recognized me no more than others had. 'Who are you?' he asked.

'Don't you remember me?'

Nna giggled, and I had to laugh myself.

'What is so funny?' he demanded. Ulan flushed angrily.

'That you should so soon forget a good friend,' I said.

'I never saw you before,' he snapped, for he knew we were making fun of him.

'You never saw Carson of Venus?' I asked; then he laughed with us as he finally pierced my disguise. 'But how did you know where to find the princess?'

'When Taman gave the required signal of acquiescence,' explained Ulan, 'one of Muso's agents told us where she might be found.'

We were soon out of the dank cellar and on our way to the palace, where we brushed past the guards under escort of Ulan and hastened through the palace to the jong's own quarters. Here Taman and Jahara sat waiting for word from the last of the searchers or from the emissary the former had dispatched to Muso at the urgings of Jahara and his own heart. As the door was thrown open we sent Nna in, Ulan and I remaining in a small antechamber, knowing that they would wish to be alone. A jong would not wish his officers to see him weep, as I am sure Taman must have wept for joy at Nna's safe return.

It was but a few minutes before he came out into the antechamber. His face was grave by now. He looked somewhat surprised to see me, but he only nodded as he turned to Ulan.

'When will Muso return to the palace?' he asked.

We both looked at him in surprise. 'Didn't the janjong tell you?' asked Ulan. 'She must have told you.'

'Tell me what? She was crying so for joy that she could not speak coherently. What is there to tell me, that I may not already guess?'

'Muso is dead,' said Ulan. 'You are still jong.'

From Ulan, and later from Nna, he finally got the whole story, pieced out with what I told him of my search through the city; and I have seldom seen a man more grateful. But I expected that from Taman; so I was not surprised. He always gave fully of himself to his friends and his loyal retainers.

I thought I should sleep forever when I went to bed that morning in my apartments in the jong's palace, but they didn't let me sleep as long as I could have wished. At the 12th hour I was awakened by one of Taman's aides and summoned to the great throne room. Here I found the grand council of nobles assembled around a table at the foot of the throne and the rest of the room crowded with the aristocracy of Korva.

Taman and Jahara and Nna sat in their respective thrones upon the dais, and there was a fourth chair at Taman's left. The aide led me to the foot of the dais before Taman and asked me to kneel. I think Taman is the only man in two worlds before whom I should be proud to kneel. Above all other men, he deserves reverence for his qualities of mind and soul. And so I knelt.

'To save the life of my daughter,' commenced Taman, 'I offered my throne to Muso with the consent of the grand council, You, Carson of Venus, saved my daughter and my throne. It is the will of the grand council, in which I concur, that you be rewarded with the highest honor in the power of a jong of Korva to bestow. I therefore elevate you to the rank of royalty; and as I have no son, I adopt you as my own and confer upon you the title of Tanjong of Korva.' Then he rose and, taking me by the hand, led me to the vacant throne chair at his left.

I had to make a speech them, but the less said about that the better – as a maker of speeches, I am a fairly good aviator. There were speeches by several great nobles, and then we all trooped to the banquet hall and overate for a couple of hours. This time I did not sit at the foot of the table. From a homeless wanderer a few months earlier, I had been suddenly elevated to the second position in the empire of Korva. But that was all of lesser moment to me than the fact that I had a home and real friends. If only my Duare had been there to share it all with me!

Here at last I had found a country where we might live in peace and honor, only to be thwarted by that same malign fate that had snatched Duare from my arms on so many other occasions.

XIX

Pirates

I never really had an opportunity to more than taste the honors and respon-sibilities that devolve upon a crown prince, for the next day I started outfitting my little fishing boat for the long trip to Vepaja.

Taman tried to dissuade me, as did Jahara and Nna and all my now count-less friends in Korva; but I could not be prevailed upon to abandon the venture, however hopeless I myself felt it to be. The very ease and luxury of my new position in life made it seem all the more urgent that I search for Duare, for to enjoy it without her seemed the height of disloyalty. I should have hated it always had I remained.

Every assistance was given me in outfitting my craft. Large water tanks were installed and a device for distilling fresh water from sea water. Concen-trated foods, preserved foods, dehydrated fruits and vegetables, nuts, every edible thing that could be preserved for a considerable time were packed away in waterproof containers. New sails were made of the strong, light 'spider cloth' that is common among the civilized countries of Amtor, where spiders are bred and kept for the purpose of spinning their webs for commer-cial use, as are silkworms on Earth. They gave me weapons and ammunition and warm blankets and the best navigation instruments available; so that I was as well equipped for the journey as it was possible for anyone to be.

At last the time of my departure arrived, and I was escorted to the river with all the pomp and ceremony befitting my exalted rank. There were troops and bands and a hundred gorgeously caparisoned gantors bearing not only the nobility of Korva but its royalty as well, for Taman and Jahara and the Princess Nna rode with me in the howdah of the jong's own gantor. Cheering throng lined the avenues and it should have been a happy event, but it was not – not for me, at least; for I was leaving these good friends, as I full believed, forever and with little or no hope of attaining my heart's desire. I shall not dwell further upon the sadness of that leave-taking. The pall of it hung over me as I ailed out upon the broad expanse of that vast and lonely ocean, nor did my spirits lift until long after the distant mountains of Anlap had dropped below the horizon; then I shook the mood from me as I looked with eagerness toward the future and set my mind solely upon success.

I had set a range of from ten to twenty days for the cruise to Vepaja, depending, of course, upon the winds; but there was always the possibility of missing the island entirely, notwithstanding the fact that it was a continent in size, being some four thousand miles long by fifteen hundred wide at its greatest width. Such a supposition might seem ridiculous on Earth, but here conditions were vastly different. Maps were inaccurate. Those available indicated that Anlap was scarcely more than five hundred miles from Vepaja, but I knew that at least fifteen hundred miles of ocean must separate them. Duare and I had learned that when we had flown it. The reason their maps must be inaccurate is due to their false conception of the shape of the planet, which they believe to be a flat disc floating on a sea of molten rock, and their further belief that the antarctic region forms the periphery and what I knew to be the equator, the center of the disc. This naturally distorts every possible conception of the shape and size of oceans and land masses. These people in the southern hemisphere of Venus have not the remotest idea of the existence of the northern hemisphere.

I shall not inflict upon you the monotony of the first week of that journey. The wind held steady, and at night I lashed the tiller and slept with a comparatively peaceful mind, as I had devised an alarm that sounded whenever the boat deviated from its course a certain number of points. It was a simple device electrically controlled by the needle of the compass. I was not awakened on an average of two or three times in a night; so I felt that I was keeping fairly well on my course; but I wished that I knew what, if anything, the currents were doing to me.

Since the coast of Anlap had dropped below the horizon I had seen no land, nor had a single ship appeared upon that vast watery expanse of loneliness. The waters often teemed with fish; and occasionally I saw monstrous creatures of the deep, some of which defy description and would challenge belief. The most numerous of these larger creatures must attain length of fully a thousand feet. It has a wide mouth and huge, protruding eyes between which a smaller eye is perched upon a cylindrical shaft some fifteen feet above its head. The shaft is erectile; and when the creature is at rest upon the surface or when it is swimming normally beneath, it reclines along its back; but when alarmed or searching for food, the shaft springs erect. It also functions as a periscope as the beast swims a few feet beneath the surface. The Amtorians call it a rotik, meaning three-eye. When I first saw one I thought it an enormous ocean liner as it lay on the surface of the ocean in the distance.

At dawn of the eighth day I saw the one thing that I could have wished least of all to see – a ship; for no ship that sailed the Amtorian seas could conceivably contain any friends of mine, unless, perhaps the *Sofal* was still carrying on its piratical trade with the crew, that had followed me so loyally in the mutiny that had given me command of it. That, however, was doubtful. The vessel was some distance to starboard and was moving in an easterly direction. Within an hour it would cross my course, which was due south. Hoping to avoid detection because of the insignificant size of my little craft, I lowered my sails and drifted. For half an hour the ship held its course; then its bow swung in my direction. I had been sighted.

It was a small vessel of about the tonnage of the *Sofal*, and very similar in appearance. It had no masts, sails, stacks, nor funnels. Aft were two oval deck houses, a small one resting on top of a larger. On top of the upper house was an oval tower surmounted by a small crow's nest. At bow and stern and from the crow's nest rose staffs from which long pennons flew. The main staff, above the crow's nest, was supposed to fly the flag of the country to which the ship belonged; the flag at the bow, the city from which it sailed; the stern flag was usually the house flag of the owner. In the case of warships, this staff carried the battle flag of the nation to which it belonged. As the ship neared me, I saw but one thing – a ship without country or city was a faltar, a pirate ship. The flag at the stern was probably the personal flag of the captain. Of all the disasters that could have befallen me, this was about the worst, that I should run afoul of a pirate ship; but there was nothing to do about it. I could not escape. As I had thought it best to wear my black wig through the streets of Sanara on my way to the boat, I still had it with me; and as my yellow hair had only partially grown out and as I had a black-tipped mane reaching from forehead to nape, I put the wig on now rather than take the chance that my weird coiffure might arouse suspicion aboard the pirate craft.

As the ship came close, it lay to. I saw its name painted along the bow in the strange Amtorian characters – *Nojo Ganja*. Fully a hundred men lined the port rail watching me, as were several officers upon the upper decks of the houses. One of the latter hailed me.

'Come alongside,' he shouted, 'and come aboard.'

It was not an invitation – it was a command. There was nothing to do but obey; so I raised one sail and brought my craft under the lee rail of the pirate. They tossed me a rope which I made fast to the bow and another with knots in it up which I climbed to the deck; then several of them slid down into my boat and passed every thing in it up to their fellows above. After that, they cut my boat adrift and got under way. All this I saw from an upper deck where I had been taken to be questioned by the captain.

'Who are you?' he asked.

'I am called Sofal,' I said. Sofal was the name of my pirate ship and means 'the killer.'

'Sofal!' he repeated, a little ironically I thought. 'And from what country do you hail? And what are you doing out here in the middle of the ocean in a small boat like that?'

'I have no country,' I replied. 'My father was a faltargan, and I was born on a faltar.' I was rapidly becoming a proficient liar, I who had always prided myself on my veracity; but I think a man is sometimes justified in lying, especially if it saves a life. Now the word faltargan has an involved derivation. *Faltar*, pirate ship, derives from *ganfal*, criminal (which is derived from *gan*, man, and *fal*, kill) and *notar*, ship roughly criminal ship. Add *gan*, man, to *faltar*, and you have pirate-ship-man, or pirate; fal-tar-gan.

'And so I suppose you are a pirate,' he said, 'and that that thing down there is your faltar.'

'No,' I said, 'and yes; but, rather, yes and no.'

'What are you driving at?' he demanded.

'Yes, I am a pirate; but no, that is not a faltar. It is just a fishing boat. I am surprised that an old sailor should have thought it a pirate ship.'

'You have a loose tongue, fellow,' he snapped.

'And you have a loose head,' I retorted; 'that is why you need a man like me as one of your officers. I have captained my own faltar, and I know my trade. From what have seen, you haven't enough officers to handle a bunch of cutthroats such as I saw on deck. What do you say?'

'I say you ought to be thrown overboard,' he growled. 'Go to the deck and report to Folar. Tell him I said to put you to work. An officer! Cut out my liver; but you have got nerve! If you make a good sailor, I'll let you live. That's the best you'll get, though. Loose head!' and I could hear him grumbling as I went down the companionway to the deck.

I don't know just why I had deliberately tried to antagonize him, unless it was that I had felt that if I cringed before him he would have been more likely to have felt contempt for me and killed me. I was not unfamiliar with men of his type. If you stand up to them they respect and, perhaps, fear you, for most swashbucklers are, at heart, yellow.

When I reached the deck I had an opportunity to inspect my fellow sailors more closely. They were certainly a prize aggregation of villainous-looking scoundrels. They eyed me with suspicion and dislike and not a little contempt, as they appraised my rich apparel and handsome weapons which seemed to them to bespeak the dandy rather than the fighting man.

'Where is Folar?' I asked of the first group I approached.

'There, ortij oolja,' he replied in an assumed falsetto, as he pointed to a huge bear of a man who was glowering at me a few yards away.

Those within earshot guffawed at this witticism – ortij oolja means *my love*. Evidently they thought my apparel effeminate. I had to smile a little myself, as I walked over to Folar.

'The captain told me to report to you for duty,' I said.

'What's your name?' he demanded, 'and what do you think you can do aboard a ship like the *Nojo Ganja*?'

'My name is Sofal,' I replied, 'and I can do anything aboard ship or ashore that you can do, and do it better.'

'Ho! Ho!' he pretended to laugh, 'The Killer! Listen, brothers, here is The Killer, and he can do anything better than I can!'

'Let's see him kill you, then,' cried a voice from behind him.

Folar wheeled about. 'Who said that?' he demanded, but nobody answered.

Again a voice from behind him said, 'You're afraid of him, you sailful of wind.' It seemed to me that Folar was not popular. He completely lost his temper then, over which he appeared to have no control whatsoever; and whipped out his sword. Without giving me an opportunity to draw, he swung a vicious cut at me that would have decapitated me had it connected. I leaped back in time to avoid it; and before he could recover, I had drawn my own weapon; then we settled down to business, as the men formed a circle around us. As we measured one another's strength and skill in the first few moments of the encounter, I heard such remarks as, 'Folar will cut the fool to pieces,' 'He hasn't a chance against Folar – I wish he had,' and 'Kill the mistal, fellow; we're for you.'

Folar was no swordsman; he should have been a butcher. He swung terrific cuts that would have killed a gantor, could he have landed; but he couldn't land, and he telegraphed his every move. I knew what he was going to do before he started to do it. Every time he cut, he left himself wide open. I could have killed him any one of half a dozen times in the first three minutes of our duel, but I didn't wish to kill him. For all I knew he might be a favorite of the captain, and I had already done enough to antagonize that worthy. For the right moment to do the thing I wanted to do, I had to bide my time. He rushed me about here and there dodging his terrific swings until, at last, I got tired of it and pricked him in the shoulder. He bellowed like a bull at that; and seizing his sword with both hands, came at me like a charging gantor. Then I pricked him again; and after that he went more warily, for I guess he had commenced to realize that I could kill him if I wished. Now he gave me the opportunity I had been awaiting, and in an instant I had disarmed him. As his weapon clattered to the deck, I stepped in, my point at his heart.

'Shall I kill him?' I asked.

'Yes!' rose in a thunderous chorus from the excited sailors.

I dropped my point. 'No, I shall not kill him this time,' I said. 'Now pick up your sword, Folar; and we'll call everything square. What do you say?'

He mumbled something as he stooped to retrieve his weapon; then he spoke to a one-eyed giant standing in the front row of spectators.

'This fellow will be in your watch, Nurn,' he said. 'See that he works.' With that, he quit the deck.

The men gathered around me. 'Why didn't you kill him?' asked one.

'And have the captain order me thrown overboard?' I demanded. 'No. I can use my brains as well as my sword.'

'Well,' said Nurn, 'there was at least a chance that he wouldn't have; but there is no chance that Folar won't stab you in the back the first chance he gets.'

My duel with Folar had established me in the good graces of the crew; and when they found that I could speak the language of the sea and of the pirate ship, they accepted me as one of them. Nurn seemed to take a special fancy to me. I think it was because he hoped to inherit Folar's rank in the event the latter was killed, for several times he suggested that I pick another quarrel with Folar and kill him.

While talking with Nurn I asked him where the *Nojo Ganja* was bound.

'We're trying to find Vepaja,' he said. 'We've been trying to find it for a year.'

'Why do you want to find it?' I asked.

'We're looking for a man the Thorists want,' he said. 'They've offered a million pandars to anyone who'll bring him to Kapdor alive.'

'Are you Thorists?' I asked. The Thorists are members of a revolutionary political party that conquered the former empire of Vepaja which once spread over a considerable portion of the south temperate zone of Amtor. They are the bitter enemies of Mintep as well as of all countries that have not fallen into their hands.

'No,' replied Nurn, 'we are not Thorists; but we could use a million pandars of anybody's money.'

'Who is the Vepajan they want so badly?' I asked. I assumed that it was Mintep.

'Oh, a fellow who killed one of their ongyans in Kapdor. His name is Carson.'

So! The long arm of Thora had reached out after me. I was already in the clutches of its fingers; but, happily for me, I was the only one who knew it. However, I realized that I must escape from the *Nojo Ganja* before it touched at any Thoran port.

'How do you know this Carson is in Vepaja?' I asked.

'We don't know,' replied Nurn. 'He escaped from Kapdor with the Janjong of Vepaja. If they are alive, it is reasonable to believe they are in Vepaja; that, of course, is where he would have taken the janjong. We are going to search Vepaja first. If he isn't there, we'll go back to Noobol and search inland.'

'I should think that would be quite a man-size job,' I remarked.

'Yes, it will,' he admitted, 'but he should be an easy man to trace. Here and there inland someone must have seen him, and if anyone once saw this Carson they'd never forget him. He has yellow hair, and as far as anyone ever heard no one else in the world has yellow hair.' I was grateful for my black wig. I hoped it was on securely.

'How are you going to get into the tree cities of Vepaja?' I asked. 'They don't care much for strangers there, you know.'

'What do you know about it?' he demanded.

'I've been there. I lived in Kooaad.'

'You did? That's just where we expect to find Carson.'

'Then maybe I can help,' I suggested.

'I'll tell the captain. No one aboard has ever been to Kooaad.'

'But how do you hope to get into that city? You haven't told me that. It's going to be very difficult.'

'They'll probably let one man go in to trade,' he said. 'You see, we've picked up a lot of jewels and ornaments off the ships we've taken. A man could go in with some of these and if he kept his eyes and ears open, he'd soon find out whether or not Carson was there. If he is, we'll have to find some way to entice him aboard the *Nojo Ganja*.'

'That should be easy,' I said.

Nurn shook his head. 'I don't know about that,' he said.

'It would be easy for me, knowing Kooaad as I do,' I said. 'You see I have friends there.'

'Well, first we've got to find Vepaja,' he remarked quite aptly.

'That's easy, too,' I told him.

'How so?'

'Go tell the captain that I can pilot him to Vepaja,' I said.

'You really can?'

'Well, I think I can. One never knows, what with the rotten maps we have.'

'I'll go now and talk with the captain,' he said. 'You wait here and, say, keep a weather eye open for Folar – he's the stinkingest mistal of all the stinking mistals on Antor. Just keep your back against something solid and your eyes open.'

XX

To Kooaad

I watched Nurn as he crossed the deck and ascended the companionway leading to the captain's quarters. If the captain could be persuaded to trust me, here was such an opportunity to enter Kooaad as might never come to me again. I knew from the course that the *Nojo Ganja* was holding that she was paralleling the coast of Vepaja, but too far off shore for the land to be visible. At least I was confident that such was true. I really could not know it, as one could know nothing for certain about his position on one of these Amtorian seas unless he were in sight of land.

As I stood by the rail waiting for Nurn to return, I saw Folar come on deck. His expression was black as a thunder cloud. He came directly toward me. A man near me said, 'Look out, fellow! He's going to kill you.' Then I saw that Folar carried one hand behind him and that his pistol holster was empty. I didn't wait then to see what he was going to do or when he was going to do it. I knew. I whipped out my own gun just as he raised his. We fired simultaneously. I could feel the R-rays pinging past my ear; then I saw Folar slump to the deck. Instantly a crowd surrounded me.

'You'll go overboard for this,' said a man.

'It won't be as easy as that,' said another, 'but in the end you'll go overboard.'

An officer who had witnessed the affair came running down from the upper deck house. He pushed his way through the crowd of sailors to me.

'So you're trying to live up to your name, are you, fellow?' he demanded.

'Folar was trying to kill him,' spoke a sailor.

'And after he'd spared Folar's life,' said another.

'Folar had a right to kill any member of the crew he wanted to kill,' snapped the officer. 'You mistals know that as well as I do. Take this fellow up to the captain and throw Folar overboard.'

So I was taken up to the captain's quarters. He was still talking with Nurn as I entered. 'Here he is now,' said Nurn.

'Come in,' said the captain, rather decently; 'I want to talk with you.'

The officer who had accompanied me looked rather surprised at the captain's seemingly friendly manner. 'This man has just killed Folar,' he blurted.

Nurn and the captain looked at me in astonishment. 'What difference does it make?' I asked. 'He wasn't any good to you, anyway, and he was just about to kill the only man who can pilot you to Vepaja and get into the city of Kooaad for you. You ought to thank me for killing him.'

The captain looked up at the officer. 'Why did he kill him?' he asked.

The officer told the story quite fairly, I thought; and the captain listened without comment until he had concluded; then he shrugged.

'Folar,' he said, 'was a mistal. Someone should have killed him long ago. You may go,' he said to the officer and the sailors who had brought me up; 'I want to talk with this man.' When they had left, he turned to me. 'Nurn says that you can pilot this ship to Vepaja and that you are acquainted in Kooaad. Is that right?'

'I am well acquainted in Kooaad,' I replied, 'and I believe I can pilot the *Nojo Ganja* to Vepaja. You will have to help me get into Kooaad, though. I'll be all right after I get in.'

'What course shall we take?' he asked.

'What is your course now?'

'Due east,' he replied.

'Change it to south.'

He shook his head, but he gave the necessary orders. I could see that he was very skeptical of our chances of reaching Vepaja on the new course. 'How long before we'll raise land?' he asked.

'That, I can't tell,' I said; 'but I'd keep a sharp lookout, and at night cut your speed down.'

He dismissed me then, telling me that I'd be quartered with the officers. I found my new companions little different from the common sailors. They were all bravos and rascals; and, without exception, had been common sailors themselves. I found little in common with them, and spent most of my time in the crow's nest with the lookout watching for land.

It was right after the 1st hour the next morning that I discerned the black-appearing mass ahead that I knew to be the giant forest of Vepaja, those mighty trees that rear their heads five and six thousand feet to drink sustenance from the moisture of the inner cloud envelope that surrounds the planet. Somewhere in that black mass and a thousand feet above the ground was the great tree city of Kooaad. There, too, if she still lived, would be my Duare.

I went down to the captain's quarters myself to report sighting land, and as I reached the door I heard voices. I would not have stopped to listen; but the first word I heard was the name they knew me by, Sofal. The captain was speaking to one of his officers.

'– and when we are through with him, see that he's put out of the way. Let the men know that it was because he killed Folar. We can't let them think they can get away with anything like that. If I hadn't needed him, I'd have had him killed yesterday.'

I walked away as noiselessly as I could; and returned a moment later, whistling. When I had reported land, they both came out. It was plainly visible by now, and shortly after the 2nd hour we were close in shore. We were a little too far east; so we came about and skirted the coast until I sighted the harbor. In the meantime I had suggested to the captain that he'd better lower his pirate flags and fly something more in keeping with his purportedly peaceful designs.

'What country are they friendly with?' he asked. 'What far country, whose ships and men they might not be expected to recognize.'

'I am quite sure that a ship from Korva would be welcomed,' I told him; so the Korvan flag was run up at the bow and above the deck houses; while, for an owner's flag at the stern, he used one he had taken from a ship he had sunk. There was already a ship in the harbor, a vessel from one of the little islands that lie west of Vepaja. It was loading up with tarel. There was a strong company of Vepajan warriors on guard, for the port is quite some distance from Kooaad; and there is always danger of attack by Thorists or other enemies.

The captain sent me ashore to negotiate for entry into Kooaad as well as to assure the Vepajans that we were there on a friendly mission. I found the company in charge of two officers, both of whom I had known when I lived in Kooaad. One was Tofar, who had been captain of the palace guard and high in the confidence of Mintep; the other was Olthar, brother of my best friend in Kooaad, Kamlot. I fairly shook in my boots as I recognized them, for I did not see how it could be possible that they should fail to know me. However, as I stepped from the small-boat, I walked boldly toward them. They looked me straight in the face without a sign of recognition.

'What do you want in Vepaja?' they asked, their tones none too friendly.

'We are trading with friendly countries,' I said. 'We are from Korva.'

'Korva!' they both exclaimed. 'We had heard that the merchant marine of Korva had been destroyed in the last war.'

'Practically all of it,' I said. 'A few ships escaped because they were on long cruises and knew nothing of the war until it was over. Our ship was one of these.'

'What have you to trade?' asked Tolfar.

'Ornaments and jewels, principally,' I replied. 'I should like to take them into one of your big cities. I think the ladies of the jong's palace would like to see them.'

He asked me if I had any with me; and when I showed him some that I had brought along in my pocket pouch, he was much interested; and desired to see more. I did not want to take him aboard the *Nojo Ganja* for fear his suspicions might be aroused by the ruffianly appearance of the officers and crew.

'When do you go back to the city?' I asked.

'We leave here as soon as they finish loading that ship,' he replied. 'That should be within the hour; then we leave immediately for Kooaad.'

'I'll get all my articles,' I told him, 'and go to Kooaad with you.'

Olthar seemed rather taken aback by this, and looked questioningly at Tofar. 'Oh, I think it will be all right,' said the latter. 'After all, he's only one man; and anyway he's from Korva – that will make a difference with Mintep. He and the janjong were well treated there. I have heard him speak in the highest terms of the jong of Korva and the nobles he met there.'

I had difficulty in hiding my relief at this evidence that Duare was alive and in Kooaad. But was she alive? She had evidently reached Vepaja with her father, but she might already have been destroyed for having broken the taboo custom had laid upon her as janjong of Vepaja.

'You mention a janjong,' I said. 'I am glad to know that your jong has a daughter. He will wish to buy some of my jewels for her.'

They made no reply, but I saw them exchange a quick glance.

'Go and get your stuff,' Tovar said, 'and we'll take you with us when we return to Kooaad.'

The captain was delighted when he found what excellent progress I had made. 'Try to persuade the man Carson to return to the ship with you, if you find he is in Kooaad,' he said.

'I shall certainly find him in Kooaad,' I told him. 'I am sure of that.'

A half hour later I set out with Tofar, Olthar, and their company through the great forest toward Kooaad. We had not gone far when Olthar told me that I should have to be blindfolded, and after that a soldier walked on either side of me to guide me and keep me from stumbling over obstacles. Knowing as I did how jealously the Vepajans have to guard the secret entrances to their tree cities I was not at all surprised at this precaution, but I may say that it made most awkward travelling. At last, however, we reached a spot where I was conducted through a doorway; and after the door was closed, the bandage was removed from my eyes. I found myself in the hollow interior of a great tree, standing in a cage with Tofar, Olthar, and some of the warriors. The others waited on the ground beside the cage. A signal was given, and the cage started to rise. For a thousand feet we were hoisted by a great windlass to the street level of Kooaad. Once again I stood on the highflung walkways of the first Amtorian city I had ever seen. Somewhere near me was Duare, if she still lived. I could feel my heart throb from the excitement of the moment.

'Take me to the palace,' I said to Tofar. 'I should like to get permission to show these beautiful things to the women of the jong's retinue.'

'Come,' he said, 'I'll see if we can get permission.'

A short walk brought us to the enormous tree from the interior of which the rooms of the palace of Mintep are carved. How familiar it all was! How it recalled my first days on Venus, and that day of days that I had first seen

Duare and first loved her. Now I was coming again to the palace of her father, but with a price upon my head.

At the entrance to the palace was the familiar guard. I knew the captain of it well, but he did not recognize me. When Tofar stated my request, the captain entered the palace, telling us to wait. He was gone for some time, but when he returned he said that Mintep would be glad to welcome a Korvan merchant to his palace.

'He has sent word to the women that you will show your wares in the reception room inside the entrance,' said the captain. 'They will be gathering there soon; so you might as well come in.'

'I'll leave him with you, then,' said Tofar.

I reached into my package and selected a jeweled ring, which I proffered to Tofar. 'Please accept this for your kindness to me,' I said, 'and take it to your woman with my compliments.'

If he had only known that Carson Napier – Carson of Venus – was the donor!

The women of the palace gathered in the reception room, and I spread my jewels and ornaments out before them. I had known many of them and most of the men who came with them or followed them in to see what I had to offer, but not a one knew me.

There was one particularly lovely girl whom I knew to have been very close to Duare, one of her ladies-in-waiting, in fact; and her I sought to draw into conversation. She was much interested in one piece, but said that she could not afford to buy anything so expensive.

'But your man,' I said, 'Certainly he will buy it for you.'

'I have no man,' she said. 'I serve the janjong, and I may have no man until she takes one; or until she dies.' Her voice broke with a sob.

'Take it,' I whispered. 'I have sold many already. I can easily spare this piece; then, when I come again, if you can, you may pay me.'

'Oh, but I couldn't do that,' she cried, a little startled.

'Please,' I begged. 'It will make me very happy to know that this lovely piece, which I myself so much admire, has a setting worthy of its beauty.'

I could see that she wanted it very badly, and when a woman wants a piece of jewelry or apparel, she will stop at little to possess it.

'Well,' she said, after a pause, during which she fondled and admired the bauble, 'I suppose I might pay you some time; and if I couldn't, I could give it back to you.'

'I am glad that you have decided to keep it,' I said. 'I have another piece here that I should like very much to show to the janjong. Do you suppose it would be possible?'

'Oh, no,' she said. 'That would be quite impossible; and anyway, she – she –' Again her voice broke.

'She is in trouble?' I asked.

She nodded. 'She is going to die!' She spoke in an awed whisper.

'Die?' I asked. 'Why?'

'The council of nobles has so decreed.'

'You love her?'

'Yes, of course. I would give my life for her.'

'Do you mean that?' I demanded.

She looked at me in surprise. I had let my emotions get the better of my caution.

'Why do you take such an interest?' she asked.

I looked at her for a full minute, I guess, trying to read her soul through her eyes. I could see nothing in them but truth and sincerity and love – love for my Duare.

'I am going to tell you why,' I said. 'I am going to trust you. I am going to put my life in your hands and the life of your janjong as well. I am Carson Napier – Carson of Venus.'

Her eyes went wide and she caught her breath. She looked at me for a long time. 'Yes,' she said, 'I see now; but you have changed so.'

'Suffering and a black wig make a big change in one's appearance,' I said. 'I have come here to save Duare. Will you help me?'

'I told you once I would give my life for her,' she said. 'That was no idle speech. What do you want me to do?'

'I want you to get me into Duare's quarters in some way and hide me there. That is all I ask of you.'

She thought for a moment. 'I have a plan,' she said, presently. 'Gather up your things and prepare to leave. Say that you will return tomorrow.'

I did as she bid, making several sales at the same time. I told the purchasers that I would take payment when I came back the next day. I almost smiled when I thought of the rage of the pirate captain could he have known that I was giving his treasure away. When I had at last gathered up what remained, I started toward the door. Then Vejara, the lady-in-waiting, spoke to me in a voice that all might hear.

'Before you go,' she said, 'I wish that you would bring your things to the anteroom of my apartments. I have a piece of jewelry which I should like to match if possible. I think I saw something of yours that would answer.'

'Thank you,' I said, 'I'll come with you now,' so we walked out of the reception room, and she led me along corridors to a door which she opened with a key, after glancing quickly around to see if we had been observed. 'Quick!' she whispered. 'In here. These are the apartments of the janjong. She is alone. I have done all that I can. Goodbye and good luck!'

She closed the door after me and locked it. I found myself in a very small waiting room, empty but for two long benches, one on either side. Later I learned that it was where servants waited to be interviewed by the janjong. I crossed to a door at the opposite end and opened it quietly. Before me was a beautifully furnished apartment. On a divan, reading, was a woman. It was Duare. I entered the room, and as I did so she turned and looked at me. Her eyes went wide with incredulity as she sprang to her feet and faced me; then she ran and threw herself into my arms. Of all, she alone had known me!

Neither of us could speak for a full minute; and then, though there was so much to say, I would not let her speak of but one thing, nor would I – a plan of escape.

'It will be simple, now that you are here,' she said. 'The council of nobles has condemned me to die. I suppose they could do nothing else. They do not wish my death. They are all my friends, but the laws that govern the jongs of Vepaja are stronger than friendship or their love for me or anything in the world – except my love for you and yours for me. They will be glad if I escape, for they have done their duty. My father will be glad, too.'

'But not the jong of Vepaja,' I said.

'I think he will be a little glad, also,' she said.

'Why couldn't you have escaped without me, if it is so easy to escape?' I asked.

'Because I have given my word not to violate my arrest,' she replied. 'But I cannot help it if someone takes me by force.'

She was very serious, and so I did not smile – outwardly. Duare is very sweet.

We talked then and planned until after dark. When her food was brought, she hid me; and then she shared it with me. We waited until the city had quieted down; then she came close to me. 'You will have to carry me out of my quarters,' she said, 'for I may not go of my own free will.'

In the palace there is a secret shaft down the interior of the great tree to the ground. There is no lift there – only a very long and tiresome climb down a ladder. It was never intended to be used except in emergencies of life and death, and only the jong and his family know of its existence. Down this we clambered. I thought that we should never reach the ground, but at last we did.

Duare had told me that she had fastened the ship down not far from this tree, which is close to the edge of the forest. If it were still there, and unharmed, our escape would be assured. If it were not, we were lost. That was a chance we had to take, for Duare was to have died on the morrow. There was no time for me to investigate.

Leaving the base of the tree we groped our way through the darkness, constantly fearful of attack by one of the terrible beasts that roam the Vepajan forest. When I finally thought that we must have missed the anotar in the darkness, or that it had been taken away, I saw it looming in front of us; and

I am not ashamed to admit that tears came to my eyes as I realized that my Duare was safe at last – safe and with me.

A few minutes later we zoomed into the Amtorian sky; and, leveling off, turned the nose of the ship out over the grey Amtorian sea toward the north-west and the kingdom of Korva – our kingdom. Toward peace and happiness and friends and love.

If you've enjoyed these books and would like to read more, you'll find literally thousands of classic Science Fiction & Fantasy titles through the **SF Gateway**

✳

For the new home of

Science Fiction & Fantasy . . .

✳

For the most comprehensive collection

of classic SF on the internet . . .

✳

Visit the SF Gateway

www.sfgateway.com

Edgar Rice Burroughs (1875–1950)

Edgar Rice Burroughs was a prolific American author of the 'pulp' era. The son of a Civil War veteran, he saw brief military service with the 7th U.S. Cavalry before he was diagnosed with a heart problem and discharged. After working for five years in his father's business, Burroughs left for a string of disparate and short-lived jobs, and was working as a pencil sharpener wholesaler when he decided to try his hand at writing. He found almost instant success when his story 'Under the Moons of Mars' was serialised in *All-Story Magazine* in 1912, earning him the then-princely sum of $400.

Burroughs went on to have tremendous success as a writer, his wide-ranging imagination taking in other planets (John Carter of Mars and Carson of Venus), a hollow earth (Pellucidar), a lost world, westerns, historicals and adventure stories. Although he wrote in many genres, Burroughs is best known for his creation of the archetypal jungle hero, Tarzan. Edgar Rice Burroughs died in 1950.